William R. Holloway

Indianapolis

A historical and statistical sketch of the railroad city, a chronicle of its social,

municipal, commercial and manufacturing progress

William R. Holloway

Indianapolis
A historical and statistical sketch of the railroad city, a chronicle of its social, municipal, commercial and manufacturing progress

ISBN/EAN: 9783337293666

Printed in Europe, USA, Canada, Australia, Japan

Cover: Foto ©Andreas Hilbeck / pixelio.de

More available books at **www.hansebooks.com**

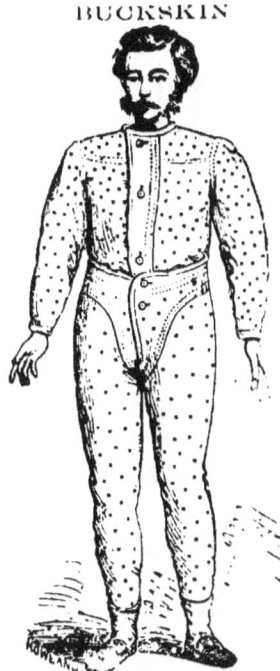

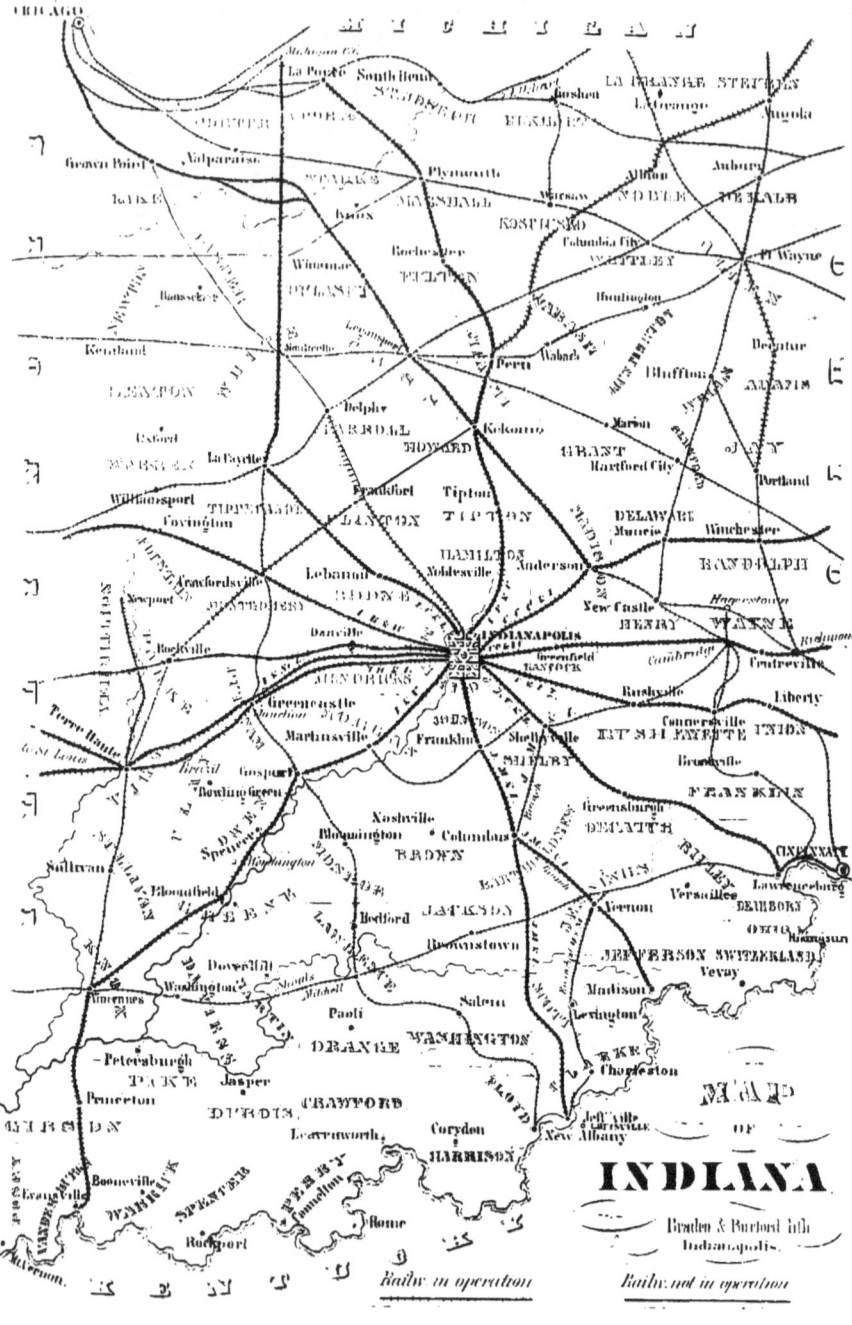

MAP OF INDIANA

Braden & Burford lith.
Indianapolis.

Railw. in operation   Railw. not in operation

STATE HOUSE

Lantet & Keep Lith. Cincinnati

INDIANAPOLIS.

A HISTORICAL AND STATISTICAL SKETCH

OF THE

RAILROAD CITY,

A CHRONICLE OF

Its Social, Municipal, Commercial and Manufacturing Progress,

WITH

FULL STATISTICAL TABLES.

BY W. R. HOLLOWAY.

INDIANAPOLIS:
INDIANAPOLIS JOURNAL PRINT.
1870.

PREFACE.

THE object of this work is to relate the rise and progress of the business of the city of Indianapolis, and give an accurate and full exhibit of its present condition· To that end no labor or expense has been spared to collect all the facts that might contribute to the formation of correct opinions on the subject by the public. Every branch of trade has been thoroughly canvassed by competent examiners, and the results systematized and tabulated, so as to give, as nearly as possible, a full view of each at a single glance. A sketch of the history of the city precedes these more particular statements, as a fitting introduction, necessary to a fair understanding of their significance.

It is not intended to be a detailed account of all the incidents, events, movements and efforts of the citizens during the time of the growth from a village full of trees to a city full of the bustle of business; but to be a history of all that relates to her progress and prosperity. It is intended rather to generalize facts, and relate results, without, however, excluding any interesting event or incident, whether directly connected with the history of business affairs or not. Whether that object has been attained, it will be for the public to judge.

Free use has been made, in this portion of the work, of the excellent history of the city by Ignatius Brown, Esq., in the Directory for 1868. It is as full a collection of all the facts as can possibly be made; but such a collection is unsuited to the purpose of such a work as this, and besides would swell its bulk beyond all reasonable limits. The present work is directed rather to use than to repeat his facts, and he is entitled to a full recognition of his efforts in this attempt to apply them to a wider purpose than a Directory.

As no similar effort to exhibit the condition and prosperity of the city has ever been made, it is hoped that this will command the interest and patronage of the public.

INDEX.

ILLUSTRATIONS.

INTRODUCTION.

General View of the Progress of the City.

THE Eastern, Southern and Western sections of the State contained many thriving, though not populous, settlements, while Central Indiana was yet a wilderness. The reason may be briefly stated to be the absence of water and the presence of Indians. Though there was water enough and to spare for ordinary purposes, there was none for navigation, and civilized men hesitate to put themselves beyond the reach of other provisions than they can procure with the rifle. Without access by a constantly navigable stream, a Central settler could never be certain of anything better than unsalted bread and venison; and he could not be certain of the bread if he depended on his own cultivation, for the country was still in the hands of the Indians. This is a second reason. A settlement could not be safe; for, though not hostile, the Indians were far from friendly. The Shawnees and Delawares had not forgotten the battle of Tippecanoe or the death of Tecumseh (who, by the way, was a native-born Hoosier, his birthplace being the Shawnee town near the site of Anderson, Madison county). This region was their favorite hunting-ground. It was full of game, and White river and its tributaries swarmed with fish. They disliked to give it up, and they did not till 1821, five years after the State Government had been created. But having agreed, by the treaty of St. Mary's, Ohio, in 1818, to cede it in 1821, the actual cession was anticipated, and settlers began to come in as early as 1820. A few came in 1819, but two of them, the brothers Jacob and Cyrus Whetzel, came by consent of the chiefs, and settled near the Bluffs of White river. George Pogue, the first who made his home on the site of the city, is generally believed to have come in the same year, but it is questioned. William Conner, the Father of Central Indiana, however, had established himself on White river, some sixteen miles north of the city, as early as 1806, and had made himself a comfortable home, with no neighbor nearer than sixty miles. He had been an Indian trader, was familiar and a favorite with them, and could venture safely where there was danger for everybody else. He and his brother John founded the town of Connersville, from which point, and its vicinity, came most of our first settlers. Indianapolis is, therefore, a sort of colony of Connersville, and, as will be seen hereafter, had to depend for some time upon the mother settlement for support. In 1820, however, a number of pioneers planted themselves on the site of the city, and from that year may be dated the beginning of its history.

Before entering upon this history, however, it will be well to present a general view of the growth of the city, which may be traced through four stages.

First. That from the first settlement in 1820, to the removal of the Capital from Corydon in 1825. This was a period of isolation, and, for a time, of struggle for existence. During this five years, no other village of the State had so much to resist, and so little to assist it. It was far from all navigable streams and all passable roads, and, for the first two years, was without clearing or adequate cultivation, without mills or means of subsistence, except what was brought on horseback through sixty miles of forest. Sickness in the second year, which prostrated nearly everybody, made its isolation more dangerous, and sickness having prevented labor, an unpleasant approach to starvation followed the ague. But the sickly settlement grew a little larger and a little healthier. It built a jail, two or three churches, patronized a few shops, and two or three of the inevitable newspapers, had a few taverns and a Sunday school, and showed evident signs that it meant to live, whether fed by State pap or not. Then, though not free from fears of the scattered Shawnees of Fall Creek, it was deemed ready for the Capital.

Second. The period from 1825, when the Capital came, to 1847, when the first railroad came. This may be said to have been a period of Legislative dependence, as the possession of the Capital was the only influence that raised Indianapolis above the position of an ordinary county town. Its central situation was nothing then, or rather it was a drawback. In the first years of this period, the recent acquisition of the Capital gave an impulse to the increase both of population and the price of town lots, but the stimulus was lost by 1827, and thenceforward growth was steady but slow, dependent on the settlement of the surrounding country, strengthened, as before remarked, by the possession of the Capital. Towards the close, the expectation of railroad communication excited a spirit of enterprise, or at least a feverish feeling of unrest, and with the impulse which the locomotive thus sent ahead of it, began a new era. During this period, business was entirely of a local character. Some little jobbing was done to country dealers, but nothing more, because, with all the enterprise in the world, nothing more was possible. Manufacturing was merely for home consumption. All trade was circumscribed by the limits of local demand. Little was expected to go farther than a farmer could drive his load of corn and get home the same day. Importations were made in heavy road wagons. Exportations in return buggies and farm wagons. An occasional flatboat, loaded with hay or chickens, went down with the spring freshets to New Orleans, if it didn't break its back on the dam at the Bluffs. An annual drove of horses went South for some years. Hogs were driven to Cincinnati or Madison, or the nearest town on a navigable stream. Woolen mills spun yarn for old women, or made jeans for country wear. Wheat was ground for the owner, or bought only to grind for home use. Corn was distilled or fed to hogs; none was shipped. Iron founding had been tried twice and failed. No business was expected to exceed a few hundred dollars per week. In this condition of things the city would have remained to the end, if the railroad had not reached it. The first stirring of this stagnation was made by the slow but steady approaches of the Madison railroad from Vernon, where it had been lying up helpless since the great crash.

Third. The period from 1847 to 1861. This was a period of new life. The railroad, like "one fool," according to the proverb, "made many." The great profits of the Madison road, the obvious benefit to the country, the fully restored financial health prostrated in 1837, with a score of lesser influences, combined to give an impetus to railroad building, which was the great feature of this new era. The enterprise thus stirred into activity showed itself in all business. Old branches were enlarged and new ones were established. The foundations of most of those which have at length proved so successful, and contributed so greatly to the growth of the city, were laid then. While business was putting on its men's clothes for manly effort, the city was doing the same. Not a few changes were made from the village character of the past. But this activity was vastly increased during the last period or stage of growth.

Fourth. The period from 1861, the breaking out of the war, to the present time. What the war might have done for a town, even as large as Indianapolis, with the muscles of its energy rendered feeble and flabby for want of vigorous exercise, it would be hard to say. It would have brought a vast increase of business, and brought out a vast addition of activity, but it might have taken both away with it, too. Indianapolis, skilled and strong, vigorous and enterprising, from the schooling of the past fourteen years, was able and prompt to use all its advantages. The concentration of troops here, with the immense demand they created for many kinds of supplies, and the flocking here of business men to meet it; the increase of the business of those already here; and the attendant smaller classes of trade which follow any crowd, maintained through four years, gave a strong impulse to the already rapidly growing prosperity of the city, and created some such feverish feeling of being able to do impossible things, as was so long prevalent in San Francisco, and still is, probably, in Chicago. But the advantages were generally safely held. They fell into strong hands, and when the war passed off, and its impulse was removed from trade, nothing was lost to the city but what was it's gain—the crowds of cormorants that followed the camps. Business was held at high water mark, or near it. In the five years since, what little, if any, was lost, has been regained, and a vast addition has been made. The growth of population and trade in all forms has gone steadily and swiftly on. In manufactures especially has the change been marked and promising. At the same time the improvements of the city have not been less marked. Whole streets of superb business blocks have been erected, and miles of streets paved and lighted. Handsome residences have spread outward further and further, till they crowd up the hunting forests of a few years ago. A system of water works is in process of construction. Business that used to swing back and forth along Washington street as some occasional impulse directed, but never left its fixed groove, has turned out, or filled up and run over, into a score of other streets. All the features of a well-grown city have supervened upon the face of the village that the first railroad entered. How far this development may continue, or how it may terminate, will be considered in another place.

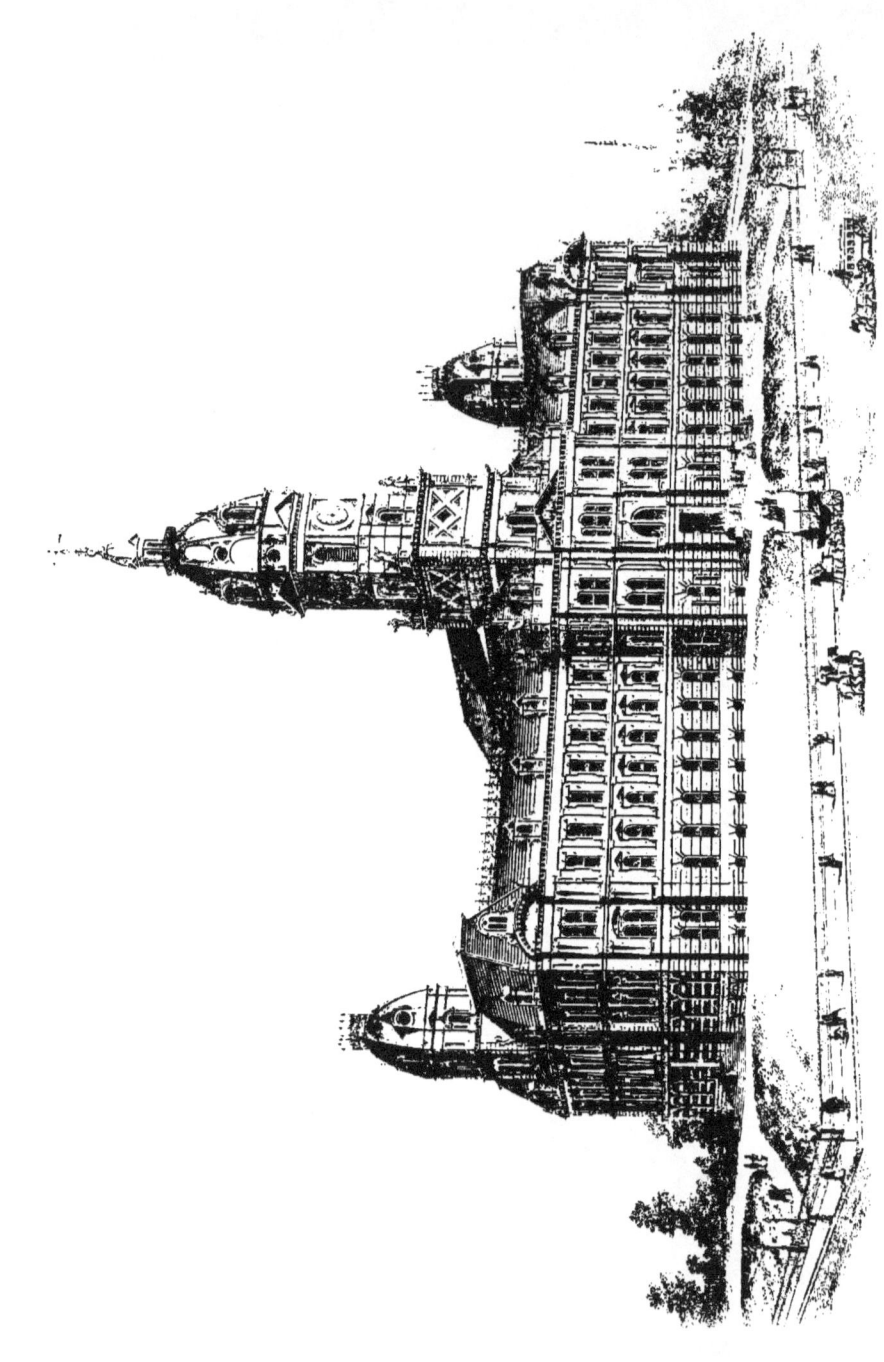

FIRST PERIOD--TO 1825.

Chapter I.

INDIANAPOLIS is situated in the slightly depressed center of a considerable plain on the east bank of White river, in latitude 39° 55′. This plain, though nowhere level for any considerable distance, is yet broken only by comparatively slight elevations, which increase its attractiveness without swelling to either the grandeur or inconvenience of hills. It lies so high above the river that it is not subject to overflow from the highest freshets, and never has been overflowed. At the time of the selection of the site of the Capital, the ground was covered with a dense growth of oak, ash, sugar, beech, walnut, hickory, and all other ordinary forest trees, and with thickets of underwood, that sheltered as much game probably as was ever found ranging the same space of country. It was traversed by a creek, subsequently called "Pogue's Creek," after the traditional first settler, and by two or three bayous or "ravines," as they were called, which proved a frequent cause of annoyance, and of occasional serious injury. The remains of the largest may yet be seen near Carey's barrel and stave establishment. The underlying stratum, consisting of sand and gravel, through which the surface water was filtered, being rarely more than twenty-five feet below the surface, formed an easily accessible reservoir of pure but "hard" water, which has until now rendered the city independent of any other supply. But to all these advantages there was a serious drawback, as the first settlers found. The dense forests sheltering the soil from the sun and compelling it to retain its moisture, the broad and swampy "bottoms," the marshes, and the frequent freshets, made it the very home of the "chills and fever," and for many a year their visit was anticipated with the unpleasant confidence of a debtor in a persevering dun. But the soil was excellent, and the promise of a "good time" sometime undoubted, and the pioneers of that day, as of all days, did not count the chances of chills against the certainty of crops and future competence.

So, into this land of remote promise, somewhere about the first of March, 1819, tradition says, came George Pogue, a blacksmith, from the White Water region, and built a cabin near the present eastern end of Michigan street. Tradition is confirmed by better evidence, but unfortunately contradicted by other evidence equally good. Probably no question of individual credit and municipal history was ever so obscured, by excess of light, as that of the origin of Indianapolis. And the obscuration began almost as soon as the town was begun. George Pogue had been dead only about a year, and the town was only two years old, when one of the second influx of settlers,

Dr. S. G. Mitchell, published a letter in the Indianapolis *Gazette*, contesting Pogue's claim to the honor of being the first settler, and giving it to John and James McCormick. Cyrus Whetzel, who settled at the Bluffs at about the same time that Pogue is said to have reached this place, concurs with Dr. Mitchell. Mrs. King, the widow of one of the McCormick brothers, now living, in good health, and with apparently unimpaired powers of memory, concurs with Dr. Mitchell and Mr. Whetzel. Her evidence would seem to be conclusive, for she not only had the opportunity to know, but the weariness of a solitary life in the woods to impress ineffaceably the memory, that she and her family were alone in this section of the State. She claims that George Pogue, with her husband and husband's brother, and some others, first came here about the time of Pogue's traditional arrival, and built cabins preparatory to the removal of their families, which was effected, in her case, in January or February following, 1820, and that no other family was known here till her husband's brother brought his, about a month later. Pogue would appear from this statement to have been only one of a company to "prospect" here, and the danger of traveling alone at that time, in a country held by unfriendly Indians, is a circumstance that would corroborate it. Up to this point Mrs. King's account of the settlement of the city may reconcile conflicting claims, but no farther. If she is right, Pogue, though he may have prepared to move out, did not settle till some time in 1820. The evidence for the McCormicks sums up with a force hard to resist. Dr. Mitchell's claim, within a year of Pogue's death, was not contested by anybody. The recollections of two living persons, one likely, and one certain, to know the truth, confirms the uncontested claim. On the other hand, the evidence for Pogue, if not strong enough to convince, is strong enough to perplex, us. In 1822, people were not so apt to rush into the papers upon any provocation, or none, as they are now, and Dr. Mitchell's letter may have been, probably was, undisputed, because nobody cared enough to remember whose pig pen was built first, or cared enough to write about it, and not because the opinion of the village concurred with him. The tradition which has always made Pogue the first settler, has never been weakened by accompanying doubts, or suggestions to include anybody else. And an unimpeached tradition of fifty years of age, is no slight proof of the truth of the matter it relates to. If Dr. Mitchell's belief had been that of his fellow-townsmen in 1822, we of this generation would never have heard of George Pogue as the first settler. That the tradition, or general belief, has outlived so early and public an attack is a fact that will weigh as heavily in a just estimate as any personal recollection. A mistake, if uncontested, might grow into tradition, but a mistake caught when it is a year old and shown to everybody's eyes could get no credit afterwards. John Pogue, son of George, who was a well grown lad, if not of full age in 1819, and well able to recollect, has stated repeatedly and unqualifiedly that his father came here on the second of March, 1819, nearly one year before the McCormicks came. The contest of his father's claim would be likely to stamp the event and date more indelibly upon his memory, and make his evidence, by that much, more important. One of the McCormick children of that date, adds his recollection of the current belief that Pogue was the first settler. There is about an equal weight of evidence, both of inference and memory, on each side, and there is no reason why there should be when there are so many persons living who can add decisive facts.

But if Pogue was not the first settler he certainly was the first martyr, if we may allow that name to one who ventures and dies in the cause of civilization. Sometime in April, 1821, early in the morning, he heard a disturbance among his horses, and believing that the Indians, a party of whom was encamped near by, were stealing them, he took his rifle and set out to see. He was last seen near their camp, where gunshots were afterwards heard, and he was never seen again. But his clothes and horses were soon after found in the hands of the Indians, so that there is no doubt of his murder by this squad of Shawnees. His name was given to the creek which was then a horror, and has ever since been a nuisance, to the citizens. So cruel an outrage of course excited the little settlement intensely, but it was too little to help itself.

If Pogue really arrived in March, 1819, he lived for nearly a year alone, with no neighbor except the Whetzels, on the south, at the Bluffs, and William Conner, on the north, sixteen miles away. But on the twenty-seventh of February, 1820, he was joined by James and John McCormick, who built themselves a house on the river near the present position of the National Road bridge. Within a few days they were followed by John Maxwell and John Cowan, who built upon Fall Creek, near the crossing of the Crawfordsville road. By the first of June, these first five had been joined by Henry and Samuel Davis, Corbaly, Van Blaricum, Barnhill, Harding and Isaac Wilson (who was the first to build on the town plat, near the northwest corner of the State House Square,) with others, making, it is supposed, about fifteen families who had settled upon what was afterwards the "donation." As the year passed on still others came, but the first comers had not been idle. They had to live through the winter and set about their preparations with the characteristic energy of pioneers.

In this duty they were providentially relieved of the hardest of their labor. A tract of near two hundred acres, west of the present Blind Asylum grounds, had been "deadened" for them by the locusts and caterpillars. They had nothing to do but clear off the underbrush. This was done, the brush used to fence in lots for cultivation, and the ground broken up and planted in corn and vegetables for the winter. Game was plenty and provisions were thus made secure for all ordinary necessities. Little more than this is known of the history of the first year of the life of the founders of the capital.

But the history does not close with this fact, however appropriate a place it might be to stop. A most important event for the little colony occurred in June. This was the selection of a site for the permanent capital of the State.

The "enabling" act of Congress, April 19, 1816, donated four sections of unsold land for a permanent capital. On the eleventh of January, 1820, the Legislature appointed the following commissioners to make the selection: George Hunt, John Conner, John Gilliland, Stephen Ludlow, Joseph Bartholomew, John Tipton, Jesse B. Durham, Frederick Rapp, William Prince and Thomas Emerson. They were to meet at the house of William Conner (above alluded to,) in the spring, and make their choice. But five of them accepted their appointment, or acted upon it. These five traversed White River Valley, making examinations as they advanced, and very naturally reached conflicting conclusions. But three points were prominent above all others; this, (called the Fall Creek location,) Conner's and the Bluffs of White River. The discussion upon meeting at Conner's was warm, if not worse, but the mouth of Fall Creek won the day against the Bluffs by three votes to two. Who the lucky or sagacious three were it is now impossible to say or they should have a conspicuous place in the celebration of the city's birth-day. The government surveys had been completed in this portion of the State, and the Commissioners were thus enabled to designate their choice in the mysterious but sensible gibberish of the survey office. They reported on the seventh of June, that they had selected sections one, two, twelve and eleven; and, section two being a fraction, enough of west fractional section three had been added to make up the grant. Thus the capital came to the mouth of Fall

Creek or near it. It was a narrow miss, but as it *was* a miss we can hardly speculate more profitably on the possible results of one more vote going for the Bluffs, than did the young lady upon the problem "where she would have been if her father had not married her mother?"

The SECOND YEAR of the town's existence began with the act to lay it off and name it. On the sixth of January, 1821, the Legislature confirmed the choice made by the Commissioners, and called the new-born city INDIANAPOLIS. The etymology of this name is evident enough and its propriety is indisputable, but it is not generally known to whom the city is indebted for it. In the Legislative Committee which prepared the bill of confirmation the point was settled, and Judge Jeremiah Sullivan, of Jefferson county, formerly of the State Supreme Court, suggested the name. In a letter replying to the inquiries of Governor Baker (kindly made at the suggestion of the author,) Judge Sullivan gives the following interesting account of the christening of the capital:

"I have a very distinct recollection of the great diversity of opinion that prevailed as to the name by which the new town should receive Legislative baptism. The bill (if I remember aright) was reported by Judge Polk, and was in the main, very acceptable. A blank, of course, was left for the name of the town that was to become the seat of government, and during the two or three days we spent in endeavoring to fill the blank there was in the debate some sharpness and much amusement.

"General Marston G. Clark, of Washington county, proposed 'Tecumseh' as the name, and very earnestly insisted upon its adoption. When it failed he suggested other Indian names, which I have forgotten. They all were rejected. A member proposed 'Suwarrow,' which met with no favor. Other names were proposed, discussed, laughed at, and voted down, and the house without coming to any agreement, adjourned until the next day. There were many amusing things said, but my remembrance of them is not sufficiently distinct to state them with accuracy.

"I had gone to Corydon with the intention of proposing Indianapolis as the name of the town, and on the evening of the adjournment above mentioned, or the next morning, I suggested to Mr. Samuel Merrill, the representative from Switzerland county, the name I proposed. He at once adopted it and said he would support it. We, together, called on Governor Jennings, who had been a witness of the amusing proceedings of the day previous, and told him what conclusion we had come to, and asked him what he thought of the name. He gave us to understand that he favored it, and that he would not hesitate to so express himself. When the House met and went into convention on the bill, I moved to fill the blank with Indianapolis. The name created quite a laugh. Mr. Merrill, however, seconded the motion. We discussed the matter fully ; gave our reasons in support of the proposition ; the members conversed with each other informally in regard to it, and the name gradually commended itself to the committee, and was accepted. The principal reason given in favor of adopting the name proposed, to wit: that the Greek termination would indicate to all the world the locality of the town, was, I am sure, the reason that overcame the opposition to the name. The town was finally named Indianapolis, with but little, if any, opposition." Indiana–polis,—the city of Indiana,—is a good name, and likely to be known as that of the largest inland city in the Union.

Christopher Harrison, James Jones and Samuel P. Booker, were, by the same act, appointed Commissioners to "lay off" the town, and directed to meet here on the first Monday of April, appoint two surveyors and a clerk, make a survey and two maps, and advertise and sell the alternate lots as soon as practicable, the proceeds of the sales to constitute a building fund.

The effect of this selection, and its confirmation, was to add largely to the slender population of the metropolis, and to bring in not a few of those who still live honored among us or have left honored names and representatives behind them. Before the lot sales took place, or soon after, there came Morris Morris, Dr. S. G. Mitchell, John Given, James Given, James M. Ray, Matthias R. Nowland, Nathaniel Cox, John Hawkins, Dr. L. Dunlap, David Wood, Daniel Yandes, Alexander Ralston, Dr. Isaac Coe, Douglas Maguire, Obed Foote, Calvin Fletcher, James Blake, Alexander W. Russell, Caleb Scudder, Nicholas McCarty, George Smith, Nathaniel Bolton, Wilkes Reagan, James Paxton, Samuel Henderson, and others less known. They came in nearly equal proportions from the south and east, or "Kentucky and Whitewater," as the divisions were then called. A population of some hundreds had been gathered by the fall, and the village might be said to have fairly entered upon its career.

The history of that first year, with a name, is a history of many annoyances, much suffering and much manly and noble exertion. A very wet summer aided the natural miasm of the region to produce such a general distribution of the chills and fever that but three persons out of the whole population escaped. Though severe, the visitation was rarely fatal to the settlers, though it came near proving so to the settlement. For rumor flew abroad with the news and dropped perilous exaggerations everewhere. But the city outlived them as the citizens outlived their cause. An unfortunate result of the general prostration was that nobody had been able to keep up the cultivation of the "caterpillar deadening," and when the bright days of October brought returning health it brought also starvation. There was no mill and nothing to grind if there had been one. Game alone was poor eating. Flour or meal could only be had by packing it on horses from the Whitewater, sixty miles off, through a pathless wilderness. But the courage of the settlers rallied to the work, and a system of horse transportation was established which furnished a meagre supply, eked out by the purchase of corn from the Indians up the river, which was brought down in boats.

The "social events" of the year were the birth of a child to Mr. Harding, who was given the name of Mordecai, and he "still lives," hearty and vigorous. This is claimed by some to be the first birth in Indianapolis ; others claim the honor for a son of Mr. Corbaly. The other, even more interesting event, was the marriage of Jeremiah Johnson, to Miss Jane Reagan, the first marriage in Indianapolis. And it would be memorable if it were the last in last week's list in the daily papers. For the gallant Jerry, with a devotion unknown in these degenerate days, *walked* to Connersville, sixty miles, for his marriage license, for Indianapolis was under the jurisdiction of the mother settlement as yet. And then he had to wait some weeks for a preacher to perform the ceremony. The first sermon was preached by Rev. John McClung, a "New Light," in what was afterwards the circle grove.

Business received a start during the year by the establishment of a store on the south bank of Pogue's Creek, in March, 1821, by Daniel Shaffer, who died in June following. John and James Given and John T. Osborn followed in the same line, near the river, and later Luke Walpole, Mr. Wilmot and Jeremiah Johnson, began business. James Linton built a saw mill on Fall Creek just above the Crawfordsville road,—some of the timbers are still standing—and a grist mill for Isaac Wilson, on the same stream near where the old "Patterson Mill" was. It had no "bolt" however, and its flour had to be sifted—a very common necessity in those days, in the backwoods. James Blake put up the first frame and plastered house, just east of where the Masonic Hall now stands. Carter, Hopkins and Nowland, all had set up taverns, and Joseph C. Read opened a school. The first market was held in the circle. And thus the metropolis started in business.

One very serious annoyance to which the citizens were subjected was the mainte- nance of the jurisdiction of Connersville over them as a part of Delaware County, which embraced all the centre and north of the State, and was attached for judicial purposes to the White Water jurisdiction. Every case had to be tried on the White Water, and the expenses of attendance would eat up any ordinary demand. Probably the effect was beneficial in repressing litigation. But it was more serious in criminal cases, for prisoners could not well be taken sixty miles through the woods for trial without allowing them many chances of escape. To obviate these difficulties the Legislature, in January, 1821, authorized the appointment of two justices of the peace for the New Purchase, with an appeal to the Bartholomew Court. Under this authority Governor Jennings appointed John Maxwell, but after a few month's service he resigned, and James McIlvain was elected by the people and commissioned by the Governor. Calvin Fletcher, who arrived in the fall of 1821, was the only lawyer, luckily, or conflict might have made litigation. As it was Mr. Fletcher was virtually the squire, and a wise one. Having no jail the citizens had no better policy to pursue towards dangerous or troublesome offenders than to scare them off, and this they practiced with good effect.

An amusing incident is related by Mr. Brown in illustration. Four Kentucky boatmen came from the Bluffs to Indianapolis for a Christmas frolic. They soon got drunk enough to be riotous, and began tearing down a little shanty of a goggery kept by Daniel Larkins. The interference of the citizens was repelled with violent threats which drove them off. But the grocery was a vital institution, and the laws must not be outraged, so after consultation it was determined to take the rioters at all hazards. James Blake, who seems to have been a leader in all enterprises of "pith and moment," proposed to take the biggest and boldest himself if his associates would take the other three. It was agreed to and the capture effected. The prisoners were taken before Squire McIlvain, who fined them heavily, and in default of payment ordered them to the Connersville jail. The idea of being taken sixty miles, in the dead of winter through, an unbroken wilderness, was too much for their courage, and they made their escape in the night, the guard understanding that *that* was exactly what was wanted.

Running along with this current of social events and progress in 1821. was the laying out and formal founding of the capital.

The Commissioners appointed by the Legislature to survey the donation. make a plat of the proposed city, and sell the alternate lots, did not meet on the first Monday of April as ordered. Only Judge Christopher Harrison attended. But he proceeded at once to execute the order. He appointed Elias P. Fordham and Alexander Ralston, surveyors, and Benjamin I. Blythe, clerk. Mr. Blythe, who became a resident of the place and was afterwards agent for the sale of lots, was well known to all old resi- dents. Ralston was a resident also, and seems to have been the active and controlling man in the survey. He had, when young, assisted in the survey of Washington city, and to the ideas obtained in that work we are probably indebted for the plan of the city, and especially its wide and regular streets. He was a Scotchman, a bachelor, and had been concerned in Burr's expedition, the failure of which left him in the West, where he chose to remain. He died in 1827, and was buried in the "old grave yard," though nobody now knows where.

The "donation" of four sections was surveyed, a fraction on the west side of the river being added to fill out one of the sections from which a corner was cut off by the eastward bend of the river. In the centre of this tract a plat of one mile square was made for the capital. It may be remarked here, however, that the donation is not exactly in the centre of the State, nor is the old plat of the city exactly in the centre of the donation. The latter is a mile or two northwest of the centre of the State. The location of the city in the donation was determined mainly by the position of Pogue's Creek. To have put the city in the centre of the donation would have taken the creek too nearly through the middle of it, and the valley of that stream was a very uninviting locality in those days. To avoid it the plat was located further north and the centre placed at the circle. A beautiful little knoll further recommended this point.

On this central knoll a circle of about four acres was laid off as the starting point, and a street eighty feet wide thrown round it. From the extreme corners of the four adjacent squares, avenues were sent out to the northeast, northwest, southeast, and southwest. The first street south was made one hundred and twenty feet wide, and called "Washington" then, and is so called now, but for many years it was called "Main" street. The remainder of the square mile was laid off in regular squares of four hundred and twenty feet, separated by ninety feet streets following the cardinal points of the compass, and divided by alleys of thirty and fifteen feet, crossing each other at right angles in the centre. The boundary streets, East, West, North and South, were not included in the original survey. The Commissioner seems to have thought that nobody would ever live on the outside of the last line of squares and made no provision to reach any but the inside. These streets owe their existence to James Blake, who represented their importance to Commissioner Harrison, and he subsequently added them to the plat. The "out-blocks," or divisions of the donation outside the original plat, were made some time afterwards. Nobody dreamed that the young town could grow all over the old plat, the "out-lots," and a great deal of the country outside of both, as it has.

The surveys having been completed and mapped as required by law, the sale of alternate lots was advertised to be held on the tenth of October, by General John Carr, State Agent. At the appointed time it was held in a cabin occupied as a tavern by Matthias Nowland, a little west of the present line of the canal, on Washington street. Although the main settlement was on the river, as new settlements always are, the sickness that had hardly yet passed away convinced the people that they must move farther off, and river lots did not sell well. The sales lasted several days and three hundred and fourteen lots were sold for $35,596 25, of which one-fifth, $7,119 25 was paid down, the remainder to be paid in four equal annual instalments. The lot on the northwest corner of Delaware and Washington streets brought the highest price, $560, and one west of the State House square sold for the next highest price, $500. Prices generally ranged between $100 and $300.

The progress made in the disposal of the town site and the adjacent out-lots of the donation, gave but a feeble promise of the future growth of the town. After the first sales, lots, as the market phrase has it, were "dull and inactive." Of the three hundred and fourteen sold one hundred and sixty-nine were forfeited or exchanged for others. The reserved lots—only alternate lots were first sold—and those that had been forfeited, were offered for sale repeatedly, but unavailingly. Money was scarce, of course, as it always is, and the reputation of the town for health was bad. The capital, though assigned to the town, might be kept away for years, as it was. The outlook was unpromising. The growth was slow, so slow that as late as 1831, *three-fourths* of the town site and donation remained unsold. In that year the Legislature, by putting a minimum price of $10 upon the lots, managed to get rid of most of them,

and when the sales were closed in 1842, it was found that the whole of Indianapolis had brought but $125,000. Out of this fund, the State House, Court House, the Governor's House, in the circle, the Clerk's office, and Treasurer's house and office were paid for. The agency for the sale of city lots was held successively by General Carr, James Milroy, Bethuel F. Morris, Benjamin I. Blythe, Ebenezer Sharpe, John G. Brown, Thomas H. Sharpe and John Cook. It was then transferred to the State Auditor.

The city as thus sold out was a forest, except where a clearing here and there had opened the ground to the light.

To get the streets cleared it was proposed to give the timber to anybody who would cut it. A man by the name of Lismund Basye took the contract for Washington street, expecting to make a "good thing" of such a superb lot of timber trees, and then began to calculate. There were no mills and his trees were of no use without them, so he rolled his splendid logs together and burned them as well as his "fingers."

The year was closed by the inauguration of a county organization. The sales made by Judge Harrison were confirmed by the Legislature, and on the last day of the year 1821, an act was passed organizing Marion county, and attaching to it for judicial purposes the territory now constituting the counties of Johnson, Hamilton, Boone, Madison and Hancock. The present Court House Square was dedicated to judicial uses, and $8,000 appropriated to build a two story brick Court House, fifty feet square, to be completed in three years, and used by the State, Federal and County Courts, and by the Legislature for fifty years, or until a State House should be built. Two per cent of the lot fund was set apart for a County Library. William W. Wick was elected the first Judge of the Circuit Court, and Hervey Bates appointed the first sheriff. Both came out early in the following year, 1822.

Chapter II.

THE beginning of the year 1822, is a convenient point from which to glance at the situation and prospects of the city. The capital had been located, the town named, its plan completed, enough of its lots sold and population collected to warrant it against dying of inanition, and the political existence of the county had just been recognized and a place within the law given it. It was ready for emigration and emigrants were ready for elections, though no representation in the Legislature had been allowed. The town was a fact, but an almost imperceptible one in the dense and limitless woods into which it had crawled. It made little more change in the face of the region than the boring of a few grubs makes in a white oak log. Scattered cabins seemed to have dropped down with no order or purpose, thickening a little near the river, and thickening still more toward the East, but they marked no street except the line of Washington, which still bore dismal testimony to the fate of Basye's speculation in timber. It was crowded with stumps and heaps of logs and limbs, which, in places, the close undergrowth of hazel, spice brush and pawpaw made impervious to all penetration. To travel along it was impossible; to cross it, except by long and devious ways, very difficult; to see across it a feat of little easier performance than looking through a stone wall. Mr. Brown notices that a spectator standing in the door of Hawkins's tavern (old Capital House site) could not see a house where Hubbard's block is on the corner of Washington and Meridian streets. No other street was visible at all, or only by patches of ineffectual clearing. Neighbors went from house to house through paths as hard to follow as a cow track in White River bottom. One could walk right over the places where are now depots, churches and four story houses, but he had to bend out of the way an intrusive root, or an inconvenient log. It is hardly a score of years since the last vestiges of this troublesome thicket disappeared, and on Pogue's Creek, near West street, there are still some honey locusts surviving the destruction.

The means of communication between the town and other portions of the State were no better than those between neighbors in the town. There were no roads. The river was useless except for such trading as necessity might create with the Indians; and the Cumberland, or National, Road, though on its way westward, came slowly and was by no means certain of being able to come beyond the Ohio State line at all. For the government was building it by contract with Ohio, with money reserved from the proceeds of public land sales in that State, and when the contract should be finished at the western boundary, there was no power to go further, except by such a construction of the Constitution as would, and did, arouse one of the warmest and most protracted political controversies in our national history, and ended by dropping the tail of the road in the mud a little west of Big Eagle Creek. The

State Legislature petitioned Congress for a continuance of the road through the newly chosen capital, within two days after the choice had been confirmed, but no attention was given the request. It was not till about Christmas, 1828, when Hon. Oliver H. Smith, then a representative in Congress from the White Water district of this State, by a resolution directing a continuance of the road westward beyond the limit of the contract with Ohio, woke up the sleeping lion of party conflict, that attention was effectively called to the matter. Even then, but for Hon. William McLean, of Ohio, the road would have left Indianapolis a tier of counties to the north, for Mr. Smith's resolution directed the "existing location to be followed" and that was tending southward. Mr. McLean changed the direction "from Zanesville, through Columbus," and sent it to this place. But this really great (for that day) work came too late to relieve the necessities of the mud and wood bound town. We got but little good of it till 1838, and by that time, though it was the only good road we had, railroads were acquiring too firm a grasp of public feeling and hope to allow its indisputable value to encourage the improvement of other roads. Its direct advantage beyond macadamizing Washington street, was not at all equal to the anticipations of the citizens. It became a thoroughfare for emigration to the Mississippi and beyond, but it left here little of the deposit that was borne along by its current. It did a vast deal for the West but not much for Indianapolis.

There were other roads, or rather places for them, laid out to the Ohio and Whitewater rivers by the Legislature, in the winter of 1821–2, and one hundred thousand dollars appropriated to build them, and still others were asked for by a petition of the citizens in the fall of 1822, but all were little better than none till long after the town had ceased to be dependent upon them. The "Michigan State Road" from the Ohio river to the new capital through Greensburg, was one of these, and at the lower end it was made a very good road, but the upper end was mud or "cross way," impassable in winter and intolerable in summer. The Madison road through Franklin and Columbus was even worse. So were all the Northern lines to Pendleton, Noblesville and Crawfordsville. And so they remained till neighborhood thrift and convenience gravelled or planked them into passability. It needs no very long memory to recall the merchant's journey to Cincinnati, consuming double the time and ten fold the comfort of a trip now to New York; or the voyages of goods wagons quite equal to an Atlantic voyage now; in the days when the Stucks, Lemasters, Perrys and their associates ruled transportation with the wagon whip as absolutely as Vanderbilt or Fisk can do with their tariffs; and those who can recall those days and scenes can easily understand what the isolation of Indianapolis was when it had no roads at all. Attempts to improve the river were made at intervals for years, but never accomplished anything but a demonstration that nothing could be done at all except upon a scale unlikely to be attempted.

The town was hidden and out of reach. We who see it the greatest railroad centre on the earth, accessible from more directions and to greater numbers than any other city that ever existed, find it hard to understand the motives that could have impelled the settlers of this period to try to get to it. Immediate profit they could not count upon, for there were no mines or promises of unusual development. Whatever they got they knew they would have to get by hard work or shrewd management, as they could anywhere else. Real estate promised a poor speculation, even in an embryo capital to which access was difficult always and almost impossible for half the year, and where sickness and starvation were visitors of most unpleasant frequency. There was not much to look to as remuneration for a great deal that must be endured. Whether it was a higher motive than personal advantage, or merely an irrepressible feeling of unrest, that sent our first settlers here, it is certain that if the upbuilding of the town had depended upon similar efforts of their descendants and successors it would have remained unbuilt. It is not necessary to look for greater virtues among pioneers than among their children to account for their contented endurance of privations, or ready daring of danger; but more striking virtues we certainly shall find. Doubtless we of this day have qualities better suited to our times, and an average of endowments and deficiencies of one generation would probably differ but little from that of the other, but those of the pioneers, whatever they were, were not ours. That is certain. No other town in the State has had to encounter so many and so serious obstacles to improvement. Those which once rivalled it had infinite advantages, either in navigable streams or easy access to other settlements. Indianapolis had nothing, and lay among hostile Indians where scalps were little safer than they are now on the slopes of the Rocky Mountains. Isolation, sickness and endless forests were serious drawbacks to a town that offered no better inducements than could be found in every township of the State. There is no just parallel between it and the cities of the far West that have sprouted out of the gold traffic. Great risks for great gains are frequent enough anywhere, and nowhere more frequent than at the faro table. There were no such chances and no such efforts here, yet no gold town can show a history of greater difficulties surmounted by more indomitable resolution.

The population at the beginning of 1822, numbering not far from five hundred, was quite as well provided with mechanical and professional skill as any young town could be, and there was very little, if any, admixture of the fierce ruffianism too often nourished by remote settlements and unforgotten Indian cruelties. All were workers, and if there were any drones they were not troublesome as well as useless. The condition of the town is exhibited accurately enough in a paragraph of one of the earliest copies of the first newspaper published here. Forty dwellings had been built during the past year; several workshops had been erected, and two saw mills and a grist mill were in operation in the vicinity, while others were in course of construction. There were thirteen carpenters, four cabinet makers, eight blacksmiths, four shoemakers, two tailors, one hatter, two tanners, one saddler, one cooper, four bricklayers, two merchants, three grocers, four doctors, three lawyers, one preacher, one teacher, and seven tavern keepers. The number of the last class seems to indicate a tendency towards speculating on the possession of the Legislature for three months in the year. There could have been but very few of the adult male population outside of this list of sixty-one working men.

In the remote and almost inaccessible situation of the little community, the want of postal facilities was, next to the supply of the necessaries of life, most keenly felt, and one of its first efforts, after settling into the form and substance of a village, was to open communication with the world they had left. A meeting of the citizens was held at Hawkins's tavern, on the thirtieth of January, to establish a private mail, which, inefficient as it must be, was better than the chance of trusting to new emigrants or occasional visitors to carry letters. A postmaster, whose chief duty was mail carrying, was chosen, in Mr. Aaron Drake, and he notified postmasters to forward Indianapolis matter to Connersville, where he would receive it and take it to its destination. He heralded his first arrival by an uproarious blowing of his horn, and though it was after nightfall the people turned out in mass to welcome him and his budget of news. The government, in a few weeks, completed the work thus irresponsibly begun, and in February sent Samuel Henderson as a regularly commissioned

(2)

postmaster, to displace Mr. Drake's enterprise. He opened his office on the seventh of March, and a month after published the first list of five uncalled for letters, a number indicating, with about equal clearness, a meagre correspondence and an eager inquiry for what there was. Henderson held the place till 1831. The office was moved about with the changes made by the growth of the town, but was, on the whole, much less vagrant than might have been anticipated even by those who could have forseen the stages in its course to its present magnitude. It was first kept near where the canal now runs, that then being a half-way point between the earlier settlement on the river and the later and larger to the eastward. It was next kept in Henderson's tavern, on the site of Glenn's block; then in what used to be called "Union Row," a line of two story brick buildings of surpassing splendor for that day, of which John Cain, the postmaster, owned one and put his office in it; later in the building on the west side of Meridian street, near Washington, now incorporated in "Hubbard's Block;" at one time it was kept on the west side of Pennsylvania street, in the same building with the JOURNAL office, and a fire which broke out in the Washington street front of the block endangered it greatly; subsequently it was removed to Blackford's building on the east side of Meridian street, opposite to a former location, and there it remained till its removal to the building which the government erected expressly for it. Of the history of its business more will be said in another place.

Almost simultaneously with the establishment of the first mail came the first newspaper of the town. It was issued on the twenty-eighth of January, and announced that its owners and editors were George Smith and Nathaniel Bolton. The former was rather a conspicuous character aside from the notoriety attaching to a magnate of the press. He wore a queue carefully tied with an eel skin string. The "old settlers" believed fully that some sort of virtue lay in such a string that no twine or strip of buckskin could boast. Old women always tied their "back hair" with eel skin, and many an eel has died a victim to this fancy that might have lived till now if only sought for his meat. Mr. Smith, moreover, had a most sonorous sneeze, which, to all the inhabitants in the vicinity of his residence on the corner of Georgia and Tennessee streets, where the Catholic institutions now stand, proclaimed the early dawn as regularly as cock-crow, and could be heard nearly as far as the arsenal gun. He was a man of some eccentricity of character, and esteemed of a rather intellectual cast in that day of material interests and influences. Mr. Bolton is better known as the first husband of Mrs. Sarah T. Bolton, not unfrequently called the "poetess of Indiana," and, unquestionably, for many years more widely known than any other literary personage in the State. He was State Librarian at one time, and subsequently Consul at the city of Geneva, Switzerland. He was more or less connected with the press for many years, but though a man of sound sense and fair attainments, he never made a very broad mark either on the press, or, through it, on the public. The first office of the *Gazette*, was a cabin near where the present Fifth Ward school stands on Maryland street. It was soon changed to the site of the Metropolitan Theatre; and thence to a building near Pennsylvania street on Washington; and later to a one-story brick on the site of Temperance Hall, which became afterwards a theatre, and the headquarters of recruiting for the Mexican war.

Very few papers have encountered or withstood greater difficulties so early in life. Its ink was compound of tar, and realized the printer's description of a paper "worked with swamp mud on a cider press." It appeared as it had a chance, for the lack of mails made it difficult to gather matter, and as for local news every tongue told that to every ear, and the accidental paper must have been as empty as a last year's bird's nest. Seven numbers were published between the twenty-eighth of January and the fourth of May, an average of one every two weeks. After that the roads and mails enabled it to appear regularly. A notice of the press of the city will give further information in regard to it, its rivals and the successors of both.

Following closely after the first mail and the first paper, came the first election. The county had been organized, but it had no officers, except the Judge and Sheriff, who served by appointment of the Governor. On the 22d of February Hervey Bates, the Sheriff, issued a proclamation ordering the election on the first of April following, of two Associate Judges, a Clerk, Recorder, and three Commissioners, and designating polling places, which show what a very extensive county we had then. One was in the town at the house of General Carr, the State Agent for the sale of town lots, on Delaware street, opposite the present county offices; one at John Finch's, near Conner's settlement, four miles south of Noblesville; one at John Page's, Strawtown, in the northern part of what is now Hamilton county; one at John Berry's, Anderson, now Madison county; and one at William McCartney's, on Fall Creek, near Pendleton. The list of candidates would have shamed even the formidable array of names that "Many Friends" announce every two years at this day. For Judges, James Page, Robert Patterson, James McIlvain, Eliakim Harding, John Smock, and Rev. John McClung announced themselves. For Clerk, James M. Ray, Milo R. Davis, Morris Morris, Thomas Anderson, and John W. Redding. For Recorder, Alexander Ralston, Joseph C. Reed, Aaron Drake, John Givan (still living), John Hawkins, William Vandegrift, and William Townsend. For County Board there were about five candidates for each of the three memberships. In a voting population of three hundred and thirty, a list of thirty-three candidates indicates that if there is any difference, we have degenerated a little from the ambition of our predecessors. Partisan differences, though resting on no questions of policy, were pretty well marked, and followed the line of nativity closely. Kentucky and Whitewater, represented by Morris Morris and James M. Ray, were the contestants, and they fought as eagerly, though hardly so unscrupulously, as later rivals for the same offices. Every voter was brought out, and pretty nearly every one was taken back drunk. In respect of temperance, later elections are a decided improvement on those of the first twenty years of our history. The Kentuckians were mainly the sufferers, from too recent residence to be entitled to a vote, and Whitewater was victorious. James M. Ray became the first County Clerk; Joseph C. Reed, the first schoolmaster, became first County Recorder; John T. Osborn, John McCormack and William McCartney first Commissioners; and Eliakim Harding and James McIlvain, first Associate Judges. James M. Ray got 217 votes, out of an entire poll of 336 in the county. At the Indianapolis precinct, 224 votes were cast, of which something over 100 belonged to the "donation." The vote shows that some addition had been made to the adult population of the town since the *Gazette's* list appeared. In August, the election for Governor was held, and William Hendricks received 315 votes, out of 317. Harvey Bates was then elected Sheriff, and George Smith, Coroner.

The County Board organized on the 15th of April, and formed thirteen townships—Pike, Washington, Lawrence, Wayne, Center, Warren, Decatur, Perry and Franklin, as at present, with four others in the outlying portions of the county—Fall Creek, Anderson, White River and Delaware. Some of these were attached to the administration of larger townships for a time. In Center, Wilkes Reagan, Obed Foote and Lismund Basye were elected Justices on the 23d of May.

The first term of Court commenced on the 26th of September, and the session was first held in Carr's Cabin, already alluded to. Judge W. W. Wick presided, assisted by his new associates Harding and McIlvain; Clerk Ray produced his first docket as

Clerk; Hervey Bates introduced business with the first official "Oyez," as sheriff; and Calvin Fletcher acted, by appointment, as the first Prosecutor. The Court, after organizing, adjourned to Crambaugh's house, west of the Canal, and there tried the first case, Daniel Bowman vs. Meridy Edwards. Richard Good, late of Ireland, was naturalized. The Grand Jury returned twenty-two indictments, six of them for unlicensed liquor-selling; and John Hawkins was granted a license to keep a tavern and sell liquor. As debtors were then liable to imprisonment, "bounds" were fixed, which allowed unfortunate poverty a chance to move about, but confined it to certain streets.

The appropriation of $8,000 and a square of ground, made by the Legislature, for a Court House, was first applied by the County Commissioners on the 22d of May, when a call was made for a plan of the proposed building. That of John E. Baker and James Paxton was selected, and the contract for erection awarded them in September. What the plan was could be seen a few weeks ago. The work was begun the following summer, and completed in the fall of 1824, at a cost of $14,000. At the same session of the County Board, Mr. Sheriff Bates was directed to procure proposals for a jail, and for clearing the Court House square. The latter was done partly by the axe and partly by the wind. A fine selection of large trees was left standing when the forest was cut away, but they were blown and broken off so badly that it was thought best to clean them out entirely. The jail, of hewed logs, two stories high, was finished early in the fall. It stood on the northwest corner of the square, a little north of the present temporary Court House. It was burned in 1833, by a negro, who a short time before had paraded the streets riding on the back of a buffalo, to the amazement of all the school children, and distinguished by a red morocco band on his cap, and the name of "Buffalo Bill." He was not burned in the jail, but it would have been little matter if he had been. A new brick jail, so long identified with Andrew Smith, Deputy Sheriff and Jailer, and with Mr. Mattingly, was then built east of the old Court House, on Alabama street, and enlarged in 1845 by an addition made of three concentric courses of hewed logs, each a foot thick, the middle one crossing the others transversely, and making quite as safe a prison, except against fire, as any stone or brick contrivance yet attempted. Both gave place, in 1852, to the present costly and inadequate structure. The Court House will soon be replaced by the building, a cut of which forms the frontispiece to this volume.

Along with other interesting first observances or inaugurations, that of the first Fourth of July celebration deserves notice. It had been arranged at a meeting at Hawkins' tavern two weeks before, and was held on the old "Military Ground," where subsequently the "Bloody Three Hundred" rendezvoused for the Black Hawk expedition. Rev. John McClung preached a sermon from Proverbs xiv. and 34, Judge Wick read the Declaration of Independence, prefaced with some appropriate remarks, and 'Squire Obed Foote read Washington's Inaugural Address, John Hawkins read the Farewell Address, and Rev. Robert Brenton, with a benediction, dismissed the meeting to a barbecue of a buck, which Robert Harding had killed the day before in the north part of the donation. The banquet was enlivened with whisky, and toasts and speeches by Dr. Mitchell and Major Redding, and the whole affair concluded with a ball at Crumbaugh's.

Militia musters were deemed important in those days, and not a few of our statesmen have won their way to national prominence through the popularity first gained with a militia plume or epaulet. James Paxton was the first Colonel of the regiment assigned to this section of the State—the Fortieth; Samuel Morrow Lieutenant Colonel, and Alexander W. Russell, Major. These titles clung to their victims to the last day of their lives, except where they were changed, as in Russell's case, for a higher one.

The first camp meeting was held for three days, beginning on the 12th of September, by Rev. James Scott, the first Methodist preacher of the town, who was sent here by the St. Louis conference. During the fall one of those singular phenomena of animal instinct, a migration of squirrels, took place. The town was filled with them, and myriads crossed the river, a feat which, except in these monstrous processions, squirrels rarely attempt. Another occurred in 1848, within the memory of many now living, when the animals were seen frequently in the remoter streets and shot out of shade trees.

Though the health of the town had been better than during the preceding year, and not worse than that of western villages usually was in those days, the ill repute of the universal prostration of 1821 clogg d its progress. The unsold lots remained unsold, and many that had been sold showed signs of a coming forfeiture. Times were hard, as they always are in a new country, and the list of tax delinquencies much longer in proportion than it is now, for sums ranging from a quarter of a dollar to three dollars, showed it unmistakably. Men who hold lots for a speculation, as well as those who hold for homes, do not willingly incur the liabilities of a tax sale. To encourage settlement, even on probation, the Legislature, early in January, authorized the unsold lots to be sold upon condition that they were cleared within four months. The tract on the west side of the river (thrown in to make up the complete four square miles of the Government donation), though it promised rather better than it does now, was thought so unlikely of settlement as a town, that it was leased in lots big enough for moderate farms, ranging from five to twenty acres. A lease was also made for three years of the ferry across White River. It ran very nearly across from the foot of Washington street to the opposite bank, some hundred yards below the National Road bridge. Two acres were also author, ized to be sold for a brick yard. Whatever may have been the effect of these encouragements, there is but one of them that has left a trace to our day, and that is the last. The brick yard furnished the material for the first brick building erected in the city, and it is standing yet, opposite the no:th end of the Post Office, on the north side of Market street. It was erected by John Johnson, begun in 1822, and completed in about a year. The first two-story frame was erected in the spring of this year, by James Linton, on Washington street, near the alley east of the Metropolitan Theatre. For a number of years it was stored full of old documents, and was occupied sometimes for public offic s, but a portion of the time as a book-bindery. The cellar under it caved in, on the street side as well as on the other, and the hogs used to wallow there. Then it was abandoned, or used for any chance purpose that it suited, till about 1840, when it was repaired and additions made to it, and a tavern for a long time known as the "Buck Tavern," from its sign, was kept there by Mr. Armstrong. It was burned down in 1847. A market house was placed in the circle grove in the spring of 1822, but was soon transferred to the present East Market place.

Though the town was the chosen capital of the State, the county had no representation in the Legislature. A petition to obtain it was adopted by a meeting in the fall, and an effort made to obtain a weekly mail from the actual capital, Corydon, by way of Vernon. Neither met with success, nor did a later effort to have the town incorporated. The citizens were not agreed about it, and no further steps were taken in that direction for ten years.

Chapter III.

Second Paper—Legislative Election—Improvements—First Drama—First Church and Sunday School — Order to Remove the Capital — the Indian Murder—Great Freshet.

THE beginning of the year 1823 was signalized by the admission of the county to the Legislature, and the preparations for the election in the following August. Two newspapers are, of course, essential to any well regulated political contest, and as there was but one (the *Gazette*), when the contest opened, another became inevitable and appeared on the 7th of March. It was called " *The Western Censor and Emigrant's Guide*," with that peculiar inverse proportion of length of name to intrinsic value that distinguishes young country newspapers everywhere. Harvey Gregg and Douglass Maguire were the proprietors and editors. Mr. Gregg has passed from the memory of all but a very few of the present generation, but he was known as a lawyer of decided ability, and like his rival, Mr. Smith, of some personal eccentricity. Mr. Maguire is still well remembered by many as one of our prominent citizens, a capable and faithful State officer (Auditor,) a true friend, and a most kindly and genial gentleman, though irritable withal, easily vexed and as easily placated. His connection with the paper, in one capacity or another, continued till 1835, but that of Mr. Gregg terminated in 1824. Mr. G. was succeeded by John Douglass, then recently from Corydon, the capital, where he had been printer to the State, Mr. Maguire acting as editor. Early in 1825 the name was changed to the " *Indiana Journal*," which it still retains, and seems likely to retain as long as a newspaper shall be published in Indianapolis. Samuel Merrill subsequently became editor. His successors and the changes in proprietorship will be noticed under their proper head.

The *Censor and Guide* took the political path that finally led to whigism, as the *Gazette's* did to Democracy; but this was the "era of good feeling," as it has been called, when parties were in a transition state, solidifying from the break up of the old Federal and Democratic parties into the future Whig and Democratic parties, and differences were less defined and less bitter then than they have become since. Parties had not been disciplined to the accuracy and unanimity of movement of armies, even where parties were distinctly formed, and elections were in a good degree contests of personal popularity. No man knew exactly what anybody else believed about politics, and was not always clear as to what he believed himself, or whom he agreed with, and his choice was naturally enough decided by personal inclination. Electioneering, though a less expensive, was a more delicate, operation than now, when a nomination gives a candidate about all the strength that any quantity of ability and personal popularity can gain. The solidity of parties is too great to be easily affected by any individual quality. But in that day a man carried himself, consequently the " ingratiating " element came powerfully into play, and was aided by the paucity of voters which made a personal acquaintance with every one not only possible but easy. The day of child-kissing, dinner-eating, wife-flattering electioneering is pretty well over now; but in 1823 and for many a year afterwards, it was a candidate's " best hold," and a good fiddler or " go d fellow"—pretty much the same thing—has beaten a good orator and a sound legislator more than once. But these were the exceptions then, as the choice of really incompetent over competent men is the exception and not the rule, whatever their personal acceptability may be, in all intelligent communities. The election made our first legislators of two men who would have done credit to any State. James Gregory of Shelby, was our Senator, and Col Paxton our Representative.

The vote showed that the town was gaining but little. At the preceding August election, when Hendricks was chosen Governor, 317 votes were cast in this county. The total vote was now but 270. *The Censor* estimated the population of the town at 600, probably quite as much as a census would have made good. A year had done nothing but settle and fix the elements already collected. But improvements were made, and a look of age and steadiness was gradually coming upon the callow capital. A woolen mill was set in operation in Wilson's mill, by Townsend & Pierce, in June. Woolen manufactures in the form of a supply of yarn for socks and thread for linsey and jeans, are among the first efforts of young communities, and apt to appear beside or close after the saw and grist mill. In this unpretending form they are as significant of a pioneer, as their larger successors are of the wealthy and well-grown, community. A new "tavern"—for the dignity of "hotel" was not claimed by the primitive establishments of those days—was built by Thomas Carter, on Washington street, opposite the Court house. It was burned in 1825, during the first session of the Legislature held in the capital. A still larger and more famous tavern was erected about the same time by James Blake and Samuel Henderson, the Post master, on the site of "Glenn's Block." It was called "Washington Hall," a name which was perpetuated by its brick successor, till the demands of business and the rise of more pretentious hotels supplanted it. Henderson's old frame was moved eastward in 1836, to make way for the brick building, and was long occupied as a shoe and tailor shop, and by Gov. Wallace as a law office. Gramling's block stands in its place now. In another place will be found a fuller notice of our early hotels. These preparations for the Legislature were not indications of equal activity in improvements in all directions. Washington street was still encumbered with trees, and the others were only chopped out in places. The town was mainly a collection of illy cleared farms, reached by cow paths; still, it seems, by the complaints of the *Censor*, to have provoked the envy or rivalry of other towns, though for what, it is not easy to see.

But the prospect of the acquisition of the capital exerted a sort of metropolitan influence, and the close of the year brought the first Theatrical entertainment ever witnessed in Indianapolis. It was given in Carter's tavern, on the night of Wednesday, the 31st of December, and consisted of the "Doctor's Courtship or the Indulgent Father," and the farce of the "Jealous Lovers." Price of admission thirty-seven and a half cents. In deference to the religious notions of the people Mr. Carter insisted on the performance only of serious music, "hymn tunes" and the like, by the single fiddle that constituted the orchestra. Several performances were given with, we are left to infer, moderate success, as the "enterprising manager," Mr. Smith—unhappily his first name is not known, or it was ".John" and might as well have not been any name at all—came back next year, and repeated the experiment with less success, as he ran off without paying the printer. The *Censor* intimated on the return of Mr. Smith in 1824, that popular feeling was not prepared for the levity of theatrical exhibitions, though its own opinion was not adverse to them. This hint explains Mr. Carter's incongruous selection of "serious music." It was a compromise between scruple and curiosity.

The religious sentiment among the early settlers of the West, even when no profession of religion was made, was always strong, and never yielded to fashionable solicitations or the hints of "Mrs. Grundy." As already noticed, the circle grove was used as a meeting house for the first attendants on public worship, and a camp meeting was held in 1822, by the Methodists, east of town; but though several denominations were fairly represented, no church edifice was erected till this year of 1823. The Presbyterians, early in the spring, held a meeting, and took steps both for a church organization and building. The former was completed in July, and the latter, at a cost of $1200 for building and lot, in the year following, though the frame was raised pretty nearly simultaneously with the congregation. It stood, till some ten or twelve years ago, where it was first placed, on Pennsylvania street, about midway of the square north of Market, on the west side. It was regularly occupied till superceded by an $8,000 brick structure, on the north-east corner of Circle and Market streets, where The JOURNAL office now stands. Both have had to make way for increased congregations and the necessities of trade, and are now represented by the superb edifice on the corner of New York and Pennsylvania streets.

This year was further marked, in its religious development, by the organization of the first Sunday School, as well as the first church. It met on March 6, in the cabinet shop of Caleb—or, as he was better known, "Squire"—Scudder, on the Washington street side of the State House Square. No attempt was made to introduce denominational differences. It was a Union School, so called, and so in fact. Its anniversary has been often celebrated with much interest, no inconsiderable number of the first scholars being still alive to relate their experiences. The attendance averaged about forty during the first year; but it was a sort of luxury not deemed necessary to be kept up through the winter, and on the approach of cold weather it was suspended till the following spring. It re-appeared on its first anniversary, and never was suspended again. After the completion of the Presbyterian church in 1824, it was held there, and continued there till the growth of other churches, and the obtrusion of denominational feelings, called off first one colony and then another, leaving to the old place little more than its Presbyterian collection. The Methodist school was separately organized April 24th, 1829, and the Baptist in 1832. After that each church formed its Sunday school to itself. But the Union lived alone six years, as useful an institution as ever was established anywhere. From an average attendance of forty the first year, it rose to an hundred an fifty before the Methodist "swarm" left the "old hive," and had a library of one hundred and fifty volumes of the now long-forgotten marble-paper covered books of the type of the "Shepherd of Salisbury Plain." To this union of Sunday schools we owe the long-prevalent fashion of celebrating the Fourth of July by a procession of all the Sunday school scholars of the town, a march to some convenient grove, reading the Declaration of Independence, a speech by some prominent lawyer or public man, and a dinner of "rusks" and water. This celebration continued till the excitement of the war banished it utterly, and it has never been replaced by any general observance. The Fourth of July in the capital has disappeared except as an idle holiday, or the occasion for some Society's pic-nic. But in 1823 the day was the great day of the year. Everybody celebrated it. A barbecue was made by Wilkes Reagan, at his residence on Market street, near the creek. Rev-

STATE AND SUPREME COURT OFFICES

Ehrgott & Krebs Lith Cincinnati

D. C. Proctor, the Presbyterian pastor, and the first regular pastor in the town, officiated as chaplain, Daniel B. Wick as reader, and Morris Morris as orator. Rev. Isaac Read closed with a benediction. The "barbecue," or roasting of a deer or beef whole, was the staple entertainment of all public assemblages of these early days. Political barbecues were frequent, and the reader may remember the noted one given on the occasion of the visit of Henry Clay in 1842, in Gov. Noble's pasture, east of town. That was about the last of those old-time festivities.

In the spring an organization of physicians was formed called the Indiana Central Medical Society, with Dr. S. G. Mitchell as president, and Dr. Livingston Dunlap as secretary. Its purpose seems to have embraced one point more than its successor of this day; for under the law of that day doctors were licensed, and this association was authorized to examine applicants and issue licenses.

Although, at the beginning of 1824, the rather disproportionate amount of hotels to other improvements indicated an expectation of the removal of the capital, the change was held off by several influences—the inaccessibility of the town, its reputed bad health, its lack of suitable buildings or any at all sufficient for the Legislature, and not least, probably, by the fact that until the session of 1824 the new county of Marion had no representative in that body. But when Senator Gregory and Representative Paxton took their places, attention was effectively directed to the matter, and on the 28th of January, 1824, an act was passed transferring the seat of Government to Indianapolis, ordering the removal, under the direction of Samuel Merrill, State Treasurer, of the offices and archives, by the 10th of January following, and fixing that day for the meeting of the Legislature in the new capitol, the unfinished Court house. This was final as far as authority went, and the transfer needed nothing but a wagon or two to be complete. Our members, upon their return home after the adjournment of the Legislature were given a complimentary banquet at Washington Hall, at which the usual enthusiastic anticipations were indulged, with the unusual fortune, however, of being at once above and below the truth. So far as the influence of the acquisition of the capital went—and the banqueters, of course, thought of no other—hope ran high over the reality. So far as the ultimate growth and importance of the city, independent of the capital, was indicated, the reality has outrun the wildest anticipations. The enthusiasm climbed too high to see clearly what was at its feet, and not high enough to see what lay a half century away. The interval, till the momentous wagon with Mr. Merrill's boxes of papers arrived, was filled up with some improvements, and some incidents that deserve to be remembered.

The streets were still in course of being opened to the light, and the Court house, a school house, the Presbyterian church, and a building for the State offices, were going up. The population had shifted considerably, and while the county grew daily larger and stronger, the town stood pretty nearly where the impetus given by the lot sales had left it. Emigrants made it a stopping place where they could look about and choose a location, and thus many came who did not stay. A census taken by the Union Sunday School Visitors—the first of a series of rather useless statistics that were regularly collected for many years—indicated that the "Donation" contained about one hundred families, an average population of six hundred, of which one hundred and seventy-two were voters, and forty-five were unmarried women.

This was not a very formidable strength if a collision should occur with the Shawnees, whom the excellence of the hunting grounds still retained near their old town on Fall Creek, in Madison county. A war could hardly be said to have been possible, but a "row" certainly was; and the town was easier to hurt, and had more to lose, than its possible assailants. Consequently a feeling of insecurity was never entirely allayed, and it was sometimes excited to a painful degree. The worst and last of these alarms occurred on the 22d of March, 1824. This was the murder of nine Seneca or Shawnee Indians, two men, one named Ludlow, three women, two boys and two girls, by five whites, Harper, Sawyer and his son, Bridge and his son, and Hudson. Hon. Oliver H. Smith, in his "Early Indiana Sketches," gives an account of the affair, and the serious commotion it excited even as far as the national seat of Government. These Indians had encamped a short time before eight miles above Pendelton, the seat of the then recently organized county of Madison, and were watched with the usual disquietude of the whites. They had been hunting and trapping only a week, Mr. Smith says, and were just ready to catch the raccoons as they issued from their winter holes to hunt frogs in the newly thawed swamps and streams. But their collection of furs excited the cupidity of Harper, who, doubtless, as did most frontiersmen, also retained the memory of some injury inflicted by the Indians to aggravate his hate, and he led his companions into the scheme to massacre the party and take their peltries. They entered the camp under the pretext of hunting their horses, and got the Indians to go out with them to help in the search. Harper took one Indian with him and Hudson took the other, and each cruelly shot his companion dead within hearing of the women and children. The whole party then went back to the camp, where Sawyer shot one of the squaws and Bridge and his son shot the other two. The children were shot with the same fiendish deliberation, but the oldest boy not being quite dead when found, Sawyer took him by the legs and knocked his brains out against a log. The bodies were thrown into a pond, where the settlers found them next day, one of the women still showing signs of life. The camp was robbed, and the murderers escaped, but not long. Harper got away to Ohio, and in those days, at such a distance, he was as safe as he would be now in Europe, and he never was caught. The others were, and caught again after an escape in July.

This terrible crime produced serious apprehensions. The people in the vicinity took refuge in the Pendleton mills, and the authorities thought it necessary to take especial measures to placate the Indians. Col. John Johnston, the Indian Agent at Piqua, Ohio, and Mr. William Conner were dispatched on a mission of conciliation. They assured the tribes that the murderers should be punished, and obtained a promise from the chief that nothing hostile should be done till they saw what the "Great Father" would do. Whatever might have been the laxity of popular notions of justice to Indians, in this case there was no escape from a rigid adherence to the law. The Government employed General James Noble, then United States Senator, to assist Calvin Fletcher, the prosecutor, in the prosecution, and General Noble brought with him his son-in-law, Philip Sweetser, a name well known in after years at the bar of Indianapolis and in the Legislature. Nearly all the prominent men of the bar were retained for the defense, among them Mr. Smith mentions Harvey Gregg, editor of the *Censor*, Lot Bloomfield, James Rariden, Charles H. Test, Daniel B. Wick, and William R. Morris, of this State, and General Sampson Mason, and Moses Vance, of Ohio. Hudson was indicted and tried in November, "in a new log building, with a puncheon floor," in Pendleton, before Judge Wick, with Associate Judges Samuel Holliday and Adam Winchell, the latter a blacksmith, who ironed the prisoners on their arrest. Mr. Smith states that W. R. Morris, for the defense, moved for a habeas corpus for the prisoners when the case was called, Judge Wick being absent. Judge Winchell, after questioning the propriety of the motion, refused it flatly with the quaint remark, "It would do you no good to bring out the prisoners. I ironed them mself, and you will never get them irons off' until they have been tried, habeas corpus or no habeas corpus." Hudson was convicted and hung in the winter, a number of Indians attending the execution. This is memorable as the *first* instance in the history of the United States of the legal execution of a white man for killing an Indian. The elder Bridge and Sawyer were hung in the following June. Young Saywer escaped with a verdict of manslaughter, and young Bridge was pardoned by Gov. James Brown Ray, an event which is still remembered as an illustration of the eccentricities of that able but wayward man. It is said that when young Bridge was placed under the rope that had hung his father, Gov. Ray, who had given no intimation of his startling design, mounted the scaffold, and after a speech on the enormity of the crime and its danger to the peace of the community, announced directly to the condemned, "No power now remains but that of the Almighty and the Executive of Indiana, to save your life," and announced to the people his pardon. The Indians were content with the justice of the whites, and gave no further trouble. Indeed, from that time Indian alarms, on any account whatever, ceased.

The spring of this murder was unusually wet, and the river rose enormously, higher than has ever been known since, except in 1828. The flood of 1847, the next highest, was not thought by Mr. Nathaniel Cox (who was thoroughly familiar with the river,) to have been quite so high. In the sparsely settled state of the country such an overflow was rather interesting than alarming, and a keel boat called the "Dandy" increased the interest the town took in the event by coming up with a load of backwoods necessaries, whisky and salt. But neither the freshet, nor the excitement caused by the Indian massacre, stopped the slow movement of such enterprises as were attempted, and religion received a full share of whatever effort was made. The Methodists held their first quarterly meeting in the Presbyrian church on the 25th of May, under James Scott, a missionary sent out, as before stated, by the St. Louis Conference in 1821. Before this the meetings had been semi-occasional gatherings, as zeal and opportunity suggested, and held at private houses. Camp meetings had been collected every year, but still the Methodist growth demanded something fixed in the fashion of settled religious communities. But though they organized their church in.1824 they were not able to get a house till the next year, when they built on Maryland street east of Meridian. In secular affairs it is to be noticed that a military school was opened in January by a Major Sullinger, for the instruction of militia officers and soldiers,—an enterprise that would seem to be about as urgently demanded as a teacher of painting in a blind asylum. A real estate agency was also established this year, by W. C. McDougal, but that seems to have been nearly as far ahead of the times as the premature West Point. But the country, as before remarked, was filling up, new farms were appearing, trade growing, and emigrants coming and scattering. The Fourth of July brought the usual celebration, and, as before, at Wilkes Reagan's. One speech was made by Gabriel J. Johnson to the citizens, and another by Major Redding to the militia. Obed Foote read the declaration, and Reagan of course furnished the barbecue. In August there was a warm contest for the office of sheriff between Major Alexander W. Russell and Morris Morris. The old rivalry between Kentucky and Whitewater had disappeared. It was Kentucky against Kentucky now. Russell was elected by 265 votes 'to 148. In November the great contest between Clay, Adams and Jackson, occurred. The Kentucky influence was paramount, and Clay got 217 votes to 99 for Jackson, and 16 for Adams. The Clay men made a regular organization on the 17th of July, with James Paxton as President, and Hiram Brown as Secretary.

In November Mr. Samuel Merrill, with the aid of a heavy wagon, traveling at the rate of twelve and a half miles a day, brought our new capital here. He put the Treasurer's office and residence in the brick building, long a well known remnant of early days, on the southwest corner of Washington and Tennessee streets, and there it remained till the little office got too small for it. The new State offices occupy its place. The Governor had to live like anybody else, where he could get a house, and this unfixed condition of the Executive household continued till the administration of Gov. Wallace, in 838, when the residence, then the finest in the town, erected by Dr. John Sanders, on the northwest corner of Market and Illinois streets. was purchased for a Governor's mansion. The Court House was not finished, but it was hurried up to allow the first meeting of the Legislature to be held there. The approach of the capital, in all the glory of the State seal, and legislative wisdom, suggested to the citizens to get a foretaste of the coming pleasure by organizing a legislature of their own. They did it, called it the Indianapolis Legislature, and, with all the leading citizens in it, made it a really entertaining assembly, and an instructive one, too. It had the same offices and rules, received messages, and discussed State measures, as the authoritative body did, and did it better The Governor's election was fixed to take place whenever a new subject of debate was needed, and his message would furnish it. When the real Legislature met, many of its members joined the other, and, as both discussed the same topics, the action of the former was not unfrequently settled in the debates of the latter.

SECOND PERIOD—TO 1847.

Chapter IV.

THE transfer of the capital to Indianapolis, though really accomplished in November of 1824, with the coming of the State offices and officers, made little more difference in the condition of the town than the arrival of any other four or five new settlers. It was not till the meeting of the Legislature, on the 1th of January, 1825, in pursuance of the act noticed in the last chapter, that the change showed itself visibly. Then the addition of nearly a hundred men, with all the hangers on of legislative bodies, the families of such as could easily bring them, or would not come without them, and the influx of those who then, as now, had "axes to grind," made such a stir in the sluggish village as one of this day can form no conception of. It was very much like doubling the population, as well as giving it new and exciting topics of talk, and incentives to speculation. Business became lively and society animated. Religion found new objects of exhortation, and literature a new audience of no trifling cultivation. The vices too had their sources of nourishment in the change, and the effect was generally an exhilaration not a little like that following a "square drink." No wonder the little town while it lay idle and unapproachable in the woods looked with longing for this change. But property was shrewder than the population, and touched speculations lightly. To the cool eye, formed of a dollar, there was not much promise in an acquisition that came for two or three months in the year, and left nothing when it went away. Crowds came in from the adjacent country to see the "big bugs," as the legislators were generally called in the Hoosier vernacular, but as they came to stare and did not stay to trade they benefitted nobody but the "grocery," the predecessor of the "saloon," and use soon made the "show" too cheap to go through the mud and snow to see. There was no permanent growing influence visible in the great acquisition, after all. So town lots stood pretty steady, and were first stirred into a fever of speculation on the approach of the Internal Improvement system of 1836. Population grew slowly. Indianapolis was merely a county town, with one unusually large and interesting session of court more than other county towns, that was all. And thus it remained till 1847, or rather till the influence emanating from the work completed in 1847, first showed itself. Thus it would have remained till the last, so far as any change depended on the possession of the capital. This advantage was something like a fairy's bad gift, which would only do one thing, and prevented the owner from doing anything with anything else. It was the town's main dedenence, after the local trade that every settlement had in an equal measure, and the meeting of the Legislature was looked to as anxiously, and made the condition of bargains, the prospect of clearing off stocks, or opening new trades, as regularly as the arrival of a caravan in a desert town, and yet it was a dependence that promised nothing more in 1870 than it had accomplished in 1825. Its first and only permanent addition to the property of the town was the location here of the Benevolent Institutions. This was not much, but it was permanent, so far as it went. These twenty-two years formed a period of legislative dependence.

The unfinished Court house (now gone), was put in such order as was possible to receive the General Assembly. The House met in the court room on the ground floor, the Senate up stairs. And here the sessions were held till December, 1835, when the new State House was first occupied. Being brought face to face with the unimproved condition of the capital, and compelled to endure its evils in their own persons, the legislators naturally enough concluded to do something to alleviate it, and on the 12th of February ordered the laying off and sale of a range of ten four-acre out-lots on the north, and another on the south, side of the town plat. Similar ranges had been ordered the year before by the Legislature, and sold at an average price of about $100 each, the highest bringing $155, and the new ranges lay outside of these. The reserved lots on Washington street were also ordered to be sold, the "bottom" of Pogue's Creek cleared out to the extent that $50 would do it, and the ferry leased for five years. The sale of out and reserved lots was made in May, at rates which indicated, as has already been said, no enthusiastic hopes of a speculation from the possession of the capital. The best Washington street lots went for $360, and the lowest at $134. Only seventeen were sold, and they brought only $3,328 into the treasury of the town agent, Mr. B. I. Blythe. The twenty four-acre out lots brought but $18 an acre, and an aggregate of $1,467. The valley of the creek was not very largely cleared, for $50 would not go far towards it, and though but a corner of the plat was cut off by it, there were trees and thickets left on it for many a year afterwards. Between its muddy borders and regular overflows, it was about as uncomfortable a stream of its size as could be found in the State. But "every little helped," and the work of the Legislature and of the citizens was slowly getting the town out of the woods, and suggesting the direction of streets to the nearest farms off Washington street. The churches were busy, and several societies for benevolent purposes were organized. On the 18th of April the Indianapolis Bible Society was formed; and, except the two churches, it is the only organization of that day that remains. It was a woman's affair mainly, and was promoted zealously by the wife of the eccentric and since greatly distinguished Oriental scholar, George Bush, the second regular pastor of the Presbyterian church. The Marion County Bible Society was also organized, with an auxiliary tract society; and these seem to have been the men's share of the same work that the women were doing in their Society. Bethuel F. Morris was the first president, and James M. Ray secretary of it. An Agricultural Society was formed, too, with Henry Bradley and Calvin Fletcher at its head; but it was, like the Medical Association and the theatre, premature, and died soon. There was not enough agriculture within easy reach of the town to have furnished the Society with a subject, if it had been ever so well attended. The land Office was removed here from Brookville, and the new capital then had the benefit of the patronage of the General Government, such as it was. The first Methodist church was built, or rather bought, in the summer of this year. It was a hewed log building on the south side of Maryland between Meridian and Pennsylvania streets. It was supplanted in 1829 by the old building on Meridian street on the site of the Sentinel office, which was succeeded in 1846 by Wesley chapel, and by Roberts chapel, on the northeast corner of Pennsylvania and Market streets, three years earlier, the original church dividing in 1842 into two congregations, Wesley and Roberts.

The indifferent progress the town evinced by the low price of the reserved lots on Washington street, sold in 1825, and the frequent forfeitures of lots bought at the first sale, induced the Legislature, in 1826, to enact a protection for purchasers, which would, without it, have lost their first payments, and probably have left the place. Besides the usual scarcity of money in new settlements, a good many purchasers were cramped by a desire to exchange their river lots for others further east, where it was thought the annual visitation of chills and fever was less severe. The act of the Legislature endeavored to meet both difficulties, by extending the time on the deferred payments, and allowing purchasers of more than one lot to surrender such as they desired, and transfer the payments to others in better situations. Under this permission river lots were rapidly abandoned, and the town moved eastward so entirely that it is only within the past ten or fifteen years that the growth of manufacturing establishments in that direction has largely filled up the site of the river settlement. A growing doubt of the navigable capacity of the river strengthened this eastward tendency. There was little probability of such river trade as would counterbalance the disadvantages of its neighborhood to residences. It was, in fact, rather a drawback than a benefit to the town; for it cut off the settlements on the west, in a measure, by crippling their means of communication. There was nothing but a ferry to connect the opposite banks, and it was a tax on the pockets as well as the patience of the people, though the Legislature did what it could to make it efficient by erecting a brick ferry house in the summer of the year following (1827) at the foot of Washington street—the National Road had not at that time come along, to turn the line of travel and residence away from the street, as it is now, and the latter was the main thoroughfare—which considerably changed and improved, is still standing, though partially burned fifteen years ago. This eastward movement of population and business is not the only fluctuation that has marked the growth of the city. The Internal Improvement system of 1836 excited a wild speculation in lots along the site of the Central Canal and drew settlement in that direction, till 1840. Then it shifted eastward again; then, with the completion of the Madison Railroad, it pushed southward, leaving business mainly along Washington street; and then, with the completion of other roads, it scattered in other directions. and began marking the outlines of that development which have been since so astonishingly filled up.

But all that the Legislature, and all that the prospects of the future capital could do, added but little to the growth attained directly after the first sale of town lots. The population in February, 1826, was seven hundred and sixty-two souls, of whom two hundred and nine were children, and one hundred and sixty-one attendants upon the Union Sunday School. The unfortunate reputation for sickness created by the epidemic of 1821 was still an active retarding influence, and occasional general attacks of other diseases kept its strength undiminished. A very wet spring, in this year, raised all the streams, stopped the mails, interfered with farming, and the influenza joined forces with the weather to resist immigration.

The local incidents of this year are few and of no special interest. An artillery company was formed under Capt. James Blake, and a cannon obtained from the Government, mainly to make a noise on the Fourth of July, and provide cripples for charity and public support. Two or three of the latter were the trophies of the suitable for the State House, it is not easy at this day to conjecture. It is large enough, it is the highest point in the original plat of the city, it is central, and it lies off the main business street with its disturbing uproar and constant crowd of passengers. But it was here that the Legislature resolved to place the Governor's house. The act making the appropriation ordered the Circle to be enclosed by an elegant and tasteful "rail" fence, by the first of May of that year, so as to be ready for the work on the house which was let on the 17th of March, to Smith, Culbertson, Bishop and Speaks. The building never was finished. It was found to be utterly unsuitable for a private residence, and no attempt was made to carry the work beyond the point necessary to suit it for public offices. It was a large square building, two full stories high, with a low slightly inclined roof, covering an attic story which was lighted by a dormer window on each of the four sides. On the roof was a "flat" about twelve feet square, surrounded by a low balustrade, which was intended for a resort in the "cool of the evening," and a pleasant place to overlook the town. The floor of the first story was raised some four feet or so above the ground, and was reached by a broad flight of steps at each side. The basement was about half cellar and half ground floor, and was for many years the resort of school boys for playing "hide-and-whoop," and "circus," and whatever fun was uppermost. One of the rooms was used by the Union Literary Society, until the State Auditor gave it permission to occupy a first-floor room. These basement vaults were used for worse purposes often, and were held by school girls and the younger boys in some dread, as a place of unclean spirits, which superstition was only so far wrong as it disallowed the spirits to be in the flesh. The first floor was divided from north to south and east to west by two wide halls, crossing at right angles, making a large room in each of the four corners. The second story was formed into smaller rooms. The attic was open, and used chiefly for a place of deposit for abandoned United States muskets and equipments, placed there at some unknown period, and plundered by the boys as they saw anything in the arms they wanted. The upper rooms were occupied as "chambers" by the Supreme Judges, and Judge Blackford kept one from the time the house was built until it was torn down. A bachelor lawyer, also, occasionally had a room there. The first floor was used by the State officers for many years, and contained, at different periods, the State Library, the State Bank, the State Engineer's office, the Clerk's office of the Supreme Court, the Common Pleas Court when first created, the Union Literary Society, Cox and Waugh's Temperance Panorama, and nobody now knows what besides. In 1829 a proposition was made to add wings to the east and west sides and turn it into a State House, but it was hardly pretentious enough for that, and the project failed. In 1857 it was ordered to be sold at auction, and in April it was sold and torn down, the material going to build the Macy House.

The Marion Fire Engine House also stood on the Circle, on the north side—if there is a side to a Circle—and was for many years a spot of no little interest to the emulous and devoted young gentlemen who ran "wid der machine." The old house was frequently broken into and occupied by prostitutes, and it was once or twice set on fire, and was finally destroyed in 1851.

The Circle was made a park by the city, but misused for a cow pasture and a play ground till its trees and grass were ruined, and then (1867) it was closely and elegantly fenced and shut out from the public entirely. Now it is a beautiful spot, and annually becoming more beautiful. It will soon be as pretty a little park as can be found anywhere. Handsome residences and imposing business houses are rising round it, and making it the center of the most impressive portion of the city.

Another appropriation of lots to public uses was made on the 26th day of January by the Legislature, that of square 25 for a State University, and square 22 for a State Hospital. This was done in connection with an order for the sale of forfeited and reserved lots and the vacation of certain alleys and squares. The history of one of these appropriated blocks, that now called University Square, has been even more eventful than that of the Circle. In the first place its dedication to a "State University," has enabled the State University at Bloomington to make a color of claim to it, and out of that claim has grown a succession of controversies that have ended in nothing but a determination on the part of the city that the Bloomington institution shall not have it, and this determination is mainly based on the sufficient argument that Bloomington has no right to it. The arguments on both sides, though interesting enough, are rather voluminous for this work, and, besides, are hardly relevant. It is enough to say that legal opinions have been expended on it at the proverbial length of legal documents, without deciding anything, and the Legislature has authorized the city to make a park of it till some better use can be found for it, and the city has done it.

The first purpose to which it was applied was as the site for the county seminary. In 1832 the Legislature authorized the lease of it to the trustees of the seminary for thirty years, with the proviso that they should build on either the south east or south west corner, and if it should be needed for University purposes before the expiration of the lease, a half acre about the building should be sold or otherwise secured to the school. In 1833–34 the trustees built, on the south west corner, the old county seminary building, which to many a man of middle age in the city embodies the best recollections of his youth. It was two stories high, fronting New York street, with a projecting lobby at each end, ostensibly for stair cases to the upper story, but really for the boys to put away their shinny clubs and ball bats. It was divided into two rooms of unequal size below, and a lecture room, and a teacher's private room, with a small room adjoining, above. The lecture room was the scene of annual terror and joy to the pupils for many a year, as there were held the examinations and exhibitions, which, in those days of primitive simplicity and few public pleasures, constituted nearly as attractive an entertainment as the opera does now. It was also the first church of Henry Ward Beecher, and of Rev. B. F. Foster, the Universalist. In fact, in very early days, the lower room of the seminary was used as a meeting place for several churches which were too weak to erect a building. The Christian congregation, or what afterwards became so, used to hold meetings in the larger of the lower rooms, and there the Rev. James McVey, who will be remembered by many of the older members of the church, as a very eloquent and rather "uncertain" preacher, first held forth in this city.

The lower rooms were first put in charge of Mr. E. Dumont in September, 1834. But then, and for several years afterwards, the school had formidable rivals, for, though owned by the county, and the teacher was appointed or approved by the trustees, it was essentially a private school. Mr. Dumont was succeeded in the following January by Mr. W. J. Hill. He by Thomas D. Gregg, in the following May. William Sullivan next took the school, in December, 1836, and Wm. A. Holliday in August, 1837. Up to this time no teacher had kept the school a year. But Mr. Holliday managed to retain it till October, 1838 and he had a formidable rival in Gilman Marston, since well known as Hon. Gilman Marston, member of Congress from New Hampshire, and as General Marston, who lost an arm early in the war, and now as Gov. Marston of one of our new Territories. He taught in the frame building erected on Circle street, on the lot next to that where Beecher's church, now the High School, was built. In October, 1838, the seminary fell into the hands of Rev. James Sprigg Kemper, destined to make it memorable as the best school the city had ever had then, or has had since, till the public schools were established. He was fresh from the Cincinnati College, a thorough scholar, and possessed of the requisite tact to manage boys and make them study. More than one prominent man now living here owes the spirit that pushed him ahead to Mr. Kemper. He left the school in 1843 or 1844, and studied for the ministry (Presbyterian), and has been for many years pastor of a church in Dayton, Ohio. He was succeeded by Rev. J. P. Safford, in 1843, who gave place to B. L. Lang in 1844. He retained it about two years, and after he retired the building was often unoccupied for the next four or five years, when it was made the City High School. It was used for that purpose from 1853 to 1859, and was torn down in 1860.

Authority was given in 1837 to lease the north west corner for twenty years to the Lutheran church, but the site was not deemed eligible, and the church was built on Ohio street, just east of where Mr. Pyle's boarding house stands now. Another abortive lease was made of the same corner for a Female Seminary in 1838. In 1850 the Governor and State Officers were authorized to sell an acre of the block to Indiana Asbury University, for the medical department of that institution, but the appraisement, $3,566, was deemed too high, and the sale was not made. The west half of the square north of the school house was reserved, or used, as the play ground of the pupils. The east half was for a long time a clover field or cow pasture. Subsequently a lumber yard was established upon the south end. In 1850 Mr. J. B. Perrine built a very high fence round the eastern half of the square, and with the addition of seats and a shed roof, made a grand show place of it for balloon ascensions and fire works. The finest exhibition of fire works ever given in the city was made there on the 4th of July, 1860. Subsequently the square was cleared and used as the drill ground of the 19th Regular U. S. Infantry, and in 1863 as the parade ground of the Home Guards, who were assembled to do battle with the redoubted John Morgan. As before stated, it is now, by authority, handsomely railed, planted with trees, and made a park, and such it is likely to remain.

The town, as heretofore stated, received an impetus from the acquisition of the capital in 1825, but a slighter one than might have been anticipated. Its growth had been but little more rapid than that of any other county town, and it was destined to expect as much, and be as grievously disappointed, in the location of the National (or Cumberland) Road, made in July, 1827, as in the possession of the capital. The year 1827 was the high-water mark of speculative growth, and what that was may be judged from an estimate, or rather inventory, of the town, made in February, 1827. The JOURNAL of that date stated that they then had a Court house (also State house); a Presbyterian church, with thirty members; a Baptist church, with thirty-six members, using a cabin as a church building; a Methodist church, with ninety-three members, just putting up a new brick building; a Sabbath-school, five years old, (the Union), with twenty teachers, and one hundred and fifty scholars. There were twenty-five brick houses, sixty frame and eighty log houses, hewed and rough, in the town; the Governor's house was going up; six two-story and five one-story brick houses, with a number of frame houses, had been built within a year; manufacturing establishments were needed. The town had received and consumed $10,000 worth of goods in the past year, embracing seventy-six kegs of tobacco, two hundred barrels of flour, one hundred kegs of powder, four thousand five hundred pounds of spun yarn, and two hundred and thirteen barrels of whisky, to which was to be added seventy-nine barrels made here. One hundred kegs of powder is such a proportion as shows that the people still largely depended on the rifle for their meat, while two hundred and eighty-four barrels of whisky shows that they did not largely depend on milk or water for their drink. A census taken in November gave a result of four hundred and twenty-nine white males, and thirty-four colored males, a total male population of five hundred and sixty three; and four hundred and seventy-nine white females, and twenty four colored females, a total female population of five hundred and three, and a total of both sexes of one thousand and sixty-six. This is a fair showing for a town only seven years old, but not by any means promising of great future results. The streets were mainly cleared on the plat, but there was no clearing on the donation outside, and many lots still retained through necessity the large trees that the owners would be glad to pay to get replaced now. Hunting was good all around the town, as proved by the sale of powder, and there were no marks of town life off Washington street. The streets were muddy, but as Mr. Brown justly remarks, the drainage was better than the engineers have since made it.

Chapter V

SUNDAY SCHOOL CELEBRATIONS—METHODIST SUNDAY SCHOOL—ARRIVAL OF THE
FIRST AND ONLY STEAMER—IMPROVEMENT OF THE RIVER—INDIANA DEMO-
CRAT—CHARTER OF RAILROADS—NEW STATE HOUSE—SMALL POX—BLACK
HAWK WAR, AND THE "BLOODY THREE HUNDRED"—FIRST MUNICIPAL GOV-
ERNMENT AND MARKET HOUSE—FIRST MURDER—CHOLERA—METEORIC DIS-
PLAY.

THE year 1828 was marked by no striking local event, except the establishment, in July, of a stage route to Madison by a Mr. Johnson. About the
same time the Indianapolis Library Association was formed, upon the very
easy plan, where the members are liberal and able, of having all the books donated
by the members. It was kept up for several years, and when it died its books remained uncared for and unclaimed—in fact few of them were worth claiming—till
about the year 1845, when the remains of them passed into the hands of the Union
Literary Society, the precursor of all the Literary and Lecture Associations we
have had. When it died the books were scattered among the members. And thus
disappeared the remains of the Indianapolis Library Association of 1825. A cavalry company was organized by Captain David Buchanan, in August. A musical
association called the Handelian Society, was also formed, and furnished the singing at the celebration of the Fourth of July, which was maintained in those early
days with a zeal in singular contrast with the observance or rather indifference to
it now. The review of them is principally interesting now from the names of the
men whose prominence gave them a place in them. In that of 1828, Hiram Brown
was President, Henry Brenton Vice President, Rev. George Bush, since so widely
known for oriental scholarship and theological vagaries, was Chaplain, Andrew
Ingram reader, and Bethuel F. Morris orator. The Sunday Schools took part in
this celebration for the first time, though subsequently, and till near the breaking
out of the war, they constituted the main part, if not the whole, of the affair. A
rifle and artillery company also took part, and ate their customary dinner in Bates'
Grove in East street, above Market, while the school children marched back to the
churches and were sent home. In 1829, the year following, the children took the
"show" out of the older hands entirely, forming a procession of two town and
five country schools on the circle, and marching, under the direction of James
Blake, who, for thirty years afterwards held the same conspicuous position, to
Bates' Grove, hearing a prayer from Rev. Jamison Hawkins, reading the Declaration from Ebenezer Sharpe, and a speech from James Morrison, and getting the
long stereotyped feast of rusk and water.

At the August election of 1828, nine hundred and thirteen votes were cast in
the county, and in the following November election nine hundred and sixty-one
were given, of which Adams got five hundred and eighty-two, and Jackson three

hundred and seventy-nine Very much of the original plat of the town, twenty-eight blocks and seventy-two lots, remained unsold in the winter of 1828. But little of the donation outside had been sold. A severe winter, with an unusually heavy snow, ushered in the year 1829.

During the year, as has been briefly noted before, the Methodist Sunday School was organized and separated from the Union School. It began April 24th, with eleven teachers and forty-six scholars, and at the close of the year it had twenty-seven teachers and one hundred and forty-six scholars. The Indiana Colonization Society was organized in the fall, with Judge Isaac Blackford as President. This, except the churches and Sunday schools, was the only association of that day that survived till ours. It seems to have been endowed with a vitality proportioned to its uselessness, for a more thoroughly useless affair was never known. The Legislature, by the exertions of a trifling little minister, Mr. Mitchell, was induced to appropriate $5,000 a year to the thing, and if any of it went for anything else than Mr. Mitchell's salary as secretary, it did *not* go to the colonization of negroes, for in twenty years the society sent to Africa from Indiana but *one* solitary negro.

There was a great deal of sickness and very little growth in the town in this year, 1829, and there was a vast deal of emigration passing *through* on its way to Illinois and Missouri. In the fall many of the contracts on the National Road were let. That for the bridge, still standing and still serviceable, was given, in 1830, to William H. Wernwag and Walter Blake, for $18,000, and it was completed in 1834. The work on the road was fitfully prosecuted for nearly ten years, and then was abandoned, at the same time the State's Internal Improvement system failed, in 1839. But one of these contracts was the direct cause of an event that startled the town and excited more enthusiasm and more reasonable hope than the arrival of the capital. This was the arrival of the steamer "Robert Hanna" in April, 1831.

General Hanna and others had taken a contract on the National Road, and to facilitate the transportation of stone and timber necessary to the work, resolved to have a steamer brought up the river to tow barges and do other like service. The result was the arrival, April 11th, 1831, of the "Robert Hanna," a small steamer, but too big for our river, as it soon appeared, for during an excursion, on the 12th, with a crowd of delighted passengers, the limbs of the overhanging trees knocked down her chimneys and pilot house and smashed a wheel-house, and when she started on her down voyage, on the next day, 13th of April, she ran aground at Hog Island, where she lay six weeks, and did not get out of the inadequate stream till fall. But as the people did not foresee all this, chiefly because they did not think of the water being considerably lower in the summer than the spring, they received the "Hanna" and a barge she was towing, with every demonstration of joy. Captain Blythe's artillery company greeted her with a noisy salute, which the crowd equalled with their shouting. All along the river, as she came up, the noise of her "scape pipe" drew spectators from both sides for two or three miles inland. She excited confident hopes of a commercial prosperity that had never been cherished before or had been given up. She confirmed for the time all that Mr. Engineer Ralston had asserted of the navigable capacity of the river. Even the most moderate anticipated that for half the year light draught boats could run, and that was but little less than is done on the Ohio, and a good deal more than is done on the Wabash. A public meeting was called, over which Judge Blackford presided, and of which James Morrison was Secretary, urging the improvement of the river, and inviting the owners and officers of the boat to dinner. This finished navigation on White river till the construction of the "Gov. Morton" in 1865, and the navigation of White river finished her after a few ineffectual attempts to run up to Cold Spring, and one to run down to Waverly. Nobody expected much of her before they saw her first trip, and after that they expected nothing but her entire loss to her owners, unless she could be converted to the ignoble use of scraping up and carrying boulders for paving the streets.

But though the navigation of the river ended thus indifferently, the arrival of the "Hanna" in 1831 was, as already said, but a confirmation of one opinion that many had long entertained. So confident was Gov. Noble of the navigability, or capacity to be made navigable, of the river, that in 1829 he offered a reward of $200 to the first steamer that should reach the town. In the spring of 1830 two steamers got pretty well up, the "Traveler," Captain Saunders, reaching Spencer, and the "Victory" reaching within fifty-five miles. As has been heretofore noticed, keel boats had several times got safely up and away. In 1822 the "Eagle" came up with fifteen tons of salt and whisky from Kanawha, the "Boxer" with thirty-three tons of goods from Zanesville, and the "Dandy," in 1824, arrived with twenty-eight tons of salt and whisky. In 1825 the Legislature appointed Alexander Ralston, the Scotch surveyor, who had done most of the work of planning the plat and laying out the town, Commissioner to survey the river, and report the practicability and cost of keeping it in navigable condition. He reported that from Sample's Mills, in Randolph county, to the Wabash, four hundred and fifty-five miles—one hundred and thirty to this place, from here to the fork two hundred and eighty-five miles, and from the fork to the Wabash forty miles—could be kept navigable for small boats, three months in the year, at a cost of $1,500. Backed by this report the Legislature memoralized Congress for the improvement of the river, and made appropriations to be expended under the direction of the authorities of the counties along its course. Some years later, one John Matthews proposed a system of slack water navigation, including dams, locks, levees, and the necessary means, and urged arguments enough for his project if the feasibility of it were left out of view. But while it was easy to prove that the navigation of the river would be a good thing, it was hard to prove that the navigation would be an easy thing. But he pressed his suggestions constantly, and in 1851 the Legislature chartered the White River Navigation Company. The company has done nothing, simply because no power less than Omnipotence can do anything with so unpromising a case as White river. It falls annually lower and lower. It has but few reaches of deep water, and very many of very rapid ripples, up which it would be no little job to tow a skiff, and an impossible job to row a skiff. These are worse every way, shallower, swifter, more impassable, than they were ten years ago. It is very doubtful if there is much more than half the water in the stream now that there was in 1840. The reasons need not be discussed here, but the fact is palpable to those familiar with the current and condition of the river. Its navigation never was practicable, except on so small a scale as to leave little chance of benefit, and now it is utterly impracticable on any scale at all.

The year 1830, like that before it, was uneventful. The town was stationary' and beyond trivial local incidents, there is little to notice. The usual Legislative session was held, with less than its usual attendance of hangers on, for a winter of great severity made traveling, always uncomfortable, a serious evil; and some compensation for customary excitements was sought in a legislative celebration of the 8th of January. A. F. Morrison, subsequently so long and well known in the politics of the State, delivered an address on the occasion. A theological debate fol lowed a week or so afterwards, between Rev. Jonathan Kidwell, a Universalist, and Rev. Edwin Ray, a Methodist, with the usual result of convincing nobody of anything he didn't believe before. No theological debate since Luther ever did. The *Indiana Democrat* was established in the spring by A. F. Morrison, and took the place of the *Gazette*, which was discontinued after eight years of the languid life of a country paper in a new town and a poor country. This paper, in 1841, was superseded by the *Indiana Sentinel*. A history of the changes in both will be found in the detailed notice of the newspapers of the city. The Fourth of July, the great event of the year, was this year made the source of dissension, that came near ending fatally. The Sunday Schools were celebrating, and so were the citizens, the former under James Blake, the latter under Demas McFarland, and each leader attempted to enlarge his own crowd at the expense of the other, by speeches at opposite street corners. The result might have been a fight, if a fortunate rain had not separated the crowds, forcing the schools into the Methodist church to complete their celebration, and sending the citizens to a neighboring grove to complete theirs. They did it by a speech from Judge W. W. Wick, and reading by A. St. Clair, under the presidency of Judge Isaac Blackford, and with the usual dinner and drinking. They attempted to enhance the divided interest of the occasion by firing a salute from the cannon, but the artillery company was Captain Blake's, and he was "in the opposite" in this case, and the gun had to be handled by raw hands, one of which, belonging to Andrew Smith, long county jailor, was blown off in the third round. The year was further distinguished by the arrival of the first "show," McComber & Co.'s menagerie, which was exhibited at Henderson's tavern, July 26-27th, and was followed a month afterwards by another. The Indiana Historical Society was organized in December, with Benjamin Parke for President and B. F. Morris for Secretary. This association "spread itself" in a fashion that promised to make it permanent and of constantly increasing value. It elected Daniel Webster, Henry Clay, Lewis Cass, John Calhoun, and pretty much all the political notorieties of that day honorary members, and received neat little autographic acknowledgments of the honor, which were a long time in the office of Henry P. Coburn, the last secretary. John Farnham gave the society its most vigorous life and power while it lasted, and enabled it to make some important collections of documents and other material of the history of the State and the Northwest. A gift enterprise by T. A. Langdon, who offered the Indianapolis Hotel as the highest prize, closed the year, which was exceedingly cold, a state of the weather that continued the whole winter, and in February covered the ground with more than a foot of snow, and brought the thermometer down to 18° below zero.

The year 1831 was marked by several events of no little importance in themselves, but promising far more in their consequences. On the 2nd and 3rd of February the Legislature chartered companies, recently formed, for the construction of no less than six railroads, to center at Indianapolis. They were the first active manifestations of the spirit of enterprise engendered by the then recent introduction of railways, exhibited in the State, and led the way for that wholesale system of internal improvements four years later, which, promising such ample benefits, at first loaded the State with such unmitigated evils. They were immature as well as premature. No adequate means had been provided, or even forseen, for their construction, and in the condition of the country at that time, there would have been no profitable use for them all. Twenty years later, with ten times the population, the country was unable to maintain even a smaller number of centralized railroads, and if these could have been built, there is no doubt they would have been disastrous failures for a time long enough to have rusted the rails off. But new settlers and settlements are enthusiastic, confident and uncalculating, and they took little heed of any consideration but that a railroad to every point of the compass from the capital would do a vast deal of good. The necessary condition—"if it can be made to pay and kept up"—was not thought of. So charters were granted for the Madison & Indianapolis, Lawrenceburg & Indianapolis, Harrison & Indianapolis, New Albany, Salem & Indianapolis, and Ohio & Indianapolis railroads. The wild character of these enterprises can be seen from the proposition to make railroads from New Albany and Harrison (Corydon) to Indianapolis, two lines that would start but a few miles apart, and inevitably "cut each others' throats." Surveys were made on four of them, the Madison, Lawrenceburg, Jeffersonville and Lafayette, but nothing more done, and their obvious impossibility caused them to be given up. But the growing favor of internal improvements impelled a new effort on a larger scale, and later they were re-chartered and some work done upon them. But in 1836 the State took several of them into her own hands, together with the combined canals and turnpikes of the great system, and carried them on till she broke down under the load.

On the 10th of February it was resolved to build a State House, on the report of a committee at the preceding session. The unsold lots of the donation, it was supposed, would furnish $58,000, and the house, it was estimated, would cost $56,000, and as a proof that the wild calculations of the railroad mania did not affect other business, it is to be noted that the house actually did cost but $60,000, a very little advance upon the estimate for a public work of any kind. James Blake was appointed commissioner to supervise the work, obtain plans and materials, and prepare generally for active operations, with an appropriation of $3,000 for these preliminaries. The plan (for which he was authorized to offer $150) was to include a senate chamber for fifty members, a hall for one hundred representatives, rooms for the Supreme Court and the State library, with twelve committee rooms and the necessary appurtenances, at a cost of $45,000. The commissioner did his work, and obtained a plan from Ithiel Town and I. J. Davis, of New York, which when reported to the Legislature of 1832 was approved, and Gov. Noah Noble, Morris Morris and Samuel Merrill, appointed to superintend the construction. The building was to be finished by November, 1838, and received upon the examination and approval of a committee of five from each house. These commissioners contracted with Ithiel Town, the architect, for the work at $58,000. He began early in 1832, and finished in December of 1835, in time for the meeting of the Legislature. The work was well done, but of bad material in the foundation. It was blue Bluff stone, far less durable than brick, but easily obtained and easily worked. It was slaty, and showed its disposition to scale in a few years after it was put into the building. It has now decayed so greatly as to disfigure, if not endanger, portions of the walls. The style of the building is Grecian, following the Parthenon, except in the preposterous little dome. If that had been left off it would have been handsome and tasteful, though the Grecian style is not fitted for a level country Its heavy architrave, low roof, square form, and lack of elevation, make it look squatty in a plain. It is intended for hilly and broken countries, where, capping natural elevations, it will harmonize with the scenery, which high and peaked buildings would not. Like all productions of real genius, it is adapted to its circumstances, and shows to less advantage anywhere else. This would have been a grave but not insuperable objection to the style of the State House. But the in congruous, contemptible dome should have condemned it utterly. It don't belong to the Grecian style, it is Roman. The Greeks knew nothing of domes or arches. And it looks just as well with the columns, pilasters, deep architrave and inclined roof of a Grecian structure, as a duck-billed cap on a Quaker coat. The stucco, too, was a bad suggestion. No plaster work will last in the extreme vicissitudes of our climate. It is wet one day, frozen the next, thawed the next, and rotting off in a few years. So the building soon looked ragged and old. Now it looks disgusting. But it was thought a fine thing thirty-five years ago. It cost $60,000, but $2,000 more than the contract. It is 200 feet long and 100 wide, or about these figures. No doubt it will be soon replaced. It is in constant need of repairs. In December, 1867, the vaulted ceiling of the Representatives' hall fell, and if there had been anybody in the "bar" it would inevitably have killed them. It made a work that cost several thousand dollars to repair completely. In 1834 a plowing-match began the work of throwing dirt from the outer side of the square to the center, and this, with a good deal of foreign addition, made the elevation on which the State House stands. The ground was raised about nine feet, and the trees, the larger ones now growing, planted the year following.

About the same time that the construction of the State House was decided, the Agent of the State was ordered to divide the donation outside of the town plat into out lots and sell them in the May following. The subdivision included about nineteen hundred acres, offered for sale in lots of two to fifty acres, at the minimum price of ten dollars an acre. A portion only was sold. As if to concentrate into the month of February all the startling events possible, Samuel Henderson, the Postmaster since the establishment of the office in 1822, was removed to make room for John Cain. And Mr. M. G. Rogers, the first artist, a portrait painter, visited the capital. The steamer "Robert Hanna," arrived on the 11th of April, producing, in conjunction with the newly awakened spirit of railroad enterprise, an extraordinary excitement, and great hopes of a commercial importance destined to be realized only in the next generation. A case of small pox, in May, created an excitement of a less pleasant kind. A public meeting was called to consider the case of Sophia Overall, a colored victim of the dreadful malady, and Dr. S. G. Mitchell, Isaac Coe, L. Dunlap, John E. McClure, C. McDougal, John S. Mothershead, Wm. Tichnor and John H. Sanders, were appointed a Board of Health, to see that the disease did not become epidemic. But the case, if it *was* small pox, was deterred by these formidable preparations for resistance from spreading, and the matter ended. The first soda fountain was put up by Dunlap & McDougal, the first elephant was exhibited, and the first three-story brick house, near the corner of Meridian street, on the north side of Washington, was erected during the summer. The August election brought out 950 votes. The first Methodist Conference was held in October, and the Indianapolis Lyceum, for the delivery of scientific lectures and debates, was organized about the same time.

The spring of 1832 brought with it nothing important. But in June came news of the Black Hawk war, and the then celebrated but now forgotten " Bloody Three Hundred," who deserve a place beside Tennyson's "Six Hundred," organized to represent Indiana in the fatal fields of that last of the Indian wars east of the Mississippi. One hundred and fifty mounted men of the fortieth regiment of militia, and as many from the regiment in the adjoining counties, were called for by Col. Alexander W. Russell, and rendezvoused in the grove on Washington street where John Carlisle's residence now stands, then part of the military ground. They came with the regular equipments of Indian fighters, backwoods rifles, tomahawks, knives, a pound of powder in each man's horn, and a buckskin "shot-pouch," with an adequate quantity of bullets. They were organized into three companies under Captains J. P. Drake, J. W. Redding, and Henry Brenton. Col. John L. Kinnard was one of the party. Col. K. was subsequently elected to Congress over W. W. Wick, and was blown up in a racing explosion on the Ohio, on his way to his second session of Congress, and scalded to death. He was one of the most popular and decidedly the most promising young man of his day in the State. He began as a school teacher. The morning before the march to Chicago the grove was full of boys throwing tomahawks, and soldiers preparing arms and knapsacks. The street (for there was but one) was full of crying women and wondering children, and Col. Russell, as he rode up with a big sword in a leather scabbard, was regarded as a second—not a third—Napoleon. The "Bloody Three Hundred" marched for Chicago, but never got any further. They met no adventures, and did no duty except marching, and came home again covered with dust if not glory. It was told of them, at the time, that one of them, who was standing guard at night up near the Lake, got frightened at a cow and fired, raising an alarm and bringing out the whole valorous host to the perilous encounter, but it was probably a calumny. The war was ended before they "got a smell." They got back on the 3d of July, and had a share of the celebration and dinner the next day, where they were regarded as "veterans." They were guided—for there were no roads up north in those days—by Mr. W. Conner, the same whose early settlement in the White River region was noted in the first chapter of this history. He was certainly capable, if any man was. The troops were paid in the January following, by Major Larned. Their departure was signalized by more blood shed than their campaign. In firing a salute from the cannon, William Warren had both his arms blown off. Injuring its gunners seems to have been about all the service that Captain Blake's gun ever did.

In August and September meetings were frequently held, under the inspiration of John Givan and Charles I. Hand and others, to build a market house at some convenient point, and it was done the year following—contracted for in May and finished in August—on the half square north of the Court house. Josiah Davis, Thomas McOouat and John Walton were charged with the supervision of the work. Dr. L. Dunlap, J. L. Hall and Demas McFarland were appointed the first Trustees of the County Seminary The first Foundry was started in August, in Stringtown, by R. A. McPherson, and continued in operation some years. The cholera created a good deal of alarm this summer, and public meetings were held and sanitary measures suggested, but the epidemic passed us by.

On the 3d of September the first steps were taken to form a municipal government for the capital. Before that it had been simply a more densely populated section of the wilderness, with no cohesion or control more than any other square mile of land. It was governed by State laws and State officers. On that day it was resolved to become an incorporated town, under the general law, and an election was held shortly after for the five Trustees provided by the law for towns thus organized. Samuel Henderson, late Post master, was made President of the Board; J. P. Griffith Clerk, and Samuel Jennison, Marshal and Collector. It was an exceedingly loose organization, but it answered well enough for a little town of a little more than a thousand inhabitants. Five wards were formed, divided by Alabama, Pennsylvania, Meridian and Tennessee streets, running the whole length of the plat. Certain ordinances were adopted, and a certain portion of townly dignity assumed. A connected history of the municipal government will be given, with all its appurtenances, in another place, and nothing more need be said of it here.

Early in the ensuing year, 1833, General Harrison visited, for the first time, the capital of the State, of which, in its territorial condition, he was so long Governor, and in which the greatest achievements of his honored career were accomplished. He was given a public dinner at Washington Hall, on the 17th of January, where he made a speech touching the exciting political issues of that day—nullification and its accompaniments—and of course for the Union. His visit, with the usual excitement created by the session of the Legislature, gave a degree of animation to social life and public feeling certainly not equaled since the arrival of the Hanna in 1831. He came back in 1835, but never afterwards.

There was engaged, at this time, either on the National Road bridge with Mr. Wernwag, or on some work on the west side of the river, a young man of good appearance and manners by the name of William McPherson. He was accused by the scandal of the day of licentious habits, and of intrigues that did him no credit. From some cause he obtained the ill will of Michael Van Blaricum, the ferryman at the Washington street ferry. There were many reports of the origin of the difficulty, and among others, one that inculpated McPherson with Van Blaricum's wife. On the 8th of May, 1833, he was crossing the ferry with the ferryman, when the latter, in the middle of the river, and in full sight of several persons, purposely rocked the boat, upset it, and threw McPherson, who could not swim, out, and drowned him. It was the first murder that had been committed in the town, and it created a great deal of excitement, which was increased by the difficulty of finding the body. Captain Blake's cannon was taken down to the bluff bank, where Merritt & Coughlin's woolen factory now stands, and it was fired to raise the corpse, ineffectually. It was recovered the next day after the murder. Van Blaricum, who belonged to the family of one of the very earliest settlers, was a bad man, but from some cause, probably the opinion that his "domestic peace" had been damaged, he was sentenced to but three years in the penitentiary, and had served but half the term, when Gov. Noble pardoned him. He returned and lived in the city, just at the west end of the bridge, for several years afterwards.

The cholera panic was renewed this year. A case or two supposed to be cholera, with its prevalence elsewhere, created so much alarm that the 26th of June was observed as a day of fasting and prayer, and in July a public meeting subscribed $1,000 to provide hospital conveniences, appointed a committee of ten—half doctors, half citizens—to act as a Board of Health, and assigned minor committees to each ward. Suitable measures were taken; the Governor's Circle building was taken for a hospital, and Dr. John E. McClure appointed to the charge of it. No case occurred, and the preparations were, happily, lost. Following the cholera came the first circus in August (Brown & Bailey's circus and menagerie), and placed itself in the open lot south of Henderson's hotel, then and for several years afterwards the only spot used for these exhibitions. It created a great deal of talk among the religious, who were willing to see the animals, but condemned the circus as immoral and irreligious. The feeling was almost universal then, and is not wholly dead yet. The "show" did a good business, as "shows" of all kinds almost invariably have done from that day to this.

The great meteoric shower of November 13th excited an alarm, not quite so general, but in some minds far more intense than did the cholera. It was deemed a portent of some great Divine display of wrath, if not the herald of the Last Day itself. It was certainly the most awful exhibition, to an uneducated mind, and the most sublime to an educated mind, that can be concieved. The sky rained fire as thickly as it ever did rain drops, apparently, till the rising day put the lights out.

Chapter VI.

N the 28th of January, 1834, the Legislature chartered the State Bank of Indiana, with a capital of $1,600,000, in $50 shares, the State taking half the stock, and private holders the remainder. The charter was to run twenty-five years. The State raised the money for her interest by the sale of what were known as "Bank bonds," and her share of the dividends, after extinguishing these bonds, it was provided should go to the establishment of a general School Fund. A Board called the Sinking Fund Board, was constituted to manage this fund of dividends, and was authorized to lend it, in any desired amounts, upon landed security, at seven per cent. interest. By this wise provision, poor borrowers, settlers who desired to buy land, and all who wanted loans on long time, were accommodated, and during the whole life of the Bank the Sinking Fund was a most important adjunct. Its loans went into every county of the State, and being amply secured, and renewable *ad libitum*, they made at once an immense profit for the ultimate school fund, and an incalculable benefit to the people. When the magnitude of the fund began to be apparent, on the recommendation of Gov. Wright its avails were ordered by the Legislature to be invested in the State's five per cent. bonds, issued in the place of those issued in 1836 for internal improvements. By this arrangement a double advantage was secured. The public debt was extinguished to the amount of the avails of the school fund, and a permanent investment of the fund was made in the credit of the State. The foreign debt became a domestic debt, at a low rate of interest, and the taxes that would otherwise go abroad remained at home to teach our children. It was paying a debt and levying a school tax both. The final yield of this fund of the State's dividends, thus vastly increased, was $3,700,000, after paying the "Bank bonds."

Of the Bank itself the history belongs rather to the State than the city, but a general sketch of it will not be out of place here. The Legislature reserved the right to elect the President and half the Directors. The stockholders elected the other half of the Directors. Samuel Merrill, late State Treasurer, was elected the first President, and Calvin Fletcher, Seaton W. Norris, Robert Morrison and Thos. R. Scott Directors. The organization was made on the 13th of February, beginning with ten branches, but ultimately increasing them to sixteen. Books for stock subscriptions were opened on the 7th of April following, and remained open thirty days. The stock was, of course, readily taken. James M. Ray was made Cashier, and he held the position till the bank was " wound up."

The Bank and its branches began business on the 20th day of November, 1834. The "mother bank," as it was called, was first kept in the Governor's Circle building. It was afterwards removed to Washington street, and kept there till 1840. In the meantime the Directors had been building a very substantial, and by no means unornamental, structure on the narrow peak between Illinois street and Kentucky avenue, on the site of an old pottery establishment, one of the first erected in the city. In 1840 a removal was made into this building, and there the bank remained during the remainder of its corporate life. The Bank of the State of Indiana—a sort of successor, or meant to be, of the State Bank of Indiana—next occupied the building, and remained till it collapsed under the National Bank act. The building has since been occupied as an insurance office and head quarters of one of the political parties. The Indianapolis Branch of the State Bank was organized on the 11th of November, by the appointment of Hervey Bates, President, and B. F. Morris, Cashier. They were succeeded in a few years by Calvin Fletcher as President, and Thomas H. Sharpe as Cashier, and these very efficient officers remained in the management of the Bank till it was wound up. Very few institutions of any kind have continued so long in the same hands as this bank. It was first kept in a building belonging to Mr. Bates on Washington Street and Virginia avenue, but in 1840 the building on the corner of Pennsylvania street and Virginia avenue was completed, and the bank removed to that. When the bank was wound up, this building (which contained the Cashier's residence as well as the bank), was sold for $16,000, to the Sinking Fund, which, though an adjunct of the bank in its origin, had an independent existence and business, and many a year to run before it could close out its wide-spread loans, and secure its mortgages. But in 1867 the Fund had worked its way through so nearly to the end that its business was transferred by the Legislature to the State Auditor, the building became unnecessary, and it was sold to the Franklin Insurance Company, for $30,000.

No Bank ever organized in the United States was managed more prudently or to greater advantage both of the borrowers and of the stockholders than the State Bank. The Indianapolis Branch would loan but $200 to any one person, except when engaged in hog or grain buying, and then it would lend liberally. This resolution caused a good deal of complaint of "narrowness" and "stinginess," but it prevented wild speculation, and saved the Bank from many a loss. The effect of it was that business men in need of immediate accommodation were accommodated, and those whose annual traffic in stock was the life of the farming interest, were supplied as far as a perfect knowledge of the trader's judgment and means indicated would be safe. In 1837, May 18th, the State Bank suspended specie payments, and resumed again on the order of the Legislature, June 15th, 1842.

In 1855, in anticipation of the expiration of the charter of the State Bank, the Legislature, by a close vote, and after a vast deal of intriguing and management, suspected to be not entirely free from corrupt elements, chartered the Bank of the State of Indiana, an institution somewhat like its predecessor in general features, but solely a stock holders' affair. The State had no interest in it. Gov. Wright, believing it to be the work of speculators, who had arranged to snatch all the stock and allow no fair competition for its possession, vetoed the bill, but it was passed over his head. When the stock books were opened for the seventeen branches, there was some appearance of the "grab game" which the Governor apprehended, and at the next session of the Legislature he made a long argument before the Senate to show that fraud had been practiced, and that the charter should be canceled. But the Bank was too strong then to be overturned, and lived till the National Bank system of Mr. Chase killed it. Its branches were generally converted into National banks. It was organized on the 1st of November, 1855, with Hugh M'Cullough, late Secretary of the Treasury, as President—he was, also, President of the State Bank during the last four years of its existence—and James M. Ray, also of the State Bank, Cashier. It began business with the beginning of the year 1857, with a capital of $1,836,000, and continued prosperously till, as before remarked, the National Bank system overwhelmed it. In 1865 it was authorized by the Legislature to "wind up," and did so as soon after as practicable. It was kept in the old State Bank building on Kentucky avenue, which it bought, and subsequently sold to the Franklin Insurance Company. Hugh M'Cullough, G. W. Rathbone and James M. Ray were Presidents, and Mr. Ray and Joseph M. Moore Cashiers. The Branch in this city was organized July 25th, 1855, with $100,000, capital, afterwards doubled, and with W. H. Talbott for President. It began business in 1857, with the "mother" bank, in the room where Cobb's drug store now is. George Tousey was then the President, and C. S. Stevenson Cashier. In 1861 Stevenson was appointed Paymaster in the army, and David E. Snyder was made Cashier. The bank was shortly before removed to the corner room of Yohn's block, Washington and Meridian streets, where it has since remained. D. M. Taylor was made Cashier in 1866, and Oliver Tousey President. As a branch of the Bank of the State it was wound up soon after this, and converted into a National Bank, in which character it still keeps its old place. A general notice of Banks will be found in another place.

In the spring of 1834 a railroad meeting was held here to obtain subscriptions to the Lawrenceburgh road, and the practice, now so general, of making county subscriptions by county Boards, to be paid by taxation, was inaugurated. The railroad fever, which reached its climax two years afterwards, was now rising fast. As stated in a preceding chapter, lines had been projected from Indianapolis, Lafayette and Madison, as well as Lawrenceburg and other points, and nothing having been done with most of them, they were rechartered in this and the following year, and in 1836 assumed by the State. Nothing came of the Lawrenceburgh line, except a little grading at one or two points.

Besides the chartering of the State Bank, and of the several railroad companies, the year 1834 witnessed the first local organization of the Whig party. The first meeting was held May 17th in the Court house—which continued to be the common political forum as long as it lasted—under Robert Brenton, familiarly known in the "unrespective" vernacular of the backwoods as "Old Bob Brenton," and speeches were made by Hiram Brown, a most unwavering Whig to the last hour of his life, and a man of extraordinary, though not persevering, talents, and by Wm. Quarles, a greatly overrated criminal lawyer, John H. Scott and John Hobart, the latter the first native poet of whom our city or its vicinity could boast. The first brewery did not grow out of this Whig movement, as we of the "lager beer period" of politics might easily conjecture, but out of the enterprise of John L. Young and Wm. H. Wernwag, and was got ready for work during this summer It was located just west of where the canal was afterwards run, at the west end of Maryland street. It did not do a very large business, and Mr. Young subsequently failed in it, when it passed into other hands. A few years ago it was abandoned. A rope-walk was also established during the year, near the market house, and the Pension Agency was removed here from Corydon.

The completion of the State House in 1835, in time for the meeting of the Legislature in December, was the most noted event of the year, though less directly connected with our municipal history than another event that sprang from it. As it approached completion, and the invaluable deposits of public laws and records which it would contain began to rise into full appreciation, the Legislature saw the necessity of protecting it, not only by insurance, but by preventive agencies, and authorized the Treasurer to procure twenty-five buckets, with suitable ladders for reaching the roof, and to pay half the expense of getting a fire engine, if the citizens would make up the other half. A meeting was held on the 12th of February to effect this object, and the existing fire-bucket company—which had done little more good than furnish the harness-making establishments with pretty fair contracts for leather buckets like small barrels, awkward in shape and unmanageable in service, for it was hard to throw water out of them on account of their contracted mouths—was reorganized as the Marion Fire Engine, Hose, and Protection Company, with Caleb Scudder as the first captain. The meeting requested the town trustees to raise their half of the cost of an engine by a tax, and to levy at the same time enough to construct five public wells. The engine called the "Marion," an "end-brake," of the best construction, by Merrick of Philadelphia, and by far the most serviceable "machine" the city ever had, was bought during the year, and received in September. It was placed, as before stated, in a small frame house on the north side of the Circle, subsequently enlarged to a two-story, and made the Council chamber, in the upper story. Thus was commenced the City Fire Department, always a prominent feature of a city government and history. A detailed account of it, and its abrogation for the present paid steam department, will be found in another place.

About the same time that the engine company was formed, the first State Agricultural Society was organized, with James Blake, Larkin Simms, John Owen and M. M. Henkle as directors, of whom Mr. Blake was President and Mr. Henkle Secretary. Steps were taken to diffuse a knowledge of, and interest in, agriculture by premiums for essays, and to organize county auxilliary societies. A State convention was held on the 14th of December, in the State House, at which little was accomplished, and not much more was done at the few meetings which followed, and the affair died. It was premature. The country was too new, the means of transportation too inadequate, to allow of Fairs and a competition and comparison of agricultural efforts, and without these practical results and illustrations a society can not hope to be more than a debating club. A county society was formed here in June, with Nathan B. Palmer as President, and Douglass Maguire as Secretary. Some money was obtained by subscription for premiums, and the Board of Justices donated fifty dollars of public money, so that, altogether, the society was enabled to distribute in premiums at the first fair, held on the last two days of October, about $180. Subscriptions to the amount of $400 were made for the next fair, and there was enough local interest manifested to warrant the hope that the exhibition would become permanent, but it failed with the State society in a few years.

The internal improvement fever was now almost at its hight. Even sober, calculating men began to see lines of railway stretching off to every point of the compass, and canals with long processions of loaded boats pouring wealth into the capital, and enterprise through every corner of the State. Speculation began to grow vigorous. Of all the projected lines of improvement, there were few that did not aim at the capital. Property was bound to rise in value as business crowded

(4)

the streets. And as imagination saw property rising, it *did* rise. It had been doing so for a year or two. Lots had doubled in value since the first projected set of defunct railroads had been chartered. On Washington street they were worth $60 to $75 a front foot. This was something promising; for a youth, with his first vote to cast, may recollect when lots on Washington street, between Illinois and Meridian, with buildings upon them—buildings now standing as incorporated parts of palatial structures—were sold for $120 a foot. The settlement which, since the great ague epidemic of 1821, had been crowding eastward, began to surge back towards the river again. Lots along the probable line of the canal became valuable, and sold rapidly, in the proportion that the canal now impairs their value. More than one family established itself close to the ditch, as a choice spot for a residence, with a blindness to unsuitability that puzzles one now. Among others, William Quarles, the lawyer, with considerable aristocratic pretensions, built a house on the east bank of the canal and south side of Washington street, under this strange delusion. The fever went off, in a few years, in a prostration that came near being fatal. This was the first speculative era in the history of the city. In the earlier years, when lots were still sold by the State's agent, there was not money enough to buy for speculation. Most of it was done with the purpose of holding on.

In November the Benevolent Society was organized, with very much the same structure that it still retains. Having little to do, and appealing for support directly to every householder by its visitors, it was kept up when more pretentious affairs failed. No small part of its sustaining influence came from the character of the contributions it asked. Like "Bill Crowder's" charity sermon, it wanted "old clothes, old coats, old hats, or any good-for-nothing old thing that nobody else would have." And these were readily given, and used with increasing benefit every year. Money was not usually solicited at the outset, or for a number of years afterwards, though it was often given, and of course, judiciously used. Now it is really a very important and indispensable institution, managing large sums of money, and vast accumulations of clothing and other benevolent material. Its system of collection and distribution has remained unchanged, and its management is in very much the same hands, except as death has removed them; that first undertook it. Visitors— a gentleman and lady of the highest respectability always—are appointed to designated portions of the city, and they apply, armed with baskets, at every house for anything that poverty and distress can make serviceable. And these collections are kept in charge of an officer, who gives them out on the order of the managers. A necessitous person has only to see any one of the score of managers and show that there is no imposition, to get adequate relief.

A literary Society was formed this year, too, taking the place of the Lyceum. It was a young men's affair, and devoted itself to the ordinary exercises of such associations, debates and essays. It was subsequently merged into, or compounded with, the Union Literary Society, organized by the elder pupils of the Seminary, and by the latter name it was known during its last and most important years, when it was incorporated under the general law (1847), and had, by much solicitation, obtained money to procure lecturers of celebrity. Its own members sometimes delivered its addresses, but the ministers of the city more frequently were the speakers, and their churches the lecture halls. Henry Ward Beecher delivered one, Dr. Samuel Johnson, the amiable and gifted Episcopal rector, delivered two or three, Dr. Fisher, of Cincinnati, was obtained for a course of four lectures in 1848. Horace Greeley delivered one lecture in 1853, in Masonic Hall, and Rev. J. C Fletcher, who was one of the members that had lectured before it in 1847, on his return from Brazil made an address in the same Hall. It was the predecessor, and an efficient one, too, of the present Y. M. C. A., and other lecturing associations.

The meteorology of 1835 is noteworthy. The spring and summer were remarkable for the frequency and volume of their rain falls. At Fort Wayne, it was reported by Mr. Jesse L. Williams, says Mr. Brown, that *ten* inches of rain fell in *two hours*. This was equal to a water spout. Hardly less remarkable was the occurrence of a severe frost on the night of the 1st of July, and the succession of a period of unusual heat and drouth. On August 18th a furious tornado swept over the country, greatly damaging houses, fences, trees and stock. And the winter of 1835-36 was almost unbroken till April.

The year 1836 is memorable both in State and municipal history, as that which gave form and active life to the wild schemes of improvement so often adverted to. The National road was in process of construction. The New York and Erie Canal, a gigantic State enterprise, had for ten years been successful and remunerative. Improvements were going on everywhere, and stimulating a spirit here which necessity created. The country was rapidly filling up, and its lands thickening with crops of grain, and teeming with hogs. But there was no outlet except through vast forests and almost impassable roads. A railroad or canal would be of incalculable benefit. This was clear. The difficulty through which very few saw clearly, or saw at all, was that every section of the State wanted a railroad or a canal, and no one would concede its claims to another, and none could be made a State work without the consent of the others. Thus when it was proposed that the State should undertake the work of internal improvement, these sectional jealousies, co-operating with the general confidence that every work when completed would pay an immense revenue to the Treasury, making taxation an obsolete necessity, forced the assumption of, or contribution of help to, nearly every enterprise that had been projected, in which there was any appearance of life or prospect of final advantage. The State took them all up, and issued $10,000,000 of bonds, to raise the money to prosecute them. The act was passed and approved on the 26th of January, 1836, but it was ascertained by a test vote on the 16th that the Internal Improvement Bill would pass, and the town was illuminated at night, and a scene of enthusiastic congratulation and jollification enacted which many now living will remember, not only for its brilliance, but for the period of suffering and stagnation to which it led so speedily and certainly. It was good while it lasted. The consequence of that measure was a State debt of some $15,088,000, on which no interest was paid for six or seven years. The great financial crash of 1837 broke down the enterprise in 1839, and at that time it was abandoned. The combined railroads, canals and turnpikes amounted to 1,289 miles, and only 281 in the aggregate had been completed, at an expense of $8,164,528 21, while the remaining 1,008 miles it was estimated would cost $19,914,244 more. The work never paid the State a cent. The whole cost was money thrown in the water. In 1846 an arrangement was made with our creditors to take the Wabash and Erie Canal with some 2,000,000 acres of land donated to it by Congress, to complete the work to Evansville, and to keep it in serviceable condition, in payment of half the debt. For the other half of the principal, 5 per cent. bonds were issued, and for the unpaid interest 2½ per cent. bonds were given. Within the present year the last of the bonds has been redeemed, and the last dollar of the burthen created by the measure for which the town was illuminated in 1836, thirty-four years ago, has been paid. The State is out of debt, and has a surplus. As remarked in the first part of this chapter, a large portion of these redeemed bonds have been paid out of the school fund, and thus the State has become the debtor of her own children instead of foreign creditors. The interest she pays now goes to the diffusion of free education instead of the pockets of plethoric capitalists.

An attempt was made at the Gubernatorial election in the year following, to stem the torrent of popular caprice, by the concentration of all opposition upon John Dumont for Governor, against David Wallace, the candidate of the Improvement party, pretty much the same as the Whig party. The Dumont men called themselves the "Modifiers," who wanted to take up a work at a time, and, carrying less weight, be more likely to get through. It was sound policy, but there were too many interests involved in the combination of enterprises to be overborne by reason, and the "Modifiers" were beaten. Gov. Wallace was eloquent and invincible on the "stump" in his exposition of the advantages of the possession by the State of these great works. Their revenue would make taxation unnecessary, the development of business they would create would give profitable employment to every man, and "two dollars a day and roast beef ' would be as little as any one would put up with. That " two dollars and roast beef" made a very effective Democratic war cry during the "hard times," from 1839 to 1844, when employment was scarce and money scarcer.

The same disaster that overwhelmed the State's credit crushed private business. Merchants owing bills for goods in the East, made unusually large by the freshet of speculation and the unhealthy inflation of trade of the preceding years, found themselves "broken," and hog speculators "went down " as fast as ever their droves did before the slaughter house hammers of the Cincinnati packing houses. The Bank, as already noted, suspended specie payment. Property bought at the big prices of the enthusiastic era could not be sold at all. Nobody had any money. Men with thousands of acres of rich land, and dozens of eligible town lots, were no better able to pay than those who had not ground enough for a grave. Several remedies were devised for this State of affairs. *First.* Eastern creditors were wise enough to see that debts pressed to execution would realize nothing, for property could not be sold; so they gave liberal terms of settlement in most cases, trusting to the revival of business and the growth of the town to put their debtors "on their feet," and enable them to pay in full, as they did. *Second.* The Legislature enacted that no property taken in excution should be sold for less than two-thirds of its appraised value, and a certain amount of household property was exempted from execution altogether. This secured debtors against the entire loss of their property with no material alleviation of their debts. *Third.* The Legislature issued bills, secured by the credit of the State, popularly known as "scrip," bearing six per cent. interest, and receivable for taxes, to supply the deficiency of currency. Two or three later issues were made, bearing a smaller rate of interest, and more largely discounted than the first. This resource afforded some relief, but less than it should, for the reason that the "scrip" had little credit or value outside of the State. This kept it below par at home. For a long time the usual question of a customer, "What is the price?" was answered by another, "Scrip or State Bank paper?" And a difference of one dollar in five was the result of the answer to it. In Cincinnati the first issues of six per cents were long worth no more than forty or fifty cents on the dollar, and it was a common speculation for our merchants to take an extra hundred or five hundred dollars along when they went to lay in stock, to buy scrip with. They could use it at home at seventy-five to eighty-five cents on the dollar, and make twenty to fifty per cent. by the speculation. Gradually, though, the "scrip" passed back in taxes to the State Treasury. Its six per cent. interest added considerably to its value, and it began to command a premium. It was worth nearly two dollars for one before it was all redeemed, fifteen years afterwards.

Business began to feel an upward impulse in 1843, but it was not till the Madi-railroad began creeping towards us from the river that a visible and active spirit of enterprise appeared.

In February, 1836, the Legislature gave the town a special charter of incorpora-tion, a new board of trustees was elected in April, and the old one retired after four years of service. Their settlement sheet showed that the revenues of the cap-ital were not enormous enough to be worth fighting for in those days. The receipts for the year ending April 1st, 1836 were only $1,610, and most of that had been collected by a special levy to pay for the "Marion" engine, for public wells, and other fire provisions. The new government inherited $124 from its predecessor, and passed some stringent ordinances against disorderly and riotous conduct. These would have been more important if they could have been enforced, for the town was full of wild, reckless, dangerous men, brought here by the work on the National Road, and increased by the influx brought by the canal.

The full fruit of the seeds of disorder sown here by these public works was not witnessed till a year or two afterwards, but from about this period till the return of "good times" and adequate employment for labor, the riotous population made so prominent a figure that a history would be incomplete without a notice of it. The central figure of the crowd was a square built, "chunky," agile and courageous man, of a naturally generous temper, and a rioter more through reckless love of mischief and adventure than real depravity, named Burkhart, and usually called "Old Dave Buckhart." He was generally seen on the street with an old slouch hat, breeches kept up by a single suspender, no coat or vest, and barefooted. His asso-ciates were like himself in appearance, but better disposed to serious outrage. They lived west of the canal, or near its line, in what is now called "Bucktown," and supported themselves mainly by stealing their neighbors' corn, pigs, poultry and potatoes. Their whisky they got by occasional jobs of rude and exhausting labor. They dug wells, excavated cellars and moved houses. When not thus engaged, they were rioting, and not unfrequently robbing outright. They were called the "chain gang," and the terror of their name was not quite lost when young men now living were born. A feud between them and the colored residents was a mat-ter of course. They were all of that political faith which holds a negro as noth-ing, and makes him a fit subject of outrage and oppression. They frequently sacked negro houses and abused their inmates, and kept the northwestern corner of the town in a perpetual turmoil. The feud culminated in a collision with "Old man Overall," a negro of rather a plucky disposition, who had some sons as willing to fight as any white man could be, and who lived on the open common near the pres-sent line of Ohio street, east of the military park. The "chain gang" gave out that they meant to "go for" the Overalls on a certain night, and the negro gathered his forces, barricaded doors and windows, loaded guns, and prepared for a siege. The assailants made a demonstration before the "colored" fortress, but a few shots and the formidable preparations warned them off, and the warfare resulted in a victory for the negroes. This was pretty near the termination of their career. It was effectually ended shortly after by a collision as novel as it was effective. The Methodists were holding a camp meeting in the military ground, and, under the ministrations of Rev. James Havens, then in the prime of his enormous physical strength and impressive but uncultured eloquence, were making many converts. On the third day of the meeting Burkhart, barefooted, and considerably drunk wandered into the woods and around the camp ground, keeping himself quite orderly and unobtrusive. An additional drink or two, however, "started" him, and he began marching around the outer line of the seats, shouting a dirty couplet of some original rhyme, at the top of his voice. The preacher several times stopped and kindly asked him to go off and not disturb the congregation, but without effect. At last he came down from the pulpit, walked right up to "old Buck"—a bit of pluck that astonished him—and asked him again to go off and leave the worshippers alone. He swore he wouldn't, and Mr. Havens at once knocked him down and whipped him till he roared. His defeat by a preacher, the object of supreme contempt to the "gang," ruined the leader's power. Shortly afterwards he was arrested for some misconduct and taken before 'Squire Scudder, where he "cavorted" and boasted furiously, till Samuel Merrill—as he used to tell the story to the writer—good humoredly took up his challenge for a scuffle, and threw him violently upon the floor of the 'Squire's office. These successive humiliations, and the growth of the moral element of the town, were too much for "Old Buck," and he moved off to the Bluffs, where he reformed and died at an advanced age. This was the end of the "chain gang;" but a number of the members remained in the town and made a hard and uncertain support by well-digging and house-moving. The leading men were "Big John Fletcher," a gigantic fellow, a perfect Hercules in form, but not as courageous as his physical powers might lead one to fancy he would be, and John Sparlan, a powerful man, of less stature but hardly less strength than Fletcher. Though they created a good deal of annoyance by irregularities and petty crimes, the "gang" was not the formidable thing it had been, and it was killed entirely less by actual resistance than discountenance. Sparlan was stabbed and killed in a street fight with John Pogue, the son of the first settler of the town. Fletcher died of dissipation, and his sons followed him, one or two by murder, one by drowning, and one by the effects of a disorderly life.

A favorite amusement of this period was running "quarter races." The course was a wide lane, covered with turf, except where an occasional wagon had cut down to the soil, bordered by a "staked-and-ridered fence" the whole length, on the east side, and a portion of the way by a similar fence on the west, and the open woods of the Military ground. It was the portion of what is now West street, lying north of the "mill race," and extending to the Michigan road (Indiana avenue), at Laquatt's residence. Crowds of idle men and truant school boys would flock out to this lane and line the fences on both sides like crows, to watch two horses, just taken out of the wagon and stripped of their "gears," run on a bet of five dollars. The races were usually, however, conducted on Saturday, so that school boys did not have to play "hookey" to see them, and they were the bulk of the spectators. "Selling races" were occasionally run on this quarter course, and provoked ugly suspicions sometimes, and sometimes desperate fights. On one occasion a gentleman somewhat known in connection with the history of the city, was thought by some of the spectators to have helped in one of these tricks, and the celebrated Nat. Vice, the pride and terror of the city, chased him home through innumerable dodges and back alleys. Nathaniel Vice was so prominent a figure of this era of the city, and so remarkable a character, that it would be improper not to speak of him a little more fully. He was a young man, not over thirty, at the time, of the middle hight, compactly though not heavily formed, with dark hair, eyes and skin, and a power of muscle absolutely unequaled. No professional acrobat or gymnast approached him, for his feats he performed with no preparation of cords or bars or years of training. He was utterly fearless, always ready for a fight, generous in temper, manly, open and honorable. He was a contractor on the canal in 1839, when the public works were abandoned by the State, and found himself with a considerable amount of arrears to his Irish employes, and with no money in the State Treasury to pay them. He called his "hands" up, explained the case to them, showed them all his money, and distributed it among them to the last cent in proportion to the amount due, promising that he would pay the balance as soon as the State paid him. For a little while the Irishmen seemed content with this arrangement, but coming up town and getting a drink or two ahead, they began to feel cheated, and resolved to punish the contractor. He came up the street shortly after, and seeing eight or ten of his "boys" round the door of the "Union Hotel" saloon, he invited them in and treated them. He left the room and they followed him. On reaching the street, they began cursing him and demanding their money. He explained to no purpose, and saw that he would have to fight. Eight of them set upon him together, and in two minutes he had whipped the whole of them so badly that they were more than willing to quit. He fought with feet as well as hands, and as he prostrated one man with a blow of his fist he sprang into the air and kicked the leader in the face so fearfully that he fell senseless and helpless, and was for a time thought to be dead. That was the biggest fight ever known in the town, though "Big Bill Crowder," the son of our first restaurant keeper, and the man who gave the name to the "Crowder farm" and "Crowder's ford" in the river, once or twice whipped three or four of the "Waterloo," crowd' a set of uncouth country cubs from the ague-infected region of what is now called "Lanergan's Lake," in the east bottom of White River.

The fighting in the early days of the capital was quite a feature in its social, or unsocial, life. No Saturday passed without one, or commonly, a half dozen. And a good deal of it was desperate and mischievous enough for the hungriest hunter of gladiatorial fun. It was not done to attract attention and create notoriety either; at least not in many cases. It is authentically related that Andrew Wilson and Zadoc Smith, while engaged in the mill on McCarty's bayou—a stream now pretty much used up—quarrelled, and agreed to go into the woods *alone* and fight it out. They did, and came back together in a half hour, with torn clothes and fearfully bruised faces, but no report as to the result of the fight. Nobody ever found out which whipped. Capt. Alexander Wiley and "big Jim Smith," the tailor, once quarrelled, and adjourned, alone, to the vacant State House square to settle the difficulty with an amicable fight. They did it, after a fearful combat, and came back together on excellent terms. A large, strong, surly fellow from "Waterloo," by the name of Bob Stevens, was for a long time the terror not only of the "bottom," but of the town, in which he invariably had a fight whenever he emerged from the mud and iron weeds, of his "native heath," to indulge his taste for Jerry Collins' whisky. He had whipped and cruelly hurt so many courageous boys who were too plucky to be "run over" by him, and not strong enough to fight him, that he was regarded as a sort of "ogre," and was allowed to "tear about" pretty much as he pleased. Finally he encountered a short, very square-shouldered, deep-chested young man by the name of Eli Glimpse, and, as usual, attempted to "ride rough shod" over him. The result was a fight, in which Stevens was nearly killed; his face was knocked to pieces, one of his eyes destroyed and his arm broken, while his antagonist had a thumb bitten round and round below the first joint, clear to the bone, as a boy bites a pawpaw stick to break it. It ruined his left hand. These will serve as specimens of the Saturday diversions of the people along about the time under consideration.

The impulse given to business and speculation by the internal improvement system soon reached its climax. The general financial convulsion of 1837 followed close upon it, and warned shrewd men of the peril of spreading more sail than was absolutely necessary to give "steerage way." Speculation was checked and soon killed outright. The costly lots on the canal were given up, and business shrank back to its old channel of Washington street, east of Illinois. But still there was a good deal of improvement going on, and some manufacturing growing into profitable proportions. The "Washington Hall," so long the leading hotel of the State, and as well known as the Whig headquarters of Indiana as Tammany Hall is as Demcratic headquarters in New York, was this year (1836) erected on the site of the frame tavern of Samuel Henderson. It was, at that time, the finest and costliest private structure that had been built or projected in the town. It was owned by a company, and opened by Edmund Browning, on the 16th of November, 1837, and by him retained till 1851. A full account of it and of our hotels generally will be found in another place.

On the 27th of April Arnold Lashley, a fiery-blooded Kentuckian, who was carrying on a carriage manufactory on the square of Odd Fellows' Hall and the Post office, fronting Pennsylvania street, quarrelled with a man named Zachariah Collins, who was hauling timber for him, or engaged in some like labor about the establishment, and in a fury struck him with a single-tree and killed him. This murder created an intense excitement. Lashley was "aristocratic," "put on style," and "held himself too high for common people," and if the population of new settlements hate any one thing more than another it is a man or woman who sets up a little social superiority. Collins was a poor man, and he had been killed for nothing. There was serious danger that the murderer would be lynched. He, however, had a preliminary examination and was held to bail, which he forfeited. He ran off and was never heard of again.

The County Agricultural Society held its second fair on the 7th and 8th of October, and Calvin Fletcher stated in his address that there were thirteen hundred farmers in the county, and that they produced an average of one thousand bushels of corn each. If he had only told us the average number of acres to a farm, or assigned to corn growing, his statement would have been of real value, as enabling us to compare the productiveness of the country at that time with its productiveness now, and to see whether there has been a material deterioration. A map of the town was published in the fall by Dr. Luke Munsell, and one of the county, by William Sullivan, surveyor, since better known as 'Squire Sullivan, who held the office of Justice of the Peace for nearly one generation, and still lives happy and honored among us. Dr. Munsell was a "queer genius," a deeply learned man, of various and valuable attainments, who yet never made all of them of half as much service as an inferior man would have made one of them. He published a map of Kentucky when he was State Engineer, before he came here. He also opened here the first, or among the first, Daguerrian establishments. A mattress and cushion manufactory was commenced by Hiram Devinney, on West Maryland street, near the canal, and a linseed oil mill was operated by his son, Frank Devinney, in the alley south of Maryland street. In February, 1836, the first home Insurance Company was chartered, with $200,000 capital, and valuable banking privileges. The charter ran for fifty years. Its direction was organized a few weeks afterwards, with Douglass Maguire as President, and Caleb Scudder as Secretary. It never did much, and died in the "hard times." In 1865 the old worthless stock was bought up, the charter renewed, and a new and vigorous company organized, as the Indianapolis Insurance Company, with Wm. Henderson as President, and Alexander C. Jameson as Secretary. The old Branch Bank building, on Virginia avenue and Pennsylvania street, was bought and is now occupied by it. Until within the past ten years, the business of Insurance, though considerable, was trifling to what it is now. The agencies were usually held by lawyers, who took them rather as accommodations than as profitable enterprizes, and no attempt was made to push business. The companies were all of the East. Now this is a vast interest, with a score or two of agencies, and some flourishing domestic companies and it plays no subordinate part in the statistics of the city's business.

Chapter VII.

AT THE time of the organization of the State Government, Indian wars were so fresh in the memories of the settlers, and the danger of their renewal, or at least of local outbreaks and murders, so evident, that a preparation for military service was wisely enough deemed indispensable, and laws were enacted constituting the State militia of all able bodied men of a certain age, forming them into regiments, usually of counties, and enjoining general "musters" for the purpose of drill and keeping alive the military spirit, from which no absence was allowed without reasonable excuse, and for neglect of which fines were imposed. The system was really too broad ever to be made very efficient, and it gradually broke down into total disuse. But for many years the annual or semi-annual "musters" were kept up, and constituted, next to the Fourth of July, the great holiday and spectacle of the season. The regiment of this county usually turned out from three hundred to four hundred men, most of them armed with squirrel-rifles, but some with hoe-handles and others with corn-stalks, a few hours were spent in elementary drills in the "manual," and in marching, sometimes in the pasture north of Market street, called "Bates Grove," and sometimes in the common south of Maryland street and west of Tennessee. The display was of little value in any respect, as the enforcement of discipline was impossible, and the attention given to drilling too slight to enable even a willing tyro to learn much. It was usually made the occasion of a great deal of boisterous fun, and the provocation to fights enough to have nourished the military spirit richly if fist-work could do it. To the boys of those days it was a very exciting spectacle to see the long line of men marching down the street with Glidden True playing the fife, and "old Peter Winchell" beating the drum, at its head, while the gallant Col. Russell, with flashing sword and brilliant epaulets, and his hat decorated with a tall plume of white feathers tipped with red, rode dashingly along, from front to rear or rear to front, shouting his orders and stirring up the dust distractingly. The utter uselessness of the militia system would doubtless have killed it sooner than it did, but for two causes: 1st, the "fun of the thing," which was no little matter to a hard-working community, with few holidays, and little opportunity to enjoy even those few; and second, the facilities afforded by it for electioneering. The militia was then about as straight a road to political preferment as the law is now, and there were few Congressmen or Legislators or county officers, who did not trace their popularity to their militia connections and positions.

The decay or desuetude of the militia parades left the town with no military attractions for some years, but still the spirit was only sleeping, not dead. Volunteer companies began to be formed, and as they were held by a constitution and laws framed expressly for each case, there was a good deal of effective attention given to the dry duty of learning elementary work. They were not large in numbers, but they were uniformed handsomely, worked and performed the manual well, and made a very different impression from the motley half armed mob of the militia days. The spirit thus rekindled never again died out so entirely but that some military organization was in existence to be stirred into occasional displays. The first of these companies was organized in February, 1837, under Col. Russell as Captain, and was called the "Marion Guards." Their uniform was of gray cloth, neat and tasteful, with black "patent leather" shakos, or high, bell-shaped hats, with short, bulbous cockades of black cotton. They were armed with the old fashioned flint-lock musket, as the cap arm had not been supplied to all the States by the General Government. They were drilled in the old stately Prussian fashion, and were really well drilled. Their monthly or quarterly parades were a time of general jubilee to the younger population. Thomas A. Morris, then recently graduated from West Point, succeeded Capt. Russell in the following summer, and under his thorough mastery of the art the company soon reached the perfection that made it so attractive. A year afterwards another company was organized and incorporated (February 14, 1838), under Capt. Thomas McBaker. It was called the "Marion Rifles" or Riflemen, and was armed with a sort of breech-loading rifle, which was among the first attempts to introduce that class of arms into the military service in any country. The lower part of the barrel next to the lock was detached from the main portion, and worked upon a hinge at the breech, which allowed the upper end to be pushed up by a rude, awkward trigger, that protruded below, and enabled the soldier to push his cartridge into the chamber with his finger. A blow with the hand pushed it back to its place, and the gun was ready for firing. But the movable breech was flat, broad and ugly, the weapon cumbrous and unhandy, and so liable, in haste or excitement, to leave the breech with the cartridge imperfectly pushed to its place, and thus fired, so as to endanger itself and the soldier, that it was not retained more than two or three years. The uniform of the Rifles was a blue fringed hunting-shirt, and blue pantaloons, with caps, a less soldierly looking but decidedly more comfortable dress than that of the "Guards." The latter, from their pepper and salt dress, were called "Grey Backs," the others were "The Arabs," a name of purely conjectural derivation. These companies sometimes, by agreement, fought sham battles along Washington street, the "Guards" marching up with stately tread and firing by platoons, while the "Arabs," practicing the "Skirmish Drill," would lie down in the dust, fire, and load, rise, retreat in a run, drop down and fire again, to the intense admiration of all beholders. In 1842 the two formed themselves into a battalion under the command of Lieut. Col. Harvey Brown, and Major George Drum. The Mexican war replaced this pacific military feeling with one more to the purpose, and company organizations languished again, with short intervals of resuscitation, till a few years before the Rebellion called for all the war spirit and skill the nation had. A more particular notice of our military companies will be found in another place.

Early in February Calvin Fletcher and Thomas Johnson were appointed commissioners by the Legislature to procure subscriptions of money from the citizens to drain the swamp on the northeast, which frequently sent very annoying streams down through the "bayous" or ravines spoken of in the first chapter of this history. Sometimes, when flooded with heavy rains, or by the overflow of Fall Creek, it became a serious mischief, filling houses along the bayous and overflowing gardens, breaking down fences, and damaging property generally. The commissioners raised the money and dug a ditch westward to Fall Creek, through Mr. Johnson's farm, and through a portion of the present Fair Ground. This answered the purpose until the extraordinary flood of 1847 occurred, which will be noticed in its place.

In 1821 the Legislature gave the town, for a west market ground, the north half of square 50, now lying north of the mill race, and between the canal and West street, but needing it for the use of the Board of Internal Improvements, an act was passed donating in its place the north half of square 48, the present West Market space, and deeds were exchanged for the lots. At this time the first appearance of a movement, which has since become quite a conspicuous feature of politics, occurred. The carpenters formed an association and fixed a day's work at ten hours, though there is no record that they expected to get twelve hours' wages for it. In this they differed from the demands of Mr. Trevallick and the venal, self-seeking, half-brained fellows like him, who are trying to make labor ridiculous by making it demand pay for what it don't do.

In the spring of the year 1837, the Episcopalians who, though not a numerous body, were among the foremost citizens of the place in wealth, enterprise and education, organized a church, with Rev. James B. Britton as rector. They had held occasional meetings since 1835, making them more frequent and with increasing attendance during the next year, and this spring concluded they were strong enough to organize and build a church. Preliminary steps were at once taken, and "ground broken" for the building, on the northeast corner of Circle and Meridian streets, in November. On the 7th of May, 1838, the corner stone was laid, the first edifice in the city, the writer thinks, that was provided with that bit of ceremonial masonry. Mr. Foster, the jeweler, then just returned from the East, deposited in the cavity of the stone some coins of the new issue, with the "Goddess of Liberty" upon them. They were the first that had been brought to the town. The usual newspapers and documents were also enclosed. The church was opened for worship in November, 1838, and used till 1857, when it was sold to the African Methodist church, removed to West Georgia street, and burned by incendiary rowdies a few years afterwards. A superb stone building of Gothic architecture, with stained windows and a chime of bells, replaced it in 1857-59. A further notice will be made of it in its place.

About the time the Episcopal church was organized the Evangelical Lutherans concluded that they were strong enough to make and maintain an organization and they held their first church meeting on the 14th of May, with Rev. A Reck as pastor. An attempt was made to put a church building on the northwest corner of University Square, as mentioned in the notice of that square, and authority was given by the Legislature for a lease of the necessary ground; but it was thought to be too far north at that time—and really there was but little of the town north of the Seminary in 1837—and the location was changed to Ohio street, near the corner of Meridian.

This year witnessed the commencement of the first female school that approached the rather indefinite grade of an Academy, that the town had known. It was called the "Indianapolis Female Institute," and was chartered by the Legislature during the preceding winter, and opened on the 14th of June by two maiden sisters of considerable attainments and capacity as instructors, Misses Mary

J. Axtell and Harriet Axtell. It flourished vigorously for twelve years, and filled about the same place among the future mothers and household managers of the town that the Seminary under Mr. Kemper did among the fathers and business managers. It was a good school, but the Misses Axtell were strongly imbued with the rather intolerant religious ideas of the old New England dispensation, and made them unnecessarily prominent in their discipline. Its reputation was so high that not a few pupils came from other towns and the adjoining States to attend it. Towards the end of its course Rev. Charles Axtell, a brother, gave his assistance in some of the departments, but no help could supply the place of the principal, whose failing health withdrew her more and more from her assiduous attention to her duties, and compelled her to close the Institute in the fall of 1849, and betake herself to a milder climate. It proved a useless effort. She died on her way to Cuba the same year.

In the fall of 1837, a school house was completed on Circle street, just north of the corner of Circle and Market, and next to the lot upon which Henry Ward Beecher's church was subsequently placed. It was a neat frame structure, divided into two rooms by sliding doors, and surmounted with a little belfry. It was first occupied by Mr. Gilman Marston, who had previously taught a little school in the second story of one of the buildings east of the Union Hotel, or Capital House—recently the *Sentinel* office—and had earned a good reputation as a faithful and painstaking teacher, whom the boys liked because he rarely whipped. Discipline with him was subordinate to acquisition, and if scholars studied well and made good progress, he did not inquire with savage strictness into the exact responsibility for the wad-throwing that covered the walls with little dabs of unfinished paper-mache, or the real sinner in the buzz that broke out of some knot of young heads and interrupted an older boy's recitation of the oration against Cataline, or Virgil's account of the way to make bees. With him, in charge of the Female Department, was Mrs. Eliza Richmond, for many years after one of the most energetic and efficient of all the workers in benevolent projects in the the city. Mr. Marston remained nearly two years. He has, as noted in a preceding chapter, since reached a position of national influence, as a member of Congress, a gallant and disabled General during the war, and now as Governor of one of our Rocky Mountain Territories. He was succeeded by Orlando Chester, who died the year following, and the school was taken by Mr. John Wheeler, afterwards a Professor in Asbury University. He retained it for several years, and on leaving it for the Professor's chair, it was discontinued. It was called the "Franklin Institute."

Preceding this school by several years, and rivaling even the County Seminary in point of age, was a school on the north west corner of Market and Delaware streets, kept by teachers who either had taught in, or were subsequently transferred to the seminary, except the last one. The house had been a carpenter's shop, and was rudely benched about with the faces fronting the wall, and provided with rough slabs with tressels, for seats. Its last occupant was Mr. Josephus Cicero Worrall, as incompetent a teacher and as accomplished a "blatherskite" as ever worried either end of a pupil. He was a very indifferent scholar and very indifferent to the progress of his pupils. His pay was all he cared for. His inordinate fondness for tobacco, which he chewed incessantly even when he smoked, his penuriousness, his making scholars help him in his household work, to carry water, saw wood, dig potatoes and do general gratuitous service, with his unremitting severity, which was as indiscriminate as it was harsh, made him the thorough detestation of every boy and girl that ever was under his care, and the ludicrous pomposity of his quarterly announcements of a new term, invariably signed with his full name "Josephus Cicero Worrall," made him the laughing stock of older persons. He was a "character" and a very unpleasant one. The first and only successful attempt at "barring out" ever made in the city, was instigated by dislike of him. His scholars of both sexes "barred" him "out" on the Christmas of 1837 and forced him to treat to apples, which all the older ones threw contemptuously away before his face. He was forced, by the general dislike he had created, to abandon school teaching about the year 1843 or '44, and leave the city. He returned ten or twelve years afterwards and was engaged in the stove and tinware trade, with little success, for a short time.

At the same time that Mr. Worrall was teaching in the old carpenter's shop, an old man by the name of Main, a Scotchman, of excellent capacity and attainments, but the most completely "distrait" and absent minded creature ever born, taught in the house near the opposite corner, on the south, where Aquilla Noe, the blacksmith, and for many years a constable of the township, had lived. At this school a pupil could learn if he chose, or play if he liked that better, and most of them did. With his head squeezed between his hands, except when one of them was shoveling great heaps of snuff, strong enough to sneeze the neck of a rhinoceros into dislocation, from an old horn "mull," into a nose that looked as if he had smeared it with molasses to make the tobacco stick in lumps and strings all round his nostrils, he would pore over Stewart or Hamilton and forget that he ever had a school. The most unruly disturbances did not disturb him. The boys could fight, play marbles, pull pins and throw books without arousing him. To run out into the back yard and play "hide and whoop" among the mustard stalks was an every day amusement. Not unfrequently he would hear but a single recitation and forget the others, unless a pupil reminded him—a bit of thoughtfulness that pupils are not given to obtruding upon a teacher—and the best of it to the boys was that if he did unexpectedly come out of his reverie, he rarely remarked anything wrong in the disorder which could not possibly have escaped his eye, if it did his mind. He might have sat for Dickens's delineation of the old schoolmaster in the "Curiosity Shop." He subsequently removed with his brother, a stone mason, to Arkansas and was never heard of here afterwards.

On May 29th a convention of the editors of the State was held in the town, in the council chamber, and the attendance evinced considerable interest in the business among the fraternity; more, at all events, than can be created now. There were twenty present, a larger proportion than has ever been collected since. Fifty-two papers were then published in the State, and no editorial convention in the past thirty years has had so nearly one-half of the whole "press gang" as it. John Douglass, the proprietor of the *Journal* was President, and John Dowling of the Terre Haute paper, the Secretary. A constitution and rules were adopted, of course, and never thought of again, and rates of advertising agreed upon and never adhered to, as has been the case ever since.

The National road was now in course of being "metaled" or covered with the broken stones of the "McAdam" plan of road making, through the town, and in June the trustees were urged to improve the sidewalks too. Something was done in this direction and a fresh advance made to something like municipal street propriety. The sidewalks were first made fifteen feet wide on Washington street and ten on the others. Afterwards the former were made twenty feet—to the intense disgust of the property owners who had to pay for the extra work—and the latter twelve feet. Since then the sidewalks of ninety feet streets have been widened to fifteen feet, making the clear roadway sixty feet. A hail storm of remarkable severity, both for duration and the size of the hail stones, occurred on the 6th day of June, and broke all the glass in the town, nearly. The Ladies' Missionary Society held a fair—the first ever attempted in the town—to raise money for their especial purpose, on New Year's Eve, in the Governor's Circle building, and obtained $230, quite equal to a contribution of $2,000 now.

Early in 1838 the town government was re-organized by an act of the Legislature of February 17th, made more effective, and extended over the whole donation for all purposes but that of taxation. Only property within the limits of the original plat could be taxed. Six Wards were formed, instead of five, and were divided by Alabama, Pennsylvania, Meridian, Illinois and Mississippi streets. Each ward elected a Trustee for one year, and a President of the body was elected by a general vote. His position corresponded so closely to that of Mayor,—though his duties did not,—that he was generally called by that title. The Trustees were required to be free-holders; four were made a quorum, and they were to be paid $12 a year for one meeting a month. They were authorized to enact all necessary ordinances, improve streets, borrow money, license liquor shops, shows and theatres, maintain a fire department, regulate markets, and levy taxes, not to exceed one-half of one per cent., nor upon territory outside of the original plat. The President had the authority and jurisdiction of a Justice, in addition to his purely municipal authority, and the Marshal had the authority of a Constable. The Secretary, Treasurer, Collector, Marshal, Supervisor, Market Master, Lister and Assessor, were all elected by the Council. The town government, thus changed, became more efficient, and prepared the way for a regular city government. On the last Saturday of March, 1838 the first election of the "new dispensation" was held, and Judge James Morrison,—one of the ablest lawyers and most estimable men the city has ever had,—was elected the first President. Ordinances were at once passed to secure quiet, order and safety. The town was full of the "hands" employed on the canal and on the National Road, and the most rigorous government possible would not be likely to do more than was needed. It was, in fact, a town for a despotism. The Irish on the canal were frequently embroiled in faction fights; and on one occasion in this year, the war assumed the proportions of a battle, all the hands on the "sections" adjoining the town hurrying from both directions to the scene, and "falling in" with their respective preferences, "Corkonians" or "Fardowns," till some three or four hundred were engaged. The ' chain gang" was busy and mischievous, and the whole community greatly unsettled.

The "sickly season" this year, was unusually fatal. From the first visitation of 1821, till within the last twenty years, that season,—extending from about the middle of July to the middle of September, or to the first frost of fall,—was a regular and dreaded visitant. This year, the large aggregation of ill-fed, ill-housed, disorderly and dirty men, doubly subject to the malarious diseases of the locality, spread the epidemic wider, retained it longer, and made it more fatal than it might otherwise have been.

In the very beginning of the year, a Mr. John Wood, who was doing a banking business in the room of the old Branch Bank, on Washington street, established a "Steam Foundry," in connection with Mr. Underhill, a Quaker, on Pennsylvania street, north of the University square. It was kept in operation for many years, and was really the pioneer of the iron business in the city. Benjamin Orr opened the first ready-made clothing, or "slop shop," in the city, during the year.

Up to the year 1839, the Governor had no official residence. He had to live in his own house, if he had one, or rent one, if he hadn't. Governor Noble resided in his own mansion, about a mile east of the town plat, during his two terms, and died there. Governor Wallace lived, when he first came here, in a two-story frame house near the west bank of the canal, south of Washington street. On the 13th of February, 1839, the Legislature ordered the State officers to purchase a suitable building for the Governor's house, furnish it, and keep it exclusively for an Executive mansion. They accordingly bought a large two-story brick house, erected some three years before, on the north west corner of Market and Illinois streets, by Dr. John H. Sanders, and at that time the handsomest and most capacious dwelling house in the town. It had the whole of the south east quarter of the square for its grounds,—three lots,—and, being within a square and a half of the State House, was as convenient as it was capacious and comfortable. It was first occupied by Governor Wallace, in 1839, and successively by Governors Bigger, Whitcomb, Dunning, (Lieutenant Governor, succeeding on Whitcomb's election to the United State's Senate), Wright, Willard and Morton. But, as the street grades were fixed and side walks made, it was found that the house was so far below the line of drainage, that in rainy weather it was surrounded with quite a pond of water, which kept the walls damp, moulded the paper, spoiled provisions, and created constant sickness. Governor Whitcomb's wife died there; so did the first and second wives of Governor Wright. Governor Willard's family was constantly afflicted, and Governor Morton's suffered so severely and unremittingly that he resolved to abandon it, whether the Legislature made any other provision for a residence or not. He left it, and took rooms at the Bates House, in 1864; and the Legislature, at the session of 1865, ordered it and the entire grounds to be sold. They were disposed of in small lots, at a good price, and furnished the money to build the State Offices on the site of the old Treasurer's Office, south west corner of Tennessee and Washington streets. The Illinois street front of the ground is now filled with a block of handsome business houses. At the time the Executive residence was ordered to be sold, the Legislature appropriated $5,000 per annum as a provision for rent and household expenses; but intended, also, to make a necessary addition to the Governor's salary, which, during the great depreciation of the currency, was quite inadequate. The Constitution forbids any increase of a State Officer's salary during the term for which he is elected; and the only way that the imperative addition to that of the Governor could be made, was by this appropriation for house rent. There has been several attempts made to build another State mansion, on some of the State's unoccupied lots, or to buy a suitable residence already built; but so far nothing has been done in this direction. Doubtless a new house will be provided before long.

In March the second election under the new municipal "dispensation" was held, and Judge Morrison declining to be a candidate, Nathan B. Palmer, one of the oldest and most respectable citizens, and formerly Treasurer of State, was chosen. The total vote was 324, indicating a population of about 2,000. The town government was not much of an affair in those days, in any respect. It had no police force, left its ordinances but indifferently enforced, and made but few street improvements. Indeed it had little to do anything with, for it was not allowed to tax over fifty cents on the hundred dollars, and that was confined to the original plat, and there were neither manufactures nor mercantile business of value enough to pay any considerable revenue. For the year ending March 27th the receipts were $7,012 the expenses $6,874, more than half of which went for the erection of the West, and the extension of the East, Market house, by Elder, Colstock

& Co. Something was paid for the repair of the public wells, and $145 went for grading and graveling streets—a sum that shows clearly enough how little was then thought of a work which, sooner or later, always makes the big item in city expenses. Printing cost $58, and Michael Shea was paid $413 dollars for clearing and fencing the "old grave yard," at that time the only burial place of the town. Portions of it were long little better than a wild forest, and many graves were irrecoverably lost during that period of neglect. Among others that of Alexander Ralston, the surveyor who "laid out" the town plat, has disappeared utterly, and it ought to have been preserved, and some monument by the city erected upon it. The town council, this year, also ordered all the streets to be opened. Several of them were still fenced up, and the ground plowed over and planted as regularly as any other part of the enclosure.

Cow pastures formed no inconspicuous feature of the town at this time, and for many a year after. Quite a number of squares in all quarters were fenced, and filled with milch cows, driven out by the boys in the morning and back again at night. "Going after the cows" was as much a regular duty of the sons then, as attending base ball clubs or concert saloons is now, and possibly a little more healthy and improving. "Sheets's pasture," composed of two squares between Georgia and South and Tennessee and Mississippi streets, was about the last of these relics of primitive fashions that disappeared from the town plat. "Van Blaricum's," south of South street, and covering the site of the Rolling mill, was another, and "Norwood's," now densely covered with residences, bordered the "Bluff road," since turned into Illinois street. In the north part of the town there were even more—so many that it would be hardly profitable to recall them. Many a middle-aged memory will travel back, in reading these lines, to the pleasantest days they can recall, when, barefooted, and with "shinny-clubs" or ball bats, they played all the way to the "pasture" and back, or left the easy-natured cows to saunter home, while they ran off for a swim in "Noble's hole," or "Morris's hole," in the creek, or at the "old snag," in the river.

These swimming "holes" were so important an element of the social economy that it is clear the citizens would have done a wise thing to provide them at any reasonable expense, if nature had not done it. They filled up healthily the spare hours of summer evenings, and the opportunities for mischief on Saturdays. They kept the most inveterate mud-sprawler clean in person, however dirty his clothes were, and they averted many a mischievous foray upon orchards and watermelon-patches that would have been bred in the heads that could not get to the water. The creek was the favorite resort of the smaller boys, those of the north and east flocking to "Noble's hole," near where Market street bridge is, and those of the centre and south to "Morris's hole," about where the creek passes out of the culvert under the Union depot. Another favorite place was a deep "elbow" near the Gas Works. "Noble's hole" was particularly affected for the advantage given its frequenters by a stratum of blue clay in the bank, which, sloping pretty steeply to the water, gave the boys a delightful slide, which their wet bodies made as slippery as greased glass. An "otter slide" was nothing to it. The facilities for impromptu imitations of Indian war paint were an additional attraction, and the pasture adjoining the creek might be seen on any pleasant evening horribly variegated with boys spotted, streaked, barred and striped in all directions, running, playing "leap-frog," and splashing into the water from the steep bank as recklessly as St. Patrick's frogs. The larger boys and stronger swimmers went to the river, usually either to the foot of Washington street, the old ferry landing, or a long snag, bending in an arc low-

(5)

over the water, about where Kingan's po k house stands. The latter was the favorite place, as the bank was covered with fine turf, the water deep, and the snug a delightful place to dive from. Very often a visitor might see, near sundown, a hundred boys at once, playing, splashing, diving, ducking each other, and laughing around that snag, with as joyous an indifference to the fact that the bottom was fifteen feet below them, and that drowning was possible, as if they had been porpoises in a tide-way. But fatal accidents did occur sometimes. Dr. Brown, a very estimable and promising young physician, went bathing on a little bar running down into the deep water at the snag, without being able to swim, and without knowing that the shallow bar made a sudden "step off." The water was thick with boys shouting and splashing about, and when the Doctor waded off the bar into drowning water, and cried for help, it was thought he was only "funning," as a score of others were at the same moment, and he drowned in the midst of a crowd any one of whom could have saved him as easily as he could turn his hand It was a very sad affair. The boys and young men built fires to give light and dived for the body a long time, but uselessly. It was found the next morning, by John Morrison, son of Judge Morrison. The very short bend in the river, below the Vincennes Railroad bridge, was, in those days, "in the woods." The town did not approach near it. The water was very deep, and the current very strong. Fatal accidents occurred here frequently. The usual resort for recovering drowned bodies was by diving. Among those always pressed into this disagreeable and dangerous service, were Rev. Amos Hanway and his younger brother, Samuel, now well known as a contractor of public works. Both were skillful fishermen, and almost lived on and in the river, and both possessed the capacity of lungs which would have made them a fortune at the Ceylon pearl banks. Samuel Hanway has frequently dived from the east to the west side of the river, at the old ferry, when the river was wider than it is now. The brothers never refused to come at call, rarely or never failed to recover the corpse, if the current had not carried it clear away, and did their inestimable work gratuitously, generally, if not always. These incidents are not important parts of the history of the city, certainly, but they will not be without interest to those who care to know something more of its early life than the records of its government and business changes.

In July 1839 the ordinances were revised, arranged, and published; and measures were taken to buy another fire engine in the fall. Three hundred dollars were appropriated for that purpose, and a committee appointed to get one for $600, if possible, and obtain donations to make up that amount.—The first sale of lots for delinquent town taxes was held on October 25th at Washington Hall by James Van Blaricum, the Marshal.—A resurvey of the donation disclosed the fact that in the first survey a mistake had been made which included eight acres that belonged to the United States. The lots had been sold in 1831, and some arrangement had to be made to save the purchasers from loss. The Legislature represented the case to Congress, and Congress donated the extra eight acres and saved a possible "Myra Gaines" case.—In November, Mrs. Britton, the wife of the Episcopal minister, opened a Female Academy near University Square, and made it quite successful. It subsequently passed into the hands of Mrs. Johnson and was changed to the building on Meridian street near the Episcopal church and called "St. Mary's Seminary."—On the 4th of November Gov. Wallace issued the first Proclamation appointing a day of Thanksgiving. He fixed the 28th, and the Thursday that is, or comes nearest, the 25th of that month, has been uniformly fixed for Thanksgiving day ever since.

The Presbyterian church of the town having, in May of the year before, 1838, followed the split that was running through the entire denomination in the United States, starting, as all church divisions did then and for long afterwards, from slavery, the "New School," consisting of fifteen adherents, formed a congregation on the 19th of November and worshipped in the lecture room of the County Seminary, under the ministrations of Rev. J. H. Johnson. In May 1839, Rev. Henry Ward Beecher was invited from Lawrenceburgh, where he had his first congregation, and took the pastorate in which he was destined to lay the foundation of the fame he has since reared so high. A year after his arrival a new church building was erected on the north west corner of Circle and Market streets, and occupied by him until he removed to Brooklyn in 1847, and by his successors, as will be elsewhere noted, till a new church was built on the corner of Vermont and Pennsylvania streets at a cost of $75,000, and the old one enlarged and improved and converted into the City High School in 1867.

The abandonment of the public works this year (1839), as noticed in the account of the adoption of the system of internal improvements by the State, gave the prospects of the town a terrible blow, which only appeared more disastrous as time developed the improbability of the completion and availability of any of the enterprises upon which so much really depended, and so much more was speculatively built. The canal was the only one that had reached the town, and as it was really in g od condition "as far as it went," to use "Mr. Nickleby's" favorite qualification, some preparation of boats had been made for the trade it might be expected to develop. It was opened from the feeder dam at Broad Ripple June 27th, 1839, by an excursion to that point. The section above to Noblesville, and that below to Martinsville, were so far advanced that a comparatively small amount of money and labor could have made a complete channel of water communication for about forty-five miles through the center of the State, and been found of very great value to the people. But everything was left, the spade in the dirt, the wheelbarrow on the plank, where the news of the State's bankruptcy overtook it, and not another lick has been struck from that day to this, except to repair the breaks and preserve the water power which the leases made obligatory upon the State or her assigns. All the way are still visible the marks of this futile improvement; in some places filled up, in some overgrown with underbrush and trees, in others still clear and capable of easy conversion to use. Below the town about three miles, the bed of the canal was turned into a country race course, and many a bet was lost there that would, but for this State provision, have been decided on the town course on West street. As far down as "Pleasant Run," where the canal was carried over that stream by an unfinished aqueduct, the water was kept a navigable depth for some years, and ran out into that creek a little way from the river, and made it a choice place for fishermen. But gradually the wooden locks south of the town decayed, the canal through the swamp then called "Palmer's Glade" became obstructed with weeds, grass and mud, and the water disappeared. A small channel was then dug from the wooden locks straight across to the river, just below the mouth of Pogue's creek, and through that the water is discharged now, and probably will continue to be for the next generation. It was in this little stream that Mary Hennerby and her little companion were drowned, or thrown after being murdered, by the villains who outraged the elder, in June 1870.

The admission of the water into the canal for the first time, in the spring of 1839, was the occasion of a general jubilee, not among the adults,—who already began to see that the eight finished miles were all we were likely to get, — but among the boys, who watched its coming away above the Fall Creek aqueduct, and marched before it, as it slowly crept down, filling the little holes, spreading out in level beds, and purling pleasantly down little descents, till it began to rise up along the banks, and its yellow tide filled the bed from side to side completely. Not much traffic was ever carried on by the canal; but a good deal of wood came down it occasionally, and some loads of grain and lumber were helped here by it. Its chief use was as a huge mill-race. An arm had been dug on the west side, near the line of Market street, which led westward about nine hundred feet, to a basin entering it in a north and south direction, at a declivity that gave a considerable fall and available power. At the north end of this basin another channel led off to the west and south, and formed a basin in the bed of one of the old "ravines," which gave ample power to mills upon the river bank below,—thus providing power upon two levels. On the 11th of June, the State leased power to one Woollen Mill, two Cotton Mills, two Paper Mills, an Oil mill, and two Grist and two Saw mills,—an addition of ten mills, and a business that could not but be a very material help to the town. But the canal was not as efficient as expected. It had too little fall for a "race," and it was grievously obstructed by an annual growth of grass, which was only imperfectly cleared out at the expense of some money, and turning off the water for a week or two. Mill-owners were dissatisfied, and refused to pay their rent. Suits were defeated by evidence showing constant loss from the failure of the State to supply water according to the contract. It is doubtful if the rent paid in the ten years that the State retained the canal, would cover the costs of her suits against the lessees. At last, on the 19th day of January, 1850, the Legislature ordered the canal to be sold. A company called the "Indiana Central Canal, Hydraulic Manufacturing and Water Works Company," bought it in October, 1851, for a trifle, from Gould & Jackson who bought of the first purchasers; and they retained it till 1859, giving no more satisfaction to lessees, and making no more profit out of it, than the State did. In 1859 a company, composed chiefly of citizens of Rochester, New York, bought it, and have been at some pains, and a good deal of expense, to keep it in serviceable condition. Several new mills have been connected with it, and now its supply of power is a very important element of city business, though most of the mills have provided steam machinery to supply any failure of water. About the first of the year 1870, the City Council chartered a company for water supply and fire protection, which is now actively engaged in completing its preparations, and it will take its forcing power from the canal. Indeed, it is now pretty evident that the demand for this power will be limited only by its capacity. Mills are thickening around it, and if it can only be assured of a constant and full current, it will be lined with machinery wherever a sufficient fall can be found. The portion below the stone lock, on Market street, will hardly be kept up long. It is a nuisance at all times; and when the water is out of it, it is a pestilence. This year, 1870, the chills and fever have infected the region along its banks so generally, that an "old settler" might be reminded of the great epidemic of 1821 and the cause is certainly the empty, feculent bed of the canal, from which a break of the Fall Creek aqueduct kept the water during the entire summer and fall. There have been many projects, and some serious efforts set on foot, to fill up this lower section, and restore Missouri street to a useful condition again; but nothing has come of them. The Company owns it, and is bound by leases to supply the old Rolling Mill and the Grist Mill called "Underhill's," near the wooden locks; and unless these obligations can be cancelled or compounded for, there is no very clear legal way to fill it up. Some miles north of the town, a freshet in the river, many years 'tb' washed off a long line of the bank, where it approaches close to the stream. Breaks below have been frequent. In 1847, during the heavy freshets, Fall Creek poured over into the "swamp" alluded to in a preceding passage of this Chapter, and sent tremendous streams down the old "ravine" beds, flooding many houses, and emptying a vast volume of water into the canal. Pogue's creek, also, rose enormously, and banked up against the mouth of the culvert under the canal, threatening to tear it away. The rising water in the canal at last burst the bank, just below the site of the old "Rolling Mill," and the whole flood poured down into the creek, swelling its torrent irresistibly, and in five minutes the culvert was torn out. This double disaster left the canal empty for a year. The culvert has since been two or three times torn out and replaced, always inadequately; and another heavy freshet in the creek will repeat the disaster and the lesson, with the same effect, probably. So much feeling was excited against the canal, by the frequent destruction of the creek culvert, that some years ago an attempt was made by a mob to resist the effort to replace it. The Company would gladly surrender this section, if they could be released from their obligation to supply water to the two mills upon it. The great State improvement has thus become a mere mill-race, so far as it possesses any value at all, and is little better than a mud-hole, and a deposit for the offal of slaughter houses, in its lower section.

The only other work tending towards the capital, upon which so much labor had been put as to make it of any use, was the Madison and Indianapolis Railroad. This enterprise was signalized by a monstrous cutting through the hills at Madison' called the "Deep Diggings," where most of the money given it by the State, was wasted; and where the use of the track was always perilous, and often fatal. It was completed to Vernon, twenty miles, in 1839, and was run regularly by the State's lessees, D. C. Branham & Co., till 1843, when a law was passed by the Legislature, authorizing its sale for a "song." The State never got anything worth mentioning for her vast outlay, and for a vast deal of really important work on this rugged section of the road. The Company, however, made a "good thing" of it. They completed the road by instalments,—first to Scipio, then to Clifty Creek, then to Columbus then to Edinburg, then to Greenwood, and finally,—in October, 1847,—to Indianapolis. And then it "coined" money. No road in any State, ever paid so well. It did all the business of the center and North of the State, with the East, South and West, at its own exorbitant rates; and, mad with prosperity, attempted enterprises which, in connection with the rivalry of the Jeffersonville and Cincinnati Railroads, broke it down so utterly, that its stock sold for two cents on the dollar, and its old rival, the Jeffersonville Company, bought it as a feeder for the upper end of its own line. So the great Internal Improvement system "ran out" and disappeared.

Chapter VIII.

THE local events of 1840 were unimportant, or so largely compounded of the political excitement of the great "hard cider" and "log cabin" campaign, that is impossible to eliminate them. From the time of General Harrison's nomination till the Presidential election, little was done or thought of but a change in the national administration and policy, which would restore the prosperity broken in the great panic of 1837. Party lines were rigorously drawn for the first time since the town was founded, and campaign papers, speeches, processions, conventions, and all electioneering arts, since so widely applied, maintained party feeling at fever heat. In March the municipal election was carried by the Whigs, in a clear party contest, indicating the result in the greater contest still to come. But the Democrats had not been "unfaithful stewards" of town interests by any means, and were washed out of office by the national tide and not by currents of local hostility. They had collected during the preceding year, to March, $5,975 and expended $4,753, leaving a balance for the use of their successors. The market houses received $1,984 of this sum, streets and bridges $1,350, the fire department $197, salaries $974, and incidentals $244. Two fire cisterns were ordered by the new administration. They were the first of a system of water supply which has since grown to be a very important department of the city government. They were of three hundred barrels capacity. A horticultural society was organized, August 22d, and maintained an active and beneficial existence for several years, under the inspiration of Henry Ward Beecher and other devotees of good taste and local improvement.

The "Palmer House" was begun this year, by Nathan B. Palmer, on the southeast corner of Illinois and Washington streets, and completed the year following, when it was leased and opened by John C. Parker, of Charlestown, Clarke county. Its site had formerly been occupied by the blacksmith shop of James Van Blaricum, which was removed to the open ground on Meridian street, south of Blackford's block. A large cabinet establishment also stood on or near its site, which is memorable for a fire that occurred there some years before, which was kept down and prevented from proving a destructive conflagration by showers of snow balls and armfuls of snow gathered up and thrown upon it by the spectators. The "Palmer House" was at first a two-story and a half building, the half story being frame. As the "Washington Hall" was Whig headquarters, the "Palmer House" became

Democratic headquarters, and has remained so ever since. The Whigs, "People's Party" and Republicans changed theirs to the Bates House, on the completion of that then magnificent edifice.

As before remarked, the principal events of the year were of a political character. As the capital and central point of the State, partisan demonstrations were frequent in Indianapolis, and not unfrequently the occasion of serious difficulties. The Whigs, especially, exceeded everything ever known before in the way of new and attractive features in their displays They hauled little log cabins in wagons, and lengthened their processions with enormous "dug-outs," arriving by some species of partisan punning, incomprehensible in rational times, at the conclusion that the battle of Tippecanoe, which was fought on a prairie and a bluff, was fitly symbolized by a "canoe." Barrels of cider were conspicuous also, and quite as appropriate. Mixed with whisky at times, they added a good deal to the excitement of the occasion, if they did nothing else. A cabin of buckeye logs was built on the site of the Bates House, and kept constantly provided with cider. Pictures of rude backwoods huts, with "puncheon" doors, and latch-strings conspicuously long and loose hanging outside, were the favorite thing for banners. Campaign songs, usually set to some negro air. for the first time became a prominent electioneering appliance. Choirs of vocalists, composed of ladies as well as gentlemen, usually did this, the most pleasing portion of the campaign work. A good singer was frequently interlarded between the orators at conventions, and the whole length of enormous processions was sometimes vocal with musical inquiries as to "What has caused this great commotion, motion, motion, the country through?" and the answer, "It is the ball a rolling on, for Tippecanoe and Tyler too, With them we'll beat little Van." Assurances that "Van, Van is a used up man," were always sure of "bringing down the house." Speeches were more violent and inflammatory, and with far less provocation, than those made during the war for the Union. Captain George W. Cutter, since widely known as the author of the "Song of Steam " and "Many in One"—the latter the finest and most original patriotic song we have— was then a young, pock-marked, fluent, unstable politician and poetaster, representing Vigo county in the lower branch of the Legislature. He had published a poem, now forgotten, called "Elskatawa," or the "Moving Fires," and was counted by the Whigs as one of their "coming men." He made a speech in the portico of the State House, in which, after repeating and intensifying all the stereotyped denunciations of the Democrats, he excited himself to such a pitch of animosity that he concluded his invective in a hoarse whisper—all the voice his violence had left him—while the foam flew from his lips, with the delightful sentiment: " D—n the Locofocos! " It tells the intensity of partisan feeling prevailing at that time, far more plainly than an elaborate description could do, to state that this bit of stupid profanity was received with hearty cheers as a choice effort of vituperative eloquence. Captain Cutter subsequently married Mrs. Drake, once a celebrated actress, but then "falling into the sere and yellow leaf," and quite old enough to have been his mother. He was a man of genius, but unbalanced and easily led astray. He ruined himself by dissipation, after many efforts to reform, and died a few years ago in or near Cincinnati.

Quite an exciting incident, and one not likely to be soon forgotten by its cotemporaries, grew out of a monster procession during the winter of 1840. As before remarked, ladies figured quite prominently in the demonstrations of both parties; but chiefly on the Whig side. In the procession alluded to, a gigantic canoe was pretty well filled with young ladies of the most estimable families in the town, and two of them, at the rear end of it, attracted especial attention, by waving a flag, or a sword, or some other apparatus symbolizing General Harrison's services. It was a trifle, and, in the general enthusiasm of the scene, neither a solecism in manners, nor a trespass on womanly propriety, but it was unusual, and a Democratic correspondent of a Terre Haute paper made an allusion to it that fell something short of courtesy, if not decency. A brother of the young ladies went to Terre Haute and got the name of the writer, and came back prepared to administer condign punishment for the insult. One cold morning, when the pavements were icy and slippery, he found one of the men concerned in the correspondence in Turner's barber shop, getting shaved, waited for him to come out, and then "pitched into" him and caned him, all hands slipping up and falling, ungracefully enough, on the ice. The names need not be told. Those who remember the affair, know who the parties were. Talk of duels and blood, and other dangerous results, was excited by the affair; but it ended with the "big thing on ice," in front of the barber shop.

Two men were prominent among the Whigs in 1840, who have since disappeared, not only from earth, but almost from the memories of their associates. Jonathan McCarty, of the White Water region, was one; and he had few, if any, superiors, on the "stump," in hard-hitting, and that sort of plain, direct talk that fires level with the heads of a mixed audience. He subsequently removed to Iowa, and was a candidate for Congress in the first State election held there in the fall of 1846. His political record was not clear of tergiversations; and, in spite of his abilities, he was never trusted or liked by the Whigs, though he served one session in Congress, on one side or the other. Joseph Little White, of Madison, was the other of this pair. He was much such a man as the more celebrated Sargeant S. Prentiss, a born orator, to whom striking phrases and impressive illustrations came as spontaneously as flowers come to an apple tree; and, like all really great orators, with a strong infusion of poetical sensibility, and disposition to put facts into the more plastic form of philosophy and generalizations. His figure was rather comical than otherwise, short, squat, fat and waddling; but his strong features and intellectual head considerably impaired the comic effect of his body, and five minutes of his speaking took it all away, and left in its place an embodied glow of eloquence. He was the finest extemporaneous speaker Indiana ever had. In the election of 1840, he was sent to Congress from the Madison district, and made a mark there, which nothing but the speedy overthrow of the Whigs, and of his aspirations, prevented from being placed well up to that of his leader, Clay. He accompanied Clay in the latter's visit to this town in 1842; and of the four speeches on that occasion,—Clay's, Crittenden's, Gov. Metcalf's, of Kentucky, and White's,—the latter's was so far the best, that the others were hardly thought of afterwards. He removed to New York a few years after he left Congress, and was prominent in the Van Buren campaign of 1848, on the "Free Soil" side. He and John Van Buren were the leading champions of the "Buffalo Platform," and were, probably, the main cause of the defeat of Cass and the Democracy.

Although the Whigs surpassed their opponents in the frequency and enthusiasm of their demonstrations, the latter made vigorous efforts to "keep even." On the 14th of October, they had an immense meeting in a Walnut grove where the Blind Asylum now stands, and were addressed by Col. Richard M. Johnson, then the Vice President, and candidate for re-election. He was the first great officer of the Government that had ever visited the town, and his coming attracted the largest crowd that had then ever been collected here. The National road was crowded with carriages and wagons, and the fences lined with spectators, for a mile or two out, waiting to catch the first glimpse of the "man who killed Tecumseh." His speech was a very wretched affair, and disclosed the fact that the Indian-killer was not a man of much ability. He moreover had the bad taste to speak, in a boasting way, of his "five wounds," and to chuckle when he said he wrote his "Sunday Mail Report" on Sunday,—as if the violation of the day were a good joke. Col. Johnson's demonstration did not help the Democrats at all. They needed better material than a warm-hearted, fat headed, jolly, hospitable old planter, with a stronger tendency to miscellaneous miscegenation than moral example, to help them out of the mire. And they had it in the speaker who followed Col. Johnson, Hon. Tilghman A. Howard, one of the noblest specimens of manhood, physically and intellectually, that ever belonged to Indiana. He was the Democratic candidate for Governor, having resigned a seat in Congress to accept the nomination. His speech was admirable, and contrasted strikingly with the mumbling imbecility of the Vice President. He was our first Minister to the young Republic of Texas, and died there. If he had lived to this day, he would have been one of the foremost men of the nation; and quite probably have been President. His personal presence was very impressive. He was tall, straight, athletic, graceful in carriage, striking in features and expression, dark almost as an Indian, with the aquiline nose that traditionally belongs to men of achievements; long, straight, black hair, and a smile indicative of unusual amiability and tenderness. He was the idol of his party, and deservedly so. He was as powerful a man as Douglas, with none of the latter's moral offsets against intellectual advantages.

The vote at the Presidential election embraced as nearly every poll in the town as it was possible to obtain. The Township,—mainly composed of the town,—gave 1,387 votes, of which Harrison had 872, and Van Buren 515. The annual Methodist Conference met here in October, and was presided over by Rev. Bishop Soule.

In March, of 1841, the town authorities procured Mr. James Wood, a Scotch surveyor, to make a plat of street grades and drainage, which was approved in 1842 by the Council, and which has since been followed with more zeal than benefit. It proceeded upon the assumption that the whole town must be drained off at the south west corner, into the creek or river; and accordingly made it an inclined plane, tilted up by high grades at one end, and sloped off at the other. The effect has been to make the upper end of some of the streets pretty nearly as high as the fences, and to turn the lots into permanent puddles. It has doubled the cost of street improvements, besides incidentally damaging city lots to an enormous amount. The only thing that can be said for it is, that the making of it and the "profile," only cost $300.

The death of General Harrison, within the first month of his administration, excited here, as every where, a great deal of feeling. A funeral celebration took place on the 17th of April, at which addresses were delivered by Governor Samuel Bigger and Rev. H. W. Beecher, and all places of business were closed. The 14th of May was kept as a day of thanksgiving and prayer.

The "hard times" bore hardest along through the years 1840, '41 and '42; and though some improvements were made, the general condition of the town was one of depression and inactivity. The resumption of specie payments by the State Bank June 16th, 1842, made no material change. Everybody put off enterprise till the "times got better." "The grass-hopper became a burden;" for though the municipal expenses of 1842 were but little more than half of those of 1839, an effort was made in '42 to abolish the town government, on account of its cost. The receipts of 1841 were but $3,197, against $5,975 two years before; the expenses $2,975 against $4,753,—salaries $767, against $974. The municipal salaries were certainly moderate,—the Council getting $12 a year, the Secretary $200, the Treasurer $100, the Marshal $100, Supervisor $200, Collector $200, Assessor $75, Market Master $140, Fire Messenger $100. But light expenses are heavy to men who have no money, and who owe more than they believe they can ever pay; and a tax of 25 or 30 cents on the $100, was a serious matter. The town government, however, was not abolished.

What newspapers call a "sensation," was produced on the 25th of April, 1842, by the attempt of a German, named Frederick Smith, to kill himself. He was keeping a grocery and beer shop in a little frame building on Washington street, near Delaware, and appeared to be doing well. But his life was troubled by some haunting horror, which he tried to tell by writing it with a piece of chalk on the open lid of his desk, but so unintelligibly, that all that could be made of it was that somebody "envied him his bread," and he resolved to rid himself of it by suicide. He blew himself up with a liberal portion of a keg of powder; but the explosion was chiefly spent upon the building, which was made a terrible wreck, leaving him blackened and senseless, but living, in the midst of it. He recovered, after a time, both his health and his senses.

T. W. Whitridge, since quite widely known as an artist, opened a Daguerreian establishment here in the summer of 1842, but soon gave it up to others, and devoted himself to painting. Henry Ward Beecher was a frequent visitor at his studio, and has several of his pictures in his house in Brooklyn. Before Mr. Whitridge came, a Mr. Brown had made an attempt to establish himself here as a portrait painter, but with little success. William Miller, the miniature painter, also came here about this time, and made his home with Dr. G. W. Mears. His success could not have been great; but still the associations formed here, brought him back for a few days every year, for several years. Joseph Eaton made the commencement of his artist life here, during that period, in a little room over Dr. Pope's drug store, near where George F. Meyers' cigar store now stands. Some of his pictures attracted a great deal of attention; but procured him more prophecies of success than patronage to assure it, and he removed to Cincinnati, where his fame and fortune grew large enough to bear transplanting in New York. Mr. Jacob Cox, a citizen and most estimable gentleman, was also working at portrait painting at such leisure moments as he could obtain from the stove and tin-ware business; and with such success, that he unquestionably holds the first place among Indiana artists, and an enviable one among those of the whole Union. His pictures, particularly his landscapes,—"compositions" of our own back-woods scenery,—were among the best attractions of the Cincinnati Art Union exhibitions, during their continuance. For nearly twenty years he has devoted himself exclusively to his art, and makes it amply remunerative.

On the 11th of June, President Van Buren visited the town, on a Western tour, and was received with as much honor as if he hadn't been ridiculed and denounced in every form of vituperation, from stump speech to doggerel songs. A procession of four military companies, the fire companies, and citizens generally, met him east of Pogue's creek bridge, and accompanied him to the Palmer House, where he made a pleasant little speech from the carriage, in reply to a formal welcome from Gov. Bigger. In the evening, he had a "reception" at the State House, and the next day, (Sunday,) attended church, once at Wesley Chapel and once at Mr. Beecher's church. He left on Monday, by the stage, for Terre Haute, and was upset near Plainfield. His appearance, and the general courtesy of his manners, weakened the dislike created by the Whig songs and caricatures for the "Fox of Lindenwald."

On the 5th of the following October, Henry Clay came. He, too, was making an exploration of the political field; and he made it to such purpose as to secure the next Whig nomination. The crowd that welcomed him, was unprecedented. Nothing approaching it had ever been seen before, and not many since have surpassed it. Thirty thousand was the estimate of those most likely not to exaggerate. The procession was three miles long, and composed of all the military and fire companies,—the trades, with appropriate banners,—several bands of music from different parts of the State, and an army of people, from all directions. Mr. Clay was accompanied by John J. Crittenden, Gov. Thomas Metcalfe, Joseph L. White, and several others, and was entertained by Governor Noble, at his mansion east of town. The crowd enjoyed itself with a barbecue of "barbaric profusion" and indifferent cooking, in a beautiful grove of Governor Noble's, east of his house. Here two or three stands were erected for speakers. Mr. Clay spoke from the main one, first of all, and for about an hour, but in no fashion to indicate his great oratorical powers. His speech was thoroughly partisan all the way through, and a little egotistical at times, as in his allusion to the "Clay men" under Jonathan Roberts in the Philadelphia Custom House. But nobody cared as much for the speech, as for the sight of the man. He was followed on the various stands by a succession of speeches, as alluded to in the notice of J. L. White, and the afternoon was pretty much consumed in oratory. The next day was devoted to a military review and parade, and the night to fire works, and the third to attending the Agricultural Fair and the races.

Although the "quarter races" on West street were still kept up, they afforded very indifferent amusement to the cultivated gambler and jockey, and an attempt was made to establish a regular course, supported by a jocky-club, here. It didn't succeed; for there was not then,—probably is not now,—the sort of spirit prevalent among the people, which makes gambling fashionable, or even tolerable: but it came nearer success than any similar effort has done since, and for one or two seasons really attracted racers of reputation from distant States. The course was located in a field belonging to David Van Blaricum, on the west side of the river, near the Crawfordsville road, and was a mile in circuit. Several "three mile" races were run here during the time of Mr. Clay's visit,—one between "Bertrand" and "Little Red;" but no "four mile" heats were attempted. Racing has now degenerated into a "moral" attraction of State Fairs.

During the fall of 1842, a Mr. Keeley lectured in the Court House on Mesmerism, and excited a great deal of curiosity, and no little credence, by exhibiting the clairvoyant powers of his subjects. He held daily levees in one of the upper rooms of the Court House, where he professed to cure some diseases of a chronic or constitutional character, and to relieve all. He had no lack of patients, and made money. He was followed by others, and several home-made mesmerists began experimenting; and among them they created an excitement about diabolical influences, that prepared the way easily enough, for the Millerite fancy of the succeeding winter. Two boys by the name of Beck, became quite notorious for their facility of handling in the mesmeric sleep, and the pleasure they took in having pins stuck through their fingers, or the backs of their hands scarred with knife-cuts. The folly lasted for several months.

Along with the "diablarie" of the mesmerists, came the Millerite excitement. Of its general history, it is unnecessary to say any thing here; but its local importance forbids a dismissal of it with a mere allusion. The capital shared the feeling of the whole country; and while few really believed the prediction of the world's destruction, very many were so far impressed by the ingenious interpretations and combinations of scriptural prophecies, as to give a closer heed to religious suggestions of a more important character, and not a few conversions date from that era. All through the winter travelling lecturers and preachers visited the town, swelling the excitement, and the circulation of the "Midnight Cry," and other papers devoted to this subject. As the spring approached, the feeling deepened. The "*dies iræ*" was coming close, and in the very crisis of the feeling, a Mr. Stevens, a young, eloquent and thoroughly informed preacher, came and delivered a series of lectures in different churches on the prophecies regarding the second coming of Christ. The first were given in the old Christian Church, on Kentucky Avenue, the last in the Lutheran Church, on Ohio street, near Market. The effect of his sermons was to nearly obliterate sectarian distinctions for a little while. All denominations thronged to hear him, and in the common interest in the catastrophe he elucidated, all sank their special interests and attachments. The lecturer professed no adhesion to any particular church, joined in the worship and communion of all alike, and was as readily received by one as the other. Though the world did not come to an end, the excitement was the origin of a great and general religious revival, probably unequalled in fervor and effect by any that have followed it. The "Second Advent" alarm died out utterly in a little while after the fated day of April passed, notwithstanding Mr. Miller fixed several other appointments for it; but the revival continued even more effectively after, than before. Probably natural phenomena lent some force to the appeals of religion. The winter was protracted far into April, and for several days, when in ordinary seasons the flowers are opening and fruit trees budding, the ground was covered with a heavy snow, upon which had fallen a hard, dense sleet, which froze so compactly, that the boys skated all over the commons, to school, and upon all sorts of errands, upon it. This unusual weather was made almost horrible, to simple apprehension, by the accompanying terterrors of the comet, one of the largest ever witnessed since man occupied the earth. Its slightly curved train, like a narrow, white cloud, stretching all across the western sky to the south western horizon, was a nightly spectacle for two months.

The "Second Advent" excitement was intensified by an accident into a ludicrous incident in the spring of 1843. Mr. Stevens had delivered at the Lutheran church, a very impressive lecture on the signs and portents that should accompany the end of the world, and his vivid descriptions, heightend by the flaming comet that glared in the west, produced a good deal of audible sobbing among the women, and some marks of feeling even among the men. The audience was dismissed, and as they passed the doors they saw the whole western sky a mass of red, angry looking light, which could be traced to no origin, and seemed spread upon, or glowing through, the thick clouds—for it was raining—and filling some of the lecturer's descriptions with alarming accuracy to minds preoccupied with that very horror. There were some suggestions of fainting, and a good many exclamations of pious terror or resignation. But the light disappeared after a while, and was found next morning to have been caused by the burning of some hemp or fodder stacks near "Crowder's farm." The position of the clouds, as is frequently the case, allowed the light to be reflected from one to another till the dreadful blaze covered the whole sky.

In February of this year, the Washington Hall took fire in the third story, upon one of the coldest days of the winter. It threatened for a time the entire destruction of the building, for water had to be passed in buckets by lines of citizens, from the well at the corner and the drug store where Haskitt's now is, and the intense cold made the work doubly difficult, and the supply for the engines very inadequate. But water and mushy ice were poured on till the lower rooms were ankle deep, and supplied the workers above as well as the engines below. Everybody worked, and everybody was coated with ice. Mr. Beecher was one of the foremost in carrying the hose-pipes right into the burning portion of the house, and, after two hours work, came out a mass of soot and dirt and ice, and blood from his cut hands, but with the fire subdued. The loss was about $4,000, much the heaviest that the town had ever suffered.

During the session of 1842-43, the Legislature took the first effective steps to establish a State Hospital for the Insane. As early as 1839 attention had been directed to the subject, but the State was in no very good condition to undertake new enterprises, and an appeal was made to Congress for a grant. Nothing came of it. The county assessors were at the same time ordered to make a return of the deaf mutes in their respective counties, as a preliminary step to a provision for this class of unfortunates. The State's financial embarrassments stopped all further effort in either enterprise for some years. Early in 1842 the Governor was directed to procure all possible information in regard to the subject of Hospitals for the Insane from the States that had them, and a year afterwards Dr John Evans lectured before the Legislature on the subject of insanity and its treatment. The result of the two efforts was a decision to "do something" at once. On the 13th of February, 1843, the Governor was directed to obtain plans and suggestions for a Hospital from the Superintendents of Hospitals in other States, for submission to the Legislature at the next session. This put the enterprise finally in motion. At the next session plans were examined, a mode of operations determined, and a tax of one cent on the hundred dollars levied to carry it out. On the 13th of January, 1845, Dr. John Evans, Dr. L. Dunlap and James Blake were appointed commissioners to obtain a site containing not to exceed two hundred acres. They selected Mount Jackson, then the residence of Nathaniel Bolton, formerly editor of the Indiana Gazette. He and his wife, the gifted "poetess of Indiana," here kept a country tavern for several years. This site, with a plan of building, was reported to the Legislature at the next session, and approved, and the commissioners ordered, February 19th, 1846, to proceed with the work. They were authorized to sell Hospital Square No. 22—alluded to in a preceding chapter—and apply its proceeds to this purpose, and an additional appropriation of $15,000 was made. The central building was begun in 1846, and finished next year at a cost of $75,000. It has since been enlarged by wings, and still other wings larger than the main building, till it now is an immense structure, supplied by its own water works from Eagle Creek, and contains the population of a very respectable country town, something over five hundred. Its entire cost has been about half a million of dollars.

At the same time that the Governor was directed to obtain plans from insane hospitals, February 13th, 1843, a tax of one-fifth of a cent on the hundred dollars was levied to provide for the Deaf and Dumb. The first work in this direction was done by William Willard, one of the assistants in the Asylum now, who was himself a mute, and had long been a teacher of mutes in Ohio. He came here in the spring of 1843, and in the fall opened a school on his own account for mutes, with an attendance of sixteen pupils. In 1844 the Legislature adopted his school as a State institution, and appointed a Board of Trustees for it consisting of the Governor, Treasurer and Secretary of State, *ex officio*, and Revs. Henry Ward Beecher, Phineas D. Gurley, L. H. Jameson, Dr. Dunlap, Hon. James Morrison and Rev. Matthew Simpson. They rented the large two-story frame building, then recently erected by Dr. G. W. Stipp, on the south east corner of Illinois and Maryland streets, and opened the first State Asylum there, in October, 1844. A site for a permanent building was selected in January, 1846, just east of the town, consisting, at first, of thirty acres, but afterwards increased by a hundred more, for the agricultural instruction of the pupils, and a building begun in 1849. It was completed in the fall of 1850, at a cost of $30,000. Meanwhile the school was removed from the Stipp house to the Kinder building, on the south side of Washington street, near Delaware, where it remained till transferred to its own building, in October, 1850. This structure has also been greatly enlarged since its erection.

The Blind were not provided for at the same time that their fellow sufferers were. The first effort on their behalf was instigated and directed by James M. Ray, to whom the Indiana Institute for the Blind is more indebted than it is to any other man living. By his efforts William H. Churchman was brought here in the winter of 1844–5. and gave one or two exhibitions in Beecher's church, with blind pupils from the Kentucky Asylum. The effect was so good that the Legislature, for whom the performances were mainly intended, and who attended them with astonishing unanimity and interest, decided to levy a tax of one-fifth of a cent on the hundred dollars, to establish a Blind Asylum. James M. Ray, George W. Mears and the Secretary, Treasurer and Auditor of State were made commissioners to apply the fund, either to the establishment of an Asylum, or to the providing for our Blind at the Ohio or Kentucky Asylums. They set Mr. Churchman to lecturing throughout the State on the subject, and gathering statistics of our blind population. On the 27th of January, 1847, James M. Ray, George W. Mears and Calvin Fletcher—the latter, declining to serve, was replaced by Seton W. Norris—were appointed to erect buildings and put the institution in operation. They were given $5,000 to pay for a site and defray other incidental expenses, and they purchased two blocks north of North street, between Pennsylvania and Meridian, and began the building in 1848. While it was in course of erection the school was opened on October 1st, 1847, in the Stipp house, where the Deaf and Dumb school had recently been kept. It had nine pupils at first, but increased to thirty during the year. In September, 1848, it was removed to the building now used as a work shop, on its own ground. The Asylum proper was finished in 1851, at a cost of $50,000, and at once occupied. A notice of the present condition and attendance of the various Asylums will be made in the proper place.

During the summer of 1843, a Mr. Robert Parmlee began the manufacture of pianos in the town, in a shop on Washington street, a little west of Hubbard's block. It could hardly have been a flourishing business, but it was continued for two years or so, chiefly by repairs on old instruments. In the fall a company called the " New York Company of Comedians," gave concerts in the upper room of Gaston's carriage shop—on the site of the Bates House—and concluded each entertainment with a theatrical performance. The leading actors were John Powell and his wife, Tom Townley, who did the dancing, and Sam Lathrop. Mrs. Drake and Augustus Adams appeared as stars during the season, which lasted pretty well through the whole session of the Legislature. The "theatre" was fronted on the east by a wide platform, where Mr. Gaston exposed his carriages to dry when varnished, and this platform was unprotected by any railing on the east and south sides. One night Mr. Corbaley, one of the settlers of 1820, coming out of the theatre in the dark, stepped off this platform and hurt himself so severely that he died in a few days. Subsequently Mrs. Drake and Mr. Adams played here when the theatre was "fixed up" in the one-story brick, where Temperance Hall now stands, which had formerly been the office of the Indiana Democrat. This was managed by Mr. Lindsay, who had conducted several theatrical seasons before this. As early as 1836 or 1837, he had opened in Ollaman's wagon shop, on Washington street, opposite the Court house, and delighted the Capitalians with the "universally popular" comic songs of the "Tongo Islands," and the

"King of the Cannibal Islands," and had been back once before the New York troupe opened in the carriage shop. These, with Mr. and Mrs. Smith's previous performances in Carter's tavern in 1823 and 1824, comprised the theatrical experience of the town until the "Thespian Corps," composed of our own young men, appeared in 1845.

In September, 1843, Miss Lesuer opened the "Indianapolis Female Collegiate Institute" in the Circle street house which the Franklin Institute had formerly occupied, and maintained it successfully for some years. During the same year, the Robert's Chapel (Methodist) congregation divided from the parent church, Wesley Chapel, and began the erection of their church on the corner of Pennsylvania and Market streets, which was completed the year following, at a cost of $10,000, or thereabout. The old building was sold in 1868, and converted into a block of business houses, and a new one erected on the corner of Delaware and Vermont streets, at a cost of $80,000. There is nothing else of consequence to note in the year 1843.

The "old grave yard," though capable of containing all the dead the town would be likely to furnish for the next ten years, was deemed inadequate in 1844, and in April a cemetery, long known as the "New Grave yard," was laid out. The old one at that time was in the woods. A dense "bottom" forest lay between it and the river on the south, and a considerable width of timber separated it from the river on the west. On the east was the Mooresville road and Dennis I. White's pasture, with an open woods stretching north from the bluff bank of the "grave yard pond." The new addition brought the living town closer to the "dead" one, and very soon monopolized the burials. Except for those who had near relatives in the old grave yard, or for those who had special reasons for not seeking, or not being allowed, participation in the new one—as the negroes—the old one soon became almost obsolete. North of the new cemetery was a superb forest and pasture extending to Maryland street. The southern portion of this was laid off into a third cemetery in 1852, extending to the track of the Indianapolis and Terre Haute Railroad, by Messrs. James M. Ray, James Blake and Edwin J. Peck. Eight years later the ground in the rear of this last addition, bordered by the river, was laid out into a cemetery, and a small section along the railway was bought by the National Government for the burial of dead rebel prisoners in 1862. This last addition was little used, and the much more eligible arrangement of the Crown Hill Cemetery superseded it entirely, so that within the present year (1870) the Terre Haute Railroad Company have obtained a release of the Government cemetery, removed all the corpses, and built there a fine and capacious engine house. The eastern half is still a cemetery, but that next the river is returned to less melancholy uses. The "grave yard pond" was once as well known a feature of the topography of the capital as the river itself. It was three or four hundred yards long by a hundred wide, and was supplied partly by springs, and partly by freshets, which made the river rise and run through it. For many years it was a favorite skating place, and was afterwards a frog's paradise. Now it has utterly disappeared. All the dirt, chips and refuse and nuisances of the city are emptied into its bed, and the new Rolling Mill has covered the upper end of its site with one of its buildings and its railway track.

On the 5th of August, 1844, a meeting was held to make arrangements for the visit of General Cass, who came on the 25th,—spoke in the Military Ground, in reply to a welcome from Governor Whitcomb,—had a reception at the Palmer House, and went on to Dayton the same evening.

The year following, 1845, was distinguished by the culmination of the only native theatrical company the capital has ever had. Some two or three years before, a large frame building had been erected on the north west corner of Market and Mississippi streets, for a foundery, that never came to any thing, and during this year the "Indianapolis Thespian Society" took it, built a stage in it, put in seats, got some fair scenery, and during the summer and fall gave some very fair performances there. The chief actors were James McCready,—afterwards Mayor,—Edward S. Tyler, James G. Jordan,—afterwards City Clerk, and first Secretary of the Bellefontaine Railroad,— Davis Miller,—once Door-keeper of the Senate,—James McVey, and, towards the close, Nathaniel Cook, a regular actor, and his younger brother John, sons of John Cook, once State Librarian. The last, and Messrs. McVey and Miller, took female parts, as there were no ladies in the Society. The first performance was of Robert Dale Owen's drama of "Pocahontas," which had little other recommendation than its Indiana authorship. The "Golden Farmer" was "run" for several weeks, very successfully. Mr. Tyler was the favorite as "Jimmy Twitcher," and Mr. McCready as "Old Mobbs," and Mr. Jordan as the "Farmer." Home's tragedy of "Douglass" was played when young Nat. Cook came out; and it has been worse played by actors of more pretensions. Cook played "Young Norval" and James Jordan "Glenalvon;" Davis Miller played "Lady Randolph." Jordan was a good actor, with unusual natural talents for the stage, and in this day could have made an enviable reputation. Young Cook was an actor by profession, but not remarkably good, and never made any figure greater than that of a "stock" actor. His brother Aquilla was afterwards connected with a theatre in Cincinnati, where he murdered the Treasurer, for some fancied insult to his wife, who was a dancing girl. The Cook family made a considerable figure in the town about this time; but it went out, as the Hoosier phrase has it, "at the little end of the horn." John Cook, the father,— who was State Librarian,— led the choir at the Temperance meetings which Mr. Hawkins, the old Baltimore reformer, held in the Court House. The favorite air was the "Blue-Tailed Fly," to which a reformatory and exhortatory song was adapted by some queer process.—This season of Temperance excitement was preceded some years before, by another and more important one, inaugurated by a Mr. Matthews, one of the Washingtonian Society. His speeches were strong, direct and very effective; and he made them more so, by singing some temperance ditty as an introduction. "What's the News?" was one of these. His cause was a new one in the capital, and his language, — though we have become used to it now,—was then considered tolerably harsh. One night he roused old Jerry Collins, the chief of doggery keepers, so greatly, that he interrupted the speech. Quite a "revival" was instituted; and many a "soaker" was arrested, for a longer or shorter time, by the good influences set to work by it.

On the 4th day of July, a negro by the name of John Tucker, was brutally murdered by a mob of white men, for no offense except his courageous defence of himself. A young man, named Nicholas Woods, began the difficulty in a drunken frolic, by abusing Tucker, who tried to avoid him. Finding that impossible, he gave Woods a thrashing. The latter followed him up, and soon collected a crowd of "roughs" and citizens, some of whom began stoning the negro. He retorted, and hurt some of his assailants. At this time he was on Illinois street, near where the Bates House now stands. Here he was driven upon the east side walk, when a saloon keeper, named Bill Ballenger, struck him down with a club. Ballenger made his escape. Woods was sent to the penitentiary, which he has since re-visited once or twice, on the solicitation of juries in larceny cases.

The celebration of the 4th was enlarged this year, by a military addition, and speeches were made, on the part of the companies, by Edward Lander, Judge of the Court of Common Pleas, and William Wallace, in Henry Ward Beecher's church.

The report of the murderous affray going on but a hundred yards from the church, greatly disturbed, and nearly destroyed, the meeting. During the summer, Washington street was graded and gravelled. The old McAdamizing was pretty well worn out, and the improvement raised the street,—too much, probably, in the middle,—and covered it with coarse gravel. The building on the south west corner of Meridian and Washington streets, was erected this summer, by Seton W. Norris. The "Locomotive," a little weekly paper, was started this summer, by Daniel B. Culley and David R. Elder. It was nothing but a boyish affair at first, and was filled with boyish "bread and butter" articles; but in 1848, after a suspension of a year or so, it was revived by Elder & Harkness, conducted by Mr. John R. Elder, and made a paper of considerable influence. Its circulation, for some years, exceeded that of any other paper in the town. The old Methodist church, built in 1828, on Meridian street, near the Circle, had, in 1845, become unsafe, as well as inadequate, and it was torn down. Wesley Chapel succeeded it, during the fall and ensuing summer of 1846. In 1869 the Chapel was sold to Mr. Richard J. Bright, and by him converted into a large and very handsome business house, mainly occupied by the "Indianapolis *Sentinel*" establishment, and that of the "*Evening News.*" A new church has just been completed on the south west corner of Meridian and New York streets.

The interest of the next year, 1846, centered in the Mexican war. Governor Whitcomb's proclamation, calling for the State's quota of volunteers, was published on the 23d of May, and was responded to with great alacrity. Three regiments were soon raised and organized, of the first of which our town furnished one company, under Captain James P. Drake, and Lieutenants John A. McDougall and Lewis Wallace. Captain Drake was made Colonel of the regiment, in the rendezvous at New Albany. This regiment was kept at the mouth of the Rio Grande, during pretty much all of its year's service, and suffered greatly from the diseases incident to the climate and camp life. A year afterwards, two other companies were raised by Captain Edward Lander and John McDougall, and were attached to the fourth and fifth regiments, which were taken by General Scott in his march upon the City of Mexico. These five regiments constituted the whole of Indiana's contribution to the Mexican war. The regiments raised during the rebellion, were numbered from these, the first being the sixth.

The Madison Railroad was now coming so close to the town, that its impulse was felt in business; and the first throbbings of the energy which was to develop such great results, began to stir the little county town with the hopes of greatness and prosperity which the visit of the "Robert Hanna" created and disappointed. The Company had selected its depot-ground on South street, east of Pennsylvania, then clear out of town. But the ground was high, and cheap, and convenient; and the first angry complaints of the citizens at this mislocation, soon died out in the bustle and excitement of the actual arrival of the road in 1847. The depot would not come to the town, so the town went to the depot,—planted heavy business houses all around it, and created, for a time, a sort of commercial center there. The creek was straightened from Virginia Avenue to Meridian street, by the property holders, and the streets graded and filled across the low muddy space of the creek "bottom."

The gamblers, who were bold and bad enough for Vicksburg, had become very offensive during the year, and the citizens held a meeting, and resolved to clear them out by constant prosecutions under the statute. A committee of thirteen or fifteen was appointed, consisting of the best and most respected citizens, to carry on the war. They began by securing the services of Hiram Brown,—one of the ablest members of the bar in the days when it was strongest,—to prosecute the scoundrels, and raised a

(6)

considerable sum of money for expenses. These preparations had their effect, and the gamblers were chased out without any prosecutions at all, or not more than one or two.   Lemuel Frazier, who kept the "Capital House," having been stirred up for allowing gambling in his hotel, retaliated by suing the committee for malicious prosecution; but nothing ever came of it.

THIRD PERIOD--TO 1860.

Chapter IX.

CONDITION OF THE CITY IN 1847—THE GREAT FRESHET—CITY GOVERNMENT—
STREET IMPROVEMENTS — MASONIC HALL — MADISON RAILROAD — SCHOOLS—
MISCELLANEOUS.

THE year 1847 marks the first great change in the condition and prospects of Indianapolis. Heretofore it had been a mere country town, which owed all its importance to the possession of the Capital. Its business was purely local. It produced little, and it distributed little that it did not produce. A small amount of "jobbing" was done in an irregular way among the smaller dealers and manufacturers of the neighboring towns, but it was neither large enough or certain enough to be considered a branch of trade. The manufacturing, except for home demand, was even more trifling than the mercantile, business. Occasional attempts had been made at iron, wool, oil, tobacco, hemp, and even ginseng manufacture, but none of them amounted to much or lasted long. The only attempt on a large scale, that of the Steam Mill Company, was a conspicuous failure. The town was isolated, and its only chance of trade was like that of the two boys locked up in a closet, who made money by swapping jackets. It lacked a way out and in. When this opening came, with the opening of the Madison Railroad, there came with it much such a change as comes upon boyhood at puberty. There was a change of features, of form, a suggestion of manhood, a trace of the beard and voice of virility. Manufacturers appeared, and would not disappear. "Stores" that had formerly mixed up dry goods, groceries, grain, hardware, earthenware, and even books, in their stock, began to select and confine themselves to one or two classes of their former assortment. Dry goods houses which kept neither coffee nor mackerel, appeared. Grocery establishments which sold neither calico nor crockery became visible. Business showed its growth in its divisions. The town itself showed the forecoming shadow of manhood in larger business houses, and the dropping down, here and there, in remote corners, of "family groceries." The price of property advanced. A city form of government was adopted. A school system was inaugurated. Everybody felt the impulse, without exactly feeling its direction, of prosperity.

In the first decided development of this change the year 1847 opened. On the 7th of January the "great freshet" reached its highest point. The river had never been so high before, except once, and has never been within three feet of the same mark since. It covered all the bottoms, and swept away miles of fences, and thousands of cattle, hogs and horses. Many fine fields were so covered with sand and seamed by the rapid currents that they were ruined, and many a prosperous farmer was nearly ruined by its devastations. So great and general were its ravages that the Legislature allowed a reduction of taxes to the sufferers. In the Capital the mischief of the river freshet was confined to West Indianapolis, or "Stringtown." It was covered entirely, from the bridge to the bluff at "Palmer's Farm." Many houses were filled nearly to the second story. The water rose high enough to cover the National Road, and in two places currents ran so fiercely that they cut through the road-way, and made ugly gaps fifty feet wide and eight or ten feet deep. On each side of the road at both breaches, the soft alluvial soil was dug out by the whirling eddies into huge holes like the craters of small volcanoes. They were fully thirty feet deep, and the southern hole, of the largest gap, was so large that a two-story frame house, which had been floated from its place by the current, was left sticking against its eastern bank, all askew, and ready to slide to the bottom at any moment. Nearly a half mile of the National Road was covered by the water. A considerable breadth of the high bank, along where the pork houses and railroad bridges now stand, was cut away, making the first approach to the change which has since brought the river to the very edge of the cemeteries. There used to be a small island a hundred or two hundred yards long, in the river, opposite the "Old Grave-Yard," and separated from the eastern bank by a narrow stream, sometimes entirely dry in summer. This island was covered with large trees, and at the head of it was a drift which for many years was a favorite place for catching "red-eyes," cat-fish, and bad colds. Between the "chute" east of that island and the Grave-Yard was a considerable breadth of forest. Now that island and that whole breadth of forest are on the west side of the river, on McCarty's sand-bar, and the water has actually cut into the Grave-Yard. The river has come one hundred yards eastward since the freshet of 1847 began the removal. Although the river did not directly damage the town, the freshet in Fall Creek and Pogue's Creek did. The former tore out the canal aqueduct, and the latter tore out the canal culvert, and between them ruined the canal for a year. Fall Creek, too, sent surplus water into the swamps north-east of town, and they poured out a flood into the "ravines" which filled a number of lots, and damaged a good many houses on their way through to the river. They emptied into the canal, and caused it to make a third break, as before noticed, below where the Rolling Mill now stands.

The news of the famine in Ireland created here, as elsewhere, a great deal of feeling, and successful efforts were made by public meetings, committees, and newspaper appeals to raise contributions for the relief of the sufferers.

As if to prepare for the material change hastening up the Madison Railroad, the town now took measures to form a city government. The Legislature on the 13th of February voted a city charter, appointing the 27th of March for an election to determine whether it should be accepted. Joseph A. Levy, a blacksmith, President of the Council, published a proclamation ordering an election on the appointed day. It was held, and resulted in a vote of 449 votes for the charter, to 19 against it. This was a very light vote, as it would indicate a population of less than 3000, and as it was 8000 in 1850, it is clear that either the town nearly trebled its population in three years, or the citizens of 1847 deemed the adoption of the charter a foregone conclusion and did not trouble themselves to vote. The population at the time of the adoption of the new charter and city form of government, and the commencement of the new era in its history, was probably about 6000. The new charter extended the government over the whole donation, except the "make-weight" fraction in Stringtown, and divided it into seven Wards, four north, and three south of Washington Street. Those north were divided by Alabama, Meridian and Mississippi Streets; those south by Illinois and Delaware Streets. The Mayor was not to preside in the Council, but had a veto power on its acts. He served two years and had the jurisdiction of a Justice in addition to his municipal authority. There was one Councilman for each Ward, who was paid $24 a year for his services. The Council elected their own President, and held monthly meetings. It had all the customary powers of such bodies, with one now taken from it, that of electing the subordinate city officers, as Marshal, Treasurer, Secretary, Street Commissioner, Attorney, and all other officers they needed. No tax could exceed 15 cents on the $100, except by authority of a special vote of the people. The first election was held on the 24th of April, and resulted in the choice of Samuel Henderson for Mayor, in favor of a tax for free schools, and of the following Councilmen: First Ward, Uriah Gates; Second, Henry Tutewiler; Third, Cornelius King; Fourth, Samuel S. Rooker; Fifth, Charles W. Cady; Sixth, Abram W. Harrison; Seventh, William L. Wingate. The new Council organized on the 1st of May by electing Mr. Rooker President, and James G. Jordan Secretary, salary $100; Nathan Lister, treasurer, $50; James Wood, Engineer, $300; Wm. Campbell, Collector, paid by fees; Wm. Campbell, also, Marshal, $150 and fees; A. M. Carnahan, Attorney, fees; Jacob B. Fitler, Street Commissioner, $100; J. B. Fitler, also, with David Cox, Messengers for Fire Companies, $25; Sampson Barbee and Jacob Miller, Market Clerks, $50; Joshua Black, Assessor; Benjamin Lobaugh, Sexton. With this crew and organization the good ship "*City* of Indianapolis" set sail on the 1st day of May, 1847.

The new city government, whatever pretentions might be involved in the title, started with as little support of metropolitan dignity as any city ever did. The tax duplicate showed a possible revenue of only $4,236, and one-fifth of that was made by past delinquencies; and street improvements had accomplished little beyond what might have been seen in any country road. Stumps and mud-holes were ugly disfigurements of the streets, and the first efforts of improvement were naturally directed to their removal. The means, no less than the unenterprising disposition of the authorities, prevented any more general or permanent effort. Side-walks were not common off Washington Street, and elsewhere were merely strips of gravel with depths of mud on either hand. Large spaces of open ground, or common, could be seen in all directions covered by "dog-fennel" of luxuriant growth. The ditches were shallow furrows, bordered, and oftentimes choked up, with "dog-fennel." Except where travel had worn away the sod, in a sinuous line that dodged a stump in one place and a mud-hole in another, the streets were masses of "dog-fennel," pleasing enough, possibly, in a picturesque point of view, but decidedly otherwise in any view that contemplated the prosperity of the new city. It is only within the past few years that this characteristic growth of the city has disappeared, and even now there are scattered patches of it clinging, like the Indian, to the territory which it once occupied alone and supreme. In any proper sense we had no streets. They were merely openings which might be used or not, as the weather made them impassable mud or insufferable dust. The town was gathered in a loose way, in the center of the donation, huddled pretty closely together for four or five streets, divided by Market Street, and sprangling off in clumps of settlement at other points, while much of the "donation" outside of the original plat was pretty good hunting ground for quails and squirrels. Only four or five years before, the woods west of Samuel Henderson's farm, where the "Home for Friendless Women" now stands, was a favorite resort for wild turkeys, and they had occasionally been driven, in the fury of the chase, clear into town. One was caught, in this way, in the Governor's Circle as late as 1841, by Mr. A. D. Ohr. On the south, the pasture where the Old Rolling Mill stands, was a capital squirrel ground, and visits of quails into the heart of the town, and their capture in back-yards and about stables, a very common occurrence. It happens occasionally even now.

Into this still half village, half forest city, the new government determined to introduce a general system of improvements. The plan of grading proposed by Engineer Wood in 1841, and adopted in 1842, was readopted, with the addition that it should be carried out systematically, by improving the central portion of the city first, and extending improvements outward as opportunity permitted. The cost of grading and graveling the streets and side-walks was taxed against the owners of the property, and, of course, caused a good deal of ill will and litigation. But as it had the advantage of making only those pay who were benefitted, it stood firmly against the numerous complaints of its injurious operation. The cost of making crossings, which consisted then, and do yet, of little wooden bridges across the gutters, was paid out of the Treasury. In this way began the improvements which have since made tolerable thoroughfares of one hundred and forty-six miles of streets, and very good ones of a number of them. Bouldering was not attempted until 1859, when Washington Street was paved in this way from Illinois to Meridian, and in 1860 from Mississippi to Alabama. This year (1870) Delaware Street has been paved with wooden blocks, upon the Nicolson plan, from Washington to North Street, and its superiority to the noisy, rough bouldering is so marked that it is possible it may be extended to all the principal streets. Notwithstanding the laudable efforts of the first city government, but little, comparatively, was done in street improvements until 1860. What is now to be seen has been mainly accomplished since then.

With the introduction of the first general system of street improvements came the free school system. The State fund yielded barely enough to maintain the schools for a single quarter, and left teachers and pupils to provide for themselves for the remainder of the year. It was hoped that a local addition might be made which would enable the schools to be kept open all, or the greater part, of the year. To this end a provision was made in the new charter authorizing a vote at the election of city officers upon the question whether a tax should be levied for school purposes. It was decided, to the credit of the citizens, almost unanimously in the affirmative. The tax having been assessed, and a provision thus made for a complete and permanent system of free education, steps were taken at once to apply the provision effectively. Donations of lots for houses, and money for tuition, were asked, to eke out the inadequate supply of both the State and city fund. The Council in the winter passed a vote of thanks to Thomas D. Gregg for the donation of $100. Others may have been more or less liberal, but no Council vote indicates it. Luckily real estate, though rising under the general impulse, was cheap, and lots were obtained for $300 to $500 in all the Wards during the following two years. Of course provision had first to be made for the erection of houses, and until that was done, by the accumulation of the city tax, the Ward schools were merely State District schools under city supervision. But the city tax came in, slowly at first, but rapidly enough by 1852 to have completed small brick houses, of one or two rooms each, but so adjusted as to allow future enlargement, in all the Wards. The yield of 1847 was $1,981; of 1848, $2,385; of 1849, $2,851. By 1850 it was $6,160 of which $5,958 had been expended upon houses and lots. Nothing being left for tuition beyond the provision of the State fund, it was paid by fees. In other words, the State provision was merely divided among the Wards and maintained in that

form until the city provision had become considerable enough to permit the inauguration of a system of city free schools. This was done in 1853. Three Trustees,
Henry P. Coburn, Calvin Fletcher, and Henry F. West, were elected by the Council to take entire control of the schools. The separate Ward Trustees were abolished, and the whole system brought together and made compact and manageable.
Calvin Fletcher drew up a series of rules and regulations, and a plan of operations,
teachers were obtained, matters set in order, and on the 28th of April, 1853, the
city free schools were really opened, with two male and twelve female teachers.
This was the beginning of what has since grown through many difficulties and em-
barassments into one of the most perfectly constructed and admirably conducted
school systems in the United States. The detailed account of the changes and difficulties through which it has passed will be found in another place.

Like all country towns, the capital had, up to this year, been compelled to hear
its lectures and concerts in churches or the Court House, with an occasional diversion to the Hall of Representatives in the State House. No special provision had
been made for so important an element of city life as a place of public entertainment.
One of the first manifestations that a new order of things was approaching, was the
resolution of the Grand Lodge of the Free Masons to erect a splendid edifice to
contain not only rooms for the Grand and city lodges, but a large hall for public
uses. In May they purchased the southeast corner of Washington and Tennessee
streets, and formed a company, of which they themselves took a large share of the
stock, to carry out this purpose. A plan of building proposed by Mr. J. Willis,
one of the first architects who became a resident here, was adopted, and measures
taken at once to proceed with the work, under the supervision of the Hon. Wm.
Sheets. On the 25th of October the corner-stone was laid with imposing Masonic
ceremonies, and the singing a song written for the occasion by Mrs. Sarah T.
Bolton. The work was not very energetically pushed, however, and it was not till
the spring of 1850 that it was so far completed that the public hall could be opened.
It was first occupied—if the writer's memory is not at fault—by Mrs. Lesdernier for
a concert or dramatic reading, and was in frequent request afterward, although the
upper or lodge rooms were still unfinished. They were completed during the fall
and winter, and the hall was dedicated by the Grand Lodge, at its annual meeting,
May 27th, 1851. The Constitutional Convention of 1850, after a few days' session
in the Representative's Hall of the Capitol, finding its accommodations inadequate,
and, moreover, having to give place soon to the Legislature, adjourned to the new
hall which had been prepared for it as fully as possible, and continued there till its
labors were completed. From its opening until the erection of Morrison's Opera
Hall, the Masonic Hall was the scene of nearly all public displays and entertainments given in the city. Political conventions, religious meetings, concerts, theatrical entertainments, lectures, balls, fairs, and panoramas, occupied it in turn. Horace Greeley, Henry Ward Beecher, John B. Gough, Theodore Parker, Ralph Waldo
Emerson, Henry Giles, lectured there, and Alexander Campbell preached there.
Madame Bishop, Bochsa, Strakosch, the now celebrated Adelina Patti, Carlotta
Patti, Ole Bull, and a long list of musical celebrities, performed there. In fact,
for fifteen years it may be considered the embodiment of the intellectual and esthe-
tic life of the city. The stock has all long been absorbed by the Grand Lodge, and
recently the building, and hall, too, have been repaired and greatly improved. For
a while after the opening of the Opera Hall, more centrally situated, and in some
respects better adapted to public uses, Masonic Hall fell into disrepute, and became
the resort of second-rate exhibitions. But since its repair, and the burning of the

Opera Hall in the winter of 1869–70, it has resumed its old position. As the Opera Hall has been left out of the new building on its site, it is likely that the old hall will retain its long supremacy a while longer.

The return of our volunteers in Mexico being anticipated, a meeting was held in May to prepare a reception for them, but as they did not come back in a body, the reception failed. Subsequently a public demonstration in their honor was made in the State House Square, at which Hon. Edward A. Hannegan made a speech, but a very rainy, inclement day spoiled it, to a great extent. A number of the volunteers came out, however, and brought their old battered and honored flags with them. In July the body of Captain Trusten B. Kinder, of this city, but who resided in one of the south-west counties of the State when he entered the army, and who was killed at the battle of Buena Vista, was brought home, and received with one of the most imposing popular displays ever witnessed in the city.

The lack of female teachers for our schools led to efforts this year to get up a sort of " Koopmanschaap " emigration scheme, to supply the deficiency, or rather it induced an application for help to Governor Slade of New Hampshire, who had for some time been conducting such a scheme. He sent on a small supply of teachers in June. They were distributed through the State, and, of course, soon married off. So the result, however beneficial in the end, left the schools little better off.

The Madison Railroad, now advancing rapidly from Franklin, would reach us on the 1st of October, and on the 25th of September a meeting of citizens was called to make preparations to celebrate the great event—really great for it realized all and more than was anticipated by the wildest enthusiasm inspired by the visit of the " Robert Hanna " in 1831. About 9 o'clock, on the morning of the 1st, the last spike was driven, just in time for the passage of two large excursion trains from below, and the locomotive came, for the first time, into the town which has since been justly enough known as the " Railroad City." Its arrival was witnessed and cheered by thousands of the " natives," most of whom had never seen a railroad or engine, and whose notions of a speed of twenty miles an hour were so indefinite as to be slightly mixed with the fabulous. Many of them improved the opportunity to make an excursion to Franklin, while the thousands who remained joined in swelling the monster procession which was to be the feature of the day's ceremonies. Spalding's circus was " showing " in the city at the time, with the band of the celebrated bugler Ned Kendall, and the whole troupe, with a cavalry company from the country, lent their attractions to the display. Governor Whitcomb made a speech from the top of a car in conclusion of this portion of the ceremony, and then all made for the hotels ' up town " for dinner. At night there were fire-works, an illumination, and a general "good time." The rejoicings were not extravagant, and if they had been they would not have exceeded the importance of the occasion which for the first time rendered the Capital independent of mud, ice and freshets. The long reign of the "wagoners"—the Peereys, Stucks and Ritchies—was ended.

The Madison Railroad depot was built, as heretofore stated, on the elevation, the site of the old " Hawkins " place, on South Street, east of Pennsylvania, then entirely out of town. The whole unoccupied "bottom" of Pogue's Creek intervened, and it was then, as it had been from the first, a muddy, unwholesome intervale, which bade fair to remain unsettled till long after the town had spread illimitably northward. Consequently, the location of the depot was generally censured as unwise. It was built during the preceding year, and speedily gathered a collection of groceries and commission houses, saloons and boarding houses, round it, and made a little city quite to itself. It has only been within the past ten years that any considerable progress has been made toward consolidating it with the parent city. But it is accomplished now, and Pogue's Creek valley has measurably disappeared under foundries, machine shops, mills, and railway tracks. The Company erected their machine shops in 1850, and built a frame car house over their track, which a hurricane blew down for them a few years afterwards. For five years the road was run upon a flat rail, a little more rapidly, but not much more pleasantly than a stage coach upon a "corduroy" road. But between 1850 and 1852 it was replaced by the T rail, and such a business, so far as profit goes, done upon it as no road is ever likely to do again. A detailed account of our railroads will be found in another place.

We may note, in concluding the sketch of 1847, that it witnessed the establishment of the first wholesale Dry Goods Store in the city—that of Joseph Little & Co., in the building, or next the building now occupied by James Sulgrove's Saddlery Hardware establishment. The firm subsequently became Little, Drum & Anderson, and in their hands the store was burned in May, 1848.

In January, 1848, Andrew Kennedy, an ex-member of Congress, and at the time a member of the Legislature, died of small pox, at the Palmer House. As his disease was not known at first, his fellow members had called upon him frequently; and, supposing themselves liable to the infection, created a panic, in which the Legislature adjourned. There was some cause for alarm; and the City Council, stimulated by a few fresh cases, set to work to provide a hospital. Universal vaccination was ordered, a Board of Health established, a hospital lot bought, material for a hospital got together, and a contract made with Seth Bardwell to erect it. But the panic disappeared, for the disease never spread widely; and the Council paid Mr. Bardwell two hundred and twenty-five dollars for his contract, and gave him the material, and thus the hospital enterprise failed. The contractor built a three-story frame house of the material, nearly opposite the Governor's House, and it is now used as a Hotel, and called the Indiana House.

The first Telegraph Company, under the charge of Henry O'Reilly, was chartered on the 14th day of February, 1848, subscriptions of stock received, and a line to Dayton built by the 12th of May, on which day the first dispatches were sent through it to Richmond. Newspaper dispatches were first published by the Sentinel, on the 24th of May. The first office was in the second story of Hubbard's block, and the first operator was Isaac H. Kiersted. Other lines have since been built, and, until recently, were all consolidated in the hands of the Western Union Company. But within the past year or so, another collection of lines, called the Pacific and Atlantic, has been made, which is operated in direct competition with the old one. Its office is on Meridian street, opposite Blackford's block, and is under the charge of E. C. Howlett. The first line, after opening in Hubbard's block, was removed to Harrison's, on Washington street,—subsequently to the rooms nearly opposite,— then to the second story of the building on the north west corner of Washington and Meridian streets, and lastly to Blackford's block, where it has an office on the ground floor, and operators' rooms above. It has been in charge of Mr. Kiersted, J. W. Chapin, Anton Schneider, S. B. Morris, J. F. Wilson, and J. F. Wallick. When the Magnetic Telegraph was first suggested as a suitable subject for Congressional encouragement, Governor Wallace, of this State, was a member of the House, and of the committee to which the matter of an appropriation was referred. His name coming last in the alphabetical order of the committee, it was his luck to decide a tie vote in favor of the appropriation. As little faith was felt by the great body, even of intelligent people, who had not seen the telegraph in operation, this vote of the Governor's was used against him with great, if not fatal effect, in his second race for Congress, with William J. Brown. But when the office here was opened, and the invention was seen to send and receive instantaneous communications with towns seventy miles away, suspicion gave place to amazement, and the general feeling was accurately and characteristically expressed by Jerry Johnson,—a very eccentric and witty old farmer who lived adjoining town on the north, and was the first man married in the town,—when he looked up at the one telegraph wire running along Washington street, and said: "Great Lord! who would ever have thought of seeing lightning driven down the street, and with a *single line*, at that?" Those familiar with the fashions of old teamsters, will understand the wit of the suggestion of the "single line." As many may not be, it may be well to explain that wagoners with three or four-horse teams, did not use a rein or line for each horse, as stage-coaches and carriages do, but used one long, heavy line, fastened to the bit of the "near leader;" and the "single line" being less easily managed, implied both more skill in the driver, and more obedience or intelligence in the horses.

In June, an attempt to form a Merchant's Exchange was made, with Charles W. Cady as Secretary, but it came to nothing. In 1853 it was succeeded by another attempt, better considered; but that failed, too, after making some effort to exhibit the advantages of Indianapolis as a manufacturing and commercial point. It was constructed by J. D. Defrees, N. McCarty, Ignatius Brown,—the author of the publication in regard to the city, and the author of a history of the city, from which most of the material of this sketch is taken—R. J. Gatling—of Gatling Gun notoriety, Austin H. Brown, and John T. Cox. The President was Douglass Maguire, the Secretary John L. Ketcham, and the Treasurer R. B. Duncan. It was succeeded in 1856 by a third failure, for want of money. In 1866 the Chamber of Commerce was formed, with Dr. T. B. Elliott as President, and J. Barnard as Secretary, and this last seems in a fair way to live. It has excellent rooms in the new *Sentinel* building.

The Indiana *Volksblatt*, the first paper published in a foreign language in the city, was established this year, by Julius Bœttcher, proprietor, and Paul Geiser, as editor. Its office was first a second floor room in Temperance Hall. But its success has since enabled its enterprising proprietor to build a house himself on Washington street, a little east of the Court house Square, and it has been published there for a number of years. It is Democratic in politics.

The Central Plank Road Company was chartered in 1848, to use the old National Road, and in 1849 laid their planks and put up two toll gates, one at the National Road bridge, and one just east of town. As this was taking an illiberal advantage of their franchise, the citizens wouldn't stand it, and the council obtained the removal of the eastern one, on condition that the company should not be responsible for the repairs of Washington street, which formed part of the National Road.

The Union Railroad Company, to which belongs the Union Depot and the city tracks connecting the different railroads centering here, was authorized by the Council on the 20th of December, 1848. There were no lines yet constructed to compete with the Madison, but several were projected, and a common passenger depot was so evidently indispensable, that it was devised as soon as the connecting roads were.

The year 1849 was little more than the record of promising but uneventful occurrences. The new life of the town was showing itself more and more plainly. Three hundred houses were built during the year, and the population was estimated at 6,500. A debt of $6,000, incurred by the street improvements of the preceding two years, was ordered, by a majority of eleven in a vote of the citizens, to be paid by a special tax, which raised the entire levy to forty-five cents on the hundred dollars. This was more than had ever been paid, and more than the State tax, and it caused a good deal of dissatisfaction with the city government. In the April election Horatio C. Newcomb was elected Mayor, in place of Samuel Henderson.— During the summer, Asbury University determined to assume something of the real character indicated by its title, and established here the Central Medical College as the medical division of the University. It was conducted by Drs. John S. Bobbs, Richard Curran, J. S. Harrison, George W. Mears, C. G. Downey, L. Dunlap, A. H. Baker and David Funkhouser, and occupied a large two-story brick buillding on the southeast corner of Washington and Alabama streets. Its first session, from November to March, was attended by twenty or more students, and a few graduates received diplomas. It continued some three years, and added to its faculty Prof. Deming, of Lafayette, who had been quite as much distinguished as a politician of the Free Soil school, and as the candidate of his party for Governor in 1846, as a physician. It lacked support.—At the preceding session of the Legislature a Court of Common Pleas was created especially for Marion county, with a jurisdiction compounded partly of the probate business of the old Probate Court and partly of the civil business of the Circuit Court, and Abram A. Hammond was made the first Judge, and was also clerk. He was succeeded by Edward Lander, who held the office till the Court was abolished or superceded by a general system of Common Pleas Courts, created in 1852, under which the Judges were elected by the people. The first was Levi L. Todd, succeeded in the following terms by Samuel Corey, David Wallace, John Coburn, Charles A. Ray, and Solomon Blair.—The Widows and Orphans' Society was organized in December of this year, to make provision for classes of distress that the Benevolent Society could not reach. Its receipts for the first year were $113.16, and its expenses $98.30. It was entirely dependent on private contributions for awhile, but has been aided since by an annual appropriation from the City Council. Allen May donated two lots to the Society, and they bought another afterwards. An asylum was built in 1855, at a cost of $3,000. Though starting with such small means and so little promise of good that few had any confidence that it would outlive the year, it has grown by the persistent efforts of the managers, and the evidences of its services, to a magnitude which would make it quite as difficult to dispense with it as it would be with one of the State Asylums.

The year 1850 was distinguished by a perceptible but not a dangerous earthquake on the morning of the 4th of April, and by the visit of Gov. Crittenden of Kentucky, with an extensive suite, on the 28th of May. This, the first official visit of one State Executive to another, was brought about by an invitation of Gov. Wright, who was desirous of drawing closer the bonds that connected the two States, and did his part in the work shortly after by marrying a Kentucky lady.— The death of President Taylor evoked a union funeral celebration in Wesley Chapel, and an eulogy by Rev. E. R. Ames.—The cholera was brought here by some German emigrants, but there was no epidemic or panic.—The Christian Church, under the influence of many of its members who lived north of Washington street, having resolved to abandon the old frame edifice on Kentucky avenue, which was built in 1836, or thereabouts, began their present chapel on the southwest corner of Delaware and Ohio streets. It has since been repaired and handsomely decorated.—E. W. H. Ellis and John S. Spann started the *Indiana Statesman* September 4th, but sold it out in 1852 to the *Sentinel.*—During the summer the Indiana Female College was organized, and the school opened in the building on the corner of Meridian and Ohio streets, now known as the Pyle House, by Rev. Thomas A. Lynch. It was suspended in 1859, but resumed in 1865 in the building of the McLean Seminary, and again suspended in 1868, when the premises were purchased for the new Wesley Chapel. It was successively conducted by Rev. Charles Adams G. W. Hoss, B. H. Hoyt, O. M. Spencer and W. H. Demotte —City receipts, ending April, 1850, were $9,327; expenses, $7,554. The total of taxable property was assessed at $2,326,185; polls, 1,243; population, by the census, 8,097— an increase of 1,500 in a year, and of $300,000 in value of property. There were 25 doctors, 30 lawyers and 120 industrial establishments.

Chapter X.

IN February, 1851, the Legislature chartered, for thirty years, with a capital of $20,000, a company originated by Mr. John J. Lockwood, called the "Indianapolis Gas Light and Coke Company." It was organized on the 28th of March, with David V. Culley as President, Willis W. Wright as Secretary, and H. V. Barringer as Superintendent. An ordinance of the City Council of March 3d gave the company a monopoly of the lighting of the streets and houses for fifteen years, authorized the laying of pipes upon certain conditions, and required that the price of gas should not exceed that paid at that time in Cincinnati. Not much confidence was felt by the public in the success of the company at first, and not much was done to deserve it. The works were defective, the officers inexperienced, and the city by a popular vote refused to light the streets. The present location of the works, on Pennsylvania street, on the south side of the creek, was that first selected, and during the fall the necessary buildings and apparatus to make a beginning were erected, and got ready for use in December. Mains were laid on Pennsylvania and Washington streets, and on the 10th of January gas was turned on for the first time, except that Masonic Hall had previously had a private gas apparatus. By the following April about a mile and a half of pipe had been laid, and 116 consumers with 675 burners had been obtained as patrons. This was not a flattering commencement, and the lack of city patronage for street lights, which is always a large source of the profit, made it worse. It was not till the fall of 1853 that street lamps were erected on Washington street between Meridian and Pennsylvania, and even then they were supported at the expense of the property owners. In the early part of 1854 several squares of Washington street, and portions of adjacent streets, were first lighted by contract with the Council, made in the preceding December. Gradual additions were made to the number of street lights, but not enough to embrace more than the most central and busiest portions of the city, and, therefore, those least likely to need their protection, till 1858-9. Then the policy of spreading the lights as widely and rapidly as practicable was adopted, and in 1860 eight and a half miles were lighted. At this time there can not be much less than forty miles of lamps. The posts were at first disposed with little regularity, but in 1859 it was ordered that there should be four to each square, one on each opposite corner, the others placed at equal distances between them. Since the addition of street lights to the patronage of the Gas Company it has prospered greatly. It began with $20,000 capital, erected its first buildings at a cost of $27,000, and finding them defective, rebuilt them in 1856 at a further cost of $30,000. In 1860, when the street-lighting policy began to show its effects fully, the new works were found inadequate and were rebuilt and enlarged to meet the demand. It began with one gas reservoir of 20,000 feet capacity. It added a second of 75,000 in 1860, and there not being enough in 1863 one of 300,000 and costing $126,000 was built on Delaware street. In 1868 a handsome three-story brick was built for the office of the Company on the south corner of the old Branch Bank lot on Maryland and Pennsylvania streets, and during the past summer another large addition was made to the works. Its capital has grown from $20,000 to $500,000, but it has expended its dividends mainly on its works. It consumes 800 bushels of coal per day, and produces about 200,000 feet of gas. Its Presidents have been David V. Culley, David S. Beatty, Edwin J. Peck, and Stoughton A. Fletcher. Its Superintendents, H. V. Barringer, C. Brown, E. Bailey, and H. E. Stacey.

The expiration in 1866 of the fifteen years' charter given by the city in 1851, opened the way for a controversy between the Council and the Gas Company which was not finally settled till 1868. As both sides had active and earnest partisans, and it is not the purpose of this sketch to take sides with either, it will be sufficient to state the steps in its rise and settlement briefly. On the expiration of the charter the Council gave notice that bids would be received for lighting the city for the ensuing twenty years. The Gas Company proposed to supply both city and citizens for $3 48 per thousand feet, and clean the street lamps for $5 48 each per year. (It had previously charged $4 50 per thousand feet, and $20 per year for each lamp, and $8 44 for lighting and cleaning.) It also claimed the monopoly of supplying private consumers under the Legislative charter for five years longer. This was the only bid received, and the Council rejected it, and disallowed the claim to monopolize the gas supply, but made a counter proposition that the Company should supply private consumers at $3 per thousand feet, and the street lamps at $28 80 each, the city to do the lighting and cleaning. Nothing came of this, and it was then proposed to capitalize the Company's property at $350,000, the city to have half the profits above 15 per cent., and continue the arrangement twenty years. The Company rejected this, but proposed to furnish gas to the city or citizens at $3 75 per thousand feet. This was not accepted, and in the spring of 1867 a rival company, called the "Citizens' Gas Light and Coke Company," formed by R. B. Catherwood & Co., of street railroad celebrity, made a proposal to take the charter for thirty years, and furnish gas at $3 per thousand feet, the city to contest the monopoly claim of the other Company. An ordinance embodying and modifying these terms, and holding the works subject to purchase by the city after ten years, was proposed on the 12th of March, 1867, and brought from the old Company a proposition to furnish gas for twenty years at $3 per thousand feet, with a number of minor provisions, and this was accepted, and the old Company re-chartered for twenty years from the 4th of March, 1867. But the controversy was not ended. It was soon found, or alleged, that the city was paying for fifteen or twenty street lamps more than existed, and paying for them whether lighted or not, and that the Gas Company was making the expense at $3 per thousand feet heavier than it was before. This produced a renewal of the difficulty, which was ended, finally, in the spring of 1868, by the election of a Gas Inspector, George H. Fleming, whose duty it is to see to the supply and quality of gas, and the interests of the city generally in regard to its gas. The cost of the city supply has been greatly reduced, and the lighting generally well attended to.

The organization and chartering of the State Board of Agriculture, mainly under the inspiration of Gov. Wright, on the 14th of February, 1851, though properly an affair of State rather than city interest, is yet too nearly identified with the development of the city to be overlooked. It has done something to encourage manufacturing by displaying our manufactures advantageously; has done quite as much, probably, by exhibiting the condition and improvements of the city to the tens of thousands of visitors annually attracted by its fairs; and has done more still by swelling our trade, as well as advertising it. Gov. Wright was the first President, and has been succeded by General Joseph Orr, A. C. Stevenson, Geo. D. Wagner, David P. Holloway, J. D. Williams, Stearns Fisher and A. D. Hamrick. The Secretaries have been John B. Dillon, W. T. Dennis, Ignatius Brown, W. H. Loomis, A. J. Holmes and Fielding Beeler. The Fairs, which have formed pretty much all the business of the Board, have been generally held here, with enough diversion to other points to demonstrate the advantages of our central location and railroad connections. Here, they were held on the Military Ground, which had been prepared by a high fence, and suitable "halls" or sheds, stalls, and other appliances, till 1860, when a large and beautiful grove north of the city, and clear beyond its limits at that time, was bought and fitted up, not handsomely, but so expensively, that what with the cost, the falling off in the interest in fairs during the war, the occupancy of the new grounds by the Government as a volunteer and prison camp, and the necessity of removing to the old ground, the Board was left with a debt on its hands which embarrassed it for several years. Since the close of the war, these [the Camp Morton] grounds have been reopened and refitted in excellent style, and during the fall of the present year [1870], the fairs both of the Indianapolis Association and the State Board, have been successfully held there. Its occupation as a prison camp during the war injured it greatly by causing the destruction of nearly all its superb trees. The General Government has, however, made some, if not full, compensation for these injuries. Fairs held at other points have either occupied the grounds of County Associations or been provided for by the citizens in consideration of the supposed benefit of having their town overrun by crowds for four or five days. The first was held for six days, in October 19—25, 1852, on the Military ground, and was very successful, the entries amounting to 1,365. The fair of 1853 was held at Lafayette, and as an additional attraction, Horace Greeley was obtained to deliver an address. Still it was not so successful as to warrant any strong hopes from the policy of making the fairs peripatetic. But the larger towns were indisposed to concede any advantages to the Capital, which they considered their rival, and demanded, as a right, that the "show" should come round to all of them in turn. The State Board decided to hold it here one year out of every three, as a compromise between the blind importunacy of other towns and its own interests, and it accordingly went to Madison in October, 1854. There its failure was so conspicuous and dismal that the Board brought it back, not only in accordance with their rule, but with the determination to keep it here. In 1855, 1856, 1857 and 1858 it was held here with decided success, especially in 1856 and 1857, when the receipts rose to $13,000 and $14,600 respectively. In 1859 the Board was forced into traveling again, and took the fair to New Albany. The receipts fell off to $8,000. It was decided to stop the traveling business and locate the fair permanently here, and here it remained through 1860—the war prevented it in 1861—1862, 1863, 1864. In 1865 it was taken to Fort Wayne, where it was quite successful—came back in 1866, and went to Terre Haute in 1867. The fair of 1869, here, was marked by a horrible catastrophe. Two saw mills were running a race on Friday, the first day of October, taking their power from the boiler in "Power Hall," and, through the culpable negligence or interest of the engineer, it was allowed to become red hot, and exploded, killing and wounding nearly one hundred people. The disaster would have been far more terrible if the great bulk of the crowd had not been drawn, at the time, to the "horse ring," to witness the trials of speed. As it was, it spread a gloom over the city exceeding any ever known in its history, and incited to the most earnest effort to provide for those who were dependent on the dead or helpless, or were too poor to secure proper assistance for themselves. A large amount of money was subscribed, and a committee of prominent citizens appointed to distribute it. A great deal of good was done by this movement, and it is but fair to state that the firm by which the ruinous boiler was made contributed with marked and prompt liberality.

At the election, in April, 1851, H. C. Newcomb was re-elected Mayor, but resigned in November, and the Council placed Caleb Scudder in the vacancy.—A special tax of five cents on the hundred dollars was, at the same election, ordered for the Fire Department.—Another election was held in September to decide the question of lighting Washington street with gas, and procuring a town clock. The first was lost, the other carried, and a clock was made by John Moffatt, for $1200, in 1853, which was placed in the steeple of Roberts' Chapel in 1854, where it remained, sometimes serviceable, and sometimes not, till 1868, when it was removed, and since then the city has had no public timepiece.—John B. Gough lectured in Masonic Hall, in May, on Temperance, the only topic he ever handled with marked ability or effect. The Hall was crowded constantly, and his last lecture, on a Sunday night, filled the street about the Hall for a considerable time before sunset.—A hurricane caused a good deal of destruction on the 16th of May, and was followed, on the 22d, by a devastating hail storm.—Gov. Wood, of Ohio, paid Gov. Wright an official visit on the 28th.—The Adams Express Company opened the first express office here in September of this year, with Messrs. Blythe & Holland as the first agents, succeeded soon by Charles Woodward, and he by John H. Ohr.—A Commercial College was commenced this year, in the building on the alley south side of Washington street, between Illinois and Meridian, by W. McK. Scott. An abortive Reading Room was attempted by the same man.—The County Agricultural Society was organized in August, and held a fair in October.—A secession of twenty-two members of the First Presbyterian church, on the 23d of September, led to the organization of the Third Presbyterian Church, with Rev. David Stephenson as pastor. A building was begun in 1852, on the northeast corner of Illinois and Ohio streets, and finished by slow degrees, so far as to allow the occupancy of the basement in 1859. The congregation in the meanwhile used College and Temperance Halls. Rev's. George E. Heckman and Robert Sloss have since been pastors.—The Church of the United Brethren, corner of New Jersey and Ohio streets, was begun this year and completed in 1852.—Madame Bishop, and Bochsa the celebrated harpist and pianist, gave the first first-class concert we had ever had, in Masonic Hall, on the 24th of May, to a delighted but not altogether appreciative audience. We did not know much of operatic beauties in those days.— An attempt was made to hold noon instead of morning markets, but it failed.— The city was making progress during this year. Charles Mayer built his iron-front house, the first in the city. We had two foundries, three machine shops and a boiler shop at work, fifty steam engines had been built, and Hasselman & Vinton had commenced making thrashing machines at their establishment. City receipts were $10,515, debt $5,407, school fund $6,199, expenses $5,935.

The most marked feature of the year 1852 was the increasing activity of railroad business, and the rapid growth of enduring improvements induced by it. So closely were these already identified that it required little sagacity to see that whatever might be the prospects of a new railroad to terminate here, it would never be unwise for the citizens to encourage it. The Madison road was in the full tide of prosperity. The Bellefontaine road was opened to the State line in November, and had already sent its share of activity ahead of it in the shops and depot erected in the northeast corner of the city. The Cincinnati road was approaching completion. The Jeffersonville road had been built to Edinburg, within railroad reach of us. The Terre Haute road was completed in May. The Peru road had been completed, with a flat rail, to Noblesville. The Lafayette road was completed in December. The Central had commenced laying track. The Union Track, connecting all these, had been completed, and the Union Depot built. We were beginning to feel our importance as a Railroad center, and exhibited our conceit in such sensible forms as new hotels, manufactures and business houses. The Bates House, the largest—subsequently greatly enlarged—hotel in the city, was built; also the Morris, now Sherman, House, opposite the Union Depot—enlarged to three times its original size a few years ago. The Washington Foundry was enlarged, and Osgood & Smith's Peg and Last Factory, Geisendorff's woolen mill, Drew's carriage establishment, Shellenbarger's planing mill, Macy's pork house, Blake's block, Blackford's first building on Meridian street, McLean's Female Seminary, school houses and Railroad shops, with many other buildings, were added to our improvements. It was a busy, bustling year, and saw the beginning of more than one establishment which has since made the fortunes of its founders.

But the very beginning of it also saw the most disastrous fire which, up to that time, had afflicted the city. East of the Capital House—since known as the Sentinel building—was a block of old buildings, by no means valuable, but filled with valuable business—extending to the alley, and on the night of the 10th of January it was burned to the ground. Among other items of destruction were the city records, in the City Treasurer's office. There were suspicions of incendiarism entertained at the time, and the insurance of one of the sufferers was contested by the Company on the ground that the fire was his own work, but the jury thought otherwise. A number of lawyers and doctors, who had their offices in the second story, were emptied into the street by this catastrophe.

On the invitation of the Legislature, particularly urged by Gov. Wright, Kossuth, the Hungarian hero and orator, visited the city on the 27th of February. A committee of fifty citizens had been appointed at a public meeting, a few weeks before, to receive him, and they went to Cincinnati on the 26th for that purpose. They accompanied him up, coming by way of Madison, and were received at the Madison depot by an immense crowd, who were at first full of adoration, but finding that the Hungarian troubled himself very little about them, and one of his suite kicking a little boy out of his way rather roughly, they changed their note and were not indisposed to think him a humbug. Ex-Mayor Newcomb made a speech to him in behalf of the city, and he was then escorted by a large procession to the State House Square, where Gov. Wright made another speech in behalf of the State. He replied in one of those wonderful efforts which commanded the admiration of all intelligent men, and was then escorted to the Capital House, where he and his suite were quartered at the expense of the city. He had a "levee" at the Governor's at night, and was introduced to the Legislature next day. On Sunday he visited Roberts' Chapel and several Sunday schools, and on Monday night delivered an address or lecture at Masonic Hall, before an association of Hungarian sympathizers. His principal object was to collect money to recover Hungary, a wild scheme which met little encouragement, though his talents

(7)

and misfortunes commanded a wide and generous sympathy. He took away about $1,000, chiefly paid for his "Hungarian notes," as keepsakes. Kossuth medals were sold in all the stores, and worn by everybody, but the Irish. Kossuth hats became the "rage," and for once the fashion was sensible. But this popularity was clouded by two circumstances: The Kossuth suite at the Capital House behaved with very considerable insolence, and ran up an enormous liquor bill; and the Irish cordially hated him, so cordially, indeed, that the Democratic convention following this event came near quarrelling seriously about him. He left on Tuesday, after a visit of four days.

During the summer the McLean Female Seminary was built by Dr. C. G. McLean, corner of Meridian and New York streets—a large and handsome three-story brick—and opened for pupils in September. It had one hundred and fifty the first year. When Dr. McLean died, in 1860, it passed into the hands of Prof. C. N. Todd, who maintained its high reputation and success till 1865, when it was discontinued and the property sold, as before noticed, to the Indiana Female College, which, after three years, sold it to the Wesley Chapel congregation, who have erected a magnificent church edifice upon the ground.

A balloon ascension was made on the 29th of July—the first ever witnessed here—by Mr. William Paullin. He was brought here by the enterprise of Mr. J. H. McKernan, but proved a bad speculation, though his ascension was fine, because the crowd could see all they cared to outside the enclosure erected round the State House Square—where he "went up"—and wouldn't pay. There was a display of fire-works at night. Several ascensions have since been made.

The Northwestern Christian University, the first and only successful attempt at the establishment of a regular collegiate institution in the city, was chartered by the Legislature in February, 1852. Stock taken on the "scholarship" plan by solicitors during the preceding year, to the amount of $75,000, was reported on the 22d of June, and on the 14th of July a Directory of twenty-one members was appointed, with Ovid Butler, the founder, manager and constant benefactor of the institution, as President. A beautiful grove adjacent to Mr. Butler's residence, in the extreme northeastern part of the city, was donated by him as a site, and a plan of building, devised by Mr. Tinsley, was adopted. This plan allowed the construction of the edifice in sections, each complete in itself, but capable of being united with the others when necessary. The style is Gothic, though not pure Gothic, but it makes a very handsome structure, which instantly commands the attention of the visitor in that quarter of the city. The west wing was built in 1854-5, at a cost of $27,000. No addition has yet been made, though the growth of the institution will soon make it necessary. It was dedicated on the 1st of November, 1855, by suitable ceremonies and an address by Horace Mann. Its first "Faculty" was composed of Hon. John Young, Rev. Allen R. Benton and Mr. James R. Challen. Its Presidents have been Hon. John Young, Samuel K. Hoshour, Allen R. Benton, O. A. Burgess, and recently Prof. Benton again. Its peculiarity is that it admits female pupils upon the same terms to the same classes as the males, and its remarkable success is a vindication of the wisdom of the plan. In 1869 Miss Kate Merrill, a lady of distinguished ability as a teacher, was elected to a regular chair, and the novel step has proved all that its advocates could wish. Within a year past Mr. Butler, to whom the University is indebted for its conception and existence, as well as its best support, has donated $10,000 more, to establish the "Demia Butler" Chair. During the present year there are about 300 students in attendance.

The beginning of the year 1853 is memorable, or should be, among a large

ODDFELLOWS HALL.
INDIANAPOLIS

class of our citizens, as the time which witnessed the permanent establishment of theatrical amusements here. Since then we have never been without a theatre "during the season." F. W. Robinson, better known as "Yankee" Robinson, whose skill as an advertiser and showman far exceeded his skill as an actor, after "operating" as a "side-show" to the first State Fair, in the fashion of English "strolling theatres," came back during the winter with his company, and opened in Washington Hall, on the 21st of January. He had a fair company, and did so good a business that the next winter he fitted up the third story of Elliott's new building on the corner of Maryland and Meridian streets as a theatre, called it the "Atheneum," and renewed his performances on a larger scale. A detailed notice of the theatres of the city will be made in another place.

Following the example of the Free Masons, the Odd Fellows, this year, took steps to provide themselves with a Grand Lodge Hall. They procured Lodge and individual subscriptions to the amount of $15,000, bought the northeast corner of Washington and Meridian streets for $17,000, and erected, during the two following years, at a cost of $30,000, a building planned by Francis Costigan, and finished with a dome by D. A. Bohlen, which Mr. Brown caustically says "is probably unlike any other on earth." Its style is certainly nondescript, a sort of cross between a Gothic chapel and the Taj Mehal, but it is the most attractive building on Washington street for all that. The ground floor rents for a handsome interest on the cost, in a bank and other business houses, and the second story is rented for offices; only the third is used for Lodge purposes. It was dedicated on the 21st of May, 1856. A notice of the city Lodges, both of the Odd Fellows and Free Masons, is appended to the general sketch of the history of the city.

In March the City Council substituted the general charter act for our special charter of 1847, which limited taxes for city purposes to fifteen cents on the hundred dollars. The revenue yielded by so slender a source was inadequate to the rapidly growing needs of a rapidly developing city, and the change was necessary. It was retained till 1857. It made elections annual, and fixed them in May, and allowed more liberty of taxation. The first election under the new law was held on the 3d of May, when 1,450 votes were cast. Caleb Scudder was elected Mayor, Daniel B. Culley, Clerk; A. F. Shortridge, Treasurer; M. Little, Assessor; Benjamin Pilbean, Marshal; N. B. Taylor, Attorney; Wm. Hughey, Street Commissioner; James Wood, Engineer. On the 6th of May, at their first meeting, the new Council created the office of Fire Engineer, for the purpose of bringing all the engine companies under such government as would enable them to work together and to advantage. Joseph Little was appointed Engineer. The receipts for the year were $10,905; expenses, $7,030. The fire tax amounted to $2,093, the expenses to $1,018; clock tax to $105; schools, $6,745; expenses for houses, $6,458 Five fire cisterns had been built, five were in progress, and six had been located. The Council Chamber was removed from Hubbard's block to the opposite building, where it remained till it was removed to Odd Fellows' Hall, then newly finished, in 1855. The city assessment showed $5,131,082 of taxables, of which $1,239,507 were personal, and $3,891,875 real property. Of "heavy" tax payers we had 35 who paid upon more than $20,000, and 59 upon $10,000 to $20,000. The assessment of 1850 was $2,326,185. That of 1853 shows that the value of city property had doubled, and a little more, in three years, though the polls had increased only from 1,248 to 1,462 Property was "going up," not because there was twice as much of it, but because what there was was held at higher figures. Besides making a Fire Engineer, the Council created a Deputy for the Marshal, and fixed the salaries of the officers as follows: Mayor, $600; Clerk, $600; Marshal $500; Engineer, $800; Street Commissioner, $400; Clerk of Markets, $350; Sexton, $80, Deputy Marshal, $400; Councilmen, $2 for each meeting.

The "Old Settlers" held a meeting in the State House on the 31st of January, to recall "old times," and meetings were held annually thereafter, sometimes at Calvin Fletcher's and sometimes at James Blake's, till 1860. That of 1855, held at Mr. Fletcher's, was reported at great length in the *Journal* of the next day, and made these assemblages much better known generally than they had been before. They were discontinued when the war broke out, and remained so till this past summer [1870], when a meeting was held on the 7th of June to commemorate the fiftieth anniversary of the selection of the site of the Capital.—The Fourth Presbyterian church, corner of Delaware and Market streets, a colony of the Second [Beecher's] church, was commenced this year, and completed in 1854 so far as to allow of its occupancy.

The arrest, May 21st, of John Freeman, a colored man, a whitewasher by trade, who had been a resident of the city for a number of years, and was known as an unusually quiet and deserving man, as a slave under the Fugitive Slave Act, created the most intense excitement that had ever been witnessed in the city. He was claimed by a Georgia planter named Pleasant Ellington, as oath was made to his identity, Justice Sullivan, acting as United States Commissioner, had really no alternative but to surrender him. The alleged slave was permitted to prove his freedom, if he could, only after he was taken back to the State whence he was said to have escaped. His claimants insisted on taking him. They were armed, and ready for resistance. But his attorneys claimed that they could prove that he was a free man, really, and demanded time to produce witnesses. The streets were thronged with a fierce and resolute crowd while this controversy was going on. All the enginery of the law was set in motion to gain time, backed by a singular unanimity of public feeling. If an attempt had been made to take him, as the United States Marshal wanted to do, without giving him a chance to prove the falsity of the claim against him, there would have been an ugly fight, and a rescue. The case was postponed, however, and Freeman, after lying three months in jail, while General Coburn, one of his counsel, went South for proof, had the tardy justice done him of being released on the 27th of August. Several planters, who knew him well, came up from Georgia and swore to his having been a free man, and the case was ended, and he was forgiven by the Fugitive Slave Act for Mr. Ellington's perjury. The presence of the planters, and the public interest in the case, caused a meeting of congratulation to be called at Masonic Hall, where some very savage speeches, of an "abolition" tendency, were made. Ellington was indicted for perjury, and sued for damages, but nothing ever came of it.

The excitement in this case was never equalled, except, possibly, in another negro affair of a different character, about the year 1838, and that was among a different class of people. A young lady organist for the Episcopal church—the first, probably, who held that position—overcome by the fascinations of a handsome mulatto, married him. The news got abroad among the rowdies, and a crowd of them attacked the house where she and her husband were lodged, dragged them out, tarred and feathered him, rode him on a rail and ducked him in the river, and abused her, though not so severely. Both were driven out of the town. This created an intense excitement for a few days. Some of the ringleaders became frightened at what they had done, and left for parts unknown, whence they have never, openly at least, emerged.

Appropos of excitements it may be noticed here that a strong temperance excitement was aroused in the summer of this year, and more general feeling enlisted than, probably, at any former time. Street speeches were frequent and fervent, and the fronts of saloons were often chosen for them. In September a committee waited on the saloon keepers, and found that a large majority of the forty-four then in the business had expressed a willingness to quit it. But they did not, till the Maine law, in 1855, forced them to do it, and that did not stop them long.—Two conventions of brass bands from different parts of the State were held during the year, one the 22d of February, under the lead of G. B. Downie, the other November 29th, under C. W. Cottom.—An attempt to establish an omnibus line from the Union Depot and on Washington street, was made this summer by Charles Garner and George Plant, but failed.—A large fire destroyed all the stables on Maryland street in the rear of the Wright House on the 10th of August.—The Indianapolis Coal Company, formed in the spring, brought the first coal to the city from the Clay county mines in the fall. John Caven, Mayor of the city from 1863 to 1867, in partnership with Robert Griffith, opened a mine near Brazil as early as did the Coal Company, and sent a few loads for use by his partner in his law office, but lack of capital prevented him from prosecuting the enterprise.—Another German paper, the *Freie Presse*, of Republican tendencies, was established in September, and the first number appeared on the 2d of that month.—Wm. Y. Wiley attempted to establish a stock auction room and exchange, but there was not enough business to keep it going.—Gavazzi, the assailant of the Inquisition and the Catholic church, which he had abandoned, lectured in Masonic Hall in October, followed by Lucy Stone in four lectures. Ole Bull gave his first concert, with Strakosch and Adalina Patti, on the 6th of December.—It was estimated that the value of buildings erected this year was $500,000.

The annual city election of 1854 resulted in the choice of James McCready for Mayor. The vote was 2,012. The Council this year determined to provide a regular police force, and in September appointed two officers to each ward—fourteen—with Jefferson Springsteen as Captain. During the summer of 1855, while attempting to enforce the Maine law against a German beer seller in the eastern part of the city, they were resisted by a large body of Germans, and the result was a terrible riot, in which several of the Germans were wounded. The police were sustained by a public meeting and by the Council, but the feeling against the law, and the expense of the force, finally induced the Council, on the 17th of December, 1855, to discontinue it and the Deputy Marshal too. But the town was riotous and unsafe, and a second force, of ten men, was created a month after, January 21st, 1856, with Jesse Van Blaricum as Captain. This was dismissed the next spring by the new Council, and the Marshal, Jeff. Springsteen, authorized to appoint one officer for each ward, with C. G. Warner as Captain. The year following this was undone, and one policeman for each ward was selected by the Council, with A. D. Rose as Captain. Two were added the next year, 1858, and Samuel Lefever made Captain. Rose was replaced in 1859. In 1861 two men were appointed for each ward, and Rose was retained. He was succeeded upon his entering the army, by Thomas A. Ramsay. John R. Cotton became Captain in 1862, two day patrolmen were added, and the force uniformed at the expense of the city. In May, 1863, the force was increased to seven day and eighteen night patrolmen, with a Lieutenant, and Thomas D. Amos as Captain. David M. Powell succeeded Amos within a week. The collection of thieves and rowdies, camp-followers and other nuisances attending the troops rendezvousing here, made it necessary to add a military guard to the police force, and the authorities did it, maintaining a strong guard at police headquarters till the close of the war. Detectives were added in December. In May, 1864, the police districts were fixed, and Samuel A. Cramer made Captain. In December, 1864, the force being deemed insufficient, sixteen men were added, to be retained till the following May. The Captain's salary was raised to $1,500, and the men's to $2.50 and $3.00 per day. Jesse Van Blaricum was made Captain again in the spring of 1865, with two Lieutenants, nine day and eighteen night patrolmen, two detectives, and sixteen special officers. He was succeeded in April, 1866, by Thomas S. Wilson, who resigned in 1869, and was succeeded by Lieut. Paul, who is the Chief now. The force now consists of 33 men, exclusive of the Captain and Lieutenant, and costs about $33,000 per year.

In September, 1866, a Merchants' Police Force was organized by Mr. A. Coquillard, which, as its name indicates, was designed merely for the protection of property. It consists of twelve men, and patrols some half dozen of the central blocks on and adjoining Washington street. It is paid by the property owners in the protected section, but is given police powers by the Council. There are also some four or five officers in the Union Depot, selected and paid by the Company, who are authorized policemen.

On the 21st of March, 1854, the Young Men's Christian Association was organized, and from the first has grown steadily in strength, influence and usefulness, till it is now inferior to no society in the State. It has maintained courses of lectures, not always profitably, has relieved the distressed systematically and constantly, and has extended its services into scores of hitherto unsuspected and untried channels of usefulness. To instance but one: It leaves stamps with the Postmaster to pay all letters carelessly or ignorantly deposited without, asking only that those who are able shall repay them. This saves probably a dozen letters every day from loss or delay. Its means grow steadily larger, and its circle of usefulness widens with them. Recently the question of erecting a building of their own has been discussed, and if it be not done now, it will be done before long. The International Convention of Y. M. C. Associations, which was held in this city this past summer, was a most impressive exhibition of the extent and power of these affiliated organizations. Delegates were in attendance from all parts of the country and from the British Provinces, and the welcome given them by the Association, as well as by the citizens, will hardly diminish their zeal much.

"Yankee" Robinson, as elsewhere noticed, opened the "Atheneum" in the fall of 1855, with a fair company, and Mrs. Sue Denin, Maggie Mitchell and J. P. Adams as stars.—The Tenth Regiment of Regulars, Col. Alexander, on their way to Utah, passed through the city in the fall, and attracted a great deal of attention, as the first body of soldiers as large as a regiment, and real soldiers too, that had ever been seen here. Capt. Bee, afterwards a Rebel General killed at Bull Run, was with this regiment when here.

Chapter XI.

THE year 1855, though it found the city prosperous, and progressing steadily in business and population, spreading rapidly in all directions over the "donation"—some sixty or eighty "additions" having been made to it by different holders of real estate since 1836, and Blake's, Drake's, Fletcher's, Drake and Mayhew's, Blackford's, and others coming in during the present year or the year before—found it also struggling with the first severe obstruction it had encountered. The Free Banks, founded on State stocks, and safe enough if prudently managed, had been allowed to multiply inordinately, and to work upon inadequate securities in some cases, and suspicion of their soundness was made certainty by a "feeler" of Gov. Wright's, who sent Mr. John S. Tarkington to a bank in the Wabash region, to "try its bottom." He found none. The bank couldn't redeem, and straightway began a movement against all the banks. It became almost a panic. The banks stopped payment; and as they furnished a large proportion of our currency the effect was disastrous. Business was checked at once. Buildings stopped half finished. New enterprises were smothered, old ones crippled or paralyzed. Everybody had money which nobody wanted to take. There was hardly any debtor so poor that he wasn't considered better than the bills in his pocket book. Nobody wanted to be paid, except at such a discount as nobody wanted to pay. To remedy this evil a convention of Free Bankers was held here on the 7th of January, 1855, to ascertain the condition and classify the notes of the different banks, that credit might be given to those that were sound, and the necessities of the public relieved as far as their circulation could do it. Up to that time the word of our city bankers was law. A man with a roll of bills took them to a banker to pass upon, and as he decided this one "good," and that one "worth eighty or ninety," and the other he "couldn't say," the roll was divided and preserved or got rid of accordingly. This was bad enough, but it became worse when these judgments varied every day or two; the good one day went to "ninety" the next, and the "uncertain" of one week came up to "fifty" the next. The convention of Bankers aimed to effect such a distinction as would relieve this embarrassment. They did what they could, and that wasn't much. Some dozen or more banks which were known all along to be safe, were classed or "gilt-edged;" a dozen or two more were put in a second class, and as many in a third, but as the data were uncertain, the classification was uncertain, and beyond the "gilt-edged," the money holder had to take the opinion of a broker or banker for what he was worth, just as before. The

Journal made a list of the different grades of banks, and changed them from day to day as the city bankers directed, and this publication did some service, and was consulted as constantly as the Union Depot time-table is by travelers. But entire relief only came with the cleaning out of the bad banks during the year 1855.

A second visit of the small pox in January of this year, continued into February, created a second panic and project to build a city hospital. On the 10th of March the Council took a decisive stand for it, and lots were purchased and plans made for a building in the extreme northwestern corner of the city, near the point where the Crawfordsville road crosses Fall Creek. There was then a vast, open, empty common between this location and the city, now almost entirely built up. The hospital was begun, but with the subsidence of the alarm came indifference about any provision for a future visitation, and the work lagged through four years, and was only finished in 1859. It cost about $30,000. During the greater part of the time from its erection till April, 1861, when the necessities of the troops compelled its restoration to its proper uses, it had been occupied by prostitutes and thieves. Several efforts were made to appropriate it to some useful purpose, but without effect. Some wanted to rent it, some to make it a prison for prostitutes. The Sisters of Charity proposed to take it, but the Council finally decided to make it a Home for Friendless Women. It was never used for this purpose, however, and was merely occupied by the person who took care of it. In May, 1861, it was given up to the use of the Government as a hospital, and retained till July, 1865, and then till the following November as a Soldiers' Home, when it was returned to the city, greatly enlarged and improved. Two large three-story ells had been added, besides outbuildings, and the grounds had been put in good condition. They were given for the rent of the hospital. A few weeks after the soldiers were removed to the Home at Knightstown, Rev. Aug. Bessonies, of St. John's Church (Catholic), asked that the Hospital be given to the Sisters of the Good Shepherd for a city prison for women, and the house of refuge (unfinished) should be conveyed to them on condition of its completion and use as a reformatory school for prostitutes. This was a rather "strong pull" in the opinion of the citizens, and they subscribed $6,000 to complete the House of Refuge and defeat the project of Mr. Bessonies. In the spring of 1866 suitable furniture and hospital supplies were obtained at the sales of the Government property at Jeffersonville, and a regular hospital was established in accordance with the original purpose. Directors and consulting physicians were selected, Dr. G. V. Woollen made Superintendent, and the hospital opened for patients on the 1st of July, 1866. It has been efficiently maintained since, at an annual cost of about $7,000.

The third prominent event of this year (1855) was the attempt to enforce the liquor law enacted during the preceding winter by the Legislature. The temperance movement assumed such formidable proportions during the years 1853 and 1854, that it could with propriety demand recognition of the political parties, and as the Democratic party repelled it unequivocally, it allied itself with the combination then forming from the ruins of the Whig party, destroyed in 1852. This combination was so heterogeneous, that a temperance mixture could, as easily as not, be stirred into it. The attempt to repeal the Missouri Compromise by the Douglas Kansas-Nebraska bill, brought the Free Soilers to the help of such Whigs as still retained a hope for their party, and both were reinforced, and largely absorbed, by the Know Nothing organization. The singular political episode presented by this association originated in a natural and proper desire to restrain the inordinate fluence of the foreign element in our country. The Democratic party had gained and retained this power by concessions that made it mischievous, the Know Nothings alleged, and it was necessary to the safety of our institutions that the predominance of the native element in our citizenship should be asserted. To this end a secret society was organized with the express object of repressing foreign influence. As the members made it a point to answer "I don't know," to every question regarding their association or its action, it obtained the name of "Know Nothing." However just may have been the object for which it was formed, it soon degenerated into an unqualified and indiscriminate hostility to foreigners of all classes. It started the wrong way to work, for a secret political society is inimical to the spirit of our institutions and government, and starting wrong, it went further and further wrong the longer it lived, and at last fell by its own weakness. But at the outset it spread rapidly, and, working secretly, the results it produced at elections startled and confounded its opponents. They were prostrated in city after city and state after state, without being able to see where the blow came from. Its career was an unbroken victory till Gov. Wise of Virginia checked it in the contest in that State in 1855. In this State, it carried the elections by sweeping majorities, and many ludicrous incidents were produced by the efforts of the Democrats to discover who their enemy was. A couple of well known citizens attempted to look into the rear windows of Masonic Hall while a State Know Nothing Convention was in session in 1855, and were discovered perched on the top of the water-closet building of the Hall, one peeping in and reporting to the other, who was taking notes, and a rough caricature of the scene, published in a little paper called the *Railroad City*, produced what Homer calls "inextinguishable laughter." The secrets of the society were, however, divulged shortly after, and published in the *Sentinel* of this city, and it soon went to pieces.

The combination of Know Nothings, Whigs, Free Soilers and Temperance men enacted a stringent prohibitory liquor law, after the Maine pattern, allowing no liquor to be sold except by authorized agents. It went into operation on the 12th of June, and Mr. Espy was appointed Agent for this township. It was enforced as far as it could be—and that wasn't far, for it was continually evaded and secretly violated—for about two months. On the 2d of July Roderick Beebee purposely violated it to test its validity. He was arrested, fined and imprisoned, and the case taken at once to the Supreme Court. The opinion being very generally entertained that the Court would decide against the law, it was soon entirely disregarded, but not until, as noticed in the last chapter, it had caused a bloody collision between the police and the Germans in the eastern part of the city. The Court, as was anticipated, decided it unconstitutional, and liquor was left without any restriction at all.

A convention of the Mayors of the cities of the State was held on the 22d of January, for nothing, so far as any result ever showed.—The first City Directory was issued this year by Grooms & Smith.—Twenty-one hundred Sunday-school children, with the Fire Companies, reinforced by the Hope Company of Louisville, celebrated the Fourth of July.—A building and Loan Fund Association was formed in the fall, and lived for some years, unprofitably, and was wound up.—A Fuel Association, formed the last of October, did better, for it furnished wood and coal to its members at fair rates.—A Women's Rights convention was held in Masonic Hall, October 22d and 23d, with Mrs. Rebecca Swank as President, and Mrs. Lucretia Mott, Ernestine L. Rose, Frances D. Gage, Adaline Swift, Harriet Cutler and Joseph Barker as leading participants.—The Black Swan sang at Masonic Hall; Powers' Greek Slave was exhibited at Masonic Hall;—Parodi sang at Masonic

Hall;—James E Murdoch attempted to play the only engagement he ever made
here, at the Atheneum, under the management of Brown & Commons, but his support was so execrable that he left after the second performance to a house consisting of just fifteen auditors.—The houses were first numbered on Washington street
this fall, but it was badly done, as was the attempt in 1858, which was superceded
in 1864 by the system which allowed fifty numbers to the square.—Park Benjamin,
David Paul Brown, Edwin P. Whipple, Henry B. Stanton, Bishop Simpson and
others lectured during the winter, before the Y. M. C. Association.

The year 1856 was ushered in by the coldest weather ever known in the city
or the Northwest. On the morning of the 9th of January the thermometer fell to
25°, some marked 28°, below zero. It has never been so cold since.—In May the
city schools had a pic-nic in the State Fair Grounds, marching out under the lead
of their teachers, in a procession that extended almost the entire length of the
town. The occasion was fearfully marred by the drowning of one of the pupils in
the basin at the west end of the grounds.

The first prominent event of the year was the meeting of the General Conference of the Methodist Church, on the 1st of May, in the Representative's Hall of
the State House. All the Bishops were present, and some of the prominent preachers of the denomination from England were also in attendance. The sessions
were daily attended by crowds of interested spectators, who never before, or since,
saw in that Hall discussions so ably and courteously conducted. The delegates
filled pretty much all the pulpits in the city, by invitation, during their stay.
This was the first national gathering that ever met here.

On the 6th of May the Democrats carried the city election for the last time.
The total vote was 2,776. The total taxables was $7,146,670, of which $1,892,152
was personal property. The receipts were $27,889, the expenses $46,105. The
city debt was growing fast. In 1854 it was $567; in 1855, $11,000; in 1856, $15,-
295. To fund the debt a loan of $30,000 was proposed to be negotiated in New
York, and Jeremiah D. Skeen was appointed the agent to negotiate it upon city
bonds. He "pawned" the whole amount to Winslow, Lanier & Co., for $5,000,
his political enemies—he was a Democrat—said, to get money to bet on the State
elections in the fall; but whatever his purpose, he kept the money, and his fraud
was not discovered till Winslow, Lanier & Co. notified the city of their possession
of the bonds and demanded payment. The city paid the New York bankers, and
twelve years afterwards, in 1868, obtained judgment against Skeen's sureties for the
whole amount with interest.

As the political contest of this year involved every office in the State or nation
of any consequence, and, besides, inaugurated the first general and organized effort
to resist the exorbitant power of the slavery party, and was doubly embittered by
the outrages of the Border Ruffians in Kansas in the effort to make the Territory a
Slave State in spite of the people, it was by all odds the most exciting conflict ever
known in the country. It was hardly equalled in intensity of feeling by that of
1860, though in extent and profusion of demonstration it was surpassed. The
Republicans on the 15th of July held a mass convention here, which, up to that time,
had never been equalled in numbers or enthusiasm, and the feeling was maintained
through the day not only by speeches, but by a singular display which "hit the sense"
of the crowd and the spirit of the occasion "point blank." This was a procession of
young men dressed to represent the Kansas "Border Ruffians" and "Buford's
Thieves," who exhibited a number of "tableaux" illustrating the cruelties and
crimes of those infamous villains. It was hailed with a continuous roar of laughter

and cheers as it passed down Washington street to the State House Square. A torch-light procession, with several thousands of torch-bearers, closed the performances at night. On the 17th the Democrats held a similar convention, little if at all inferior in numbers to the other, and closed with a torch-light procession equally magnificent. The Democrats carried the elections, if they did not the honors of lamp-wick and grotesque dresses, but so far as the city was concerned their success was short-lived. Henry F. West, the Mayor, elected in May, died on the 8th of November, and an election for his successor was held on the 22d to fill the vacancy, and that of City Clerk, created by the death of Alfred Stevens on the 26th of October. The Republicans carried it by a decided majority, and rejoiced over it with a degree of enthusiasm rather difficult to understand in view of the fact that the Mayor's power did not amount to much, and the Democrats had ten Councilmen out of fourteen. W. J. Wallace was elected Mayor, and Frederick Stein Clerk.

During the preceding winter the firm of Dunlevy, Haire & Co., established themselves here in the interest of Cincinnati bankers and brokers, who bought our bank bills at a big discount and "run" them back for the gold, to the serious injury of the business of the State and the city, both. Remonstrances, by both press and tongue, were loud and earnest, but had no effect on the Cincinnati blood-suckers, who would have "run" a depreciated bill back upon a blind beggar, if they knew he would starve if he redeemed it. The effect was that a convention of business men was held here in April to take steps to divert our Cincinnati trade to other points, where more liberality was promised, and, doubtless, would have been practiced, as Cincinnati was, beyond all question, the meanest city on the face of the earth. D. K. Cartter, of Cleveland, and a number of the leading men of that city, Toledo, Louisville and St. Louis attended, and exhibited the advantages of their several cities in speeches that gave us a great deal of valuable information, and lost Cincinnati a great deal of business.

An Art Association, of the fashion of the old Art Union, was formed, and continued for some years, to distribute pictures, contributed by Jacob Cox, Peter Fishe Reed, James F. Gookins and other artists, to the subscribers. The pictures were purchased at a fair price by the Association, with the money paid for chances by the members.—The Y. M. C. Association had George Sumner (brother of Charles), Elihu Burritt, the learned blacksmith, S. S. Cox and others to lecture during the winter.—Ole Bull played at the Atheneum, and Paul Julien, Parodi, Tiberini and others gave concerts, and Geo. F. Root had a musical convention.

The year 1857, though a year of great and increasing prosperity, was singularly uneventful. Everthing moved on in that steady, undisturbed pace which betokens the best possible condition, but gives the records little to fill up with. The United States building, corner of Pennsylvania and Market streets, was in progress, but encountering unexpected difficulties in the character of the soil. There had once been a swamp there, and though the surface was "healed over," the original disease remained below, causing a vast deal of pumping and "filling in" with broken stone and cement, before it could be trusted with the foundation of the massive stone structure intended for the Post office and the Federal Courts. The Episcopal church, the first Gothic edifice in the city, and the first church of stone; the Third and Fourth Presbyterian churches, the Metropolitan Theatre, and the large block of handsome buildings opposite the Court house, on the site of Gov. Ray's old tavern, where he intended to have the central depot of all the railroads of the United States, were in progress, with a number of less pretentious business structures and residences in all parts of the city. The increase of population and business had become so decided that calculating men began to see the way clear to make the city the centre of supply and purchase for a great part of the State, instead of allowing Cincinnati to occupy that position. A meeting was held in July to consult upon this subject, and determine upon the practicability of establishing wholesale houses. A committee appointed by this meeting reported that we had seventy-five houses and thirty-two manufactories which carried on wholesaling to some extent, in connection with what might be called their regular business, but had no exclusively wholesale establishment. Blake, Wright & Co. opened a wholesale dry goods house, to test the soundness of the theories of the "progressives," and found that they we a little too early. They soon closed it up.

The schools were improving with the general advancement of the city. There were nine houses—two rented—and the old Seminary used as the High School, which would properly accommodate but 1,200 pupils, about two-thirds of the number actually crowded into them. From that day to this, except during the time the schools were suspended under the operation of a decision of the Supreme Court against local school taxes, the accommodations, doubly and trebly enlarged, have remained still about as far behind the demand for them. Twenty-five teachers are employed, and 2,730 children, less than half the number in the city, were enrolled, of whom about three-fourths attended regularly. The houses in the 1st, 2d and 5th Wards had been raised to two stories. The house in the 8th Ward was built this year. The trustees were D. V. Culley, John Love and Napoleon B. Taylor. The fund in the past year had reached $27,050, the expenses $19,428. The Germans, by a petition to the Council in 1855, had urged that the school fund be divided proportionally, that they might support separate German schools. The Trustees, to whom the matter was referred by the Council, reported against it, early in 1857, on the ground that there was not enough money or school room for the scholars as it was, and to divide both would ruin the regular schools without benefiting the Germans.

The general charter law adopted in 1853, was amended by the Legislature in 1857, so as to make the terms of the city offices two years instead of one, and the amended act was accepted by the Council on the 16th of March of this year (1857). The first election was held in May, with a total poll of 3,300 votes, each party electing a portion of its ticket. Andrew Wallace was made Chief Fire Engineer. The salaries of officers were fixed as follows: Mayor, $800; Clerk, $600; Marshal, $500; Deputy, $400; Attorney, $400; Street Commissioner, $450; Engineer, $600; Clerk of Markets, $300; Sexton, $80; Fire Engineer, $175; Treasurer, 4 per cent. of current, and 6 per cent. of delinquent, taxes; Councilmen, $2 for each meeting. The city assessment was $9,874,700.

On the 22d of May the Turnverein had a festival, in which they turned out in procession with banners, music and other customary decorative effects, aided by some of their brethren from Cincinnati and other cities. Addresses were made, gymnastic exercises practiced, and target shooting rather ineffectually attempted, upon the Fair Ground. Among those present was the editor of the Turners' paper in Cincinnati, who gave at night, in Washington Hall, some astonishing exhibitions of his power of memory.—Heavy rains and a freshet in the river on the 10th, 12th and 16th of June.—The Fourth of July was celebrated by the union of Sunday-schools for the last time this year.—Firemen's riots in July, "cleaning out ' brothels on East Washington street, near the creek, and on West street. This sort of missionary work was attempted by the firemen several times, more to indulge a spirit of deviltry than to remove the nuisance of this class of houses.—The County Fair was a failure—the State Fair an astonishing success. The entries, as before noted, exceeded 3,000, and the receipts were $14,600.—A fugitive slave was arrested in December, made his escape by the help of the crowd, and was recaptured after a hot chase, and carried back to Kentucky.—Dodworth's band, with ninety instruments, gave a concert in the Fair Ground the last day of June, but it was a failure.— Edward Everett delivered his Washington lecture, for the benefit of the Mount Vernon Association, on the 4th of May, in Masonic Hall.—Thalberg, Parodi and Mollenhauer gave a concert on the 7th of May. Greeley, Dudley Tyng, Gov. Boutwell and others lectured to the Y. M. C. Association.—German theatrical performances were given at the "Apollo Garden," corner of Tennessee street and Kentucky avenue, by Mr. Kunz and his daughters.—The Atheneum was re-opened by Stetson & Wood.—Cameron and McNeeley started the *Daily Citizen*, at No. 10 Pearl street, and continued it for a little more than a year.—The Bidwell Brothers, Andrew and Solomon, started the *Western Presage*, as a literary and political weekly, on the 3d of January, and abandoned it in April.

The year 1858 opened with a disastrous blow at the city school system. It was firmly established, provided with good houses and adequate means, and promised to realize the expectations of the most sanguine. The citizens taxed themselves readily and heavily to support it, and took a just pride in its excellence and its benefits. But during the preceding year a case came up to the Supreme Court from Lafayette, where a system of local taxation in aid of the State Fund existed, involving the question of the constitutionality of local taxes. The constitution required that the school tax should be "uniform," and the point was made that if cities or townships were permitted, even by a general law, to add a tax to the fixed state tax, which other cities and townships did not choose to assume, there was no "uniformity," and therefore no conformity to the constitutional requirement. The Supreme Court sustained the opinion in a decision made in January, 1858, and killed our admirable schools as dead as last year's flowers. An attempt was made by the citizens, at the request of the Council, to supply the deficiency created by the abrogation of the city school tax, by individual subscriptions, but it failed of any but a temporary effect. Some $3,000 were subscribed to complete the current quarter, but the dependence was found to be greatly inadequate as well as uncertain, and at the end of the quarter the schools were closed, the teachers sought other places where "uniformity" of taxation would be construed liberally when it could be done as justly as otherwise, the houses were abandoned, and our beneficent system was a ruin. For a few weeks in each year the feeble "uniform" supply from the State fund permitted the schools to be re-opened free, but this was little better than nothing. Private schools were kept by some of the old teachers in the houses, but they made a lamentable contrast in attendance and efficiency with the system they followed. It was a disastrous blow at the future lives and culture of thousands of children, for the years lost under the operation of that decision could not come back to be filled with the instruction and improvement of the era of revived free schools and universal education. The State fund has, since the overthrow of our first system, increased so greatly as to permit its renewal and extension with the rapid growth of the city, and now there are no better schools in the United States than ours.

The increase of buildings in 1858 was estimated at $600,000. The total of tax-ables was $10,475,000. The total poll at the May election, 3,343. The Republicans improved the victory of November, 1856, by electing a majority of the Council

They have held the control of the city government ever since. The election of a Chief Fire Engineer impelled the first steps towards abolishing the volunteer Fire Department, and substituting one of paid workmen, with steam engines. Joseph W. Davis, the new Engineer, was excessively unpopular with the majority of the companies, and both he and they were constantly "in hot water" about some difference or other. The Department became greatly "demoralized," and did little except carry on its own contentions. It thus happily prepared the way for an early substitution of steam, a measure which Mr. Davis urged with great persistency and effect.

Heavy rains during the spring and early summer of this year made damaging freshets in the river and Pogue's creek. The latter flooded the lower part of the city on the 12th of April, washed off several bridges, injured the Central Railroad bridge so that a locomotive broke through it, and washed out the culvert under the canal, besides doing a good deal of mischief to the houses in its vicinity. The former, on the 14th of June, covered the bottoms and damaged the adjacent farms greatly.—A class for the investigation of the Bible was formed during the summer, and held at the Court house, on Sundays, interesting meetings, participated in by men of all creeds, and none, and lived for a year two.—The Church of the Hebrews was organized in August, and met in an upper room of Judah's block, opposite the Court house, till 1866, when the Synagogue, on Market street, east of New Jersey, which was commenced in 1865, was occupied. It was dedicated in 1857. It cost about $25,000.—The laying of the Atlantic cable, in August of this year, was celebrated by an impromptu glorification, followed by a more elaborate one on the 17th, at which Gov. Wallace made the last public address of his life. The decisive part he had taken in giving Congressional aid to the telegraph in 1841, and the penalty of defeat which he paid for it, made his selection appropriate and just, and the Governor's own admirable oratory made it pleasing to the vast crowd that gathered in the Circle to hear him.—An Academy of Sciences was formed during the summer, and held meetings for hearing essays and discussions, in Judah's block, and made quite a collection of minerals and other objects of scientific value, but the interest in it was too limited to allow it to live long, and it died in 1860.—In the way of lecturing the astronomical lectures of Prof. O. M. Mitchell, of the Cincinnati Observatory, (afterwards distinguished as a Union General in the Rebellion), to the Library Association, were the feature of the year. He delivered some ten or twelve, which, in spite of their purely scientific character, were made so interesting that Masonic Hall was crowded every night to hear them, and the *Journal* reported them regularly every day at considerable length. Thomas F. Meagher and Prof. E. L. Youmans, the celebrated chemist, Bayard Taylor, Dr. John G. Holland (Timothy Titcomb), were also among the distinguished lecturers of the season.' A. J. Davis, the prophdt of a new sect of fools, gave some of his spiritual inculcations, beginning December 10th.—The Metropolitan Theatre was completed, and opened under the management of E. T. Sherlock, with indifferent success. It was our first theatre. The corner stone was laid in August of the year before. The first performance was a series of remarkably fine tableaux, September 27th, 1858. The theatrical portion of our history will be found in another place.

The year 1859 was another year of unbroken progress, but of meagre interest in its history. All that can be told of it may be condensed into a dozen words. Buildings going up, the city spreading in every direction, business increasing. The City Council, on the 1st of March, again changed the charter by adopting the amendment of the current session of the Legislature, which made the terms of the city offices two years and of the Councilmen four. A proposition to divide the 1st and 7th Wards, forming the 8th and 9th, was voted down at the election May 3d. It was carried in 1861, however, and councilmen elected, but owing to some informality or defect in the election, the "elect" were not admitted to the Council. The total taxables was $7,146,677, more than $3,000,000 less than the year before. As the city had been steadily growing, it is not easy to understand this sudden collapse of one-third of its wealth. The receipts were $71,211, all spent, and a debt of $9,-317 added; this is the City Clerk's statement. The Treasurer reported the receipts at $59,168; expenses at $56,442. This discrepancy is as inexplicable as the other. The Fire Department cost $10,232; gas, $4,771; police, $4,882. Washington street was bouldered—the first work of the kind—between Illinois and Meridian in May. The tax was made 60 cents on the $100. There was some talk of building a City Hall adjoining the former Journal building, corner of Meridian and Circle streets, but it came to nothing. The city offices remained in Odd Fellows' Hall till 1862, when the completion of Glenn's block from the old Washington Hall and Wright House afforded an opportunity to obtain more convenient quarters, and a lease of the two upper stories was made for ten years. This year (1870), the lease was forfeited, the unexpired portion compounded for, and the offices moved to Cottrell & Knight's new building. A station house, just completed, at a cost of about $10,000, on Alabama street, south of Washington, gives the city its own prison for the first time. The use of the county jail for city offenders was enormously expensive, and crowded that "institution" unhealthily, and the station house is a most necessary and valuable addition to the city's police provision.

An attempt was made in January to organise a University and obtain the University Square from the Legislature, but it failed, partly because there was not force enough behind it, and partly because the Legislature, not feeling sure that University Square did not belong to the city, refused to make any grant in connection with it. The city has it now, and has made a handsome park of it, as noticed heretofore.—A Gymnastic Association was formed this year, and the Atheneum obtained for its apparatus and exercises, Simon Yandes being President, and Thos. H. Bowles, Secretary. Some $1200 were expended in fitting up bowling alleys, swings, ladders, bars, and other appliances, and public exhibitions occasionally given, but it died out in a couple of years. An effort had been made in 1854 to maintain such an association, and a room was rented for it in Blake's block, but it died out in three or four months.—Some miles of streets were lighted with gas for the first time, this year, the Council having adopted a general and uniform plan for placing and providing lights.—The "old Underhill property," corner of Pennsylvania and Michigan streets, was bought in April by Rev. Gibbon Williams, a Baptist clergyman, and the building, subsequently enlarged and improved into one of the handsomest edifices in the city, converted into the Indianapolis Female Institute. It is one of the best schools in the West. It can accommodate 200 boarders and 300 day pupils. After Mr. Williams left, in 1863, it passed into the hands of Mr. C. W. Hewes.—The General Assembly of the Old School Presbyterian church met on May 18th, in the Fourth Presbyterian church, and sat till June 2d. Dr. Thornwell, of South Carolina, Dr. Palmer, of New Orleans, Dr. N. L. Rice of St. Louis, Dr. Alexander, of Princeton College, Dr. McMasters, of this State formerly, and a number of other distinguished men of the denomination were in attendance.—The City Council appropriated $500 this year, to help celebrate the Fourth of July. A procession two miles long, composed of artillery, cavalry and infantry companies, the Turners, Butchers, Fenians, Firemen, some Catholic associations and Firemen from Madison, with three brass bands, was the feature of the day. Caleb B. Smith, afterwards Secretary of the Interior under President Lincoln, delivered the address on the Fair Ground. There were fire-works and a masquerade procession at night, and at midnight a march of the mysterious "Sons of Malta." This last was patiently waited for by an immense throng that lined both sides of Washington street far along above and below Military Hall, where the society met. Its demonstration was a success, so far as the shouts and enjoyment of the spectators could make it so.—Adam Dietz, drank a keg of lager beer (eight gallons), on a wager, inside of twelve hours, on the 23d of August.—The *Daily Atlas* was started by Jon D. Defrees. The *Brookville American* removed to this city by Mr. T. A. Goodwin, its proprietor, and subsequently converted into the *Daily Evening Gazette.*—George D. Prentice lectured in Masonic Hall, on the 6th of February, and H. S. Foote, formerly Governor of Mississippi,, lectured in Robert's Chapel. Mr. Lincoln spoke in Masonic Hall on the 19th of September, and Gov. Tom. Corwin, of Ohio, spoke at the American House on the 6th of July—all in preparation for the decisive and final battle with slavery of the next year.— Richard Cobden, the great English Free Trader and Statesman, passed through the city on the 5th of May.

An election was held in February, 1860, to decide whether the Council should appropriate $5,000 to assist the State Board of Agriculture in purchasing new Fair Grounds, the old having been found too small. As the Board proposed to locate the State Fair here permanently, it was thought a judicious operation to give them the necessary ground, and an attempt was made to form an association for that purpose, but the association came to nothing, and though the people authorized the $5,000 subsidy to the Board, it was deemed of doubtful legality, and never given. Subsequently the Railroads joined with the Board and bought the grove north of the city, where the State Fairs are now held. During the last fall (1870), there was some talk of obtaining still other grounds, west of the city, and removing the Fair to them, but, unless the destruction of the trees on the present ground be the objectionable feature, no reason for a change is very clearly visible.

A plan to supply the city with water was proposed by a Mr. Bell of Rochester, in the spring of 1860, but it was discussed without result. The company owning the Central Canal renewed the proposal in 1864, but with no better success. In the fall of 1865 the subject was revived by a recommendation of Mayor Caven, which suggested Crown Hill as a suitable elevation for a reservoir. The City Council resolved that the city wanted water-works, but should not build them. No company came forward to undertake the work, and it fell out of sight till the spring of 1866. The Mayor again brought it up, with illustrations derived from an examination of Mr. J. B. Cunningham, a civil engineer, but nothing practical was elicited till November, when R. B. Catherwood & Co., afterwards prominent in competing for the city gas contract, and in the street railway project, were granted a charter for a water supply company, which required the water to be taken from the river several miles above the city; that a certain sum be expended in a certain time; fire-plugs to be located where ordered at a certain price; and that the city should have the privilege of purchasing the works after twenty-five years. The Company was organized with R. B. Catherwood as President, and John S. Tarkington as Secretary, the charter accepted, a few feet of pipe laid on North street, and the thing died out. In the winter of 1868-9 some effort was made by the Central Canal Company to induce the Council to adopt the Holly system of water supply and fire protection, which dispenses with a reservoir, and ' : ces the water by machine pressure instead of gravity. They wanted to make a joint stock company, into which they would put the canal at a fair valuation, and take both the water supply, and the power to distribute it, from that unfortunate bit of State enterprise. But the Council would not listen to the scheme. A year after, in the fall of 1860, Mr. Woodruff of Rochester, organized a company to supply the city with water upon the Holly plan, as in Auburn, N. Y., Peoria, Ill., Dayton, O., and a number of other cities. He was given a charter, after a good deal of contention, and under pretty rigid limitations, and the works are now well on the way to completion. The building, near the foot of Washington street, is up and enclosed, several miles of pipe are down, a flume to operate the water machinery by a supply from the canal—the charter allowing water power, but requiring steam, too—has been laid, and an artesian well sunk seventy or eighty feet to a reservoir of pure soft water, which will be made available as soon as possible. The water works will be noticed more fully hereafter.—Street Railroads were projected in November of 1860, but nothing was done till 1863.

The political excitement of this year was so absorbing that there is little else to tell, and of that there is nothing but speeches, processions, monster demonstrations, and miles of torch lights. Each party seemed to feel that its success in the election depended mainly upon impressing people with the idea that it was strongest in lamps and banners, and long trails of dusty footmen and wagons full of women and walnut limbs. The feeling was not more intense than in 1856, for by both sides the success of Mr. Lincoln, in view of the division between Douglas and Breckenridge, was deemed pretty much a foregone conclusion, and this probability allayed excitement to a considerable extent, but it seemed more nearly universal. The Democrats, whatever they thought of their chances, were in no degree surpassed by their more hopeful opponents in the glory of torches and crowds and speeches. The demonstration on the day that Mr. Douglas spoke in the old Fair Ground, September 28th, was quite equal to that of the Republicans on the 29th of August. A month after the election political issues began passing from the stage of discussion to that of battle, and opened a new era in the history of our city.

A destructive storm, accompanied by a phenomenon somewhat resembling the cloud end of a water spout, occurred on the 29th of May, a little while before sundown. It passed along the south end of the city, sweeping a little north east at the end of Virginia avenue, tearing out a path through roads, fences, houses and whatever interposed. It twisted the residence of Gardner Goldsmith, a horticulturist on Virginia avenue, half way round on its foundations, and tore one end of it entirely away, breaking Mr. G.'s leg in the ruins. Trees two or three feet through were uprooted, broken short off, or twisted round as if the water spout had wrung them like a wet rag. It was the most fearful tornado experienced here for many years. The spout was described at the time as a long narrow bag, or tongue, hanging down from a small cloud that passed swiftly below the other clouds, swaying about and thrashing up and down violently, and tearing up everything which it passed.

A fine display was made on the Fourth of July by the firemen and military, trade societies and citizens, and a superb display of fire-works given in the coliseum, which was merely a high fence round the southeastern portion of University Square, with a shed roof and roughly seated.—Bayard Taylor, Henry J. Raymond, Lola Montez, Prof Youmans, John B. Gough, Dr. R. J. Breckenridge, George W. Winship, lectured during the year, and a fool walked a rope stretched from Blackford's block to Yohn's.

(8)

THIRD PERIOD--TO 1871.

Chapter XIII.

THE Fourth Period in the history of our city, embraced in the decade from January, 1861, to January, 1871, is the most important, not only as regards events affecting the whole country, in which it bore a conspicuous part, but in those affecting its immediate development and prosperity. It saw us rise from a more flourishing inland town and prominent railway station to the condition of a manufacturing and commercial centre, increasing our population 130 per cent.; spreading far around beyond the lines of the "donation;" reaching out to every quarter of the State for business; displacing whole blocks of handsome residences for huge ware houses; tearing away the inadequate buildings of earlier years for palatial stores and banks; paving and lighting scores of miles of streets every year; supplying water, and providing sewerage; bearing heavy taxes for war purposes, and paying large debts without serious oppression, under the impulse of rapidly accumulating wealth. It saw Indianapolis a town, with a prospect of steady but not unusual development, and it sees a city with commanding power and position, with prosperity established, and the future beyond the reach of accident. Up to this time, though slowly "forging" ahead of its former rivals, Madison, New Albany, Evansville, Lafayette and Fort Wayne, and recognized as the largest and wealthiest town in the State, its position was not so fully assured but that the advantages exposed in the coal fields and other sources of industry, might equal the start it had, and ultimately leave it behind. But the close of the decade sees it hopelessly ahead of all rivalry, the metropolis of the State, the seat of the most numerous, varied and productive manufactories, and the distributing centre of a trade probably unequaled by any city in the Union of the same population. Instead of being endangered by the development of the coal and iron interests, its position has been made certain by them. It has four, and will soon have five, railroads penetrating the coal fields in as many directions, and bringing to us, at the centre, from which they all radiate, our choice of coal for all uses. The consequence is a growth of the iron interest that surprises the most sagacious and sanguine of our business prophets. And with long, if not equal, steps, cotton and woolen mills, grain and saw mills, pork houses, breweries, lumber yards, stave factories, furniture works, wholesale grocery, dry goods, drug, book, shoe, hat and other houses, have kept close by its side, or close behind. The enormous influx of troops during the war, not only from our own State in preparation for the field, but from other States in passing back and forth as the exigencies of the time required, and the flood of trivial and temporary trade that always follows a crowd, gave an impulse to solid business and permanent development less in degree, but like in kind, to that experienced by San Francisco twenty years ago. Everybody was in a fever of enterprise, and nobody seemed to think that anything was impossible. Illinois street, which had previously known little business except what a saloon or two and a few millinery establishments at one end, and a hotel at the other, could do, became crowded with clothing stores, restaurants, cheap jewelry stands, saloons, grocery stores, boarding houses, gambling hells, and all that kind of traffic, decent and indecent, honest and rascally, that pursues an army as albicores do a flock of flying fish. Wholesale houses began pushing up from the Union Depot and down from Washington street, along Meridian. Pennsylvania thickened with machine shops in the creek bottom, and heavy houses sprang up on Delaware. Business which had previously been confined to Washington street, except as scattered butcher shops and family groceries had dribbled it about on other streets, now began to "swell beyond the measure of its chains," and locations on cross streets were deemed quite equal to the best on Washington, and on Meridian street better. The city was actually burthened with population and trade. It was like a man breathing oxygen, living too much to last. The close of the war and the disbanding of the army, though it dropped us back to a healthy condition, in which there were elements of safe calculation, and left us a little exhausted by over exertion, was nevertheless so gradual a depletion that the change was effected without a violent or dangerous shock. And our temporary advantages had been so promptly and judiciously improved that much upon which we had laid our hands was held fast. We had made a great and irreversible step forward. The impulse of the war was weakened but not lost, and there was never any fear that we should have to begin as 1861 found us, and build over again, in better fashion, what the "flush time" had built for itself. The drift, like the sediment left by the Nile flood, fertilized enterprise for new crops of achievements. With this glance at the changes produced by the war, and the influences set in operation by it, the connection of the city with military affairs may be introduced.

The split in the Democratic convention at Baltimore in 1860 gave plain warning that the Slave States would abide by no action or election that they did not control. It therefore caused no surprise when South Carolina passed an ordinance of secession and was speedily joined by other States. The subject had been fully discussed here on the stump and by the press, and public opinion had reached, as usual, two conflicting, but very well defined, conclusions. On the one side it was held that the Union should be preserved at all hazards, and the recusant States forced, by invasion and power of arms, to obey the will of the majority. On the other, it was contended that if the Government began a war of coercion, struck the first blow, shed the first blood, and stood before the world the military aggressor, while the South confined its action to ordinances and paper demonstrations, the effect would be an union of all the Slave States, border and sea board, the enlistment of the sympathies and aid, if not actual alliance, of our European rivals, and a serious danger of losing our own Government as well as the States that had abandoned it. For this reason it was suggested that a National convention, elected directly by the people, should be called to consider the difficulty, and if no adjustment could be made, it would be better to let the South try a separate government, allied by interest and kindred to ours, than to risk the chances of an aggressive war with a people better fitted by tastes and modes of life for military service than we then were. If the proposition should be rejected, the South would be placed so clearly in the wrong that a resort to coercion would be less likely to repel the border States or European sympathy. Governor Morton, then recently elected Lieutenant Governor, set forth the grounds of the first of these opinions fully and effectively in a speech at the Court house a short time after the Presidential election. The other was advocated by the *Journal*, conducted by B. R. Sulgrove. The debate, though earnest, as beseemed so vital a question, was never angry or discourteous. It was protracted till the first gun was fired at Fort Sumter. That shot scattered all causes of difference between the coercionists and the conventionists. The South had begun the war, and the conventionists were relieved of all fears as to the effect of aggression by the Government. It was no longer a question of taking the offensive and making invasions, but a question of self-defense and preservation of the Government. If the South had remained quiet, and left it with the North to decide whether there should be war or not, and to begin the war, it is not clear, even now, what the issue might have been. The factious spirit at home was dangerously strong, even against a defensive war. Strengthened by the effect of an offensive war, and the union of all the Slave States, with European help more openly and unrestrictedly given, and it might have defeated, as it did seriously cripple, the Government from 1862 to the summer of 1864. The great majority of the people, both of the city and the State, followed the lead of Governor Morton, and gave their "voice for war" as heartily as "Sempronius." Feeling being thus pretty well prepared for hostilities, and the mad fury of the South removing all grounds of difference in the North, it would have caused no astonishment to a reflecting man to see a strong outburst of resentment at the attack on Fort Sumter. But the universal uproar of rage and uprising of armies passed all the conclusions of logic and all the anticipations of patriotism. It was a phenomenon. The State was a chaos of military spirit and patriotic zeal, out of which it was nearly as hard to bring order and organization as it was for Frankenstein to make a man of a confusion of leather, beef bones and sheep's entrails. But, if we may believe Mrs. Shelley, Frankenstein did make a man of his material, and Gov. Morton made an army of his.

The Union of the coercionists and their opponents, produced by the attack on Fort Sumter, was facilitated by two occurrences that foreshadowed war. The Star of the West, while trying to carry provisions to Fort Sumter, was fired upon by the rebel batteries near Charleston and driven off; and Mr. Lincoln, in passing through this city on the 12th of February, 1861, on his way to Washington to assume the Government, made a little speech of five minutes, indicating his line of action, which had a very decided effect. Every word of it was carefully weighed, and it was evident that what he said would be done. Suggestively, rather than positively, he stated that it was his duty to protect and preserve the property of the nation, and he must do it. It was the first authoritative intimation of the policy of the new administration and the new order of things. Differences began to fade away on the side of the Union men after this. The line of support or hostility to the Government began to show through party organizations. A violent upheaval was breaking through old party crusts. It was completed the day the news came of the attack on Fort Sumter. The excitement in the city was intense. The streets were thronged and the corners blockaded by eager crowds, waiting for fresh news, discussing consequences, and magnifying every chance of resistance by Major Anderson. At night a meeting was held at the Metropolitan Theatre, surpassing in numbers and interest any in the history of the city, at which old party lines were utterly obliterated. Democrats and Republicans were equally officers, speakers, committees, and authors of resolutions. About half past nine o'clock the news came to the meeting that Major Anderson had surrendered, and then it would not have been safe for any man to have avowed sympathy with the South. "War," was everybody's cry, except a few who said nothing. For once all the inveteracy of political feeling, and all the natural hesitation to fight of a people to whom war and all that belongs to it are unknown, were broken down. All seemed to feel the greatness of the crisis, and though there was indescribable excitement there was not much boisterousness. Hundreds remained out of bed all night waiting about the telegraph or newspaper offices, or collected in knots in saloons or on the corners. The next day several of our military companies began recruiting. The next, though Sunday, was given more to battles than the God of battles. On Monday morning the proclamation of the President calling for 75,000 volunteers, and the order of the War office assigning six regiments as the quota of our State, appeared, and the excitement was given a practical direction. For a year the unanimity and enthusiasm of the first meeting at the Theatre were a type of every demonstration in Indiana and the Northwest. The conquest of Western Virginia, largely effected by Indiana soldiers and generals—for McClellan got the credit of what Gen. Thomas A. Morris planned and executed—encouraged effort, and the defeat at Bull Run stimulated it. There was no lack of volunteers. Governors were annoyed by requests to get regiments accepted, and when done, it was accorded by the War office, and received by the applicants, as a favor. The sagacious and impeccable Cameron could not see any use in other troops than infantry, or other arms than the old smooth-bore musket. So he refused cavalry and artillery, and was seriously troubled with too much infantry. He did not know the value of taking the tide at the flood. His successor learned it by finding the tide at dead low water. During this flush time of war feeling volunteers were at a discount. Not less than 30,000 men were tendered Governor Morton for the 6,000 demanded. Six regiments of three-months men were organized in a week, and rendezvoused at the old Fair Ground, where the city companies, the Grays, the Guards, the Zouave Guards, and the Independent Zouaves, had taken up their quarters the day the Governor's proclamation was issued in execution of that of the President. They were visited there and addressed by Stephen A. Douglas about a week after. Every day, and almost every hour of the day, for two weeks, companies could be seen marching up from the Union Depot, with the fife and drum that had not seen service since the old militia musters or the campaign of the Bloody Three Hundred. Recruiting flags were thick along the streets, and the rattle of drums incessant and deafening. Crowds of boys, sometimes swelled by admiring country girls, followed the recruiting squads in their progress, and people flocked from their houses to witness for the first time the "pomp and circumstance" of war, such as it was. Seven companies were organized here, most of which were incorporated in the Eleventh (or Zouave) Regiment, Col. Lewis Wallace. The six regiments were numbered, from the concluding number of the five regiments raised during the Mexican War, the Sixth, Seventh, Eighth, Ninth, Tenth and Eleventh. The last, being, as already remarked, mainly composed of our city companies, was presented a flag by the ladies of the city, in the State House Square, on which occasion the gallant Colonel practised a *coup de theatre* which was about as impressive as "Puff's" unanimous prayer in the "Critic." He took the flag, and, raising it above his head, called on his men to kneel and "swear to remember' Buena Vista." But he made one of the best disciplined and most efficient regiments in the service out of them. They were sent to Evansville, May 8th, to protect the border, but subsequently removed to Maryland, where, while stationed at Cumberland, a squad of their scouts had a skirmish with a band of rebel cavalry, and fought pluckily. As it was the first real fighting in which Hoosiers were concerned, it gave the Eleventh regiment a prominence in the State which it never lost, and its gallant conduct entitled it retain. The other five regiments were the first in Western Virginia. They drove the rebels from all their advanced posts, protected the railroads, fought at Rich Mountain, and defeated and killed General Garnett at Carrick's Ford. The volunteers beyond the six regiments of our quota, were formed into six regiments of one year State troops, under an act of the Legislature at the extra session then in progress, but subsequently all except one enlisted for three years, and were transferred to the United States service. The places of the men who did not like to engage for the long term were rapidly filled. They were reviewed by General McClellan on what was then a large common, north of the Fair Ground, on the 24th of May. It can serve no purpose to introduce here the history of the troops of the State or city. That belongs to a work of wider scope than this. It will be enough to sketch the city's connection with the war, through its camps, prisons, Soldiers' Home, and provision for bounties and soldiers families.

The first camp, afterwards called Camp Sullivan, as already noted, was on the old Fair Ground. The new Fair Ground was rapidly converted to the same uses and called Camp Morton, and it was the complaints of the men there that induced the Legislature to censure the first State Commissary, Isaiah Mansur. They had been accustomed to good food and plenty of it, at home, and they made an unreasonable fuss about their rations in camp. Mr. Mansur took the office without pay, furnished all the meat in his own packing house—the best in the market—supplied fresh baker's bread, butter and sugar, advanced his own money, and did better than any one who blamed him could have done, and he was paid for it by as unjust a censure as was ever inflicted. Public opinion, in which the *Journal* led the way by defending him with irrefutable proofs and arguments, reversed the hasty judgment of the Legislature. Ill feeling and violent demonstrations are frequent incidents of the transition from the freedom of home-life to the discipline of efficient soldiers. Camp Morton was the scene of many such, in which sutlers were generally the sufferers. Camp Burnside, south of Camp Morton, on Tinker street, was made a very neat and attractive little town for many months, first by the volunteers under Col. Biddle, and next by the "Invalids" or "Veteran Reserve Corps." Camp Carrington, subsequently, was made the largest and best arranged camp in the State. It lay beyond the extreme northwestern corner of the city. The artillery camp, called Camp Noble, was fitted up by Col. Fryberger, and occupied by the Twenty-Third Battery for a time. The Eleventh regiment had a camp, while re-organizing for the three years' service, on the west bank of White River, near Cold Spring. The camp of the Second Cavalry, Col. John A. Bridgeland, was near Fall Creek, four miles north of the city. The colored regiment, Col. Charles Russell, was collected at Camp Fremont, in the woods at the southeast extremity of the city, to the left of Virginia avenue. The practice ground of the artillery was about three miles south of the city, near Mr. Paddock's residence, west of th'

Bluff road. The Nineteenth Regulars, Lieut. Col. King, were stationed here for several months, in 1861-2. Camp Morton was used exclusively as a prison camp after the organization of the first regiments. The prisoners brought from Fort Donelson, early in the spring of 1862, were placed there, and guarded first by different volunteer regiments, but finally by the Veteran Reserves. The exposure to which these prisoners had been subjected created an epidemic, and the citizens opened hospitals for the sick in the old Atheneum room and in Blackford's old building on Meridian street. The ladies did the nursing, and did it as tenderly and perseveringly as if the patients had been their own relatives. But the mortality was very severe, and the little grave yard, now emptied, along the Terre Haute Railroad track near the river, made a promise of growth which was happily not fulfilled.

But the institutions of most consequence in the connection of the city with the war, were the Arsenal and the Soldiers' Home. The first was the result of Gov. Morton's determination to see that the Indiana troops were supplied with good ammunition. The General Government could furnish but little, and that not always good. The materials were supplied by the Quartermaster, the workmen by a detail of the 11th regiment, and on the 27th of April, 1861, the Arsenal was inaugurated by moulding bullets in hand-moulds in a blacksmith's furnace, and packing the cartridges in the next room. Subsequently it was enlarged till it employed several hundreds of hands, and supplied a large portion of the ammunition of the troops west of the mountains. In October, 1861, the Secretary of War, Mr. Cameron, and the Adjutant General, L Thomas, visited the Arsenal, approved it, paid for its work, and recommended it highly. Herman Sturm was its Superintendent. For a time it occupied Ott's building south of the State House; then the buildings north of the State House Square, and was afterwards removed to vacant ground east of the city. It was discontinued on the 18th of April, 1864, after three years' service. Its entire business in three years amounted to $788,838.45, upon which the State made a profit of $77,457.32, or nearly 10 per cent. The Arsenal has since been succeeded by regular a Government establishment, in the northeastern suburbs, where ample and admirable buildings have been erected, and the grounds handsomely laid out and ornamented.

The Soldiers' Home, like the Arsenal, was the result of obvious necessity, which the Governor had the decision to provide for. The city was not only the great State rendezvous, but it was the halting and recruiting post of most of the troops passing east or west to the "front." They came always hungry, dirty and tired, and very often sick. A night's rest, or a wash, or good meal, might often be worth a man's life. So the Soldiers' Home was started. The Sanitary Commission had agents at the Union depot to provide meals for the men, and help for the sick, at the hotels, but this was expensive and unsatisfactory, and a camp was established, with hospital tents, on the vacant ground south of the Union Depot. But in 1862, the Governor, seeing the increasing tide of troops, and the inadequacy of the provision made for them, resolved to establish a permanent Home This was done by Qartermaster Stone, in July, 1862, who erected buildings in the grove on West street, just north of the Terre Haute Railroad. These buildings were afterwards added to and enlarged, till it could lodge 1,800 men and feed 8,000 every day. From August, 1862, to June, 1865, it furnished 3,777,791 meals. During 1864 it furnished an average of 4,498 meals per day. The bread was supplied by a bakery under the charge of the Quartermaster, so well conducted that all the soldiers needed, and thousands of loaves for the poor, were provided out of the rations of flour the men were entitled to. The savings in the rations of other articles amounted to $71,130.24. The savings of flour, a sutler's tax, and the sale of offal, paid $19,-042.19. So that this beneficent institution was sustained almost entirely by the rations of the troops sheltered by it. The ladies of the city, on all holidays, or noted occasions, provided excellent dinners for all at the Home, cooked them, waited at the table, and did all the service themselves. A Ladies' Home for the benefit of soldiers' wives and children, was opened in a building near the depot in December, 1863. An average of 100 a day was taken care of till its close.

After the departure of the three years' troops, there came, for a time, a calm, upon the domestic aspect of the war, broken only by the clamor of the newsboys "*Journal* Extra!" "'nother battle!" and the Morgan raid, till the return of the re-enlisted veterans. As each old regiment re-enlisted at the end of its term for three years more, it was allowed a furlough to come home, and thirty days to remain in the State. It was received with salutes of guns, processions of all the troops in the city, addresses by the Governor and its own officers, and given a good dinner at the Home.

The Morgan raid, early in July, 1863, produced a good deal of excitement, but it ended in nothing worse than calling the citizens to University Square to drill for a few days, and the sending away of the specie reserves of some of the banks. The day the news of the fight near Corydon reached here, a Michigan battery which had been stationed here for some time, was ordered to take the Jeffersonville cars to meet the adventurous rebel. As it passed down Tennessee street, at the crossing of Indiana avenue, a caisson exploded, blowing two men over the tops of the adjacent shade trees, horribly mutilating them and killing them instantly, and mortally wounding a man and boy who happened to be passing near at the time.

The gathering and organizing of troops during the continuance of the war formed the most conspicuous feature of the city's history, but there were many incidents growing out of the war, more political than military, which demand some notice. During the first ebullition of patriotic feeling which followed the attack on Fort Sumter, there was hardly a sound of dissent heard, no appearance of slack loyalty was tolerated. The *Sentinel* proprietors failed for some reason to hoist a national flag on their building, and the mob of uncompromising patriots threatened violence if they did not. They and the editor, with several other citizens, who were, or were believed to be, sympathizers with the South, were made to take an oath of fidelity to the Government. They were for a while in serious danger of personal violence. Subsequently, as the war lagged and prospects grew dark, opposition became more open and decided. It assumed a party shape, and added to the usual hostility of parties all the rancor of civil war. The minority were treated as enemies of their country, and repaid what they thought oppression with resentment that did not always discriminate between the justice of the war and the justice of the action by which they suffered. At a county convention held in the Court house square on the 2d of September, 1862, some of their speakers, notably among them Mr. Robert L. Walpole, spoke bitterly of the Government and the soldiers, and justified or palliated the rebellion. Many soldiers in the crowd were exasperated, and retorted angrily. A row resulted which came near ending fatally. The obnoxious speakers were driven off, and had but a narrow chance for their lives. If caught, some of them would most probably have been killed. At the following election the suspected opponents of the war were often excluded from the polls, and not a few were beaten away from the ground and otherwise maltreated. "Traitor" was the mildest epithet given to the rebel sympathizer or the less obnoxious Democrat who censured the war policy of the Government. At one time, while a veteran regiment was encamped here, some allusion to the participation of a portion of its members in a political procession of the day before, made by the *Sentinel*, brought down an angry crowd who attempted to "clean out" the office. But for the resolute and prompt action of Gov. Baker, then Provost Marshal of the State, it would have been done. In some other towns of the State it was done. In the fall of 1863 a State Convention of the same class of men was held in the State House yard, and arms were so generally exhibited or detected that no little alarm was excited, and preparations made by the military to either meet an attack or suppress a riot. Several were arrested and fined for carrying concealed weapons. As the trains left the depot in the evening, returning, the crowds upon them began firing their revolvers in a sort of defiance or triumph, and scattered shots recklessly in all directions. A child was said at the time to have been killed, and two or three persons wounded, but it was not true. The eastern trains were speedily stopped, and every man compelled to give up his arms. Some hundreds were captured, and many more thrown away, and found by the boys next day. This senseless act gave a color to the damaging assertions of the "loyalists" as to the dangerous character of the party, and provoked harsher feelings and more intolerant action. Probably it is not a matter of astonishment that thus "overcrowed" and put under, the opponents of the war should resort to secret and oath-bound associations as a means of protection or vengeance. At all events they did it, and during the winter of 1862-3, when the session of the Legislature was approaching, the air was full of rumors of organized bodies of "Knights of the Golden Circle," and what not, combining here to support the anti-war majority in that body in an effort to overthrow the State Government, and take the State out of the war and out of the Union. A secret society was formed to resist it, and here were the first movements of the Union League on one side and what became the Sons of Liberty on the other. With the conflicting assertions of each as to its own and its enemy's purposes this sketch has nothing to do. It deals merely with the facts developed by their efforts. Among these are, 1st. The presentment by the Grand Jury of the United States Court, in May, published in August, 1862, in which the existence of secret treasonable associations is declared to have been abundantly proved by the confessions of members. 2d. The developments made by detectives of the ceremonies, oaths and purposes of the Sons of Liberty, which was published in 1864. This disclosure pretty nearly ruined the Order for a party machine, and it was utterly ruined shortly after by the next and most important political event of the war in which the city was concerned. 3d The "Treason Trials." A conspiracy to combine large rebel forces from Missouri and Kentucky, aided by rebel sympathizers at home, and by the rebel prisoners in the Northwest who were to be provided with arms by the plunder of the Government arsenals, to overrun this and adjoining States and fatally embarrass the Government, was, through the efforts of leading Democrats of this city, frustrated, but not so far deprived of dangerous vitality but that secret efforts to form anew and reknit the broken links of the scheme were made, mainly through H. H. Dodd, the most active of the leaders of the S. O. L. On the 20th of August, 1864, Gov. Morton received a letter from New York, dated the 18th, notifying him of the shipment of a large number of revolvers and cartridges to this city to Mr. Dodd, the boxes marked as "Stationery," or "Sunday-School Books." Mr. Dodd's office was searched, and the weapons found exactly as described. He made his escape for a time, but, returning, was arrested on the last day of August. Subsequently L. P. Milligan, William A. Bowles, Stephen Horsey

Andrew Humphreys, Horace Heffren and some others were arrested for participation in this and other treasonable efforts. Dodd was tried, convicted and condemned to death by a military commission, but escaped from the Government building—over the Post office—by the help of friends, on the night of the 6th of October. Milligan, Bowles and Horsey were subsequently tried in the same way and received the same sentence, commuted to imprisonment in the Ohio Penitentiary. Humphreys's sentence was commuted by the General of the District, A. P. Hovey, to confinement within a specified region of the country. All were released under a decision of the United States Supreme Court.

The military zeal which, at the outbreak of the war, made recruiting not only easy but troublesomely abundant, slackened as the progress of the war developed clearly what military service meant. Volunteers had to be bought, at last, at prices corresponding to the sacrifices required. Patriotism dropped out of the calculation, and entering the army became a business affair, in which wages and bounties were set against the cost of maintaining families, the loss of time, and the possibilities of battle. But other influences combined with this natural tendency of a protracted war, to make military service a business divested of sentimental attributes. First among these was political opposition. When the first fury of indignation at the aggression of the rebels had expended itself in war and words, this opposition began to show itself, cautiously at first, but boldly a little later. The national tax was denounced, and organizations formed to resist it and any attempt at conscription. McClellan's failure before Richmond, brightening the prospects of the rebellion, strengthened it. The war was legislated against by every possible means during the winter of 1862–3. Naturally accompanying or following this political effort, were movements to discourage enlistments, to encourage desertion, and organizations to protect deserters and resist their arrest. So effectual were these that during the single month of December, 1862, no less than two thousand three hundred Indiana deserters were lured home, to their own disgrace and the infinite injury of the service. Letters from relatives politically adverse to the war, urging desertion and promising protection, were one of the most powerful of these disloyal appliances. The papers of that time published hundreds of them, revealed by the soldiers themselves. An inadequate conception of the obligation they had incurred facilitated these treasonable efforts. To them an engagement to serve in the army was like a bargain to do any other job. If they didn't like it they could leave it by merely forfeiting unpaid wages. Deserters, of course, brought home terrible stories of destitution and suffering, and hostile newspapers made the most and worst of every reverse and every discouraging circumstance. Thus recruiting was diminishing while desertion was increasing. The withdrawal of tens of thousands of the most industrious and productive of our population from their various industries created a great demand for labor. Wages rose, and, with the depreciation of currency, everything else rose, too. The recruit, with the certainty of employment and good wages at home, was not to be obtained for the meagre pay of a soldier. If he had a family, it had to be provided for, and if he hadn't, no discrimination could be made against him, and he was paid as if he had. Thus came bounties and heavy burthens, far beyond the expenses which appeared in the settlements of the national treasury, or the aggregate of the national debt. As the war made heavier draughts upon labor, wages advanced further, and with them bounties advanced, till, with national, county and city bounties, and advance pay, the recruits under the last call of 300,000 men, December 24th, 1864, were paid nearly $1,000 each, before they had gone into camp.

The first appropriation by the city for war purposes was one of $10,000, made on the 20th of April, for the support of our three-months volunteers. Others were frequently made for the purchase of wood, provisions, and other necessaries of destitute families. In August, 1864, a purchase of two hundred cords of wood was made, and in the winter $3,500 was appropriated. Contributions of fuel and food were occasionally made all over the State by the famers, who appointed a day to move in procession through streets of the chief towns, with wagons loaded with wood, flour, potatoes, meats, vegetables and fruits, to some point of deposit. Tens of thousands of dollars worth were thus collected and distributed by duly appointed agents. Very many farmers vied with each other who should give most, and make the most striking display, and wagons carrying five and even ten cords of wood, and others with mountains of food, were no unfrequent sights. Several of these were witnessed in Indianapolis. Large sums both for soldiers and their families were raised by fairs, and by private contributions. Those for the former were managed by the State Sanitary Commission, directed by Wm. Hannaman and Alfred Harrison. The others were distributed as the occasion prompted. A State Sanitary Fair was held in the old Fair Ground, at the time of the State Agricultural Fair of 1864, at which $40,000 were raised. During the continuance of the Sanitary Commission there were raised and distributed $606,570.78. Besides the sum of $16,049 50 contribted to the United States Sanitary Commission from Indiana, $4,566,898 06 was paid by counties, townships and towns for like purposes, making the total of contributions of this character, in this State, about $5,200,000.

Expenses incurred for the support of soldiers' families, though in the aggregate of private and public contributions larger than the expenses for recruiting volunteers, yet form but a small part of the accounts of the city treasurer. The heaviest items there were made by bounties. Until the political opposition to the war began to make itself formidable, and desertion had diffused discouraging feelings, and the large diversion of labor to the army had raised wages, nobody thought of bounties Families were left to the care of neighbors and the irregular assistance of the paymaster. But war was found to be a very serious business, and began to be viewed with a business eye. The soldier had to be assured of something safer than a neighbor's care of his family. He looked out for it himself, and the bounty was the provision for it which he exacted. At first it was light. In the fall of 1862 the city appropriated $5,000 for bounties, which lasted till May, 1863. Considerable expense was incurred for the city regiment during the alarm created by Morgan's raid. On the 14th of December, 1863, an appropriation of $25,000 was made for bounties, and additional sums were raised by committees in the different wards. A draft was avoided by thus filling our quota with volunteers. During the summer of 1864 the old regiments which had re-enlisted for three years more, as nearly all from this State did, were allowed to return home on a furlough, and their receptions, sometimes of daily occurrence, were one of the most interesting features of the war as it could be seen in this latitude. The Seventeenth Regiment, one of these, upon re-enlisting, credited itself to this city, that is, enlisted as coming from the city, and, to the number composing it, made a set off against any subsequent draft. No bounty was asked at the time. But subsequently, as some of the men complained, naturally enough, that they got nothing, when others, raw recruits, got hundreds of dollars, the Council gave them $5,355. On the suggestion of Gov. Morton, the Governors of Ohio, Illinois, Wisconsin and Iowa met in this city April 24, 1864, and urged the President to accept the services of a large body of men, 85,000, from these States, for one hundred days, to guard General Sherman's communications during his "march to the sea." The President consented, and the city's quota of the

7,115 assigned to this State, was raised at once. The Council appropriated $5,000 for the support of their families. Our regiment, under Col. Sam. C. Vance, Lieut. Col. Cramer and Major Hervey Bates, Jr., did good service. Under the call for 300,000 men, of October 17, 1863, increased on the 1st of February, 1864, to 500,000, and, on the 14th of March, to 700,000, no draft was made. The State's volunteers filled her quota, with 2,493 men to spare. On the 18th of July, 1864, a call for 500,000 more men was made, and the city's quota was fixed at 1,258. For the first time our citizens had to bestir themselves to avoid a draft. Meetings were held during the summer to raise subscriptions for bounties, and to procure volunteers, with considerable but not sufficient success. Some $40,000 was subscribed, and about 800 men enlisted, but the draft on the 28th of September found us 450 men short. The drafted men raised a considerable sum to procure substitutes, but, the prospect looking dark, the City Council made two appropriations, one September 28th for $92,000, and one October 3d, for $40,000, to assist them, and during October and November the quota was filled, at an expense of $180,000. On December 20th, 1864, another, and the last call, for troops was made. The whole number demanded was 300,000, and the State's quota was 22,582, of which 2,493 had been paid by over-enlistment on the preceding call. The Mayor, Mr Caven, made repeated recommendations of appropriations for bounties, to fill the city's quota, and the Council responded by giving, first, the unexpended balance of a preceding appropriation, $2,500, and next $20,000. This didn't amount to much, and in January, 1865, the Mayor urged further appropriations and drafting by wards. The Council ordered $125,000 to be paid in $150 bounties, with $10 premium for recruits. Three days after they raised the bounty to $200, and sent an agent to Washington to obtain an order for drafting by wards. This order was made, and in February the Council appropriated $400 to every man who should be drafted, if he had purchased a $50 city order. Petitions were presented, February 22d, 1864, from 4,400 citizens asking that $400,000 be raised by city bonds, to pay bounties and fill the quota. An ordinance to this effect was passed, and the bonds prepared and sent to New York, but none were sold. On the 6th of March $100,000 was borrowed of five banks, in $20,000 divisions, on our bonds, at 12 per cent., and this was appropriated in $4,00 bounties. The quota was at last nearly filled, when it was ascertained that a blundering blockhead of the War Department had made a big mistake in assigning the city's credits for volunteers, and that the quota was full, with hundreds to spare. Over a fourth of the loan was thus saved. The war expenses from May, 1864, to May, 1865, which included the bulk of bounty appropriations, amounted to $718,179. The entire war expenditure was about $1,000,000.

These heavy appropriations necessarily left heavy debts. But, as the city was flourishing with amazing vigor, heavy taxes were imposed, usually running from $1.50 to $1.75 on the $100, and paid, and at the close of the war the debt was $368,000. This has since been paid off, but a new one has recently been contracted for the construction of sewerage and other expenses, the amount of which is about $400,000. Our debt in 1849 was $6,000. It was nearly paid by a special tax in 1850, but in 1851 it was $5,400, all paid but $557 in 1854. In 1855 it was $10,000, and in 1856 $15,300. A loan was ordered to be made in New York to pay it, and Jerry Skeen appointed agent to negotiate it. An account of his defalcation has been given. The effect of it was that the city debt rose to $23,740 in 1857. In 1859 it was reduced to $9,300, raised to $11,500 in 1860, and to $46,000 in 1861. In 1862 it was reduced to $16,500. In 1863 it was reduced to $11,250, and subsequently paid off. The city was virtually out of debt that year. The war and the

INDIANA REFORMATORY INSTITUTE FOR WOMEN & GIRLS

increased expenses created by higher wages, salaries and prices made the debt, as before stated, $368,000 in 1868.

The improvement of the city may be judged from the reports of building permits and street work. In 1865—the first full statement under the ordinance of 1864—there were issued permits, in the city and its additions, for 1,621 buildings, costing $2,060,000; 9 miles of streets and 18 miles of sidewalks were graded and and graveled, 1 mile of streets bouldered, 4 miles of sidewalk paved, and 3 miles of streets lighted. In 1866 there were erected 1,112 houses, at a cost of $1,065,000; 8½ miles of streets and 16 of sidewalks were graded and graveled, the third of a mile bouldered, 2 miles of sidewalk paved, and 3 miles lighted. In 1867 the houses built and repaired were 747, costing $902,520; of streets 4½ miles and of sidewalks 9 miles were graded and graveled, less than half a mile bouldered, 2½ miles of sidewalk paved, and 4½ miles of streets lighted. Since 1867 improvements have increased in number and value largely, as will be seen by the table appended to this chapter.

Besides these indispensable improvements others have been made of the character which add either to the beauty or convenience of the city, and the possession of which is usually considered the test of public spirit and genuine city development. First among these is Crown Hill Cemetery. After the old cemetery had been extended to the river on the west, and the Terre Haute Railroad on the north, it was found that before many years the space would be insufficient, and the pressure of business would probably displace the dead and cover their graves with shops, factories and mills. To provide against this certain though remote difficulty an association was formed on the 25th of September, 1863, with James M. Ray as President, Theodore P. Haughey as Secretary, and Stoughton A. Fletcher, Jr., Treas'r, with seven directors. S. A. Fletcher, Sr., proposed to advance the money necessary to purchase a site, and a committee selected the nursery farm of Martin Williams about three miles northwest of the city on the Michigan road. At one end of it rises a very steep hill, the highest anywhere near the city, at the foot of which, at that time, lay a wide stretch of cleared land bordered by a heavy forest. Two hundred and fifty acres, embracing this hill, and several adjacent tracts, were bought for $51,500. Mr. F. W. Chislett was made Superintendent, and early in 1864 he began laying out the grounds. In 1864 the cemetery was dedicated, Hon. Albert S. White, formerly United States Senator, delivering the oration. Lots were rapidly bought by leading citizens, and beautiful and costly monuments, some of marble, some of Aberdeen granite, others of ordinary stone, have been erected. It is now a beautiful place, and a constant resort on fine days. The cemetery pays no dividends; every lot owner is a stockholder. The profits on lots sold are expended in beautifying the grounds.

The war brought its evils, and not a few of them, along with its benefits. Among these the worst was the inundation of prostitutes. They flaunted their gay shame in every public place. They crowded decency, in its own defense, out of sight. Their bagnios polluted every street. The military camps were not always, with all the vigilance of sentries and rigidity of discipline, safe from their noisome intrusion. The jail was nightly filled with them and their drunken victims. And the remuneration of their vice was so ample and constant that a fine was a trifle. Even of it could not be paid, the alternative of a few days' confinement only restored them in better health, with stronger allurements and appetites, to their occupation. To secure some alleviation of this evil, and some chance of making punishment effectual towards reform, the Mayor, in May, 1862, recommended a house of refuge where abandoned women could be confined alone, and subjected to a discipline impossible in a common jail. Nothing was done, however, till the summer of 1863. On the 27th of July Stoughton A. Fletcher, Sr., proposed to give the city a lot of seven acres of ground, just beyond the southern suburbs, on the "Bluff road," if suitable buildings for a House of Refuge were put upon it. Plans and estimates were made by Mr. D. A. Bohlen, architect, and an effort made to entrust the establishment to the "Sisters of the Good Shepherd" The donation was accepted on the 10th of August, and $5,000 appropriated to the building, which was to be used both as a refuge and reformatory school, and as a city prison for women. A committee was put in charge of the enterprise, and contracts made in the fall. Within a year the basement, solidly and handsomely built of stone, at a cost of about $8,000, was completed, but there the work stopped. The contractor broke down under the great advance in the cost of labor and materials, and abandoned it. The start was excellent, the location is admirable, the work done worthy of any structure that can be put upon it, the institution needed, the condition of the donation binding, and the city ought to fulfill its bargain and complete the house. One part of the object with which it was undertaken, it is true, has been assumed by another institution, the Home for Friendless Women, but there is enough for it to do yet to make it well worth completion. The Home, just mentioned, was the work of an association formed in 1866, for the reformation and care of prostitutes. Experience had proved, by repeated successes in other cities, that there were many of this forlorn class who honestly desire to lead a better life, but, repelled by society at every approach, they were compelled to continue in shame to avoid starvation. To provide for these both a home and a school, an advance into purity and a means of access to pure society, as well as to furnish temporary protection to meritorious but necessitous women, the association established their Home. They at first rented a building in the Second Ward, but subsequently, by means of donations, and appropriations from the Council, erected a capacious and handsome building on North Tennessee street, at the verge of the city. This was placed in charge of Mrs. Sarah Smith, a Quaker lady, who had long been active, both with tongue and pen, in every benevolent work, and was admirably adapted by superior intellect and firmness of character to the duties imposed upon her. In her hands the Home was successful beyond expectation. But on the 22d day of September, 1870, the building was almost destroyed by fire, and a serious check given to its operations. But the press urged immediate effort by the citizens and Council to rebuild it, and examination showing that much of the standing walls could be safely used, an adequate appropriation was made by the Council and a considerable sum procured by donation, and the Home will soon be as beneficently at work as before.

The undoubted convenience, and almost uniform success, of Street Railways had caused the suggestion of a system of them here, as early as November, 1860 but nothing was done till June 5th, 1863, when a company, the "Indianapolis," was organized under the State law, with General Thomas A Morris as President, Wm. Y. Wiley, Secretary, and Wm. O Rockwood, Treasurer, for the purpose of constructing one. They applied to the Council for a charter on the 24th of August, and while their proposition was under discussion, another company, the "Citizens'," organized by R. B. Catherwood of New York, with John A. Bridgeland as President, and a number of our capitalists as stockholders, made another proposition, embracing more immediate operations and a greater length of serviceable track within a given time. The contest was hard, and not free from hard words and injurious insinuations. Among these was the charge that the latter company had not the means to perform its contract. The managers put down $30,000 in cash, and offered a bond of $200,000, as security. But the Council gave the charter to the "Indianapolis" Company December 11th. It was declined on the 28th. Mr. Catherwood of the Citizens' Company was notified, and he agreed to take the charter and reorganize his company. On the 18th of January the Citizens' Street Railway Company was given a perpetual charter, with an exclusive right to the streets and alleys, for thirty years, with R. B. Catherwood as President, E. C. Catherwood as Secretary, and H.H. Catherwood as Superintendent. The Company were permitted to lay a double or single track in, or on each side of, the centre of any street or alley of the city or its subsequent additions were to use horse cars only; to put the tracks on the level of the street grades; to boulder between them and two feet on each side; to change tracks if street grades were changed; to charge five cents only on any route; to complete and equip three miles by October 1, 1864, two miles more in a year more, and two miles additional by Christmas, 1866. After the completion of these seven miles the Council retained the right to order further extensions, the Company forfeiting any route it failed to build on such an order; and the right to take the tracks at an appraisement, or give them to another company, if ten miles were not completed within ten years. The Company began work at once, but the Government's occupancy of the Railroads delayed the arrival of the rails, and, on their request, the Council extended for sixty days the time for the completion of the first section of the system. The first track was laid on Illinois street, from the Union Depot, and this was opened in June, 1864, by the Mayor driving a car on it, with the Common Council and city officers as freight. A double track was laid on Washington street from Pennsylvania to Illinois, and a single track to West street, running north on the latter to the Fair Ground, and was largely used during the Fair. A track was laid on Virginia avenue in the fall; another run up Massachusetts avenue in the spring of 1865, and that on Washington street continued to the river. In 1866 the latter was carried eastward to Pogue's creek, and the Illinois street track extended to Tinker street, and to Crown Hill Cemetery. In 1868 a line was run down Kentucky avenue and Tennessee street, by which all the northern lines, the Washington street lines, and those entering either, connect, through a track on Louisiana street, with the Illinois street line, thus enabling passengers to run round the whole circuit of the railway system without shifting cars. Thirty-two cars, mostly for two horses, long, capacious and superb, were first put upon the tracks, and kept till 1868. But two horses, with the double expense of conductor and driver for each car, was too much, and single horse cars were substituted April 3d, 1868, with only a driver and a box for fares. Simultaneously with, or shortly after, the commencement of the tracks, the Company began erecting stables, car houses and shoeing shops on the northeast corner of Tennessee and Louisiana streets, and the establishment now covers a half square in length, and a hundred feet or more in breadth, with handsome and durable brick buildings.

As above remarked, this Company encountered serious obstacles in the beginning of their enterprise, in the cost of iron, in the difficulty of getting it here at any price with the Government occupancy of the railroads, and in the high price of labor. They further increased their expense, disproportionately to all prospect of speedy remuneration, by extending their lines to thinly populated portions of the city. The convenience of access to remote sections, thus afforded, has added greatly to their value, but not much to the revenues of the Company. Undoubtedly a profit will come from the outlay as the city grows, but for the present they have benefited the city far more than themselves. The estimate that they have added to the value of real estate in those quarters more than the amount of their capital stock (a half million of dollars), is moderate. The embarrassments resulting from this policy have compelled an application to the Council, once or twice, for relief from taxes and the charges of street improvements, and the Council have, fairly enough, granted some advantageous exemptions, until the increase of population shall supply remunerative patronage. It is believed that the extension of one of the present lines, and the construction of one other short line, will afford ample street railway facilities for a population of one hundred thousand, the mark set by many for the census of the city in 1880. Then the enterprise will be an unequalled investment. Few cities present so many advantages for a system of street railways at once efficient and cheaply maintained, as Indianapolis. Its streets are so level that one horse or mule can do the work of two where the grades are heavier. Besides, the teams are changed four times a day, so that no animal is overtaxed, unless, as will sometimes happen in spite of the vigilance of men and officers, a careless or brutal driver does it by reckless driving, and the losses from abuse or exhaustion are proportionably light. There are now seven lines in operation, with an aggregate of fifteen miles of track, fifty cars, one hundred and fifty horses and mules, and from fifty to seventy-five drivers and other employes. They make an average of one thousand trips per day, at a cost of $60,000 to $75,000 per year. The principal stockholders are William H. English and E. S. Alvord of this city, and Winslow, Lanier & Co. and J. B. Slawson of New York.

On the 19th of April, 1864. the Council created a Board of Public Improvements, consisting of three members, with the City Clerk as Secretary. They take charge of all public works of whatever kind, and permits are obtained of them to erect private buildings. This allows the compilation of building statistics, previously impossible.—In 1865 city aid was voted, upon petition of many citizens, to the amount of about $200,000 to four lines of railroad, the Vincennes, $60,000; Indiana and Illinois Central, $45,000; Indianapolis, Bloomington and Western, $45,000; Indianapolis and Cincinnati Junction $45,000 These roads have all been completed and are in full operation, except the I and I. Central. The Cincinnati Junction road received its appropriation upon the express condition that it should place its machine shops in this city. The condition has been utterly disregarded. What can be done about it is not clear, as the road has the money, but there certainly ought to be some remedy for such dishonesty as this.—The project of building a station house was urged in 1866, but came to nothing. It has since been built on Alabama street, as noticed in the last chapter.—In 1867 the corner stone of the Catholic Cathedral, South Tennessee street, near Georgia, the largest sacred edifice in the State, and the costliest, was laid with imposing ceremonies in the presence of a vast multitude on the 20th of July. The Cathedral is of Gothic architecture, two hundred and three feet long, and seventy-five feet wide, in the form of a Latin cross, with vaulted ceiling sixty feet high, a row of chapels on each side of the nave, a rose window eighteen feet in diameter over the main door' and a tower at each corner of the front one hundred feet high. These are to be surmounted by spires adding another hundred feet, but it is doubtful if the building will look the better for the addition The southwest quarter of that square, with half the southeast quarter, is covered with buildings devoted to the uses of the Catholics, including a splendid school house, St. John's church, Bishop's residence, the female school of the Sisters of Providence, and the Cathedral. St. John's

Infirmary, on Maryland street, in the former residence of James Sulgrove, belongs to the same collection, as does the adjoining lot on the east. With the corner lot on Tennessee and Maryland streets, the church would have the entire west half of that square, with a portion of the other half. It is Catholic headquarters in Indianapolis.

In 1864 the Kingan Brothers, who were largely engaged in packing and shipping meats, not only in this country, but in Belfast, Ireland, Liverpool, England, and Melbourne, Australia, desiring a Western slaughtering and packing establishment, determined to locate it here, on the river, at the foot of Maryland street, instead of in Cincinnati. They built what was then, and probably is yet, the largest single building devoted to that business in the United States. They opened it with a very successful season in the winter of 1864–65, but in the spring it caught fire and was almost entirely destroyed, with an immense amount of lard, bulk meat and hams in it. The loss was about $240,000, the heaviest ever incurred in our city. The structure was immediately rebuilt, on the uninjured portions of the walls, of the same dimensions as before, except that it was left a story or two lower. It has since been in constant use, summer as well as winter, in slaughtering and packing cattle, hogs and sheep.—In 1868 Mr. J. C. Ferguson, one of the oldest of the city packers, built a house but little less than that of the Kingans, just south of it, and has done, probably, more pork packing than any other establishment. These, and all the pork houses of the city will be noticed more fully in the chapter assigned to that subject.—In 1868 Mr. Valentine Butsch and Mr. Dickson bought Miller's half finished block on Illinois and Ohio streets, and changed it into a large, commodious and beautiful theatre, inferior to few in the largest cities, and called it the Academy of Music. It was opened in the winter of 1868–69. It will be noticed more fully in the chapter upon "Amusements."—In 1868, 1869 and 1870, the ceremony, first instituted by the women of the South, of decorating the graves of soldiers with flowers on the 30th of May, was observed here, in 1869, especially, with a degree of unanimity never witnessed since the end of the Fourth of July celebrations. It was conducted by the ladies, under the suggestion of the Society of the Grand Army of the Republic, and was made a holiday by the entire community.

In the spring of 1868 the heirs of Calvin Fletcher, Sr., who died in 1866, proposed to donate to the city thirty acres of land, at its northeastern corner, for a park, upon condition that it should be forever kept as a park, that $30,000 should be expended upon it within a given time, and the heirs be allowed to designate one of the commissioners to improve it. For no better reason than a belief that the donation was prompted by a desire to draw fashionable residences in that direction, and thus enhance the value of the vast tract of Fletcher property in the vicinity, the proposal was declined. Parks have been made in the old Fair Ground and University Square, however, and though far too inadequate, they will be a great relief to the monotony of walls and pavements. The Military Park, as it is called, is finely laid out with walks and drives, entirely covered with luxuriant grass, studded with some fine old trees, and recently set with plenty of young ones, and has a large basin in the centre, with a fountain spouting from, and tumbling its waters down upon, an imitation of a natural rocky summit, which rises out of the little lake. George Merritt, the Commissioner, has the merit of the laying out of this park. Last summer a band of music performed there on Thursday evenings, and were paid by subscriptions obtained mainly by the efforts of Mr. Henry E.

(9)

Church, who had the concerts in his charge. It is a place of constant resort, and will become more a necessity as the city grows.

In 1867 a new rolling mill company was formed, and a mill built as soon as practicable afterwards, to roll bar, rod and ordinary merchantable iron. It was controlled by Dr. Winslow S. Pierce and Jas. H. McKernan. It did well for a time, but failed in a year or less, and was bought by Messrs. Butsch and Dickson, who, after running it successfully for a few months, sold it to a company mainly composed of German citizens. Steel rails and bars have been made in it of excellent quality.—In 1869 a company of six German residents was formed to make glassware here. In the fall and winter their building was erected and furnace prepared, and they began blowing bottles, vials and fruit jars, with such entire success that they soon got an order from Philadelphia for $40,000 worth of fruit jars. The sand was brought at first from the Fall Creek bluffs, near Pendleton, and was a friable sand-stone needing to be "stamped" to be used, but latterly river sand has been successfully used, and is cheaper. During the past summer they have erected another blowing house, and have just put up an extensive warehouse for the storage of their goods. The works cover nearly a half square on Kentucky avenue and Merrill street.—During the spring and summer of 1870 the County Board, with the assistance of a considerable sum subscribed by the citizens interested, erected a handsome iron bridge over the river, at the foot of the extension of Merrill street, near the old cemetery. Each span will bear without risk seventy-five tons, or a great deal more than will ever be piled upon it.—During the past year Mercer, Nash & Co. have erected buildings and begun operations in making car wheels on Merrill street, north of the new rolling mill. They began with ten wheels a day, but are now making eighteen. They have more demands than they can fill.

The two chief improvements of the city, since the introduction of gas and street railways—water supply and sewerage—are now in progress, and belong to the year 1870. The first, as already noticed, was a project of several years standing. It became a reality during the winter of 1869. The sketch of the struggle through which it passed need not be repeated here. It is enough to say that it was strenuously, and not altogether disinterestedly, resisted, mainly on the ground that it was merely a "fetch" to enable the owners of the canal to force its sale upon the city at their own price. It was to supply the water for distribution as well as for motive power, and with the system once established, it would be indispensable, let its price be what it might. The water company met this charge by proposing to take water for distribution from wells supplied by percolation from the river, to use the canal only for motive power, and even for that only as the alternative of steam, binding themselves to maintain both, and the steam at all events; and, finally, if the city wished in time to buy the works, the canal should not be included. These propositions demolished all objections and the charter was granted.

The sewerage system had been suggested scores of times in the past score of years, but in 1865 three engineers, James W. Brown, Frederick Stein and Lazarus B. Wilson, were appointed by the Council to devise a general system and make the necessary surveys. In 1868 a tax of fifteen cents was levied for sewerage purposes, and a small sewer constructed on Ray street, from Delaware street to the creek, into which it empties a square east of West street. It cost $16,500. A year after an attempt was made to construct a sewer on South street, but the plan of it was objected to, injunctions obtained against it, and it was abandoned. During the winter of 1869-70 Mr. Moses Lane, an eminent engineer, who has made sewerage a specialty, was invited by the Committee on Public Improvements to examine the city with reference to its drainage, and after a survey of a few days, he furnished a plan (charging the trifling sum of $1,800 therefor), which was adopted, and contracts let in the summer for a trunk sewer from Washington street to the river on Kentucky avenue, on South street from Kentucky avenue to Noble street, down Noble to Fletcher avenue, at the city boundary, and on Illinois street from Washington to South. The sewer on Illinois street is in progress, and is laid of heavy drain pipe. The trunk sewer is eight feet in diameter, faced at the river with dressed stone, provided with " man holes " for each square, and " catch basins " at all street crossings to collect the gutter water and clean it of sediment before allowing it to enter the sewer, It is made of brick, three widths of a brick (a foot) thick, laid in hydraulic cement, and plastered heavily with cement on the outside as it is finished. The work, so far, has been admirably done. The contractors are Wirth & Co., of Cincinnati. It was publicly charged, while the contracts were pending under a motion to reconsider the letting, that corruption had been used to obtain support, and overcome the difference in favor of the bids of Symonds, Hyland & Co., of this city, but as the contract was confirmed, and the work energetically begun and thoroughly well done, the affair was dropped and nothing came of it but a good deal of newspaper objurgation. The contracts now unfinished amount to about $180,000.

In the winter of 1870 large "additions " of some of the best built parts of the city were made by the Council, against the strong protests of the residents, who wanted to enjoy city advantages without paying city taxes. Something like two thousand inhabitants were added by this accession. It embraced a large section of suburban villas on the north, south, west and east. An attempt to do this in 1865 was defeated.

In 1870 preparations were made for the erection of the new Court House. Many objections were made to the plan (shown in the illustration), as too costly; many complaints were made of the attempt of the Commissioners to secure a heavy loan to build it; an injunction was obtained prohibiting them from issuing the bonds as they proposed; and many wanted the south half of the Square sold (for it would have brought an immense sum), and the proceeds applied to the erection of a house on the north half. Nobody seemed entirely satisfied, but so many were dissatisfied with different features that no opposition could be made effective, and the work was "placed on the stocks" about as the County Board designed it. The old house, associated with the history of the State from 1825 to 1835, and with that of the city during nearly its whole career, was torn down, and the excavation of the cellar begun. A description is unnecessary, as the admirable engraving will give a better idea of the completed structure than any description could do.—The Reformatory School for Females, authorized by the Legislature in 1869, has been commenced just beyond the eastern boundary of the city, near the National road, and will soon be one of the most attractive edifices we have. It is intended to be for girls what the House of Refuge is for boys. The latter, authorized by the act of 1865, is now in full operation at Plainfield, fifteen miles west of the Capital. It has over 200 inmates, managed upon the "Family system," and is successful beyond all anticipation. It is under the experienced superintendence of Mr. Frank B. Ainsworth.

Chapter XV.

THE history of the Government of Indianapolis, like the general history, may be divided into four periods. 1st. The period from the first settlement to 1832. This, to make a pardonable "bull," was the period of "No Municipal Government," the general laws of the State, and the officers created by them, sufficing for the limited necessities of the village. 2d. The period of "Trustee Government," from 1832 to 1838, when the town was managed by five Trustees. 3d. The period of "Town Government," by the Council alone, from 1838 to 1847. 4th. The period of "City Government," with a Mayor and Council, from 1847 to this time. Several minor changes in each of these periods will be briefly noticed. Of the *first* period nothing need be said.

Second. The first incorporation was resolved upon by a meeting of citizens held at the Court House on the 3d of September, 1832, and the day for an election fixed. It was made under the general law, not by a special act. Five Trustees were elected by a general vote, and the town divided into five wards, all contained within the original plat. The 1st Ward embraced all east of Alabama street; 2d, from Alabama to Pennsylvania; 3d, from Pennsylvania to Meridian—this single tract of a square in width shows where the densest portion of the town lay; 4th, from Meridian to Tennessee; 5th, from Tennessee westward. Samuel Henderson, whose death in California was recently announced, was elected by the Board of Trustees as their first President. A general ordinance of portentous length (thirty-seven sections) for the magnitude of the town, was published on the 1st of December. Offenders were prosecuted by the Board, in its own name, before Justices of the Peace, and proceedings were required to be commenced within twenty days. Licenses were required for shows and liquor shops, and the usual prohibitions were made of dangerous or disturbing acts, either of omission or commission, such as firing guns, flying kites,—this latter little regarded and never enforced—racing horses, driving over walks,—there were none in those days that could be injured much—leaving cellar doors open, teams unhitched, hogs at large, wood piles on Washington street over twelve hours, or shavings anywhere over two days; keeping stallions on Washington street, and the like. Markets were held on Wednesdays and Saturdays, for two hours after daylight, regulated by a special ordinance enforced by a Market Master. Hucksters were prohibited. Elections were held in September. The officers were President, Clerk, Treasurer, Assessor, Marshal and Market Master. On the 5th of February, 1836, the Legislature, by special act, incorporated the town and legalized the work of the Trustees. Taxes were limited to fifty cents on the hundred dollars of real estate, and their collection to the original town plat, though the whole donation was under the jurisdiction of the Trustees. No other change of any consequence was made. In the settlement of the old and the new Board, April 1st, 1836, the receipts for the year preceding were shown to be $1,610, and the expenses $1,486, of which $1,150 was paid on the first fire engine, the Marion. The balance, $124 was passed to the new administration.

Third. On the 16th of February, 1838, a new act of incorporation was passed by the Legislature, making no change in the power of taxation, or its limit of application, but authorizing sales of property for delinquent taxes, and increasing the wards to six. The first three were left unchanged, with Alabama, Pennsylvania and Meridian streets as boundaries, but the 4th was cut off at Illinois street, making it, like the third, a single block in width, across the plat; the 5th was limited to Mississippi street, and the 6th extended from Mississippi westward. The principal change was in the election and power of the President, and the constitution of the Council. The former was chosen by a popular vote, the members of the latter by the votes of their respective wards, and both for a year. The President had a Justice's jurisdiction, and the Marshal a Constable's. The Council was empowered to borrow money, levy taxes, (up to a half per cent. on realty), establish licenses &c., and the members were paid $12 per year. The other town officers were elected, as before, by the Council. The new Government differed, essentially, but little from the present City Government. It opened the four streets bounding the original plat, elected officers, and arranged the fire department, licenses, &c.

Fourth. On the 13th of February, 1847, a city charter was granted by the Legislature, and adopted by a vote of 449 to 19, on the 27th day of March. A free school tax was authorized by about the same vote at the same time. This charter created seven wards, which remained unchanged till the addition of the 8th and 9th in 1861. The new arrangement divided the town, including the whole donation east of the river, by Washington street. The section north of the line was divided into four wards by Alabama, Meridian and Mississippi streets, the numbers running from east to west; the section south was divided into three wards by Illinois and Delaware streets, the numbers running from west to east. Elections were held in April. The Mayor was elected by popular vote every two years, and one Councilman from each ward every year. The former had the jurisdiction of a Justice as before, with a veto upon the acts of the Council. The latter elected their own President and all other officers, and were paid $24 per year. They could not levy a tax exceeding fifteen cents on the hundred dollars, except by authority from the people, given in a special election. Samuel Henderson, the first President of the Town Board of Trustees, was elected the first Mayor. This charter remained essentially unchanged till 1853. The limit to the power of taxation was found to be mischievous, and a proposition was made to remove it, but without effect, in 1852. In March, 1853, the general charter law was adopted by the city. This changed elections to May, where they have since remained, made the terms of all offices a single year, gave two Councilmen to each ward, and all elections to the people, and made the Mayor the President of the Council, as he has since continued to be. In 1857. March 16th, the amended general charter, passed by the Legislature, was adopted, This made the terms of all officers two years, one half the Council going out every year. In 1859 the general charter was again amended so as to make the terms of Councilmen four instead of two years. In 1861, the 1st Ward was divided, and the 9th made of the eastern half, and the 7th divided, the 8th being formed of the eastern section. The Councilmen were elected from the new wards, but political influences, supported by alleged defects in the election, kept them excluded for several months. On the 20th of December, 1865, this charter gave place to another, which made all terms of office two years, allowed the office of Auditor, and gave the election of Auditor, Assessor, Attorney and Engineer to the Council. On the 14th of March, 1867, this was again changed so as to make a City Judge, and give the election of Mayor, Clerk, Marshal, Treasurer, Assessor, and Judge to the people. John N. Scott was elected City Judge, in May, 1867, and served two years. John G. Waters was elected City Auditor, at the creation of the office, and served four years. Both offices were abolished in 1869, the duties of Judge being transferred to the Mayor, and those of Auditor to the Clerk. The minor offices, as Sexton, Printer, Clerk of Markets, Wood Measurer, and the like, are filled by the Council.

The following tables of officers under the various forms of municipal govern" ment, are taken from Mr. Brown's work. They are incomplete simply because the city records were all burned up in 1851, and have been but indifferently kept the greater part of the time since. A good deal of inquiry and investigation have elicited nothing more than he has collected:

TRUSTEES FROM 1832 TO 1838.

Year	1st Ward.	2d Ward.	3d Ward.	4th Ward.	5th Ward.
1832	John Wilkins	Henry P. Coburn	John G. Brown	Sam'l Henderson	Sam'l Merrill
1833	" "	" "	Sam'l Henderson	John Cain	" "
1834	Alex F. Morrison	L. Dunlap	Joseph Lefevre	J. Van Blaricum	Nath'l Cox
1835	Jas. M. Smith	Jos. Lefevre	Chas. Campbell	H. Griffith	N. B. Palmer
1836	G. M. Lockerbie	John Foster	Sam'l Merrill	" "	John L. Young
1837	Lost	Joshua Soule	Lost	Lost	Lost

The town authorities, during this period, had little to do, and could have done but little if they had been charged with more. The streets were lumpy with stumps. Trees were still standing full sized in many of them a little way from Washington street. Mud-holes, circumvented by roundabout tracks close to the fences, and by foot-passengers by climbing along fences past the deepest places, were common. The remains of more than one or a dozen of these may still be detected by a heavy rain. The "ravines" tore through the town in two fierce torrents in wet seasons, flooding houses and lots from New Jersey street to the river. The southern one, of which some marks may still be seen east of Alabama street, near the present City Hall, and near the river at Kingan's pork house, was the largest; but the northern one, which left marks from east of Mr. Hervey Bates' residence along down to the West Market, did more mischief, as it ran through a more densely populated section. The valley of Pogue's Creek was a swamp and thicket, and all south of it was "country." Much north of it, to Maryland street, was made up of corn fields and cow pastures. There were no sidewalks and no improvements that amounted to anything.

COUNCILMEN FROM 1838 TO 1847.

Year.	1st Ward.	2d Ward.	3d Ward.	4th Ward.	5th Ward.	6th Ward.
1838	Lost	Lost	Lost	Lost	Caleb Scudder	Nathaniel Cox
1839	G. M. Lockerbie	W. Sullivan	J. E. McClure	P. W. Seibert	Geo. Norwood	S. S. Rooker
1840	M. Little	S. Goldsberry	Jacob Cox	"	"	A. A. Louden
1841	"	"	"	A. A. Louden	"	C. H. Boatright
1842	Joshua Black	"	J. R. Nowland	P. W. Seibert	T. Rickards	A. A. Louden
1843	"	"	"	A. A. Louden	"	S. S. Rooker
1844	"	"	"	"	H. Griffith	"
1845	W. Montague	"	"	"	C. W. Cady	{Wm. C. Van-Blaricum}
1846	"	"	A. W. Harrison	"		

TOWN OFFICERS FROM 1832 TO 1847.

Year.	Pres't Council.	Clerk.	Marshal.	Treasurer.	Assessor.	Engineer.	Street Sup'r.
1832	S. Henderson	J. P. Griffith	Sam'l Jenison	None	Glidden True	None	None
1833	"	"	"	None	G. M. Lockerbie	"	"
1834	A. F. Morrison	Jas. Morrison	John C. Busic	T. H. Sharpe	"	"	"
1835	N. B. Palmer	Joshua Soule	R. D. Mattingly	"	John Elder	"	W. Ballenger
1836	G. M. Lockerbie	"	Wm. Campbell	"	None	Wm. Sullivan	Thos. Lupton
1837	Joshua Soule	Hugh O'Neal	"	"	A. G. Willard	Luke Munsell	{James Van-Blaricum}
1838	Jas. Morrison	Joshua Soule	"	Chas. B. Davis	"	R. B. Hanna	R. C. Allison
1839	N. B. Palmer	Herrey Brown	J. Van Blaricum	H. Griffith	Henry Bradley	James Wood	
1840	H. P. Coburn	"	"	Chas. B. Davis	T. Donnelan	"	T. M. Weaver
1841	Wm. Sullivan	"	"	"	"	Luke Munsell	None
"	D. V Culley	"	R. C. Allison	"	J. H. Kennedy	"	W. Wilkinson
1842	"	. . .	Benj. Ream	"	Thos. Donnelan	"	
1843	"	W. L. Wingate	J. Van Blaricum	J. L. Welshans		James Wood	
1844	Laz. B. Wilson						
1845	Jos. A. Levy	Jas. G. Jordan	N. N. Norwood		John Corn		
1846	"	"	Jacob B. Fitler	Gro. Norwood			Jacob Fitler

Besides these more important offices, there were several others, either filled many years by the same men or only temporarily filled, which can be presented in this note. The office of Market Master or Clerk was filled for the first five years, till 1837, by Fleming T. Luse, a cabinet maker, whose shop formerly stood where the Branch of the State Bank Building is. It was subsequently held for nine years, from 1837 to 1845, by J. Wormagen. During 1845 it was held by J. Wormagen for the East and Jacob Miller for the West Market, and in 1846 by Miller for the West, and J. B. Fitler for the East. The office of "Collector" was held by the Marshal till 1844, with the exception of the year 1837, when it was.held by Wm. Smith. From 1844, to the change in the charter, it was held by Henry D. Ohr. During two years, 1834 and 1837, James Morrison was City Attorney. In 1838 the office was held by Hugh O'Neal, and in 1846 by John L. Ketcham. It was not so much an office as an occasional appointment. The office of Weighmaster was held by John F. Ramsey in 1836, and by Adam Haugh from 1840 till the change of the charter. There was no Sexton till 1843. John Musgrove was the first, succeeded in 1844 by John O'Connor, and he again by Musgrove in the two following years, till the City Government came in. Thomas M. Smith was made Fire Engineer in 1846, but the office expired with the charter, and was not renewed till 1853. The "Messengers" of the Fire Companies were officers selected to take charge of the apparatus, and were, for the Marion, David Cox, from 1843 to 1846, and for the Good Intent, Jacob B. Fitler, for 1845 and 1846.

CITY OFFICERS FROM 1847 TO 1871.

The office of President of the Council is omitted from this list, because it was little more than nominal, and was abolished by the Amended Charter of 1852. It was held successively by Samuel S. Rooker, C. W. Cady, (both in 1847,) Geo. A. Chapman, Wm. Eckert, A. A. Louden and D. V. Culley, (both in 1850,) and by D. V. Culley till abolished.

Year.	Mayor.	Clerk.	Treasurer.	Marshal.	Engineer.
1847	Sam'l Henderson	James G. Jordan	Nathan Lister / Henry Ohr	Wm. Campbell	James Wood Sr.
1848	" "	" "	James Greer	John Bishop	" "
1849	H. C. Newcomb	" "	J. H. Kennedy	Sims A. Colley	" "
1850	" "	J. T. Roberts	John S. Spann	Benj. Pilbean	" "
1851	Caleb Scudder	D. B. Culley	A. F. Shortridge	Sims A. Colley	" "
1852	" "	" "	" "	Elisha McNeely	" "
1853	" "	" "	" "	Benj. Pilbean	" "
1854	James McCready	Jas. N. Sweetser	" "	" "	" "
1855	" "	Alfred Stevens	H. Vandegrift	Geo. W. Pitts	Amzi B. Condit
1856	H. F. West / W. J. Wallace	Fred. Stein	Francis King	Jeff. Springsteen	D. B. Hosbrook
1857	" "	Geo. H. West	" "	" "	" "
1858	S. D. Maxwell	John G. Waters	J. M. Jameson	Aug. D. Rose	James Wood
1859–60	" "	" "	" "	Jeff. Springsteen	" "
1861–62	" "	" "	J. K. English	D. W. Loucks / Jno. Unversaw	James Wood Jr.
1863–64	John Caven	C. S. Butterfield	" "	" "	" "
1865–66	" "	" "	W. H. Craft	" "	Joshua Staples / R. M. Patterson
1867–68	Daniel McCauley	D. M. Ransdell	Robert S. Foster	" "	" "
1869–70	" "	" "	" "	George Taffe	" "

Year.	Attorney.	Assessor.	Street Comm'r.	Market Master.	Sexton.
1847	{ A. M. Carnahan { N. B. Taylor	Joshua Black	Jacob B. Fitler	{ S. Barbee { Jacob Miller	Benj. F. Lobaugh
1848	Wm. B. Greer	Charles I. Hand	John Bishop	" "	Jos. I. Stretcher
1849	Edwin Coburn	Henry Ohr	George W. Pitts	" "	" "
1850	Wm. Wallace	Samuel P. Daniels	G. Youngerman	" "	None
1851	Albert G. Porter	L. Vallandingham	Joseph Butsch	" "	Phillip Socks
1852	" "	Jacob S. Allen	Hugh Slaven	" "	" "
1853	N. B. Taylor	Mat. Little	Wm. Hughey	Henry Ohr	" "
1854	" "	John G. Waters	" "	Jacob Miller	George Bisbing
1855	" "	Jas. H. Kennedy	Jacob B. Fitler	Richard Weeks	John Moffitt
1856	John T. Morrison	John B. Stumph	" "	Geo. W. Harlan	A. Lingenfelter
1857	Benj. Harrison	" "	Henry Colestock	Richard Weeks	John Moffitt
1858	Samuel V. Morris	D. L. Merriman	" "	Charles John	" "
1859-60	Byron K. Elliott	R. W. Robinson	" "	" "	Garris'n W. Allred
1861-62	Jas. N. Sweetser	John B. Stumph	John A. Colestock	Thomas J. Foos	" "
1863-64	Richard J. Ryan	{ " " { Wm. Hadley	John M. Kemper	J. J. Wenner	" "
1865-66	Byron K. Elliott	" "	August Richter	Charles John	" "
1867-68	" "	" "	" "	Sampson Barbee	" "
1869-70	" "	" "	August Brumer	G. B. Thompson	Elisha Hedges

Year.	Fire Engineer.	Seal'r W'ts & M's.	Printer.	Chief Police.
1847	None	None	None	None
1848	"	"	"	"
1849	"	"	"	"
1850	"	"	"	"
1851	"	"	St's'm'n & Loc'm'tve	"
1852	"	"	Sentinel &	"
1853	Joseph Little	Joseph W. Davis	Locomotive	Jeff. Springsteen
1854	Jacob B. Fitler	John T. Williams	Elder & Harkness	" "
1855	Chas. W. Purcell	" "	Charles G. Berry	" "
1856	Samuel Keeley	H. J. Kelley	Larrabee & Cottom	{ J.M.VanBlaricum { Chas. G. Warner
1857	Andrew Wallace	J. M. Jameson	Journal Company	Augustin D. Rose
1858	Joseph W. Davis	J. G. Hanning	" "	Samuel Lefevre
1859-60	{ J. E. Foudray { Jos. W. Davis	C. S. Butterfield	" "	Augustin D. Rose
1861-62	" "	James Loucks	" "	{ Thos. A. Ramsey { Thomas D. Amos { David Powell
1863-64	Chas. Richmann	" "	Ellis Barnes	
1865-66	" "	{ " " { Joseph Bishop	James G. Douglass	Jesse Van Blaricum
1867-68	{ G.W. Buchanan { Chas. Richmann	Aug. Bruner	" "	Thomas S. Wilson
1869-70	" " Daniel Glazier.	Sam. B. Morris	{ " " { M. G. Leo	{ " " { Henry Paul

In the list of Printers, Ellis Barnes and James G. Douglass are substitutes for the Journal proprietors. The office of Weigh Master was created in 1847, and first filled by John Patton. From 1848 it was held by Adam Haugh till 1855. It has not been filled since.

TABLE OF VOTES, TAXABLES, RECEIPTS AND EXPENDITURES.

Year.	Vote.	Taxables.	Receipts.	Expenses.	Str'ts &c	Fire D'p.	Police.	Gas.	Salaries
1847	468	$1,000,000	$4,000	$1,800					
1850	1,143	2,326,185	9,237	7,554					
1852	1,300								
1853	1,460	5,131,682	10,096	7,030					
1854	2,012	....	20,500	20,000					
1855	2,090								
1856	2,776	9,146,670	27,889	46,105					
1857	3,300	9,874,700	32,697	31,003					
1858	3,343	10,475,000							
1859	3,390	7,146,607	50,168	56,442	....	$10,232	$4,882	$4,771	
1860	....	10,700,000	87,202	80,172	28,790	11,353	5,986	6,445	
1861	3,468		84,508	84,508	15,653	16,249	6,300	7,648	$10,180
1862	....	10,250,000	79,132	79,132	2,744	12,510	9,693	8,966	10,662
1863	2,880	18,578,683	97,115	97,487	18,809	12,668	10,687	10,988	11,524
1864	....	19,723,732	125,011	156,444	33,222	21,202	18,473	12,505	12,040
1865	2,341	20,013,274	507,831	854,391	20,240	21,612	27,990	15,220	14,618
1866	....	24,835,750	409,704	404,713	33,880	20,332	23,416	3,051	9,638
1867	6,135	25,500,605	445,253	331,525	52,186	27,207	37,511	38,164	17,452
1868	....	24,000,000	431,669	224,941	36,018	33,049	27,509	37,100	27,528
1869	5,640	22,000,000	426,586	234,408	31,204	24,927	27,194	29,423	15,183
1870	....	24,656,460	429,355	405,016	62,410	35,925	23,633	20,046	
1871		30,000,000							

There was paid for jail fees, the city having no prison of its own, in 1863, $2,842; 1864, $5,509; 1865, $7,686; 1866, $11,113; 1867, $8,116; 1868, $6,336; 1869, $2,871; 1870, $4,197. Bounties paid in 1863, $5,010; 1864, $35,155; 1865, $718,170; 1866, $151,197; 1867 $70,575.

MAYOR'S VOTE SINCE 1859.

Year.	Republican.	Democrat.	Rep. Maj.
1859	Samuel D. Maxwell................... 1,895	James McCready...................... 1,495	400
1861	Samuel D. Maxwell.................... 2,076	James R. Bracken..................... 1,390	686
1863	John Caven........................... 2,899	No Opposition...............................	2,899
1865	John Caven........................... 2,341	No Opposition...............................	2,341
1867	Daniel Macauley..................... 3,317	B. C. Shaw........................... 2,818	499
1869	Daniel Macauley..................... 2,843	John Fishback, (Independent)..... 2,797	46

BUILDINGS.

Previous to 1865 there are no data upon which to base even an estimate of the value of the buildings annually erected in the city. But in 1864 a Board of Public Improvements was appointed by the Council, a permit from which was required for every building, the estimated cost of which was given. The first report was in 1865.

Year.	No. Houses b'lt & rp'rd.	Value.	Miles Str'ts.	Cost.	Miles Sidew'ks.	Cost.	Bridges.
1865	1,621	$1,860,000	10	....	22	....	....
1866	1,112	1,065,000	9	....	18	....	....
1867	747	902,520	5	....	11	....	....
1868	530	805,796	4½	$27,172	2½	$10,058	$2,332
1869	720	947,086	6½	40,740	4½	26,669	1,584
1870	840	1,213,879	10	147,813	7 4-5	37,893	19,693

CITY SALARIES.

Mayor $3,000	Gas Inspector.............. $800	Fire Engineer............$1,400 00
Clerk............................ 1,800	Attorney......................... 500	Chief of Police......... .. 1,400 00
Marshal............Fees and 600	Street Commissioner... 1,400	Lieut. Police...per day 3 50
Dep'ty Marsh'l, Fees and 500	Assessor...................... 2,000	Market Clerk.............. 600 00
Treasurer...1½ per cent. and 5	Engineer...................... 1,800	Sexton..........Fees and 50 00
per cent. on distraints	Wood Measurer........... Fees	Sealer W'ts & Meas'rs, Fees

THE FIRE DEPARTMENT.

The first organization for protection from fires was made on the 20th of June, 1826, with John Hawkins as President, and James M. Ray as Secretary. Its implements were ladders, axes and buckets, and the church and hotel bells rang the alarm. The first regular fire buckets were curiosities. They were made in the town, of heavy harness leather, painted green inside, bound with a leather-covered rope around the mouth, handled by a leather strap for a bail, and shaped somewhat like a lager beer keg, bigger in the middle than anywhere else. They held a half bushel or thereabouts. The town ordinance required one or more to be kept in every house, and the owner's name to be painted upon them. Their awkward shape made them of little value for use directly upon a fire, for with the narrow mouth, obstructed by a broad strap, it was impossible to throw more than a third or half of the contents out at once, and the effort usually resulted in deluging the enthusiast who made it. But they did well enough to supply engines, by means of lines of men who passed them full, from hand to hand, from the nearest pump to the engine, while an opposite line passed them back empty, and about all the service they ever did was in this way. Resort was occasionally had to this primitive water supply where there was no cistern or accessible well, till three or four years before the adoption of steam fire engines in 1860. The best service of bucket lines was done at the fire in the Washington Hall, in February, 1843.

The Legislature, on the 7th of February, 1835, authorized the State Treasurer to procure twenty buckets, for fire purposes, and suitable ladders, and to pay half the cost of a fire engine if the citizens would pay the other half. The citizens on the 12th met and requested the Trustees to subscribe the money, and levy a tax to pay it, and the Bucket Company was reorganized as the Marion Fire, Hose and Protection Company. The engine, the Marion, was bought in the Summer and brought here in September. It was an "end-brake," made by Merrick, of Philadelphia, and was never surpassed, or fairly equalled, by any of the costly "machines" afterwards purchased. It was permanently housed in 1837, in a two story frame house on the north side of the Circle. The Council subsequently sat in the upper room. The house was carelessly guarded, and often used by prostitutes, and in 1851, after having been on fire once or twice before, it was burned, with the city records in it. The fire was attributed to the members of the Company, at the time, and their resentment at being required to "put up" with so shabby an affair was the supposed motive. It is certain that many of them refused to work when ordered by their captain, and other companies did what was done, but it may be fairly doubted whether they did more than entertain a decided disposition to see it go. In 1855 a brick house was built on the corner of Massachusetts Avenue and New York street, and in July, 1858, a splendid new "side-brake" engine was purchased, but never did much service. The town of Peru bought it, in April, 1860, for $2,130. The first officers and members of the Marion Company were the most prominent and respectable citizens of the place. Caleb Scudder was the first Captain. He was succeeded by James Blake, John L. Mothershead, and other leading citizens. But in a few years the town grew larger, and the members of the Company grew older and more indis- posed to run long and work hard, and younger blood took their places. By 1848, they had all become "honoraries," and passed practically from the Company. After serving ten years, a member was entitled to claim his "honorary certificate," which gave him to all the privileges of a fireman, such as exemption from city taxes, and from service in the militia and upon juries, without any obligation to pay dues or do duties, and in 1845-6 this limited time of the founders of the Company expired. A considerable change was then made in its composition. It became less respectable, and a good deal more efficient. In 1859 it, like all the other compa- nies, became dissatisfied with Chief Engineer Davis, and the Council, strongly disposed anyhow to introduce steam apparatus and paid firemen, was not at all urgent to have it kept up, and it was disbanded February, 1860, after a life of a quarter of a century.

In 1841, the Marion Company divided, and the seceders took the "Good Intent," a second-hand engine, of rather uncertain quality, which had, from the Spring of 1840, been kept and used with the Marion. The new Company, afterwards known as the Independent Relief, like the old one, was made up of the best citizens, but with a rather larger infusion of "fast" men than the old one. It was changed with the same steps as the other. John H. Wright, the first merchant who opened a "cash store" here, and the first to begin pork packing systematically, was the first Captain. In 1849 the old engine was taken by a new company and replaced by a sort of "row-boat" apparatus, then in the flush of its ephemeral glory, and the "boys" for a long time made vigorous rivalry with the Marions. But they were beaten usually, for their engine "took water" badly, and had nearly always to be "primed," a process that lost time and gave their vigorous rivals an advantage never thrown away. In August, 1858, they raised some money by subscription to buy another engine, and the Council helped them, and this, an end-brake, they used till they were disbanded in November, 1859. They had a severe controversy with the city about their apparatus, but in February gave up everything except their old "row-boat," which they broke up and sold the following Spring. Their house was a two story brick on the west side of Meridian street, in Hubbard's block. Its upper room was used by the Fire Association, as well as by the Company.

In November, 1849, the Western Liberties Company was organized, and took the old "Good Intent." They kept it in a small frame house, on the point between the National road and Washington street, and used a big triangle for a bell. In 1857 the brick building on the south side of Washington street, west of West street, was erected for them, and a new engine, the Indiana, given them. The Company was disbanded in 1859, and the engine sold.

The "Invincibles," usually called "Wooden Shoes" by the older companies, organized in May, 1852, and obtained a little iron box engine, called the "Victory," with which, being light and easily handled, and their numbers strong, they did good work, and made good time to fires in all parts of the city. In March, 1857, they got a new engine, the Conqueror, and used it till they were disbanded in Au- gust, 1859. Their house was on the east side of New Jersey street, a half square north of Washington. After the inauguration of the Paid Department, in 1860, the Invincibles formed part of it for a few months. They were then finally disbanded, and their engine sold to Fort Wayne.

The Union Company was organized in 1855, and a handsome house built for them the year following, on South street, between Delaware and Alabama. In April, 1856, a first class engine, called the "Spirit of 7 and 6," a name the significance of which is about as hard to guess as the interpretation of the "arrow-head" inscriptions of Nineveh, was purchased for them. The Company was disbanded in November, 1859. A fruitless effort was made to reorganize it in the Paid Depart_ ment next year, and the engine was taken at $600 in part pay for the steam engine since stationed in their house.

A Company called the "Rovers". was organized in the northwestern part of the city, in March, 1858, a house and one of the old engines given them, and measures taken to procure them a new engine, but before it had reached the stage of efficient existence the old volunteer system was tottering, and nothing was done. The Company was disbanded in June, 1859, and the house sold the year after.

The "Hook and Ladder Company" was organized in 1843, and did good service till the 14th of November, 1859, when they were disbanded with the other companies. A one story brick house was built for them on the west end of the East Market space.

Besides these regular companies, there were two companies of boys, the "O K Bucket Company," and the "Young America Hook and Ladder Company." The former was organized in December, 1849, and did good service in providing buckets for "lines" to supply the engines, and in keeping down or extinguishing fires in the start. They used the old buckets for a time, but were soon supplied with a neat light wagon and new buckets by the Council. Their house was on the northeast corner of Meridian and Maryland streets, where the Opera House was afterwards built. They were disbanded in 1854, but reorganized next year for a little while, and then, being finally disbanded, changed to a sort of Engine Company, and, in 1857, were given the "Victory," the little iron engine first used by the "Invincible" Company. The young "Hook and Ladder" Company got their apparatus in June, 1858, but did little, and were disbanded November, 1859.

There was never any effective separation of Engine and Hose Companies. Each engine had its own hose reel, and for a long time the members served indifferently with either apparatus. Hose Directors were especially assigned, but they were under the command of the Captain of the Company. In the latter years of the system, a separation was partially effected, and members were classed as "engine" and "hose" men, but separate organizations, houses and service never existed. The officers were, usually, the Captain, Secretary, Treasurer, two Engine Directors, two Hose Directors, a Messenger, and a "suction hose" man, the last a position rather than an office, assigned to the most experienced member, as much of the efficiency of an engine depended on the accuracy and rapidity of the "suction" man's work. The "Messenger" kept the apparatus in order, looked to the repairs of hose and the like, and was paid about $50 a year by the Council—the only office with a salary. It was usually held by a mechanic acquainted with the construction of engines.

Until about 1852 or 1853, the annual cost of the volunteer system was slight and made up of hose repairs, occasional repainting of apparatus, and similar expenses, but after that time larger demands were made, the independent character of the companies was changed, and they became less associations of citizens for a special purpose, and more a sort of gratuitous servants of the Council. There was no union or co-operation among them, however, and the consequences were sometimes mischievous. In 1853 it was determined to subject them to a common authority, and the office of Chief Fire Engineer was created. Joseph Little was first appointed to it, with B. R. Sulgrove as First Assistant, and William King as Second Assistant. Obedience to these officers was the condition of appropriations by the Council, and refractory companies were ruled by the fear of being left to bear their own expenses. To enable them to exert their power most effectively, and counter-check the despotism of the purse in the hands of the Council, the Fire Association was organized in 1856, with B. R. Sulgrove as the first President. This body was composed of delegates from each company, and held its meetings in the hall of the Relief Company on Meridian street. Its existence and functions were recognized by the Council, and it became the authoritative representative of a very large, active and politically formidable body of about four hundred voters. No appropriations were made to companies but upon its recommendation, and all company action that affected the general interests of the Department was subjected to its supervision. It was, in fact, the Legislature, as the Engineer was the Executive, of the Fire Department. For a time its business was well conducted. But its political power was too obvious to allow it to remain free from partisan solicitations, and the tenacity with which the firemen stuck to each other made its authority even more formidable than it appeared. From the time the companies began to assume closer relations with the Council, they began to act together in certain elections which they deemed concerned them most directly, and, until the system began to fail in 1858, they were virtually conceded the office of city clerk. Daniel B. Culley, of the Marion, held the office three successive years, from 1851 to 1853. Jas. N. Sweetser, of the Marion, next took it, then Alfred Stevens, of the Relief, for two years—dying in the last half of the second year, and succeeded by Fred. Stein, and then it was given to Geo. H. West, of the Marion. The Fire Association concentrated and directed this feeling of fraternity, and as its power became more apparent, its demands became more exorbitant. The Council felt that it had taken an "Old Man of the Sea" on its back, and the citizens murmured at the unaccustomed expense. Power and money produced their inevitable effects, and the Association, in its second year, showed signs of internal discord and unmanageable jealousies. The Presidency began to be intrigued for, and measures canvassed outside and "log-rolled" for, with about as little moderation and not much more honesty than is seen in the Legislature or Congress. More than one violent disruption was attempted, and reconciliations were not easily made. At last the crash came with the election of Joseph W. Davis, formerly Captain of the "Invincibles," as Chief Fire Engineer, in 1858. He had been a prominent, active and peremptory member of the Association, with decided opinions, strong prejudices, and no particular disposition to conceal either. Of course he was liked heartily by those who agreed with him, and cordially disliked by everybody else, and the latter were by far the stronger party. Nothing but the union of the firemen had preserved their power so long, for the city was restive under their burthen, and now their union was broken. It was evident that the volunteer system was approaching its end. An attempt was made the year following, 1859, to restore harmony and efficiency by the election of John E. Foudray, who had never been a fireman, or had not for many years been actively connected with any company, and was therefore free from the partialities imputed to Mr. Davis; but a few months showed that the disease was incurable. The city had grown so large, and steam engines had been made so light, that the stage of fitness of one to the other was reached, and in August, 1859, the Council declared against the volunteer, and proposed to establish a paid, department, with steam apparatus, which, as Miles Greenwood, First Chief Engineer of Cincinnati under the paid system, used to say, possessed the valuable quality of "neither drinking whisky nor throwing brick-bats." On the 4th of September the Committee on the Fire Department reported in favor of the purchase of a small steam engine, and the sale of the "Relief" and "Good Intent." A Latta engine was exhibited here in the latter part of September, but it was thought too heavy for our unimproved streets, and a Lee & Larned rotary-pump engine, which was exhibited October 15th and 22d at the canal, and proved quite equal in the strength of its stream to the heavier Latta, was purchased and received on the 30th of March, 1860. Its location was a point of hot dispute in the Council and by the press, but it was at last, through the efforts of Mr. G. W. Geisendorff, Captain of the "Westerns," and a member of the Council, placed in the engine house of the "Westerns," at the extreme west end of the city, where it still remains. The new paid department was composed of the steam engine, with Frank Glazier as Engineer, two hand engines under Charles Richmann and William Sherwood, and a hook and ladder company under William W. Darnell. Joseph W. Davis received the reward of his efforts for the new arrangement in the position of Chief Engineer with a salary of $300. In August, 1860, a third class Latta was bought and placed in the Marion house on Massachusetts avenue; Charles Curtiss was appointed Engineer. In October a Seneca Falls engine was bought, after a competitive trial, and stationed in the Union house on South street, with Daniel Glazier as Engineer. In 1867 a second Seneca Fall engine was bought and stationed in the western house, with G. M. Bishop as Engineer. The other of the same make was sent back for repairs. The Latta has also been repaired, and the Lee & Larned. Engines and reels are kept constantly ready for service, and are both drawn by horses. The men are paid and usually do little else than their fire work.

In 1863 a central alarm bell was procured and placed in an open frame work tower in the rear of Glenn's block. It is rung by means of apparatus from a tower on the block, where a watchman is on duty day and night. For five years the locality of a fire was vaguely designated by striking the number of the ward; but in February, 1868, a telegraph system was adopted and put in operation in April, at a cost of $6,000, which provides locked boxes, the keys kept at designated places, which contain an apparatus that by a simple motion enables anybody to send an alarm to the central station. The places of these boxes and the signals belonging to them, are published.

The water supply was long uncertain and inadequate. As already stated, it was usually furnished by "lines" of spectators, if a well could not be easily reached by an engine. The canal and the creek were ample, but fires rarely occurred in those sparsely settled sections of the town. Several large wells were dug, one on the point between Kentucky avenue and Illinois street, another on Washington at the junction of Virginia avenue, and others in other places; but these were not to be depended on, and in 1860 two 300-barrel cisterns were made. But they did little service, and until 1852 the city was without any regular or reliable water supply for fires. In that year a tax for cisterns was assessed and sixteen constructed in about two years. There are now, scattered about in the most available places, 78 cisterns of 300 to 1,800 barrels capacity. The introduction of the Holly system of water works, which aims to provide streams for fires by direct pressure from the pump through the fire-plug, may affect our fire department ultimately, but it is not thought now that it will. Steam engines will hardly be dispensed with, and we must have cisterns for them. An attempt was made in 1868 to bore an artesian well, on the northwest corner of University Square, to fill the fire cisterns, and a good deal of money spent upon it, but it has been abandoned. A steam pump to fill cisterns was made in 1864 at a cost of $1,000. The hose is all gutta percha.

PRESENT CONDITION OF DEPARTMENT.

The following statement of the present condition of the Fire Department has been kindly furnished by the Chief Fire Engineer, Dan. Glazier:

No. 1.—C. B. Davis—Cost $4,800—out of service.

No. 2.—William Henderson—Cost $5,500—located on corner of Massachusetts avenue and Delaware street. This engine was rebuilt last season at a cost of $2,600. Engineer, Cicero Seibert.

No. 3.—Cost $3,500—located on South street, between Delaware and Alabama streets—Engineer, John R. Belles.

No. 4.—Cost $6,000—located on Washington street, between West and California streets. Engineer, George M. Bishop. Takes place of No. 1—is run by the No. 1 Company.

No. 5.—John Marsee—Cost $6,000. Not located—new engine in reserve.

The city has purchased grounds and will build new houses this coming summer, consequently the location of some or all the engines will be changed.

No. of Hose Reels—5. Total cost $1,800.

No. of feet of Hose—5,000. Cost about $7,000.

No. of men engaged in Fire Department—1 Chief Fire Engineer, 3 Engineers, 1 Superintendent of Telegraph, 2 Watchmen on the Tower, one Hook and Ladder man, 3 Firemen, 6 Drivers, and 12 Hosemen.

Wages of Men.—Chief Fire Engineer, $1,300 per annum; Superintendent of Telegraph, $35 per month; Engineers, $90 per month; Firemen, Drivers and Watchmen, $2.50 per day; Hosemen, $180 per annum.

No. of horses—14. No. of cisterns—78.

Total cost of Hose since organization of paid Department—$16,000.

SIGNAL STATIONS AND NUMBERS.

2   Engine House, cor. Massachusetts avenue and New York street.

3   Corner East and New York streets.

4   Hook and Ladder House, New Jersey, near Washington.

5   Spiegel, Thoms & Co's Factory, on East.

6   Washington and Noble.

7   Davidson and New York.

1-2   Noble and Michigan.

1-3   Noble and Massachusetts avenue.

1-4   East and Massachusetts avenue.

1-5   New Jersey and Ft. Wayne avenue.

1-6   Delaware and Ft. Wayne avenue.

1-7   Pennsylvania and Pratt.

1-8   Blind Asylum.

2-1   Tennessee and St. Clair.

2-3   Michigan, between Meridian and Illinois.

2-4   Tennessee, bet. Vermont and Michigan.

2-5   Illinois street and Indiana avenue.

2-6   New York and Canal—Helwig's Mill.

2-7   West street and Indiana avenue.

2-8   Frink & Moore's Novelty Works.

3-1   282 Indiana avenue.

3-2   Blake and Michigan.

3-4   Douglass and New York.

3-5   Cotton Factory, near river.

3-6   Geisendorff's Woolen Factory, near river.

3-7   No. 1. Engine House, Washington, bet. West and California.

4-1   West street and Kentucky avenue.

4-2   Georgia and Mississippi, Coburn & Jones Lumber Yard.

4-3   Washington and Tennessee.

4-5   Illinois and Louisiana, Spencer House.

4-6   Illinois and Garden—Osgood & Smith.

4-7   Illinois and McCarty.

5-1   Bluff Road and Ray.

5-2   Delaware and McCarty.

5-3   East and Bicking.

5-4   Virginia avenue and Bradshaw.

5-6   Virginia avenue and Noble.

5-7   Georgia and Benton.

6-1   16 Fletcher avenue—Chief Engineer's res.

6-2   No. 3 Engine House, South street, between Delaware and Alabama.

6-3   Gas Works.

6-4   Penn'a and Georgia—Farley & Sinker.

6-5   Glenn's block.

6-7   Delaware and Washington.

7-1   185 New Jersey street, cor. Virginia avo.

POLICE.

The Police force was first established in 1854. Its changes and the general features of its history are related in chapter X, and need not be repeated here.

Chapter XVI.

LTHOUGH Indianapolis holds a high place in the estimation of showmen, and is invariably marked for every traveling exhibition, from an operatic star to a double-headed baby, a considerable portion of its respectable patronage has been directed by a peculiarity of taste, compounded partly of Puritan traditions and partly of backwoods culture, which, even to this day, makes certain classes of entertainments "unclean." Menageries are illustrations of natural history, and the schools are dismissed to see them. Circuses are "devil's devices," and church members are, or were, "called over the coals" for visiting them. Concerts are bearable, and even the opera is not altogether abominable, but a theatrical performance is beyond moral toleration. This feeling used to be much stronger and more generally diffused than it is now, when the growth of population and ungodliness has provided ample patronage for everything, and moral antipathies, finding themselves practically powerless, have thinned greatly from inanition, and weakened from want of exercise. But in their greatest strength they could not subdue the open rebellion of many, and the secret disobedience of others, to the purity that closed the circus canvass on them, or shut them out of Ollaman's wagon-shop, or the old "hay press" foundry. It would be hard to determine whether the religious opposition of the "fathers" of the Capital injured the tabooed performances more than the additional allurement of doing a forbidden thing benefited them. At all events, though deprived of the advantage of the "family attendance" of old settlers, circuses, negro minstrels and ballet pieces have been quite as well patronized as "animal shows," lectures and concerts. "Shows," the generic Hoosier name for all sorts of exhibitions under canvass, may be considered the favorite weakness of the Capital. A circus of fair average pretensions will fill its seats in spite of weather, mud or money, and a half dozen in close succession will keep doing it, as if people went to see how much better or worse one was than another. Other exhibitions are little less attractive. Negro minstrels will suck all the patronage from an opposition lecture or charity fair. The theatre, alone, of the old-time "immoral" class of exhibitions has had a fluctuating patronage and an accidental prosperity. During the war, and since, under the impulse of some famous actor, it has done very well, but averaging all the seasons before 1861, with all those since 1865, it will be found that the profits might be turned in upon the National debt without sensibly diminishing the necessity of a tariff. Those familiar with the business might explain this exceptional sterility; it is enough for this sketch to state the fact. As concerts, lectures and "shows" have no especial connection with the city or its history, it would be an impertinent enlargement to say more of them here. The theater, however, having "a local habitation and a name," bringing population here, diffusing its earnings here, and ornamenting our streets with imposing edifices, is a part of the city, and cannot be properly omitted.

(10)

As has been stated in the general history of the city, the first theatrical performance was given here on the night of the last day of the year 1823, in the dining room of Major Carter's tavern, opposite the Court house, by a Mr. and Mrs. Smith, imposingly announced as "late of the New York theatre." Two pieces were played, "The Doctor's Courtship, or the Indulgent Father," and the "Jealous Lovers." The price of admission was "three levies"—the popular abbreviation in early times of three "elevenpence," in later years changed, by more frequent intercourse with the South, to the Mississippi "patois" of three "bits,"—and the orchestra was composed of Bill Bagwell and his fiddle. Mr. Carter was largely imbued with the prejudices against the stage, to which allusion is made above (and which recently sent a dead actor of excellent character "round the corner" for christian burial, in New York), and he objected to the use of so profane an instrument as a fiddle in his house, as an auxiliary to a performance which his conscience could illy tolerate in its least offensive form. He was finally pacified by the assurance that the obnoxious instrument was a "violin," and by the performance thereon of the air of a favorite hymn. Several exhibitions were given, with sufficient success to attract the adventurous Mr. Smith here again in June, 1824. But he failed then, and ran away without paying his bills, a trick that wandering showmen have practised frequently since.

The next attempt at theatrical entertainment was of a higher order altogether. A full company was engaged and a building fitted up expressly for it. A Mr. Lindsay was manager. Mr. Ollaman's wagon-shop, on Washington street, opposite the Court house, was the theatre, and two or three musicians composed an attractive orchestra for that day. Among other pieces, Kotzebue's "Stranger" was produced several times, and "Pizarro," the "Loan of a Lover," "Swiss Cottage," and a number of the old dramas and farces which even yet hold possession of the stage against half naked women and bloody melo-dramas. Songs were given in the "wait" between the first and second pieces, and some of them became quite as popular as S. C. Foster's plaintive negro melodies of a later day. The "Tongo Islands," with its interminable and inextricable tangle of gibberish for a chorus, "Jinny git your hoe cake done," and some of the songs made famous by Jim Crow Rice, may even yet be recalled by old residents with good musical memories. This was about the year 1837 or 1838.

During the winter of 1840–41 Mr. Lindsay returned with a really superior company, and fitted up the one-story brick building, formerly occupied as the office of the Indiana *Democrat*, where Temperance Hall is now. Mrs. Drake, and A. A. Adams, whose irregularities had prevented him from getting an Eastern engagement and forced him here to support himself, were the chief attractions. Neither of them ever played better, and the little house, which would not seat more than three hundred, was nearly always full. This was Mr. Lindsay's last appearance here.

It was here that a ludicrous scene occurred "not set down in the bills." Captain George W. Cutter, a leading Whig orator, from Terre Haute, and a poet who subsequently attained a national reputation, fell in love with Mrs Drake, who was several years his senior. She returned his passion with theatrical, if not sincere, demonstrations, and the billing and cooing of the oddly mis-mated lovers was the standing joke of the city during the session of the Legislature. One night, in some performance, Mrs. Drake, who was affectionately watched from the wings by her Wabash adorer, in making a "stage" fall, made a real one, and hurt herself, or Cutter thought she did, and he rushed upon the stage, to the horrible disorder of the scene, and the infinite fun of the audience, and tenderly lifting up his rather ponderous inamorata, audibly condoled with her, and led her off with all the touching sweetness of the honey moon. The crowd roared, cheered the gallant Captain "to the echo," and made fun of him for the next six weeks. He and Mrs. Drake were married that winter at Mr. Browning's Hotel. This love passage was the "sensation" of that season.

In 1843 "The New York Company of Comedians" opened a theatre in the upper room of Gaston's carriage-shop, where the Bates House now stands, and gave series of concerts closing with stage performances, during the better part of the winter. Mrs. Drake and Mr. Adams, Mr. Brown's history says, appeared here, but the writer has an impression, not definite enough to place against anybody's actual recollection, that they played together but one season, and that was during Mr. Lindsay's occupation of the Democrat office.

Another theatrical demonstration was a home-made affair, and by no means the worst given us. During the winter of 1839-40 an old foundry building called the "hay press," from an "institution" of that kind established in its rear to bale hay for transportation to New Orleans in flatboats, was fitted up with a stage and scenery, and used by the "Indianapolis Thespian Corps" to present Robert Dale Owen's play of "Pocahontas." The leading actors were James G. Jordan, as "Captain John Smith;" James McCready, as "Powhattan;" William Wallace, as "Pocahontas;" John T. Morrison, Davis Miller and James McVey in other characters. Though but an indifferent acting piece, and utterly forgotten as anything else now, its novelty made it entertaining enough to "run" for sometime at irregular intervals. Two or three years later the "Corps" was revived, and strengthened with the addition of Mr. Edward S. Tyler, and produced several standard plays with decided merit and success. The "Theatre" was opened, usually, once a week, but sometimes twice, in the summer and fall of that and the succeeding year. (It is but just to say that there is a good deal of discrepancy as to the dates in the history of the "Corps." The writer has fixed those given by the memories of the gentlemen belonging to the Corps, who concur unanimously in placing their performances at least as early as 1844, and the first presentation of "Pocahontas" is fixed positively, by one of the leading actors, in the winter of 1839-40.) The best paying performance, and the best dramatically regarded, was the "Golden Farmer," with Mr. Jordan as the "Farmer," Mr. McCready as "Old Mob," and Mr. Tyler as "Jimmy Twitcher." The last was a "hit." In the first scene, where "Jimmy" overhauls his booty and "takes an account of stock," and in that in which he falls off a fence and hangs by the seat of his breeches to one of the spikes, the audience never failed to "come down" with furious applause. The "Brigands," with Jordan in the song of "Love's Ritornella," was also popular. Towards the close of the season of 1842 or 1843, probably the latter, Mr. Nat. Cook, eldest son of the then State Librarian, who had been playing subordinate parts in a Cincinnati theatre, came out here, and a big demonstration was made. The town was full of rumors of his talents, his wonderful wardrobe, his fame abroad, and of all other inducements to make him the "lion" of the theatre-going society—not the highest in the city at that time—and to bring a big crowd to hear him. Home's tragedy of "Douglass" was announced, with Mr. Cook as "Young Norval," Mr. Jordan as "Glenalvon," and Mr. Davis Miller as "Lady Randolph," to be followed by the "Two Gregories," with Mr. Cook as one of the "Gregories," Mr. Jordan as the Frenchman, and Mr. John Cook, Jr., as the sweetheart of "Gregory." There was a full house, and rap-

turous applause when "Young Norval" came on for the first time, resplendent in
scale armor of tin chips, and impressive in all the rant and strut and grunt of
traditional stage propriety. But he didn't hold up. Mr. Jordan made a decidedly
better character of the villain. This was the dying blaze of the Thespians. They
expired in October, after Mr. John T. Morrison, as per programme, attempted
to declaim Dimond's "Sailor Boy's Dream," and forgot the third stanza and all
behind it. He could have done admirably if his memory hadn't tricked him, but
"stage fright" was too much for him, as it has been for many a man who has
become famous on the stage since.

(There is a long blank in theatrical history, between the Thespians and the
next stage exhibition, of too little consequence to deserve notice.)

Early in 1853, January 21st, Mr. F. W. Robinson, calling himself "Yankee
Robinson," located in Washington Hall for the winter, with the company he had
been exhibiting as a "side show" at the State Fair the fall before. To evade the
license for theatrical performances, he announced concerts by the Alphonso troupe,
and a vocal annoyance was followed by a very fair play, sometimes two. The leading actor was Henry W. Waugh, afterwards clown in Robinson's circus under the
name of "Dilly Fay," and more widely, as well as more honorably, known as a
young artist of very great promise. He painted all the scenery, and it was well
done. During the following year he assisted Mr. Jacob Cox in painting a "Temperance Panorama" in the Governor's Circle, which, never adequately managed,
failed as a traveling exhibition, though it did well in the city at Masonic Hall. He
went to Italy ten or twelve years ago, and died of consumption on his way home,
in England. Mr. and Mrs. Sidney Wilkins did the "heavy business," and Mr.
James F. Lytton the Irish characters. He sang well and with good comic effect,
and he made Irish songs very popular. "The Low Backed Car," "Billy O'Rourke,"
"The Flaming O'Flannigans," "Finnegan's Wake," and several other songs owe
their Indianapolis popularity to him. Robinson closed his season the 7th of March.
Mr. H. W. Brown then took the Hall, and, with Mr. Wilkins and wife, Mrs.
Mehen, and some others, first produced "Uncle Tom's Cabin" and with success.
He ran only four weeks, closing July 26th, 1853. Mr. Wilkins then took the
place and company, and made a brief season of a few weeks.

During the summer and fall of 1854, Mr. C. A. Elliott, having built and enclosed
his large liquor house, on the corner of Meridian and Maryland streets, Mr. Robinson
rented the third story, and had it turned into a moderately capacious and comfortable theatre, still better than Washington Hall, called "The Athenaeum." His
company consisted of R. J. Miller, who, subsequently taking the line of "Yankee"
characters—the most abominable caricatures that ever disfigured any stage in the
world, whoever the actor might be—called himself "Yankee Miller," his wife, Mr.
Bierce, another stage "Yankee" called "Yankee" Bierce, and "Yankee" Robinson himself and his wife, F. A. Tannehill, George McWilliams, his sister, Mary
McWilliams, J. F. Lytton and H. W. Waugh. This was a profitable enterprise.
The theatre was always well filled, and the plays given with no inconsiderable
share of force and scenic effect. It was here that Indianapolis was introduced to
the first "star" ever seen on White River. Miss Susan Denin, of moderate his-
trionic talent, very considerable personal beauty, and a reputation that did not
repel admirers of other attractions than her acting, appeared in "Fazio," and in the
farce of "Good for Nothing," the latter the better performance of the two, and
made a sensation which has hardly been equalled in intensity even by Kellogg and
Nilsson, though it must be admitted that the sensation did not pervade precisely

the same classes, or run upon the same level of respectability. She appeared in the same place in the year following, with her sister Kate, and played " Romeo " to Kate's " Juliet." This exhibition in tights was especially attractive to the sappy juniors of the masculine persuasion, and though her acting was not improved, her success was decided. In the spring of 1855, Maggie Mitchell, who had made her first appearance in Chicago but a few days before, appeared here, and gave no very striking indications of ability to achieve a marked success. The papers treated her kindly, however, and she left with some money and some encouragement. J. P. Addams also played during this season.

On the closing of Robinson's season, April 14th, 1855, Austin H. Brown and John M. Commons took the Atheneum, and engaged several of the best actors in the country. Mr. C. J. Fyffe was manager. The "support" was wretched and patronage fell off, though Harry Chapman and his wife, Mrs. A. Drake—reappear-ing for the first time since 1842—William Powers, a disastrous failure, and James E. Murdoch, then confessedly at the head of the profession in the United States in genteel comedy, drama, and skill as a reader, were among the attractions. Mr. Murdoch played to less than twenty persons, the unbearable heat of a close room, so near the roof, in midsummer, repelling hundreds who would have gladly heard him anywhere where they could sweat without being scalded. He threw up his engagement for the benefit of the managers after the second performance, which was the "Stranger," and left in a big disgust, which he has never so far conquered as to come back, except to lecture or give a reading. On the 15th of September, 1855, Mr. Commons reopened the theatre, and ran it till the 8th of December, with Miss Eliza Logan, Joseph Proctor and wife, Susan and Kate Denin, Peter and Car-oline Richings, and W. J. Florence and wife,. Thomas Duff was stage manager. In March, 1856, W. L. Woods opened it again for a month, Mr. W. Davidge, low comedian, being the star. Vance and Lytton ran it from May 16th to June 3d, with Eliza Logan, Miss Coleman Pope and Miss Richings as attractions. Maddocks and Wilson opened spasmodically during the summer, as a chance crowd made an appearance of pay possible. During the State Fair Wilson and Pratt used it, and Yankee Bierce and the Maddern sisters, in the early part of December. From the 16th of December till the 9th of March it was run by J. F. Lytton & Co., with Yankee Miller, Mr. and Mrs. Lacey, Tannyhill, Lytton and others as company, and Susan Denin, Dora Shaw, John Drew, Charlotte Crampton, Mrs. Drake and Miss Duval as stars. In March, 1857, Cal. J. Smith attempted to do something with the now dilapidated affair, but he couldn't do much at best, and he did noth-ing with this but ruin it outright. It should be stated that Miss Eloise Bridges, appeared in the early fall of 1865. In August 1858, a German company played at the Atheneum for a little while, and in January of that year and February of 1859 the Germans ran two theatres, one at Washington Hall and one at Union Hall. Kate Denin and her husband, Sam. Ryan, opened Washington Hall in April, 1858 for a few days, to no advantage to anybody ; and Harry Chapman, with his wife and his wife's mother, Mrs. A. Drake, and the admirable comedian John K. Mortimer, opened the Atheneum during the State Fair. This completes the sketch of makeshift theatres, halls temporarily fitted up, companies temporarily collected, and of seasons sporadically scattered through the year. From this time there is to be noticed only a regular theatre, built on purpose, and worthy of the population and prosperity of the city.

Up to this time the Theatre, though a denizen, was not a citizen, of the Capi-tal. It was a tenant, not a proprietor, and moved about with little improvement of accommodations. But in 1857 Mr. Valentine Butsch built the Metropolitan Theatre, corner of Tennessee and Washington streets, opposite the Masonic Hall, expressly for stage performances, and gave this class of amusements permanence and character. The corner stone was laid in August, 1857, and in a little more than a year the house was finished. It is one of the handsomest in the city, three stories high, eighty-two by one hundred and twenty-five feet, stuccoed to resemble stone, with niches in the second story front for symbolical statues, and a balcony which furnishes a place for the band to play alluring airs, before the rising of the curtain. The ground floor is divided into large business rooms, with two stairways to the theatre entrance. The auditorium will seat about twelve hundred persons, and could seat more if the gallery were not so indifferently arranged that the stage is visible only from the lower seats of the centre and from the two ends The dress circle under the gallery is separated from the "pit" or parquette by a descent of a foot or so, bounded by an iron balustrade, through which there are two openings from the dress circle, the only means of entrance. The vaulted ceiling is neatly decorated with fresco work. The stage, though not large, is quite adequate to any ordinary exhibition. The scenery was painted by S. W. Gulick, who was succeeded by Thomas B. Glessing, an artist of marked talent, who has provided both the Metropolitan and the Academy with as good scenery as can be found in any theatre in the West. It cost, with the lot, about $60,000.

The Metropolitan was opened under the management of E. T. Sherlock on the 27th of September, 1858, with an exhibition of the "Tableaux Vivants" of the Kellor Troupe, if the writer remembers correctly. A number of "stars" of greater or less magnitude appeared during the season, which closed on the last day of February, 1859. Among them were Sallie St. Clair, the leader of the "naked school," in such displays as the "French Spy," Hackett, the great—in all senses—"Falstaff," the Florences, J. B. Roberts, Mrs. J. W. Wallack, Mrs. Sinclair (Forrest), Adah Isaacs Menken, another of the "stripping" class, Eliza Logan, Mr. and Mrs. Waller, Matilda Heron, then in the flush of her recently acquired renown as the great "realistic" actress, and the Cooper English Opera Troupe and other stars. The season was pecuniarily a failure. Large expenses were incurred without the presentation of striking inducements to patronage, except in a few cases, and the houses did not "pay." There was, moreover, no little remnant of that antipathy to the theatre alluded to in the opening of this chapter, to encounter, and it was the more damaging as being directed by the oldest, wealthiest and most respected citizens. The manager sought to conciliate it once by offering a benefit to the Widows and Orphans' Society, then sadly in need of help, but after much discussion the offer was declined under the advice of the leading male directors, and a probable donation of five hundred dollars thrown away. The ground of refusal was distinctly stated to be the Society's doubt of the moral tendency of stage exhibitions. The city press, with scarcely an exception, exposed the insufficiency of the reason, and the impropriety of looking too nearly into the means by which money properly offered was gained. The same scrutiny might repel donations from speculators in family distress and the poverty of the very class for whose relief the Society was organized. A charitable association does all its duty when it honorably obtains means which it benificently applies. The discussion was warm for a while, the "moralists," as they were called, standing resolutely by their creed that money for pure purposes must come from pure sources, though the starvation of the suffering were the consequence of refusing that of doubtful acquisition. The city has outgrown this opinion now, if one may judge from the fact that a theatrical exhibition, by amateurs, was made on two successive nights in the Opera Hall for the benefit of this same Society, and an amateur opera was given in the Academy of Music two or three times for a similar benevolent object. The moral difference between an amateur and a professional exhibition is not a wide one, and in these instances the artistic difference was not much wider. The performances were quite as good as the average of stage exhibitions, and the only feature that the societies seemed to lament was that they did not pay better.

The failure of Mr. Sherlock did not deter Mr. George Wood from re-opening the theatre in April, 1859, for a few nights, nor John A. Ellsler from attempting a two months season immediately after. He was the first to produce ballet pieces with some approach to the scenic splendor, the tinsel, flowers, naked girls, and gorgeous tableaux of Eastern theatres. He opened it again during the fall and winter, but with little success. On the 25th of April, 1861, its management was undertaken by Mr. Butsch himself, with Felix A Vincent as stage manager, and the crowd brought here by the demands of the war made it pay. From this time to the close of the war the Metropolitan was the most profitable investment in the city. It was crowded all the time, whatever might be the attraction, though the "stock" was nearly always good enough to merit good patronage, including, as it did, Mr. Vincent, in some respects one of the best comedians ever seen here; Miss Marion McCarthy—who subsequently became insane and died here—a good actress in nearly all classes of characters from farce to high tragedy, and a pleasing singer as well; Mr. F. G. White, a broad low comedian of unfailing popularity with "the boys;" Mr. Ferd. Hight, an excellent "old man" and fair comedian, Miss Phillips, the best "old lady" we have had, and several others. Vincent continued as manager under Mr. Butsch till 1863. He was succeeded by Wm. H. Riley, who played leading parts as well as manager, and made himself deservedly popular, not more by his judicious enterprise in one capacity than his correct and effective performances in the other. His wife also appeared frequently and successfully in such parts as "Desdemona," "Juliet," "Mrs. Haller," and the lighter characters of tragedy and serious drama. Mr. Riley remained in charge of the Metropolitan till 1867, when he removed to New Orleans, to take the management of the St. Charles Theatre, of that city. He died there within a month after his arrival, regretted alike for his professional excellence and social character. The season of 1867-8 was managed by Mat. V. Lingham, and that of 1868 by Charles R. Pope. The latter, besides his own acting, which has rarely been equalled by any "star," gave us a succession of the best performances we have ever had, including a week of John E. Owens, and another by Edwin Forrest, in which he appeared as "Virginius," "Spartacus," "Richelieu," and "Othello." Madame Ristori, appeared one night, the 25th of March, 1867, under Gran's management. Mr. Pope has since taken the St. Charles Theatre in New Orleans. In 1868 Mr. Butsch closed the Metropolitan and transferred his personal management to the Academy of Music. Since then the Metropolitan has been opened as a sort of "Varieties" and "Minstrel" hall, though it has always inclined more or less to the drama. Mr. Sargeant had it in 1870, and Mr. Fred. Thompson in the spring of 1871.

In 1868 Mr. Butsch, perceiving the inadequacy of the Metropolitan to the rapidly growing population of the city, and resolved to "keep even" and retain his long mastery of amusement resources, bought the incomplete structure called "Miller's block," on the southeast corner of Illinois and Ohio streets, paying $50,000 therefor, and completed it into one of the largest and handsomest edifices in the

West, making a theatre of the second and third stories, and business rooms of the first, with an entrance on both streets. This he called the Academy of Music. The auditorium will seat about 2,500, and in completeness of arrangement, elegance of finish, comfort of accommodations, and general pleasantness of effect, it will compare with any of the smaller theatres of the United States. The dress circle is separated from the parquette by a line of boxes, and there are two well arranged galleries, the lower a better place than the parquette to hear music. The upper is usually reserved for "citizens of African descent." The Academy was opened in the fall of 1868 under the management of Mr. W. H. Leake, with a fair stock company, containing Mr. White, Mr. Hodges, and one or two others familiar to the theatrical public in past times; his wife, Miss Annie Waite, being the leading lady, and one, in all respects of careful study, conscientious effort, pleasing appearance, and versatility, unsurpassed in the city. Mr. Leake has had Mr. Owens, M-. Forrest, the Richings Opera Troupe, the German Opera Troupe, the Blondes, "Rip Van Winkle" Jefferson, Mr. Leffingwell, Mrs. Lander, Fanny Janauschek, and other distinguished performers in the Academy during his administration. In the fall of 1870 he and Mr. James Dickson leased it, with the Metropolitan, of the proprietors, Butsch & Dickson, and have since been running it, with the Terre Haute Opera House—the Metropolitan being leased, as before stated, for a Varieties establishment—with what success in money remains to be seen.

Besides these regular theatres there have been several places of amusement of a more questionable character opened from time to time. A Mrs. English kept up a cheap museum on Washington street for sometime, several years ago, and another, the greatest merit of which was its sign, was maintained in a shed on the corner of Illinois and Georgia streets. The Exchange building on Illinois street was converted into a "music hall" in 1869, which did pretty well with "minstrels" and dances of doubtful decency. In 1870 it was reopened with a similar "show," and drew full houses through the winter till it was closed up by the Young Men's Christian Association, which bought the building for its own use and emptied the theatre, ballet girls, "can-can" and "oil room" into the street. In the winter of 1869, before the Exchange was first opened for this sort of entertainment, a " Varieties" affair of the vilest kind was maintained for a while in Court street, south of the Post office.

Both the Masonic Hall and Morrison's Opera Hall have been converted into temporary Theatres at times, and a notice of them will be found in the general history of the city.

Among the amusements of earlier days may be mentioned the first " Pleasure Garden," corner of Tennessee and Georgia streets—the site of the present Catholic block—laid out and maintained by John Hodgkins, one of our old restaurant keepers, and earliest ice cream and confectionary makers, who kept on Washington street where Blackford's block now stands. The ground was well set with apple and other fruit trees, and under these seats were made, and bowers built, and flower beds were planted, and a very handsome resort created, which was well patronized for two or three summers. It was far superior to anything in the beer garden way we have since had, though the Apollo Garden, on Kentucky avenue, with its trees, bowers, open air theatre, and other attractions, made an approach to it at the outset.

Although not exactly an "amusement," no more appropriate place occurs to mention our city brass bands, of which we have had several. Though in these later days they have become a regular occupation and passed out of the province of history, the earlier ones were admired if not cherished objects of city enthusiasm, and were quite as much of an "institution" as any place of amusement. The first that ever attained skill enough to be entertaining was the old Indianapolis Band, taught and led by Mr. Protzman, a soap boiler. Its leading members were Edward S. Tyler, the bugler, James McCready, trombone player, Thos. Mc. Baker, another trombone performer, Aaron D. Ohr and James McCord Sharpe, clarionet player. The instruments were obtained by a subscription of the citizens. This band stuck together for some years, and achieved the reputation of considerable proficiency. It played for the Thespian Corps at one time, and provoked some harsh comments thereby from some of the preachers. Later, in 1850, or thereabouts, another band was formed by Mr. George Downie, a more accomplished musician than Mr. Protzman, and was maintained for a time with considerable success. Mr. Downie was the manager of a great band convention held here in 1853, which gave concerts and held a sort of musical tournament for some prize or other. Since that time bands have ceased to be such prominent features of city history, and there is no occasion to trace them further.

Chapter XLII

PROBABLY no town in the United States ever allowed a newspaper to strike root so speedily and deeply as Indianapolis. It was laid out in 1821, and the first sale of lots were held in October of that year. The population was only about 400, possibly 450. There were no mails, no roads, no water routes, no access to the outside world, and there were no improvements and no population in the adjoining country. The promise of the means to make a paper either interesting or profitable was about as feeble as can be imagined. But, as stated in the beginning of this history, the Indianapolis *Gazette* was started early in the succeeding year, January 28, 1822, and under one name or another remains here to-day, with a reasonable certainty of lasting as long as the city lasts. A sketch of its early history is given in the place where its establishment is noticed and need not be repeated here. Its proprietors were George Smith and Nathaniel Bolton, the latter well known to the citizens of the "middle era," but the former is remembered now only by a few of the oldest settlers or their oldest descendants. Mr. Bolton's wife Mrs. Sarah T. Bolton, now Mrs. Reese, was for many years the only literary character of whom Indiana could boast, and her fame was by no means as wide as her worth, though it has extended since. In 1829, the proprietors, after dissolving partnership in 1823 and reuniting in 1824, separated finally, and Mr. Bolton maintained the paper alone until the fall of 1830. In the spring of that year the Indiana *Democrat* had been started by Alexander F. Morrison, and the *Gazette* was sold out to it and consolidated with it, retaining the new name, however. Mr. Morrison was long the most prominent and able editor in the State. Though not a polished, he was a clear, forcible and pungent writer, and particularly effective in the use of sarcasm and personalities, in which he has had few equals. A newspaper in his day was merely a vehicle for the promulgation of political opinions and diatribes, and he was admirably adapted for its work. News was but a little part of its interest or value. Few expected or cared to find any thing more in it than its editor's or correspondents' notions. For the present duty and aim of a paper he might not have been so well suited, though as leading editor of the *Sentinel* in 1856, or thereabouts, he showed no lack of the ready ability necessary to the production of a daily sheet. He alone maintained and conducted the *Democrat* for some years. Subsequently he was joined by Mr. Bolton, and after a period of joint management he retired, and was succeeded by Mr. John Livingston, who finally purchased Mr. Bolton's interest and took the entire control himself. It was published the greater portion of the time during these changes, in a little brick building, on the site of Temperance Hall, erected for it. This building was fitted up as a theatre in 1841, Mr. Adams and Mrs. Drake played there as noted in the chapter on "Amusements." During the time of Mr. Livingston's sole ownership it was published in the upper story of the frame building where

INDIANAPOLIS JOURNAL BUILDING,

George F. Meyer's tobacco store is. In July, 1841, George A. Chapman and Jacob Page Chapman, who had previously published a Democratic paper in Terre Haute, bought out Mr. Livingston, removed the office to a one story frame, on the site of Blake's block, east of Masonic Hall, and changed the name to the Indiana *Sentinel*. The *Sentinel*, under the vigorous management of the Chapmans, speedily became the leading paper of the State, and its strong, racy editorials, mainly the work of Page Chapman, exercised an influence in the party it represented never before attained by any sheet, and probably not surpassed by any since. It was one of the main influences in reversing the political condition of the State. Only weekly and semi-weekly editions were published at first, but on the 6th of December 1841 a daily sheet was issued and maintained through the session of the Legislature. The following year the daily was resumed and continued through the session as before, and in 1843 the experiment was repeated, but it was not until April 28th, 1851, that this feature was made permanent. During this time the proprietary management remained with the Chapmans, though Mr. John S. Spann became a partner in November 1846. A new two story brick building was erected purposely for the paper in 1844. on Illinois street, (now occupied by a saloon), and the publication, with an extensive job establishment, continued there till about June, 1850, when, Chapmans and Spann dissolving their connection, Mr. William J. Brown became the owner of the paper and removed it to a building on West Washington street, near Meridian. The job office was, at the same time, sold to E. W. H. Ellis and John S. Spann, and retained in the old building. In April, 1852, Mr. Brown passed the paper over to his son, Mr. Austin H. Brown, remaining as leading editor, however, and it was removed to the Tomlinson building, on East Washington street, opposite the Glenn Block, then the Wright House. On the 2d of March, 1855, John C. Walker and Charles W. Cottom bought out Mr. Brown but retained the old location. Messrs. Walker and Holcombe were the editors. John S. Norman, of the New Albany *Ledger*, with Mr. John S. Spaun, bought out Walker & Cottom, December 4th. 1855, Mr. Norman assuming the editorial control. But he did not like the position of "party organ," and returned to New Albany in about six weeks, the paper passing into the hands of William C. Larrabee and C. W. Cottom, with A. F. Morrison and Mr. Larrabee as leading editors, January 24th, 1856. Seven months afterwards Mr. Joseph J. Bingham, then of Lafayette, purchased an interest, and the firm of Larrabee, Bingham & Co. held the concern till January 13th, 1857, when it was taken by Mr. Bingham and John Doughty and moved to the old Capital House building, which had been fitted up in first rate style, making the most commodious office then in the State. But here, just as it was starting off with every promise of success, it was overtaken by an appalling catastrophe. A new boiler for the engine of the press-room, placed at the rear end, exploded a little after dark on the evening of the 7th of April, 1857, tearing the eastern room of the building to pieces; precipitating type, cases, imposing stones, and all the apparatus of the office down upon the press-room; breaking the presses, setting fire to the woodwork, and creating a scene of horror never before or since witnessed in this city. One of the press hands, by the name of Homer, was killed instantly and several others injured. Publication was suspended and appeals for assistance, though by no means so liberally responded to as the ability and value of the paper demanded, brought out contributions which the energy of the proprietors made sufficient to allow a resumption of work on the 21st. But the embarrassment caused by the calamity hung upon the proprietors for a long time. The *Sentinel* Company, which then took the establishment, retained it till July 31st, 1861, when Mr. John R. Elder and John Harkness, of the *Locomotive*, joined with Mr. Bingham and purchased it, removing it to the *Locomotive* office on South Meridian street, near Washington, in Hubbard's block. In 1863 a new three story brick building was erected for it, on the other side of Meridian street, and a little further south, and it remained there till 1865. Then Mr. Charles W. Hall bought it and took it back to its old Capital House location and changed the name to the *Herald*. With Hall & Hutchinson as proprietors, and Judge Samuel E. Perkins as editor, it continued there till October 1866, when it was put into the hands of a receiver and bought in January 1867, by Lafe Develin, of Cambridge City. He was bought out by the present owner, Mr. Richard J. Bright, in April 1868, the name changed back to the *Sentinel* and Mr. J. J. Bingham installed as editor, a post he has held with but a very brief interruption since 1856. The paper owes much to Mr. Bingham's ability, industry and sagacity as a political writer, and the party owes him no less as a shrewd and indefatigable leader. Mr. Bright removed the office in December 1869 to the :ew building, corner of Circle and Meridian streets, which he had enlarged from Wesley Chapel. It is now one of the largest and best in the West. On the 4th of September 1850, Messrs. Ellis & Spann began the publication of the *Indiana Statesman*, in the old *Sentinel* office on Illinois street, and made it both a handsome and good paper for two years. It was sold to and merged with the *Sentinel* in September 1852.

A little more than a year after the appearance of the *Gazette*, the history of which has just been traced, on March 7th, 1823, the *Western Censor and Emigrant's Guide* was established by Harvey Gregg and Douglass Maguire, in a building opposite Henderson's tavern, near the spot where the *Sentinel* was afterwards located so long. Its history is given in the chapter covering the date of its first appearance, and only its later changes need notice here. On the 11th of January, 1825, its name was changed by the proprietor, Mr. John Douglass, to the *Indiana Journal*, a name it has since retained through all changes of proprietorship, and fully entitle it to the honor of being the oldest paper of the Capital. Its career has been unbroken from that time till the present, and no other paper can claim a longer life than twenty-four years. The *Journal* is now forty-six years old. Douglass Maguire was editor under Mr. Douglass' administration — the latter rarely attempted to manage the editorial department himself—till 1826. Then Mr. Samuel Merrill occupied the "tripod" till 1829. Messrs. Douglass & Maguire renewed their connection in the fall of 1829, with the old arrangement of duties, and continued together till 1835, when Mr. S. V. B. Noel purchased the interest of Mr. Maguire, and the firm of Douglass & Noel was formed, lasting till February, 1842. Then Mr. Noel, who had been editor, retired and was succeeded by Theodore J. Barnett, a man of decided talents and respectable attainments, an eloquent speaker, and well adapted by temper and tastes for his duties. In his time there was the bitterest newspaper quarrel that had been known in the Capital. The campaign of 1844 between Clay and Polk was warm, and personalities were freely thrown about. The editors, of course, came in for a large share, and they were unusually offensive. The consequence was a close approach to a fight between Mr. Barnett and George A. Chapman in the Post Office, one day, in which pistols were drawn, or supposed to be, and a furious excitement created. But before this collision, Mr. Noel had purchased the paper, and Mr. Douglass retired for good and all from the business he had followed for twenty years here. Mr. Kent succeeded Mr. Barnett as editor, in Mr. Noel's administration, but remained only a few months. John D. Defrees, of St. Joseph, then recently a State Senator from that county, removed here and became editor in March 1845, and in February 1846 purchased the concern and retained the sole control of it till the fall of 1854, when he sold out to the *Journal Company*, composed of Joseph M. Tilford, James M. Mathes, Ovid Butler and Rawson Vaile, the last recently editor of a free soil paper in Wayne county. Mr. Vaile became editor. Berry R. Sulgrove became its editor in 1852, and remained so up to 1864. For multifarious knowledge, indomitable industry, brillaint composition and power of condensation, he stands confessedly at the head of journalists of the past or present day. Since Mr. Sulgrove's return from Europe in 1867, he has been a frequent contributor to the editorial pages of the JOURNAL, as well as its temporary editor during two sessions of the Legislature. Mr. Barton D. Jones obtained an interest in 1856, and became local editor. The company sold to William R. Holloway & Co., in the summer of 1864, Mr. Holloway assuming the editorial control with Mr. H. C. Newcomb as political editor. Mr. James G. Douglass and Mr. Alexander H. Conner became associated with Mr. Holloway in February 1865, under the name of Holloway, Douglass & Co. In the winter of 1866 Mr. Samuel M. Douglass—he and James are sons of the old proprietor, John Douglass—joined with his brother and Mr. Conner and bought out Mr. Holloway, and the firm of Douglass & Conner retained the establishment till June 1870, when it was purchased by Lewis W. Hasselman and William P. Fishback. Mr. Holloway repurchased a sixth interest in 1867 and still holds it. Some weeks ago Mr. Thomas D. Fitch purchased of Fishback a sixth interest, and Mr. Hasselman gave his eldest son, Otto W. Hasselman, a sixth of his interest, and these five now constitute the proprietorship of the *Journal* establishment.—In the summer of 1864, Mr. Horatio C. Newcomb became editor of the *Journal* and continued till December 1868, making, by all odds, the ablest and most successful editor the paper had ever had. As a writer he was lucid, coherent and logical, little given to brilliance of effect, but never mistaken in his facts, or unsafe in his conclusions. He was an eminently safe party guide, and never set the "key note" of attack or defence from which he or his party had to abate a jot of pitch or force. His successor, Mr. Fishback, though less experienced in his duties, gives ample promise of needing little else, if he needs any thing, to attain the same enviable position and influence.—The *Journal* office at the start was on Washington street—near the Capital House site as before stated—subsequently it was on the south side of the same street in the frame building west of Hubbard's block; then in the three story brick on the north side near Meridian street; then on Pennsylvania street where it remained till the fall of 1860. Here the first steam press was erected, and here, in the spring of 1849, the office was seriously damaged by fire which involved the Post Office, then in the same building, and the "McCarty corner." During the spring and summer of 1860 the *Journal* Company erected the building on the corner of Circle and Meridian streets expressly for it, and had the best office in the State. In 1866, however, the proprietors, Holloway, Douglass & Co. purchased the First Presbyterian Church building and lot, corner of Circle and Market streets, and there erected a superb five story structure which is now the *Journal* Building, and likely to stay so. Semi-weekly editions of the paper were published during the session of the Legislature for a long time, the first appearing December 10th, 1828. A tri-weekly was first issued December 12th 1838. A daily edition was first published during the session of the Legislature in 1842, beginning with the 12th of December, and repeated at the same season thereafter, till the assembling of the Constitutional Convention in 1850. Then the publishing of daily verbatim reports of the proceedings of that body made a bigger effort necessary, and a larger sheet-appeared on the 7th of October of that year, and in one size or another, with several varieties of "heads" and arrangements of matter, finally settling into the quarto form and plain letter head, it has continued till now, with a probability of lasting as long as daily papers are needed here.—The *Sentinel* bought and absorbed the *Statesman*. The *Journal* has bought and absorbed two or three evanescent dailies. The first of these was the *Atlas*, started by John D. Defrees, on south Meridian street, in Van Blaricum's block, with an Erricson hot air engine to run its presses, in July 1859. He maintained it till after the election of 1860, and sold in March 1861 to the *Journal* Company. In 1867 Holloway, Douglass & Co. bought the *Daily Gazette*, another weakling that fell by the way. It was at first the Indiana *American*, a weekly removed here from Brookville by Rev. T. A. Goodwin in 1857. He sold it to Downey & Co., who changed it to a daily evening paper and sold it to Jordan & Burnett, who called it the *Gazette* and made it a good paper. They sold it in 1868 to Smith & Co.; they to Shurtleff, Macauley & Co., and they to C. P. Wilder who sold it to the *Journal* men.—The *American*, as a weekly issue, has been resumed by the original proprietor, Mr. Goodwin, within the past year.

The daily press for the first few years of its existence was not distinguished by amazing energy or enterprise. The amount of reading matter rarely exceeded four or five columns, and of this a column of original matter would have been rather an unusual proportion. Telegraphic dispatches, though published when the first line was finished, were not made a permanent feature for some years, the dispatches of the Cincinnati papers being copied usually as a substitute. In fact it was not until the seige of Sevastopol made telegraphic news particularly interesting that much attention was given this now overshadowing feature of all daily papers. Even then the reports were received by the old "recording" process of dashes and dots on a long strip of narrow paper, written out in skeleton by the operator, and copied by the editors, each for himself filling up the skeleton as he thought best. Enterprise in other respects was not ahead of this exhibition in the telegraphic way. No attempt was made to report a night meeting for the next morning's paper. The reports of Council proceedings were usually copied from the Clerk's minutes the next day, and published the day after. On the night that Hasselman & Vinton's machine shop was burned the first time, it was thought a notable bit of enterprise in J. H. McNeely, the local of the *Journal*, to stop the press and put in a five line item announcing the catastrophe and probable loss the next morning. Editorial comments on late news were rare, and no thought was entertained of making a telegraphic item the text of a leader. The nearest approach to it that had ever been attempted were the leaders in both papers on the acquittal of Matt Ward for the murder of a school teacher in Louisville. The news came by the noon Cincinnati mail, and the articles appeared the following morning. In 1855 the *Journal* published a five column report of the proceedings and speeches of a meeting of "Old Settlers" at Calvin Fletcher's house, in which the language of the speeches was followed with some approach to accuracy, the parenthetical "cheers" and "laughter" of Eastern papers indulged mildly, and a general effect of verbal daguerreotyping attempted, with considerable success. It was a novelty of domestic manufacture, and the demand for "extra copies" was heavy for several days after. It was the first decided achievement in the way of newspaper enterprise, and was followed up by attempts to report, or at least notice, night meetings in the next morning's paper, and generally to substitute city fashions for the old time-ways of weekly papers. A single incident will show the condition of things into which this reform obtruded better than any description. The paper was put to press as soon as the day's "composition" was finished, usually about sun down or a little after. One Saturday the *Journal* for Monday was put to press pretty late in the afternoon, but in time to be sent to Cincinnati by the night train, and the *Columbian*, then edited by Albert D. Richardson, since so tragically notorious, came out on the same Monday with a quizzical notice of the Indianapolis paper that had so strangely managed to discount the almanac. If the Capital had tumbled into the gape of an earthquake, or a live angel had sailed across the State proclaiming the result of the next election, the paper would have had no mention of it. In the *Sentinel* the reform was made mainly by Mr. Bingham, in the *Journal* by Mr. Vaile, the principal and working editors of their respective papers.

Besides the two earliest and best known papers, and those which they have absorbed, there are others without some notice of which this sketch would be incomplete. Somewhere about 1850, possibly before, a little paper called the *Daily Dispatch* was published for some months by W. Thompson Hatch, a gentleman of considerable enterprise but restricted in pecuniary and intellectual resources. Its leading feature was a series of sketches of members of the Legislature of the current session. There is an impression in the writer's mind that an effort was made both before and after, to establish a neutral daily of a milk-and-water complexion, but without success.—On the 14th of May, 1857, Messrs. Cameron & McNeely started the *Daily Citizen*, and made a very sprightly and valuable paper of it, but a year's experience proved it unprofitable and it was dropped in June 1858.—In July 1859, the *Daily Atlas* was started by J. D. Defrees, as before noted. The *Evening Gazette*, changed from the *American*, transported from Brookville, has been noted.—The *Telegraph*, a German daily, was established by the *Freie Presse* Company in 1866. It is in existence and doing well yet.—The *Evening Commercial* was established by Dynes & Co., in 1867, in the place of the sold out and swallowed *Gazette*. It was printed at first at Downey & Brouse's place, in the *Sentinel* building, on Washington street; afterwards in the *Journal* building on Meridian street. Then it was sold to M. G. Lee, the present proprietor and editor, who removed it in 1868 to the corner of Washington and Illinois streets, opposite the Palmer House, and within the past year has taken it back to Circle street.—The Daily *Evening Mirror*, in 1868 developed from the *Saturday Mirror*, a weekly paper established by George C. Harding and Marshall Henry, December 22d, 1867. Although it was not allowed the use of telegraphic dispatches, its local matter was so piquantly written and its general tone so different from that of the party organs, that it attained a very good circulation. But the establishment of the *Evening News*, in December 1869, with a full supply of afternoon dispatches and market reports, and with an editorial conduct as independent as the *Mirror's*, proved too much for the latter, and in February 1870 it was sold to the proprietor of the *News* and was absorbed by it. Judge Fabius M. Finch was associated with Harding and Morton during the greater part of the life of the Daily *Mirror*, and during the last four months it was edited by Mr. John Finch.—The Daily *Evening News* was established by John H. Holliday, in December 1869, and the first number appeared on the 7th of that month. It was the first evening paper that anticipated any of the material news of the morning papers, and its low price—two cents—speedily introduced it into houses where a paper had never been taken before. Its circulation within the city now equals that of its older morning cotemporaries, and its position is as firmly fixed. It is published in the new *Sentinel* building.—In June 1870, Messrs. Dynes & Cheney started the Daily *Times*, a morning paper in the Reform interest, which announced its "mission fulfilled" with the sale of the *Journal* establishment to Messrs. Hasselman & Fishback, and died after a short career of a week, selling its material to the *Journal*. It had nothing else to sell.

In distinguishing between Daily and Weekly papers the line of separation must not be pushed too far, for all the dailies have published weekly editions, made up almost wholly of matter kept standing from the several daily issues of the preceding week. But there have been weekly papers that had no daily connections or off-shoots at all. The first of these that attained any position or reputation, if not the very first after the pioneer papers, was the *Locomotive*, a little sheet not much larger than the page of this volume, published by John H. Ohr, Daniel B. Culley and David R. Elder, three apprentices in the *Journal* office, which was then on the north side of Washington near Meridian street. The first number appeared on the 3d of April, 1847. It ran through one volume of three months and disappeared for six months. It was made up of selections, and contributions of school boys and young gentlemen of immature powers, and didn't die a day too soon. It was revived on the first of January 1848, by Douglass & Elder, and enlarged about an inch all round, from seven to eight in width, and from ten to twelve or thirteen inches. It was made of much the same material as before, but devoting itself wholly to local matters, gossip, business and improvements, which were clear below the range of the stately political papers, it became a sort of family necessity. In March 1850, John R. Elder and John Harkness took it—then published in Hubbard's block on Meridian street—and without changing its local character, put a new force not only into its editorial matter but its contributions, which sprung clear above the puerile level of its former life, and made it a "power" in the town. Its circulation for some years was the largest in the county and entitled it to the Post Office advertisements. In July 1861, the proprietors bought the *Sentinel*, as before stated, and amalgamated the *Locomotive* with it.

In 1846 or thereabout, an anti-slavery paper, called the *Indiana Freeman*, or some such name, was started by a Mr. Depuy and maintained, with decided ability but little profit or popularity, for a year or two. Dr. Ackley assisted the editor at times, but "abolitionism" had but few friends in those days, and no amount of talent could have maintained it. The owner's sign was stolen one night and placed upon an out-house, and the office was besmeared with dirt and tar. Threats of mobbing were made at times, and more than once Mr. Depuy watched all night long for marauders, but the threats never exceeded the infliction of puerile malice.

In September 1848, Julius Boetticher attempted the hazardous experiment of publishing a German paper here, and the *Volksblatt* made its appearance, from one of the second story rooms in Temperance Hall. Mr. Boetticher and his daughter did most, if not all, the type setting, and he did all the writing, and worked the hand-press upon which it was printed. Nothing but the most untiring industry and perseverance could have saved it. At any other time it would inevitably died any how, but the universal European revolution, with the succeeding war in Hungary, gave an interest to foreign, and especially to German, news, which enlarged the circle of readers and advertising patronage at the same time. How important to it were little influences, which two or three years later it could have kept or lost almost without knowing it, may be judged from the fact that Mr. Boetticher attributes his determination to persevere, after the first disheartening effort, to the

PROVIDENCE BOARD OF TRADE BUILDING.

accession of a considerable list of cash subscribers brought by Prof. Hoshour's class in German, who had been recommended by their teacher to take and read a German paper. The *Volksblatt* is now a "fixed fact," with a large and remunerative business. It was edited, after the first fierce struggle with adversity was over, by Mr. Paul Geiser, a German of unusual attainments, and decided talents, but of very uncertain or unsettled principles. Later it fell into the hands of Mr. Adolph Seidensticker, who was editor for several years. It is now published in Mr. Boetticher's own building on East Washington street nearly opposite the City Hall.—In September 1851, Ellis & Spann started the *Statesman*, as related in the account of the *Sentinel* and its "tributaries." It lasted just one year.—On the 15th of August 1851, the *Hoosier City*, a neat little folio, about the size of a "foolscap sheet" squared, was commenced by Samuel H. Mathers, Francis M. Thayer, now editor of the Evansville *Journal*, and Henry C. Ferguson, another triplet of *Journal* apprentices, like those that originated the *Locomotive*. Its leading articles were sprightly and well written, and attracted a good deal of attention. Two of them, "Apology for Tobacco" and "A Short Plea for Ugliness," were copied all over the country at the time, and one, the former, was republished in England. Mr. Thayer was generally supposed to be the author, though he never frankly—notwithstanding his name—admitted it. It was closed at the end of its three months volume and never renewed.—About the same time, 1851, Rev. B. T. Kavanaugh started a temperance weekly here called the *Family Visitor*. It subsequently became the *Temperance Chart* and was edited by J. W. Gordon, Esq.—On the 3d of September 1853, the *Freie Presse* was established by an association of Germans of free soil tendencies, to counteract the influence of the *Volksblatt* which was given decidedly and effectually to the Democrats. The same company, or its successor, published the Daily *Telegraph*. The editor of the *Freie Presse* who became most widely known as connected with it was Mr. Theodore Bielscher, a German of the wildest speculative kind, who never had a moderate opinion about any thing, but withal a man of ability and scholarship. He remained in direction of the paper for some years.—In 1855 Mr. Charles Hand began a miscellaneous sort of Weekly called the *Railroad City*, but it died in a few months. It wasn't intended to live long.—Somewhere about this time the *Western Universalist* was established here by Mr. Manford and Dr. Jordan, and maintained for two or three years.—The *Witness*, a paper in the Baptist interest, conducted by Dr. M. G. Clarke belonged to the same period. It was published at the *Journal* office.—On the 3d of January 1857, the Bidwell brothers, Andrew and Solomon, began the publication of a remarkably well printed, but decidedly radical, weekly, called the *Western Presage*, at No. 86 East Washington street. It lasted three months.—The Indiana *American*, late of Brookville, was brought here by Rev. Thomas A. Goodwin, as heretofore stated, and kept up for a time with a good deal of energy, but it was sold in about two years to Downey & Co., who changed it to a Daily, and it subsequently became the evening *Gazette*, and still later a meal for the *Journal*.—The period of the war, though favorable to most other enterprises did not nourish new growths of newspapers. The times were too feverish for Weeklies, and it took too much money to establish Dailies. One wouldn't and the other couldn't be done. The first important effort after the close of the war, was that of the *Sunday Mirror*, started by George C. Harding and M. Henry, in the building of the Franklin Printing Company on West Maryland street near Meridian street, December 22d, 1867. Mr. Harding was the sole editor for a time, but was subsequently joined by Mr. William B. Vickers. John R. Morton supplanted

(11)

Mr. Henry, and the establishment was removed to Meridian street, its present location. Its success, with the writing especially the local and miscellaneous, of the two editors and of several admirable contributors, with the soliciting skill of Mr Morton, was soon made apparent, and encouraged the perilous effort of growing a Daily *Evening Mirror*, with the result already related. After the sale of the Daily to the *News*, the Weekly was abandoned, and Mr. Vickers began the publication of *Town Talk* in its place, with much of the old spirit of the *Mirror*, and a good promise of success. But Mr. Harding, after some weeks of silence, revived the *Mirror*, effected a reunion with Mr. Vickers and an absorption of the new paper, and the old name was filled up with the old paper in every important feature. In the latter part of May 1870, Mr. Harding sold out and the *Mirror* has since been owned and edited exclusively by Mr. Vickers. It is the only exclusively literary Weekly in the city, and stands at the head of its class in the State.—Shortly after the suspension of the *Mirror*, Mr. John R Morton established the *Journal of Commerce*, a Weekly devoted to the business interests of the city and State. It was at first edited by Enos B. Read, late of Cincinnati, but subsequently by Dr. Winslow S. Pierce, a gentleman well known in the business circles of the State. The office is now on Washington street, opposite the Trade Palace.—The *People*, started by Enos B. Read, late editor of the *Journal of Commerce*, Mr. Schollman and George J. Schley, is a Sunday paper, the only one we have, given to illustrations, sensations and intellectual spice and pepper generally. It is published on Circle street. With these may be mentioned the *Little Sower*, and *Little Watchman*, Children's Sunday School papers, edited by Rev. W. W. Dowling. They are handsomely printed, well conducted and very widely circulated.

The first monthly publication was the *Indiana Farmer*, established by Osborn & Willotts. It had not a very promising field, and accomplished little. It died somewhere, about 1830 or '40, or came so near it that its revival, with Henry Ward Beecher as editor, was like making a new affair. Mr. Beecher was hardly so profound an agriculturist as Mr. Greeley, for his experience did not extend beyond his lot on Ohio and New Jersey streets, where he raised more flowers than fruit, but he could ring endless changes and pleasant ones on the primary necessity of good ploughing and sound seed, and they were really more needed than instructions in "drainage" or "humic acids" or "constituent elements." One of his "squibs" on the unusual effect of a "well polished plow" in producing good crops, which explained in the conclusion that the polish would do no good unless made by constant rubbing in the earth, was widely copied and hardly ever properly credited. In very recent times the *North Western Farmer*, by Dr. T. A. Bland, succeeded by Messrs. Caldwell & Kingsbury, has taken the place, or a higher one, of the old monthly. The *Christian Record*, a monthly organ of the denomination of Christians, started at Bloomington, was removed to this city by the proprietor, James M. Mathes, in 1854 or '55, and it has continued here ever since. It is now in charge of Rev. Elijah Goodwin. The following list of the publications now published here is all that need be said:

DAILY.—Journal, Sentinel, Commercial, News, Telegraph, (German.)

WEEKLY.—American, Journal of Commerce, Mirror, People, Independent, (Temp.,) Little Sower, Volksblatt, (Ger.) Spottsvogel, (Ger.) Zu Kunft, (Ger. Turner.)

MONTHLY.—Masonic Advocate, Odd Fellows' Talisman, Western Journal of Medicine, North Western Farmer, School Journal, Benham's Musical Review, Willard's Musical Visitor, Christian Record, Phonic Advocate, Little Chief, Bee Journal, American Housewife, Ladies' Own Magazine, Morning Watch.

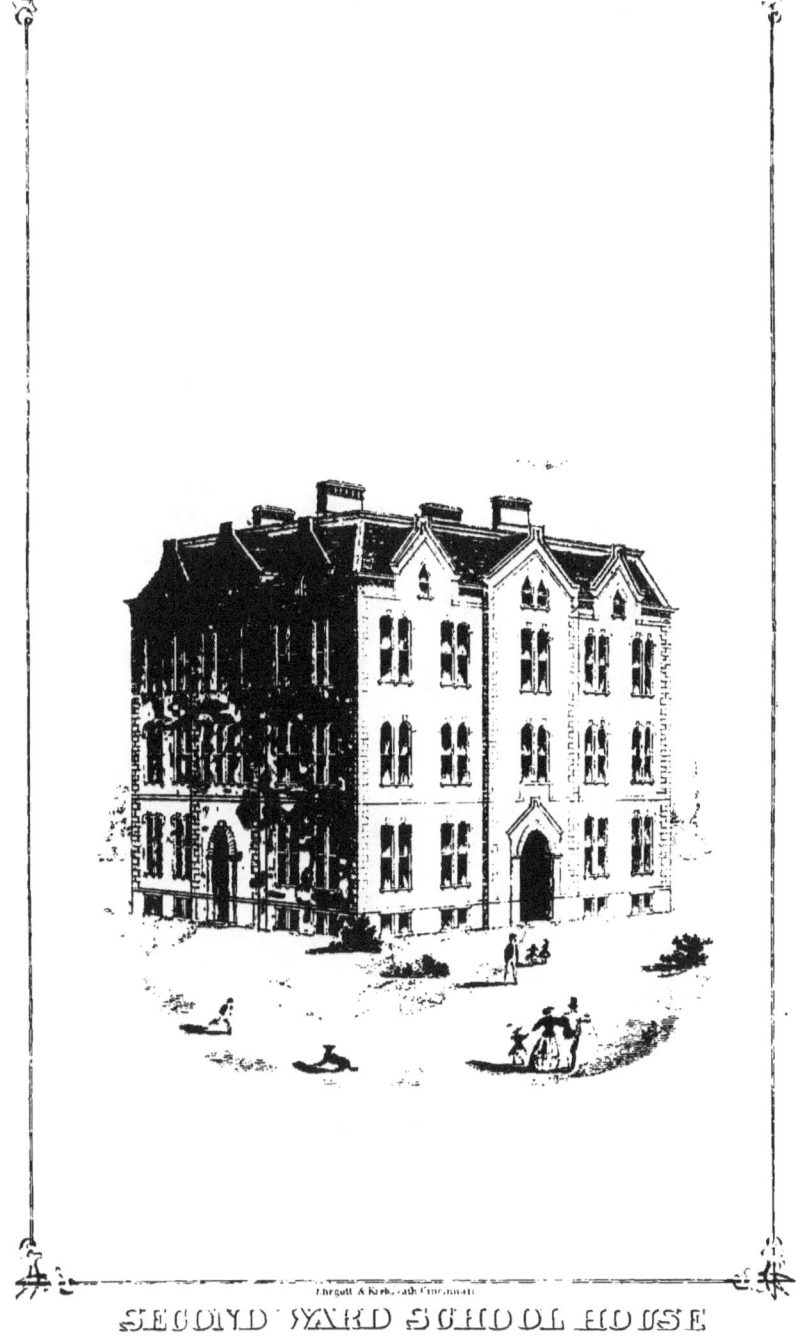

Ehrgott & Krebs, 7th Cincinnati

SECOND WARD SCHOOL HOUSE

EDUCATIONAL.

The Schools of Indianapolis have, from the early days of the city, been in good standing and repute.

For thirty-three years after the founding of the town, the schools were all private or denominational; but many of them were characterized by strong points of excellence, of which pleasant memories are cherished by many of the older citizens.

Our object is to give a brief narration of some features of interest connected with the public schools of the city, and our plan necessarily excludes any other than a casual reference to the private schools which ante-dated the organization of the common school system.

In the year 1821, one year after the selection of the site for the capital, the first teacher appeared. With a very limited number of poor pupils, the income arising from his enterprise was not encouraging; the school was soon given up, and the teacher left to practice his profession in more fruitful fields.

Several citizens, now living, received their first knowledge of letters from the instruction of the late venerable James Blake, in the well-remembered Sunday school conducted by him in Caleb Scudder's cabinet shop.

During the years 1822, 1823 and 1824, there were private schools started, of moderate success and usefulness. In the Spring of 1825, the year after the removal of the capital from Corydon to Indianapolis, the number of children had multiplied in the town, and no one was found willing or able to instruct them. The necessity becoming urgent, Samuel Merrill, then Treasurer of State, was induced to open a school in a log Methodist church building, on Maryland street, between Illinois and Meridian. The school was much needed, and did a good work in starting aright the lives of many of our useful citizens.

In the Autumn of 1826, Mr. Ebenezer Sharpe came to the town, with his family, from Kentucky; and, in November of that year established a school in the school-room of the old Presbyterian Church, on Pennsylvania street, between Market and Ohio. Mr. Sharpe at once took a position as a citizen of the first order of merit, and a teacher of rare ability and worth. He was a man of culture and accomplishments; and, by his excellent qualifications as a teacher, gave tone to popular education in the minds of the public. Many of our most estimable citizens are indebted to his moral and religious counsels, as well as to his instructions in literature and science, for their success in after life. He was well adapted to lay broad and deep the foundation of a popular system of education. In his school duties he was assisted by his son, Thomas H. Sharpe, now living, an honored and well-known citizen of Indianapolis.

At a later period, in 1830 and after, Thomas D. Gregg taught an excellent school on the corner of Market and Delaware streets.

Rev. Wm. A. Holliday will be well remembered as a worthy and successful teacher.

After the County Seminary was finished on University square, a series of excellent schools were taught there, from 1845 to 1854, under the charge of James S. Kemper, Ebenezer Dumont, J. P. Safford, Benjamin L. Lang, E. P. Cole, and other successful teachers. During this period there were also a number of other private schools of merit.

How THE PUBLIC SCHOOLS WERE STARTED.—It was not until the Winter of 1846-7 that any attempt was made to establish a system of free schools for the city. The measures then taken grew by slow degrees, until six years afterward a free school was opened for two months; but it was nine years after the initiatory steps were taken before free schools for the full school year were actually established.

From the Report of the Trustees of the Public Schools, for the school year ending September, 1866, we extract the following "historical sketch of the schools:"

"During the Legislative session of 1846-7, the first city charter, prepared by the late Hon. Oliver H. Smith, for the town of Indianapolis, was introduced into the General Assembly. It would have passed without opposition as a matter of course and courtesy, had not a well-known member from this town, Mr. S. V. B. Noel, presented as an amendment Section 29, which provided that the City Council should be instructed to lay off the city into suitable school districts, to provide by ordinance for school buildings, and the appointment of teachers and superintendents; and, further, that the Council should be authorized to levy a tax for school purposes, of not exceeding one-eighth of one per centum of the assessment.

"The amendment met with a vigorous and determined opposition from several influential members, * * whose arguments carried weight; and the amendment was in peril, when a prudent and useful member, who advocated all sides on vexed questions, moved to still further amend by providing that no tax should be levied unless so ordered by a vote of a majority of the town, at the ensuing April election, when the ballots should be marked 'Free Schools,' and 'No Free Schools.'

"The charter, thus amended, became a law.

"An animated contest ensued in the town, and at the first charter election the school question became the overshadowing issue. The opposition was thin and noisy. The friends of free schools were quiet, but resolute; and on the day of election were by no means sanguine of the result.

"A citizen, who was to a considerable degree a representative of the learning, jurisprudence and capital of the town, the late venerable and eminent Judge Blackford, was earnestly cheered as he openly voted a ballot endorsed 'Free Schools.' The cause of impartial education triumphed by an overwhelming majority.

"The population of Indianapolis was then about six thousand. City lots and building material were cheap and abundant; but the valuation of property was low, and twelve and a half cents on a hundred dollars produced but a slender revenue. The proceeds of the tax were carefully husbanded, and economically invested, from time to time, in school lots and buildings. Lots were purchased and houses built in seven wards of the city, and teachers appointed, who received their limited compensation from the patrons of the schools.

THE PUBLIC SCHOOLS, FROM 1853 TO 1871.—"For a period of six years the records show payments made by the city treasurer for lots and buildings, but none for teachers' salaries. Previous to 1853, the schools were managed by trustees in each of the school districts into which the city was divided. The schools had no central head, and no organization outside of the several districts. In January, 1853, the Council appointed Messrs. H. P. Coburn, Calvin Fletcher and H. F. West, the first Board of Trustees for the city schools. At their first meeting, March 18, 1853, they elected ten teachers for the city schools, and ordered that they receive $2.25 a scholar for the term, to be paid by the parent or guardian. April 8, 1853, it was ordered that the sixth ward lot be graded. It is interesting to note that thirteen years elapsed before the grade was made. April 25, 1853, the first free schools were opened for a session of two months. On this date a code of rules and regulations, prepared and reported by Calvin Fletcher, was adopted. These rules were comprehensive and well matured, and constitute the basis of the code now in force in the schools. May 14, 1853, occurs the first record of the payment of salaries to teachers.

"From this time forward, the receipts from city taxation and the State school fund, by slow degrees increased, and the schools flourished and grew in favor with all good citizens.

"Early in 1855, Mr. Silas T. Bowen was appointed superintendent of the schools, with instructions to visit and spend a day in each school every month, and to meet the teachers every Saturday for review of the work done, instruction in teaching, and classification. His contract with the Board called for about one-third of his time in the discharge of these and other duties. It is clear, from the arduous labor performed, that the schools got the best of this bargain.

"March 2, 1856, Mr. George B. Stone was appointed superintendent. All his time was given to the schools, and they were conducted with vigor and success. * * * The schools were fully and generously sustained by the public. The revenue, in great part derived from local taxation, was sufficient to sustain them prosperously during the full school year. But this period was of short duration. Early in 1858, the Supreme Court of the State decided that it was unconstitutional for cities and towns to levy and collect taxes for the payment of tuition. The effect was most disastrous. It deprived the city schools of the principal part of their revenue, and in spite of generous efforts on the part of a portion of the public, the free-school graded system, which had taken ten years to build up, was destroyed at a blow. The superintendent and many of the teachers emigrated to regions where schools were, like light and air,—common and free to all; with no constitutional restrictions or judicial decisions warring against the best interests of the people.

"Then commenced the dark age of the public schools The school-houses were rented to such teachers as were willing, or able from scant patronage, to pay a small pittance for their use. The State fund was only sufficient to keep the schools open one feeble free quarter each year; and, in 1859, even this was omitted for want of money. * * * * * * * *
At length the Legislature made provision for more efficient and prosperous schools and fuller taxation for their support.

"During the last five years, the schools have been rapidly gaining in length of term, and in general prosperity and usefulness. We cannot here give even a condensed statement of the successive steps by which this improvement has been accomplished. The schools, during the last two years, have been in session the usual school year of thirty-nine weeks. Considering the ten years required to develop an efficient system of schools, previous to the judicial blotting-out, and the slow growth of the nine subsequent years, it is hoped that no further disaster will occur to set them back another decade, but that they may go on increasing in strength and vigor, and each succeeding year be stronger and better than the last."

In April, 1854, an enumeration of the school population was taken by order of the Board of Trustees. The number of persons in the city between the ages of five and twenty-one was found to be three thousand and fifty-three. At that time there were enrolled in the schools eleven hundred and sixty pupils, with an average daily attendance of eight hundred and one, nearly equally divided between the then seven wards of the city. There were also in attendance at the High School in the Old Seminary, on University square, one hundred and fifteen pupils, under the charge of Mr. E. P. Cole as principal, who enjoyed the moderate salary of $250 a quarter.

The course of study in the high school was about the same as in the A and B intermediate grades of the present day, and embraced instruction only in reading, writing, spelling, arithmetic, geography, and grammar.

The above is the first record to be found, as regards either the school population, enrollment, attendance, or the grading of pupils. The public school statistics, therefore, date back from the present time only seventeen years.

During ten of those years, from 1853 to 1863, the record is very imperfect, in respect of the working and grading of the schools and the enrollment and attendance of pupils. It is impossible to learn, with any accuracy, how many pupils were in the schools, or what methods of instruction were carried out.

All the material facts to be found of record are embraced in the table of the statistics of the schools appended to this sketch. From April, 1857, to May, 1858, a period of thirteen months, the minute book of the School Board shows no record whatever.

In June, 1858, the Trustees ordered their first levy for school purposes, of fifteen cents on the hundred dollars of valuation, for the purpose of building school houses and for the current expenses of the schools. In December of the same year, the Trustees resolved that, "as circumstances have occurred since the levy of the above tax, making it difficult for the tax-payers to meet the requisition in full; and whereas the building in the northwestern part of the city can be postponed; therefore, resolved that the County Treasurer be instructed to collect but seven and one-half, instead of fifteen cents, of that levy." The school-house alluded to, the new Fourth ward house, was commenced seven years, and finished nine years, after the above action of the Board.

During the long vacation of the schools, for the two years ending February, 1860, the school property was cared for, and the School Board exercised some supervision over the private schools, which were kept in the rented school-houses. The quarterly rental of ten to thirty dollars a term for the small and large buildings, was moderate; but the payments were more moderate, as the schools receiv ed but limited patronage, and the rents were generally either excused or unpaid.

In June, 1858, Mr T. J. Vater was employed to care for the school property; and in September of the same year, James Greene was appointed School Director, at a salary of $250 a year during vacation, and $500 a year during "term time," when he was to give one-half of his time to the schools.

The school fund fell to its lowest ebb in June, 1858, when the balance in the city treasury, belonging to the schools, was $28.93. In April, 1859, there was in the Treasury $3,547, for the current expenses of the schools, being the proceeds of the levy of 1858; and in June, $3,377, belonging to the tuition fund, and available for teachers' salaries. The opening of the schools, however, was postponed until February, 1860, in order that the free schools might then remain open twenty-two weeks. Twenty-nine teachers were appointed, at salaries ranging from $50 to $100 a quarter. Of those then selected but one now remains in the schools—Miss Eliza Ford, the accomplished principal of the Ninth district.

The average professional life, in this most useful vocation, is less than ten years; few die, but nearly all resign.

In August, 1860, the City Council ordered the removal of the old, decaying County Seminary building, on University square. The High School had for some years been abandoned, but its home was now destroyed.

November 26, 1860, the schools were reopened for the session of 1860-61, with twenty-nine teachers; among them Miss Ford and Miss Alice Gray, of the present corps.

In June, 1861, the first Board of Trustees, elected by the people, one from each ward, organized.

After the close of the Winter session in 1861, the free schools were not reopened until February 3, 1862. They then continued in session for a period of twenty-two weeks.

Professor Geo. W. Hoss was appointed School Director, to serve during the school term, giving one-half his time to the schools, at a salary of $500 per annum. Twenty-nine teachers were appointed, at the following rates of pay, being an increase on the previous salaries: Principals of grammar schools, $150 a term of eleven weeks; assistants of same, $75. Principals of intermediate departments, $75 to $85 a term; and teachers in the primary schools, $50 to $68. The aggregate compensation of teachers for the two terms was $4,658. The name of Miss Nebraska Cropsey, the present competent principal of the primary departments of the schools, first appears on the roll of teachers for 1862.

Owing to the pressure of taxation, by reason of the war of the rebellion, the annual levy, made in March, 1862, was reduced to three cents on each one hundred dollars valuation, and thirty cents on each poll.

The same Spring, by order of the Trustees, shade-trees were planted on all the school property; and the present appearance of the grounds, and the summer shade, promoting the comfort and well-being of the pupils and teachers, attest that the measure was useful and well timed.

In October of this year Professor Hoss was appointed Superintendent. He was required to give one-fourth of his time to the schools, for the quarterly pay of $62.50; and never was a modest salary more industriously earned.

The next term of the schools opened in November, 1862, with twenty-eight teachers. The salaries were fixed at the following prices " for each day's services actually rendered ": Principals of grammar schools, $2.50 per day; assistants, $1; principals of the 1st, 3d, 4th, 6th and 7th wards, (one-story buildings), $1.25 per day; principals of the 1st, 2d, 5th and 8th wards, (two-story buildings), $1.50 per day; primary and secondary principals, $1.10; and all assistants, 85 cents a day. A few months later an increase of twenty per cent. on the above salaries was voted.

In the Spring of 1863 the Trustees levied a tax of fifteen cents on the $100. The pay-roll of twenty-nine teachers, for the quarter ending May 2, 1863, amounted to $2,834.

In May, 1863, a new Board of nine Trustees, elected by the people, organized; and in August following elected twenty-nine teachers, with salaries varying but little from those of the previous year. The schools opened for the session of 1863-4 on the first Monday of September, 1863.

On the 29th of August, the Trustees, by resolution, defined at length the duties of Superintendent, fixed the salary at $1,000 a year, and elected to the position Professor A. C. Shortridge. The wonderful growth, vigor and success of the schools, during the last eight years, show how prudent was the selection, and how efficiently Professor Shortridge has discharged the duties of this important trust.

From this time forward the income arising from special taxation, and the apportionment from the State Tuition Fund, rapidly increased; so that the schools, although the number of pupils multiplied with each succeeding year, were still kept open during the usual school year of thirty-nine weeks.

In August, 1864, the High School, which died out in the crash of 1858, was again organized in the school-house on the corner of Vermont and New Jersey streets, and placed in charge of W. A. Bell, the present Principal, at a salary of $900 a year.

In the Spring of 1865, the income from the Special Fund was $15,963, and from the Tuition Fund, $14,489. In April of that year, under the new Common School Law of the State, a Board of three Trustees was elected by the Common Council, and organized on the 23d day of May.

In July, the School Board adopted plans for two new school-houses, with capacity for one thousand pupils; one on the corner of Michigan and Blackford streets, and the other on the corner of Vermont and Davidson streets; and appointed Joseph Curzon, who designed the buildings, as architect and superintendent. One of these buildings was completed and opened in the Winter, and the other early in the Spring, of 1867. The two buildings, fitted and furnished complete, with enclosures and out-buildings, cost $71,000.

In February, 1866, the lot, 223 by 160 feet, on Union street, on which the Sixth district house was afterward built, was bought at a cost of $5,500.

The same month, the first Board of Visitors was appointed by the Trustees—two competent persons being selected from each ward of the city. Their services were cheerfully rendered, and their periodical visits to the schools did much to acquaint the public with the movements and progress of the schools, and to stimulate both teachers and pupils to increased diligence.

In June, 1866, the largely increased attendance in the schools, and the urgent want for more school-room, warranted the Board in making the annual levy for building and current expenses, to the full amount allowed by law, viz: 25 cents on $100 valuation of property, and 50 cents on each poll.

The same season the salaries were ordered, as follows: Superintendent, $2,000; Principal of the High School, $1,250; Teacher of Vocal Music, $1,500; and Teachers of the Ward Schools, from $400 to $625 per annum. Thirty-nine teachers were employed.

Early in the Fall of 1866, an "Annual Report of the Public Schools, for the year ending September 1, 1866" was published in a pamphlet of ninety-four pages. It contains much useful information with regard to the schools, statistics of permanent value, and a *resume* of the early history of the schools; to which we are indebted for many of our facts.

In January, 1867, the first Evening Schools were established, and have been continued during the Winter months to the present time. These schools have accomplished great good; but the attendance has not been at all equal to the needs of the class most requiring such privileges.

In December, the Second Presbyterian Church property, on the corner of Market and Circle streets, was purchased for the High School, and for the offices of the

Trustees and Superintendent. The cost of the property, refitted and furnished for its new uses, was $18,000.

In February, 1866, a Training School was organized in the new Fourth district school-house. Miss A. P. Funnelle, a graduate of the Model School, of Oswego, N. Y., and of the N. Y. State Normal School, at Albany, was appointed principal. The object of this school was, to furnish persons desiring situations as teachers in the Indianapolis schools with the requisite instruction and training in the whole science and art of Education, so as to fit them to successfully perform their duties in any primary or intermediate grade. The results accomplished by the culture and discipline of this school have been most satisfactory.

In the report for 1869, the Superintendent says:

"The good influences of our Training School have permeated every part of our school system. Not a single one of the five thousand pupils, from the senior class of the High School, to the lowest primary grade, has failed to receive, directly or indirectly, some of the benefits of its organization. Twelve young ladies graduated the first year, fourteen the second, eleven the third, and ten the fourth; making a total of forty-seven, all of whom at once became teachers in the public schools; thus securing earnest, cultivated, and thoroughly competent teachers, for the most part brought up by our own firesides and in our own homes, and educated in our common schools."

Owing to want of room suitable for the purpose, the Training School was not continued for the year 1870-71, but it is understood it will be recommended for the year 1871-2.

Immediately after the dedication of the new school-house on Michigan and Blackford streets, the old Fourth Ward House, on Market street was assigned to the use of Colored Schools, but without provision for the payment of teachers, as the law establishing such school had not then been enacted.

June 16, 1867, a report from the School Trustees was presented to the Common Council, recommending a supplementary levy by the city of ten cents on the hundred dollars, for tuition. In this report it was estimated that the annual expense for teachers' salaries, for the next year, would be $40,000; while the annual revenue derived from the State fund was about $20,000. The levy called for was adopted by the Council.

In September, 1868, the new building on Union street, in the Sixth Ward, which had been commenced in the spring of 1867, was opened for the reception of pupils. This School House was built from the designs, and under the superintendence, of Joseph Curzon, and has capacity for eight hundred and forty pupils, (though by crowding all its space and seating the attic story, nearly one thousand pupils have been admitted.) Its cost, including enclosure, furniture and out-buildings, was $44,000.

In August, 1868, sixty-eight teachers, and in July, 1869, seventy-six teachers, were elected to positions in the Schools.

In April, 1869, a new Board of Trustees, elected by the Common Council, organized. The usual full levy was made by the Board in August, and the Council was petitioned for a supplementary levy of eleven cents, and twenty-five cents on each poll.

The report to Council showed an expenditure for instruction of $44,470 for the year just closed, and an estimated cost for teachers' wages for the year 1869–1870, of $55,000.

In October, 1869, a lot one hundred and eighty-eight by one hundred and ninety-eight feet, on the corner of Walnut and Delaware streets, was purchased for the sum of $18,000, and the old Second Ward School House property sold for $9,000.

Measures were immediately taken to build a suitable School House on the new lot. Enos and Huebner were selected as architects. The erection of the building was vigorously prosecuted, and it was finally opened for the reception of pupils during the winter of 1871. It is, like the Sixth District House, four stories high, and has capacity for 728 pupils. Its cost, including all fixtures, improvements, enclosures and furniture, was $70,000.

In the Fall of 1869, the "Eighth Annual Report of the Public Schools, for the year ending August 31, 1869," a volume of one hundred and thirty-nine pages, was published. This report contains much valuable information with regard to the schools and a full record of their movements during that year.

In a report of the School Board to the Common Council, of June 18, 1870, we find the following compact exhibit, to which we add the statement for 1871. There were, at the close of the school years ending with the dates mentioned, the following results:

Year Ending	Pupils in the Schools.	Annual Cost for Tuition	Number of Teachers.
June, 1868,	4,949	$34,007	62
" 1869,	5,160	44,470	78
" 1870,	5,795	54,092	29
" 1871,	6,449	60,480	103

During the school year commencing September, 1869, schools for colored pupils were established in the old Fourth and Sixth Ward school-houses. The schools rapidly filled up with pupils, eager to learn; and the accommodations becoming too small, the capacity of the Fourth ward house was doubled, by the addition of a second story, during the Summer of 1870. An Evening School for colored youth was also opened during the Winter of 1871, and was popular and very fully attended.

THE EVENING SCHOOLS.—October 31, 1870, the Superintendent reported a total number of three hundred and seventeen pupils attending the Night Schools for the Winter of 1869-70. The average number was one hundred and sixty-one; and the cost, $507—being $1.59 each on the enrollment, and $3.15 on the average attendance. The previous year the cost was $2.15 per capita on the number enrolled, and $1.10 on the average number.

From an unpublished report of the School Board we extract the following remarks with regard to the Evening Schools:

"Their instructions have been eminently useful to a class of persons who have no other opportunities for obtaining useful learning; but their numbers should be largely increased from that class of untaught boys and girls, who, as at present situated, are subjected to the worst influences during the long nights of Winter. The Evening Schools have been even too respectable: containing few youth who are not of confirmed steady and industrious habits. We earnestly commend these schools to all good citizens, as worthy of their best endeavors to increase the interest in them, by frequent visitations, and to add to their numbers by solicitations, watchfulness, and missionary effort among those young persons who can hardly escape becoming bad citizens, unless rescued by the influences thrown around them in these schools, by exciting a thirst for knowledge which shall overcome the fascinations of idleness and vice."

THE NEW GROWTH OF THE CITY SCHOOLS—Dates back only seven years, to the school year 1863-4, previous to which time, as will be seen, the schools were feebly supported, and kept open as free schools but a short period in each year.

Seven years ago, there were in the city not less than nine thousand persons of legal school age, while there was room in the schools for less than fourteen hundred. Not a school-house in the city was well adapted to school purposes, or to the best approved graded system of conducting schools. No complete classification was possible. The school-houses were generally badly ventilated, uncomfortably seated, and some of them were situated on low and unwholesome sites. More than fifty per cent. of the children between six and fifteen years had no room in the schools.

At that time, and previously, a modest tax of three to fifteen cents was levied, which yielded scarcely more than enough revenue to cover current expenditures, without any considerable balance for building purposes. With half the children of the city practically excluded from school privileges, and no possibility of material relief without a much larger fund and more and better school-houses, the burden and responsibility resting upon the school officers were very great. The work neglected or delayed during many previous years had to be crowded into a short period, beside the necessities of the hour.

The time, during the closing years of an exhausting war, was not propitious for heavy and unusual taxation. But the Trustees did not hesitate to use, to the utmost limit of the law, all the power in their hands to remedy the evil. During this period, additional permanent room and seats were provided in new buildings, and by rearrangement of the old, for thirty-six hundred pupils, at an expense of about $185,000; yet, even now, the most urgent, pressing duty devolved upon the school officers is to provide for not less than fifteen hundred pupils, who are needing the advantages afforded by our schools, but are prevented for want of room. While the schools have thus largely increased in accommodation, the need has augmented in even greater ratio We know of but two ways, in this rapidly-growing city, for preventing increased expenditure on account of the schools, from year to year: First, by permitting the schools to become feeble and unpopular, so that the children will stay out; secondly, by providing no further accommodations, so that they cannot get in.

THE PUBLIC SCHOOL FUNDS.—The revenue for the support of the Indianapolis Public Schools is derived from two separate and distinct funds.

First, the TUITION FUND. This fund is derived, in part, from the general school fund of the State, and in part by taxation under the provisions of the Common School law of the State, and is apportioned to the different counties by the Superintendent of Public Instruction, on the basis of the number of persons of legal school age (six to twenty-one years) in each county. The County Auditors, on the same basis, apportion the fund to the different towns and cities of each county.

Under the provisions of the law the counties which are richest in children receive the largest revenue. The effects of this apportionment on the county of Marion will be seen by the following table:

DATE.	Amount of school revenue collected in Marion County.	Am't apportioned to Marion County.	Net loss to Marion Co. under the apportionm't.
May, 1869..............	$62,693	$35,662 ⎰	
October, 1869.........	12,912	10,532 ⎱	$29,411
May, 1870..............	59,231	40,710 ⎰	
October, 1870.........	13,739	10,943 ⎱	21,317
Total for two years.	$148,575	$97,847	$50,728

Over thirty per cent. of the School revenue collected in this county under the State tax, is distributed over the State, and aids in educating the youth of poorer counties. Perhaps, however, there is no basis of apportionment more equitable than that of the school population, provided the census of persons of legal school age is fairly taken in all parts of the State. There are reports of irregularities and frauds in some localities in the taking of this census, which, if true, make the apportionment most unjust and oppressive; and the unequal distribution is contrary to the intent and meaning of the law.

The Tuition Fund in this city is not limited to the revenue derived from the above apportionment, but is complemented by local taxation for teachers' salaries. This tax has heretofore, since 1867, been levied by the Common Council; but hereafter, under the provisions of the law approved March 3, 1871, the authority for all supplementary taxation will rest with the Board of School Commissioners.

The second source of revenue for the City Schools is the SPECIAL SCHOOL FUND.

This Fund can be used only for the current expenses of the schools, including school lots, buildings, repairs, fuel, and all items of expenditure except teachers' salaries. It is derived from a tax levied by the Trustees and placed upon the county duplicate, of "not exceeding 25 cents on each $100 of valuation, and 50 cents on each poll." The amount of revenue raised by this tax is fully stated in the general table of statistics annexed.

THE SCHOOL OFFICERS.—From 1853 until the spring of 1861 the Trustees were elected by the Common Council. From 1861 to 1865, owing to a change in the law, the Trustees were elected by the people, one from each ward. In 1865 the law was again amended, and the Trustees were elected by the Council, until the passage of a law, approved March 3, 1871, providing for a Board of School Commissioners, to be elected by the people, one from each "School District." At present the school districts are the nine wards, but the Commissioners are authorized to re-district the city for school purposes. They are also authorized to levy such additional taxes as may be necessary for the efficiency of the schools, and to provide suitable buildings.

The annual report of receipts and expenditures of school revenue is made by the School Board to the County Commissioners, with whom all accounts and vouchers are filed and settlement made in March of each year.

The Superintendent of the Schools is the acting executive officer of the Board of Trustees or Commissioners. He is entrusted with the general organization and management of the Schools. The School Board elect the teachers annually, but all reports from them with regard to their duties, or the condition of their schools, are made to the Principals, or directly to the Superintendent, who is responsible for

SIXTH WARD SCHOOL HOUSE

the efficient grading and successful working of the whole. The Superintendent is assisted by two Principals, one for all the schools north of Washington street, and one for the schools south of that street. There is an additional Principal, who has the general supervision of instruction in the Primary grades. There is also a teacher for all the schools in each of the departments, of vocal music, drawing and gymnastics. A competent mechanic is also employed, who has general charge of supplies and of all minor repairs to the school property. As the value of the school property exceeds $300,000, it requires constant attention and care. The judicious custody of this valuable estate, situated as it is in twelve different locations of the city, keeping it in repair, fit for its uses, comfortable for the children, and free from unnecessary wear and tear, form no small part of the duties of the School Trustees.

CLASSIFICATION OF THE SCHOOLS.—The schools are divided into three Departments—PRIMARY, INTERMEDIATE, and HIGH SCHOOL. Each Department is subdivided into four Grades, known, counting in order from the least advanced, as D, C, B and A, Primary; D, C, B and A, Intermediate; and the First, Second, Junior, and Senior years of the High School.

The regular time required to complete the course of study in each department is four years, and for each grade one year. The twelve grades, from D, Primary, through the Senior year of the High School, will therefore occupy twelve years. A pupil commencing in the Primary at six years of age, would, if "in course," graduate from the High School at eighteen. Many ambitious and industrious pupils are able to pass the examinations and finish their grades in a shorter period. Some rare pupils can pass two grades a year; more can accomplish three grades in two years. But without "cramming" or overwork, any ordinary child can finish the regular course within the time prescribed. "All the scholars in the same grade in the different schools are pursuing like studies at the same time, and all are supposed to be equally anxious, at the next annual or semi-annual examination, to graduate into the grade next higher."

THE METHODS OF INSTRUCTION.—If our Common School System is a machine, it is a self-adjusting invention, and adapts itself to the wants of the individual child as well as to the requirements of the mass of children. The individuality of each pupil is preserved, and yet all in each grade work in accord and harmony in the same general routine of study. The key-stone of the system is the idea that the child teaches himself. He is neither taught, instructed nor „crammed." His teacher directs his attention from one object of interest to another. He is so led that he observes, thinks and comes to correct conclusions by the exercise of his own powers. What is learned is thoroughly learned, because it is *thought out*, not conned by rote. That teacher is most successful whose power is greatest in securing the attention and directing the observation of the pupil.

THE RANGE OF INSTRUCTION—PRIMARY DEPARTMENT.—*The First Year*, the pupils learn objects first, then words representing and describing objects. They next learn to read, and afterward to spell, both by letter and sound. The slate is introduced in the beginning, and the pupil learns to print, to write and to combine numbers, by the use of objects. He also learns the size, form color and uses of familiar objects, and the simple elements of drawing, both inventive and by imitation. Physical exercises, of a few minutes duration, occurring at stated periods during each day's session, are commenced this year and continued through the years in all the grades.

The Second Year.—Reading, writing and spelling are continued. The words of the spelling lesson are written on the slate. Lessons in language are introduced, and further progress is made in numbers and drawing.

The Third Year.—The pupil now reads fluently and understandingly, and both tells and writes readily in his own language the substance of his reading lessons. Writing, both on slate and paper, is continued, and spelling is advanced. The four fundamental rules of arithmetic, where results do not reach thousands, are studied. Drawing is continued, and progressive lessons in language, geography, plants, animals, and objects.

The Fourth Year.—Reading, spelling, definition, sentence-making, writing, geography, arithmetic, oral lessons in language, natural history, inventive and map drawing, are the leading exercises of the year.

INTERMEDIATE DEPARTMENT.—*The First Year*, reading is further advanced in the number and difficulty of the objects read, and pupils answer questions based on the lessons. They spell all important words in their reading lessons and several hundred selected words and a limited number of pages from the spelling book in use; and the above, together with punctuation, definition, penmanship, arithmetic, abbreviations, geography, map drawing, inventive drawing, compositions, with oral instruction in language, and classification of plants, are the principal studies of the year.

The Second Year.—The same general exercises by advanced steps are continued. The intermediate arithmetic and the first book of algebra are completed and reviewed, and considerable advance made in the second book of geography; further progress is made in map drawing and in composition. Oral arithmetic, with progressive lessons in language and miscellaneous topics, and drawing of leaves, plants, curved lines, etc., are continued.

The Third Year.—Reading is further advanced, and the pupil is required to explain the reading lessons and answer questions based on them. Spelling, punctuation, definition, arithmetic to per centage, and penmanship are continued, and Guyot's Common Geography is completed and reviewed. Cutter's First Book of Physiology is completed and reviewed. The practice of English composition, from incidents, or elements, given by the teacher, continues; and the important lessons in language, which, by this time, have become a thorough elementary analysis of the English tongue, are made a leading part of the course.

The Fourth Year.—The fourth reader and the spelling book are completed. Three hundred selected words are spelled; and five hundred are defined and placed correctly in English sentences. Arithmetic is continued to mensuration. A text-book on grammar, following and illustrating the language lessons, is completed and reviewed. Anderson's grammar-school history of the United States is completed and reviewed. The analysis of the language, with compositions, is continued. The pupil, having thoroughly mastered the above course, is prepared for

THE HIGH SCHOOL.—*The First Year.*—The range of instruction embraces algebra, Latin, German, the science of common things, composition, book keeping, reading and spelling, and advanced English grammar, and a further analysis of Language.

The Second Year.—Reading and spelling, arithmetic, Latin or German, the the analysis of English words, United States history, book-keeping, natural history, and geometry, are the most important exercises.

The Junior Year.—This, and the succeeding year, the studies are more or less elective, and embrace a course in geometry, trigonometry, physiology, Latin, German, universal history, natural philosophy, English grammar, botany, and physical geography. Rhetorical exercises and composition are continued.

The Senior Year.—The range of studies embraces physical geography, rhetoric, chemistry, Latin, French, Constitution of the United States, astronomy, mental philosophy, English literature, and geology, together with regular exercises in composition and declamation.

MUSICAL INSTRUCTION.—In February, 1866, instruction in vocal music was introduced as one of the regular branches of education, and was placed under the control of Mr. George B. Loomis, who has continued in charge of this important department to the present time. All the pupils are taught to sing, and the more advanced pupils to read music.

The primary teachers are instructed by the music teacher in the art of teaching music, and by them daily instruction is given to their pupils. In grades above the primary the work is done exclusively by the teacher of music, who gives to each school, in most of the buildings, two half hour lessons each week, and, owing to the number of rooms, but one in some of the intermediate grades. The benefits of the instruction in vocal music during the last five years, are abundantly recognized by all who are acquainted with the progress of the schools.

THE HIGH SCHOOL.—This important school is worthy of especial care by reason of its eminent province, as the cap-stone of our school system. Five thousand pupils in the lower schools look to this institution as the summit of their ambition. Many never reach it, but all reach *toward* it. The present range of study will be seen above.

To the minds of many friends of education, its course of instruction is incomplete. The foundation is probably broad enough, but the structure built thereon admits of further improvement. One of the problems of our school system is whether we shall go beyond the present limits. Must the city of Indianapolis forever say to her young men and young women, who have successfully finished the four years course prescribed in the High School, and who have prepared a strong foundation for future useful acquirements: "This city can be of no further service to you in obtaining an education—go elsewhere?"

Must these pupils, the pride and future hope of our city, be banished from home if they desire to complete a more liberal course of instruction?

In addition to the expense and other evils attending the removal of our cultivated pupils from home, and the injustice, in that the rich can go and the poor can not, there is an additional grievance of no small moment. It is, that there is no course of study in our higher institutions of learning which fills out the course of our High School. That course is not designed, primarily, to fit our youth for the regular classes of a college course; but to give them the greatest amount of practical and useful knowledge, adapted to their wants in *any* position in life. As very few of its students have opportunity, or contemplate taking a regular college course after graduating at the High School, it was deemed best to incorporate into the studies of that school several important branches belonging to each collegiate year. Without this a majority of the pupils would have no opportunity of acquiring a knowledge of some of the most useful and indispensable principles of science, ethics and general literature; in the absence of which the culture so much desired in the High School would be fragmentary and incomplete.

As the office of the Common School embraces only that elementary instruction which is indispensable to all; so the High School should afford to the full that higher education in science, art and literature, which gives special qualification for the more eminent and responsible vocations in life.

During the last two years of the present course the studies are in part *elective.* To these should be added from year to year, as needed, such other elective studies as may fit the pupil for his special life work.

Indianapolis should be willing, able and proud, to prepare her pupils to enter the sharp competition of business life, and all the varied industries of this busy age, thoroughly fitted to achieve success and distinction. There should be a school of science and art, with a course thorough, rigid, exhaustive, and fully adequate to the instruction of students in the sciences and mechanic arts.

The schools are always open to visitors. They belong to the public, and both school officers and teachers expect and desire citizens and strangers to look into them at any time. The public are welcome at all hours; and frequent visitations encourage both pupil and teacher.

The appended statement presents in tabular form, all the important movements of the schools which can be found in the records for eighteen years, from 1853 to 1871. We regret that for the first ten years the record is so incomplete. We also present an interesting exhibit showing the value of the school property and capacity of the buildings:

TRUSTEES AND SUPERINTENDENTS FROM 1853 TO 1871.—From 1853 to 1861, the Board of Trustees was elected by the Common Council. From 1861 to 1864, the Board was elected by the people, one from each ward; and from 1865 to 1871, the Trustees were again appointed by the Council. In June, 1871, a Board of School Commissioners, one from each School District, was elected by the people.

1853.—Henry P. Coburn, Calvin Fletcher, H. F. West. School Director—The City Clerk

1854.—H. P. Coburn, Calvin Fletcher, John B Dillon, William Sheets. Director—The City Clerk.

1855.—Calvin Fletcher, David Beaty, James M. Ray. School Superintendent —Silas T. Bowen.

1856.—Calvin Fletcher, David Beaty, D. V. Culley. Superintendent—George B. Stone.

1857.—D. V. Culley, N. B. Taylor, John Love. Superintendent—George B. Stone.

1858–1859.—D. V. Culley, John Love, David Beaty. Director—James Greene.

1860.—Caleb B. Smith, Lawrence M. Vance, Cyrus C. Hines. Director—James Greene.

1861–1862.—Oscar Kendrick, D. V. Culley, James Greene, Thomas B. Elliott, James Sulgrove, Lewis W. Hasselman, Richard O'Neal. Director—Geo. W. Hoss.

1863–1864.—James H. Beall, D. V. Culley, I. H. Roll, Thomas B. Elliott, Lucien Barbour, James Sulgrove, Alexander Metzger, Charles Coulon, Andrew May, Herman Lieber. Superintendent—A. C. Shortridge.

1865–1866–1867–1868.—Thomas B. Elliott, William H. L. Noble, Clemens Vonnegut. Superintendent—A. C. Shortridge.

1869–1870.—William H. L. Noble, James C. Yohn, John R. Elder. Superintendent—A. C. Shortridge.

THE SCHOOL PROPERTY.—The estimated value of improvements includes buildings, fences and furniture.

First District School House—Corner of Vermont and New Jersey streets. Capacity for 232 pupils; value of lot and improvements, $13,500.

Second District School House—Corner of Delaware and Walnut streets. Capacity for 728 pupils; value of lot and improvements, $70,000.

Third District School House—New York street, between Illinois and Tennessee. Capacity for 296 pupils; value of lot and improvements, $13,000.

Fourth District School House—Market street, between West and California. Capacity for 220 pupils; value of lot and improvements, $10,500.

Fourth District New School House—Corner of Michigan and Blackford streets. Capacity for 592 pupils; value of lot and improvements, $38,000.

Fifth District School House—Maryland street, between Mississippi and the Canal. Capacity for 280 pupils; value of lot and improvements, $13,000.

Fifth District New School House ("*Colony*"—Root street, between West and White River. Capacity for 100 pupils; value of lot and improvements, $5,500.

Sixth District School House—Pennsylvania street, between South and Merrill. Capacity for 110 pupils; value of lot and improvements, $10,000.

Sixth District New School House—Union street, between Merrill and McCarty. Capacity for 848 pupils; value of lot and improvements, $51,500.

Seventh District School House—East street, north of Louisiana. Capacity for 112 pupils; value of lot and improvements, $7,500.

Eighth District School House—Virginia avenue, corner of Huron street. Capacity for 396 pupils; value of lot and improvements, $15,500.

Ninth District New School House—Corner of Michigan and Davidson streets. Capacity for 550 pupils; value of lot and improvements, $38,000.

High School Building—Corner of Circle and Market streets. Capacity for 270 pupils; value of property, $25,000.

Value of school property recently added to the city, $25,000.

Total valuation, $336,000. Total capacity of buildings, 4,734 pupils.

12

SUMMARY OF STATISTICS OF THE PUBLIC SCHOOLS FOR EIGHTEEN YEARS FROM 1853 TO 1871.

DATE	Income from the Tuition Fund	Income from the Special Fund	Census of School Population*	Number of weeks of Free Schools	Number of Teachers	Number of different Pupils enrolled	Average whole number belonging	Average daily attendance	Per cent. of attendance	Quarterly Pay Roll of Teachers	Salary of the Superintendent, 2	Salary of the Principal of the High School, 1	Salary of Principals of District Schools, 1	Salary of other Teachers, 1
1853	$3,377			8	10	1100		801		$2,573	†$475	$1,000	$500	$250
1854	4,522	$3,547	3053	11	19					2,825	†475	1,000	500	300
1855			3901	22	34					3,037	400		500	300
1856			4504	30	28						1,300			300
1857			4328	39	30					2,815	1,300			
1858			4739	†						2,565	250			
1859	4,161		4934	††	31					2,353	500		400	200
1860			5178	20	29						500		400	200
1861			4803	21	29						500		400 to 600	200 to 340
1862			4965	22										
1863	9,744	5,590	6863	30	29	2040		1096		2,834	1,000		300 to 600	240 to 290
1864	11,366	4,532	11,907	36	30	2374	1260	1096	64.86	3,250	1,200	900	300 to 700	240 to 360
1865		15,976	12,455	38	28	2533	1428	1365	92	3,721	1,500	1,000	500 to 620	360 to 376
1866	18,923	29,111	‖9177	39	34	3242	1753	1600	91.2	3,578	2,000	1,000	500 to 620	400
1867	28,016	36,045	9025	40	44	4149	2562	2361	94.2	6,197	2,000	1,250	500 to 621	400
1868	31,512	45,824	9092	40	62	4949	3250	3629	95.	10,500	2,000	1,500	600 to 700	400 to 600
1869	40,568	51,638	11,251	40	78	5100	3549	2375	94.9	11,117	2,000	1,600	1,200	400 to 600
1870	46,570	51,430	22 13,213	40	92	6795	3907	3759	94.7	12,806	2,400	1,700	1,300	460 to 600
1871	57,569	58,142	13,213	40	93						2,400	1,600	1,300	400 to 600

* The Census from 1854 to 1865, included all white persons between five and twenty-one years; from 1866 to 1871, all between the ages of six and twenty-one; and since 1870, all white and colored persons between the last mentioned ages.

† City Clerk, acting School Director.

1 Salaries are based on the rate per annum for a full School year of forty weeks.

‡ Superintendent was also Principal of the High School.

* High School suspended until 1864.

† No free Schools—School Houses rented.

2 From 1858 to 1865, the Executive Officer of the Board was called the "Director." His pay was $250 during vacation and $500 during term time.

‖ This falling off in the Census is ascibed to the minimum age being increased by one year (six and twenty-one years,) and in part to incomplete returns.

|| Two Principals only appointed; one for the Districts North and one for the Districts South of Washington street.

22 Includes the first enumeration of Colored persons of School age, being 12,382 white and 831 colored.

NORTHWESTERN CHRISTIAN UNIVERSITY.

The site of this institution is in the northeastern suburb of the city, near the terminus of the Street Railway, and about two miles from the Circle Park. It is conducted under the auspices of the Christian denomination.

The charter of the University was granted by the General Assembly of Indiana in January, 1850, and provides for the formation of a joint stock company, with a capital of not less than $95,000, nor more than $500,000; to be divided into shares of $100 each; two-thirds of the amount of the stock to be set apart for an endowment fund. Under this charter the requisite amount of stock was subscribed; and in July, 1852, the company was organized by the election of the first Board of Directors.

The institution was opened on the 1st of November, 1855; and has had a steady, sure growth.

The capital stock of the company now amounts to about $170,000; of which, in accordance with the charter, two-thirds is in the endowment fund, and is advantageously invested, so as to sustain the institution.

The collegiate year begins about the middle of September, and closes about the last of June; being divided into three terms of about thirteen weeks each.

The system of instruction consists of a Collegiate Course of four years; a Preparatory Course of two years, in which students are prepared for the collegiate course; and a Primary Department, called the "Academic Course," of which Mrs. E. J. Price is Principal.

The regular Course is substantially that of the o'dest and most efficient Colleges in the East.

The Law Department was recently organized, and its first term commenced the 16th of January, 1871. This Department has three chairs, filled by Hon. Byron K. Elliott, Charles P. Jacobs, Esq., and Hon. Charles H. Test.

The institution also has a Commercial Department, to qualify students for business pursuits; of which C. E. Hollenbeck, Esq., an accomplished teacher in this important branch of instruction, is Principal.

The Musical Department, in which students are taught the principles of vocal and instrumental music, is under the charge of Prof. H. J. Schonacker, a gentleman of superior qualifications as a musical instructor.

The number of students in attendance during the present term is about three hundred.

One of the first colleges in the West to abandon the old-time policy of excluding female students from collegiate advantages was the *Northwestern Christian University.* During the year just closing about sixty female students have attended the University; and all its students enjoy equal rights, privileges and opportunities, irrespective of sex.

There are four Societies, composed of members of the institution, each having handsome halls: the Mathesian, Pythonian, Athenian (the members of which are female students,) and the Philocurian. Of these the first three are literary, and the last is religious.

The edifice, (of which a large portion of the original design is yet unbuilt,) is in the Gothic style of architecture. Its principal material is brick, handsomely trimmed with dressed stone, and the whole building is at once tasteful and commodious. It is proposed to commence the erection of the remaining portions of the building, and so complete the original design, during the present year; which will make it perhaps the largest and most elegant college edifice in the West. The completed building will have the following dimensions: Length, three hundred and eighty feet; greatest depth, one hundred and forty feet; height, four stories. The site of the institution embraces an area of twenty-five acres, the whole forming a large and beautiful grove, within the corporate limits of the city, and valued at $100,000. Stately forest trees adorn the site and assist in making the institution pleasant and attractive—a persuasive and congenial spot to the student of even ordinary appreciation of beautiful surroundings. The value of the present building is about $75,000; that of the completed buildings will be more than double this amount.

Faculty.—Rev. W. F. Black, A. M., President, and Professor of Hebrew and Syriac; W. M. Thrasher, A. M., Vice President, and Professor of Mathematics; S. K. Hoshour, A. M., Professor of the Greek Language and Literature, and of Biblical Literature; A. Fairhurst, A. M., Professor of Natural Science; H. W. Wiley, A. M., M. D., Professor of the Latin Language and Literature; Miss Catharine Merrill, A. M., Professor of English Literature, (Demia Butler chair;) M. Manny, A. M., Professor of French; Professor H. J. Schonacker, Principal of the Musical Department; Professor C. E. Hollenbeck, Principal of the Commercial Department; J. W. Lowber, A. B., Tutor in Greek; D. L. Thomas, A. B., Tutor in Latin; E. T. Lane, A. B., Tutor in Latin; J. Q Thomas, A. B., Tutor in Mathematics; J. H. Roberts, A. B., Tutor in English Literature; Mrs. E. J. Price, Principal of the Academic Department. Law Department,—Hon. Charles H Test, Judge Byron K. Elliott, and Charles P. Jacobs, Esq., Professors.

INDIANAPOLIS YOUNG LADIES' INSTITUTE.

This Institution is advantageously located, on the northeast corner of Pennsylvania and Michigan streets

The Institute was founded, and is conducted, by the Baptist denomination. It was founded in 1858, in the belief that there was a need for such an institution under the auspices of that denomination in this State; and that Indianapolis possessed, in its extent and most accessible location, in its intellectual and social aspects, and in its healthfulness, the best advantages for such an institution. The success of the enterprise has justified this belief and action of its founders.

To establish the Institute a joint stock company, called the "Indianapolis Educational Association," was formed in 1858, who secured the above site. The Association being as yet without financial standing, it was found necessary that personal credit be pledged for the fulfillment of the contracts entered into; and Revs. J. B. Simmons and M. G. Clarke, with Messrs. J. R. Osgood and James Turner, of this city, became personally responsible for the payment of $16,000, the purchase money, ten years from that time, with annual interest until maturity. The work of building up the Institute was at once vigorously begun. The Association generously resolved that the proceeds of the school, if any, should be devoted, after the school was placed on a firm foundation, to the gratuitous education of the daughters of indigent clergymen. The stockholders retained for themselves only the right to determine the general management of the Institute, without thought of personal gain.

Rev. Gibbon Williams, a man of large experience and proven worth, was selected as the General Superintendent; and his daughter, Miss Emily Williams, an accomplished educator, was the first Principal of the school. Under their direction, with the aid of very valuable assistants, the school advanced, with varying fortunes, for four years. But its legitimate income was small. The money paid by subscribers was soon exhausted by accruing interest and necessary improvements; and the work moved slowly, as such enterprises, however worthy, are apt to do.

In the year 1862, Rev. C. W. Hewes, a graduate of Brown University, and a gentleman of nearly twenty years experience in public life, became virtually the proprietor of the school. Under the management of Professor Hewes, the Institute prospered to such a degree that its accommodations soon became inadequate; and it was found necessary to enlarge the building, at a cost of nearly $8,000.

Soon afterward the site was enlarged, at an additional cost of $5,000. In 1866, the growth and prosperity of the institution demanded a further enlargement of the building, at a cost of $14,000: making the total cost of the buildings and site to that date, $53,000.

The friends of the Institute take pleasure in knowing that all this expenditure has been eventually a profitable investment; for, leaving out of consideration the benefits of the enterprise as an instrument of education, the property would, to-day, bring an increase over what it has cost.

On a beautiful site of one and one-fourth acres, in one of the most valuable localities in the city, the Association now have an institution of learning creditable to themselves and to the city.

More than $40,000 have been paid on the property; and the Association expect soon to extinguish the remainder of the debt.

Under the administration of Professor Hewes the Institute attained a high state of efficiency and popularity. It has graduated many accomplished young ladies, who furnish in their own attainments convincing evidences of the excellence of the Institution.

The Trustees, not content with the success already secured, are laboring to increase the advantages and enhance the popularity of the Institute. They propose that it shall no longer be conducted as a private enterprise in any sense; feeling that it will be more largely useful when administered solely in the interest of the great cause of education.

In the belief that educated ladies are better adapted to the duties of preceptors in female colleges, the Trustees engaged a corps of competent lady instructors; and now feel more fully justified than ever before in inviting patronage of their institution, as one capable of satisfying in an eminent degree the requirements of a first class Female College.

In the language of Professor J. R. Boise, of the University of Chicago, the conditions of a superior institute, "which shall be as nearly like a well-regulated home as possible; where my daughter, above all, shall be safe; where she will be kindly treated; where only kind words are heard, and where courteous manners, without affectation, prevail; where the instruction in all branches of learning is thorough; and where Christian influences are constant and all-pervading, are very fully realized in the Young Ladies' Institute of Indianapolis."

The Institute is at present under the control of the following

Board of Trustees—Rev. Henry Day, President; Samuel C. Hanna, Secretary; H. Knippenberg, Treasurer; E. C. Atkins, Esq.; Rev. W. Elgin; E. J. Foster,

Esq.; John A. Ferguson, Esq.; Dr. H. C. Martin; Aaron McCrea, Esq.; J. R. Osgood, Esq.; Wm. C. Smock, Esq. And the following

Board of Instruction—Rev. L. Hayden, D. D., Superintendent; Mrs. M. J. P. Hayden, Principal; Miss C. F. Barney, Miss Rebecca I. Thompson, Miss H. M. Williams. Miss Esther Boise, Teacher of Ancient and Modern Languages; Mrs. Sarah S. Starling, Teacher of Painting, etc.; Miss Leonora Cole, Teacher of Music; Miss L. D. Hawley, Matron.

ROMAN CATHOLIC SCHOOLS.

St. John's Academy for Girls, under the charge of the Sisters of Providence of the Catholic Church, located at the corner of Tennessee and Georgia streets, was established in 1859. It is a graded school, conducted by Sister Ann Cecelia Buell, as Superior, and ten teachers. The course is comprehensive, including the usual English studies, practical mathematics, the various branches of natural science, French and German, music, drawing, etc. The year is divided into two terms; beginning on the first Monday in September, and ending with the month of June. The school has now about three hundred and twenty-five pupils.

St. John's School for Boys, is conducted by the *Brothers of the Sacred Heart;* with Brother Aloysius, as Superior, assisted by five teachers. The average attendance is about two hundred.

Saint Mary's School for Boys has about one hundred pupils.

Saint Mary's Academy for Girls, is under the charge of the *Sisters of St. Francis;* has seven teachers and about two hundred pupils.

St. Patrick's School for Boys, under the care of the *Brothers of the Sacred Heart*, has four teachers and one hundred and fifty pupils.

Connected with St. Patrick's parish is, also, the *Novitiate of the Brothers of the Sacred Heart*, a training school for teachers, open only to members of the Brotherhood; having three preceptors and twenty students at this time.

St. Patrick's School for Girls, is conducted by Mrs. L. A. Kealing, and has about sixty pupils.

GERMAN PROTESTANT PAROCHIAL SCHOOLS.

Zion's church, one hundred and eighty pupils; St. Paul's (German Evangelical,) two hundred and forty pupils; Second German Reformed, one hundred pupils.

GERMAN ENGLISH SCHOOLS.

A very extensive institution of this description is located at 122, East Maryland street, and is now in its twelfth year. It was founded, and is supported, by German citizens of Indianapolis; and its object as stated by the Principal is, that the children of German citizens may have the requisite facilities for instruction in the German as well as the English language. Its corps of instructors consists of one Principal and six assistant teachers. The principal is Professor George A. Schmidt. The present number of pupils is about three hundred. The school is sustained by the subscriptions of about one hundred German citizens, constituting an Association, and by the tuition fees. The school property of the Association is worth about $25,000.

Professor Mueller is also proprietor of a large and flourishing German-English school, located on East Ohio street.

BUSINESS COLLEGES.

The Indianapolis Practical Business, Military, and Lecture College—Is the title of an institution consolidated with the *Bryant & Stratton* Business College a few months ago, and organized by an association of prominent citizens of this city. It is in successful operation, and, when it has fully occupied its proposed field of instruction, as it gives good promise of doing, will be a most important institution. Its general plan comprehends "a college of specialties, or a number of special institutions under one management; a large business school, and shortly a scientific school, a law school, and perhaps other special schools. The intention is to extend the field of the business college so as to give instruction in everything relating to the business transactions which may arise in connection with any pursuit of life, all kinds of business records, forms, calculations, correspondence, and the customs and laws of business; also instruction in all the purely practical branches, physical training by military drill, and a system of daily lectures."

The Board of Directors is constituted as follows:—Dr. R. T. Brown, William C. Tarkington, Esq , Col. James P. Harper, Calvin A. Elliott, Esq., Alexander L. Southard, John Fishback, Esq., Austin H. Brown, Esq., Hon. Byron K. Elliott, Hon. Daniel Macauley.

The officers are:—Dr. R. T. Brown, President; Calvin A. Elliott, Esq., Vice President; Alexander L. Southard, Secretary and General Superintendent of College; Austin H. Brown, Esq., Treasurer.

Location, corner of Meridian and Maryland streets.

Professor C. Koerner & Co. are the conductors of a Business College, located in Glenn's block.

BENEVOLENT INSTITUTIONS AND SOCIETIES.

Brief mention has already been made, in the general historical portion of this volume, of the various Benevolent Institutions located in or near this city. The ensuing pages will now give a more particular description of these.

THE INDIANA HOSPITAL FOR THE INSANE,

One of the most efficient and successfully administered institutions of the kind in the country, is beautifully located two and a half miles west of the city, on the continuation of Washington street. It was founded by an act of the General Assembly of the State in 1847.

The administration of the institution is under the general direction and supervision of a Board of Commissioners, now composed of three gentlemen, namely: Dr. P. H. Jameson, of Indianapolis, President; and Dr. James H. Woodburn, and John M. Caldwell, Esq., of Indianapolis. The other principal officers consist of a Superintendent, two Physicians, a Steward and a Matron.

The institution was opened for the reception of patients in 1848.

The main building consists of a central building and two wings. The latter extend from each end of the center structure laterally and backward, giving to the front a broken, receding range. The entire linear extent of the edifice is 624 feet. The three principal parts of the building, as it now stands, were erected at as many different periods: the center, in 1847-8; the south wing in 1853-6; and the north in 1866-9. Each addition has had the effect to somewhat impair the architectural symmetry and unity of the original design.

The structure is built of brick, trimmed with dressed stone. Its architecture, though it cannot strictly be classed with any distinct order, may appropriately be termed a modification of the Plain Doric. The Doric is dimly shown in the square columnar projections on the corners and faces of the walls, rising from the basement story to the entablature, and surmounted by capitals in imitation of that order.

The architrave, frieze, and cornice more nearly correspond with the Doric than any other style. All the principal elevations, though modified in the details of the wings, have the same general features. The cornice elevation of the center and of the first principal sections, is 57 feet. The center building is surmounted by an octagonal belvidere 17 feet in diameter; and in height 36 feet from the superior line of the roof. The elevation to the top of the balustrade on the belvidere, is 103 feet.

The center building has five stories, inclusive of basement and a superior or half story. The basement is used for store rooms, etc.; the second story for offices, public parlor, dispensary, officers' dining room, etc.; the third and fourth stories for private rooms for the Superintendent and other officers; and the fifth story is occupied by the female employes.

The wings are three and four stories in height, and are entirely occupied by

INDIANA HOSPITAL FOR THE INSANE.

wards for the patients. The entire capacity of the wards is about five hundred patients.

Forty-four feet in the rear of the center building, and connected with it by a wooden corridor three stories in height, is the chapel building, 50x60 feet, the first floor of which contains the general kitchen, bakery, dining rooms for the employes, etc.; the second, the steward's office, sewing room, rooms for employes, etc.; and the third floor is entirely occupied by the chapel, having seating accommodations for three hundred persons.

Immediately in the rear of the chapel building is the engine building, 60x50 feet; the first floor of which contains the requisite boilers for heating all of the buildings throughout, and the pumps of the water-works—connected with which are six fire-plugs to furnish hose attachments in case of a fire breaking out. The second floor is occupied by the laundry, and the third by rooms for the male employes.

Additional to the foregoing buildings, is a carpenter shop, 30x50 feet, and two stories in height, containing the ordinary machinery, etc.

The north wing was constructed under the direction of the present Board of Commissioners, and is superior in its style, workmanship and adaptation to its uses

The south wing and portions of the center would bear some remodeling and improvements.

The entire building is lighted by gas. It has complete water works, of the Holly system, for supplying water throughout the institution, and for the extinguishment of fires, should occasion arise; also, an approved apparatus for forced upward ventilation.

The grounds of the institution consist of 160 acres—the buildings being situated near the center, on a slight eminence. Of this area, about 40 acres are set apart for the immediate grounds surrounding the buildings; they are liberally adorned with shade trees, shrubbery, etc.; and are suitably laid out with walks, drives, etc. Twenty acres are contained in a forest grove; and the remainder is used for agricultural purposes, being tilled by the patients.

The original cost of these grounds was but $4,000. They are now worth, at a low estimate, $50,000.

Under its managment for several years past, the institution has attained a superior degree of efficiency and usefulness—"worthy alike of the wealth, intelligence and humanity of its patrons, the people of the State."

During the year ending October 31st, 1870, 792 patients were under treatment—a much larger number than during any previous year; and indicative, not so much of an unusual increase in insanity, as of the increased capacity of the institution. During the same time, 317 patients were discharged; of whom 187 were restored; 19 improved; and 59 not improved. There were 51 deaths during the year.

The increasing demands on the institution necessitate the enlargement of the south wing at an early day, at an estimated cost of $50,000.

The expenditures during the past year were $122,745.96.

During the past 22 years, 4,431 patients have been treated in the institution; in regard of whom the following statistics are of interest:

Former Occupation—Males.—Bakers, 6; Bankers, 2; Brewers, 2; Brickmakers, 5; Blacksmiths, 39; Butchers, 7; Clerks, 49; Carpenters, 56; Coopers, 21; Clergymen, 18; Contractor, 1; Cabinet makers, 10; Cigar makers, 3; Confectioner, 1;

Chair makers, 4; County officers, 5; Daguerrean artists, 3; Dentists, 3; Druggist, 1; Editors, 2; Engineers, 4; Farmers, 1,291; Fullers, 5; Foundrymen, 4; Gunsmiths, 8; Hatters, 3; Hotel keepers, 3; Hunters, 2; Harness makers, 4; Laborers, 226; Lawyers, 9; Locksmiths, 2; Mechanics, 9; Merchants, 61; Miners, 4; Musicians, 2; Machinists, 7; Manufacturers, 34; Millers, 19; Millwrights, 2; No occupation, 64; Physicians, 17; Plasterers, 22; Pump makers, 3; Printers, 9; Painters, 15; Peddlers, 6; Potters, 3; Railroad men, 7; Shoemakers, 30; Slater, 1; Stone masons, 3; Saloon keepers, 3; Steamboatmen, 2; Saddlers, 8; Soldiers, 36; Students, 16; Tanners, 3; Telegrapher, 1; Teachers, 28; Tailors, 24; Tinners, 6; Traders, 9; Tragedian, 1; Upholsterers, 1; Wagon makers, 15; Weavers, 7; Watchmakers, 5; Watchmen, 3.

Females—Actress, 1; Housework, 1,982; Mantua maker, 16; No occupation, 52; Paper makers, 2; School girls, 33; Tailoresses, 29; Teachers, 41.

Ages of Patients when Admitted—Under 20 years, 396; from 20 to 25 years, 688; from 25 to 30 years, 723; from 30 to 35 years, 624; from 35 to 40 years, 558; from 40 to 45 years, 428; from 45 to 50 years, 404; from 50 to 55 years, 277; from 55 to 60 years, 144; from 60 to 65 years, 106; from 65 to 70 years, 50; from 70, to 75 years, 32; from 80 to 85 years, 4; from 85 to 90 years, 2.

The present officers are: President of the Board of Commissioners, Dr. P. H. Jameson; Commissioners, John M. Caldwell and Dr. James H. Woodburn; Superintendent, Dr. Orpheus Evarts; Physicians, Drs. W. W. Hester and W. J. Elstun; Steward, Charles H. Test; Matron, Mrs. Mary Evarts. The officers and employes number nearly one hundred.

The succession of Superintendents has been as follows: Dr. John Evans, Dr. —— Patterson, Dr. James S. Athon, Dr. James H. Woodburn, Dr. Wilson Lockhart, Dr. Orpheus Evarts, the present Superintendent.

The whole cost of the buildings and grounds has been about $375,000—a much less sum than their real value to-day. It would require $600,000, perhaps, to purchase the site and erect and furnish such a hospital, if required at this time.

THE INDIANA INSTITUTE FOR THE EDUCATION OF THE BLIND,

Is situated very nearly in the center of the most beautiful section of the city. Its site occupies the space of two city blocks, an area of eight acres; bounded on the south by North street; on the west, by Meridian; on the north, by Walnut; on the east by Pennsylvania.

The Institute was founded by an Act of the General Assembly, in 1847, and was first opened, in a rented building, on the first of October of that year. The permanent buildings were completed, and first occupied, in the month of February, 1853. The original cost of buildings and grounds, was $110,000; their present valuation is $300,000. The principal edifice is composed of a center building, having a front of ninety feet, and a depth of sixty-one feet, and is five stories in height; together with two four story wings, each thirty feet in front, by eighty-three feet in depth: making a total frontage of one hundred and fifty feet. Each of these sections of the building is surmounted by a handsome cupola, of the Corinthian order of architecture. The building is mainly constructed of brick, stuccoed in imitation of sand-stone: the basement story being faced with sand-stone ashler, rustic-jointed. The portico of the center building, and verandas on the fronts and sides of the wings, are of sand-stone: the former thirty feet wide by thirty five feet deep, and extending to the top of the third story. The portico and cornices of the building are of the Ionic order.

In addition to the main structure and usual out-buildings, there is a plain three story brick building, forty by sixty feet, containing the work-shops for the several trades of the pupils.

The number of pupils in attendance during the past year was one hundred and seven; of whom forty-six were males, and sixty-one females.

The corps of officers and instructors is composed as follows:

Trustees.- P. H. Jameson, President, John Beard, Cass Byfield; Secretary, H. W. Ballard; Superintendent, W. H. Churchman; Teachers in Literary Department, Albert Stewart, Miss S. A. Scofield, Mrs. C. C. Wynn, Miss Kate C. Landis, Miss Mary Maloney; Teachers in Music Department, R. A. Newland, D. Newland; Teachers in Handicraft Department, J. W. Bradshaw, Mrs. S. J. Ballard; Household Officers, J. M. Kitchen, M. D., Physician, H. W. Ballard, Steward, Mrs. A. C. Landis, Matron, Mrs. S. J. Ballard, Girl's Governess.

The Superintendents of the Institution have been: W. H. Churchman, from October 1, 1847, to September 30, 1853; George W. Ames, from October 1, 1853, to September 30, 1855; William C. Larrabee, from October 1, 1855, to January 31, 1857; James McWorkman, from February 1, 1857, to September 10, 1861; W. H. Churchman, the present Superintendent, reappointed October 10, 1861.

The annual appropriation for its maintainance, is about $30,000.

The grounds are handsomely adorned, the government of the Institution excellent, and its efficiency second to none of the kind in the country.

The engraving on another page gives a correct view of the building.

INDIANA INSTITUTE FOR THE DEAF AND DUMB.

This Institution was authorized by an Act of the General Assembly in 1844.

Its location is particularly beautiful, in the eastern suburb of the city, just south of Washington street.

The Institute, proper, consists of three buildings connected by corridors. Two of these buildings were erected in 1848-9; the third in 1869-70.

The front building has a facade of two hundred and sixty feet; and contains the offices, library, general study rooms, officers' and teachers' rooms, and the dormitories for the pupils. The center of this building is eighty by fifty-four feet, and five stories high; the lateral wings sixty by thirty feet, and three stories in height; the transverse wings, thirty by fifty feet and four stories high. The middle building contains the store-rooms, kitchen, laundry, bakery, dining-halls, servants' rooms, hospital, and several school-rooms. It is three stories high: the center being forty by eighty feet; and the wings thirty-two by seventy feet. The rear building contains the chapel and ten school-rooms. It is two stories high; the center being fifty feet square; and the wings forty by twenty feet.

In addition to the above described buildings there are others, detached from them, containing the engine house, wash-house, and the shops for the Industrial Department. The aggregate cost of the buildings has been $220,000.

The grounds comprise one hundred and five acres, worth $1000 per acre. The grounds more directly surrounding the buildings are beautifully laid off in walks, and drives, and are elaborately ornamented with shrubbery and forest trees; and contain, also, a flower garden with conservatory. Appropriate spaces are devoted to the purposes of an orchard, a vegetable garden, and play grounds for the pupils. The remainder, and principal area, is laid off in pasture and farm lots.

Altogether it is one of the most beautiful spots in or about Indianapolis; and must go far to make those for whose benefit it was ordained forget their misfortunes, in the scenes of beauty about them; It reflects the largest credit on the State that founded and has maintained this noble charity; and on the efficiency of the successive managements that have so beautified and adorned the place. Nor have the efforts of officers and teachers to make the Institution useful—in respect of the intellectual and moral welfare of those committed to their care—been less successful, than the pains taken to make the grounds ornamental.

The number of pupils in attendance during the past year was two hundred and sixty-four.

The principal officers of the Institute are: Dr. P. H. Jameson, President; Dr. J. M. Kitchen and W. R. Hogshire, Trustees; Thomas Mac Intire, Superintendent; Dr. F. S. Newcomer, Physician. The following are the Instructors in the Intellectual Department: Horace S. Gillett, A. M., William H. Latham, A. M., M. D., Walter W. Angus, Sidney J. Vail, H. N. Mac Intire, William N. Burt, A. M., John L. Houdyshell, Naomi S. Hiatt, Eugene W. Wood, Sarah C. Williams; Teacher of Articulation, Joseph C. Gordon, A. M.

The first Instructor in the Institution was William Willard, a deaf mute, who was employed in 1844, at a salary of $800 per annum. Mr. Willard had previously conducted a small school for the instruction of deaf mutes in this city. He acted as Principal to the Institution until July, 1845; and was succeeded by J. S. Brown, who served as Principal until July 7, 1853. The latter was succeeded by the present Superintendent, Thomas Mac Intire; who, for seventeen years, has most efficiently discharged his responsible duties.

The annual appropriation for its support has for several years been $44,000.

INDIANA FEMALE PRISON AND REFORMATORY.

This Institution is one of the fruits of the recent agitation for Prison Reform, and of the progress lately made in that field. It had its origin in that wise benevolence that having long noted the defects of the prison system, in its relation to the management and care of female inmates, in 1869 began that agitation for reform in this respect, which resulted in attracting considerable attention to such defects, and in stimulating philanthropy to labor for their correction. The attention of Governor Baker was attracted to the subject of Prison Reform, in which he became very much interested; and to the interest and investigation given the subject by him, is due the first practical step taken toward realizing the idea of the present Indiana Female Prison and Reformatory. To this end he drafted a Bill; and the Legislature endorsed the Governor's recommendation by giving it the authority of a statute. The following extracts from the Act of the Legislature are here quoted, as best explaining the nature and objects of the Institution:

"As soon as the Penal Department of the institution created by this act shall be ready for the reception of inmates, it shall be the duty of the warden of said State Prison, upon the order of the Governor, to transfer and convey to the institution created by this act all the female convicts who may then be confined in said prison, and deliver them to the Superintendent of said institution, with a certified statement in writing, signed by such warden, setting forth the name of each convict, the court by which, and the offence of, and for which she was convicted and sentenced, the date of the sentence, the term of the court at which sentence was pronounced, and the term for which said convict was sentenced, which certified statement in writing shall be sufficient authority for the confinement of such convict in the institution created by this act, for the portion of the term of such convict which may be and remain unexpired at the time when she shall be transferred to said institution as aforesaid."

The provisions with regard to the Reformatory Department declare that:

" Whenever said institution shall have been proclaimed to be open for the reception of girls in the Reformatory Department thereof, it shall be lawful for said Board of Managers to receive into their care and management, in the said Reformatory Department, girls under the age of fifteen years, who may be committed to their custody, in either of the following modes, to-wit:

First.—When committed by any Judge of a Circuit or Common Pleas Court, either in term time or in vacation, on complaint and due proof by the parent or guardian, that by reason of her incorrigible or vicious conduct, she has rendered her control beyond the power of such parent or guardian, and made it manifestly requisite that from regard to the future welfare of such infant, and for the protection of society, she should be placed under such guardianship.

Second.—When such infant shall be committed by such judge as aforesaid, upon complaint by any citizen, and due proof of such complaint, that such infant is a proper subject for the guardianship of said institution, in consequence of her vagrancy or incorrigible or vicious conduct, and that from moral depravity or otherwise of her parent or guardian, in whose custody she may be, such parent or guardian is incapable or unwilling to exercise the proper care or discipline over such incorrigible or vicious infant.

Third.—When such infant shall be committed by such judge as aforesaid, on complaint and due proof thereof, by the Township Trustee of the township where such infant resides, that such infant is destitute of a suitable home, and of adequate means of obtaining an honest living, or that she is in danger of being brought up to lead an idle and immoral life."

By authority of the Act creating the institution, the Governor appointed Hon. E. B. Martindale, of this city, (who has been succeeded by James M. Ray, of this city,) Ashael D. Stone, of Winchester, (who has been succeeded by Dr. Armstrong, of Carroll county,) and Joseph I. Irwin, of Columbus, a Board of Managers. These gentlemen secured the service of Isaac Hodgson, of this city, who drafted a plan for the proposed prison, which was accepted; but by reason of the fact that the appropriation for the purpose of carrying out the provisions of the act, amounted to only $50,000, the entire plan could not be fully carried out at present.

The building, now nearly completed, is situated just north of the Deaf and Dumb Asylum, between it and the Arsenal, and presents quite a commanding appearance when viewed from the National road. It is a two story brick, with a basement and Mansard roof. It will be one hundred and seventy-four feet long, and is composed of a main building with side wings, and traverse wings at either end. The latter are to have a length of one hundred and nine feet. Standing in front of the central portion of the building, is a dwelling house three stories high, with a basement, which will be occupied by the Superintendent and officers of the Institution, and connects with the Reformatory by a passage way on the first floor.

A building in the rear, and connecting with the Reformatory in the basement and first story by passage ways, will be occupied by a large boiler room and bath rooms. A brick ventilating stack seventy feet high will be located here. The style of architecture is " Utilitarian," and exhibits excellent taste on the part of the architect, and practical knowledge of the requirements of such an institution.

Although the present edifice does not embrace the entire plan for the completed building, it is perfect in itself, and contains all that is necessary for the proper working of the institution. The complete plan is for a building with an extreme length of five hundred and twenty-five feet. But several years will necessarily pass before the entire building can be finished, or indeed, before it will be needed.

Owing to the premature adjournment of the last General Assembly, the necessary appropriation for finishing the building, for furnishing it, and for carrying on the institution, was not made. The inauguration of the institution has, therefore, been delayed. The Committees of both Houses of the late General Assembly, however, unanimously approved the expenditures already made, the work that has been performed, and the estimates submitted for future appropriations; so that the opening of the institution has only been deferred for a brief period, by the default of the General Assembly.

INDIANA HOUSE OF REFUGE.

The Legislature of Indiana, by an Act approved March 8, 1867, authorized an institution to be known as "A House of Refuge for the Correction and Reformation of Juvenile Offenders."

To carry out the provisions of this Act the sum of $50,000 was appropriated. The general supervision and government of the Institution is vested in a Board of Control, consisting of three Commissioners, to be appointed by the Governor, by and with the advice and consent of the Senate. The members of the first Board hold their offices for the respective terms of two, four, and six years, and after this one member of the Board to be appointed in the same manner, every two years, whose term of office shall continue for six years.

The following gentlemen were the first Board, viz: Charles F. Coffin, Esq., of Wayne county, Hon. A. C. Downey, of Ohio county and General Joseph Orr, of Laporte county.

The Board held their first meeting in the Governor's rooms in Indianapolis, Ind., on the 23d day of April, 1867, and organized by electing Charles F. Coffin, President. The Board then resolved to visit and examine the Reform School at Chicago, Ill., the House of Refuge at Cincinnati, O., and the Ohio State Reform Schools, at Lancaster, O. After a full examination and consideration of the merits of these institutions for the reformation of juvenile offenders, the Board unanimously adopted what is known as the "Family System," (in imitation of the Ohio State Reform Schools,) as contra-distinguished from the "congregate plan." This system divides the inmates of the Institution into families of fifty boys each—each family having a separate house and proper family officers. The officers to each family are a House Father (who has the immediate charge of the family of boys) assisted by an Elder Brother; all the families are under the jurisdiction of a common Superintendent.

It was contemplated by the founders of the Institution, and by the legislature calling it into existence, that it should be located at some suitable point near Indianapolis, combining the several necessary conditions. Manifestly it should not be located so near a large city as to allure unruly and truant inmates from the quiet and discipline of the Institution to the temptations of the city. In view of this and other essential considerations controlling its location, Governor Baker selected and established a site for the institution, three-fourths of a mile south of Plainfield,

SYLVANIA HOUSE OF REFUGE,

in Hendricks county, on the line of the *Indianapolis, Terre Haute, Vandalia and St. Louis Railway,* fourteen miles west of Indianapolis. The site is a very eligible one: being easy of access from all parts of the State.

The farm upon which the institution is located contains two hundred and twenty-five acres; combining beauty of location with fertility of soil; and particulary favored with running streams affording an abundant and unfailing supply of water for the use of the institution, and for the needs of the live stock on the farm. The site of the buildings is a beautiful plateau, about eighteen feet above the level of the adjacent valley.

The engraving on another page will serve to give a good general idea of the appearance of the buildings and grounds.

The Board, with the approval of the Governor, adopted a plan for the grounds and buildings, with a view to the ultimate erection of one main building and eight family houses, besides one house for a reading room and hospital, and two large shops for mechanial labor, intended to accommodate four hundred boys.

On the 27th of August, 1867, the Board, with the approval of the Governor, appointed Mr. and Mrs. Frank B Ainsworth, Superintendent and Matron. They immediately entered upon the discharge of their duties, which they have ever since discharged with great credit to themselves and to the institution.

On the first of January, 1868, three family houses and one work shop were completed and ready for occupancy, and the Governor issued his proclamation declaring the Institution ready for the reception of inmates. During the past year the main building and one additional family house have been completed,

The plan of the buildings is an elongated octagon. All the family houses front to the center of the plateau save the two on the east side, which front to the east. The main building stands east of the centre, fronts to the east; it is sixty-four by one hundred and twenty-eight feet, external measurement, and is three stories high above the basement. In the basement are the vegetable cellars, wash room, ironing room, furnace room and kitchen. On the first floor are the office, reception room, officers and boys dining rooms, pantry and store room. On the second floor are the Superintendent's family rooms, private office, and five dormitories for officers, etc. On the third floor are the Assistant Superintendent's rooms, a store room and library, the chapel and hospital.

The family houses are uniform in style, and are thirty-six by fifty-eight feet external measurement. The basement contains a furnace room, a store room, and a large wash room, which is also used for a play room in stormy weather. On the first floor are two rooms for the House Father and his family; and a school room, which is also used for a sitting-room for the family of boys. On the third floor are the boys' dormitory, a clothes room and a room for the Elder Brother, etc.

These buildings are erected on a plan suggested by an experienced reformer, and admirably serve the purpose for which they were designed.

The first boy was received January 23d, 1868, into the institution, from Hendricks county. A few days after this ten boys were transferred from the Northern Prison. Since the opening of the institution twenty-two boys have been received to its guardianship. There are at this time one hundred and seventy-eight inmates remaining in the institution; two having been indentured; one having died, and the rest having been discharged. Notwithstanding that there are no high fences, walls, or physical contrivances, to prevent the boys from escaping, not a single boy has succeeded in getting away, and although the inmates are of the most hardened and desperate classes, not one has been subjected to corporal punishment.

The plan of instruction is that of the most approved common school system. All the boys attend school one-half of each day and are engaged at some useful employment, either on the farm, or in the garden, or shoe-shop, or tailor-shop, or chair-shop, or some other division of the domestic department, the other half. This discipline is mild and firm, and eminently parental—the higher sentiments of the boys being appealed to.

The institution is a success beyond all expectations, and it has already demonstrated its value to the State by converting to a life of usefulness and respectability, many neglected children who would, but for its saving influence, have been miserable waifs among the scum of society.

THE COUNTY INFIRMARY.

This institution is situated about three miles north-west of the city, and was established in 1832. It is a well-managed and efficient institution. The "farm," consisting of 160 acres, was purchased in 1832. At this date the only building on the site was a log cabin of two rooms. Buildings were erected from time to time, as the demand for accommodations increased, of which the principal structure was erected in 1845. To this an addition for the accommodation of the insane paupers was made in 1858. These buildings were soon found inadequate to the demand upon them; and in 1869 was commenced the erection of the present capacious and appropriate structure. The corner stone of the building was laid on the 28th of July, 1869; and it was dedicated in October, 1870, under the auspices of the Young Men's Christian Association.

The principal building is in the Norman style of architecture. Its front is two hundred and four feet; extreme depth, one hundred and eighty-four feet; height, four stories. The building presents a fine architectural appearance. The plan of the interior is excellent; securing neatness, convenience, and plentiful light and ventilation.

In the rear of the main structure is another building twenty-eight by seventy feet, and two stories in height.

The increased room thus obtained has afforded opportunities for introducing a much more thorough and efficient system than before existed. The contrast between the system of management of the Marion County Infirmary of to-day and that of the past, is as striking as the contrast between the present buildings and those they superseded.

Now the institution is so conducted as to secure the well-being of the inmates; then it was merely a receptacle, into which was thrust that inconvenient class in the community who, being unable to help themselves, were thus stuck away out of sight and dismissed from public concern. Now the management conforms to common morality and propriety by separate accommodations for the sexes ; then no adequate separation of this kind was practicable. Now the insane are cared for apart from the others, and humane and adequate means employed to ameliorate their condition and conduce to their cure; then they were hidden away and confined in repulsive quarters and surroundings calculated to craze the sane, and with nothing but the rudest diet for eking out a miserable existence. Then the institution was unsightly, the quarters unclean, the *regimen* scant and unwholesome, the medical assistance inadequate, because of inadequate compensation; no regard was paid to the education of the children, or to the moral instruction of either old or young. Now the converse of all these conditions prevails: cleanliness pervades the buildings, and is enforced on the part of the inmates; religious services are regularly held in the chapel; a "nursery department" has been provided for the children, where they are separately kept, and given the needful attention in respect to their education, their morals and their health; the insane are appropriately provided for; and the due distinction between the sexes is observed. This contrast, so favorable to the present condition of the asylum, does not signify that it was formerly in a worse state than most similar institutions of to-day; on the contrary it only illustrates the superiority of the Marion County Infirmary over most pauper asylums. Neither is any reflection on past officials intended; nor is it charged that they could have done better with the means with which they were furnished. The improvement in the condition of the asylum is principally due to the attraction of the attention of the community to the need for reform in the institution, and to the enlistment of the benevolent and humane sentiment of the people in its behalf.

The first Superintendent was Peter Newland. From 1832 to 1839 the office of Superintendent was discontinued, and its functions were discharged by a Board of Directors. The records show the following to have served as Directors: Wm. McCaw, Cary Smith, James Johnson, Isaac Pugh, Samuel McCray, George Lockerbie, and Thomas F. Stout.

The office of Superintendent was revived in 1839; since which time the following have served in that capacity: Aquilla Hilton, James Higgenbottom, Nelson McCord, Henry Fisher, William H. Watt, John Adams, Levi A. Hardesty, Parker S Carson, Joseph L, Fisher, and William H. Watt, the present Superintendent.

The office of Physician to the Infirmary was created in 1840, previous to which date the Superintendent was authorized to call in a physician whenever the services of one might be required. Since the creation of the office the following have successively served the county as Physician to the Infirmary: Drs. Parry, Yeakle, Dunlap, Mothershead, Dunlap, John S. Bobbs, Sanders, John M. Gaston, M. H. Wright, H. C. Brown, Michael Lynch, R. N. Todd, Milton Phipps, J. K. Bigelow, Wm. Wands, and H. H. Moore, the present Physician. The office of Physician was for years an unattractive trust. The salary was the merest trifle; The duties considerable and forbidding. Recently the salary has been increased; but is still too small to possess any pecuniary temptation to any competent physician to undertake the discharge of the duties.

It was during Dr. Wand's term as physician that the new buildings were instituted and completed. It is due to this gentleman to give him large credit for agitation of the question of reform, for urging the necessity for the improvements that have since been made, and for the present beneficent system of the Infirmary.

At this time there are about 38 children in the nursery department, which is under the charge of Mrs. Durham.

In the department for the insane there are about 58 patients, under the immediate charge of Nicholas Daly.

The whole number of inmates at this time is about 185.

The new buildings were erected at a cost of about $120,000, and the value of the site is about $32,000.

INDIANAPOLIS CITY HOSPITAL.

A visitation of the small pox in 1855, first suggested the idea of a City Hospital in Indianapolis. The result was, that early in March, 1856, the establishment of such an institution was authorized by the Common Council. A site was secured.

(13)

in the north-western part of the city, containing nine and one-half acres; and the Hospital building was completed in 1859.

To the efforts and influence of Dr. Livingston Dunlap, an estimable citizen, an eminent physician, and a member of the Council, is the establishment of this institution so largely due, that he has been appropriately called the "Father of the City Hospital."

For about two years after its completion the Hospital was an idle piece of property. First it was proposed to sell the property; then various uses were suggested; and a proposition from the Catholic Church to conduct it as a hospital was defeated, because of denominational objections. Finally the property was placed in the care of a keeper; in which condition it was found at the beginning of the Rebellion. The concentration of troops at this point dictated the employment of the institution as a hospital for military purposes; and to this end Drs. Kitchen and Jameson were appointed by the State authorities to the charge of the hospital in May, 1861.

Under the zealous and very efficient direction of Dr. Kitchen, the institution was used as a military hospital until July, 1865; during which period its great usefulness vastly more than compensated for the outlay incurred in its establishment and maintenance. From July, 1865, to April, 1866, the institution was used for a Soldiers' Home, under Dr. M. M. Wishard, in which capacity it again subserved in a large degree the causes of philanthropy and patriotism.

During Dr. Kitchen's administration extensive improvements in buildings, as well as in the hospital system, were made; so that at the close of the war, when the institution was surrendered to the city, the latter found itself the possessor of a hospital organized at the expense of the United States Government.

About 13,000 patients were treated in the hospital during the war. Under Dr. Kitchen's administration, also, the grounds were ornamented by shade trees, further adding to the usefulness and attractiveness of the place—another result of his constant concern and efforts for the improvement of the institution.

April 27th, 1866, Dr. Kitchen published a card in the *Journal* calling attention to the neglected state of the institution, and to the necessity for putting it into an efficient condition for use by the city. A meeting of the citizens was immediately held, and Hon. J. D. Howland appointed to present the subject to the Council. April 30th a committee of the Council, consisting of Dr. Jameson and Messrs. Kappes and Emerson, were appointed to meet the Board of Health and perfect a plan for the improvement and management of the hospital, and to report the necessary ordinance for that purpose. At a special meeting, May 2d, an ordinance was introduced authorizing the purchase of materials sufficient to equip a hospital with accommodations for 75 patients. William Hannaman was appointed the agent of the city to make purchases. An ordinance for the management of the hospital was also passed at the same time. These efforts were greatly accelerated by a threatened visitation of cholera, then prevailing in Europe.

The ordinance for the management of the hospital provided for the election of a Board of Directors, in which each ward was to be represented, who were invested with full control of the management of the institution. The Board organized June 12th, 1866, by the election of Dr. J. M. Kitchen President, and L. B. Wilson, Esq., Secretary. June 28th, 1866, Dr. G. V. Woolen was elected Superintendent for one year, also the following Medical and Surgical Staff:

Surgeons—Drs. J. S. Bobbs, J. S. Athon, J. A. Comingor, and L. D. Waterman.
Physicians—Drs. J. H. Woodburn, T. B. Harvey, R. N. Todd, and J. M. Gaston.

Dr. Woolen opened the hospital on the 1st of July, 1866. To the requisite attainments in medical science he added great energy and much previous experience in like responsibilities; and it was not long before the hospital was placed in good condition for the reception of patients. Large repairs and some important additions were made during his administration. Great care and economy were necessary during the first year of its existence, in order to inaugurate and maintain the charity without making it oppressive financially. Its officers found much ignorance prevailing as to the nature and wants of such an institution, encountered many perplexities unknown to the people generally, and certainly are deserving the thanks of the public for their industry, and patience, and good management.

Dr. Woolen was Superintendent of the institution until July 1st, 1870, when when he was succeeded by Dr. E. Hadley, the present Superintendent, who is serving the hospital well and acceptably.

Since his retirement from the superintendence of the institution, Dr. Kitchen has remained the President of the Board of Directors; and still continues to take his old interest in the success of the hospital.

During the official year ending July 1st, 1870, the number of patients treated was 245; number of births 27; number of deaths 25. During the same period the total expenditures of the institution were $6,606.97; and the average expense *per capita* was $0.50.

The present number of patients is 48; the whole number treated in the institution from the beginning, 1,180.

The officers for the current year are: President of the Board of Directors, Dr. F. S. Newcomer; Superintendent, Dr. E. Hadley; Assistant Superintendent, Dr. R. D. Craighead; Matron, Mrs. E. M. Porter. The Medical and Surgical Staff is composed as follows: Consulting Officers—Drs. George W. Mears and James S. Athon; Surgeons—Drs. J. A. Comingor, L. D. Waterman, G. V. Woolen and J. K. Bigelow; Physicians—Drs. Thomas B. Harvey, R. N. Todd, D. H. Oliver and A. W. Davis.

HOME FOR FRIENDLESS WOMEN.

Location: Tennessee street, just beyond city limits.

In 1863, Stoughton A. Fletcher, sr., donated to the city of Indianapolis, seven acres of ground lying southwest of the city, near White river, on condition that within a certain time a house should be built for abandoned women, to serve as a prison for the vicious and intractable—as a home for the more mild and teachable. The gift was accepted, and the house commenced. Seven thousand dollars had been expended on a foundation, when the work suddenly came to a stop; all the means in the public treasury being required for bounties for the soldiers. The building was never completed, nor the site occupied for the use for which it was donated, being too far from the city.

The Young Men's Christian Association cooperated with the active friends of the enterprise; committees of the Association canvassed the city for funds; and finally a building of nine rooms was obtained for a temporary Home, situated on North Pennsylvania street. The early efforts of the Home were directed to the amelioration of the condition of the prisoners in the county jail, from which its first inmates were taken: all of whom were more or less benefitted, and many of them greatly.

But the publicity of the location, as well as other reasons not necessary to be stated here, was an obstruction to the highest usefulness of the institution; and steps were soon taken to obtain the necessary means for a permanent Home in a more suitable location. For this purpose the city and county appropriated $7,500 each.

A location on North Tennessee street, just outside the city limits was secured; and by means of the city and county appropriations, money donations, and donations of city lots by James M. Ray, William S. Hubbard and Calvin Fletcher, of Indianapolis, and by Stillman Witt, Esq , of Cleveland, Ohio, and early in May, 1870, a suitable building had been erected. The Home was dedicated on the 21st day of May, 1870, the religious services on the occasion being conducted by Rev. Drs. Scott, Holliday, Day, and others.

The building thus completed and dedicated was in the Renaissance style of architecture, of brick, fifty-seven by seventy-five feet, three stories high, with forty-nine pleasant rooms and chambers, having a capacity for one hundred inmates, and was a neat, convenient, and commodious structure.

In this building for several months, the institution was conducted with the most commendable philanthropy. It was conducted not as a prison, but as a Home, to which the inmates should become attached. Pains were taken to learn the workings of similar institutions elsewhere; for which purpose some of the Managers traveled extensively.

It has been indeed, what its name signifies—a "Home for Friendless Women." Not alone as a refuge for Fallen Women; but also for the needy and helpless of the sex, irrespective of the causes of their misfortunes.

The success of the Home has exceeded the expectations of its benevolent founders. "Lost" girls—"lost" in the dreariest sense of the word—"lost" in their own reckless abandonment to vice—"lost" in the judgment and estimation of society—shelterless and utterly depraved—whose only home was the jail, the low brothel, or the open air—have found in the Home a refuge, and a restoration to the community's and their own respect.

The institution was suddenly interrupted in its mission of usefulness by a fire on the 23d of September, 1870, which laid the building in ashes, save a portion of the walls. By this calamity, a loss of several thousands of dollars over insurance was sustained. A building for a temporary Home was secured at No. 476 North Illinois street; where the inmates have been provided with a home, while the managers and the community set themselves busily to work to rebuild the institution on its old site. It was found that the walls of the burned building were available for use in erecting the new; appropriations were again obtained from the city and county; and by these aids and individual donations, the work of rebuilding the Home was prosecuted with such vigor and success, that the new building, on the site of the old, was recently dedicated and occupied—a building as commodious, as convenient, and as attractive as the one destroyed.

The results of the institution attest its usefulness, and speak the praise of its management. The Home was opened on the 22d February, 1867. During that year it had 70 inmates; during 1868, 140; during 1869, 133; during 1870, 225. Its management has been as economical as it has been useful. During the first three years of its existence, its aggregate expenses were $5,612.19. Conspicuous in the administration of the institution from the first have been James Smith and his wife, Sarah J. Smith—members of the Society of Friends Both have been faithful and efficient. Mrs. Smith as City Missionary, has blended decided energy with philanthropy.

The limits of this sketch do not admit of mention of all those, dead and living, who have given important aid and encouragement to this enterprise. Conspicuous among these has been James M. Ray, Esq.; and it is justly claimed that to him more than to any other one person is the establishment of the institution indebted. The late Col. Blake was also a fast and useful friend of the enterprise. Both of these citizens—the one yet living, and the other gone to his reward—have been permanently connected with many benevolent institutions and enterprises in the city and county.

The present officers of the institution are: James Smith, Superintendent; Sarah J. Smith, City Missionary; Miss Sarah M. Alcorn, Matron.

Officers of the Board of Managers.—Mrs John S. Newman, President; Mrs. J. L. Ketcham, Mrs. Hannah Hadley, Vice Presidents; Mrs. C. N. Todd, Treas'r; Mrs. Charles W. Moores, Corresponding Secretary; Mrs. J. H. Kappes, Recording Secretary; Mrs. J. M. Ray, Auditor.

Officers of the Board of Trustees.—James M. Ray, President; William S. Hubbard, Treasurer; Samuel Merrill, Secretary; D. E. Snyder Auditor.

ORPHAN'S HOME.

Location: Corner of Tennessee and Fifth streets.

The movement for the erection of this institution was started in the year 1849, by the Indianapolis Benevolent Society. At the annual meeting of this association, in that year, the destitution among the widows and orphans in the city was a prominent subject of consideration; and committees were appointed to enlighten the public as to the extent of such destitution, and to enlist popular charity for its amelioration. At a called meeting of the same society in November of the above year, a society for the relief of the classes stated, was organized, by the election of a President, three Vice Presidents, a Treasurer, a Secretary, a Depositary, thirteen Managers, and a Visiting Committee,—all of whom were ladies; and an Advisory Committee of gentlemen.

In January, 1850, this society obtained a legislative charter for the establishment of the Home. The first officers were as follow:

Mrs. A. W. Morris, President; Mrs. Alfred Harrison, Mrs. William Sheets, Mrs. Judge Morrison, Vice Presidents; Mrs. Phipps, Treasurer; Mrs. Hollingshead, Secretary; Mrs. Wilkins, Depositary; Mrs. Calvin Fletcher, Mrs. Graydon, Mrs. McGuire, Mrs. I. P. Williams, Mrs. Cressy, Mrs. Williams, Mrs Willard, Mrs. Underhill, Mrs. Irvin, Mrs Dr. Dunlap, Mrs. I. Hall, Mrs. Bradley, Managers; Mrs. Duncan, Mrs. Ferry, Mrs. Paxton, Mrs. Dunn, Mrs. Campbell, Mrs. A. F. Morrison, Mrs. M'Carty, Mrs. Myers, Mrs. Brouse, Mrs. Wiseman, Visiting Committee; Messrs. N. M'Carty, A. Harrison, Judge Morrison, William Sheets, J. R. Osgood, Butler, A. G. Willard, Ohr, and Wilkins, Advisory Committee.

In 1854, the association was enabled to purchase two city lots for a site for the Home; a third being then donated for that purpose by James P. Drake, Esq. In 1855, the first building on this site was erected, costing $1,200. In 1869, the building was greatly enlarged and improved, at a cost of $3,000; all—as well as the sums previously expended—having been raised by popular donations. The property and improvements are now worth about $14,000; and the institution is in a prosperous condition. It has an average family of thirty-five children. While the necessaries of life are provided for the children, their education is not neglected:

in the institution a school is conducted three hours each day, by a competent governess.

The domestic arrangements, which are managed in a most excellent manner, are administered by a matron, governess, nurse, cook, and a man-of-all-work.

The Home is one of the most useful and efficiently conducted permanent charities in the city. It has no endowment, and its successful establishment and maintainance is due to the unwearying philanthropy of those who have had its interests in charge—sustained, of course, by popular contributions. Of late years the County has come to the assistance of the institution with a quarterly allowance for the board of each child.

Prominent in the infancy of the institution, and during their whole lives, for valuable services and persevering benificence in this field, were Mrs. Alfred Harrison, Mrs. A. G. Willard, Mrs. Richmond, and Mrs. John H. Bradley.

The donations in support of the Home have been many, and, in the aggregate, large. Among these we find record of the following: A lot, donated by W. S. Hubbard, Esq., from which $800 was realized; a legacy, of $1,200, from Mrs. Bryant; considerable donations from Calvin Fletcher, Sr., Mrs. Givan, and Mrs. John H. Bradley; and $600 worth of provisions from the Society of Friends.

The number of children cared for at the Home during the past year was 120.

The Presidents of the Society, so far as record of them is found, from the beginning, have been, Mrs. A. W. Morris, Mrs. A. G. Willard, Mrs. W. T. Clark, Mrs. Wilson, and Mrs. Hannah T. Hadley.

At the last meeting of the Managers, held on the first Tuesday of May, 1871, the following officers were elected for the ensuing year:

Mrs Hannah T. Hadley, President; Mrs. Dr. J. H. Woodburn, Mrs. John S. Tarkington, and Mrs. John Bradshaw, Vice Presidents; Mrs. Fred. Baggs, Treasurer; Mrs. Benj. Harrison, Secretary; Mrs. John C. Wright, Corresponding Secretary.

Board of Managers.—Mrs. William Mansur, Mrs. Joseph E. McDonald, Mrs. John C. New, Mrs. David Macy, Mrs. Rachel Clarke, Mrs. John I. Morrison, Mrs. William D. Hawk, Mrs. Cyrus Boaz, Mrs. J. T. Wright, Mrs. R. M. Pattison, Mrs. Margaret Evans, and Mrs. John Fishback.

Advisory Committee.—His Excellency Governor Baker, Alfred Harrison, Esq., Hon E. B. Martindale, J. R. Osgood, Esq., John M. Lord, Esq., General Daniel Macauley, Hon. Jos. E. McDonald, Jacob T. Wright, Esq., Thomas H. Sharpe, Esq., W. H. Morrison, Esq., William Jackson, Esq., Hon. John W. Ray, James M. Hume, and Gen. George F. McGinnis.

INDIANAPOLIS ASYLUM FOR FRIENDLESS COLORED CHILDREN.

This institution is located in the north-western quarter of the city.

The Articles of Association for its establishment were filed for record on the 28th of February, 1870. The building was erected and completed, during that year.

The management of its affairs is vested in a Board of Directors, now composed as follows:

William Hadley, President; Solomon Blair, Treasurer; William C. Hobbs, Secretary; James Kersey, of Hendricks county; Joseph Morris, Plainfield; Allen Hadley, Mooresville; B. C. Coffin, W. L. Pyle, Enos G. Pray, Indianpolis; Charles Reeve, Friendswood.

INDIANAPOLIS BENEVOLENT SOCIETY.

On page 50, mention is made, in a general way, of this society. Its antiquity; its large usefulness; the honored names, living and dead, connected with it in the past and present; make appropriate a fuller sketch of its history in this place.

The society was organized on Thanksgiving evening, in November, 1835. The movement was participated in by representative Christian citizens of the city generally, irrespective of denomination; and the usual religious services on the above mentioned evening, were dispensed with in all the churches, to enable the members to participate in the work of organizing this society. Each succeeding anniversary has been celebrated on Thanksgiving evening; on which occasions, it is well understood that the usual Thursday evening services are not to be held in the churches, that their members may attend the Anniversary meeting of this society. Its plan is simple, as its work of charity is great.

For the purposes of the society, the city is divided into districts, now thirty in number. The officers consist of a President, Secretary, and Treasurer. Whoever contributes to the charities dispensed by the society, is a member of it. At each anniversary meeting officers are elected for the ensuing year, donations are collected and a canvassing committee (consisting of one gentleman and one lady) is appointed for each district.

The officers, and these committees, constitute the whole Executive authority of the society. The committees canvass their respective districts for contributions of money and clothing. The money goes into the care of the Treasurer; the clothing, etc., into a depository.

The committees draw on the depository as occasion arises, for the articles there deposited, for the benefit of the destitute in their respective districts. To prevent the misappropriation of the money thus raised, a contract is made with one or more, (generally two) grocers, to supply groceries on the order of the members of the committees. The usual weekly allowance thus made is $1.50 for each family; increasable, if required, in cases of sickness. A committee is also empowered to relieve the destitution of transient persons, and aid in securing them transportation to their homes or friends.

The first President of the society was the late James Blake, Sr.; who held that trust continuously, to the period of his death, November 26th, 1870. Calvin Fletcher, Sr., was its Secretary from the time of its organization, until his death, May 26th, 1866; and James M. Ray, was its Treasurer, from the beginning, until Mr. Blake's death, when he became President. The present officers are:

James M. Ray, President; Ebenezer Sharpe, Treasurer; Rev. Elijah T. Fletcher, Secretary.

LADIES' SOCIETY FOR THE RELIEF OF THE POOR.

This society was organized on the 10th of February, 1869, by a few Protestant and Catholic ladies of this city. Its object, in a word, is benificence. Its means are derived by such methods as fairs, donations, etc.

The society is strictly undenominational in its membership, and its charities are dispensed without reference to creeds. In an unostentatious manner, it has accomplished a great deal in the way of practical philanthropy. The officers are:

Mrs. J. H. McKernan, President; Mrs. John A. Reaume, Treasurer; Miss Julia Cox, Secretary.

GERMAN PROTESTANT ORPHANS' ASSOCIATION.

This body was permanently organized on the 11th day of August, 1867, with Frederick Thoms, Esq., as the first President.

Like every other young organization of a benevolent character, unaided by appropriations from the public treasury, its progress was at first slow; while obstacles were abundant and difficult. The society, has, however, been superior to all discouragements and come to be an important instrumentality in the work of benevolence. In the absence of a building for an asylum for those for whose benefit the society was organized and has labored, its benefactions have been performed in such other ways as were practicable.

The society has purchased a site of six and three-quarter acres, at the terminus of Virginia avenue, on which will be erected, as soon as possible, a suitable building for an Orphans' Home. The association has about one hundred members. Its present officers are:

Conrad Russe, President; J. J. Wenner, Vice President; Tobias Bender and Fr. Hillman, Secretaries; Henry Helm, Treasurer; Frederick Thoms, J. Helm, H. H. Koch, T. Sander, William Teckenbrock, and Henry Mankedick, Trustees.

LADIES GERMAN PROTESTANT ORPHANS' HOME ASSOCIATION.

This is an auxiliary to the foregoing society, and its stated meetings are held at the same times and place. It was founded in the month of October, 1870. Its officers are:

Mrs. Ruschaupt, President; Mrs. Schoppenhorst, Vice President; Mrs. Reinheimer, Secretary; Mrs. Reiher, Treasurer.

THE INDIANAPOLIS SOCIETY FOR THE RELIEF OF THE CRIPPLED, RUPTURED, AND DEFORMED.

The system of Benevolent Institutions of this State, caring so liberally and extensively for the Insane, Blind, and Deaf and Dumb, makes no provision for a class at least as large as either of these, as helpless, and that would seem to be also entitled to similar assistance from the State—its crippled, impotent and deformed population.

To remedy the condition of this class of unfortunates, a number of the liberal and benevolent citizens of this city, incorporated the above named Society on the 7th of September, 1870. The proposed capital stock of the society was $100,000, subject to enlargement. "Over that sum has been promptly subscribed for the object here, mostly by citizens of the Capital, but that this foundation may be enlarged, so as to provide for the aid of the afflicted and needy in all parts of the State the co-operation of the friends of such an effort, in the several counties, is needful and is earnestly solicited.

"The whole management of the association is in the hands of the subscribers thereto, each sum of $25 entitling the subscriber to membership and an equal voice in all its control, while the payment of ten dollars entitles to membership without voting.

"The subscription of $25 also entitles the subscriber to nominate a patient for treatment. $100 entitles the subscriber to the annual nomination of a patient. $1000 entitles to the nomination of a patient for a free bed annually. $5000 entitles the subscriber, and his heirs or assigns, to the nomination of a patient to a perpetual free bed from the society.

"The aim of the society is to provide comfortable homes and boarding in the City of Indianapolis, at low rates or free of charge, as the necessities of the poor may require—also, surgical treatment, and mechanical apparatus, appliances, supporters, etc., for relieving deformities, paralysis, and other affections destroying the usefulness of their limbs or bodies."

The articles of association provide that no salary shall be attached to any office held in the society.

All apparatus and appliances to be furnished at the cost only of the time and materials required for their manufacture.

The society is, as yet, without a building of its own; but the patients are provided with suitable board. The surgeons are Drs. Allen and Johnson, of the Surgical Institute; and the superior facilities of that institution are thus afforded the patients.

"Sixty patients have already received gratuitous treatment, aid, and relief, through the society. Twenty cases have required and been provided with apparatus or mechanical appliances for deformity. Twelve cases have required and been relieved by surgical operation. Fourteen of these patients reside in this city, but the benefits of the society are designed to extend to sufferers of this class in every part of the State, and already patients have been received, cared for, treated and relieved, from the counties of Ripley, Jennings, Blackford, Franklin, Miami, Marion, Floyd, Morgan, Tipton, Vigo, Wayne, Warren, Fountain, Parke, Putnam, Madison and Dearborn."

It is the expectation of the society, that the State will finally make appropriate provision for this class of its helpless population.

Its management is vested in a Board of Directors, an Executive Committee, and the following officers:

James M. Ray, President; Barnabas C. Hobbs, Addison Daggy, W. P. Johnson, A. L. Roache, Vice Presidents; William H. Turner, Recording Secretary; K. H. Boland, Corresponding Secretary; John C. New, Treasurer.

RELIGIOUS.

PROTESTANT EPISCOPAL.

CHRIST CHURCH,

Located on the north-east corner of Meridian and Circle streets, is an artistic speci-men of the early English, or plain-pointed, architecture; and is, as all edifices erected to the worship of the True God should be, *true* throughout. Where it looks like stone, it *is* stone; even to the mullions of the windows. Its floor consists of a tower porch, nave, and shallow north and south transepts; which, together, will seat about five hundred worshipers. The chancel—sixteen feet deep, and raised four feet—is lighted by a triplet window, adorned with rich glass, filled with Christian symbols. The other windows of the Church, many being memorial, are less elaborately decorated. The altar—memorializing the one perfect and sufficient sacrifice, propitiation and atonement—is prominent in position, and superior in orn-amentation. It is placed high against the east wall of the chancel. The font is on the level of the nave, at the steps of the chancel. An oaken lecturn stands just outside the chancel, on the north side. The pulpit, situated at the left side, is an octagonal oaken structure, supported on a pedestal, all plainly but handsomely fin-ished. The roof is open, heavily timbered, and the ceiling is colored with ultra marine blue.

Outside, the whole building presents a beautiful, true, and churchly appear-ance, with its lancet, triplet, and trefoil windows, appearing along the side, among the buttresses, and up in the gable angles. The gray lime-stone walls, well laid in irregular shapes and varying tints, are relieved by prominent buttresses, with water-sheds and caps, high above the eaves. The roof is of blue and purple slate, laid in square and octagonal courses.

The chief feature, however, of the building, is the fine tower and spire, which occupies the south-west angle, and is the centrally prominent object in the city. The tower proper, is about seventy-five feet high, heavily built, and boldly but-tressed. Two doors open, one west, and the other south, into the lower story, forming a vestibule; the one south being decorated with appropriate carvings and inscriptions. Windows mark the stories above, until four bold stone gables pierced by triplets, with open blinds, complete the stone work. Within the last story a chime of nine bells is placed, which ring out joyfully or plaintively, in the success-ive seasons of festival and fast. Above the stone-work a timber octagonal spire, slated like the roof, pierced with four windows, and having the angles covered with a moulding of galvanized iron, rises sixty feet higher. This is surmounted by a finial, which gives the name of the Church in monogram. It is formed by a combination of the first two Greek letters in the name of CHRIST; and has been since early in the fourth century, a well known symbol of Christianity, signifying "Christ."

The parish and congregation of Christ Church, have been in existence nearly a quarter of a century. The Rev. Melancthon Hoyt, first resided in Indianapolis,

INDIANAPOLIS

as a Missionary of the Protestant Episcopal Church. No records of his work are preserved. The Rev. Jehu C. Clay, (late Dr. Clay, of Philadelphia,) had also visited the place, and had been requested to settle, after Mr. Hoyt left. The Rev. Mr. Pfeiffer, had preached here some fourteen years before, and baptized an infant; and the Rev. Henry M. Shaw, had also appeared here as an Episcopal Clergyman. On the 4th of July, 1837, the Rev. James B. Britton, (now of Ohio,) took up his residence as Missionary, and on the Sunday following, July 9th, the regular services of the Church in Indianapolis, commenced. In April, 1837, a few persons started a movement, which, in July, of that year, resulted in the following agreement and association :

"We, whose names are hereunto affixed, impressed with the importance of the Christian religion, and wishing to promote its holy influence in the hearts and lives of ourselves, our families and our neighbors, do hereby associate ourselves together, as the Parish of Christ Church, in the town of Indianapolis. township of Centre, county of Marion, State of Indiana, and by so doing, do recognize the jurisdiction of the Missionary Bishop of Indiana, and do adopt the Constitution and Canons of the Protestant Episcopal Church in the United States of America."

Indianapolis, July, 13, 1837.

(Signed)—Joseph M. Moore, D. D. Moore, Chas. W. Cady, T. B. Johnson, Geo. W. Mears, Thomas McOuat, Janet McOuat, Wm. Hannaman, A. St. Clair, Mrs. Browning, Miss Howell, Miss Gordon, Mrs. Riley, Miss Drake, Mrs. Julia A. McKenny, G. W. Starr and Mrs. Starr, James Morrison, A. G. Willard, M. D. Willard, Jas. Dawson, jr., Edward J. Dawson, Jos. Farbos, Nancy Farbos, Joseph Norman, Joanna Norman, Stewart Crawford, Jno. W. Jones, Edward Boyd, Mrs. Stevens.

The first vestry, elected under this organization, (21st August, 1837,) consisted of five persons, to wit:

Arthur St. Clair, Senior Warden ; Thos. McOuat, Junior Warden ; James Morrison, Joseph M. Moore, and Wm. Hannaman.

On the 7th of May, 1838, the corner stone of the Church was laid by the Rector, and the work progressed with such rapidity that the building was opened for Divine Worship on the 18th of November following, and consecrated December 16, by the Right Reverend Jackson Kemper, D. D., Missionary Bishop of Indiana and Missouri. This church was a plain, but neatly finished and strongly built Gothic edifice, of wood, which, while it made no pretensions to architectural beauty, was very far superior to any house of worship then erected in the place, and, undoubtedly, gave impulse to the building of other places by the several denominations, as its successor, the present beautiful Christ Church, did again, twenty years later. It was, indeed, strange as it may seem in these days of architecural taste, considered to be the handsomest church in Indiana; and many letters were received, from various parts of the State, requesting drawings of the "spire," as it was called ; the said spire, being merely a belfry stuck upon the front gable of the church. This building stood for twenty years, and was removed in 1857, to make room for the new church. It was sold, afterwards, to the African Methodist Congregation, and subsequently was destroyed by fire.

The succession of rectors in Christ Church, has been as follows, viz:

Rev. James B. Britton, three years, from 1837 to 1840 · Rev. Moses H. Hunter, one year, form 1842 to 1843; Rev. Samuel Lee Johnson, four years, from 1844 to 1848; Rev. Norman W. Camp, D. D , three years, from 1849 to 1852; Rev. Joseph

C. Talbot, seven years, from 1853 to 1860; Rev. Horace Stringfellow, Jr., two and one-half years, from 1860 to 1863; Rev. Theodore J. Holcomb, one and one-half years, from 1863 to 1864; Rev. J. P. T. Ingraham, four years, from 1864 to 1868; Rev. Benjamin Franklin, 1868, the present Rector.

Of these all are living, save one—the Rev. Samuel Lee Johnson, who died in office.

The present church was begun and nearly completed under the rectorship of the Rev. Joseph C. Talbot, D. D. (now Assistant Bishop of the Diocese.)

The chime of bells was hung in the spring of 1861; and the spire erected in the autumn of 1869.

The list of communicants numbers about two hundred and fifty. On the 15th of October, 1869, the seats in this church were declared free; and reliance for support is made successfully upon the Sunday offerings.

The Sabbath-School is in a flourishing condition, and has about two hundred and twenty-five members.

The value of the church property is about $70,000.

SAINT PAUL'S CATHEDRAL.

Location: Corner of Illinois and New York streets.

This parish was organized on the 10th of July, 1866, a vestry elected, and the Rev. Horace Stringfellow, Jr., called to the rectorship. For a brief period, beginning September 2d, 1866, the regular services of the parish were held in Masonic Hall. Meanwhile the present church site was purchased, on the rear of which a brick chapel was erected. The first services in the chapel were held on Christmas day, 1866.

The erection of the Cathedral was commenced in the spiring of 1867. It was opened for Divine worship at the meeting of the Diocesan Convention, in June, 1868.

The Rev. Mr. Stringfellow resigned the rectorship, in June, 1869, and was succeeded by the Rev. Treadwell Walden, the present rector, in February, 1870.

The parish was organized with six communicants; the number in June, 1870, was one hundred and ninety-seven.

The dimensions of the Cathedral are sixty-five by one hundred and fifty feet; the extreme dimensions of the entire building, sixty-five by one hundred and eighty-three feet.

The style of the architecture is the rural English Gothic, of the twelfth century. The exterior aspects of the building are striking, and well illustrate the sharp, bold, outlines and details of the Gothic style. Its greatest length is on New York street. The superior elevation of the roof is sixty feet; and the height of the tower one hundred and twenty feet.

The interior of the Cathedral consists of a central and two side naves, with three aisles. West of the auditorium is the baptismal font and section room. In the transept are the chancel, vestry-room, library, etc.. The chancel, thirty by forty feet, containing the Bishop's seat and sixteen stalls, is very elegant. It has fifteen windows, of stained glass, and is artistically ornamented with appropriate, emblematical designs. The windows of the auditorium are also of stained glass, but less ornamental than those of the chancel. The window of the baptismal font is likewise richly ornamented. The ceiling of the auditorium is of the ornamental

INDIANAPOLIS

open-roof construction. The seating capacity of the auditorium is about one thousand.

The principal material of the walls is brick, tastefully trimmed with dressed stone and Milwaukee yellow brick.

The Cathedral is furnished with a splendid organ, worth about $8,000.

From Saint Paul's parish has sprung a flourishing Mission in the north-western portion of the city, elsewhere spoken of.

The vestry is composed of the following: W. H. Morrison and T. A. Hendricks, Wardens; Joseph E. McDonald, John M. Lord, E. S. Alvord, John W. Murphy, David E. Snyder, W. J. Holliday, and J. A. Moore.

The Sabbath-School is in a prosperous condition; numbering, (including the Sunday School Mission,) about two hundred and fifty pupils.

The cost of Saint Paul's Cathedral, and value of site, are about $75,000.

GRACE CHURCH.

Location: Corner of Pennsylvania and St. Joseph streets.

This parish was organized in January, 1854. The membership of Christ Church, having become very large, and it being believed that there was a field for a new enterprise, Messrs. Deloss Root, J O. D. Lilly, and Nelson Kingman, with their families, withdrew, and organized the present parish of Grace Church.

The present house of worship of the parish was built without delay, and dedicated in the summer of 1854. Shortly afterward, the Rev. M. V. Averill, was called to the rectorship of the parish, who remained about two and a-half years. Mr. Averill was an energetic, as well an able rector; and the prosperity of the parish during his rectorship, is attested by the fact that in that period, the number of communicants increased from ten to sixty. Mr. Averill was succeeded by the Rev. Dr. C. B. Davidson, who remained with the parish about three years; at the end of which time the number of communicants was about seventy-five. Dr. Davidson retired on the 10th of October, 1870. For several months the parish was without a rector. On the 1st of January, 1871, the Rev. James Runcie was called to the rectorship; who entered upon his duties on the 1st of March, 1871.

The present membership of the church is about seventy-five.

The Sabbath-School, of which George W. Geiger, Esq., is Superintendent, has one hundred and ten members.

The church edifice is a frame building, of the modified Gothic style, and is particularly neat and tasteful in its *ensemble*, finish, and appointments. It is doubtful if at a like expense, a better effect in respect of a house of worship, could be produced. The aspects of the interior are inviting and suggestive of comfort. The windows are of stained glass; the ceiling, of the open-roofed construction. The chancel, in the ornamentation of its triple windows, and its appointments, is artistic; the symbols typifyng, with fine effect, the idea expressed in the name, *Grace Church*. The church has a fine organ.

The value of the building and site, is about $11,000.

CHURCH OF THE HOLY INNOCENTS.

Location: Corner of Fletcher avenue and Cedar street.

This parish was organized as a " Mission Sunday School of Christ Church," in July, 1866, at the residence of James Meade, No. 50, Forest avenue, by Rev. C. C. Tate, Assistant Minister of Christ Church. The attendance upon the services of the young society augmented to such an extent, that increased accommodations soon became necessary. Steps were accordingly taken to build a chapel on the north-east corner of Fletcher avenue and Cedar street, which had been donated for that purpose by S. A. Fletcher, Jr. The required amount for building the chapel, $1,800, was raised by the members of Christ Church—mainly through the exertions of the Rev. C. C. Tate, and of that earnest worker, the Rev. J. P. T. Ingraham, Rector of Christ Church, who was the moving spirit of the enterprise.

The chapel, in size, twenty-five by forty feet, beside the chancel and robing-room, was opened for public worship on the afternoon of the Epiphany Sunday, January, 6, 1867, the services being conducted by the Revs. J. P. T. Ingraham and C. C. Tate. The singing exercises were assisted by a cabinet organ, the gift of Miss C. J. Farrell. The chapel then took the name of the *Holy Innocents*. Regular afternoon services were held by Rev. Mr. Tate, until the following July, when he resigned as Assistant Minister of Christ Church, to accept the Rectorship of St. Paul's Church, Columbus, Ohio. At the latter date, Mr. Willis D. Engle, was elected Superintendent of the Sunday School, the afternoon services being conducted by the Rev. J. P. T. Ingraham, assisted by a lay-reader. During this time the chapel building was further improved through the exertions of the few who labored there.

January 1st, 1868, the Rev. George B. Engle, as Assistant Minister of Christ Church, took charge of the Mission, and continued to serve in that capacity, until January 4th, 1869, when, with the consent of the Bishop, and the concurrence of the other parishes in the city, the *Church of the Holy Innocents* was organized, with a membership of about thirty. The first officers of the Church were:

A. Willis Gorrell, Senior Warden; William A. Taylor, Junior Warden; Ansel B. Denton, George Davidson, Daniel S. Moulton, David B. Hunt, Edwin Vickers, Thomas V. Cook, and Willis D. Engle, Vestrymen; Willis D. Engle, Secretary and Treasurer.

A call was extended to the Rev. George B. Engle to become the rector of the church, and was accepted.

On Easter Monday, March 29th, 1869, the same officers were re-elected, except John Boswell, whose place as vestryman, was filled by the election of Joseph Thompson. Willis D. Engle was elected as delegate to represent the parish in the Diocesan Convention.

On Easter Monday, April 10th, 1871, the following officers were elected:

A. Willis Gorrell, Senior Warden; William A. Taylor, Junior Warden; Ansel B. Denton, John Algeo, George Davidson, D. B. Hunt, James Meade, Daniel S. Moulton, and Willis D. Engle, Vestrymen. Willis D. Engle, Secretary; William A. Taylor, Treasurer; and Willis D. Engle, delegate to represent the Parish in the Diocesan Convention.

During the fall of last year, considerable expenditures were made in improvements on the church building, in neatly inclosing it, and in adorning the grounds with shrubbery and shade trees.

The membership at this time is about sixty. The Sunday-School numbers eighteen teachers, and one hundred and forty pupils. The seats are all free. The rector's salary is paid by subscription, and the current expenses by the offertory.

EPISCOPAL MISSION.

A flourishing Mission, sustained by *St. Paul's* Parish, has been established in the north-western part of the city. A suitable site has been purchased; and du-

ANNAPOLIS

ring the present year, *Saint Paul's Chapel* (Second) will be completed; the site and building to cost about $5,000.

Pending the appointment of an Assistant Minister of *Saint Paul's* the Mission will continue to be served by the Rector, the Rev. Mr. Walden; who conducts its regular religious services every Thursday evening, in the temporary building occupied by the Mission. Of Sundays its members attend the services in *Saint Paul's Cathedral*.

The Sabbath-School, of which Mr. S. R. Lippencott, is Superintendent, and Mrs. Harriet Preston, Lady Manager, is in a flourishing condition.

Summary.—Total membership of the Episcopal denomination, in Indianapolis, five hundred and eighty-two; total Sabbath-School membership, seven hundred and forty-three; total value of church property, $168,000.

PRESBYTERIAN.

FIRST CHURCH.

Location: Corner of Pennsylvania and New York streets.

The *First Presbyterian Church* is one of the religious landmarks of this city, and with its early history is associated the early history of Presbyterianism in this State. The foundation of this church society was half a century ago, when this was the "Far West," and when the church was following closely in the footsteps of pioneer civilization. Of those who took an active part in the organization of this church there yet remain a very few to tell the story of its early history.

In 1820, the future city of Indianapolis was mapped out and its lots offered for sale. In August of 1821 Rev. Ludlow G. Gaines preached the first Presbyterian sermon in the city, in a grove south of the present State House square. In 1822, Rev. David C. Proctor, of Connecticut, was engaged as a missionary for one year.

In 1823 a subscription of $1,200 was raised and a house of worship erected on Pennsylvania street, near the corner of Market. On the 5th of July of the same year, a Presbyterian church was organized and the names of fifteen members enrolled.

In 1842, a second house of worship was erected, on the corner of Market and Circle streets, at a cost of $8,300, and on the 6th of May, 1843, it was dedicated.

In 1864, the foundations of the present church edifice were laid. The chapel, containing a lecture room, a social room, Sabbath-School rooms and pastor's study, was erected and opened for service in 1866. The present audience room was opened for service December 29th, 1870.

Since the organization of the society in 1823, a period of nearly 47 years, the congregation has built three church edifices and one mission church—now the Seventh Presbyterian Church—and has had the following pastors: Rev. Geo. Bush, Rev. John R. Moreland, Rev. James W. McKennan, Rev. Phineas D. Gurley, D. D., Rev. John A. McClung, D. D., Rev. Thomas Cunningham, D. D., Rev. J. Howard Nixon, and Rev. R. D. Harper, D. D. Dr. Harper recently resigned the pastorate to accept a call from Philadelphia, and the church authorities have not, at this writing, selected his successor.

The only surviving pastors are Rev. Dr. Cunningham, of San Francisco; Rev. J. Howard Nixon, of Springfield, Missouri, and Rev. Dr. Harper, of Philadelphia.

At different intervals the following persons have served the church with great acceptance as stated supply: Rev. Ludlow G. Gaines, Rev. David C. Proctor, Rev. Isaac Reed, Rev. William A. Holliday, Rev. Samuel Fulton, Rev. Charles S. Mills and Rev. J. F. Dripps.

The following persons have served as elders in this church from its organization until the present time: Dr. Isaac Coe, Caleb Scudder, John Johnson, Ebenezer Sharpe, John G. Brown, Col. James Blake, Hon. Samuel Bigger, George S. Brandon, Charles Axtell, H. C. Newcomb, James M. Ray, Thomas H. Sharpe, William Sheets, Thomas McIntire, General Benjamin Harrison, Myron A. Stowell and William R. Craig.

In December, 1838, fifteen members of this church were granted letters of dismission to organize the Second Presbyterian Church of this city; and in 1851, thirteen years subsequently, letters of dismission were granted to twenty-one persons, including three Elders, Caleb Scudder, James Blake and H. C. Newcomb, to organize the Third Presbyterian Church of this city. These little bands, who separated from the parent society, have grown into full, well-equipped organizations, and are doing good service in the cause of Christianity.

The church has a membership of three hundred and fifty one. The Sabbath-School has four hundred and twenty-five members. The principal officers of the church are:

Ruling Elders—James M. Ray, Thos. H. Sharpe, Wm. Sheets, Thos. McIntire, M. A. Stowell, Benj. Harrison, Robert Browning, James W. Brown, Jere. McLene, Isaac C. Hays, H. L. Walker, A. M. Benham.

Deacons—Wm. J. Johnston, J. A. Vinnedge, Henry D. Carlisle, E. P. Howe, Carlos Dickson, Charles Latham.

Trustees—E. B. Martindale, Robert Browning, James W. Brown, William Braden, Upton J. Hammond. Superintendent of Sabbath School, E. B. Martindale.

The church edifice is in the Gothic style of architecture, and is an artistic and elegant structure. The main building, sixty by one hundred feet, fronts on Pennsylvania street; and in the rear, on New York street, is the chapel building, fifty by seventy-five feet. The audience room, in its design and appointments, is one of the finest in the country. Its pews are arranged in curved lines; the windows are of beautiful stained glass; the ceiling is very ornamental, "rafter finished," and finely frescoed. The tower is one hundred and seventy-six feet in height.

The building is built of pressed brick, trimmed with dressed stone. The chapel is divided into three rooms: two for social meetings, and one for the pastor's study. The second story contains the Sabbath-School room. The dimensions of the building are sixty-five by one hundred and fifty-five feet. The cost of building and site was $104,117.74.

SECOND PRESBYTERIAN CHURCH.

Location: Corner of Pennsylvania and Vermont streets.

The materials for the ensuing sketch of this organization have been chiefly obtained from a discourse preached at the opening of the present chapel, by Rev. Hanford A. Edson, the pastor.

The society was formed, with fifteen members, November 19, 1838, in the Marion County Seminary, a small brick building standing, until 1860, at the south-west corner of University Square. The Rev. Henry Ward Beecher, the first pastor, entered upon his work July 31st, 1839. Worship was continued in the Seminary for a year. Afterward the congregation removed to their own edifice, the present High School building, on the north-west corner of Circle and Market streets, occupying at first the lecture-room. This house was dedicated to the worship of the Most High, October 4th, 1840. On the 19th of September, 1847, the pastorate of Mr. Beecher closed, and he removed to Brooklyn, New York, where he has since gained the reputation as a pulpit orator, with which the world is familiar. He was succeeded by Rev. Clement E. Babb, at the time a student in Lane Seminary, now associate editor of the *Herald and Presbyter*, of Cincinnati. He commenced work May 7th, 1848, and continued in the pastorate until January 1st, 1853. It was under his supervision that a colony, now the Fourth Presbyterian Church, was established, with twenty-four members. This occurred November 30th, 1851. The third pastor, Rev Thornton A. Mills, began his work January 1st, 1854, and remained with the Church three years, the relation between pastor and people, being dissolved by the Presbytery, February 9th, 1857. Dr. Mills having been elected Secretary of the General Assembly's Committee on Education, went at once to New York. He is the only one of the pastors of the Church not now living. He died suddenly June 19th, 1867. Rev. George P. Tindall was his successor, called to the pastorate August 6th, 1857, and continuing in the field until September 27th, 1863. During his ministry, in 1858 and 1859, large numbers were added to the Church. The present pastor, Rev. Hanford A. Edson, has occupied the place since January 17th, 1864. On the 15th of May of that year, a building was dedicated at the corner of Michigan and Blackford streets for a Mission Sunday School, which had been established by members of the Second Church, and which has now grown into the "Fifth Presbyterian Church." November 20th, 1867, another colony, the "Olivet Presbyterian Church," was formed with twenty-one members, a house of worship having been dedicated for them a month previous.

For the beautiful stone edifice at the corner of Pennsylvania and Vermont streets, of which we present an engraving, ground was broken in the spring of 1864. The corner stone was laid May 14th, 1866; the chapel occupied December 22d, 1867; and the completed edifice dedicated January 9th, 1870. Mr. Joseph Curzon, of this city is the architect. The entire cost of the property is about $105,000. The present membership of the church is considerably above four hundred. The Sabbath-School is in a flourishing condition, and has three hundred pupils enrolled.

Besides the pastor, the officers of the society are as follows:

Ruling Elders.—William N. Jackson, Samuel F. Smith, Enoch C. Mayhew, Edwin J. Peck, John S. Spann, William S. Hubbard, Thomas A. Morris, Moses R. Barnard, and Frederick W. Chislett.

Deacons.—Sandford Morris, Edward S. Field, Clement A. Greenleaf, George W. Crane, William W. Wentz, Richard M. Smock, David W. Coffin, and Willis H. Pettit.

Trustees.—William P. Fishback, William M. Wheatley, John S. Spann, James M. Bradshaw, and William Mansur.

The church edifice is massive and imposing. It is built, from foundation to spire, of rubble limestone; the corners, buttresses, and other projecting angles, being artistically faced with dressed stone. Its architecture is the Gothic style of the twelfth century. The auditorium is seventy-eight feet in length by fifty-seven feet in width; thirty-seven feet high in the center, and twenty-six and one-half feet at the side walls; with a recess for the choir twelve by thirty-two

(14)

feet, and another for the pulpit, five by fourteen feet. The ceiling is finished in ash and black walnut; with plastered panels separated by stucco mouldings. The pews, pulpit, and other wood work, in the interior, are also, richly finished in walnut and ash. The windows are highly ornamented. The chapel, session room, and pastor's study, are in keeping with the elegance of the auditorium; as is, also, the Sabbath-School room, now in the second story. The auditorium is lighted by silvered reflectors. The main tower is one hundred and sixty-one and one-half feet in height, and eighteen feet square at the base. A smaller tower at the entrance to the chapel, is ninety-five and one-half feet in height. Without, the structure is massive and artistic; within, it is elegantly and tastefully finished and furnished.

THIRD PRESBYTERIAN CHURCH.

Location: Northeast corner of Illinois and Ohio streets.

This church was organized on the 23d September, 1851, at the residence of Caleb Scudder, Esq., in this city, by the Presbytery of Muncie; twenty-one person withdrawing for the purpose from the First Church.

Prominent among the founders of this association were James Blake, Caleb Scudder, John W. Hamilton, H. C. Newcomb, Nathaniel Bolton, Dr. W. C. Thompson and C. B. Davis. The congregation first met for religious worship in Temperance Hall; and afterward erected the present church building, which was completed and dedicated in 1859.

The Third Church has for many years been a prominent religious power in the community. Its present membership is four hundred and fifty. The Sabbath-school numbers two hundred and thirty-three pupils.

In 1867 a colony went out from this congregation and formed the Fifth Presbyterian Church; which has since been sustained in part by the parent church.

The Third Church has had the following pastors: The Rev. David Stevenson, from 1851 to October, 1860; the Rev. George C. Heckman, D. D., from 1861 to 1867; the Rev. Robert Sloss, the present pastor, since June, 1868.

, Prominent among the earlier members and officers of this church are the names of James Blake, Caleb Scudder, Hon. H. C. Newcomb, John W. Hamilton, Chas. N. Todd, Dr. W. C. Thompson, the Rev. C. G McLean, D. D., Wm. M. Blake, William Stewart, Silas T. Bowen, Dr. Theophilus Parvin, J. D. Carmichael, L. N. Andrews, William Glenn and H. W. Keohn.

The church edifice, though not so imposing or elegant in its architectural aspects, as several others in the city, is nevertheless a commodious and substantial structure, built of brick, with stone facings, in the modified Norman style of architecture. Its external dimensions are eighty by forty-eight feet. The size of the audience room is seventy-one by forty-five feet; and it has, including the gallery, seating capacity for about six hundred persons. The value of the property is about $50,000.

The present officers of the church are:

Pastor.—Rev. Robert Sloss.

Elders.—H. C. Newcomb, S. T. Bowen, J. D. Carmichael, Dr. T. Parvin, C. N. Todd, L N. Andrews, A. S. Walker.

Deacons.—James Muir, James Wilson, Wm. M. Blake, Chas. G. Stewart, D. H. Wiles, R. Frank Kennedy, Wm. Judson, James D. Brown.

Trustees.—Thos. D. Kingan, W. W. Woollen, D. H. Wiles, R. F. Kennedy, Wm. Judson, James Hasson, Frank Landers.

FOURTH PRESBYTERIAN CHURCH.

Location: Corner of Delaware and Market streets.

The Fourth Presbyterian Church was formed by a colony from the Second Presbyterian Church.

On the 30th of November, 1851, twenty-four members of the latter society withdrew by letters, and proceeded at once to organize under the name of the *Fourth Presbyterian Church of Indianapolis.* Two elders were elected, Alexander Graydon and Samuel Merrill. A call was extended to the Rev. George M. Maxwell, of Marietta, Ohio, with the offer of a salary of $800. The call was accepted, and Mr. Maxwell commenced his services as pastor early in the year 1852.

After nearly six years of struggle, the society, on the 13th of September, 1857, was enabled to dedicate the present house of worship to Divine service. The number of members at that date was one hundred and fifteen.

In the spring of 1858 a religious revival resulted in a large increase of the membership.

In November, 1858, Mr. Maxwell's health failing, he resigned, much to the regret of his congregation.

In October, 1859, the Rev. A. L. Brooks received a unanimous call, which he accepted, at a salary of $1,500.00, and commenced his labors immediately. Rev. Mr. Brooks labored with the church until March, 1862, when he accepted a call from Chicago.

In July, 1862, the Rev. Charles H. Marshall accepted a call to the pastorate of the Fourth Church. His salary, at first $1,000, was gradually increased during his stay to $2,500.

Many additions were made to the church during the revival of 1869.

In October, 1870, Mr. Marshall was compelled by failing health to sever his pastoral relation with the church, to the general regret of the membership. During his pastorate the war for the Union began and ended; and at one time the Fourth Church demonstrated its patriotism by sending to the field not only its pastor, as chaplain, but some forty of its young men.

On the 1st of January, 1871, Mr. Marshall was succeeded by the Rev. J. H. Morron, of Peoria, Illinois, the present pastor.

The church membership numbers one hundred and eighty-five; that of the Sabbath-Schools, about one hundred and seventy-five.

The church edifice presents a somewhat ancient and time-worn aspect externally. It is quite commodious, having seating accommodations for about six hundred persons. The building is of stuccoed brick, and is surmounted by a high tower. The value of the property is about $50,000, and it is free of debt.

The elders of the church since its organization have been:

Alexander Graydon, Samuel Merrill, Horace Bassett, John L. Ketcham, Henry S. Kellogg, Alexander H. Davidson, Charles W. Moores, David Kregelo, Robert Evans, Emanuel Haugh, John McKeehan, Samuel Merrill, J. H. Brown, Robert M. Stewart. Col. Samuel Merrill is Superintendent of the Sabbath-schools.

The officers for the current year are:

Elders.—David Kregelo, Robert Evans, John McKeehan, Samuel Merrill, Robert Stewart, James H. Brown.

Deacons.—William H. Comingor, Joseph R. Haugh, Hervey Bates, John L. Ketcham, Robert W. Cathcart, Daniel W. Grubbs.

Trustees.—Wm. A. Bradshaw, Joseph K. Sharpe, David Kregelo, Joseph R. Haugh, John D. Condit.

FIFTH CHURCH.

Location: East side of Blackford street, between Vermont and Michigan streets.

A frame chapel, erected on the above stated site in 1864, for the purposes of a Mission Sabbath-School, was purchased in the autumn of 1866, by the Third Church, into whose control the School then passed. In October, 1867, it was organized by the authority of the Indianapolis Presbytery, as the *Fifth Presbyterian* Church, with eighteen members: twelve from the Third, and one from the First Presbyterian Churches of this city, and five from churches elsewhere located. The exercises incident to the organization were conducted by Revs. George C. Heckman, L. G. Hay, W. W. Sickles; and Elders James Blake and Charles N. Todd.

The first, only, and present pastor of the society, is the Rev. William B. Chamberlain, who began his labors as such in the summer of 1869; was ordained in October of that year, and installed in October, 1870.

The chapel is a frame building; cost, with site, $2,000; and will seat two hundred persons.

The growth and prosperity of the society have been such as to demand and warrant a better and more commodious house of worship. For this purpose a desirable site has been secured on the south-west corner of Michigan and Blackford streets; where excavation is now being made for a new building, to be of brick, cruciform, with a fine tower; having a basement for Sabbath-School and other purposes; and an audience room with a capacity to seat four hundred and fifty persons. The cost of the new structure will be from $12,000 to $15,000. The society expect to occupy the basement by the fall of 1872, and hope to complete the building within two or three years.

The number of members is about one hundred and fifty. The Sabbath-School has two hundred and fifty members.

OLIVET CHURCH.

Location: Corner of Union and McCarty streets.

This church was established by a colony from the Second Church. A few members of the parent body, met with their pastor, on the 22nd of June, 1867, and instructed a committee to buy a suitable site in the south-western quarter of the city. The corner of Union and McCarty streets was selected for that purpose; the present church building was erected without delay, and was dedicated on the 20th of October, of the same year, by the Rev. H. A. Edson, pastor of the Second Church. On the 20th of November, 1867, a church organization was effected. The first pastor was the Rev. J. B. Brandt; the second the Rev. Luman A. Aldrich; the third, and present, the Rev. Joseph E. Scott. The house of worship is a plain, comfortable frame building. The property is valued at $2,500, and is free from debt. The Church membership numbers over one hundred persons; that of the Sunday-School about one hundred and twenty-five.

SEVENTH CHURCH.

Location: Elm street, near Cedar.

Originally established as a mission enterprise, by the First Church, and in its infancy conducted and sustained by the parent body, the Seventh Church has now about attained the stature of a full grown and self-sustaining organization; able and entitled to manage its own affairs. Of the maxim that "Christianity is the greatest civilizer," the results of this enterprise are a triumphant exemplification.

One Sabbath day, early in the year 1865, Wm. R. Craig, a resident of the south-eastern part of the city, was much disturbed by a rude and lawless troop of boys, outrageously wanting in that training which inspires a decent respect for the Sabbath day. Their repeated and flagrant violations of the Sabbath, and unruly conduct generally, had often outraged the feelings of the staid old Scotchman, but never to such a degree as on this occasion; and now, for the first time, he began to seriously debate with himself the question of a remedy. He thought of applying to the police; and then dismissed that recourse, as being an inadequate measure of relief, and not sufficiently radical. Finally he decided that a Sabbath-School, by reaching the consciences of the offenders, would, in the course of time, effect a thorough and lasting cure. Mr. Craig, who was a member of the First Church, proceeded at once to prepare for the application of his remedy.

The pastor and elders of that church concurred in his proposition, and called a meeting of the pastors and elders of the four principal Presbyterian churches, to consult upon a plan for opening the campaign; a meeting of the officers and pastors of the First and Third Churches was shortly afterward held to consider the question; and finally it was agreed that the First Church should take suitable steps to provide spiritual instruction for the south-eastern quarter of the city. Wm. R. Craig and N. M. Wood were shortly afterward appointed a committee to establish a Sabbath-school there; for defraying the expenses of which work of organization, $130 was voted. A room in an old carpenter shop, belonging to Peter Routier, on Cedar street, was rented for the purpose. The school was organized by Messrs. W. R. Craig and Thomas McIntire, and successfully conducted through the summer of 1865 under the superintendence of N. M. Wood, Esq.

The rude building then occupied by the mission proving too small and uncomfortable for the purpose, it was decided to erect a suitable building for Sabbath-School and other religious services. Through the exertions of James M. Ray, a member of the First Presbyterian Church, a site was secured in Fletcher's Addition, donated by Calvin Fletcher, Sr., A. Stone, W. S. Witt, Elisha Taylor and James M. Hough. The Board of Church Extension pledged $500 to aid in the erection of a building, and the First Church took upon itself the responsibility of seeing to it that the new enterprise should not fail. To this end Elder Thomas McIntire and James W. Brown, Esq., were appointed a committee to superintend the work of erecting the new building. Subscriptions to the amount of over $3,200 were collected, and the building was completed and occupied by the Sabbath-School early in December, 1865. The parent church supplied the Rev. W. W. Sickles to preach for the young congregation for a period of six months. The dedicatory exercises were held on the 24th December, 1865, and were conducted by the Rev. J. H. Nixon, pastor of the First Church. The Rev. Thomas Galt, licentiate, of Chicago, preached for the congregation from May to September of 1867; and was succeeded by Rev. C. M. Howard.

At 7½ P. M., on the 27th November, 1867, the church was formally organized by order of the Presbytery; the committee consisting of the Revs. J. H. Nixon and William Armstrong, and Elders Thomas McIntire and William R. Craig. Twenty-three persons, either by examination or by letter, were admitted into the new organization. Wm. R. Craig was chosen the first elder, and the Rev. C. M. Howard was invited to become the pastor. Mr. Howard was a gentleman of extraordinary religious enthusiasm and industry. The field was forbidding, and a pastor in search of a pleasant sphere of labor, where the wilderness had been subdued by Christian cultivation, would have avoided the pioneer duty assumed by Mr. Howard. The latter labored with such patient and persevering industry, that great success followed his efforts, and the church rapidly increased in numbers. Worn out by hard service, he was obliged to ask a release from his pastoral duties, and he retired from that position in October, 1869.

In November, 1869, the Rev. John B. Brandt was called to supply the congregation. At the end of the year he was compelled to discontinue his pastoral relation to the church, on account of the demands on his time by the Young Men's Christian Association of this city, of which he was the Superintendent.

During the year 1869 Samuel E. Kennedy, Edwin G. Barrett and Alexander Craig were elected elders; Messrs. J. W. Kolwes, Lewis H. Decker and James Duthie, deacons; C. A. Griffith, Robert J. Pedloe, John R. Childers, Jacob Beltz, Hiram C. Husted, J. W. Brown, Edwin G. Barrett, and John Jolly, Trustees.

Rev. L. G. Hay took charge of the church November 1st, 1870, remaining about six months. He was specially qualified for this post by many years of experience in similar fields, and by a happy union of religious zeal with practical sagacity, and the society flourished during his pastorate.

Rev. Charles H. Raymond has recently assumed pastoral charge of this church, and entered upon his work with the hearty co-operation of his people.

The Scotchman's remedy for the cure of disorder in his locality has proven successful.

The present number of communicants is over one hundred. The Sabbath-School reckons about two hundred and fifty members and twenty officers and teachers. The success of the latter is largely due to the Superintendent, Mr. Ebenezer Sharpe, who lately retired from this position to take charge of the North Street Mission School. The present Superintendent is Mr. Alexander Craig.

The value of the property is about $2,000.

PRESBYTERIAN MISSIONS.

North Street Mission.—Location: On the corner of North and Delaware streets.

This flourishing mission of the First Presbyterian Church, was established in July, 1870. The mission building had been occupied for Sabbath-School purposes before this time, being known as the "Saw Mill Mission," but for several months the field had been abandoned. The leading spirits in the new organization were Gen. Ben. Harrison, Dr. C. C. Burgess, Ebenezer Sharpe, Capt. E. P. Howe, I. C. Hays and others, all members of the First Presbyterian Church.

The Sabbath School has an average attendance of over two hundred, sometimes reaching nearly two hundred and fifty. Regular religious services are held of Sunday evenings, and a prayer meeting, conducted by the officers of the mission, is held on each Wednesday evening.

Rev. L. G. Hay has been appointed to take charge of this mission, and it is expected that a church will be established in the course of the present year.

The laborers in this work have been active and zealous, and it has been a successful enterprise from the start. The chapel occupied by the mission, was purchased for that purpose by James W. Brown, Esq., a citizen noted for his munificence in regard to religious enterprises in this city. The mission has thus had a chapel furnished free of rent—an assistance of no small moment to a young organization.

From the importance of this field and the encouragement which the enterprise has received, it is confidently predicted that the *North Street Mission* will, at no greatly distant day, develop into one of the largest and most prosperous churches of Indianapolis.

The value of the property is about $2,500.

Memorial Chapel is located on the corner of Christian avenue and Bellefontaine street; and was founded, as it has since been maintained, by the Second Presbyterian Church. A Sabbath-School, under the charge of Mr. M. R. Barnard, as superintendent, was immediately organized, and has steadily increased in prosperity ever since. George Crane, Esq., succeeded Mr. Barnard, in October, 1870. His labors in building up the mission have been both zealous and successful; so that the average attendance is about seventy-five. From the first, weekly prayer meetings have been held; which have also been well attended—the citizens in that vicinity taking an active interest in the success of the mission. Should the enterprise continue to prosper in the future as in the past, (of which there is no reason to doubt,) the result will be the early admission of this mission into the Presbytery as a full grown church.

The building in which the services of the Mission are held, is a neat frame structure, with seating room for about two hundred persons, and was erected in the spring of 1870, at a cost, including that of site, of about $3,500.

West Street Mission.—Location: West street, near Georgia.

This mission was established on the 25th of July, 1869, by a colony of young men from the First Church, assisted by two or three other persons; who secured, for their purpose, a building formerly used as a Soldiers' Barracks, located as above.

The field was not inviting, and the building anything but elegant or attractive; but the founders of the enterprise, with little but their own zeal and persistence (of which they have certainly expended an extraordinary amount) to aid them in the work, succeeded in establishing and conducting a useful and growing mission of the Presbyterian Church, in a locality where there was great need of such an undertaking.

They began by organizing a Sabbath-School, with Henry D. Carlisle as superintendent. The school was successful from the beginning. The average attendance of pupils is about seventy-five; any material increase of which number is hindered by the limited capacity of the building. Mr. Carlisle has, with the exception of an intermission of a few months, been the superintendent ever since. The young men who founded the mission have, with the assistance of an additional helper or two, continued to sustain it; and have managed to accumulate a handsome Sunday-School library, and an organ, besides fitting up the room and paying the rental.

During the past summer, out-door meetings, largely attended, were held every Sabbath in front of the building; and when the cold weather put a stop to those, and forced the "Colony" to adjourn to the inside, these meetings were not discontinued. These religious services have been conducted by the five young men in charge of the Sabbath-School, (Henry D. Carlisle, P. L. Mayhew, R. D. Craighead, Leroy W. Braden, and Charles Meigs;) who—as they express it—"being too poor to secure a regular minister, have had to do their own preaching,—with what help they could get from laymen of the different churches of the city.'

The attendance at these Sabbath evening meetings has generally been as large as the limited capacity of the building would admit of.

Indianola Mission.—The location of this mission is in Indianola, on Washington street, half a mile west of the White River Bridge. The property was, for a number of years, occupied as a Methodist church. Having fallen into disuse by the latter denomination, a mission Sabbath-School was started there on the 15th of July, 1870, by three of the young members of the Third Presbyterian Church; H. H. Fulton, E. G. Williams, and John G. Blake. The field for the mission was large and necessitous; and it has had a good degree of success. Beside the usual Sabbath-School exercises, religious services of Sabbath evenings, have for some time been regularly held—chiefly by laymen.

Arrangements for the purchase of the property by the Presbyterian denomination, will, it is expected, be concluded shortly; and thus another addition to the list of Presbyterian churches in this city, is far advanced in its developement.

The mission is directed by John G. Blake, as Superintendent, with an Assistant Superintendent, ten teachers, and the usual additional officers. The number of members is about one hundred. The value of the property is about $1.000.

Summary—Total membership of the Presbyterian Denomination in Indianapolis, 1,736; total Sabbath-School membership, 2,008; total value of church property, $320,117.74.

BAPTIST.

FIRST BAPTIST CHURCH.

Location: North-east corner of New York and Pennsylvania streets.

The first assemblage of Baptists in Indianapolis was nearly fifty years ago. An old record, still preserved, quaintly states that "The Baptists at, and near Indianapolis, having removed from various parts of the world, met at the School House in Indianapolis, in August, 1822, and after some consultation, adopted the following resolution: *Resolved*, that we send for helps, and meet at Indianapolis, on the 20th day of Sept'r next for the purpose of establishing a regular Baptist church at s'd place. That John W. Reding write letters to little Flat Rock & Little Cedar Grove churches for help. That Samuel McCormack write letters to Lick Creek and Franklin churches for helps—then adjourned."

The next meeting was pursuant to adjournment. Elder Tyner attended from Little Cedar Grove church and "after Divine service went into business." "Letters were received and read from Brothers Benjamin Barns, Jeremiah Johnson, Thomas Carter, Otis Hobart, John Hobart, Theodore V. Denny, John McCormack, Samuel McCormack, John Thompson, and William Dodd, and Sisters Jane Johnson, Nancy Carter, Nancy Thompson, Elizabeth McCormack, and Polly Carter, then adjourned until Saturday morning 10 o'clk."

Saturday morning:

" Met according to adjournment and after Divine service letters were rec'd from John W. Reding and Hannah Skinner. Brother B. Barns was appointed to speak and answer for the members—and Brother Tyner went into an examination, and finding the members sound in the Faith pronounced them a regular Baptist church, and directed them to go into business."

FIRST BAPTIST CHURCH,

"Brother Tyner was then chosen moderator, and John W. Reding clerk 1t agreed to be called and known by the name of the First Baptist Church, at Indianapolis, then adjourned until the third Saturday in Oct'r 1822.

J. W. REDING, CK."

Benjamin Barns appears to have been rather the most prominent among the early membership, for on the third Saturday of June, 1823, the record recites: "agreed that Bro. B. Barns be called to preach to this church once a month until the end of this year: to which Bro. Barns agreed."

The first deacon was John Thompson, who was, by a unanimous vote of the church, called to that office on the third Saturday of December, 1822.

In May, 1823, Samuel McCormack was "ordered to be a singing clk. to this church."

A committee appointed to secure a place for worship, consisting of J. Carter, H. Bradly, and D. Wood, reported that "the School house may be had without interruption." This was a new log school house, situated on the north side of, and partly in, Maryland street, between Tennessee and Mississippi streets.

On the third Saturday, in November, 1824, a committee of three was appointed "to rent a room or repair the school house for a meeting house the ensuing season, to report at the next meeting." At the next meeting, in January, 1825, the committee reported "that $1.25 had been expended in repairing the school house,—and the deacon is requested to pay the same out of the joint funds, and that each Brother pay the Bro. deacon a small sum on to-morrow." At the same meeting it was, "on motion, agreed that the church petition the present Gen'l Assembly for a site to build a meeting house upon; and that the S. E. half of the shaded block 90 be selected,—and that Bro. J. Hobart, H. Bradley and the clk. be appointed to bear the petition." In due time the committee reported that the petition had "failed."

In the spring of 1825, Major Thomas Chinn invited the church to use his house as a place for worship during the summer; which invitation was accepted.

In June, 1825, the church purchased from Wm. Wilmott, Esq., lot 2, in square 50, for use. There was a small frame house on the lot, which was not plastered, and arrangements were made to finish it, which were afterwards "postponed *sinadi*," and the house left as it was. An apportionment was ordered to pay for the house and lot, and a committee reported an assessment of $48, divided among the fifteen male members of the church.

In January, 1826, Rev. Cornelius Duvall, of Owen county, Kentucky, was called to the pastorate. Nothing resulted from this call, so far as appears upon the records, and in December, 1826, Rev. Abraham Smock was called as pastor for one year; he accepted and soon began his labors. Soon afterward, the church disposed of the lot purchased from Wilmott, and lot 3, in square 75 (where Schnull's block now stands) was purchased for $100, and a meeting house erected in 1829.

In July, 1830, Rev. A. Smock resigned, and for some time the church was without a pastor.

In September, 1831, of two members received into the church, by letter, one was "Bro. Mosely Stewart, (man of color.")

In May, 1832, Rev. Byron Lawrence was "requested to preach for us as frequently as he can on Lord's day for six months."

In April, 1833, Revs. Jameson Hawkins, Byron Lawrence, and Ezra Fisher, were "invited to preach for this church statedly, on each Lord's day, making their own arrangements."

In August, 1833, "Bro. Anthony A. Slaton, (man of color,) was rec'd by letter."

In February, 1834, Rev. Ezra Fisher was called "to be the stated preacher of the church." He served in this capacity some months, and in January, 1835, T. C. Townsend was requested to preach by the church, until a regular pastor should be settled.

In July, 1835, Rev. J. L. Richmond was called to the pastorate and accepted.

The house of worship first erected on the new lot was replaced in due time by a more pretentious frame edifice, which was occupied by the church as a place of worship, for a number of years.

In 1843, the Rev. George C. Chandler took the pastorate and remained until 1847. He was succeeded by Rev. T. R. Cressy, who continued until 1852. He, in turn, gave way to Rev. Sidney Dyer, who labored until 1857, and was followed by Rev. J. B. Simmons, who preached from 1858 to 1861. On the morning of the first Sunday, in January, 1861, the church building was destroyed by fire, and for a time after that, the congregation worshiped in Masonic Hall. Mr. Simmons resigned the pastorate in 1861, and Rev. Henry Day, of Philadelphia, was called to the vacant pulpit. Mr. Day accepted the call, has been the pastor of the church ever since, and has fully earned his high place in the public estimation, without as within his congregation. To repair the destruction caused by the fire, the church at once purchased a desirable site on the north-east corner of New York and Pennsylvania streets, and in 1862, began the erection of the commodious and handsome brick edifice shown in the accompanying engraving.

Under the ministration of Rev. Mr. Day, the church has enjoyed an uninterrupted progress; so that to-day, in respect of the extent and character of its congregation, and of influence, it occupies the front rank in the numerous religious societies of Indianapolis.

The present number of members is five hundred and fifty-eight.

The Sabbath-School is also in a highly prosperous condition. For a period of over twenty years, it was under the charge of the late J. R. Osgood, to whose eminent zeal, piety, and efficiency, a large measure of its prosperity is due. The school now numbers over six hundred scholars.

The church building, though not strictly homogeneous and "true" in respect of its architecture, is nevertheless, a commodious and elegant edifice; and its internal appointments are of the first class. It cost about $50,000; and will readily seat twelve hundred people. It has a fine organ that cost $2,500. Its erection was one of the fruits of that quite recent spirit of rivalry in splendor of church architecture, that has resulted in making Indianapolis eminent for the number of its elegant church edifices.

The officers for the present year are as follow:

Pastor.—Reverend Henry Day, D. D.

Deacons.—E. C. Atkins, H. S. Gillet, and J. M. Sutton.

Trustees.—C. P. Jacobs, J. W. Smither, E. J. Foster, H. Knippenberg, H. C. Martin, J. M. Sutton, S. C. Hanna, and W. C. Smock.

SOUTH STREET BAPTIST CHURCH.

Location: Corner of South and Noble streets.

The "Home Church" (as the First Baptist Church is called) purchased a lot on the corner of South and Noble streets, erected a neat brick chapel thereon, and began a mission in that part of the city. A Sunday-School was at once established, which developed a deep interest, and in 1869, seventy-six of the members of the First Church withdrew by letter, and formed a new society known as the *South Street Baptist Church*, receiving from the parent body a free gift of the chapel building and grounds. This church now enjoys a happy prosperity under the pastorate of Rev. William Elgin.

The number of members is about one hundred; Sabbath-School membership, two hundred and fifty.

The value of the property is about $10,000.

GARDEN MISSION.

Location: Corner of Washington and Missouri streets.

A second mission interest was established by the First Church, in 1866, in the old German theater, on the corner of Tennessee street and Kentucky avenue. It now occupies the building at the corner of Washington and Missouri streets, and sustains a weekly prayer meeting, and a Sunday-School of one hundred and fifty scholars. · Henry Knippenberg, Esq., is the Superintendent.

NORTH BAPTIST MISSION.

In April, 1870, a third mission interest was established on the corner of Cherry and Broadway streets, and is now known as the *North Baptist Mission*. This interest sustains a Sunday-School of about one hundred and seventy pupils, under the charge of C. P. Jacobs, Esq., Superintendent. Preaching every Sunday, a weekly prayer meeting on Tuesday evening, and an adult Bible class. A neat chapel, thirty-two by forty-five feet, has been erected and furnished, and a church will doubtless be organized here during the coming year.

The value of the property is about $6,000.

SECOND BAPTIST CHURCH—(COLORED.)

Location: M'chigan street, between Indiana avenue and West street.

This church was founded in the year 1846, by the Rev. Mr. Sachel, a missionary of Cincinnati. The services of the congregation were first held in a school house on Alabama street. In 1849, they built their first house of worship, on North Missouri street, between Ohio and New York streets. It was a small building, twenty by thirty feet; and was burned in the winter of 1851. The building was not insured, and the congregation for some time afterward, worshiped in a house near the corner of North and Blackford streets, owned by John Brown, Esq., (now deceased), who was a deacon of the church, and a prime mover in building the first and second houses of worship of the congregation.

In the latter part of the year 1852, the church building was rebuilt, on the site occupied by the building that had been burned. It was a cheap, one story structure, twenty-six by thirty-six feet; and was enlarged in 1864. The congregation seem to have always been both prosperous and enterprising; and accordingly we find them commencing the erection of a more commodious house of worship, in September, 1867.

It will, when completed, be a neat and capacious building, reflecting great credit on the congregation, considering the means at their disposal and the obstacles they had to overcome. The dimensions are sixty-three feet square. The basement has been completed and occupied, and the building will be completed in due time.

The auditorum will occupy an entire story, with a ceiling twenty-two and one-half feet in height, and a gallery all around. The extreme elevation at the top of the belfry, will be one hundred and five feet. The cost of the completed structure will be about $16,000. The congregation has been served by the following pastors.

Joshua Harmon, (since deceased), 1848–51; Jesse Young, 1852–53; J. J. Fitzgerald, (since deceased,) 1853–5; George Butler, 1855–6; Pleasant Bowles, 1857, (for six months); and Rev. Moses Broyles, the present pastor, who is now in the fourteenth year of his pastoral relation to the congregation. For the want of method and system in the administration of its affairs, the church underwent many trials and vicissitudes during the first eleven years of its existence. When Mr. Broyles took charge of affairs in 1857, the membership was not more than twenty-five; now it is four hundred and thirty-five, and steadily increasing. The usual Sabbath and week day religious services, are regularly held in this church. Its affairs are now methodically administered, and it has all the officers of a well appointed, thoroughly organized church. The Sabbath-School, of which Andrew Lewis is superintendent, has two hundred and sixty-five members, and is divided into twenty classes, with as many teachers.

Summary—Total membership of the Baptist Church in Indianapolis, one thousand and ninety-three; total Sabbath-School membership, one thousand two hundred and sixty-five; total value of church property, $76,000.

CONGREGATIONAL.

PLYMOUTH CHURCH.

Location: Meridian street, near Circle Park.

This church was organized August 9th, 1857. The original membership consisted of thirty-one persons, a majority of whom joined by letter from other churches in this city. For several months previous to the organization, these members supported religious worship and a Sabbath-School in the Senate Chamber of the State House. There the church continued to worship (except for a short period, during which services were held in Ramsey's Hall on Illinois street), until their removal to their present edifice on the north-west corner of Circle and Meridian streets. For a few months after the organization, Rev. W. C. Bartlett officiated as minister.

The original officers of the church were as follow:

Trustees.—A. G. Willard, E. T. Sinker, W. W. Roberts, E. J. Baldwin.

Deacons.—Horace Bassett, Albert G. Willard, Edward T. Sinker, Benjamin M. Ludden.

Clerk.—E. Montgomery.

Treasurer.—Albert G. Willard.

Rev. N. A. Hyde, the first pastor, entered upon his duties in October, 1868, and resigned the pastorate in August, 1867, to become Superintendent of the American Home Missionary Society for Indiana.

Rev. E. P. Ingersoll, the next pastor, commenced his labors March 1st, 1868, and resigned January, 1870.

Rev. Joseph L. Bennett, the third and present pastor, entered upon his duties in January, 1871.

The officers at the present time are the following:

Trustees.—S. A. Fletcher, E. T. Sinker, (died April 5th, 1871), N. R. Smith, S. A. Fletcher, Jr.

Deacons.—H. S. Rockey, A. G. Willard, I. S. Bigelow.

Clerk.—Jared M. Bills.

Treasurer.—Albert B. Willard.

The membership of the church now numbers about two hundred. The Sabbath-School, John Martin, superintendent, numbers about one hundred and twenty-five.

The house of worship occupied by this church was commenced in the fall of 1858; the front part, containing the lecture room, pastor's study and social rooms, was completed in September, 1859; this was occupied as the place of worship by the congregation until the main audience room was erected, in 1866.

Of the church building extensive improvements, both external and internal, were commenced in October, 1870; and the reconstructed and improved edifice was dedicated on the 30th of April, 1871, at which time the present pastor, the Rev. Joseph L. Bennett, was installed.

The house of worship, if surpassed by others in size and architectural splendor, is nevertheless one of the most pleasant and convenient in this city of elegant and costly church buildings.

The value of building and site is about $38,000.

MAY FLOWER CHURCH.

Location: Corner of St. Clair and East streets.

A Sabbath-School, organized by the Young Men's Christian Association, at a small private house on the corner of Jackson and Cherry streets, resulted in the organization of the present Mayflower Congregational Church, on the 23d May, 1869. The original membership consisted of thirteen members, who united with the church by letter: five from the Plymouth Congregational Church of this city; two from the Third Street M. E. Church; one from Roberts Park M. E. Church; three from the Fourth Presbyterian Church.

The church building, located as above, was dedicated in January, 1870. It is a frame building, forty by sixty feet, and simple and neat in its architectural aspects. From the time of organization as a church until November, 1870, the Rev. C. M. Sanders was pastor. He was succeeded on the 1st April, 1871, by the Rev. G. W. Barnum, the present pastor.

Forty-three members have united with the church since its organization.

The present number of members is about thirty-five. The Sabbath-School has about two hundred and twenty five pupils.

The present officers are: M. S. Whitehead and J. R. Irving, Deacons; Andrew Fisher, Treasurer; E. D. Olin, Clerk; S. A. Fletcher, Andrew Fisher and E. D. Olin, Trustees.

The value of the church property is about $5,000.

Summary—Total membership of the Congregational Denomination in Indianapolis, two hundred and thirty-five; total Sabbath-School membership, three hundred and fifty; total value of church property, $43,000.

CHRISTIAN.

CHRISTIAN CHAPEL.

Location: South-west corner of Ohio and Delaware streets.

This society was organized on the 12th January, 1833. Dr. John H. Sanders and Peter H. Roberts were its first ruling elders. The number of names enrolled at the time of organization was twenty. Eld. John O'Kane may appropriately be considered the Father of this church. He visited the city in the latter part of 1832, and started the movement that led to the organization of the society, of which he was the first preacher.

During the early history of the church, and when it most needed aid, Ovid Butler, Esq., Robert A. Taylor, (since deceased, and father of Hon. Napoleon B. Taylor, of this city), Dr. John H. Sanders, (father of Mrs. Governor Wallace, Mrs. R. B. Duncan and Mrs. Dr. Gatling, of this city), and Mr. Charles Secrest were fast and liberal friends of the enterprise, and contributed freely to its support.

Elder O'Kane, J. L. Jones, M. Combs, L. H. Jameson, A. Prather and others visited the city during the early years of the church, to hold protracted meetings, which were generally successful. B. K. Smith, and Elder Chauncey Butler were resident laborers in this service. Through these instrumentalities the church gradually grew in strength; and a house of worship was built in the summer of 1836, on Kentucky avenue.

On the 1st October, 1842, at the instance of Elder O'Kane, Elder L. H. Jameson became resident evangelist, in which service he continued until 1853. During the latter year the congregation occupied the present church edifice. At this date the membership had increased to three hundred and seventy-five.

The succession of pastors thenceforward was: Elders James M. Mathes, for one year; L. H. Jameson, one year; Elder Elijah Goodwin, three years; Elder Perry Hall, three years; Elder O. A. Burgess, seven years; Elder W. F. Black, the present pastor, who has served the church for two years.

Christian Chapel ranks among the leading churches of the city. The present number of members is about six hundred. The Sabbath-School has about two hundred members.

The church building is quite plain externally; but is attractively furnished and appointed within.

The value of the building and site is about $35,000,

SECOND CHRISTIAN CHURCH (COLORED).

Location: First street, between Mississippi street and the Lafayette Railway.

This society was established in the spring of 1867, as a mission of the First Christian Church of this city, Prominent in its establishment and support during its infancy were Messrs. W. W. Dowling and J. M. Tilford. As soon as possible, and in a short time, a house of worship was secured at the above stated location. It is an unpretentious frame building, but sufficient to meet the present wants of the society; having capacity for about two hundred and fifty persons.

The society consists of about one hundred members. The Sabbath-School is in a prosperous state, having about one hundred and twenty-five members.

Rev. Rufus Conrad, the present pastor, has served the society in that relation ever since its organization.

The value of the building and site is about $2,000.

THIRD CHRISTIAN CHURCH.

Location: Forest-Home avenue, near Ash street.

In the spring of 1867 a Sunday-School was organized at the North-western Christian University, and placed in charge of Prof. A. C. Shortridge, who was mainly instrumental in its establishment. Out of this grew the organization of the Third Church, which took place in the chapel of the University on the first Sabbath in January, 1869. For the first year of its existence the congregation had no regular minister, but maintained the usual weekly meetings, with preaching by various ministers as their services could be obtained. The second year the services of Austin Council were secured as pastor. Since then Elder Elijah Goodwin has been serving in that capacity.

The church has built a comfortable house of worship on Forest-Home avenue, near Ash street,—a frame building, sixty feet long and thirty-four wide, with a baptistry under the pulpit platform, and dressing rooms in the rear. The society numbers something over one hundred members. The Sabbath-School has about one hundred and seventy-five members.

The value of the property is about $8,000.

The present officers are:

Elders.—E. Goodwin, J. M. Tilford, J. M. Bramwell, R. T. Brown.

Deacons.—A. C. Shortridge, H. C. Guffin, R. M. Cosby, J. P. Elliott.

FOURTH CHRISTIAN CHURCH.

Location: Corner of Fayette and Walnut streets.

This organization began as a Mission Sabbath-School on Sunday, 28th June, 1868, at a dwelling on Blake street. Here the school continued to meet every Sabbath day until the following November, when the place of meeting was changed to a room on the corner of New York and Blake streets. In the following winter the mission was organized as a church society by Elder J. B. New as pastor, with W. W. Dowling as superintendent of the Sabbath-School. In the summer of 1869, the place of worship was changed to a small hall on Indiana avenue, where the services were held until the close of the year 1870. On the 1st of January, 1871, the present house of worship was dedicated.

The chapel is a neat wooden structure, capable of seating about three hundred persons; and cost, including the site, about $4,000.

The present membership of the society is about one hundred; that of the Sabbath-School, about one hundred and twenty-five.

Elders John B. New, L. H. Jameson, W. W. Dowling and others have filled the pulpit from time to time. The society is yet without a regular pastor.

SALEM CHAPEL.

Location: Corner of Illinois and Fifth streets.

This is a prosperous mission of the First Church. The house of worship was dedicated on the 25th December, 1870, by Elder W. F. Black. The Sabbath-School, under the superintendence of Geo. W. Snyder, has about two hundred members. The prospects are excellent that this mission will, at no distant day, be discharged from its wardship to the parent organization, and become a separate and flourishing church. The value of the present building and site is about $4,000.

OLIVE MISSION.

Location : Corner of Tennessee and Fourth streets.

This is also a mission of the First Church, and was founded in 1869. Its services are now held in a rented building; but its members expect (an expectation warranted by the growth of the enterprise) to build a suitable edifice at an early date for the use of the mission.

The Sabbath-School, of which Jasper Finney is superintendent, numbers about one hundred and seventy-five members.

Summary—Total membership of the Christian denomination in Indianapolis, about nine hundred; total Sabbath-School membership, one thousand. Total value of church property, $53,000.

GERMAN REFORMED.

There are two societies of this Denomination in Indianapolis: the First and Second German Reformed Churches.

This denomination is a branch of the church of the great Reformation inaugurated in Germany in the sixteenth century, and the source of the present numerous family of Protestant denominations. Among the fathers of the German Reformed Church were Zwingle, Melancthon and Calvin, whose creed differed in several respects from that of the Father of the German Reformation, Luther.

The Lutheran and German Reformed denominations originated about the same time (A. D., 1519): the former in Northern Germany; the latter in Switzerland, whence it spread into Southern Germany, France, Holland and England.

The German Reformed Church first obtained a foothold in this country in the year 1740, in Pennsylvania, where the Rev. Mr. Schlatter labored as the first German missionary of that church in North America. Thence arose the German Reformed Synod of the United States, and the other Synods that labor through the Board of Domestic missions of the German Reformed Church

This much by way of preliminary observations upon the denomination in general.

THE FIRST GERMAN REFORMED CHURCH OF INDIANAPOLIS

Is located on Alabama street, between Washington and Market streets.

In the fall of 1851 the Board of Domestic Missions sent to this city, to labor as its missionary, the Rev. George Long. He began by preaching every Sabbath day in the Court house. Before long he had succeeded so well that he was enabled to organize a congregation, who in the spring of 1852, began the erection of a house of worship on the above location, which was dedicated in October of the same year. In November, 1856, Mr. Long resigned his pastorate, and on the 25th of the following month the Rev. M. G. I. Stern was elected his successor. During the ministry of Mr. Stern his church ceased to be a missionary enterprise, and became a self-supporting society. The debts of the church were all paid, and it steadily grew in membership and in the attendance upon its services.

On the 26th July, 1865, the Rev. Henry Echmeier succeeded Mr. Stern, and became pastor of the church. During his pastorate the church building was enlarged to its present dimensions and otherwise improved.

Mr. Echmeier resigned after serving the church over three years as its minister; and the Rev. J. S. Barth is now the supply of this congregation.

The house of worship is a plain but neat brick building. The present membership of the church is about two hundred; that of the Sabbath-School, nearly the same number.

Some of the founders and prominent early supporters of this church are still active members. Among these are J. W. Brown, at present elder and superintendent of the Sabbath-School, Henry W. Tenneman, William Stolte, Frederick Kortepeter, Frederick Schowe, Henry Kruse and Herman Kortepeter.

The value of the property of the society is about $12,000.

SECOND GERMAN REFORMED CHURCH.

Location: South side of East street, south of Merrill.

This society was organized in the summer of 1867, by several members of an extinct church organization, living in the south-eastern quarter of the city. The Rev. Mr. Steinbach, who had labored here as a Lutheran missionary, took charge of the young society thus established. He served for a brief period, resigning at the close of the year 1867.

At a meeting of members held on the 1st January, 1868, the Rev. M. G. I. Stern was selected as Mr. Steinbach's successor in this missionary field. The result was the organization, in the autumn of 1869, of a second church of the German Reformed denomination in Indianapolis.

Mr. Stern is still the pastor of this church; which has been a prosperous society from the first. The present number of members is about one hundred, and the average attendance upon Sabbath-day services about two hundred and fifty to three hundred.

Connected with this church is a German-English parochial school, with an average attendance of about one hundred pupils, and having two instructors. The Sabbath-School membership is about two hundred and fifty.

The church building is a plain neat, frame structure, having capacity for five hundred communicants.

The property of the church is valued at about $9,000.

Summary—Total membership of the German Reformed Church of Indianapolis, three hundred; total Sabbath-School membership, about four hundred and fifty; total value of church property, $21,000.

THE SOCIETY OF FRIENDS.

There is but one church of this denomination in Indianapolis. The house of worship is located on the corner of Delaware and St. Clair streets.

The church was organized in the year 1854. For two years the small congregation held their religious services in the old Lutheran church building, on North Pennsylvania street, near St. Clair. The officiating minister during this period was Mrs Hannah Pierson, from Lockport, New York. In 1866 the society built their present house of worship, located as above stated. The next ministers of the church were David Tatum and Hannah B. Tatum.

In 1865 the society organized a "monthly meeting," and has had the following resident ministers: Jane Trueblood, W. G. Johnson, Barnabas C. Hobbs, and Enos G. Pray.

The present number of members is about two hundred and forty-six. The Sabbath-School has about eighty members. The value of the property is about $12,000.

(15)

METHODIST.

MERIDIAN STREET M. E. CHURCH.

Location : South west corner of Meridian and New York streets.

This church society, long known as *Wesley Chapel M. E. Church*, was the pioneer organization of the Methodist denomination in this city, and occupies toward the numerous family of Methodist churches in Indianapolis to-day, the relation of a tree to its branches.

To begin with the beginning of the history of this church, it is necessary to go back to the year 1822, when the Indianapolis Circuit of the Indiana District of the Methodist Episcopal Church was organized by Rev. William Cravens, who had been appointed to this circuit at the session of the Missouri Conference.

In 1825, the Missouri Conference was divided, the Illinois Conference was created, and the Indiana District became a part of the latter body.

In 1829, Indianapolis Station was formed. This station subsequently passed within the limits of the Madison District, created in 1830; of the Indiana Conference, created in 1832; and of the Indianapolis District of the latter Conference, created in 1833.

At the session of the Indiana Conference, held in Centerville, on the 19th of October, 1842, the Indianapolis Station was divided into two charges: The Western (Wesley Chapel), and the Eastern (Roberts Chapel).

At the session of the Indiana Conference, held in Madison, on the 16th October, 1845, the charge was again divived, forming the central charge, (Wesley Chapel), and the western charge (Strange Chapel).

In 1870, the society took the name of Meridian street M. E. Church, from the location of their elegant new church edifice, now nearly completed.

For many years, the society, of which the present Meridian Street Church is the development and continuation, occupied as a house of worship the well-remembered *Wesley Chapel* building, on the south-west corner of Meridian and Circle streets. This familiar and weather-scarred structure, gave way, in the year 1869, for the erection on its site of the present *Sentinel Building*.

The society purchased a site on the south-west corner of Meridian and New York streets; on which a costly and artistic house of worship is now near completion. The basement has for sometime been occupied, and the edifice will be completed and dedicated during the present summer.

Between the dates of the abandonment of the Wesley Chapel building and of the occupation of the yet unfinished structure, the congregation worshipped in the building of the Second Universalist Church.

The circuit preachers, stationed preachers, and presiding elders, have been as follows:

1821—Rev. William Cravens, Circuit Preacher. 1822-3, Samuel Hamilton, Presiding Elder; James Scott, Circuit Preacher. 1823-4, William Beauchamp, Presiding Elder; Jesse Hale and George Horn, Circuit Preachers.

In 1825, on the division of the Missouri Conference, John Strange become Presiding Elder, and John Miller, Circuit Preacher. 1825-6, John Strange, Presiding Elder; Thomas Hewston, Circuit Preacher. 1826-7, John Strange, Presiding Elder; Edwin Ray, Circuit Preacher. 1827-8, John Strange, Presiding Elder; N. Griffith, Circuit Preacher 1828-9, John Strange, Presiding Elder; James Armstrong, Stationed Preacher. 1829 to 1832, Allen Wiley, Presiding Elder; Thos.

Hitt, Stationed Preacher. 1832-3, John Strange, Presiding Elder ; Benj. O. Stevenson, Stationed Preacher. 1833, Allen Wiley, Presiding Elder; C. W. Ruter, Stationed Preacher. 1833-4, James Havens, Presiding Elder; C. W. Ruter, Stationed Preacher. 1834-5, Jas. Havens, Presiding Elder; E. R. Ames, Stationed Preacher. 1835-6, James Havens, Presiding Elder; J. C. Smith, Stationed Preacher. 1836-7, James Havens, Presiding Elder; A Eddy, Stationed Preacher. 1837-8, A. Eddy, Presiding Elder; J. C. Smith, Stationed Preacher. 1838-9, A. Eddy, Presiding Elder; A. Wiley, Stationed Preacher. 1839-40, A. Eddy, Presiding Elder; A. Wiley, Stationed Preacher. 1840-1, James Havens Presiding Elder ; W. II. Goode, Stationed Preacher. 1841-2, James Havens, Presiding Elder; W. H. Goode, Stationed Preacher.

1842-3—"Indianapolis station " having been divided into two charges, James Havens was appointed Presiding Elder, and L. W. Berry Stationed Preacher, of the Western charge (Wesley Chapel).

1843-4—Same appointments. A building committee, consisting of Alfred Harrison, Thos. Rickards, and Bentley Alley, was appointed to erect a parsonage building on the church lot.

1844-5—L. W. Berry, Presiding Elder, and W. W. Hibben, stationed preacher, Superintendent Sabbath-Schools, J. J. Drum, A. W. Morris and Mrs. Eliza Drum.

1845-6—L. W. Berry, Presiding Elder; Wm. V. Daniels, Stationed Preacher.

1846-7—Rev. E. R. Ames, Presiding Elder, and W. V. Daniels Stationed Preachers. Salary of Stationed Preacher, $550.

1847-8—Rev. E. R. Ames, Presiding Elder; Rev. F. C. Holliday, Stationed Preacher. Same salary.

1848-9—Same appointments. Salary of Preacher increased to $600

1849-50—Rev. E. R. Ames, Presiding Elder; Rev. J. S. Bayless, Stationed Preacher. Salary of latter, $500.

1850-51—Rev. C. W. Ruter, Presiding Elder; Rev. B. F. Crary Stationed Preacher. Salary, $600.

1851-2—James Havens, Presiding Elder; Giles E. Smith, Stationed Preacher.

1852-3—B. F. Crary, Presiding Elder; John Kurns, Stationed Preacher. Salary of preacher, $700.

1853-4—B. F. Crary, Presiding Elder; J. P. Linderman, Stationed Preacher.

1854-5—B. F. Crary, Presiding Elder; James H. Noble, Stationed Preacher.

1856-7—W. C. Smith, Presiding Elder; James Hill, Stationed Preacher.

1858-9—Wm. C. Smith, Presiding Elder; E T. Fletcher, Stationed Preacher.

1860-2—Jas. H Noble, Presiding Elder; C. D. Battelle, Stationed Preacher.

1862-4—Jas Hill, Presiding Elder; S. T. Gillett, Stationed Preacher.

1864-6—James Hill, Presiding Elder; Wm. McK. Hester, Stationed Preacher.

1866-7—S. T. Gillett, Presiding Elder; Wm. McK. Hester, Stationed Preacher.

1867-8—S. T. Gillett, Presiding Elder; C. N. Sims, Stationed Preacher.

1868-70—B. F. Rawlins, Presiding Elder; C. N. Sims, Stationed Preacher.

1870-71—B. F. Rawlins, Presiding Elder; R. Andrus, Stationed Preacher.

The present membership of the church numbers five hundred and four; that of the Sabbath-School, four hundred and eighty-nine.

The pastoral labor is performed by Rev. Reuben Andrus.

The following persons constitute the "Official Board," who, in their respective departments, supply the work of the church:

Trustees—Oliver Tousey, Ingram Fletcher, A. Ballard, V. T. Malott, Daniel Stewart, J. H. Ross, Jacob P. Dunn, Dr. H. E. Carey, C. W. Smith.

Stewards—J. F. Ramsey, J. C. Yohn, T. P. Haughey, Jason Carey, Aaron Ohr, J. M. Ridenour, F. A. W. Davis, J. H. Colclazer, J. H. Osborn.

Class Leaders.—R. Ferguson, T. P. Haughey, A. Ballard, R. S. Carr, I. Taylor, B. V. Enos

Local Preachers.—E. T. Fletcher, T. A. Goodwin, J. C. McCoy, R. Ferguson.

Committees. Missionary.—J. M. Ridenour, C. W. Smith, Charles Dennis, Wilson Morrow.

Sunday-School.—Dr. H. G. Cary, C. W. Smith, R. S. Carr.

Tract Cause.—R. Ferguson, J. H. Ross, Aaron Ohr.

The principal officers of the Sabbath-School are:

Superintendents.—Wilson Morrow, H. G. Carey, Mrs. Theo. P. Haughey.

Secretaries.—J. H. Colclazer, Miss Annie Dunlop.

Treasurer.—J. S. Carey.

Fifty per cent. of the entire school are adults, and about one-half of the membership of the church, including twenty-one out of twenty-three of the active members of the official board, are engaged in the Sabbath-School.

The church edifice has a front of seventy-three feet on Meridian street, and a depth of one hundred and twenty-one feet on New York street. Its walls, towers and buttresses are built of a bluish-looking lime stone, with cut-stone trimmings, and irregularly laid and neatly pointed. The style of its architecture is the Modern Gothic; after designs of Messrs. Enos & Huebner, of this city. Externally the principal feature of the building is the front, the center of which is flanked on either side by a graceful, buttressed tower, terminating in a lofty spire (not yet completed). The center terminates in a high gable, surmounted by the Rock of Ages—the Cross of Christ. On each side of the center are wings, whose corners are strengthened and ornamented by buttressed turrets. The sides of the walls are also buttressed.

The entrance is by three large doors, whose arches are supported by richly ornamented columns. Above the entrance is a large and very beautiful rose window, elaborately ornamented. The entrance is into a spacious vestibule, leading into the lecture room in the first story, and into the audience room in the second story. The first story contains the lecture room, sixty-two by forty-six feet; two infant class rooms, ladies' parlors, the class room, and the pastor's study. The windows of this story are all of beautiful stained glass. From the rear of the first story a long winding stairway leads to the audience room.

But it is in the decorations and appointments of the audience-room that this edifice especially excels. Its dimensions are sixty-six by eighty-seven feet. Its height at the sides is twenty-six feet; at the center, forty-three feet. The ceiling is highly ornamented. The pews, which are of elegant pattern and finish, are curvilinearly arranged. The most artistic features are its elaborately ornamented windows, each one of which typifies in its design, some one of the prominent attributes of the Christian religion. This room will easily seat one thousand persons.

The total cost of the property will be about $100,000.

ROBERTS PARK M. E. CHURCH.

Location: Corner of Delaware and Vermont streets.

This society was organized in October, 1842, by a division of the Meridian Street congregation (then called "Wesley Chapel," and worshiping on the corner of Circle and Meridian streets)· The new congregation was called "The Eastern

'Charge"—the city being then divided by the Conference into two charges separated by Meridian street.

The first pastor was the Rev. John S. Bayless; the first place of worship, the Court house. At the end of the first year the membership numbered three hundred and twenty-two.

The society was active and energetic from the first; and within a short period after its organization, it had erected a commodious church building on the northeast corner of Pennsylvania and Market streets, which was christened *Roberts Chapel*, in honor of the famous Bishop Roberts. This building, so long a religious landmark of the city, gave way in 1868 to the encroaching march of commerce; and the same reasons that made its site valuable to the uses of trade, also recommended the purchase of a new site for the church, less surrounded by the noise of business, and more appropriate for Divine worship. So the venerable building disappeared, and on its site a business block was erected.

The congregation purchased an acre of ground, fronting on Delaware and Vermont streets; and in the center of this ample space a splendid and substantial edifice is rising. Pending its erection the congregation have been worshiping in an old frame building, near the location of the new edifice, which has been aptly named Roberts' Chapel Tabernacle.

The elegant structure now in process of erection is in the *Renaissance* style of architecture, one hundred and twenty-three by seventy feet, and will be surmounted by a lofty spire. The walls will be of white magnesia lime stone.

The entrance to the main audience room is from the west, fronting on Delaware street. The entrance to the lecture room is from the south side of the church, fronting on Vermont street; the entrance is into a short hall, on the east side of which is the Sabbath-School and church library room. There are two large double doors from this hall, one opening into the lecture room, and the other into the church parlor and infant class room. Its dimension are fifty by sixty-two feet, and including the church parlor and infant class room, which connect with it by large folding doors, will be capable of seating eight hundred persons. The wood work is of oiled ash. The ceiling is divided into nine large pannels, with elegant wooden cornices; and from the center of each pannel hangs a chandalier. The room is lighted by six double windows. All the windows of the church are of ground glass; the body of each light is plain, with a vine border around the edge. The upper part of each window is semi-circular, and furnished with a beautiful emblem or motto. The main audience room will seat one thousand three hundred persons. A gallery will encircle the auditorium around its entire extent. The organ loft and singers' gallery will be in the rear of the pulpit. The estimated cost of the building, including the site, is $150,000.

The congregation has been characterized by great spirituality and energy as a religious organization, and has set off several flourishing colonies: Asbury Church, on South New Jersey street; Trinity, on the corner of North and Alabama streets; and Grace Church, on the corner of East and Market streets, are all offshoots from Roberts, Chapel.

The church membership numbers five hundred and twenty-seven; that of the Sabbath-School, three hundred and fifty-two.

Roberts Park Church has been served by the following pastors, in the order given:

Revs. John S. Bayless, John L. Smith, George M. Beswick, Samuel T. Gillett, John H. Hall, William Wilson, Samuel T. Cooper, William H. Barnes, J. W. T.

McMullen, C. W. Miller, W. Wilson, H. Colclazer, John V. R. Miller, A. S. Kinnan, W. II. Mendenhall, F. C. Holliday. The present pastor, the Rev. Dr. Holliday, now in the third year of his pastorate, is widely known, as well without as within his denomination, as an able and effective minister—a conspicuous light, for many years, in the Methodist church of Indiana.

The principal officers of the church are: Rev. F. C. Holliday, D. D., Pastor; John B. Abbett, Local Elder; Thomas A. Nelson, Local Preacher; George W. Ackert, Local Preacher.

Church Trustees—Dr. L. Abbett, John W. Ray, A. G. Porter, George Tousey, Frederick Baggs, J. F. Wingate, W. II. Craft.

Sunday-School Superintendent, John W. Ray; Assistant Superintendent, W. L. Heiskell; Female Superintendent, Mrs. Anna C. Baggs.

ST. JOHN'S M. E. CHURCH.

Location: Corner of California and North streets.

This society was organized under the name of the Western Charge (west of the canal), in the year 1845. The first minister appointed to the charge was the Rev. Wesley Dorsey.

A frame building for the use of the congregation was built on Michigan street, west of the canal, and christened *Strange Chapel*, in honor of Rev. John Strange, an eminent and honored pioneer of the Methodist church in Indiana, whose remains lie in the old cemetery of this city. This building soon proved to be disadvantageously located, and it was accordingly removed to a site on Tennessee street, near Vermont.

At a quarterly meeting conference, held January 12th, 1869, the following resolution was adopted and put upon the minutes:

"*Resolved*, That it is the sense of this Quarterly Conference, that the prosperity of the charge, spiritually and financially, will be promoted by its adherence to the old usages of the church, especially in the seating of the congregation, and singing; and that the Conference hereby pledge the charge to stand by these usages."

This resolution was passed to accommodate some wealthy members, who did not believe in promiscuous or pew sittings, nor in choral or instrumental music. The result was the withdrawal of about one-half of the membership from the church by letter, and the addition of but four or five other members to the church during the ensuing quarter.

During the year 1869 the church property on West Michigan street was sold, and a new house of worship built, located on the corner of Michigan and Tennessee streets. This building, erected at a cost of $13,000, was dedicated on the 9th of January, 1870. To secure the further religious exercises of the congregation against all innovations on "old fashioned Methodism," provisions to that effect were incorporated in the body of the conveyance of the site. The edifice dedicated to these principles stood but one year, and was consumed by fire on Sunday, the 8th January, 1871.

Several months prior to the latter date, the membership had become divided on the question of receiving the pastor appointed by the Conference. The majority, but least wealthy, of the members were worshiping in Strange Chapel at the time of its destruction by fire. The other division, the lesser in numbers, the greater in wealth, had been worshiping in the building of the Second Universalist church congregation, over the way from Strange Chapel.

The church property—that portion which had not been destroyed by fire—was sold; and the remainder of the congregation, at length a unit in belief and action, have since held their religious services in Kuhn's Hall, with Mr. Walters as pastor.

The third quarterly conference, held March 6th, 1871, appointed a committee to purchase a lot on which to erect a house of worship. A building committee consisting of D. B. Hosbrook, Rev. G. Morgan and J. A. Gregg, were appointed and invested with plenary power to devise plans and erect a suitable building for the use of the congregation.

By a unanimous vote the name of the church was changed to *St. John's M. E. Church*, and the leaders' and stewards' meetings, and boards of trustees, were authorized to transact business hereafter under that name.

The purchasing committee has selected a lot on the corner of California and North streets, sixty by ninety-five feet, for which $1,400 was paid, and on which a church is to be built, in the Norman style of architecture, to cost from $12,000 to $15,000. The church is to be completed by the 1st of July, 1871, with the Rev. L. M. Walters, as pastor.

The society, dating from the last schism, is reported to be in a flourishing condition. The present membership numbers about one hundred and forty. The Sabbath-School has one hundred and fifty members.

From Strange Chapel sprung a flourishing local mission enterprise, which has since become the Third Street M. E. Church, elsewhere mentioned.

The following is a list of the pastors who have served Strange Chapel since its organization:

Rev. Wesley Dorsey, Rev. D. Crawford, Rev. Wm. Morrow, Rev. T. G. Beharrell, Rev. Frank Taylor, Rev. E. D. Long, Rev. T. S. Webb, Rev. G. M. Boyd, Rev. Griffith Morgan, Rev. William Graham, Rev. N. L. Brakeman, Rev. J. C. Reed, Rev. James Havens, Rev. J. W. Green, Rev. C. S. Burgner, Rev. G. W. Telle, Rev. J. W. T. McMullen, and Rev. L. M. Walters.

ASBURY M. E. CHURCH.

Location: New Jersey street between Louisiana and South streets.

This church was organized in 1849, under the name of the Depot and Indianapolis East Mission. It was a colony of Roberts Chapel Church, to which congregation collectively, and to the Rev. William H. Goode, Presiding Elder of the Indianapolis District of the Northern Indiana Conference especially, it owes its existence as a church. The original membership was composed entirely of Methodists residing in the southern part of the city, and who had previously been members of Roberts Chapel Church.

During the period of its wardship to Roberts Chapel, Asbury Church was controlled and sustained by the quarterly conference of that body, aided by a small missionary appropriation from the North Indiana Conference. Its first pastor, the Rev. Samuel T. Cooper, was a member of Roberts Chapel Quarterly Conference.

The first stewards of the Depot Mission, John Dunn, Theodore Mathews, John E. Ford, Miles J. Fletcher, and Richard Berry, were elected by the quarterly conference of Roberts Chapel Church, on the 17th of November, 1849. The connection of the mission with the parent body, and its dependence thereon, continued until the 9th of November, 1850.

The members of this young organization seem to have had their full share of difficulties and deprivations to encounter in rearing the infant charge to the stature of a grown-up and self-supporting church. In default of a better, they used as a place of worship an upper room in the freight depot of the Madison and Indianapolis Railroad Company, until the erection of their present church building, which was dedicated in the summer of 1852. Henceforth, the obstacles were few, and the progress was more rapid and less interrupted. The church is now in a prosperous condition, having a membership of two hundred and fifty, and a flourishing Sabbath-School of two hundred members.

The pastors of the church have been as follow, in the order given:

Rev. Samuel T. Cooper, Rev. J. B. De Motte, Rev. Samuel T. Gillett, Rev. Samuel P. Crawford, Rev. J. W. T. McMullen, Rev. Joseph Cotton, Rev. Asbury F. Hester, Rev. E. D. Long, Rev. John G. Chaffee, Rev. R. M. Barnes, Rev. W. W. Snyder, Rev. J. W. Mellender, Rev. F. C. Holliday, Rev. John H. Lozier, Rev. Samuel T. Gillett, and Rev. Charles Tinsley.

The present officers are:

Pastor.—Rev. Charles Tinsley.

Trustees.—Joseph Marsee, William Hannaman, George W. Hill, Valentine Rothrock, and William L. Wingate.

Stewards.—George W. Hill, R. L. Lukens, George W. Crouch, Andrew May, W. K. Davis, James Fisler, Isaiah G. Shafer, and Jacob Coffman.

Sabbath-School Superindent—James H. V. Smith.

The value of the church building and site is about $15,000.

The church owns a valuable lot on the south-east corner of South street and and Virginia avenue, valued at $10,000, on which it is proposed to erect a house of worship next year.

TRINITY M. E. CHURCH.

Location: North-west corner of North and Alabamba streets.

On the 17th May, 1854, a class of sixteen members of Roberts Chapel, led by J. W. Dorsey, Esq., met and organized as the "Seventh Church." The place of meeting then, and during the remainder of the year, was "Dorsey's School House," a small frame building, on the west side of North New Jersey street, north of Walnut.

The Sabbath-School was at first larger than the church membership, and in a short time the house of worship became too small for the society. The present location was then purchased; on one side of which, by the end of the year 1854, a plain brick church building was erected. Here the society, young and feeble, looking unpropitious circumstances resolutely in the face, began an earnest struggle for existence; and in the succeeding years has made gradual and sure progress over a way hedged up with formidable trials and obstacles.

The first pastor was Rev. Mr. Griffin, who served six months. At the end of his term, the name of the society was changed to *North Street M. E. Church.*

Following Mr. Griffin, as pastor, came Revs. William Holman, for three months; John C. Smith, one year and nine months; Frank A. Harding, one year and six months; John Hill, two years; C. P. Wright, one year; Charles Martindale, six months. Rev. Elijah Whitten filled out the remainder of Mr. Martindale's year, as supply.

For the years 1862 and 1863, the charge was left to be "supplied," various local preachers officiating, until Rev. George Betts, for a brief period, and after him, Rev. William Wilson, were regularly employed. In April, 1864, the Rev. W. J. Vigus was appointed to the charge. The Missionary Society appropriated $300 in payment of his salary. Mr. Vigus served three years.

In the spring of 1867 the Rev. R. D. Robinson succeeded Mr. Vigus; and it was during his pastorate that the church for the first time became self-sustaining.

By the action of the General Conference of 1868 on the question of boundaries, this church was transferred from the jurisdiction of the Northern to that of the South-Eastern Indiana Conference. In September of the same year the Rev. J. Monroe Crawford, the present pastor, was appointed. Mr. Crawford has been more than a pastor, simply, of the church; he has at the same time labored unremittingly, and with great success, to rescue the church from financial embarrassments.

The following clergymen have served the charge as Presiding Elders: Revs. James Hill, Augustus Eddy, H. Barnes, J. V. R. Miller, and R. D. Robinson, the present Presiding Elder.

The Sabbath-School has flourished from the first; now having an average attendance of two hundred and twenty-five, and an enrolled membership of three hundred and fifty. Its present Superintendent is Eli. F. Ritter, Esq.

The church has a total membership of two hundred and twenty-three, including the members on probation.

The present house of worship was dedicated on the first Sabbath in January, 1867, by the Rev. T. M. Eddy, D. D. The society now took its present name of *Trinity M. E. Church.*

The building—yet in an unfinished condition—is built of brick, with stone trimmings; dimensions, fifty by eighty feet; is pleasantly located; and is provided with permanent sittings for six hundred and twenty-eight persons. The property is valued at about $20,000.

The officers of the society are: John G. Smith, Local Elder; Christian Spiegle, John S. Dunlop, Eli F. Ritter, W. H. Smith, Rev. Henry Wright, Trustees.

AMES M. E. CHURCH.

Location: Corner of Madison Avenue and Union street.

The history of this church, though brief in chronology, is abundant in peculiar interest. Its establishment to-day on a firm and prosperous footing is not due to the liberality of an opulent membership, nor to any considerable extent to extrinsic assistance, nor to propitious chance; but pre-eminently to the persistent energy of a few persons of limited means.

Ames Church was organized by Rev. Joseph Tarkington, while he was city missionary for the four Annual Indiana Conferences, whose boundaries meet at Indianapolis. The field of the young church being within the limits of the Indiana Conference, a few members of Wesley Chapel purchased a lot on the corner of Norwood and South Illinois streets, upon which a small, rude tabernacle was placed, in July, 1866. In this humble structure Mr. Tarkington held services fortnightly; until the cold weather forced him to abandon the place. But "where there is a will there is a way;" and accordingly we find the young congregation worshiping for the next three months in an unoccupied grocery building, on Madison avenue. While thus situated, in February, 1867, a society, comprised of twelve members, was organized; a series of meetings followed; and a number of additions to the church, on probation, were made. A Sabbath-School was organized on the 1st of February, 1867.

On a lot, purchased for the purpose by members of Wesley Chapel, an unpretending place of worship for the congregation—twenty-four by forty feet—was meanwhile being erected. This was completed in March, 1867, and was occupied by the congregation during the same month.

In September, 1867, the Indiana Conference made an appropriation of $650, from the missionary funds, for the partial support of a pastor for the young church, and Rev. L. M. Walters was appointed to the charge. On entering upon his duties he found a congregation consisting of but twenty-one available members, and five probationers. The first fruit of his pastorate was a revival of religion, during the following winter, resulting in the addition of nearly one hundred members. The church now began to flourish; the house was insufficient; an addition was built in the summer of 1868, and this, too, was shortly filled. The increase of membership was so considerable, that the winter of 1868, found the building still inadequate. But the members were more abundant in exemplary zeal, than in this world's goods; and were unable to build the sort of an edifice their numbers and needs required. External aid was sought to no purpose; the time was unpropitious; the wealthier Methodist Churches of the city, were too much occupied with their own enterprises, to aid the young and struggling church. Its prospects were anything but promising. Here was a house full of poor members, unable to support the present establishment; no space for the necessary increase of accommodations; and no means at hand, or prospect of aid from without, to obtain a suitable site and erect a suitable building.

So discouraging was the prospect, that many of the members had about come to the conclusion to disunite with the church, and join some other society, better established, and free from unusual financial difficulties, as a means of ridding themselves of present and prospective church burdens.

The pastor, seeing that the church must take prompt and energetic action, if it was not to perish untimely, opened a vigorous campaign against the discouraging forces, and, over considerable opposition, effected the purchase of the Indianapolis Mission Sunday-School property, on the corner of Madison avenue and Union street. The price was $5,000; for the payment of which a period of five years was allowed. This gave the church a substantial brick building, forty by seventy-two feet; which they have occupied ever since June, 1869. The congregation, in addition to the purchase money, have expended $1,500 on repairs and improvements.

By an advantageous sale of their church property, on South Illinois street, for $4,000, the congregation have almost liquidated the debt incurred in obtaining their present church property, and the remainder of the debt will not mature for four years. The church, meanwhile, has flourished and become stronger; and, at length, after a succession of financial embarrassments, and a steady progress from a small beginning, Ames Church, in the fourth year of its age, is a fixed and flourishing society. Within the past three years there has been expended for the support of the church an aggregate of about $8,750; of which about $7,000 was raised within the church.

The membership now numbers about two hundred persons. The audience room will seat comfortably about three hundred; and if the church will not compare in splendor or magnitude with the older and more pretentious ones in this city, it can challenge any of them to show better results in proportion to the means of each. The Sabbath-School has about two hundred and twenty-five members. The present pastor is Rev. Joseph W. Asbury.

The church is under many obligations to *Wesley Chapel* for aid and encouragement in its darkest days. To the Rev. Mr. Walters praise is due for his unwearying patience and disinterested labors in an untempting field, to rescue the church from its manifold difficulties, and establish it on a firm and enduring basis, when so many embarrassments and discouragements combined against the struggling society.

GRACE M. C. CHURCH.

Location: North-east corner of Market and East streets.

At a meeting of the friends of a missionary movement for the planting of a Methodist church in the eastern part of Indianapolis, held on the 10th September, 1868, the following memorial was adopted:

" We, the undersigned, members of the M. E. Church, residing in and near Indianapolis, respectfully represent:

1. That there is a large field ripe for the harvest, embracing the eastern part of our city, occupied by our denomination, and which only requires vigorous cultivation to produce much fruit for our beloved Methodism.

2 That we hereby pledge ourselves to sustain to the best of our ability, a missionary movement for the occupancy of this inviting field, both by personal identification with such organization, and the contribution of our means.

3. That we promise to pay the amount set opposite our names, to sustain a missionary appointed for this work.

4. That we believe the sum of $5,000 can be raised to build a house of worship, and we pledge ourselves to go forward at once in the enterprise of building a church for the use of such congregation."

The memorial asked for the appointment to this work of a minister of "zeal and experience," and was signed by Willis D. Wright, Charles W. Brouse, W. H. McLaughlin, Arthur L. Wright, William Moffitt, John H. Frazier, John Berryman, J. W. Hossman, Charles Potts, J. M. W. Langsdale, James Ballenger, W. J. West, W. Q. Smith and S. T. Beck. J. M. W. Langsdale, Wm. H. McLaughlin and Arthur L. Wright were appointed a committee to lay the memorial before Bishop D. W. Clark, then presiding over the Southeastern Indiana Conference, in session at Franklin, Indiana.

In compliance with the request of the memorialists, the Rev. W. H. Mendenhall, who had served Robert's Chapel as its pastor, was appointed to the new charge.

The first quarterly meeting was held on the 19th and 20th of September, 1868; at the close of which one hundred members from Roberts' Chapel had united with the mission. The first quarterly conference was organized September 22d, 1868.

A suitable site for a house of worship was at once obtained; the building was rapidly erected, and on the 21st February, 1869, it was dedicated by Bishop D. W. Clark.

Rev. M. H. Mendenhall was reappointed by Bishop Simpson at the session of the South-eastern Indiana Conference, September, 1869, and served the charge until April, 1870, when he was transferred to the North Indiana Conference, and Rev. J. W. Locke, D. D., was appointed to fill the vacancy until the close of the Conference year. The present pastor, the Rev. Thos. H. Lynch, was appointed to the charge September 7th, 1870.

Highly successful revival services have been held in this church from time to time, and there is not in the city a congregation that has made better progress, considering its age.

The entire cost of the building, including site, furniture, and other appointments, has been about $20,000. The building is pleasantly located, is inviting in appearance without and within, and has seating accommodations for about six hundred persons.

The church membership numbers about two hundred and forty; that of the Sabbath-School, over three hundred.

THIRD STREET M. E. CHURCH.

Location: Third street, between Illinois and Tennessee.

In July, 1866, a class was organized, with Jesse Jones as leader, and a membership of thirty-six persons, to meet at the residence of Mr. Ellison Brown.

This class was the origin of *Third Street M. E. Church.*

In the spring of 1866, a site was purchased on Third street, and the erection of a building commenced, under the direction of the Ames Institute, intended for a mission church. Not receiving the necessary support, the young men of the institute were unable to finish the building; and Jesse Jones, a member of Strange Chapel, completed the work at his own expense

At the session of the North-Western Indiana Conference, in September, of that year, the church was placed under the control of Rev. J. W. Green, of Strange Chapel.

Soon after this, the Rev. A. L. Watkins, was made associate pastor with Mr. Green, and labored successfully in the new church for four months, when his failing health compelled him to abandon his work. The services of R. N. McKnig, a student of Asbury University, were secured for the remainder of the conference year.

The church building was dedicated September 8th, 1867, by the Rev. Thomas Bowman, D. D.

At the session of the North-Western Indiana Conference, September, 1867, Third Street Church was made an independent charge, and Rev. S. J. Kahler was appointed pastor.

The boundaries of the Indiana Conferences having been changed by the General Conference of 1868, Third Street Church fell within the limits of the South-East Indiana Conference.

Rev. S. C. Noble was the pastor during 1868-9; and Rev. L. M. Wells, during 1869 '70. The Rev. Frost Craft, the present pastor, was appointed in 1870.

The church edifice is a neat frame building, and its auditorium has seating capacity for about three hundred and fifty persons.

The membership numbers one hundred and thirty; the Sabbath-School, about one hundred and twenty-five.

The value of the building and site is about $6,000.

GERMAN M. E. CHURCH.

Location: Corner of New Jersey and New York streets.

This congregation was organized in the year 1849, with fifteen members.

The first house of worship was built in 1850, on Ohio street, between New Jersey and East streets. The first Trustees were: Wm. Hannaman, Henry Tutewiler, John Koeper, Frederick Truxess, John B. Stumph.

The growth of the society rendered a more capacious house of worship a necessity, and on the 19th of December, 1868, the site of the present church building, corner of New York and New Jersey streets, was purchased. The erection of the building was much delayed by the want of the requisite means. The basement was occupied on Christmas day, 1869; and through the persistent energy of the pastor, the Rev. G. Trefz, and the liberality of his congregation, the building was finally completed. The dedicatory exercises took place on the 17th day of April, 1871. Sermons were preached on the day of dedication by Professor Loebenstein, of Beren College, Ohio; Dr. William Nast, and the Rev. H. Liebhart.

The building is fifty-three by seventy-six feet in size, outside dimensions. The style of architecture is Byzantine, and the material of the structure is stone and brick. From the middle of the roof rises a tower, fifteen feet square, terminating in a spire one hundred and fifty-eight feet in hight. The interior is furnished in artistic style, and is neatly and comfortably appointed. The room is lighted by twelve Gothic windows, having ground glass centers and colored side pieces. The seating capacity, including galleries, is seven hundred and fifty, although a thousand could probably gain admittance. The room is lighted at night by a ceiling gas reflector, seven feet and a half in diameter, containing forty-two burners—the largest single reflector in the city.

The pastors have been: Rev. John Muth, 1849 to 1850; Rev. John H. Barth, 1850 to 1852; Rev. John H. Bahrenberg, 1852 to 1854; Rev. G. A. Braunig, 1854 to 1855; Rev. John Bier, 1855 to 1856; Rev. John H. Luckemeyer, 1856 to 1857; Rev. Max Hohans, 1857 to 1858; Rev. G. F. Miller, 1858 to 1850; Rev. John Hoppen (who died in 1861, and was one of the most zealous and effective ministers in the conference), 1860 to 1861; Rev. John Schneider, 1861 to 1862; Rev. William Ahrens, 1862 to 1863; Rev. G. A. Braunig, 1863 to 1864; Rev. A. Loebenstein, 1864 to 1866; Rev. H. G. Lich, 1866 to 1868; Rev. G. Trefz, the present pastor, who entered upon his duties in 1868.

The present Trustees are: Frederick Thoms, Peter Goth, Frederick Rapp, George Albright, Joseph Long, George Hereth, Gustave Stark.

The present membership numbers two hundred and twenty-five; the Sabbath-School has twenty-four officers and teachers, and two hundred pupils.

The cost of the building and site was $27,500; and the society is virtually out of debt.

MASSACHUSETTS AVENUE CHURCH.

Location: Corner of Massachusetts avenue and Oak street.

This society was organized in the summer of 1870, under the pastoral direction of Rev. B. F. Morgan, with about eighty members.

The Rev. Amos Hanway, the present pastor, was appointed by Bishop Scott, in September, 1870.

The number of communicants is now about one hundred and eighty; the Sabbath-School has about two hundred and fifteen members, and is in a growing condition.

The church site and building are worth about $4,000.

ALLEN CHAPEL (COLORED).

Location: On Broadway street, between Christian Avenue and Cherry street.

This society was organized August 6th, 1866, by Bishop Campbell; and began with only eight members. In the same year the conference appointed Elder W. S. Lankford a missionary for the north-eastern portion of the city. He began his labors by holding religious services at a private house in that quarter of the city. Here he organized a Sabbath-School. Steps were early taken to procure a site and erect upon it a house of worship for the society. By the aid of a small contribution from the conference, and larger ones from individual friends of the enterprise, the above site was secured, upon which a neat frame building—thirty-six by forty-four feet, having a seating capacity for about two hundred and fifty persons, and creditable in its style and appointments—was promptly erected. By Christmas, 1866, the society had occupied their new building.

Elder Lankford was succeeded in the pastorate, at the expiration of one year, by Elder Henry Brown, who remained one year. The latter's successor was the Rev. Henry DePugh, the present pastor, now in his third year.

The society has shown great energy from the first, and has had a corresponding prosperity. Its membership now numbers about two hundred, and the Sabbath-School has one hundred and twenty-five members. The value of the property is about $5,000.

BETHEL CHAPEL (COLORED.)

Location: Vermont street, between Missouri and West streets.

This society was organized in 1836. The colored population of the city at that time, and for many years following, was inconsiderable in number and limited in means. Consequently the society prospered indifferently, and contended against many difficulties. For several years the religious services were held in such buildings as the means of the society enabled them to secure—in private houses, etc. Finally a site was secured on West Georgia street, between Mississippi and the Canal, to which was removed the discarded building formerly used by the congregation of Christ Church. In this building the society worshiped for several years; when it was destroyed by fire, July 9th, 1862.

Several years later the property on Georgia street was sold, for which $3,000 was realized.

The society secured their present church site, on Vermont street, between Missouri and West, and energetically proceeded to erect thereon a far more costly and pretentious building than the one that the fire had destroyed. Pending its erection and dedication the congregation worshipped in the old Strange Chapel, on North Tennessee Street.

Though their new house of worship is not yet completed, the audience room has for some time been occupied by the congregation. To complete it and extinguish the debt of the society will require several thousand dollars.

It is quite a neat and commodious structure, and will seat from six hundred to eight hundred persons. The property includes a parsonage, adjacent to the church building. When the improvements shall have been completed, the value of the property will be from $25,000 to $30,000.

Owing to the deficiency of the records of this church, and of the other sources of information that have been accessible for the present purpose, it has not been

Ehrgott & Krebs Lith Cincinnati

CATHEDRAL.

practicable to obtain a list of the past pastors of this society. The present pastor is Rev. W. C. Trevan; and particularly prominent, energetic and efficient among his predecessors, was the Rev. W. R. Revels—a brother of Ex-Senator Revels, of Mississippi—who served the congregation from 1861 to 1865.

The present church membership is about four hundred; that of the Sabbath-School, two hundred.

Summary—Total membership of the Methodist Denomination in Indianapolis, three thousand two hundred and nineteen; total Sabbath-School membership, two thousand eight hundred and six; total value of church property, $391,500.

ROMAN CATHOLIC.

OUTLINE OF ROMAN CATHOLIC CHURCH HISTORY IN INDIANAPOLIS.

The year 1836 may be given as the date of the initiatory steps in the formation of the first Roman Catholic society in this city. Prior to that date several Catholic families had settled in this city and in its vicinity, who were visited once or twice a year by priests from a distance. The earliest of these visitors was the Rev. Father Francois, who was living and laboring among the Indians near Logansport, Indiana. Another pioneer minister of the church was the Rev. Theodore Badin, the first priest ordained in the United States, who held religious services a few times in Indianapolis and Shelbyville, Indiana. There being no house of worship dedicated to the Roman Catholic faith anywhere in this section, the visiting clergymen were content to say mass at the residences of Joseph Laux, Michael Shea, John O'Connor, and of other of the early Catholic settlers.

Some time during the year 1837, the Rt. Rev. Simon Gabriel Brute, appointed the first Bishop of Vincennes in 1834, assigned the Rev. Vincent Bacquelin to the charge of the Catholic settlement near Shelbyville, Indiana. The latter laid the foundation of St. Vincent's Church, which was soon after completed. Once or twice each month he visited the infant Catholic society here; who, for want of a church building of their own, now rented a small room which they used for church purposes for nearly three years.

In 1840 a lot was purchased beyond the canal, opposite to the old "Carlisle House," on which a small frame church called The Holy Cross Church was erected. This building is still standing, but is now used for trade purposes. The pastor, Father Bacquelin, a zealous and earnest evangelist, continued to attend alternately St. Vincent's, Shelby county, and the Holy Cross, Indianapolis, until August, 1846, in which year he was accidentally killed, and was buried at St. Vincent's. For several months after his death, the church was served by Rev John McDermott; who was succeeded by Rev. Patrick J. R. Murphy, who, in March, 1848, was located elsewhere; and the charge was then given to Rev. John Gueguen. At the time of the accession of the last named minister to the pastorate, the congregation had outgrown the capacity of their church, and steps were taken for the erection of a suitable edifice. Accordingly work was commenced on the present St. John's Church, which was completed in 1850. Father Gueguen officiated here until the year 1853, and was succeeded by Rev. Daniel Maloney, who, in 1857, enlarged the church building.

In the same year the Roman Catholic Germans, whose minister was Rev. L. Brandt of Madison, commenced building the present St. Mary's Church, on Maryland street, near Delaware. The enlargement of St. John's church had scarcely been completed when Father Maloney was removed, and Rev. Aug. Bessonies appointed pastor. The appointment was made in October, 1857, and on the 5th November following Rev. Mr. Bessonies began the pastoral labors which he has ever since performed with unremitting zeal, and in a most exemplary Christian spirit.

In January, 1858, the German Roman Catholic congregation were assigned a settled pastor, in the person of Rev. J. Seigrist, who officiated a short time in St. John's, until, by extraordinary effort, the erection of the German church was so far advanced as to permit its use for Divine service on August 15th of that year. In 1858 the members of St. John's congregation began building a Young Ladies' Academy on the corner of Georgia and Tennessee streets, which was completed and opened by the Sisters of Providence in 1859, and was enlarged in 1861. During the four years succeeding 1859, several purchases of real estate were made, and a number of buildings for church uses erected: among which may be specified the Catholic Cemetery, in 1862, and St. John's Pastoral Residence, in 1863. In 1862 Rev. J. M. Villars was appointed assistant pastor of St. John's, and was succeeded by R. F. Gouesse.

In 1865 St. Peter's Church, at the end of Virginia avenue, was built by the Rev. Aug. Bessonies, and was opened for Divine service on the 29th of June, (Feast of St. Peter). Rev. Joseph Petit was the first pastor. In 1865 the large school building for boys adjoining St. John's Pastoral residence, was begun. It was completed in 1866; and in 1867 the Brothers of the Sacred Heart took charge of it and began their educational labors. At the same time the German Catholics built school houses for boys and girls, and in 1866 the Sisters of St. Francis, from Oldenberg, opened their academy.

The house of worship of St. John's Church, notwithstanding the formation of the two new parishes—St. Mary's and St. Peter's—was now too small; and the erection of a splendid cathedral, fronting on Tennessee street, between Maryland and Georgia streets, was commenced in 1867. The foundation, which cost over $7,000, having been finished, on July 21, 1862, the corner stone was laid by the Rt. Rev. Maurice de St. Palais, Bishop of Vincennes, in the presence of the Governor and officers of State, the members of the City Council, and an immense concourse of the inhabitants of the city and neighborhood, such as was never before gathered together in the city on any similar occasion.

The general style of the cathedral is the French Gothic of the thirteenth century, and the front will be very imposing and elegant. The extreme dimensions of the building are seventy-five by two hundred two and a-half feet. The center nave is fifty feet wide and fifty-three feet high at the highest point. The transept is to be fifty by sixty-seven feet. The three principal entrances are on the west, the center one being double. Also north and south side entrances.

The sanctuary is forty by thirty and a-half feet, with the vestry rooms on either side. There will be a chapel for the baptismal font on the north side of the church, near the entrance; and four smaller chapels on each side of the nave, for side altars and confessionals. The pulpit will be at the south-west corner pillar of the transept.

The elevation comprises two towers surmounted by spires, similar in general outline and finish, and two hundred feet high. The three front portals are trimmed with cut stone. One leads through each tower. The central portal is thirty-two feet in height and eighteen feet in width. The others are sixteen feet in height and eight in width.

Above the chancel, there is a large rose window. eighteen feet in diameter. filled with cut stone tracery. The glass will be stained and filled with emblematic figures.

There will be a gallery for an organ and choir, thirty feet in width, and extending across the front of the church; but no other gallery.

The foundation of stone is very heavy; and the window and doorways will be set in cut stone. Two large furnace and coal cellars underneath are arched. and heating pipes will be enclosed with iron cylinders, so that the building will be fire proof.

On the occasion of the laying of the corner stone, the sermon was preached by the Jesuit Father Smarius.

The Rev. Father P. R. Fitzpatrick. who succeeded Father Gonesse. in 1866. was appointed to make the requisite collections for con inuing the work of erecting the edifice. and Rev. D. McMullen was sent here to assist in the parochial duties and to attend to adjoining missions. In 1868, the pastor, Rev. Aug. Bessonies, took charge of the building, and, with Father Fitzpatrick, collected funds to carry on the work. In June, 1869, the latter was assigned to St. Peters Church to take the place of Rev. Father Petit. who visited Europe. In October. 1869. Father Brassart was sent to assist at St. John's. until January 1st, 1870, when Rev. Father Petit returned and was located at St. John's until the Bishop's return from Rome. St. John's new church, better known as the Cathedral, in expectation that the Bishop of Vincennes, will remove to this city, or that a new See will be created at Indianapolis, is now completed as to the exterior: and work on the interior is steadily progressing. The interior finish and appointments will be in keeping with the artistic elegance of the general design. The cost of the completed edifice will be about $120,000.

In 1870, Father P. R. Fitzpatrick, then pastor of St. Peter's church. finding that building to small to accommodate his fast increasing congregation, laid the corner stone of a new church building, called St. Patrick's. It is a fine brick structure, and will be completed sometime in August, 1871, when the old church will be used for a school house by the Brothers of the Sacred Heart. for the instruction of the boys of the congregation.

St. John's Home for Invalids, whose character and purposes are sufficiently indicated by its name—is located on Maryland street, between Illinois and Tennessee, and is under the charge and administration of the Sisters of Providence In place of this institution, the erection of a hospital on East street is proposed —for which purpose an appropriate site has been secured.

House of Refuge.—The erection of a building for this purpose is proposed : and to this end suitable property has been donated to the Sisters of the Good Shepherd, by the city of Indianapolis, and by S. A. Fletcher, Esq.

The Catholic population of the city, including children, is estimated at ten thousand, distributed among the parishes as follows :

St. John's, five thousand; St. Mary's three thousand; St. Peter's two thousand.

The pastors now in charge are: St. John's,—Rev. Aug Bessonies, and Rev. Joseph Petit; St. Peter's,—Rev. P. R. Fitzpatrick; St. Mary's,—Rev. S. Siegrist.

Summary.—Total number of communicants of the Catholic Denomination in Indianapolis, about four thousand ; total Sabbath-School membership, about one thousand ; total value of church property, $300,000.

(16)

HEBREW.

The Hebrew population of Indianapolis numbers about five hundred. The Judaic faith has one church society in this city; whose house of worship is located on the south side of Market street, between New Jersey and East streets. Prior to 1833, the families of Moses Woolf and Alexander Franco, constituted the entire Hebrew population of this city. With these for a nucleus, the number slowly increased; and in the winter of 1855, a congregation was organized, who purchased three and a-half acres near the city and dedicated it to the uses of a cemetery. The constitution and by laws of the society give the following list of officers and members at the date of organization:

Mr. Moses Woolf, President; Dr. J. M. Rosenthal, Vice President; Mr. Max Glaser, Treasurer; Mr. Ad. Dessar, Secretary; Mr. Ad. Rosenthal, Mr. Max Dernham, Mr. Mr. Julius Glaser, Trustees; Mr. Peter Harmon, Mr. Josesph B. Dessar, Mr. Selig Weil, Mr. Jacob Maas, Mr. S. Sloman, Mr. H. Bamberger, Mr. Simon Wolff, Mr. J. M Altman, Mr. H. A. Jessel, Mr. F. Ullman, Dr. N. Knepfler, Mr. Fred. Knefler, Mr. Henry Kittner, Mr. Moses Heller, (Knightstown,) Mr. H. Rosenthal, (Kokomo.)

Of these Mr. Woolf and four others are the only members still connected with the society. No minister was engaged until the autumn of 1856; when a small room in Blake's Row was rented and fitted up for religious services, and the Rev. Mr. Berman was engaged as pastor during the holidays.

The congregation increased very rapidly during the next few years, and in 1858 was able to provide a more suitable place of worship, a hall in Judah's Block, which was dedicated by the Rev. Dr. Wise, of Cincinnati. During the same year the energetic congregation engaged the Rev. J. Wechsler, a minister of eminent zeal and ability, as pastor; who served until 1861.

During the latter year the society was without a pastor and was on the brink of dissolution—the membership at one time having been reduced to thirteen. In 1862, the society rallied, and made a forward movement by the election of Rev. M. Moses as pastor. Meanwhile, several innovations were made in the old-time ceremonies and tenets of the Jewish faith, and the worship was not a little modified and altered, in accordance with the spiritual progress of the age. Thus a life-giving spirit and harmonious zeal were infused into the society. Among the changes made at this time was the organization and employment of a choir. Henceforth the society had a more rapid growth.

Mr. Moses retired from the pastorate in 1863, and was succeeded by the Rev. Dr. Kalish, a learned divine who rendered general satisfaction. The membership had now increased to over fifty, and the society began to seriously consider the necessity of obtaining suitable church property of their own. To secure the success of this enterprise, the Rev. Mr. Wechsler, who was a second time chosen, persistently labored. To impress its importance upon his congregation he made nearly every sermon an occasion; and, finally, in 1864 subscriptions were started. During the same winter a sufficient sum was subscribed to authorize the purchase of a site on East Market street, and on the 7th day of December, 1865, the corner stone of the present temple was laid, with the impressive ceremonies of the Jewish Church, the Rev. Dr. Lilienthal, of Cincinnati, delivering the oration. But before the building had been completed the subscriptions were exhausted, and work was suspended for over a year. The society was again in the midst of a crisis, from which the prospects of escape were anything but encouraging; and it was abundantly predicted and readily believed, that the property would have to be sold to pay the incumbrances upon it.

From this dilemma the liberality of a few members rescued the imperiled enterprise. These went into the money market and raised the requisite means for completing the building.

The temple, erected and furnished at a cost of $22,000, was dedicated on the 30th of October, 1863. The dedicatory exercises were of an imposing character: embracing a large procession, an address by H. Bamberger, Esq., the President of the congregation; a dedicatory sermon by the Rev. Dr. Wise, and a banquet at night.

In the autumn of 1867, Mr. Wechsler was succeeded by the Rev. Morris Messing, the present pastor.

The congregation has certainly shown great perseverance in the face of formidable discouragements; and may be pardoned for no small degree of pride, in the building of so handsome a house of worship by a membership so small.

The society now has fifty-eight members, and sustains a Saturday and Sunday-School of fifty-four pupils.

The temple is in the *Renaissance* style of architecture, and is a tasteful structure in its exterior aspects and interior finish and appointments. It is built of brick, with an elegant stone front. Its dimensions are forty by eighty feet; and the auditorium has seating capacity for about four hundred persons.

The value of the building and site is about $27,000.

LUTHERAN.

FIRST ENGLISH LUTHERAN CHURCH.

Location: Corner of Alabama and New York streets.

This association was organized in January, 1837, by the Rev. Abraham Reck; and was at that time composed of twenty members, among whom were the heads of the Brown, Haugh, Ohr, and other families,—well-known names in the city.

Of the primary organization but seven members are now living; and these are still connected with the church.

The founder, and first pastor, died in 1869, in Lancaster, Ohio.

The first church building,—a one-story brick—was erected in 1838, on the south-east corner of Meridian and Ohio streets.

The Rev. Mr. Reck resigned the charge in 1840, and was succeeded by the Rev. A. A. Timper, (now of Illinois,) who served until 1843. He was shortly afterward succeeded by the Rev. Jacob Shearer, (since deceased,) who was the pastor until 1845. From 1845 to 1850, the Rev. A. H. Myers, (now of Ashland, Ohio,) was pastor of the congregation. His successor was the Rev. E. R. Guiney, whose labors were closed by his death, in 1853, and whose remains lie in Crown Hill Cemetery. The next pastor was the Rev. J. A. Kunkleman, (now of Philadelphia,) whose ministry covered a period of over eight years; during which period the present church edifice was built, (completed and dedicated in 1861.) After the retirement of Mr. Kunkleman, in 1866, the congregation was served successively by the Rev. J. H. W. Stuckenberg, (now of Pittsburgh,) for about eighteen months; and Prof. H. L. Baugher, (of Gettysburg, Penn.,) for nearly a year. The present pastor, the Rev. W. W. Criley, accepted the charge in 1869.

The society now numbers over two hundred members; the Sabbath-School, one hundred and fifty.

The church edifice is a neat brick building, having capacity for about three hundred persons. Connected with the church is a parsonage.

The value of the church property is about $18,000, and the society is entirely out of debt.

ST. PAUL'S GERMAN EVANGELICAL LUTHERAN.

Location: Corner of East and Georgia streets.

This association was organized on the 5th June, 1844, at a meeting held in the old seminary building. Pursuant to the action of that meeting, a site was purchased on Alabama street, between Washington and Louisiana streets; on which a brick church edifice was built, and dedicated on the 11th day of May, 1845. The first pastor was the Rev. Theodore J. G. Kuntz; who was succeeded in 1851 by the Rev. Charles Frinke. Under the energetic and wise administration of the latter pastor, the congregation increased to such an extent that the capacity of their church-building became insufficient, necessitating the erection of another and larger edifice.

For this purpose the requisite site was secured at the corner of East and Georgia streets; where a house of worship, fifty by one hundred and seventeen feet was erected, and was dedicated November 3d, 1860, by the Rev. Dr. Wyneken, President of the Evangelical Lutheran Synod.

The completion of this commodious structure was a source of appropriate pride and satisfaction to the congregation that had labored so assiduously and harmoniously to that end; and whose success, considering the difficulties to be overcome, had been as conspicuous as it had been speedily attained.

On the same site, immediately in the rear of the church edifice, two buildings for school purposes were also erected by the congregation; who, since their first organization, have sustained a parochial school, which is now conducted by three teachers: Messrs. Contselmann, A. Krome, and William Brueggemann.

The Rev. Mr. Frinke, having accepted a call from Baltimore, Md., was succeeded by the present pastor, the Rev. Chr. Hochstetter, called from Pittsburgh, and installed in his present pastoral relation on the 24th of April, 1868.

Under the pastoral charge of Mr. Hochstetter the church has had great prosperity; and the number of members, as well as of pupils in the parochial school, has largely increased.

In 1869, a site for a parsonage was purchased on the corner of East and Ohio streets, and a neat residence was erected upon it.

In 1870, ten acres of ground were purchased in the south-eastern suburb of the city, and dedicated to the purposes of a cemetery for the Lutheran population of Indianapolis.

The number of voting members of this church is two hundred and ten.

A capable choir and a large organ furnish a good quality of music at the religious services of this society.

The present number of pupils in the parochial school is two hundred and sixty.

The governing authorities of the church for the current year, are as follow:

Rev. Chr. Hochstetter, Pastor; Frederick Ostermieer, William Cook, and Charles

Prange, Trustees; Louis Meier, and William Roeber, Elders; Ernest Roeber, and Charles Stiegman, Presbyters.

The value of the property is about $50,000.

ZION'S CHURCH.

Location: Ohio street, between Meridian and Illinois.

This society was founded in 1840. The first pastor was the Rev. J. G. Kunz; who served the church until 1842. The church had no regular pastor until 1844, when the Rev. J. F. Isensee was called to the charge.

The first house of worship, located on the site of the present church building, was dedicated on the 18th of May, 1845. The society now took the name of the German Evangelical Zion's Church—the first German Protestant church organization in Indianapolis.

The Rev. Mr. Isensee retired from the pastorate in 1850; since which time the church has been served by the following pastors:

The Rev. A. Rahn, 1850–51; the Rev. Mr. Riley, 1851–52; the Rev. C. E. Zobel, 1853–54; the Rev. A. E. Knester, 1854–59. The Rev. H. Quinius, the present pastor, has served the congregation since 1859.

In 1860, the society built a two story brick building, for parochial school purposes.

In 1866, was begun the erection of their present house of worship. The corner-stone was laid on the 1st of July, of the same year; and the building was dedicated on the 5th of February, 1867. The church now has four hundred communicants; the Sabbath-School two hundred pupils, and the parochial school one hundred and eighty.

The church property is valued at $30,000.

Summary—Total membership of the Lutheran Denomination, in Indianapolis, eight hundred and ten; total Sabbath-School membership, three hundred and fifty; total value of property, $98,000.

GERMAN EVANGELICAL ASSOCIATION.

SALEM CHURCH.

Location: New Jersey street between Market and Ohio.

This society was organized on the 19th day of June, 1855, with twenty-one members, under the name of "Immanuel Church of the Evangelical Association of Indianapolis."

The first Trustees of the organization were, M. W. Steffey, Samuel Dickover, and George Klopfer.

The society has had to contend against great financial embarrassments, but the liberality and energy of the members have been superior to all emergencies.

The present house of worship, located as above stated, is a plain, substantial brick building, in size thirty-six by sixty feet, of the value (with site) of about $9,000. The auditorium has seating capacity for about three hundred persons. The society has been served by the following pastors:

The Revs. M. W. Steffey, Henry Kramer, Matthew Hoehn, Michael Krueger, A. B. Shaefer, G. G. Platz, J. M. Gomer, John Fuchs, F. Wiethaup, I. Haufman, and Conrad Tramer, the present pastor.

On the 23d of August, 1870, the name of the society was changed to Salem Church.

The organization is in a prosperous condition; numbering one hundred and eighteen members; the greater portion of whom are of mature age and heads of families.

The Sabbath-School is likewise in a flourishing state, and has about one hundred and fifty members.

UNIVERSALIST.

FIRST UNIVERSALIST CONGREGATION.

The organization of the first Universalist Church Society in this city, was as early as 1844. The society, owing to the limited number of adherents to the Universal faith living here at that time, had but a feeble and brief existence.

In 1853 a church was organized under the name of the "First Universalist Church of Indianapolis." Of this society, the Rev. B. F. Foster, was the first pastor, continuing in that relation until 1860. His successor, for something over one year, was the Rev. W. C. Brooks, who was succeeded by the Rev. B. F. Foster, who was followed, in 1866, by the Rev. J. M. Austin, of New York. Mr. Austin remained about six months, at the expiration of which period, Mr. Foster, being at that time State Librarian, and a resident of Indianapolis, took temporal charge of the church, continuing in that relation until the close of his term as State Librarian, in 1869. Since then the church has been without any settled pastor, though occasional services have been held.

An effort is being matured for the re-establishment of the church on a permanent basis.

The society has never had a house of worship of its own, and its services have been held in the following places: In the old Seminary building (on the site of the present University Park,) in the Court House, in Temperance Hall, in Masonic Hall, in College Hall, and in the Hall of Wallace's block.

SECOND UNIVERSALIST CONGREGATION.

The organization of this society grew out of a schism in the First Universalist church, in the year 1860; not on account of doctrinal differences, but of individual differences.

About $3,500 was obtained by subscriptions; of which sum $1,000 was subscribed by John Thomas, Esq., the leader of the movement. A site was secured, and a house of worship erected, on the corner of Michigan and Tennessee streets.

By the foreclosure of a mortgage on the property, and by discharging an indebtedness of nearly $5,000, Mr. Thomas afterward became the exclusive owner thereof.

With the exception of the first twelve months after the dedication—during which time the Revs. C. E. Woodbury and W. W. Curry officiated as pastors—the building has not been used for religious purposes by the Universalist denomination. It was occupied for some time by Wesley Chapel (Methodist Episcopal) congregation, pending the completion of their new building, and afterwards by one wing of the Strange Chapel (Methodist Episcopal) congregation, called the Congregational Methodist Church, with the Rev. J. W. T. McMullen as pastor

The latter organization has also disbanded; and the premises are now unoccupied for religious uses.

UNITED BRETHREN IN CHRIST.

This denomination is represented in this city by but one church; whose house of worship is located on the south-east corner of Ohio and New Jersey streets.

This society was organized in 1850; and the present church building was erected in the year following. Until a few years since the organization had a steady growth in prosperity. During the late war the membership had increased to three hundred and fifty-three; but the withdrawal by letter, at the close of the war, of a number of the soldiers who had attached themselves to this church while in camp here, reduced the membership to about two hundred.

In the autumn of 1869 a schism occurred in this society, resulting in a new organization under the name of the Liberal United Brethren, and embracing a majority of the original body. The Liberals held possession of the church property, closing its doors against the other body.

A resort to the courts resulted in placing the original society again in possession of the property on the 31st August, 1870.

The Liberals disbanded their organization, and its members generally united with the Methodist Episcopal denomination.

The society was then re-organized, and now numbers forty-two active members. The Sabbath-School, which had been disbanded by reason of the dissensions, has also been re-organized, and now reckons about eighty members.

The church building has capacity for about four hundred persons; and the property is valued at $5,000.

The society has been served by the following pastors, beginning with the first in the order stated: Revs. J. D. Vardaman, two years; A. Long, one year; A. Davis, one year; M. Wright, one year; D. Stover, one year; C. W. Witt, four years; P. S. Cook, two years; William Nichols, one year; L. S. Chittenden, one year and a half; J. S. Wall, six months; Thomas Evans, two years; A. Hanway, on year; B. F. Morgan, one year; and W. J. Pruner, the present pastor.

UNITARIAN.

FIRST UNITARIAN SOCIETY OF INDIANAPOLIS.

On the 13th of February, 1868, pursuant to a call signed by George K. Perrin, J. B. Follett, and others, a small company met in this city to consider the feasibility of forming a Unitarian Society. The late Judge David McDonald presided at this meeting. It was decided to open correspondence with various Unitarian clergymen with a view to securing the services of a regular pastor; and Morrison's Opera Hall was engaged as a place for holding the services of the society. In this hall on the 12th of April, 1868, were held the first public services of the society, Dr. G. W. Hosmer, of Antioch College, Ohio, officiating. Thereafter, until the following summer vacation, services were held regularly at this hall; after which the society met for a time at the office of Judge McDonald.

On the 14th of May, 1868, the society was formally organized, and a president, an executive committee and secretary were elected.

In October, 1868, the Rev. Henry Blanchard, by invitation delivered a sermon before the society in the Academy of Music; and a call was at once extended to him to become the pastor of the society. He accepted, entered upon the work in January, 1869, and remained for about two years. Mr. Blanchard was the only regular pastor the society has had; and since his resignation the pulpit has been irregularly filled by ministers from other cities.

The following is the Declaration of Belief adopted by the society:

"Reverently recognizing our dependence on Almighty God, the one God and Father of us all, who is above all, and through all, and in us all, and believing in the usefulness of public worship; accepting Jesus of Nazareth, who taught the Absolute Religion of love of God and Man, as the world's greatest Teacher and Example, and desiring to imitate his life and study his words, we, the undersigned, agree to unite ourselves in a religious association to be known as the First Unitarian Society of Indianapolis, Indiana."

Mr. Blanchard was a popular pulpit orator and generally attracted large congregations. The largest attendance at his meetings was about twelve hundred; the average, about five hundred. The greatest number of enrolled Sabbath-School pupils was about one hundred and twenty.

RECAPITULATION.

The following table shows the Church and Sabbath-School membership of each Denomination in this city, and the value of the church property held by each Denomination, according to reports furnished, in most instances, by the pastors of the several churches:

CHURCHES.	Church Membership.	Sabbath-School Membership.	Value of Church Property
Protestant Episcopal...............	582	743	$16,800
Presbyterian........	1,736	*2,208	320,117
Baptist................,....	1,093	†1,435	‡116,000
Methodist........................	3,219	2,806	₹391,000
Roman Catholic....................	4,000	1,000	300,000
Congregational	235	350	43,000
Christian........................	900	1,000	53,000
Lutheran........................	810	350	98,000
German Reformed..................	300	450	21,000
German Evangelical Association..	118	150	9,000
United Brethren..................	42	80	5,000
Universalist‖.........			
Unitarian........................	500	100	
Jewish..........	58	54	27,000
Friends	246	80	12,000
Total.................	**13,839**	**10,806**	**$1,529,117**

* In the Summary on page 216, the number 2,608 should be 2,208.

† In the Summary on page 220, the number 1,265 should be 1,435.

‡ In the Summary on page 220, the amount $76,000 should be $82,000.

₹ Includes the estimated cost, when completed, of buildings in process of erection.

‖ No reports. See page 246.

UNDENOMINATIONAL RELIGIOUS SOCIETIES.

YOUNG MEN'S CHRISTIAN ASSOCIATION.

The *Young Men's Christian Association*, of Indianapolis, had its organized beginning on the 12th December, 1854, about five years after the first organization of this kind was founded, in London, England. The history of its work of beneficence and charity—like that of kindred organizations the world over—cannot be written to advantage, as in the case of a separate religious congregation, worshiping at stated periods and in a particular edifice. The latter is a conspicuous object, and its work is done in ways and manners so regular and methodical as to be "seen of men." On the contrary, the real extent of the services performed by the Young Men's Christian Association of Indianapolis can be fully appreciated only by the workers in that organization, and by Omniscience.

The number of persons who have been the recipients of its benefactions would amount to thousands. Its charities and ministrations are contracted or limited by no form of sectarianism. To serve God by benefiting man is its only faith—its comprehensive creed. While it has regular spheres of labor, it also claims the world for its field, and to the best of its means, aids the destitute and ministers to the neglected, wherever found. Subordinate to the church in one sense, its effect is to extend the influence of the church to individuals, and into the waste places. For the benefit of the destitute and neglected classes the Association was particularly intended.

Chief among the more comprehensive labors of the Association in this city, from time to time, have been the establishment and maintenance of mission Sunday-Schools, and religious services in destitute parts of the city—principally conducted by laymen.

The quarters of the Young Men's Christian Association—until recently, located in Vinton's block, opposite the Post office—contain, beside the offices, a reading and library room, with current files of the principal religious periodicals, for perusal by citizens and strangers whenever they choose. The rooms are open every night and day for the accommodation of strangers, of both sexes, who may be inclined to call; and for the large number of applicants for assistance. Not the only recipients of its charities are these applicants. The destitute and sick are invited, wherever they may be—all possible aid given them.

Besides the prayer meetings held at the rooms every morning, there are some missions and other places of worship where regular religious services are held by the Association. During the summer season from six to fifteen open-air meetings are held under its auspices every Sunday.

The amount of money expended in these charities, in the first year of the Association, was $370.00; and for the year just closed, $4,681. The latter sum by no means embraces all the material charities of the Association. To this should be added a larger amount, in the shape of articles of clothing distributed by the Association, and donated to them by citizens. Considering that its resources are entirely made up of voluntary offerings, it is seen by the above figures that the work and influence of the Association have greatly increased; and that it has now a firm hold in the consciences and upon the purses of the people.

The following are names of its Presidents from the beginning: E. J. Baldwin, to March, 1856; Miles J. Fletcher, from March, 1856, to March, 1857; S. T. Bowen, from March, 1857, to March, 1858; J. W. McIntire, from March, 1858, to March,

1850; Benjamin Harrison, from March, 1859, to March, 1860; Theophilus Parvin, from March, 1860, to March, 1862; F. A. W. Davis, from March, 1862, to July, 1865; W. P. Fishback, from July, 1865, to September, 1866; J. A. Kunkleman, from September to October, 1866; W. H. Hay, from October, 1866, to September, 1868; W. A. Bell, from September, 1868 to September, 1869; John W. Ray, from September, 1869, to September, 1870; and the latter was succeeded by Wilson Morrow, the present President.

From 1862 to 1865, by reason of the extraordinary demands of the war, the Association was comparatively neglected. Beginning with Mr. Fishback's administration—peace having returned—the vigor of the Association renewed itself; and it has steadily grown in efficiency and power ever since.

The principal part of its early work was performed by volunteers, until early in 1868, when Rev. Wm. Armstrong was elected to the post of City Missionary and Superintendent of the work of the Association. In this capacity he zealously served until July, 1863, when he was succeeded by Rev. J. B. Brandt, the present incumbent, an industrious, zealous and competent gentleman for the place.

Lectures are occasionally given under the auspices of the association, by the more prominent public lecturers, serving the double purpose of giving the outsiders the benefit of the lectures, and the association the assistance of its portion of the net profits of the engagement.

The membership of the association, at this time, numbers about three hundred and seventy-five.

The above is, necessarily, the merest outline of the history of the association. As stated in the beginning of this sketch, the magnitude of the good it has done cannot be known by any one person in this world. Yet thousands of men and women can testify to benefits received through its ministrations. Hardly a church has been organized here since the existence of the Association but is more or less indebted to it. It is gratifying to know that the Association is in a more prosperous condition than ever before. It is now one of the permanent institutions of the city, with every promise of continually increasing usefulness.

On the 1st of March, 1871, the Trustees purchased, for the occupancy and use of the Association, the building on the west side of North Illinois street, between Washington and Illinois streets, known as the Exchange Theatre.

The purchase price was $24,000; which sum has nearly all been raised or subscribed. The building has been refitted and renovated, and the Association now has accommodations more commensurate with its needs.

The officers for the current year are: Wilson Morrow, President; Ed. S. Field, Vice President; Charles C. Dennis, Recording Secretary; M. R. Barnard, Corresponding Secretary; Joseph McDowell, Treasurer; Rev. J. B. Brandt, Superintendent.

Board of Trustees—William S. Hubbard, President; E. C. Mayhew, Treasurer; Wm. C. Smock, Ingram Fletcher, Benj. Harrison, R. Sedgwick, John H. Ohr, Theo. P. Haughey.

Executive Committee—Joseph McDowell, Chairman; C. C. Dennis, Secretary; Wilson Morrow, M. R. Barnard, W. H. Hay, E. S. Field, Mrs. Anna Baggs, Mrs. Delitha B. Harvey, T. H. K. Enos.

STANDING COMMITTEES.—On Finance—D. H. Wiles, R. Sedgwick, Wm. C. Smock.

Library and Rooms—J. G. Kingsbury, D. H. Wiles, E. A. Cobb.

Lectures and Sermons—W. A. Bell, M. R. Barnard, Joseph McDowell.

Meetings—R. Frank Kennedy, C. C. Olin, C. P. Wilson.

Temperance—John W. Ray, W. H. Hobbs, Mrs. Dr. Siddall.

Hotels and Boarding Houses—E. A. Cobb, Edward Gilbert, G. W. Alexander.

Ladies' Working Committee—Mrs. Anna Wilson, Mrs. Martin Byrkit, Mrs. L. L. Jackson.

Ladies' Missionary Committee—Mrs. Mary E. Carey, Mrs. Rebecca Newland, Mrs. Dr. James Braden.

Missionary—W. S. Wooten, D. W. Coffin, Joseph Sutton.

Statistics—John B. Brandt, Joseph R. Perry.

THE WOMEN'S CHRISTIAN ASSOCIATION.

This auxiliary of the Young Men's Christian Association was organized in October, 1870. Its principal sphere is to secure homes and employment for homeless women, and to visit and care for the indigent sick. It also has charge of a Sabbath-School for newsboys, boot-blacks, &c. The society has about one hundred members, of whom about thirty are on the active list.

YOUNG MEN'S CHRISTIAN ASSOCIATION, GERMAN.

This Association, similar in its character and objects to the Young Men's Christian Association of Indianapolis, was organized on the 5th of January, 1870.

An organization of this character, dependent entirely for support on the voluntary aid of individuals, cannot, in the space of a little more than one year, become great and powerful; yet, considering its age, the Association has made good progress.

The present membership numbers about sixty.

Each member pays a yearly contribution of one dollar into the treasury; the payment of $20.00 secures a life membership.

The regular meetings of the Association are held every Tuesday evening.

It is proposed to open, at an early day, suitable rooms for the purposes of a library, reading rooms, and offices.

The officers of the Association are: President, J. J. Wenner; Vice Presidents (one from each of the German churches), Christian Schmidt, Second German Reformed Church; J. J. Wenner, German Methodist Church; Adam Helm, Zion's Church; William Braun, First German Reformed Church; Chas. Aldag, German Evangelical Church.

INDIANAPOLIS FEMALE BIBLE SOCIETY.

This association is an auxiliary of the *American Bible Society*, and was organized in 1830. The object of the Society is shown by its title, and is known by its works: The distribution of the Bible to the destitute who cannot afford to buy it, and in public places where its reading is neglected. The jurisdiction of the Society is the city of Indianapolis and Marion county.

The funds of the Society are derived from the voluntary donations of the churches and citizens generally. During the war the Society gave an aggregate of fifty-one thousand four hundred and ninety-one Bibles and Testaments to soldiers and prisoners of war stationed at this point. The total number gratuitously distributed since 1853, is fifty-eight thousand one hundred and sixty-nine.

The affairs of the Society are directed by a president, a vice president, treasurer, secretary and board of managers. The present officers are:

President, Mrs. Jane M. Graydon; Vice President, Mrs. John Wilkins; Treasurer, Mrs. C. W. Brouse; Secretary, Julia A. Bassett.

MEDICAL.

INDIANA MEDICAL COLLEGE.[*]

This institution is located on Delaware street, on the west side of the Court House square.

A description of the institution necessitates a brief recital of the instrumentalities that led to its establishment.

Previous to 1863, the only organization of physicians, in this city, was the Indianapolis Medical Association. This was as much social as professional. Its meetings were held at the offices or residences of now one and then another member; in fact, it was not an organization in the true sense of the term, nor was it highly useful to the cause of medical science. This association became extinct in the course of a few years, and was succeeded, in 1863, by another organization similar in name, but much more efficient and useful in point of fact. In 1864, the Marion County Association was formed. These two organizations were merged into the Indianapolis Academy of Medicine, a corporate body under the laws of the State, founded on the 3d of October, 1865. The Academy has ever since held stated meetings once each week, at which regular exercises, in the interests of medical science, have been held—such as an essay by some appointed member, discussions of pathological, physiological and therapeutical questions, etc.

The benefits of the organization to medical science and to the members—who thus interchange views and obtain the advantages of the peculiar experiences or observations of one another—are sufficiently obvious, without further explanation. The Academy was the parent of the Indiana Medical College.

This institution was organized in May, 1869. The first movement looking to its establishment, was started by the Academy in February of that year. The original plan was, a State institution as a department of the Indiana State University, and thus to obtain the aid of the State in behalf of the enterprise. The committee of the Academy appointed to make an investigation into the feasibility of this plan, consisting of Drs. George W. Mears, John S. Bobbs and J. H. Woodburn, reported unfavorably on the project.

The report was concurred in by the Academy and a resolution adopted, that a committee of five be appointed to report upon the propriety of an effort, on the part of the profession in Indianapolis, for the establishment here of a medical college; and also to report a plan for that purpose.

This committee, consisting of Drs. Waterman, Harvey, Todd, Kitchen and Gaston, reported in favor of the enterprise, and submitting a plan of organization. The plan was accepted, and subsequently another committee was appointed to select a faculty: the professors so selected to organize themselves into a college of medicine, to be known as "The Indiana Medical College;" to devise the means for its maintenance; secure suitable building accommodations; in short, to manage the business concerns, generally, of the institution.

The first Faculty was composed as follows:

---

[*] Of the establishment, nature and brief existence of the "Central Medical College," mention is made on page 91.

INDIANA MEDICAL COLLEGE

J. S. Bobbs, M. D., Pres't., Principles and Practice of Surgery; G. W. Mears, M. D., Obstetrics; R. T. Brown, M. D., Chemistry and Toxicology; R. N. Todd, M. D., Vice President, Principles and Practice of Medicine; L. D. Waterman, M. D., Descriptive and Surgical Anatomy; T. B. Harvey, M. D., Treasurer, Diseases of Women and Children; W. B. Fletcher, M. D., Physiology; F. S. Newcomer, M. D., Professor of Materia Medica and Therapeutics; J. A. Comingor, M. D., Surgical Pathology, Orthopedic and Clinical Surgery; C. E. Wright, M. D., Demonstrator of Anatomy.

At a meeting on the 4th of May, 1869, Dr. Bobbs reported articles of association, which were approved and signed by the other members of the Faculty; and, at the same meeting, Hons. Samuel E. Perkins and John D. Howland were elected members of the Board of Trustees, with the Faculty.

The Academy of Medicine subscribed liberally to the support of the institution, to make up the excess of expenses over the inadequate receipts from tuition, during the infancy of the college; and a number of the members bound themselves to pay annual subscriptions, for this purpose, for five years.

In this way the Indianapolis Medical College was founded. The first session was opened in October, 1869.

The College building is now complete. Its lecture rooms are adapted to the accommodation of over two hundred students. All the departments, especially those of Anatomy and Chemistry, are well supplied with material for illustrations. A laboratory for students has been opened under the charge of Prof. Stevens, where superior facilities are provided for the practical teaching of Analytic Medical Chemistry.

The city hospital affords ample opportunities for the study of clinical medicine and surgery. Cases were presented to, and operations performed before, the class during the past winter, representing almost the entire field of Medicine and Surgery.

The Chemical department is now furnished with a full line of apparatus, which enables the teacher of this branch to give a thorough and illustrative course in chemistry and toxicology.

Candidates for the degree of Doctor of Medicine, must have attended two full courses of lectures—the last one being in this college; and have studied three years under the direction of a regularly educated physician.

The present Faculty is composed of the following gentlemen:

J. A. Comingor, M. D., President and Prof. of Principles and Practice of Surgery; G. W. Mears, M. D., Prof. of Obstetrics; Thad. M. Stevens, M. D., Professor of Chemistry and Toxicology; R. N. Todd, M. D., Professor of Principles and Practice of Medicine; L. D. Waterman, M. D., Prof. of Anatomy and Clinical Surgery; T. B. Harvey, M. D., Prof. of Diseases of Women and Children; W. B. Fletcher, M. D., Prof. of the Institutes of Medicine; Dugan Clarke, M. D., Prof. Materia Medica and Therapeutics; J. M. Dunlap, M. D, Demonstrator of Anatomy.

THE BOBBS DISPENSARY.

This is an institution in the building of the College, and is so named in honor of the late Dr. John S. Bobbs of this city, who, at his death, left a bequest of $2,000, to be employed by trustees named in his will, for the benefit of the poor of Indianapolis. The Faculty of the College, of which Dr. Bobbs was President at the time of his death, suggested, as the means of most advantageously and most appropriately carrying out the intentions of the deceased, that the bequest be used in establishing and aiding in the maintenance of a Dispensary for the benefit of the poor of the city. The plan was so appropriate that it was put into effect; and the result is the Bobbs Dispensary, by means of which poor people in need of medical assistance, and unable to pay for it, receive the necessary treatment. Those incapable of attending the Dispensary are visited by some one of the corps of attending physicians, composed of members of the College Faculty.

In addition to the bequest of Dr. Bobbs, the county makes an annual appropriation of $700, and the city a similar appropriation of $600, in support of the institution. The bequest could in no other way have been employed so beneficially and so appropriately.

In April last the Resident Physician made the following report to the City Council:

Whole number of patients treated.. 331
Number of visits made... 468
Number of post mortem examinations made... 4
Number vaccinated.. 29
Number of surgical operations.. 37
Number of prescriptions filled at Dispensary....................................... 880

THE INDIANA SURGICAL INSTITUTE

Is located on the corner of Illinois and Georgia streets.

This Institute was incorporated July 24th, 1869, with a capital stock of $150,000.00, for the treatment of deformities of the spine and limbs, and all descriptions of surgical cases. For ten years prior to the time of its establishment in Indianapolis, this enterprise had been carried on in Illinois, and it was then removed to this city because of its more central and more easily accessible location.

The building will accommodate about three hundred patients, and is capable of affording treatment to about three thousand cases annually. The number of patients treated is generally equal to the greatest capacity of the institution.

In respect of the capital invested, of the mechanical and other appliances for the treatment of patients, of capacities and facilities generally, this institution has no superior in the United States. Its patronage is correspondingly great in number, and is distributed over a corresponding area of territory.

Patients from twenty-five States have resorted to this institution for treatment. During the past year more than ten thousand people have visited Indianapolis because of the Surgical Institute, paying to the various railroads over $100,000 in the way of fares, and expending in the city, for board, merchandise, treatment, etc., nearly $400,000.

The Institute gives employment to over fifty persons, including surgeons mechanics and nurses. The buildings, which were at first considered ample, have since proved to be too small to accommodate the demand.

The institution is provided with the various kinds of baths: the Turkish, Russian, electro-thermal, &c.; also, a large machine-shop, with a steam engine, and the requisite machinery for the manufacture of the apparatus and appliances employed in the treatment of deformities.

The superior facilities afforded by the institution are attested by the results. Numerous cases of the more hopeless descriptions, of children and adults afflicted with deformities ordinarily considered incurable, have been successfully treated here. Paralysis of the young, crooked feet, legs, hands and arms, hare-lip, deformities of the face, tumors; such are the chief phases of deformity and affliction that—defying ordinary curative powers—find their way to this institution, and there are proven to be tractable and curable.

Victims of accidents upon the railways, of explosions, runaways, or whatever cause, are frequently taken to the Institute for treatment, on account of its admitted superior facilities for surgical treatment.

While the Institute is an individual enterprise, it is in no small sense a benevolent institution. Patients who are able to pay, are required to do so; but many indigent sufferers are treated gratuitously.

The object of the institution is the treatment of that large class of sufferers, that can obtain no benefit from the general practitioner of the healing art, because of his want of the necessary adjuncts in the way of surgical appliances. Here all the approved adjuncts are at hand. Mechanical contrivances adapted to the varied types of deformity and essential to work cures, baths suited to the patient's case and constitution, here make corrigible what without them would be hopeless. And should the attending surgeon require the assistance of some peculiar apparatus not at hand, he has the requisite machinery and skilled workmen to make what is wanted.

With such facilities and capacities, the Surgical Institute has very naturally great success in treating the afflicted.

TEMPERANCE SOCIETIES.

This city is the headquarters for the State of the following Temperance organizations: The *Indiana State Temperance Alliance, Sons of Temperance, Good Templars, Temple of Honor.*

The *State Temperance Alliance* was organized in this city December 11th, 1867. Its first annual session was held here on the 26th February, 1868; the second, on the 2d and 3d February, 1869; the third, on the 2d and 3d February, 1870; the fourth, on the 1st and 2d February, 1871.

The *Alliance*—as its name implies—is a union of all the advocates of total abstinence from the use of intoxicating liquors in the State. Its membership is, therefore, largely—but not exclusively—composed of members of the other Temperance organizations. The administration of the society is vested in a Board of Officers and a Board of Managers. The present Board of Officers is as follows:

R. T. Brown, President, Indianapolis; N. W. Bruice, Vice President, Lafayette; C. Martindale, General Agent and Corresponding Secretary, Indianapolis; T. A. Goodwin, Recording Secretary, Indianapolis; J. B. Abbett, Treasurer, Indianapolis.

With reference to the Board of Managers, the State is divided into three divisions, each having a Board of ten members.

Subordinate to the State Alliances, there are five "District" Alliances in the State, holding Conventions quarterly; also an Alliance in each county.

During the past two years about one hundred thousand persons have become members of this society; and the sum of nearly $40,000 has been raised and expended under the direction of its managers.

Briefly stated, the object of the society is to discourage the use and sale of intoxicating liquors; to repress the traffic therein, by the enforcement of existing laws, and the speedy enactment of more stringent and prohibitory legislation in that regard. Prominent among the means employed, are the copious distribution of Temperance literature, the efforts of lecturers (of whom six are employed), &c.

The city Alliance has about two thousand members.

The " *Temperance Alliance* " is the name of the official organ of the State Temperance Alliance. It is published monthly in this city. Its editor is Rev C. Martindale, Corresponding Secretary of the organization.

INDEPENDENT ORDER OF GOOD TEMPLARS.

This is the most numerous and influential secret Temperance organization in the State The Grand Lodge meets in Indianapolis once in each year.

In this city there are eight lodges, with a membership of about eight hundred. Four of these Lodges meet at the "Good Templars' Hall," one at the "Temperance Alliance Hall," and the others in different parts of the city. There about three hundred Subordinate Lodges in the State, and about fifteen thousand members.

The present officers of the Grand Lodge are: E. B. Reynolds, Esq., G. W. C. T.; Rev. S. B. Falkenburg, G. W. C.; Miss A. M. Way, G. W. V. T.; Sylvester Johnson, G. W. S.; H. F. Underwood, G. W. T.; John W. Buttriss, G. W. M.; Miss Ella Rex, G. W. D. M ; Miss Sarah Reeves, G. W. I. G ; M. W. Jackson, G. W. O. G. Rev. E. Gaskins, G. W. Chaplain.

The number of members "in good standing," in this city, is about one thousand.

SONS OF TEMPERANCE.

This order, considered as to North America, embraces in its organization National, Grand and Subordinate Divisions.

The National Division of the Sons of Temperance was organized in the city of New York on the 17th June, 1844. At the present time the order has been carried into nearly all the States and Territories of the Union, and in all the British North American Provinces. During the twenty-seven years of its existence there have been admitted into the Order, in this country, more than two millions of members.

The Indiana Grand Division of the Sons of Temperance, of which this city is the headquarters, was organized May 2d, 1846. In 1861, there were about four hundred and ninety Subordinate Divisions in the State. Since then the order, considered as to this city and State, has retrograded in numbers, owing to the war and other causes, until now there are but forty Subordinate Divisions in the State. This decline appears to have been arrested; and the membership in this city and State is reported to be again increasing steadily.

The order in this city is represented by *Washington Division No.* 1; which has a membership of about fifty.

TEMPLE OF HONOR.

The Subordinate bodies of this order are called *Temples*; the State body is called the *Grand Temple.*

The order is represented in this city by one *Temple*, organized on the 27th March, 1870, and having about fifty members.

The *Grand Temple* meets annually, on the fourth Monday of May; it has no fixed place of meeting.

The Grand Officers are: Joseph A. Williams, W. C. T., New Albany; J. J. Young, W. V. T., Evansville; Will. A. Quigley, W. R., Madison.

The Supreme Council, the head of the Order for North America and the British Provinces, meets annually in July—this year at St. Louis, Mo.

ST. PATRICK'S TEMPERANCE BENEVOLENT SOCIETY.

This is the title of an Irish Temperance Society, organized in 1870. It now numbers about one hundred and fifty members.

UNITED STATES ARSENAL.

One of the prominent "objects of interest" is the United States Arsenal building and grounds, situated on a commanding eminence east of the city, about half a mile north of Washington street, and one mile and a-half east of Circle Park.

The location of an Arsenal at this city was authorized by act of Congress, early in the Rebellion. Its establishment here was in March, 1863, and, pending the erection of the present buildings, a rented building, on the corner of Delaware and Maryland streets, was used for the purposes of the Arsenal, Captain William Y. Wiley O. S. K., in charge. Captain Wiley resigned his commission on the 14th of October, 1870.

The site of the Arsenal was selected by General Buckingham, and work on the buildings was commenced in August, 1863. These, with the exception of some minor details, have been completed and occupied some years.

Of these buildings the following is a brief description :

Main building—Three stories high, one hundred and eighty-three feet long, and sixty-three feet wide; for the storage of arms, &c.

Artillery Store-house—Two stories high, two hundred and one feet long, and fifty-two feet wide; for the storage of artillery, &c.

Magazine—One story high, fifty feet long and thirty-four feet wide; for storing powder.

Office—One story high, forty-three feet long and twenty-two feet wide.

Barracks—Two stories high, one thousand one hundred and five feet long and thirty-two feet wide; for the enlisted men.

Two Sets Officers' Quarters—Two and a half stories high, eighty feet long and forty feet wide.

One Set of Officers' Quarters—One story and a half high, forty-seven feet long and twenty-eight feet wide.

All of these buildings, with the exception of a portion of the officers' quarters, are built of stone and pressed brick, and are both substantial and imposing in appearance.

The grounds consist of seventy-six acres, and have great advantages in respect of beauty as well as of utility. Nature has given the site a commanding elevation, an undulating surface and numerous forest trees. To these art has added the beautifying auxiliaries of shrubbery, fine drives and walks, &c. A stream of running water passes through one corner. About twenty-five acres are used for pasturage and garden purposes; the rest for the buildings and surrounding grounds.

The grounds and improvements—especially in summer and autumn-time—unite in forming one of the most picturesque and attractive localities in the vicinity of the city.

(17)

The several commandants from the beginning have been: William Y. Wiley, Captain and O. S. K.; T. J. Treadwell, Captain of Ordnance; James M. Whittemore, Captain of Ordnance; William II. Harris, Captain of Ordnance and Brevet Lieut. Colonel U. S. A.; and R. M. Hill, Captain of Ordnance and Brevet Major U. S. A., the present commandant.

UNION DEPOT.

Location: On Louisiana street, between Illinois and Meridian streets.

The eleven railways centering in this city, all converge in the Union Depot. No equal convenience of a like character is found anywhere else in this country. The ends of the earth, so to speak, are here brought into connection under one roof, and long transfers from one depot to another, involving expense, inconvenience and delay, are avoided.

The building, and so much of the tracks leading into it as lie within the city limits, belong to the *Union Railway Company;* that is, to an association composed of the following railway companies: Jeffersonville, Madison & Indianapolis; Terre Haute & Indianapolis; Bellefontaine; Indianapolis & Cincinnati; Indiana Central. The remaining six companies occupy the depot as tenants.

The *Union Railway Company* was formed in 1850, and was at that time composed of the Madison & Indianapolis, Bellefountaine, and Terre Haute & Richmond Companies; of which John Brough, Oliver H. Smith and Chauncey Rose were, respectively, the Presidents. These three men, since famous in history, and of whom Mr. Rose alone is yet living, were thus the founders of the *Union Depot.*

Gen. T. A. Morris, as Chief Engineer, superintended the erection of the building, which was completed in 1853. At that time only the Madison, Bellefontaine, Terre Haute, and Peru Railways were in operation Soon after the Indianapolis & Cincinnati, and the Indiana Central Railways were admitted into the association, and therefore into the Depot. The Indianapolis & Peru Company never had any interest in the Depot, and but a slight interest in the tracks, which it subsequently sold to the association. The Lafayette & Indianapolis Company was admitmitted, with tenant rights, in 1854; the Jeffersonville & Indianapolis Company in 1855; The Cincinnati & Indianapolis Junction in 1858; the Indianapolis Bloomington & Western, and the Indianapolis & Vincennes in 1869; and the Indianapolis & St. Louis in 1870.

Mr. William N. Jackson, Secretary and Treasurer of the *Union Railway Company,* has had charge of the Union Depot ever since its opening in September, 1853.

The dimensions of the building are four hundred and twenty by two hundred feet.

The expansion of our railway system has greatly exceeded even the liberal anticipations of the projectors and founders of the *Union Depot;* and extensive as are its provisions, it has grown to be insufficient for the great demands upon it. Its available space is entirely taken up by the net-work of tracks of which it is the focus—presenting at times, during the day, a scene of apparent confusion very like a tangled skein, having neither beginning nor end to it, but which the care and efficiency of its management always unravels in good order. The number of trains daily arriving in, and departing from, the *Union Depot* now averages about seventy-six, many of them of great length. It is estimated that the annual number of arrivals and departures of passengers at this depot amounts to two millions.

But, as before remaked, the demands upon the Depot have outgrown its capacities, large as they are, and the want of room entails greatly increased responsibilities upon the management.

The erection of a similar building and on a larger scale, now urgently demanded, must ere long become a necessity, if the great convenience of one passenger depot for all our railway lines is to be continued.

The cost of the site and improvements of the *Union Depot* property has been about $275,000.

THE COUNTY COURT HOUSE.

Location: Court House Square, on Washington Street, between Alabama and Delaware streets.

As the present rude structure, that has for so many years sufficed for the purposes of the courts and offices of the county, is in process of gradual dismemberment, to give way to a new and more becoming structure; it is the latter, as it will be when completed, that is to be described here. The building will front on Washington street; the lineal extent of the front will be two hundred and seventy-five feet; the depth of the main building is two hundred and thirty feet; and that of the two wings, one hundred and four feet each. The elevation of the main cornice will be eighty-one feet; and of the tower, two hundred feet. The building will consist of three stories, with a basement and a Mansard roof. Two minor towers, one at the extremity of each wing, will be about one hundred feet in hight.

The style of architecture is the *Renaissance*. The ground floor will contain the several county offices; the second story, the courts, consultation, library, and witnesses' rooms; the third (a mezzanine), the jury rooms, &c. The basement will be devoted to general utility purposes. Beneath the basement floor will be the heating apparatus.

There will be three main entrances to the building; on the south, west and east. The court and other rooms will be spacious, and appropriate in the style of their finish, with ceilings of great elevation. The whole building will be traversed by spacious halls and corridors, and will be supplied with an abundance of light. The ground plan is rectangular in form, and its entire linear extent is one thousand six hundred and eighty feet. The plan makes due provisions for a jail building, jail yard, and Sheriff's residence in the rear, and comprehends two entrance gates on each side—the two on the north side being designed for carriages.

The plans are perfected, and the foundation is now rising. It is calculated that the building will be completed in about four years, at an estimated cost of about $500,000.

CEMETERIES.

CROWN-HILL CEMETERY.

Location: Two miles north-west of the city limits.

The dates of the establishment, dedication, etc., of Crown-Hill Cemetery, with the names of the incorporators and managers, are stated in the general historical sketch, page 125.

The total area of the grounds is three hundred and forty-nine acres. The location is the most beautiful and appropriate for the purpose in the vicinity of the city; and its superiors anywhere are very few. It takes its name from that of the only considerable eminence near the city. The grounds would appear to have been especially ordained by nature for the purposes of a last resting place. They combine the attractions of a rural cemetry with convenience of distance from the city—yet not so near as to be in danger of encroachment from the extension of the city limits. A turnpike road is on the west line, and another on the east; while a street railway to the main entrance brings it within a half hour's ride of the city. The grounds are cut by small ravines into undulations of convenient size for sections; and the carriage-roads are so surveyed and laid out as to take advantage of this feature. The sections, therefore, vary in size and figure, and the winding roads aid in producing a picturesque effect.

It has been the usage, in other principal cemeteries, to lay off the space in square or rectangular lots, without regard to the configuration of the ground; imparting a certain monotony of aspect, which is obviated here by sections of multiform figures, and various size. This not only varies the aspect of the grounds, but brings about "that true fraternity and comity of interests between the rich and poor which should especially prevail in the city of the dead."

Large and magnificent lots, valued at thousands of dollars, are joined by small plots which are within the means of the humblest citizen; and the elaborate and costly monuments on the former add greatly to the beauty of the more unpretentious memorial stones on the latter. Every section contains its large lots, and small and cheap ones also; and each presents attractions for all classes, so that there can never be a separation of the Cemetery into divisions for different classes.

A section of the cemetery, on a beautiful and commanding knoll, is set apart for a resting place for the Union soldiers who died while on duty in this city, or whose remains have been brought here for interment.

To the natural beauties of the grounds, in their picturesque undulations and abundance of forest trees, individual taste and affection have added (under judicious regulations by the managers), the ornaments of evergreens and flowering plants. Inclosures of lots have been forbidden, as marring the appearances of a cemetery, and tending, with the rust and decay of time, to disfigure rather than to beautify.

The tendency, in so many cemeteries, to too great a profusion of shrubbery and shade trees, which excludes sunlight and makes the grounds dark and damp, is confined within judicious limits here.

The Cemetery is a public instititution in which every person who purchases a burial plot has as great an interest as any of the incorporators or managers—the second of the articles of incorporation being as follows: "The distinct and irrevocable principle on which this association is founded, and to remain forever (except as hereinafter allowed), is that the entire funds arising from the sale of burial lots and the proceeds of any investment of said funds, shall be and they are specifically dedicated to the purchase and improvement of the grounds for the Cemetery, and keeping them durably and permanently inclosed, and in perpetual repair through all future time, including all incidental expenses for approach to the Cemetery, and the proper management of the same; and that no part of such funds shall, as dividends, profits, or in any manner whatever, inure to the corporators."

The exception provided for in the foregoing article is the provision of the thirteenth article, that "after twenty-five years shall have expired from the organization of this corporation, by a vote of twenty-five of the corporators living in the county of Marion, Indiana, and after a fund has accumulated which will amply and permanently provide for the preservation, sustaining and ornamenting the

Cemetery, such alteration may be made, at any annual meeting, in the principles and limitations of these articles as that out of the surplus funds of this Cemetery or association, contributions and appropriations may be made by the managers in aid of the poor of Indianapolis."

The success of the enterprise will appear from a comparison with other well known cemeteries. The receipts from the sale of lots in Greenwood Cemetery, during the first five years after it was opened, were $54,298.17, and the like receipts in Spring-Grove Cemetery, during the first twelve years, $128,892.49. The like receipts in Crown Hill Cemetery, from the date of its dedication to January 1st, 1870 (four years), were $172,060.70.

The Crown Hill Street Railroad, built chiefly by the Cemetery Company, at a cost of $17,000, was permanently leased to, and is now operated by, the Street Railway Company, of Indianapolis.

Crown Hill Cemetery has been under the immediate care of F. W. Chislett, as Superintendent, ever since its establishment; and its condition is the best evidence he could desire, of his efficiency.

The number of interments to January 1st, 1871, aggregated two thousand one hundred.

It contains many elegant monuments; and, whether in respect of natural beauty of site or added ornaments, ranks conspicuously among the cemeteries of the country.

CITY CEMETERY.

Location: On Kentucky Avenue, between West street and the river.

Of the establishment of this Cemetery, and other principal facts of its history mention is made on page — of the historical sketch in the first part of this volume.

It was, until the opening of Crown Hill Cemetery, the principal burial ground of Indianapolis.

The original tract consisted of but four acres. As need arose for more space, several additions were made by incorporated companies, the City having only a sort of general administrative supervision over these additions, and the expenses of of keeping the grounds in repair being borne by the proprietors and lot owners.

The site is a favorable one, and the added ornaments, in the matter of shade trees, shrubbery, drives, etc., extensive; but since the opening of Crown Hill Cemetery, the City Cemetery has fallen into comparative disuse.

The names of many of the prominent citizens of by-gone days are recorded on the memorial stones here; among others that of Ex-Governor Whitcomb.

With the exception of about one hundred, the lots are all sold; but less than half of them are occupied, as yet, by graves.

There is no record of the number of interments in this cemetery.

Of the additions to the cemetery, the principal are as follows:

The *Union Cemetery*, consisting of five acres, laid off in February, 1834, by Nicholas McCarty, Sr., Isaac Coe, James Blake, James M. Ray and John G. Brown.

The next addition, consisting of seven and one-half acres, was laid off by E. J. Peck, Esq., President of the Terre Haute and Indianapolis Railway Company, in February, 1852.

In September, 1838, a Philadelphia company, under the name of Siter, Price & Co., laid off a third addition, embracing two out-lots of the city, which was called *Green Lawn Cemetery*.

The original grounds and the several additions above mentioned, are in one inclosure, and are collectively called *The City Cemetery*. The entire area of this cemetery is about twenty-five acres.

THE HEBREW CEMETERY.

Location: Three miles south of the center of the city.

The grounds consist of three acres. As its name implies, this cemetery is devoted to the uses of a burial place for the Jewish population.

It was established in 1856, and was the first property purchased by the Hebrew congregation of Indianapolis.

It handsomely laid off in lots, but a small proportion of which have been required for interments, the Jewish population of the city being proportionably small.

The grounds are appropriately inclosed, and if not picturesque either by nature or art, are nevertheless maintained in a neat and tasteful condition.

THE CATHOLIC CEMETERY.

Location: Two miles south of the city.

The grounds of this cemetery consist of eighteen acres; of which five acres belong to the German (St. Mary's) congregation, and the remainder to the other Catholic congregations. The whole tract was purchased in the year 1860, by the Rev. Aug. Bessonics, pastor of St. John's Church, at a cost of about $2,500. The value of the tract to-day would be about $4,000.

The grounds have no striking natural aspects. The site is sufficiently undulating for all essential purposes, and art has done much to ornament the spot, in the way of evergreens, shade trees, &c. The whole is neatly inclosed, and contains a number of elegant monuments.

LUTHERAN CEMETERY.

On the first of May, 1870, the Trustees of St. Paul's German Evangelical Lutheran Church purchased ten acres of ground, situated a short distance south of the city, on the Three-notch road, between the Madison and Bluff roads, for a cemetery for the members of that society. The grounds have been laid off in rectangular lots, generally forty by sixty feet. The number of interments at the date of this writing is five hundred and five.

LAW COURTS.

The pricipal law courts located here are:

The United States Circuit and District Courts; the Supreme Court of Indiana; the Criminal Circuit, the Civil Circuit, and the Common Pleas Courts of Marion county, and the Superior Court.

UNITED STATES COURTS.

The United States District and Circuit Courts are held in the Government building, corner of Pennsylvania and Market streets.

District Court.—The United States District Court, for the District of Indiana, was constituted by an act of Congress, approved March 3d, 1817. Under this act the District Court had Circuit Court jurisdiction, and the judge's salary was fixed at $1,000 a year, which has since been increased, from time to time, to $3,500 a year. The following have been judges of this Court: Benjamin Park, 1817 to 1825; Jesse L. Holman, 1835 to 1842; Elisha M. Huntington, 1842 to 1863; Caleb B. Smith, 1863 to 1864; Albert S. White, March to September, 1864; David McDonald, December 13, 1864. to August, 1869; Walter Q. Gresham, the present incumbent, since 1869.

Circuit Court.—The judges of this Court have been John McLean, Noah H. Swayne, David Davis and Thomas H. Drummond. Judges McLean, Swayne and Davis presided in the Circuit Court by virtue of their offices as Associate Justices of the Supreme Court of the United States. Judge Drummond presides as Judge of the Circuit Court of the United States for the Seventh Judicial Circuit, composed of the States of Indiana, Illinois and Wisconsin; a recent law of Congress having created a circuit judge for each judicial circuit.

District Attorneys—Thomas Blake, 1817 to 1819; Alexander Meek, 1819 to 1822; Charles Dewey, 1822 to 1829; Samuel Judah, 1829 to 1837; Tighlman A. Howard, 1837 to 1840; John Pettit, 1840 to 1842; Courtland Cushing, 1842 to 1844; Daniel Mace, 1844 to 1848; Lucien Barbour, 1848 to 1850; Hugh O'Neal, 1850 to 1853; Benjamin M. Thomas, 1853 to 1856; Alvin P. Hovey, 1856 to 1858; Daniel W. Voorhees, 1858 to 1861; John Hanna, 1861 to 1866; Alfred Kilgore, 1866 to 1869; Thomas M. Browne, the present Attorney, from May term, 1869.

Clerks of Circuit and District Courts—Henry Hurst, from 1817 to 1835; Horace Bassett, from Nov. 30, 1835, to May 24, 1853; when John H. Rea was appointed District Clerk. Mr. Bassett continued Circuit Clerk to December 20, 1860, when Mr. Rea was appointed to that place. He continued to hold both offices to September 15, 1863, when Watt. J. Smith was appointed District Clerk. These gentlemen remained in office until April 18, 1865, when J. D. Howland was appointed to both clerkships.

Marshals—John Vawter, 1817 to 1829; William Marshall, May 4, 1829, to 1830; Gamaliel Taylor, May 7, 1830, to 1840; Jesse D. Bright, May 18, 1840, to 1841; Robert Hanna, November 15, 1841, to 1845; Abel C. Pepper, November 17, 1845, to 1849; Solomon Meredith, May 21, 1849, to 1853; John L. Robinson, May, 1853, to 1860; Elisha G. English, 1860 to 1861; David G. Rose, April 1, 1861, to 1865; Benjamin Spooner, the present Marshal, April 24, 1865.

Branch Courts—During the present year, what may be termed Branches of the Circuit and District Courts have been established at New Albany and Evansville, by authority of a late act of Congress.

THE SUPREME COURT OF INDIANA,

Created by the Constitution, was organized by an act of the first General Assembly of the State, approved on the 23d December, 1816. The first term began on the 5th May, 1817. Up to 1852 the Supreme bench consisted of but three Judges, who were appointed by the Governor. Since then there have been four Judges, elected every six years by the people. The following shows who have been Judges of the Supreme Court from the time of its establishment, and the period of service of each:

The first bench consisted of James Scott, John Johnson and Jesse L. Holman. At the December term, 1817, Isaac Blackford was appointed successor of John

Johnson, deceased. On the 28th January, 1831, Stephen C. Stevens and John T. McKinney succeeded Judges Scott and Holman. On the 30th May, 1836, Charles • Dewey was appointed successor of Judge Stevens, resigned, and Jeremiah Sullivan, successor of Judge McKinney, deceased. On the 21st January, 1846, Samuel E. Perkins succeeded Judge Sullivan. On the 29th January, 1847, Thomas L. Smith was appointed the successor of Judge Dewey.

October 12th, 1852, the bench having been increased to four Judges, by an amendment of the State Constitution, and made elective by the people, Samuel E. Perkins, Andrew Davison, William G. Stewart, and Addison L. Roach were elected—Judge Blackford holding over, as a fifth Judge, until the expiration of his appointment. Judge Blackford retired from the bench on the 3d January, 1853, having been a Judge of the Court thirty-six years. On the 18th May, 1854, Alvin P. Hovey was appointed to succeed Judge Roache, resigned, and on the 10th October following Samuel B. Gookins was elected the successor of Judge Hovey.

December 10th, 1857, James M. Hanna was appointed to fill the unexpired term of Judge Gookins resigned; and on the 16th January James L. Worden succeeded Judge Stewart, resigned.

On the 11th October, 1864, Charles A. Ray, Jehu T. Elliott, James S. Frazer, and Robert C. Gregory were elected to the Supreme Bench, and served until the expiration of their term, January 3d, 1871; when the present Court was sworn in: Samuel H. Buskirk, John Pettit, Alexander C. Downey, and James L. Worden,.

The Reports of the decisions of this Court, from the date of its organization to the present time, consist of forty-one volumes.

The office of official Reporter of the Decisions of this Court was created in 1852, and made elective every four years. The reports of the decisions of the Court up to May, 1848, were published by Judge Blackford in eight volumes, and are styled *Blackford's Reports*. Another of the Judges, Smith, published a report of the decisions rendered between May, 1848, and May, 1850, in one volume—not in general circulation among the profession—called *Smith's Report*. The first official Reporter was Horace Carter, whose reports are comprised in the first and second volumes of the *Indiana Reports*—beginning chronologically where *Blackford's Reports* terminate. Albert G. Porter was Reporter of volumes three, four, five, six and seven; Gordon Tanner, of volumes eight, nine, ten, eleven, twelve, thirteen and fourteen; Benjamin Harrison, of volumes fifteen, sixteen and seventeen; Michael C. Keer, of volumes eighteen, nineteen, twenty, twenty-one and twenty-two; Benjamin Harrison, of volumes twenty-three, twenty-four, twenty-five, twenty-six, twenty-seven, twenty-eight and twenty-nine; James B. Black, the present Reporter, of volumes thirty, thirty-one and thirty-two.

MARION CIVIL CIRCUIT COURT.

The Civil Circuit Court for this county was established in 1821. Up to the creation of the Criminal Court, it had jurisdiction of criminal as well as civil actions; since then, of civil actions only. Its present jurisdiction may be briefly stated thus:

Exclusive jurisdiction of actions for slander and libel.

Concurrent jurisdiction with the Common Pleas and Superior Courts, in all causes where the amount exceeds $50; and with the Superior Court in causes involving the title to real estate, and in those charging breach of marriage contract·

Appellate jurisdiction of civil causes arising in the justices courts, and of contested wills appealed from the Court of Common Pleas.

The following have been Judges of this Court from the time of its organization: Wm W. Wick, Bethuel F. Morris, Wm. W. Wick, Stephen Major, Wm. J. Peaslee, Wm. W. Wick, Fabius M. Finch, John Coburn, John T. Dye, Cyrus C. Hines, and John S. Tarkington, the present Judge.

SUPERIOR COURT.

This Court was established by an act of the last General Assembly. It has no exclusive jurisdiction.

Concurrent jurisdiction with the Circuit Court in all manner of civil causes of which the latter has jurisdiction, except actions for slander.

Appellate jurisdiction of all civil causes arising in the justices courts.

The Court has three Judges, who each try causes as a separate Court, at what is called the *Special Term,*; and who jointly determine at the *General Term* appeals from the special term.

The bench consists of Judges H. C. Newcomb, Frederick Rand and Solomon Blair.

THE MARION CRIMINAL CIRCUIT COURT,

Was created, by an act of the Legislature, December 20, 1865. There are six courts of this description in the State. They were established in a few of the more populous counties to relieve the crowded dockets of the Civil Courts of all criminal causes, and thus expedite the disposal of litigation.

This Court has original, exclusive jurisdiction of all felonies and misdemeanors, except such as may arise in the justices' courts and Mayor's court; and appellate jurisdiction of criminal causes arising in the justices' courts and Mayor's court.

The first Judge of this Court was Gen. George H. Chapman, who was succeeded in 1870 by Byron K. Elliott, the present Judge.

MARION COUNTY COURT OF COMMON PLEAS.

This Court was established in 1852, absorbing the Probate Court, which had existed from the early history of the county up to that time.

The recent creation of the Superior Court, has relieved the Common Pleas of much of its business, and will probably have the effect to make the latter chiefly a Probate Court.

Its jurisdiction, as qualified by successive statutes, is, in brief, as follows:

Exclusive jurisdiction of all probate matters.

Concurrent jurisdiction with the Civil Circuit and Superior Court in all civil causes except actions for libel, slander, breach of marriage contract, and those involving title to real estate.

Appellate jurisdiction of all civil causes appealable from the justices' courts.

The Judges of this Court have been: Levi L. Todd, David Wallace, John Coburn, Charles A. Ray, Solomon Blair, and Livingston Howland, the present Judge.

JUSTICES' COURTS.

These are inferior courts, having limited jurisdiction in civil and criminal causes.

Civil jurisdiction in causes where judgments are confessed, in any sum not exceeding $300. They may try any action where the amount claimed does not exceed $200, where the suit is founded on contract or tort.

Criminal jurisdiction—Exclusive, original jurisdiction where the fine assessed cannot exceed $3.00; concurrent jurisdiction with the Criminal Court, to determine all cases, punishable by fine only, where the fine may not exceed $25; and preliminary jurisdiction of felonies generally.

CITY COURT.

This Court is coeval with the incorporation of Indianapolis as a city. It has exclusive jurisdiction of violations of city ordinaces, and preliminary jurisdiction of felonies.

MUSICAL SOCIETIES.

The capacities of the musical societies and of the musical professionals in a community, form a good measure of the position of that community in the scale of civilzation and refinement.

A comparison of results attained in this city, shows a progress in musical science commensurate with the city's material progress.

That a great improvement has been made in the character of our musical compositions, in the capacities of our musical organizations for vocal and instrumental execution, in the qualifications of our musical teachers, in the general diffusion of musical knowledge, in the patronage accorded the higher grades of musical talent, are facts quite evident to those who have taken an interest in these subjects during the past few years.

The first musical society of any prominence in this city, of which any record is preserved, was organized about the year 1850. Mr. A. G. Willard was its leader, and Professor P. R. Pearsoll (a musical pioneer of the city, but who has kept even pace with, and often in advance of, musical progress, and who might be termed the Nestor of our home musicians), principal musician. Among its members were Mr. John L. Ketcham, Mr. Davidson, Mrs. Dr. Ackley, and other well known names of the past and present days of Indianapolis. This society was short lived.

Other societies, neither comprehensive in their objects nor animated by the conditions favorable to longevity or success, were formed, lived their brief periods, and were disorganized.

In 1863, the *Musicale*, a select society, composed only of musical experts, was organized, with Mr. J. A. Butterfield as leader. The meetings were held in the parlors of some of the members, among whom were Mrs. John W. Ray, Mrs. Holcomb, Mr. R. R. Parker and Mr. A. M. Benham. This society was devoted to classical music only, and appeared in public but once during its organization, which lasted two years.

In the summer of 1864, Professor Benjamin Owen came to this city, and soon gathered together a large number of pupils in vocal music; whom, with the amateur musicians of this city, he organized into a class, of which he which he was the leader and pianist. This organization was largely efficient in educating the public taste as to music; their public appearances were frequent; they successfully essayed difficult selections from the great masters. Among the prominent solo singers of this society were Miss Croft (now Mrs. A. M. Benham), Miss Amelia Heinrichs, Mrs. Dora Patterson Swift (since deceased), Miss Helen M. Dodge, Mr. L. D. Goldsberry, Mr. and Mrs. Owen, and many others whose names do not now occur to the writer. The period of the existence of this society was about three years, when it, too, yielded to the common lot.

The next considerable musical society in this city, was the *Mendelssohn Society*, which was organized at Benham's music store, on the 23d of September, 1867. Its officers were: W. H. Churchman, President; General Daniel Macauley, Vice President; C. P. Jacobs, Secretary; Thos. N. Caulfield, Director. The sessions were held at the Institute for the Blind. Mr. Caulfield was the conductor until his removal from this city in 1868, when Professor Bergstein was elected leader, which position he filled until the society was discontinued, in 1870. This organization was by no means in vain. Its members studied good music and attained superior excellence in execution, and certainly contributed materially to the cause of musical culture.

This necessarily brief and imperfect record of our past musical history, brings us up to the organization of existing musical societies.

Before dismissing these general observations, it may be worthy of mention, that the first pianos offered for sale in this city were manufactured by T. Gilbert, of Boston, and consigned to the Rev. Charles Beecher, in 1844. Some of these instruments are still in use, and present a picturesque contrast with the improved pianos of to-day. The first piano brought to this city was the one still in the possession of Mrs. James Blake.

THE MAENNERCHOR.

The Indianapolis Maennerchor, in respect of its age, prominence, and musical capabilities, is the chief German singing society of this city. It was founded in 1854. Its first leader was E. Longerich, who was succeeded by A. Despa; he by C. J. Kantman; he by Professor C. H. Weegman, and he by Professor Carl Bergstein, the present leader. In the great National Saengerfest held here in 1867, the Indianapolis Maennerchor was the inviting society and the directing one. The net proceeds of that festival aggregated $2,500; all of which was donated for the benefit of the German-English School, of the Indianapolis Benevolent Society, and of the German Benevolent Society of this city.

The Maennerchor now numbers about sixty active members, of whom about twenty-five are ladies; and three hundred honorary members.

In addition to the occasional public appearances of the Maennerchor, its members hold a "Social" once each month, during the winter season, on which occasions fine vocal and instrumental concert programmes are performed, and the best and most difficult compositions are excellently rendered. Recently the society has leased the entire Turner-Hall building, where its meetings for the transaction of business, rehearsals, and practice, are held.

THE HARMONIE,

A German singing society, was organized on the 1st of October, 1869, and is the result of a consolidation of three former German societies of this city, the *Liederkranz*, the *Harmonia* and the *Frohsinn*. These three societies joined together, under the direction of Professor Bergstein, in September, 1869, to celebrate the Humboldt centennial.

The temporary union of these societies was followed by their permanent consolidation, under the name of *Harmonie*, on the date above mentioned. This union, suggested, and in a great measure secured, by Professor Bergstein, made the *Har-*

monie a very large society. Its objects are similar to those of the *Maennerchor*, and its organization also, save that ladies are not admitted as members, as in the *Maennerchor*.

The members meet twice a week, in Marmont's Hall, for rehearsals and practice.

The President of the society is Henry Elft, and the Director C. B. Lizius. The number of active members is forty-five.

THE DRUID MAENNERCHOR.

This German singing society was founded in 1868. As its name implies, none but Druids can be admitted to membership, and it has no lady members. In other respects, its organization and character are similar to the *Maennerchor* society; but, being much younger than the latter, it has not attained to the prominence or skill of that organization.

Its meetings for the transaction of business, rehearsal, practice, and so forth, are held twice each week, in Mozart Hall.

It has about one hundred members, of whom thirty-two are on the active or singing list. The President is Philip Reichwein; and the Director, Professor August Mueller.

THE CHORAL UNION,

This is a select society, having for its objects mutual progress in musical culture and the advancement of musical science in this city. It is composed chiefly of amateurs, directed and leavened by skill and trained talent. It numbers many of the best amateur singers in the city.

The Union was projected and has been sustained by certain enterprising citizens, in the hope of making it a fitting musical exponent of the city of Indianapolis.

Need often arises, in a city of this size, for the services of a musical organization capable of rendering the better and more difficult musical productions, and this desideratum is is now found in the Choral Union. From its large membership and its abundant practice and competent training, the organization appears to particular advantage in choruses, while it also embraces a good proportion of singers of marked and peculiar excellence for solos and concerted pieces. The recent public appearances of the Union attest the great capabilities and promise of this organization. The society has already accumulated a large musical library. The Union is not devoted to vocal music alone, but embraces an orchestra also. The number of members is about one hundred and twenty-five.

The officers are: M. R. Barnard, President; Wm. C. Smock, Secretary; Prof. J. S. Black, Director; E. C. Mayhew and Prof. G. B. Loomis, Leaders.

THE PHILHARMONIC ORCHESTRA.

This organization is composed of a number of the more proficient amateurs of this city. It contains the elements and capabilities of a first class orchestra. The members meet once each week for study and practice. The field of their study and practice is classical music, as opposed to the wish-washy and tasteless productions which are thrown upon the market in such lavish abundance, and find multitudes of interpreters and patrons. The leader and conductor is Dr. R. A. Barnes.

Benham's *Musical Review* (a handsome and well edited monthly periodical of twenty-four pages), now in the sixth year of its publication, must be reckoned prominently among the agencies that have done much to organize and develop our musical talent, and advance musical interests in this city. Its pages embrace each month much valuable original and selected matter, correspondence, musical compositions, etc. Its list of contributors comprises some first class talent, in this country and in Europe, whose contributions are frequently widely reprinted.

The *Musical Visitor*, a monthly periodical of twenty pages, published by A. G. Willard & Co., yet in the first year of its publication, is also growing into deserved favor and consequence.

Within the past three or four years Professor J. S. Black, as an instructer of vocal music, has done much to inspire greatly increased interest in musical culture.

Among other prominent instructors are Professors Bergstein, Reitz, Leckner and Pearson.

PUBLIC LIBRARIES.

The *State Library* was called into existence by an act of the General Assembly in 1843. It was created and is maintained by Legislative appropriations. Including battle-flags, war relics, and so forth, the Library occupies the entire west half of the first story of the State Capitol.

The present number of volumes, of all descriptions, is about twenty-five thousand: of which ten thousand are literary and miscellaneous works; seven thousand, public laws and documents; two thousand, bound volumes of newspapers and periodicals; four thousand, duplicate volumes of public laws and documents; and two thousand, pamphlets and unbound documents.

The Library is in charge of the State Librarian, who is elected biennially by the General Assembly. The following have been the Librarians: Samuel P. Daniels, to 1844; John B. Dillon, 1844 to 1851; Nathaniel Bolton, 1851 to 1853; Gordon Tanner, 1853 to 1857; James B. Bryant, 1857 to 1859; James Lyon, 1859 to 1861; Deloss Brown, 1861 to 1863; David Stevenson, 1863 to 1865; Benjamin F. Foster, 1865 to 1869; M. G. McLain, 1869 to 1871; and James De Sanno, the present Librarian.

For the support of the Library, and for meeting the expenses incident to its maintenance, there is a standing appropriation of $400 per annum, and a yearly specific appropriation of $1,000. These amounts do not admit of extensive additions to the Library; and to make it all it should be, in respect of the literary and scientific collection, larger appropriations are requisite.

THE INDIANAPOLIS LIBRARY.

The city is yet without a general circulating Library. The want of such a Library has led, in past years, to the inception of a number of unsuccessful movements looking to that result. As a preliminary movement to this end, in March, 1869, one hundred citizens organized, under the style of the *Indianapolis Library Association*. The conditions of membership were, and are, a subscription for library purposes of $150, to be paid in annual installments of $25; thus affording an annual revenue of $2,500, for five years, for the maintenance and increase of the Library.

The Association proceeded with promptness to carry out its object. Suitable rooms were secured in Martindale's building, north-east corner of Pennsylvania and Market streets; and the paid up portion of the subscriptions have, from time to time, been devoted to the purchase of books and the support of the Library. The management of the enterprise has been excellent, and the funds of the Association have been invested to the best possible advantage. Already a collection of about three thousand volumes has been obtained; which number will be increased during the present spring to about four thousand five hundred; and it may justly be said that a better selection of like magnitude, than the three thousand volumes now on the shelves, could hardly be made. For the present the privileges of the Library are restricted to members—those who subscribe $150 to the Library fund—and to such others as may be allowed the use of the books by the payment of $5.00 annually.

This limitation of the use of the books to subscribers was, and is yet, manifestly necessary to the creation of a Library at all; and it has been the intention from the first to convert it into a Public Circulating Library as soon as it shall have attained a suitable magnitude and endowment.

The officers of the Association are: John D. Howland, President; William P. Fishback, Vice President; D. W. Grubbs, Secretary; William S. Hubbard, Treasurer.

MARION COUNTY LIBRARY.

This Library now numbers about two thousand volumes. The records show the first meeting of the first Board of Trustees of the Library to have been held in April, 1844. The Trustees are appointed by the County Commissioners. The first Board consisted of D. L. McFarlin, George Bruce, Henry P. Coburn, John Wilkins, James Sulgrove, and Livingston Dunlap.

The present Trustees are Powell Howland, L. M. Phipps, Charles N. Todd, William Hadley, John Duncan, and George W. Parker.

The interest on a fund of $2,000 is expended, as it accrues, in the purchase of books, &c.

The payment of a small sum annually entitles any citizen of the county to the use of the books.

THE TOWNSHIP LIBRARY,

Is in the keeping of the Township Trustee, whose office is on North Delaware street, opposite the Court house.

The collection is an indifferent one, numbering, all told, about one thousand volumes; and the appropriations for its support are too limited to admit of any considerable additions.

TELEGRAPH COMPANIES.

WESTERN UNION TELEGRAPH COMPANY.

Location of Indianapolis Office: In Blackford's Block, south-east corner of Washington and Meridian streets.

The first Telegraph office in this city was opened on the 12th of May, 1848—an office of the *Ohio, Indiana* and *Illinois Telegraph Company*—better known as the

O'Reilly line, from the name of its principal owner, Henry O'Reilly, one of the early builders of telegraph lines in this country, and owner of the right to construct lines in a large extent of western territory, purchased from S. F. B. Morse, the inventor of the Electro Magnetic Telegraph.

The *O'Reilly line*, as originally constituted, was from Dayton to Chicago, and ante-dating all of the numerous railways diverging from this city at the present day, was built along ordinary highways. Richmond, Indianapolis, and Lafayette were the intermediate points of prominence on this line. A branch of this line extended from Lafayette down the Wabash river, and through Terre Haute to Evansville; and these embraced all the telegraphic facilities in the State at that time, except a line through the northern counties, from Cleveland to Chicago.

In 1853, the *Cincinnati & St. Louis* line was built, and an "opposition" office was opened in this city.

About January, 1852, the "opposition" line had been sold to a new company, and rechristened as the *Wade line*.

On the 1st of May, 1853, the "opposition" office was consolidated with the O'Reilly office, and its interests were merged into the latter. This step was in consequence of the light receipts of the offices; for it was only a few years ago that the use of the telegraph was a comparative rarity when contrasted with the general and extensive use of that agency at the present day. The consolidation applied only to points where both companies had been maintaining separate offices.

During the spring of 1854, the Wade company constructed a new line from Cincinnati to St. Louis, *via* the *Ohio & Mississippi Railway*, which resulted in the discontinuance of that company's line between the same points, *via* the ordinary highways through this city.

The next line built was from Indianapolis to Union City (along the *Bellefontaine Railway*), and extended from the latter point to Dayton, Ohio; on the completion of which the line along the ordinary road, between Dayton and Indianapolis *via* Richmond, was discontinued.

In the summer of 1854, the *Western Union Telegraph Company* built a line from Cincinnati to Indianapolis, over the *Indianapolis & Cincinnati Railway*, and maintained a separate office in this city for a short time. About the first of October, 1856, the office of the *Western Union* and *O'Reilly* lines, in this ci y, were consolidated, giving to the former company control of the consolidated interests, with John F. Wallack) the present district superintendent) as manager. The *Western Union Telegraph Company* now operated four lines: one to Cincinnati; one to Dayton, Ohio, *via* Union City; one to Madison; and the old line, *via* the ordinary road, from here to Lafayette.

In 1856, was inaugurated the present arrangement between the *Western Union Telegraph Company* and the *Associated Press* of Indianapolis, in regard to telegraphic news reports—an arrangement since expanded and perfected; existing at nearly every point in this country where daily newspapers are published, and enabling the latter to furnish their readers with the news of the day in all parts of the New and Old Worlds.

It will, perhaps, be sufficient to give an idea of the magnitude of this business of furnishing "Press Reports," to state that the transmission of these reports occupy the lines almost exclusively from six o'clock in the evening till from one to three (as a rule) on the next morning. The aggregate of such reports, received at and sent from this city, is now about eight thousand five hundred words per day, paid for at lower rates, of course, than ordinary messages, on the basis of contracts between the several united Press associations and the Telegraph companies.

It may be worthy of note, in this connection, to state, that the first press report sent to this city by telegraph, appears to have been in the month of December, 1851, according to an entry in a record of that date, charging Wm. J. Brown (of the *Sentinel*) $11, on account of services in telegraphing the President's message (a very slight abstract or statement of its points, evidently). Henceforth the growth of the business of the office was rapid, and new lines multiplied as new railroads were built.

In December, 1864, the *United States Telegraph Company*—an association that promised at one time to be a strong rival of the *Western Union Company*—opened an office here; but, from the first, the policy of the managers of the *Western Union* has been that of absorbing rival enterprises; and so, in 1866, the *United States* line shared the general fate; and its lines here, nine in number, passed under the control of the *Western Union* Company.

By a recent re-division of the Territory of the *Western Union Telegraph Company* (which operates seven-eighths of all the lines in the United States, and a considerable portion of the lines in New Brunswick and New Foundland), Mr. Wallick's jurisdiction, as Superintendent of the Sixth District of the Central Division, comprises the lines radiating from Indianapolis, and the lines intersecting therewith, south to the Ohio river; east to Columbus and Crestline, Ohio; west to Alton, Illinois; and north to Chicago.

The number of Telegraph offices within the area of Mr. Wallick's district, of which Indianapolis is the principal office, is one hundred and sixty; with two thousand two hundred and eighteen miles of poles, and four thousand four hundred and fifty-eight miles of wire. In the main office in this city twenty-nine separate wires are worked.

The business having out grown the accommodations of the former location of the office, it was removed in 1865 to Blackford's Block, south-east corner of Meridian and Washington streets; where it is now located, and occupies four rooms: one in the basement, called the "battery room;" one on the ground floor, for the business office—where messages are received and delivered; one on the second floor, used for the Superintendent's office; and a large room on the third floor, called the "operating room," containing twenty-four sets of the best instruments, and with superior appointments in every other respect; and another on the third floor, used as a "local battery" room.

The offices in this city operating the *Western Union Company's* lines are as follow: The main office in Blackford's block, and auxiliary offices at the Union Depot, at the rooms of the Board of Trade, and at each of the railway depots— about eighteen or twenty in all.

The present organization of the office is as follows: John F. Wallack, District Superintendent; C. C. Whitney, Manager of the main office in Indianapolis; and fifty-one operators and other employes, including those at the branch offices.

It is an instructive commentary on the progress of Indianapolis, as well as on the increasing patronage of the Telegraph, that for several years after the establishment of the first office in this city, one operator, (without the assistance of even a messenger), had no hard task in transacting all the business, besides keeping a section of the line in repair; while about fifty-six persons are required to direct and perform the business of to-day.

The growth of this business will also appear by the following exhibit of the annual receipts of the main office (exclusive of the receipts from press reports, the extent of which has already been mentioned), since the establishment of the first office in Indianapolis: 1848, $530.33; 1849, $1,105.08; 1850, $1,161.08; 1851, $1,619.28; 1852, $1,869.88; 1853, $1,808.18; 1854, $2,433 90. 1855, $2,788.47; 1856, $2,524 04; 1857, $4,29.33; 1858, $33,855.18; 1859, $4,078.72; 1860, $5,202.61; 1861, $16,098.25; 1862, $23,192.33; 1863, $22,158.32; 1864, $31,978.85; 1865, $33,-418.31; 1866, $26,981.51, 1867, $23,916 75; 1868, $29,037.59; 1869, $24,854.47; 1870, $22,271.19.

The slight reduction of the receipts for the past year from those of several previous years, is on account of the extensive employment of the telegraph for military purposes during the war—which inflated the business of the Telegraph Company, as it did nearly every species of business.

THE PACIFIC AND ATLANTIC TELEGRAPH COMPANY.

Location of the Indianapolis office: No 21 South Meridian street.

On the 15th December, 1869, the *Pacific and Atlantic Telegraph Company* opened an office at No. 22 South Meridian street, in this city, with E. C. Howlett, Esq , as manager. This company was organized as an opposition to the *Western Union* Company; and has thus far avoided the fate of previous opposition companies in the West: which have been either absorbed into that powerful corporation, or, after a while, have ceased to exist.

The usual result of competition has followed the establishment of the opposition office here: a large reduction (almost 66 per cent.), in the rates of telegraphing to all points reached by the lines of the competing companies.

The new company gives every external evidence of a good degree of prosperity and growth, considering its youth and the great wealth and power of the *Western Union* company.

The lines have been extended as rapidly as patronage has seemed to justify; and the reduction in tolls caused by the establishment of competing lines, appears to have increased the volume of business to such a degree as to sustain a healthy opposition to the *Western Union* Company; in which opposition the *Pacific and Atlantic*, the *Atlantic and Pacific*, and the *Franklin* Companies are combined and mutually interested. The business of the office here shows a favorable improvement: the receipts for the month of December, 1870, being tenfold those of the corresponding month in 1869. The office now employs the services of a manager and two operators, and operates wires as follows: One to Pittsburgh, two to Chicago, two to Dayton, and one to Cincinnati. This company also has communication with St Louis, *via* Chicago.

On the 1st February, 1871, a fire partially destroyed the building at that time occupied by the office of this company. The office was promptly re-opened at No. 21 South Meridian street, its present location.

EXPRESS COMPANIES.

The increase in the carrying trade by express companies, at this point, has been in proportion to the multiplication of railways, and, consequently, has been very great.

The *Adams* Express Company was the first to open an office here, upon the completion of the Madison Railway, in 1847. The first agent of the company was M. M. Landis, Esq. As other railway lines were opened, new routes were also opened over them.

(18)

The *American* Express Company's office, here, was established in 1852.

This latter event resulted in a division of territory, as follows: the *Adams* having routes over the Bellefontaine and Terre Haute & Richmond Railways, and on all the railway lines running south of the lines named; the *American* also having routes over those two lines, and on lines running north of them.

This division of territory remained in force until the establishment here of an office of the *United States* Express Company, in 1854. This new competitor acquired a portion of the routes previously operated by the *American*, the *Adams* still retaining all of the territory acquired in the division with the *American*.

This arrangement remained in force until 1866, when a new competitor, the *Merchants' Union*, opened an office here, establishing routes over such lines of railways as granted the requisite permission. This *status* continued about two years. Then, to prevent unprofitable competition, the several companies above named made a new division of territory. By this arrangement the *Adams* Express Company's office here disappeared early in 1838.

In the latter part of the year 1868, by consolidation of the two companies, the offices and business of the *American* and *Merchants' Union* Express Companies, at this place, were united.

By virtue of a new arrangement between the companies, the office of the *Adams* Company was reopened March 12th, 1870. As a result of the previous arrangements, above noted, the business of the *Adams* has been very much diminished, and restricted to fewer routes than formerly; for which concessions here, corresponding advantages were gained elsewhere.

The present division of territory is as follows:

The *American* has exclusive routes on the Indianapolis, Cincinnati & Layfayette Railway; the Martinsville; the Jeffersonville, Madison & Indianapolis; the Indianapolis & St. Louis; the St. Louis, Vandalia, Terre Haute & Indianapolis; the Louisville, New Albany & Chicago (north of Greencastle); The Evansville & Crawfordsville (north of Terre Haute); the Evansville, Terre Haute & Chicago (north of Terre Haute); the Pittsburgh, Cincinnati & St. Louis (from Indianapolis to Dayton); the Chicago and Great Eastern (from Richmond to Chicago).

The *United States* has exclusive routes over the Cincinnati & Indianapolis Junction Railway; the Indianapolis, Peru & Chicago; the Indianapolis, Bloomington & Western; the Pittsburgh, Cincinnati & St. Louis (from Richmond to Columbus); the Cleveland, Columbus, Cincinnati & Indianapolis (from Indianapolis to Crestline); and the White Water Valley of the I., C. & L.

The *Adams* has exclusive routes over the Indianapolis & Vincennes Railway; the Louisville, New Albany & Chicago (south of Greencastle); the Evansville & Crawfordsville (south of Terre Haute). This company has also the right to do *through* business over the eastern lines leading from this city.

The earnings of the Indianapolis offices of the several companies, last year, were as follows:

American Merchants' Union..$100,335 00
United States.. 46,600 00
Adams (est.)... 25,000 00

    Total..$171,935 00

Number of employees: American Merchants' Union and United States, 80; Adams, 7.

The offices are located as follows: American Merchants' Union and United States, J. A. Butterfield, Agent, north-west corner of Meridian and Maryland streets; Adams, John H. Ohr, Agent, No. 17 North Meridian street.

AGRICULTURE.

INDIANA STATE BOARD OF AGRICULTURE.

Indianapolis, as the Capital, from its central situation, and as the commercial metropolis of the State, is so identified with the agricultural interests of Indiana, that a sketch of the State Board of Agriculture is proper in this volume.

The Indiana State Board of Agriculture was organized by a special act of the Legislature, entitled "An act for the Encouragement of Agriculture," approved February the 14th, 1851.

In this act we find, as incorporate members of the Board, the names of such prominent men as Gov. Jos. A. Wright, Dr. A. C. Stevenson, Putnam county; Gen. Joseph Orr, Laporte county; David P. Holloway, Wayne county; Geo. P. Lane, Dearborn county; and others who have taken conspicuous parts in matters appertaining to the general advancement of agriculture and manufacturing interests in Indiana.

Prior to the passage of this act, and in no small degree instrumental in securing its passage, societies for the promotion of agriculture and the mechanic arts had been formed, by individual enterprise, in a few of the counties. Of these the most noteworthy were those in Wayne and Marion counties; the former, attributable to the efforts of Gen. Sol. Meredith, W. T. Dennis, David P. Holloway, J. M. Garr, and others; the latter, to the efforts of Rev. Henry Ward Beecher, Wm. S. Hubbard, Dr. G. W. Mears, and others.

Through this means a stimulus was given to agriculture and manufacturing in Indiana, and especially to the latter at this point, that in all reasonable probability, in the absence of this legislative enactment, would not have been attained for many years to come.

The State Board was industrious and efficient. Dr. A. C. Stevenson, of Putnam county, visited England while a member of the Board, and brought home numerous specimens of the finest short-horns. In eastern Indiana, more particularly, are the fruits of these instrumentalities conspicuously apparent. General Meredith, George Davidson, and others, of Wayne county, and Hon. I. D. G. Nelson, of Allen county, soon followed in this line of progress, until the ambition to offer first class products in the markets of the East from Indiana, became general; and whatever credit may have attached to Indiana in this regard is, in the main, directly traceable to this Act of our Legislature and the efforts made by our Board of Agriculture.

The following have been Presidents of the Board: Gov. Joseph A. Wright, Gen. Joseph Orr, Dr. A. C. Stevenson, Gen Geo. D. Wagner, Hon. D. P. Holloway, Maj. Stearns Fisher, Hon. A. D. Hamrick, and Hon. Jas. D. Williams, present incumbent. The following have been Secretaries: John B. Dillon, William T. Dennis, Ignatius Brown, W. H. Loomis, A. J. Holmes, Hon. Fielding Beeler, and Jos. Poole, present incumbent.

The Eighteenth Annual State Fair, under the auspices of the State Board, was held in October, 1870. The First was held on the site of the present western City Park, October 28th, 1852. The State Board have paid in premiums more than one hundred and thirty thousand dollars at these several Fairs. But the amount ex--

pended in premiums is a very small portion of the great assistance agricultural interests in Indiana have received by the law to which we have referred. For it not only brought into existence the State Board of Agriculture, but we find that in the brief period of five years (1857), sixty-eight County Societies had been organized under and by the provisions of this act.

February 17th, 1852, the first or original act was amended, allowing County Societies to draw from the county treasuries certain funds arising from licenses to menageries, &c.; and subsequently the Legislature passed laws empowering the State Board of Agriculture and County and District Societies to purchase and hold real estate.

In 1864 W. H. Loomis, then Secretary of the Board of Agriculture, was mainly instrumental in securing the passage of an act exempting Fair Ground property from taxation, and directing County Treasurers to refund taxes paid on real estate so held.

It is due to Mr. Loomis, in passing, to state he has been something more than merely an efficient officer in the Board. His zeal and interest in securing the highest usefulness of that organization, have been extraordinary and efficacious; and for many years he has been a valuable aid to agricultural progress in Indiana.

The supreme efforts of the State in aid of subduing the Rebellion absorbed the attention of Legislatures and people, agricultural progress was retarded in consequence, and very many local Agricultural Societies were discontinued. Subsequently the attention of the public returned to the arts of peace; and agriculture reasserted its high claims upon the attention of the authorities.

Previous enactments having been found defective, the Legislature enacted a law authorizing "Joint Stock Associations for the promotion of Agricultural, Mechanical, Mining and other industrial pursuits." Under this latter law many contiguous counties in various portions of the State, have united and organized "Joint Stock Associations," have purchased fine grounds, pay larger premiums than the old societies, and have proved more useful to the advancement of home industry than the older organizations.

To the success of all laudable efforts in the promotion of these enterprises, whether under the auspices of our State Board of Agriculture, or of Joint Stock, County, or District Associations, the Capital has contributed liberally. State Fairs— like any other public gatherings that assemble at Indianapolis—while they may, and do, bring profit to its tradesmen and patronage to its hotels, are, nevertheless, proportionally beneficial to the State at large; and the Capital has not been the recipient of any undue share of the benefits growing out of these enterprises. While the State has appropriated $37,752.71 for the State Board of Agriculture, since its organization, in 1851; the citizens of Indianapolis have contributed to the Board $28,946.95, in addition to their proportion of legislative appropriations. Thirteen of the eighteen annual exhibitions of the State Board have been held at this city; and of these but one was, in any sense, a failure.

This exception was the exhibition of 1860, one of the finest displays made at any of the whole series, but called a "failure," financially, because at its conclusion the Board found itself several thousand dollars in debt. But inasmuch as it was the first exhibition held in the new Fair Ground, (Camp Morton having just been purchased by the Board for that purpose), on which large sums had been expended by way of improvements, the Fair could not justly be called a failure, because its receipts were unequal to such extraordinary expenses.

On the contrary, all but one (that at Terre Haute), of the five Fairs held at other points, in the State, were financial failures, because of their unfavorable locations for a general attendance from all sections of the State.

By excellent management the debt of the Board has since been extinguished.

The Fair Grounds, situated in the northern suburb of the city, consist of thirty-six acres; of which thirty acres were purchased by the railway companies, and the remainder by the State Board. These grounds are excellently adapted to the purpose, and possess all the requisite improvements for the convenience of exibitors and visitors.

THE INDIANAPOLIS AGRICULTURAL AND MECHANICAL ASSOCIATION.

In the year 1870 a Joint Stock Association with the above title was formed in this city, for the encouragement of Agriculture, the Mechanic Arts, and Stock-growing. The first Board of Directors, elected on the 28th of March, 1870, was composed of Lewis W. Hasselman, E. S. Alvord, Hon. Fielding Beeler, John Fish-back, Richard J. Bright, John T. Francis, W. C. Holmes, Jos. D. Patterson, and Hon. T. B. McCarty.

At the first meeting of the Board of Directors they elected the following officers:

President, Lewis W. Hasselman; Vice President, E. S. Alvord; Treasurer, E. J. Howland; General Superintendent, John B. Sullivan; Secretary, J. George Stilz; Assistant Secretary, William H Loomis. The latter gentleman, until his recent removal to Colorado, performed all the active duties pertaining to the office of Secretary.

The Association held its first exhibition—and a very creditable one—on the State Fair Grounds, last September; at which more than $14,000 in premiums was awarded and paid. Owing to the value of the premiums thus paid, to the fact that this was the Association's first exhibition, and to the erroneous impression prevailing throughout the State that it was merely a local exhibition, the attendance was disproportionate to the merits of the Fair.

So far as the display was concerned, it was incontestibly a great success; and in live stock and manufactures, it was preeminently so. The merits of this initial exhibition, and the liberal award of premiums, if not at the time remunerative, have given the Association a wide-spread popularity, and will insure adequate attendance upon its future exhibitions.

Though the first exhibition resulted in a loss of several thousand dollars, for the reasons stated, the Association is confident of future success, and is determined to deserve it. Its officers and principal stockholders have the requisite enterprise, public spirit and financial ability to successfully conduct a much graver undertaking.

At the second annual meeting of Stockholders, held at their office in the Indianapolis Board of Trade Room, March 28th, 1871, the following gentlemen were elected a Board of Directors: John Fishback, Indianapolis; Col. Wm. M. Wheatly, Indianapolis; Gen. Sol. Meredith, Cambridge City; Owen Tuller, Terre Haute; Hon. Fielding Beeler, Indianapolis; John T. Francis, Indianapolis; Wm. C. Smock, Indianapolis; Eli Heiny, Indianapolis; John H. Kenyon, Indianapolis.

The following officers were elected for the current year: President, John Fishback; Vice President, Col. Wm. M. Wheatley; Treasurer, Joseph R. Haugh; Secretary, Wm. H. Loomis*; Superintendent, Elisha J. Howland.

---

* Since appointed Register of the Land Office at Fair Play, Colorado; whither he has removed.

At this meeting steps were taken to purchase suitable grounds for the use of the Society, and eighty-six acres, directly south of the city, on the line of the Jeffersonville and Indianapolis Railroad, two miles from the center of the city, at the southern terminus of East street, were subsequently secured. The grounds are abundantly supplied with clear, perpetually running water, and abundance of shade.

The capital stock of the Association has been increased to one hundred thousand dollars; thus making it an easy matter for the Society to improve their grounds in a substantial manner, by the building of permanent halls for the exhibition of machinery and manufactured articles of all kinds, of stalls for live stock, and by putting into proper condition a fine one-mile time-track for the exhibition of horses.

MISCELLANEOUS SOCIETIES.

THE INDIANAPOLIS TURN-VEREIN.

The society of the Indianapolis *Turn-Verein* was organized on the 31st December, 1864, with the following members: John F. Mayer, Fred. Steffens, Charles Hœhne, F. Erdelmeyer, C. Koster, P. Lieber, J. Blosh, H. Hartung, F. Balweg, T. Moesch, L. Maas, E. J. Metzger, P. Kretsch, C. Steffens, B. Bannwarth.

The objects of the Association, stated briefly, are the mental and physical improvement of the members. Stated more fully, they were originally meant to embrace a wide field of intellectual exercises, as well as theoretical and practical gymnastics; stated meetings for hearing lectures on all subjects of human thought; literary and gymnastic exercises by the members; and methodical instruction, intellectual as well as physical.

This comprehensive programme, never fully carried out, is less than ever adhered to at the present time. In fact, beyond the gymnastic exercises of the youth, and the exhibitions of skill therein by them, the society is chiefly social in character.

The Hall is furnished with the requisite appliances, for gymnastic exercises; in which a high degree of skill has been attained by many of the German youth.

Occasionally, at public entertainments, festivals, etc., the members give exhibitions of their proficiency in the performance of difficult gymnastic feats; illustrating that the organization has been and is a success in respect of at least one of its objects,—that of physical improvement.

To have succeeded so well in this particular more than justifies the establishment and maintenance of the society; for an organization that has been so effective in conducing to good health and vigorous and muscular bodies, which invites so successfully the youth to spend their leisure time for the benefit of their health, instead of in idle and dissolute ways, is certainly a beneficent and commendable organization.

The Indianapolis *Turn-Verein* belongs to the *American Alliance* of *Turners* (the *Turner-Bund*), and subscribes to the platform of the latter.

The society numbers about fifty members, and occupies the first story of the *Turn-Halle* building.

The present officers are: Adolph Frey, First Speaker (President); Adolph Bauer, Second Speaker (Vice President); Paul Krauss, First *Turnwart* (Director of Gymnastic Exercises); F. W. Wachs, Second *Turnwart;* F. Rassfeld, Recording Secretary; J. Martin, Corresponding Secretary; F. Wenzel, Treasurer; C. Frische,

Zeugwart (Keeper of the Arms, &c.); C. Krauss, Librarian; J. Hunter,* Charles Steffens, and Louis Maas, Trustees.

THE SOCIAL TURN-VEREIN.

Political differences in the *Indianapolis Turn-Verein* resulted in a schism; a number of the members withdrawing and organizing an independent society called the *Social Turn-Verein*, on the 18th July, 1866. This independent organization is devoted, as its name implies, to social and gymnastic cultivation; and forbids the introduction of the discordant elements of sectarianism or party creeds into its councils and proceedings. It is fashioned, in its objects and methods, after the regular organization from which it withdrew; but, refusing to comply with the constitution of the National Alliance, in the respect of according support to political parties according to the measure of their advocacy of liberty and progress, it is not recognized by the *American Turn-Bund*. It has not, as yet, attained to the prominence and influence of the *Indianapolis Turn-Verein*, although it now enjoys a good degree of prosperity.

The present Speaker of the society is Francis Schneider; and the present number of members is about sixty-five. During the present month (June 1871), measures, looking to a reunion of this organization with the *Indianapolis Turn-Verein*, have been instituted, with a strong probability of success.

THE ASSOCIATION OF FREE-THINKERS.

This German Association was founded in April, 1870, by Prof. Charles Beyschlag, of this city; who framed its constitution, and was its head and Speaker until his resignation, in November, 1870.

The Association, as set forth in its constitution, and illustrated by its practice, is founded on the basis of free thought, is independent of every sectional creed or ecclesiastical belief, and accepts as true only such conclusions as are confirmed by the elucidations of science, and established by the light of reason.

The ordinary methods by which the Association proposes to carry out its objects are: lectures on popular, scientific and moral themes; a Sunday-school, in which are taught the history and character of the different systems of religion and morals, according to the best authorities; social meetings, in which all free-thinking people and their families are invited to participate; and appropriate observances by the Speaker at funerals, and on other serious and solemn occasions.

The Association now numbers about one hundred and fifty members. For its support each member is required to pay one dollar into the treasury quarterly.

UNITED IRISH BENEVOLENT ASSOCIATION.

Mention of this organization was inadvertently omitted from the chapter relating to Benevolent Societies; it is therefore inserted here.

This society was organized on the 24th of November, 1870. Its objects, as stated in its constitution, are: to promote the social welfare of Irish citizens; to create a fraternity of sympathy, an identity of interest, and a union of power among them; and benevolence.

Membership of the society is limited to those who are of Irish birth or extrac-

---

* Deceased.

tion, who are between the ages of eighteen and fifty years, and who are free from bodily infirmities calculated to abbreviate life.

The vitality and prosperity of the society are shown by the fact that its membership, at the end of five months from the date of organization, numbered one hundred and fifty. It was recently incorporated under the laws of the State.

THE FENIAN BROTHERHOOD.

The Indianapolis Circle of the Fenian Brotherhood was organized in the year 1859; by the Rev. Edward O'Flaherty. The first officers were: R. S. Sproule, Centre; J. G. Keatinge, Secretary; Dr. Lynch, Treasurer.

Up to the time of the breaking out of the rebellion, the workings of the order were in a quiet, preparatory sort of way, and but little was known or heard of it, in a public sense, compared with its subsequent notoriety. About this time Mr. John Simpson became Centre of the Indianapolis Circle.

The split of the order into the O'Mahoney and Roberts factions took place late in 1865. A majority of the Indianapolis Circle voted that President Roberts was the true chief of the Brotherhood; on which the minority withdrew and organized a Circle in the O'Mahoney interest. Thomas Nash was chosen Centre of the latter body, which died out after an existence of about one year.

On the 19th of March, 1866, President Roberts visited this city, and his reception at the old Tabernacle building, in the court house square, was one of the largest mass meetings ever held in Indianapolis. At this meeting a large sum of money was subscribed. After this all was quiet in Fenian Circles here till the latter part of May of the same year, when orders were received to March to Canada. In three days about one hundred and thirty men were armed, equipped, and sent to the rendezvous at Buffalo, N. Y., under command of Captain James Haggerty.

The engagements near Fort Erie followed, in which the Indianapolis contingent bore a prominent part. After the fiasco in which this raid resulted, Fenianism, in this city, fell into decay; and late in 1866 it ceased to exist as an organization. In the spring of 1867 it was reconstructed, and recovered much of its lost strength.

On the 3d of June, 1868, a State Convention of the Brotherhood was held here, when the State was divided into the *Northern* and *Southern Districts*, and E. F. Hart, of this city, was appointed Centre of the latter district. For a while the Circle here prospered anew; but internal dissensions breaking out again, resulted in its dissolution.

The Indianapolis Circle has not since had an existence as an organization. Out of its disorganized material grew the present military company called the *Emmet Guards;* and in 1870 was organized the *St. Patrick's Temperance Benevolent Society*, now numbering about one hundred and fifty members, and much more effectual in reclaiming the subjects of intemperance from their moral degradation, than was the Fenian Circle in recovering the lost independence of Ireland.

Of the resuscitation of the Fenian organization in this city there is now next to no prospect. The experiences of the past have taught many the impracticability of achieving the independence of Ireland by unlawful forays into Canada; while the mismanagement of the affairs of the order, and misuse of its resources, have produced a general distrust and lukewarmness among its former members.

THE WATER WORKS.

Of the different unfulfilled movements contemplating the building of water works in this city, an account is given on pages 112 and 113, of the general history.

After much previous consideration and investigation of the subject, the City Council, in January, 1870, granted a charter to the *Water Works Company of Indianapolis*, to build works for supplying the city with water; providing, among other conditions, that the works should be of the *Holly system;* that fifteen miles of pipe should be laid before the close of the year 1871; and that, in addition to the requisite supply of water for the cisterns, etc., the works should furnish the necessary quantity of water and power for the extinguishment of fires.

The company, with a capital stock of $500,000, was at once organized, and the following officers and directors were chosen:

President, James O. Woodruff; Secretary, Alex. C. Jameson; Treasurer, William Henderson; Directors, William Braden, William Henderson, Thos. A. Hendricks, Deloss Root, Harmon Woodruff, Henry R. Selden, Aquilla Jones, Sr., and James E. Mooney.

The *Holly System*, as most readers are aware, dispenses with the reservoir, and forces the water directly from its source into the pipes by means of immense force pumps; at the same time furnishing ample power and abundance of water for suppressing fires—doing away with the cost of purchasing and maintaining fire engines.

The available portion of the *Indiana Central Canal* was purchased, for propelling power for the machinery of the works. A site for the water supply, buildings, &c., was secured on the east bank of the river, and south of Washington street a huge well has been sunk; the pumps and machinery have been put in position, and over them a suitable building has been erected.

The fifteen miles of pipe required to be laid by the end of the year 1871, had been laid by the early part of that year. The area supplied by the works, at this time, is one mile square.

The extension of the system throughout the entire area of the city will require sixty miles of pipe.

The machinery is substantial and powerful. There are three engines—two piston and one rotary, from the Holly manufactory at Lockport, New York; and three Turbine water wheels. The combined power of the engines and water wheels is eleven hundred horse power. The provisions for the suppression of fires are of the most ample character. Of fire hydrants connected with the fifteen miles of pipe already laid, there are two hundred; and when the system is extended to all parts of the city, the estimated number will be about six hundred. The company guaranty to throw six streams of water, at one time, to an elevation of one hundred feet, in any part of the city reached by the system. The cost of the works, as far as completed, has been about $350,000; that of the complete system will be about $650,000.

The supplying capacity of the machinery is about 6,000,000 gallons daily.

The present officers of the Company are: John R. Elder, President; William Henderson, Treasurer; Alex. C. Jameson, Secretary; C. N. Lee, Superintendent.

SECRET ORDERS.

THE MASONS.

GRAND LODGE.—The Grand Lodge of Indiana was formed at Madison, January 12th, 1818. Alexander A. Meek being the oldest Past Master present, was called to the chair. On the next day an election for officers was held, and Alexander Breckner was elected Grand Master.

For a number of years the annual communications were held at various points in the State, viz: Jeffersonville, Corydon, Madison, Salem, Vincennes, New Albany and Indianapolis; but, s'nce 1833, they have been held at Indianapolis. The Grand Lodge Hall is located at the south-east corner of Washington and Tennessee streets. The corner stone was laid October 25, 1848, and the building was erected during the years 1849-50, at a cost of about $20,000., and was dedicated by the Grand Lodge May 27, 1851. The Grand Officers for the years 1870-71 are:

M. W. Martin H. Rice, of Plymouth, Grand Master; R. W. George W. Porter, of New Albany, Deputy Grand Master; *R. W. William T. Clark, of Indianapolis, Senior Grand Warden; R. W. Christian Fetta, of Richmond, Junior Grand Warden; R. W. Charles Fisher, of Indianapolis, Grand Treasurer; R. W. John M. Bramwell, of Indianapolis, Grand Secretary; Rev. John Leach, of New Carlisle, Grand Chaplain; Bro. George H. Fish, of Evansville, S. G. Deacon; Bro. W. B. McDonald, of Orleans, J. G. Deacon; *Bro. J. Sharpe Wisner, of Bluffton, Grand Lecturer; Bro. Thomas B. Ward, of Lafayette, Grand Marshal; Bro. William M. Black, of Indianapolis, Grand Tyler. The stated communications are held at Indianapolis, on the Tuesday next succeeding the fourth Monday in May.

SUBORDINATE BODIES IN INDIANAPOLIS.—There are six Lodges of Master Masons in the city, the oldest being *Center Lodge*, No. 23. A dispensation, for this organization, was issued March 27, 1822, Harvey Gregg to be the first Master, Milo R. Davis the first Senior Warden, and John T. Osborn the first Junior Warden; and on the 7th of October, 1823, a charter was granted, Harvey Gregg to be the first Master, Harvey Bates to be the first Senior Warden, and John T. Osborn the first Junior Warden. In 1834, its charter was surrendered and a new charter granted, dated December 17, 1835. On the first of January, 1871, this Lodge had two hundred and forty-eight members. The officers for 1871 are Joseph Solomon, W. M.; Nicholas R. Ruckle, S. W.; Henry H. Langenberg, J. W.; Henry Daumont, Treasurer; Charles Fisher, Secretary; Robert P. Daggett, S. D.; John Vanstan, J. D. Stated communications, first Wednesday of each month.

Marion Lodge, No. 35, was chartered May 27, 1847. The number of members on the 1st of January, 1871, was one hundred and fifty-three. The officers for 1871 are: Jackson Saylor, W. M.; Thomas C. Rout, S. W.; Henry C. Sailors, J. W.; John F. Conwell, Treasurer; John G. Waters, Secretary; H. C. McFarland, S. D.; John Ingles, J. D. Stated communications, on the third Wednesday in each month.

Teutonia Lodge, No. 178, (German).—The charter of this Lodge is dated May 29, 1867. The number of members January 1, 1871, was eleven. The officers for 1871 are: Charles Lauer, W. M.; Christian Karle, S. W.; Joseph Bernauer, J. W.; Frederick Meyer, Treasurer; Chas. Dehne, Secretary; Frederick Klare, S. D.; Louis Halle, J. D. Stated communications, on the second Friday of each month.

Capital City Lodge, No. 312.—The charter of this Lodge is dated May 24, 1865. Number of members January 1, 1871, ninety-one. The officers for 1871 are: Wm. H. Ireland, W. M.; A. H. Stoner, S. W.; Hiram Seibert, J. W.; Frederick Baggs, Treasurer; Geo. H. Fleming, Secretary; Henry D. Pope, S. D.; John A. Miller, J. D. Stated communication, on the first Tuesday of each month.

Ancient Landmarks Lodge, No. 319.—Charter dated May 24, 1865. Number of members January 1, 1871, one hundred and thirty. The officers for 1871 are:

* Dead.

James W· Hess, W. M.; Joel O. Martin, S. W.; Charles E. Cones, J. W.; Wm. W. Woolen, Treasurer; Ephraim Hartwell, Secretary; Wm. S. Armstrong, S. D.; Robert B. Cowen, J. D. Stated communication on the first Tuesday of each month.

Mytic Tie Lodge, No. 398.—Charter dated May 25, 1869. Number of members January 1, 1871, fifty-three. The officers for 1871 are: John Caven, W. M.; Erastus J. Hardesty, S. W.; Joseph W. Smith, J. W.; Ebenezer Sharpe, Treasurer; William S. Cone, Secretary; Willis D. Engle, S. D.; Alfred E. Miller, J. D. Stated communication, on the fourth Wednesday in each month.

The total number of Master Masons affiliated with Lodges in Indianapolis, on the 1st of January, 1870, was six hundred and eighty-two. Total number on the 1st of January, 1871, six hundred and eighty-six. Increase during the year, four; or, about three-fifths of one per cent.

The number of deaths during the year 1870, was eight; or one and one-sixth per cent.: being an average of life of sixty-five years.

THE CHAPTER.—*Indianapolis Chapter, No. 5, Royal Arch Masons.*—Charter dated May 25, 1846. Number of members September 1, 1870, one hundred and forty-eight. Present officers: Benjamin C. Darrow, H. P.; Ephraim Colestock,* K ; Ephraim Hartwell, S.; John Ebert, C. H.; Wm. H. Valentine, P. S.; Charles F. Pleslin, R. A. C.; Isaac Thalman, G. M. 3 V.; Alfred L. Webb, G. M. 2 V.; W. S. Cone, G. M. 1st V.; Henry Daumont, Treasurer; Charles Fisher, Secretary; Wm. M. Black, G.

Time of regular meeting, on the first Friday of each month. Died during the year, one. Increase of members during the year, one.

Keystone Chapter, No. 6, Royal Arch Masons.—Dispensation granted September 3, 1870. Charter dated October 20, 1870. Present number of members thirty-six. Present officers: Martin H. Rice, H. P.; Joel O. Martin, K.; Daniel Martin, S.; Wm. S. Cone, C. H.; Wm. H. Ireland, P. S.; James Peacock, R. A. C.; John J. Palmer, G. M. 3d V.; Wm. O. Stone, G. M. 2d V.; George Cumming, G. M. 1st V.; Wm. W. Woolen, Treasurer; Ephraim Hartwell, Secretary.

THE COUNCIL.—*Indianapolis Council, No. 2.*—Charter dated October 18, 1855. Number of members September 1, 1870, one hundred and four. The present officers are: Roger Parry, T. Ill. G. M.; *Ephraim Colestock, D. Ill. G. M.; Wm. S. Cone, P. C. W.; Charles F. Pleslin, C. G.; Henry Daumont, Tr.; Charles Fisher, Rec'r.; Wm. M. Black, S. and S. No deaths during the year. Decrease during the year, three.

Time of regular meeting, on the first Monday of each month.

THE COMMANDERY.—*Raper Commandery, No. 1.*—Charter dated May 14, 1848. The number of members on the 1st of January, 1871, was seventy-six. Officers: Roger Parry, E. C.; Nicholas R. Ruckle, G.; Alfred T. Webb, C. G.; John Ebert, P.· George H. Fleming, S. W.; W. S. Cone, J. W.; Henry Daumont, Treasurer; Charles Fisher, Rec'r.; Oliver B. Gilkey, St. B.; Charles F. Pleslin, Sword B.; Isaac Thalman, Warden; Wm. M. Black, Sentinel. Time of regular meeting, on the fourth Wednesday of each month.

Died during the year, one. Increase of members during the year, one.

SCOTTISH RITE A. & A. M.—*Adoniram Grand Lodge of Perfection*, was instituted in February, 1864, under a dispensation granted by the Supreme Council to Hon. Caleb B. Smith, and others.

The number of members April 1st, 1871, was two hundred and fifteen. The officers for 1871 are: John Caven, T. P. G. M.; Jehiel Barnard, D. G. M.; Joseph

---

*Died June 27, 1871.

W. Smith, S. G. W.; James M. Tomlinson, J. G. W.; Russell Elliott, G. O.; L. R. Martin, G. Treasurer; Ephraim Hartwell, G. Secretary; A. Sidney Chase, G. M. of C.; Max. F. A. Hoffman, G. Organist; Charles Lauer, G. C. of G.; C. H. G. Bals, G. H. B.; Charles John, G. Tyler.

Meeting for business and work, every Wednesday evening. Died during the year, two. Increase of members during the year, eleven.

Seraiah Council of Princes of Jerusalem, was instituted in February, 1864, under a dispensation granted to Caleb B. Smith, and others.

The number of members April 1, 1871, was one hundred and sixty-six. Present officers: P. G. C. Hunt, G. M.: Jehiel Barnard, Dept. G. M.; Jos. W. Smith, Sen. G. W.; ·A. Sidney Chase, Jun. G. W.; Ephraim Hartwell, G. Secretary; L. R. Martin, G. Treasurer; Cyrus J. Dobbs, G. M. of C.; Joseph B. Phipps, G. M. of E.; Charles John, G. T.

Died during the year, two. Increase of membership during the year, two.

Indianapolis Chapter of Rose Croix.—A dispensation to open this Chapter was granted November 2, 1864, to Theodore P. Haughey and others.

The number of members April 1, 1871, was one hundred and twenty-four. The officers for 1871 are: Jehiel Bernard, M. W.; Nicholas R. Ruckle, Sen. W.; Joseph W. Smith, Jun. W.; John B. Brandt, G. O.; L. R. Martin, G. Treasurer; Ephraim Hartwell, Secretary; Gilbert W. Davis, G. H.; Wm. H. Valentine, M. of C.; Cyrus J. Dobbs, Captain of G.

Died during the year, one. Increase of membership during the year, six.

Indiana Consistory.—A dispensation to open this Body was granted November 2, 1864, to Edwin A. Davis, and others.

The number of members April 1, 1871, was one hundred and seven. Officers for 1871: Nicholas R. Ruckle, Commander in Chief; Cyrus J. Dobbs, First Lieutenant Commander; P. G. C. Hunt, Second Lieutenant Commander; Max. F. ·A. Hoffman, M. of S.; Nathan Kimball, G. C.; E. Hartwell, Secretary L. R. Martin, Treasurer; S. A. Johnson, G. E. and A.; Charles H. G. Bals, G. H.; Algernon S. Chase, G. M. of C.; Joseph W. Smith, G. S. B.; S. T. Scott, G. C. of G.; Charles John, G. S.

Died during the year, one. Increase of members during the year, five.

The Thirty-Third Degree. — Persons in possession of the Thirty-third Degree, and Members of the Supreme Council, N. J. U. S., residing in Indianapolis, are: James W. Hess, thirty-third degree; John Caven, thirty-third degree; Phineas G. C. Hunt, thirty-third degree; Nicholas R. Ruckle, thirty-third degree. Deputy of the Supreme Council for the District of Indiana, John Caven, thirty-third degree.

COLORED MASONIC ORGANIZATIONS.

The African Grand Lodge of Indiana was organized in this city in 1855, and now numbers eighteen effective Subordinate Lodges, in good standing. The first Grand Master was J. G. Britton, of Indianapolis. Present Grand Officers: William Walden, Grand Master; C. A. Roberts, Deputy Grand Master; G. W. Robinson, Grand Secretary; James Van Horn, Grand Treasurer. Stated Communication in June Annually, at Indianapolis.

The Subordinate bodies in this city are the following:

Union Lodge No. 1—Organized in 1847—has forty members.

Gleve's Lodge No. 2—Organized in 1866—has about forty-five members.

Pythagoras Lodge No. 9—Organized in April, 1869—has fifty members.

Zerubbabel Chapter No. 2, R. A. M.—Organized in September, 1869—has thirteen members.

INDEPENDENT ORDER OF ODD FELLOWS.

This city is the seat of the Indiana Grand Lodge and Indiana Grand Encampment of the Independent Order of Odd Fellows, and of four Subordinate Lodges and three Subordinate Encampments of that Order. The charter for the first Subordinate Lodge in this State—New Albany Lodge No. 1—was granted by the Grand Lodge of the United States, on the 9th of October, 1835. Monroe Lodge, No. 2, Madison, was chartered sometime in 1836.

THE GRAND LODGE OF INDIANA.—On the petition of New Albany Lodge No. 1, and Monroe Lodge No. 2, the Grand Lodge of Indiana was instituted at New Albany, by Deputy Grand Master Henry Wolford, of the Grand Lodge of Kentucky, on the 14th August, 1837. By a warrant dated October 19th, 1841, the Grand Lodge of Indiana was removed to Madison.

September 19th, 1845, the Grand Lodge of the United States authorized the reference of a proposition to remove the Grand Lodge of Indiana to Indianapolis, to a voteof all the Subordinate Lodges in the State. The vote was in favor of such removal, and the first meeting of the Grand Lodge in this city, was held on the 19th of January, 1846. It has ever since been located here. At the time of its removal to this city, the Grand Lodge comprised twenty-seven Subordinate Lodges, with an aggregate membership of seven hundred and sixty-eight.

The first Grand Officers were: Joseph Barkley, Grand Master; Richard D. Evans, Deputy Grand Master; Jared C. Jocelyn, Grand Secretary; Henry H. West, Grand Warden; John Evans, Grand Treasurer.

The successive Grand Masters, for the period of one year each, except where it is otherwise stated, have been: Joseph D. Barkley, from August, 1837; Richard D. Evans, from August, 1838 (deceased in February, 1847); William Ford, from August, 1839 (deceased October, 1860); Christan Bucher, from August, 1840; John Neal, from August, 1841; James W. Hinds, from August, 1842; Noah H. Cobb, from July, 1843; William Cross, from July, 1844; John H. Taylor, from July, 1845 (deceased in August, 1858); Joel B. McFarland, from July, 1846 (deceased in April, 1861); John Green, from July, 1847; Philander B. Brown, from July, 1848; Job B. Eldridge, from July, 1849; Milton Herndon, from July, 1850; Oliver Dufour, from July, 1851; Joseph L. Silcox, from July, 1852 (deceased in May, 1856); William K. Edwards, from July, 1853; Oliver P. Morton, from July, 1854; J. B. Anderson, from July, 1855; James H. Stewart, from November, 1856; P. A. Hackleman, from November, 1857 (deceased in October, 1862); A. H. Mathews, from November, 1858 (deceased in April, 1862); Thomas Underwood, from November, 1859; Solomon Meredith, from November, 1860; William H. Dixon, from November, 1861 (deceased in April, 1865); Jonathan S. Harvey, from November, 1862; Dennis Gregg, from November, 1863 (deceased October, 1865); Harvey D. Scott, from November, 1864; Thomas B. McCarty, from November, 1865; Jos. A. Funk, from November, 1866; John Sanders, from November, 1867: Samuel L. Adams, from November, 1868 (deceased August 23, 1869); James A. Wildman, from November, 1869; W. H. DeWolf, from November, 1870.

The present Grand Lodge Officers are: W. H. DeWolf, M. W. Grand Master, of Vincennes; J. W. McQuiddy, R. W. D. Grand Master, of New Albany; Platt J. Wise, R. W. Grand Warden, of Fort Wayne; E. H. Barry, R. W. Grand Secretary, of Indianapolis; T. P. Haughey, R. W. Grand Treasurer, of Indianapolis;

Thomas Underwood, G. Representative, G. L. U. S., of Lafayette; J. A. Wildman, G. Representative G. L. U. S., of Kokomo; Philip Hornbrook, alternate G. Representative G. L. U. S., of Evansville; C. L. Cory, alternate G. Representative G. L. U. S., of Fairfield; Rev. C. A. Munn, W. G. C., of Kendallville; E. H. Wolf, W. G. M., of Rushville; Reddick Harrell, W. G. C., of Petersburg; H. C. Milice, W. G. H., of Kosciusko; H. D. Milns, W. G. G., of Terre Haute.

The Grand Lodge now numbers three hundred and thirty-eight effective Subordinate Lodges, having an aggregate membership of about twenty thousand. The Annual Communication is held in Grand Lodge Hall, in this city, on the third Tuesday in November; the Semi-annual Communication is held at the same place on the third Tuesdays in May and November.

Of the elegant "Grand Lodge Hall," on the north-east corner of Washington and Pennsylvania streets, a brief description is given on page 99. It is only necessary to supplement what is there written, with a corrected statement of the cost of the building and site,—in round numbers, about $62,000, instead of $47,000, as there given.

THE GRAND ENCAMPMENT OF INDIANA.—This body was instituted at Indianapolis on the 10th of January, 1847, by Jacob Page Chapman, by virtue of a warrant granted by the Grand Lodge of the United States. The first officers were: Christian Bucher, M. W. Grand Patriarch; Philander B. Brown, M. E. Grand High Priest; Jacob Page Chapman, R. W. Grand Senior Warden; A. W. Gordon, R. W. Grand Junior Warden, Willis W. Wright. R. W. Grand Scribe; Edwin Hedderly, R. W. Grand Treasurer; David Craighead, R. W. Grand Sentinel.

The successive Grand Patriarchs, for one year each, have been: Christian Bucher, from July, 1847; Thomas S. Wright, from July, 1848; Isaac H. Taylor, from July, 1849; Job Eldridge, from July, 1850; Jacob Page Chapman, from July, 1851; Daniel Moss, from July, 1852; Edward H. Barry, from July, 1853; Marshall Sexton, from July, 1854; Lewis Humphreys, from July, 1855 to November, 1856; Jonathan S. Harvey, from November, 1856; Chris. Miller, from November, 1857; John H. Stalley, from November, 1858; Thomas B. McCarty, from November, 1859; N. P. Howard, from November 1860; L. M. Campbell, from November, 1861, David Ferguson, from November, 1862; Leonidas Sexton, from November, 1863; James Burgess, from November, 1864; F. J. Blair, from November, 1865; C. P. Tuley, from November, 1866; William M. French, from November, 1867; William C. Lupton, from November, 1868; James Peirce, from November, 1869; Thomas G. Beharrell, from November, 1870.

The present officers are: Thomas G. Beharrell, M. W. Grand Patriarch, of Moore's Hill; W. Y. Monroe, M. E. Grand High Preist, of North Madison; Samel Raymond, R. W. Grand Senior Warden, of Indianapolis; Reuben Robertson, R. W. Grand Junior Warden, of New Albany; Edward H. Barry, R. W. Grand Scribe, of Indianapolis; T. P. Haughey, R. W. Grand Treasurer, of Indianapolis; Christopher Toler, W. Grand Sentinel, of Madison; Joseph S. Watson, W. Grand Deputy Sentinel, of Indianapolis; James Peirce, G. Representative G. L. U. S., of New Albany; G. W. Jordon, of Attica, and John F. Wallick, of Indianapolis, alternate G. Representatives G. L. U. S.

The present number of Subordinate Encampments, is one hundred and seven; with an aggregate membership of about four thousand five hundred.

The Annual and Semi-annual Communications of the Grand Encampment, are held in Grand Lodge Hall, in this city, at the same dates as those of the Grand Lodge, before stated.

SUBORDINATE BODIES IN INDIANAPOLIS.—These are: Center Lodge, No. 18; Philoxenian Lodge, No. 44; Capital Lodge No. 124; Germania Lodge, No. 129; Metropolitan Encampment, No. 5; Marion Encampment, No. 35; Teutonia Encampment, No. 57.

Center Lodge, No. 18, was instituted on the 24th of December, 1844, with the following members: William Sullivan, Edgar B. Hoyt, Jacob Page Chapman, William A. Day, Enoch Pyle, Jacob B. McChesney, and John Kelley. William Sullivan was the first Noble Grand of this Lodge, and its first Representative to the Grand Lodge.

The membership, on the 31st of March, 1871, numbered one hundred and fifty-six. The present officers are: L. W. Hetselgesser, Noble Grand; George C. Strachan, Vice Grand; George P. Anderson, Permanent Secretary; John W. Miller, Recording Secretary; John G. Waters, Treasurer.

Philoxenian Lodge, No. 44, was instituted on the 8th of July, 1847, with the following members: Harvey Brown, D. P. Hunt, Willis W. Wright, J. J. Owsley, Wm. Robson, George D. Staats, D. T. Powers, Lafayette Yandes, William Mansur.

The first officers were: Harvey Brown, Noble Grand; D. P. Hunt, Vice Grand; Willis W. Wright, Secretary; John J. Owsley, Treasurer.

The present officers are: J. H. McClosky, Noble Grand; E. R. Wood, Vice Grand; D. De Ruiter, Recording Secretary; George D. Staats, Permanent Secretary; Joseph Staub, Treasurer

The present membership numbers one hundred and ninety.

Capital Lodge, No. 124, was instituted on the 20th of January, 1853, with the following principal officers: John Dunn, Noble Grand; John Cottman, Vice Grand; William Wallace, Recording Secretary; George F. McGinnis, Treasurer. The present number of members is one hundred and ninety-five.

The present principal officers are: W. H. Hazleton, Noble Grand; J. H. Miller, Vice Grand; G. S. Webster, Recording Secretary; John F. Wallick, Permanent Secretary; John McElwee, Treasurer.

Germania Lodge, No. 129, was instituted on the 24th of February, 1853, with ten members and the following officers: Charles Coulon, Noble Grand; Alexander Metzger, Vice Grand; Julius Boetticher, Secretary; Henry Schmidt, Treasurer.

The membership, at the end of the first year, numbered thirty-five. The present number of members is two hundred and sixty-nine.

The present officers are: Henry Geisel, Noble Grand; Henry Vogt, Vice Grand; Nicholas Hofmeister, Secretary; Charles Richman, Treasurer; Tobias Bender, Permanent Secretary.

Metropolitan Encampment, No. 5, was instituted on the 20th of July, 1846, with the following officers: Jacob Page Chapman, Chief Patriarch; Edwin Hedderly, High Priest; George B. Warren, Senior Warden; W. B. Preston, Junior Warden; Benjamin B. Taylor, Scribe; A. C. Christfield, Treasurer; John H. Taylor, Sentinel. The present membership numbers one hundred and forty.

The present officers are: L. W. Hetzelgesser, Chief Patriarch; D. De Ruiter, High Priest; August Smith, Senior Warden; E. A. Hardy, Junior Warden; L. P. Creasey, Recording Scribe; George D. Staats, Permanent Scribe; John Reynolds, Treasurer; David Anderson, Sentinel.

Marion Encampment, No. 35, was instituted on the 24th of March, 1853. The first officers were: Obed Foote, Chief Patriarch; J. K. English, High Priest; A. Defrees, Scribe; D. Yandes, Jr., Senior Warden; Wm. C. Lupton, Junior Warden

G. G. Holman, Treasurer; J. M. Kemper, Sentinel. This Encampment has about ninety members.

The present officers are: O. D. Butler, Chief Patriarch; H. Nicolai, High Priest; E. Cullum, Senior Warden; J. Holmes, Junior Warden; J. W. Smith, Recording Scribe; Henry Adams, Permanent Scribe; John F. Wallick, Treasurer; Paul Sherman, Sentinel.

Tentonia Encampment, No. 57, (German).—Instituted August 1st, 1858, with thirty-two members. The first officers were: G. F. Meyer, Chief Patriarch; Chas. Coulon, High Priest; John B. Stumph, Senior Warden; Charles Bals, Junior Warden; F. Tapking, Scribe; Alexander Metzger, Treasurer.

Present officers: Charles Kuetemeyer, Chief Patriarch; G. M. Wagner, High Priest; William Schmidt, Senior Warden; H. Elstrod, Junior Warden; W. Banse, Recording Scribe; Tobias Bender, Permanent Scribe. Number of members, one hundred and twenty-four.

KNIGHTS OF PYTHIAS.

As this Society is of comparatively recent origin, a brief mention of its rise and general history, is here prefixed to its history in relation to this city. The order of the *Knights of Pythias* was instituted in Washington, D. C., on the 19th of February, 1864, by J. H. Rathbone, by the organization of Lodge No. 1. The establishment of other Lodges followed; and on the 8th of April, of the same year, the *Grand Lodge of the District of Columbia* was organized.

The order now entered upon a critical period of its history, threatening its early extinction. Before long, all the Lodges but one had faded out of existence. The exception was Franklin Lodge No. 2, Washington, D. C., which continued to act as the Grand Lodge of the District of Columbia, and was the rallying point for the recovery of the lost ground, and the future advance of the order.

On the 23d of February, 1867, *Excelsior Lodge No. 1,* of Pennsylvania, was established in Philadelphia. This movement was followed by the establishment of Lodges in other States; and on the 11th of August, 1868, the *Supreme Lodge of the World* was organized, at Washington, D. C. — representatives being present from the District of Columbia, Pennsylvania, Maryland, New Jersey and Delaware.

On the 10th of March, 1869, the *Supreme Lodge* met in Annual Session in the city of Richmond, Va., with eight Grand Lodges represented, as follows: District of Columbia, Pennsylvania, New Jersey, Maryland, Delaware, Virginia, New York and Connecticut. At the second Annual Session, held in New York on the 10th day of March, 1870, the following additional States were represented: Ohio, Kentucky, West Virginia, Massachusetts, California, Indiana and Illinois,—or, sixteen Grand Lodges in all. At the third Annual Session, held in the city of Philadelphia, additional States were represented, namely: Georgia, Louisiana, New Hampshire, Rhode Island, Wisconsin and Iowa, — or twenty-two Grand Lodges in all, on the 18th of April, 1871.

The order has also been established in North Carolina, South Carolina, Alabama, Mississippi, Missouri, Minnesota, Vermont, Maine, Florida, Wyoming Territory and Canada, (but in these, except Missouri, Grand Lodges have not yet been organized,)—making thirty-one States and provinces in which it has an existence on this Continent.

Petitions have been received for the establishment of the order in Germany, Italy, England and France, and even in South America. This outline shows that the order has had a rapid growth and extension, in the face of internal troubles and dissensions in several localities, severely crippling its progress.

The growth of the order is shown by the subjoined comparison:

January 1 1865,...............	3 Lodges,...............................	78 members.
" 1, 1866,...............	1 Lodge,...............................	52 "
" 1, 1867,...............	4 Lodges,...............................	379 "
" 1, 1868,...............	48 "	6,847 "
" 1, 1869,...............	194 "	34,624 "
" 1, 1870,...............	465 "	54,289 "
" 1, 1871,...............	700 "	84,000 "

The diminished ratio of increase during the year last past, is attributed to internal troubles; which now, it is stated, are satisfactorily arranged, and will not hereafter retard the progress of the Society.

THE ORDER IN INDIANA.—The order was introduced into this State by P. G. C. Charles P. Carty. The first Lodge, in Indianapolis, Marion Lodge No. 1, was instituted on the 12th day of July, 1869. By October 12th, of the same year, six Lodges had been organized,—three in this city, and three in Fort Wayne.

The Grand Lodge of Indiana was organized in Indianapolis, on the 20th of October, 1869, with the following officers: Charles P. Carty, V. G. P., Indianapolis; Hon. John Caven, G. C., Indianapolis; John L. Brown, V. G. C., Fort Wayne; George H. Swain, G. R. and C. S., Indianapolis; George F. Meyer, G. B., Indianapolis; John B. Ryan, G. G., Indianapolis; W. A. Root, G. I. S., Indianapolis; Charles Johns, G. O. S., Indianapolis.

At the Annual Session of the Grand Lodge, January 11th, 1870, the following officers were elected: John B. Stumph, V. G. P.; Hon. John Caven, G. C.; John L. Brown, V. G. C.; Charles P. Carty, G. R. and C. S.; George F. Meyer, G. B.; John B. Ryan, G. G.; George H. Swain, G. I. S.; Charles Johns, G. O. S.

During the year 1870 Lodges eight, nine, ten, eleven and twelve, were organized at different points in the State. On the 1st of May, 1871, there were nine effective Lodges in the State, with an aggregate membership of about seven hundred. The present Grand Officers are: Hon. John Caven, V. G. P., Indianapolis; Wm. H. Hazelton, G. C.—*office, 24½, East Washington Street, Indianapolis;* James A. Hughes, V. G. C., New Albany; Charles P. Carty, G. R. and C.S.—*office at Martin & Hopkins' Insurance office, Sentinal Building, Indianapolis;* J. W. Smithers, G. B., Indianapolis; N. R. Bennett, G. G., Cambridge City; John Beard, G. I. S., Franklin; Charles Johns, G. O. S., Indianapolis.

THE ORDER IN THIS CITY.—The Order in this city is represented by the following subordinate Lodges: Marion No. 1, organized July 12th, 1869; Olive Branch Lodge No. 2, organized July 12th, 1869; Koerner Lodge No. 6, (German,) organized October 12th, 1869; Star Lodge No. 7, organized February 1st, 1870. The present officers of the city Lodges are:

Marion Lodge No. 1.—M. McKeon, V. P.; H. Slusher, W. C.; B. R. Binkley, W. V. C.; H. L. Burt, R. and C. S.; Jas. Shephord, F. S.; C. P. Carty, B.

Olive Branch Lodge No. 2. — George C. Webster, V. P.; W. H. Roll, W. C.; N. C. Potter, W. V. C.; J. H. Batty, R. and C. S.; Jesse De Haven, F. S.; W. C. Burk, B.

Koerner Lodge No. 6.—Otto Boetticher, V. P.; Philip Reichwein, W. C.; William Banse, W. V. C.; Fred. Gausepohl, R. & C. S.; Charles F. Schmidt, F. S.; Michael Steinhauer, B.

Star Lodge No. 7.—Joseph Kingan, V. P.; H. C. Chandler, W. C.; J. Neumeyer, W. V. C.; S. E. Perkins, Jr., R. & C. S.; Walter Hartpense, F. S.; W. H. Pitzer, B.

(19)

On the 1st of July, 1871, the membership of the city Lodges was as follows:

Marion Lodge No. 1 85
Olive Branch Lodge No. 2 170
Koerner Lodge No. 6 70
Star Lodge No. 7 120
                                                                                  ———
Total 445

The several Lodges in this city have fitted up a spacious and handsome hall in the fourth story of the Citizens' Bank Building, where they meet once a week, as follows: Marion Lodge No. 1, Wednesday evening; Olive Branch Lodge No. 2, Saturday evening; Koerner Lodge No. 6, Monday evening; Star Lodge No. 7, Tuesday evening.

THE DRUIDS.

Octavian Grove No. 1.—This body ("working" in German,) was instituted in November, 1856, and now has about two hundred members. The present officers are: David Wechsler, N. A.; August Hermuth, V. A.; August Mueller, Secretary. Stated meetings every Monday evening.

Humboldt Grove No. 8. — This Grove also "works" in the German language. It was instituted in April, 1868, and its present membership numbers one hundred and thirty. The present officers are: Charles Franke, N. A.; William Weiland, V. A.; Henry Voigt, Secretary. Stated meetings every Wednesday evening.

The *Grand Grove of Indiana* was instituted in Indianapolis, in 1860. The Annual meetings are held on the second Tuesday in May, but at no fixed place.

IMPROVED ORDER OF RED MEN.

Palmete Tribe No. 17, (German,) was instituted on the 2d day of May, 1870, with twenty members. The number of members at this time is sixty-five. The present officers are: John Burkart, Sachem; Lawrence A. Geis, Senior Sagamore; A. Kaiser, Junior Sagamore; B. Bernauer, Prophet; Henry Albersmeier, Secretary; Joseph Raible, Keeper of Wampum. Stated meetings, every Monday evening.

Red Cloud Tribe No. 18.—This body "works" in English. It was organized on the 10th day of August, 1870, with six members. The present membership numbers eighty-five. Present officers: W. C. David, Sachem; Joseph R. Forbes, Senior Sagamore; O. N. Ridgeway, Junior Sagamore; F. W. Hamilton, Prophet; George C. Miller, Keeper of Wampum; Wm. H. D. Merrill, Secretary. Stated meetings, every Wednesday evening.

INDEPENDENT ORDER OF RED MEN.

Pocahontas Tribe No. 141.—This Tribe was organized October 3d, 1869, with forty-eight members. The membership now numbers one hundred and sixty-two. Present officers: J. L. Beeler, O. C.; F. W. Schliebitz, U. C.; John Ihntris, 1st Secretary; August Haeffner, 2d Secretary; H. Geisel, Treasurer; Philip Lehr, Priest. Stated meetings, every Tuesday evening.

SONS OF HERMANN.

Schiller Lodge No. 1.—This is the only Lodge of this Order in Indiana, and was chartered in July, 1870. It numbers between fifty and sixty members. The present officers are: Charles Coulon, ex-President; Wm. Schoeneman, President; Henry Miller, Vice-President; Frederick W. Schliebitz, Corresponding Secretary; R. Steinhauer, Recording Secretary; William Banse, Treasurer. Stated meetings, every Thursday evening.

HARUGARI.

The Grand Lodge of Indiana held its first session in Jeffersonville, on the 27th of June, 1860. Its Annual meetings are now held in Indianapolis, on the first Wednesday in August. The Grand Lodge now comprises fourteen subordinate Lodges, with an aggregate membership of about six hundred. The present Grand Officers are: Aegidius Naltner, of Indianapolis, G. B.; Franz. Flaiz, Deputy G. B.; August Schreiber, G. A.; Edward Mueller, Grand Secretary; John Stein, Grand Treasurer.

Freya Lodge No. 68, Indianapolis, was the second Lodge instituted in this State, and numbers about one hundred and twenty members.

HEPTASOPHS.—(SEVEN WISE MEN.)

Indianapolis Conclave No. 1, was organized November 1st, 1870, and has ninety-five members. Present officers: John H. Gruenert, Archon; Benedict Fischer, Chancellor; Herman Altman, Provost; H. H. Langenberg, Chaplain; Henry Speckman, General Inspector; Dietrich M. Muegge, Treasurer; Henry Dipple, Financial Secretary; Wm. Schoeneman, Herald; N. Emerich, Secretary. Stated meetings, every Tuesday evening.

Gayo Conclave, No. 1, was organized May 26th, 1871, by the election of the following officers: Wm. S. Cone, Eminent Archon; S. T. Scott, Chancellor; W. D. Engle, Provost; John G. Waters, Secretary; Russell Elliott, Treasurer; John C. Miles, Inspector General; Joseph W. Smith, Herald; Wm. Logan, Prelate; James E. Shepard, Warden, Charles E. Brigham, Outside Sentinel. Number of members, eighteen. Stated meetings, every Friday evening.

THE POST OFFICE.

The early history of the Indianapolis Post Office, its different locations, etc., are briefly stated on pages 17 and 18.

It is now located in the Government building—popularly called the Post Office building—on the south-east corner of Pennsylvania and Market streets. Of this building the lower story and basement are occupied by the Post Office; the second and third stories, by the United States Collector, Assessor, District Attorney, Marshal, the Federal Courts, the Judges and Clerk of the United States Courts.

The erection of the building was begun in 1857, and it was completed in 1860. The building cost $165,000; a low figure, considering its size and quality.

Its style is uniform with that of the more recently erected government buildings throughout the country. Its leading features conform to the Grecian style of architecture. Its principal materials are stone and iron, and it is fire proof.

The Indianapolis Post Office is one of the first class distributing offices in the United States. The mails, for an extensive area of surrounding country, are sent here to be again distributed and forwarded to their destination. About two years ago the free delivery or carrier system was introduced, by which mail matter is delivered at the residences or places of business of citizens, and is collected for mailing from street boxes placed at convenient intervals throughout the city.

The successive post masters have been: Samuel Henderson, from March, 1822, to February, 1831; John Cain to 1841; Joseph M. Moore to 1845; John Cain to 1849. Alexander W. Russell succeeded Mr. Cain for the term ending in 1853, but dying in office, he was succeeded for the remainder of his term by his son, James N. Russell. Wm. W. Wick 1853 to 1857; John M. Talbott to 1861; Alexander H. Conner to 1866; D. G. Rose to 1868; William R. Holloway, the present incumbent, since April, 1869. The total number of employes connected with the Post Office is now fifty.

The annexed statement shows the extent of the business transacted at the Indianapolis Post Office during the year 1870:

Stamp Statement.—Received for sale of postage stamps.................. $70,101 81
Received for the sale of stamped envelopes....................................... 14,086 65

Total.. $84.188 46
Money Order Department.—Received for money orders sold......... $85,762 55
Received deposits from Postmasters on money order account............. 408,624 00

Total.. $494.286 55
Amount paid out for money orders drawn on the office..................... $222,118 80
Registry Department.—Number of registered letters received for distribution... 19,120
Number of registered letters received for city delivery....................... 8,376
Number of registered letters received for mailing............................... 1,240
Number of registered packages of stamps and stamped envelopes received for mailing.. 6,120
Number of registered packages of envelopes used............................... 13,910
General and Box Delivery.—Number of letters delivered from boxes and through general delivery... 306,000
Number of letters advertised and sent to Dead Letter Office.............. 18,400
Carriers' Department.—Number of mail letters delivered.............. 2,276,134
Number of local letters delivered.. 1,472,640
Number of newspapers, etc, delivered.. 376,704
Number of letters collected... 1,349,943

Total delivered and collected by carriers........ 4,150,045
Domestic Mails.—Number of letters received for distribution........ 9,403,200
Number of letters deposited in office and collected from the street boxes for the mails.. 1,331,457

Number of letters sent from the office... 10,734,657

Number of city letters mailed which were sent to the Dead Letter Office   6,000
Number of letters held for better direction, and sent to Dead Letter Office   7,200
Number of letters addressed in initials and fictitious names, which were sent to the Dead Letter Office........ 500
Not Deliverable.—Number of letters returned from hotels and sent to the Dead Letter Office... 800
Number of letters returned to writers.. 7,000
Number of bags of newspapers mailed, received, and distributed, making an aggregate of 70,200 bushels.. 42,570
Number of lock pouches and mail boxes despatched.......................... 28,600
Number of lock pouches and mail boxes received................................. 28,500

MILITARY ORGANIZATIONS.

Company A, of the *Indianapolis National Guards*, and the *Emmet Guards*, are the only organized representatives of the military spirit of the city. The former is a remnant of a full battalion styled the "National Guards," which was organized after the close of the war, and attained a high degree of proficiency in drill exercises. At present, all the companies but "A" company are disbanded.

H. H. LEE,

Established in 1860.

The China Tea Stores.

ACADEMY OF MUSIC CORNER;
No. 7 ODD FELLOWS' HALL;
MADISON AVENUE.

COFFEE AND SPICE MILLS:

SOUTH MERIDIAN STREET, ONE SQUARE FROM UNION DEPOT.

From the Journal of Commerce, July 14th, 1871.

H. H. LEE'S COFFEE AND SPICE MILLS.

The Tea, Sugar and Coffee Trade of Indianapolis.

The success which is sure to follow a careful, systematic course of efforts in a given direction, has a happy illustration in the business career of H. H. Lee, who, appreciating the wants of Indianapolis in that direction, saw a comparatively unoccupied field in the tea, sugar, coffee and spice trade, which he has cultivated to his own interest and that of the city until he stands at the head of three as fine establishments as the country can boast, alike a credit to his own enterprise and that of the Hoosier Capital. This prominence has been achieved by a strict attention to the business in hand and a mastering of all its details, which places it in the power of the operator to understand the controlling influences of the market, and enables him to select first-class goods at the most advantageous rates, which advantage is shared with the consumer. By dealing only in goods which thoroughly stand the test of trial, and prove in every point equal to representation, the card of H.H. Lee upon a package has become the synonym of genuineness, and guarantees that they who once purchase at his establishments will duplicate the same as often as required by family necessity.

Mr Lee's reputation as a merchant from the start was rested upon the quality of the goods vended by him, which has stood the test of time, constantly increasing his business, requiring greater facilities for meeting the demand, until he has been compelled to open a coffee and spice mill in the city, in addition to his extensive stores on North Pennsylvania street and corner of Ohio and Illinois. This new establishment is situated at the intersection of Madison avenue with South Meridian street, and has been fitted up as might have been expected from the well-known taste and liberality of its proprietor. In the basement an eight-horse power engine works a coffee roaster, with a capacity of eighteen hundred pounds per day, with two large spice, and the same number of coffee mills. A patent coffee cooler stands ready to receive the berry as it comes from the roaster. Taken all together, the establishment is complete in all its appointments, and cannot fail to largely add to the already extensive trade of its enterprising proprietor.

The organization known as the *Emmet Guards,* consisting of one company, is composed of Irish citizens, and is the exponent of the martial spirit of the Fenian Brotherhood in this city.

If these organizations fail to do the city justice in point of numbers, they certainly do it credit in point of quality and proficiency in executing the manœuvres of the drill and the manual of arms.

INSURANCE.

FOREIGN COMPANIES.

The number of Foreign Life, Fire and Marine Insurance Companies, having agencies in this city, is ninety-two, and of Accident Insurance Companies, three. Of these, many are State agencies. All the prominent companies of this country, and several large European companies, are represented here. The aggregate annual business of these agencies, is very large, but cannot be stated. The Insurance laws of Indiana do not require the companies doing business in the State to annually report to the State authorities the amount of business done, as in several other States; and an effort to obtain the information from the agents, by an application to each, was successful in too few cases to furnish even a basis for an approximation of the aggregate business done. The annual receipts of all these agencies, on account of premiums, may safely be placed at $3,000,000.

FRANKLIN LIFE INSURANCE COMPANY OF INDIANAPOLIS.

The pioneer and only Indiana Life Insurance Company, (except the Masonic Mutual Benefit Society, undermentioned,) is the *Franklin Life Insurance Company,* of Indianapolis, organized under the laws of the State in 1866.

The founders of this enterprise, if they were controlled in their undertaking by the prospect of its proving remunerative, were influenced also by another consideration, of more concern to the community in general, namely: the keeping in this city and State of a portion of that large sum of money annually drawn therefrom by the representatives of Eastern Insurance Companies.

The enterprise was vigorously prosecuted, and the company was soon formed, and prepared for business. It was started on a purely mutual basis, without capital stock, and as its only assets were the accumulation of the premiums over losses and expenses, its progress was necessarily slow. Added to this, was the opposition of the agents of foreign corporations that had long enjoyed a monopoly of the business in Indiana. The *Franklin* was in the hands of men who were capable and resolute, and being liberally sustained throughout the State, it has steadily grown in the confidence and favor of the people. It is now firmly established, and is making good progress toward the front rank of Life Insurance institutions. The assets now amount to more than $200,000, and the annual income is over half of that sum. The company has paid over $30,000 to the widows and orphans of its deceased members; and as it has been managed with great prudence and economy, the dividends have been large—aggregating more than $40,000.

The number of new policies issued in 1870, was four hundred and twenty-three; and for the present year, the indications are that more than double that number will be issued.

In 1868 the company purchased the building so long occupied by the old State Bank, where it has very pleasant and commodious offices.

FRANKLIN
ORGANIZED, 1866.

Life Insurance Co.

W. S. HUBBARD, President.

W. D. WILES, Vice-President.   E. P HOWE, Secretary.

FREDRICK BAGGS, Treasurer.   L. G. HAY, Actuary.

DIRECTORS.

James M. Ray,
W. D. Wiles,
R. S. Foster,
Frederick Baggs,
Ingram Fletcher,
William Braden,
Nicholas McCarty,
Nathan Kimball,
Preston Hussey, Terre Haute,
A. R. Forsyth, Greensburg,

Austin B. Claypool, Connersville,
Leonidas Sexton, Rushville,
John W. Burson, Muncie,
William S. Hubbard,
L. G. Hay,
Valentine Butsch,
Benj. C. Shaw,
M. L. Bundy, Newcastle,
C. S. Hubbard, Knightstown,
Ezra G. Hays, Lawrenceburg.

GENERAL OFFICE:

Corner Kentucky Avenue and Illinois Street,

INDIANAPOLIS.

THE ONLY INDIANA COMPANY.

ASSETS, OVER - - - - $200,000.00

ANNUAL DIVIDENDS.
NO RESTRICTION ON TRAVEL.
ALL KINDS OF POLICIES ISSUED.

SOLVENCY!   ECONOMY!   SECURITY!

SUSTAIN HOME INSTITUTIONS.

Since Life Insurance, in addition to the benefits it assures to those dependent upon policy holders, has now come to be an important power, in a public, commercial sense, the success of the *Franklin*, as being a "home" institution, cannot be regarded here with feelings of unconcern. If it shall attain the magnitude already reached by many American Life Insurance companies—whose assets in some cases reach from $10,000,000 to $40,000,000—its influence upon the finances of the State will be decidedly felt, and to the public advantage. The effect would be to reduce the rate of interest;. to provide additional funds for manufacturing and other investments requiring long time and low interest: and so large an addition to the supply of loanable funds, would do away with what is known as a "tight money market."

The company is efficiently managed, the officers for the present year—1871—being: Wm. S. Hubbard, President; Wm. D. Wiles, Vice President; E. P. Howe, Secretary; Fred. Baggs, Treasurer, and L. G. Hay, Actuary. These are all gentlemen of acknowledged ability and integrity, as are also the entire Board of Directors.

MASONIC MUTUAL BENEFIT SOCIETY OF INDIANA.

This Society was incorporated on the 5th day of August, 1869.

Its object is to give financial aid to the widows, orphans and dependents of deceased members. Its membership is confined to Master Masons of Indiana in good health at the time of admission. The members are divided into four classes; those from 21 to 30 years of age constitute the first class; from 31 to 40, the second; from 41 to 50, the third, and from 51 to 60, the fourth class.. Each member pays an admission fee of $6, and an assessment upon the death of a member, ranging from 90 cents to $1,80, according to the class to which he belongs. The heirs of a deceased member receive a benefit amounting to $1 for each member of the Society. The membership is now (July 1st., 1871,) about four thousand. The Society has paid twenty-two benefits, amounting to over $50,000. These figures illustrate the popularity of the plan of this Society with the Masonic Fraternity in this State; and the plan has been adopted by the Masons of several other States..

The office of the Company is at No. 24 Kentucky Avenue.

GERMAN MUTUAL FIRE INSURANCE COMPANY.

This organization, the only "home" Fire Insurance Company doing business in this city, was instituted in May, 1853. It has had a steady and sure growth from the period of its birth. It is constituted and conducted on the *Mutual* plan. Beginning operations with a subscribed insurance amounting to $100,000, the Company is now carrying an aggregate insurance of $4,000,000. The average of the *reserve fund* is about $35,000; the average value of *premium notes* held is about $350,000. The reliability of the Company is a matter of uncontradicted repute, and is attested by the fact that during its entire existence—over eighteen years—it has never been sued for the payment of a policy.

Policies are issued in this Company for a period of six years; *premium notes* are taken for the whole amount of the premiums for that period; and each policy-holder is subject to an Annual assessment, averaging about $7\frac{1}{2}$ *per centum per annum* of the amount of the premium rates held against him by the Company: thus the policy holder will, at the end of six years, have had six years of insurance, for about 45 *per centum* of the premium he originally agreed to pay.

The operations of the Company are limited to Indiana.

The management of the affairs of the Company is vested in a Board of Directors and in a Board of Officers, as follows:

Directors.—Valentine Butsch, A. Seidensticker, A. Naltner, George Koeniger, Chas. Grobe, Joseph Deschler, John Stumph, Charles Brinkman, Julius Boetticher.

Officers.—A. Seidensticker, President; Valentine Butsch, Vice-President; A. Naltner, Treasurer.

BANKING INSTITUTIONS.

STATE AND PRIVATE BANKS.

The plan of the State Bank and its several branches, called into existence by a legislative charter in 1834, and discontinued by the expiration of that charter in 1857; how the State, through its connection with and interest in that institution, incurred a debt of $1,390,000, in order to obtain a loan of the requisite funds; and how, from the use of the loan thus obtained, the State, in the space of twenty-five years, extinguished that loan, interest and principal, and netted about $3,700,000 (which has now grown to be nearly $5,000,000), for a permanent school fund; are sufficiently described on pages forty-six and forty-seven of the general historical sketch.

On pages forty-seven and forty-eight are also briefly sketched the origin and decline of the *Bank of the State*, with its several branches. As there stated, the introduction of the National Bank system superseded this extensive institution. Since then it has been in process of gradual extinction. Ten of the branches have been discontinued; while the other ten have, for several years, been retiring their circulation, but still continuing, though generally in a limited degree, to do a general banking business in other respects. Practically, it may be said that the *Bank of the State* is an institution of the past.

We have only space for a brief mention of the banking establishments of this city that antedate in their establishment the National Banking System.

The Indianapolis Branch of the State Bank was organized November 11, 1834, with Harvey Bates, as President, and B. F. Morris, as Cashier. Two or three years later, Mr. Bates was succeeded by Calvin Fletcher, and Mr. Morris by Thomas H. Sharpe, who served until the expiration of the bank's charter.

The *Indianapolis Branch of the Bank of the State* was organized on the 25th of July, 1855, with a capital of $100,000, which was afterwards increased to over $200,000. Its first President was W. H. Talbott. In January, 1857, Geo. Tousey became President, and C. S. Stevenson, Cashier. Mr. Stevenson resigned in 1861. He was succeeded by D. E. Snyder, who served until November, 1866, when he was succeeded by D. M. Taylor, the present cashier. George Tousey was succeeded as President in 1866, by Oliver Tousey, the former having resigned to accept the Presidency of the *Indiana National Bank*.

The first private banking institution, of which there is any record, was the *Indianapolis Insurance Company*, which was chartered early 1836, with a capital of $200,000; a corporation having authority to do both an insurance and a banking business. This institution suspended business in 1840, but was reorganized by Messrs. Defrees, Morris and others, about the year 1853. In 1858 or 1859, it suspended business a second time. In 1865 it was again reorganized, passed into the control of a new corporation, the capital was increased to $500,000, and the business was resumed. Under the last mentioned change it is still conducted, and occupies the old Branch Bank building. It no longer does an insurance business, but is a banking institution exclusively.

BANK.

INDIANAPOLIS INSURANCE CO.

Bank of Discount and Deposit.

PAY INTEREST ON DEPOSITS.

Buy and Sell Exchange, Deal in Commercial Paper, and make Collections in all Parts of the United States.

OFFICE IN COMPANY'S BUILDING,

Corner of Virginia Avenue and Pennsylvania Street,

INDIANAPOLIS, IND.

WM. HENDERSON, President.

Alex. C. Jameson, Secretary.

WM. HANNAMAN.   R. L. WHITTEN.   H. G. HANNAMAN.

HANNAMAN & CO.,

DEALERS IN

Drugs, Paints, Oils, &c.

100 EAST WASHINGTON STREET,

Indianapolis, Ind.

JOHN WOODBRIDGE & CO.,

Importers and Wholesale and Retail Dealers in

China, Glass and Queensware,

TABLE CUTLERY and PLATED WARE,

GOLD FISH AND AQUARIA.

12 WEST WASHINGTON STREET,

INDIANAPOLIS, IND.

The present private banking house of Fletcher & Churchman was established by S. A. Fletcher, Sr., in 1839, occupying an indifferent and primitive structure on the present site of No. 8 East Washington street. Timothy R. Fletcher was a partner in this house from its beginning to 1858. On the 1st of June, 1864, S. A. Fletcher, Sr., retired and was succeeded by S A. Fletcher, Jr., and F. M. Churchman. On the 1st of January, 1868, S. A. Fletcher, Sr., again became the head of the house, S. A. Fletcher, Jr., retiring. This house now occupies the most elegant building of all the banking houses in the city—No. 30 East Washington street. It began business with a capital of but $3,000. Its increase will appear from the exhibit of its present magnitude, further on.

E. S. Alvord & Co. opened a banking establishment in 1839, and discontinued it four years later.

John Wood began business as an exchange broker and banker in 1838, and failed in 1841—to the considerable detriment of many who held the irredeemable shinplaster currency he had put into circulation.

The *Bank of the Capital*, J. Wooley & Co., proprietors, having a nominal capital of $400,000, began business in 1853 and failed in 1857, with a considerable excess of liabilities over assets. W. S. Pierce and John H. Bradley were Presidents, in turn, of this institution, and J. Wooley was its cashier.

The *Farmers and Mechanics Bank* was instituted in February, 1854. Its successive Presidents were Allen May and G. Lee; it successive Cashiers, William F. May and O. Williams. Cashier May absconded in May, 1855, taking with him $10,000 of the bank's funds. This shock was fatal to the existence of the concern.

The two concerns last named were organizations under the Free Banking Law of 1852, as were also the following:

The *Traders Bank*, Messrs. Wooley & Wilson, proprietors, established in 1854; the *Central Bank*, established in July, 1855, having a nominal capital of $500,000; the *Metropolitan Bank*, also established in 1855. Of the *Central Bank* Ozias Bowen and J. D. Defrees were successive presidents; Sidney Moore and W. H. McDonald, successive Cashiers. The proprietors of the *Metropolitan Bank* were A. F. Morrison & Co.; its president was J. P. Dunn, and its cashier the notorious Jerry Skeen. These institutions were short-lived. Their chief result was the emission of a large circulation of notes, after which they supended payment, and then their proprietors or the State Auditor closed up their offices, leaving the holders of their circulation to suffer the losses.

Thus it was that the Free Banking System was, as a rule, a benefit only to the bankers thereunder, the holders of their circulation sustaining great losses by its depreciation.

The present banking house of A. & J. C. S. Harrison was established in 1854, by its present proprietors.

In February, 1856, Dunlevy, Haire & Co., brokers, began business in this city. As agents for Cincinnati banks, they had sent to them for redemption, during the brief existence of their firm, some $2,000,000 of the circulation of our State and Free Banks, for which they drew the specie. This extensive depletion of our banks of their specie, brought Dunlevy, Haire & Co., and their principals, into great disfavor here, and led to the commercial convention of 1856.

Wm. Robson, A. L. Voorhees, and others, established a Savings Bank, in Odd Fellows' Hall, in 1854; of which Robson became the proprietor in 1857. The collapse of the *Bank of the Capital* involved Robson's enterprise in the wreck, on the

HASKIT & MORRIS,

Wholesale and Retail Druggists

AND DEALERS IN

DRUGGISTS' SUNDRIES,

No. 20 West Washington Street,

INDIANAPOLIS, - - INDIANA.

MISS M. CUSTAR,

CONFECTIONER,

No. 189 East Washington Street,

INDIANAPOLIS, INDIANA.

Ornamental Cakes, Pyramids,

ICE CREAM, WATER ICES, JELLY,

And every article pertaining to the trade will be served in the neatest style.

Private Parties Furnished with Oysters, Meats, Ice Cream, Etc., on the Shortest Notice.

MEALS AT ALL HOURS.

17th of September. 1857, leaving his depositors victims to the amount of $15,000. This indebtedness was all, or nearly all, paid by the receiver in April, 1858.

In 1856, G. S. Hamer established an enterprise devoted chiefly to "note shaving," and the emission of "shinplaster" currency. After an inglorious career of some six months, Hamer was arrested for passing counterfeit money, his enterprise faded out of existence, and he out of the community.

The present private banking house of Fletcher & Sharpe, the "Indianapolis Branch Banking Company," was established January 1st, 1857, by Calvin Fletcher, Sr., and Thomas H. Sharpe. Calvin Fletcher, Sr., died on the 26th of May, 1866. The present house consists of Thomas H. Sharpe, Ingram Fletcher and Albert E. Fletcher.

In the autumn of 1862, Kilby Ferguson established the *Merchants Bank.* Disastrous gold speculations terminated Mr. Ferguson's banking career in somewhat less than one year. His liabilities were not settled until several years after his failure.

At the beginning of the year 1860, it is estimated that the banking capital of the city did not exceed $500,000. The statistics at the close of this sketch will exhibit the great increase since then.

The *Indiana Banking Company,* a private bank, and a reliable and flourishing institution of to-day, was established March 1st, 1865, with a capital of $100,000.

The present private banking house of Woolen, Webb & Co., was established in March, 1870; the Savings Bank of J. B. Ritzinger, March 26, 1868.

This completes our mention of the State, Free and Private Bank enterprises of the city to the present date; and we will now retrace our chronology to the time of the introduction of

THE NATIONAL BANKING SYSTEM.

The war of the rebellion wrought its familiar revolution in the paper currency circulation of the country, superseding the circulating notes of State and private banks by a currency founded on the credit of the nation. Thus was inaugurated the era of a better founded and more correct system of banking—as relates to circulation, at least—than the country had ever known: The National Banking System, established by Congress in 1864.

The first National Bank in this city, and one of the first in the United States, was organized on the 11th of May, 1863, by Wm. H. English and ten associates, under the name of *The First National Bank of Indianapolis.* The paid in capital, in the beginning was $150,000, which amount has been increased, from time to time, until it is now $1,000,000, with a surplus fund of $200,000,—being the largest bank in the State, and one of the largest in the West. The First National occupied this field exclusively until the fall of 1864, when the Indianapolis National was organized, and others followed, until we now have five, with an aggregate capital of $2,500,000, being about one eighteenth of all the wealth on the tax duplicate of the county. It is the boast of the stockholders of the First National Bank that one-fortieth of all the taxes flowing into the treasury of Marion county is derived from the tax upon the stock of that bank.

The dates of the organization of the other National Banks in this city were: *The Citizens' National Bank,* November 28, 1864; *The Indianapolis National Bank,* December 15, 1864; *The Fourth National Bank,* January 23, 1865 (consolidated with the *Citizens'* in December, 1865); *The Merchants' National Bank,* January 17, 1865; *The Indiana National Bank,* March 14, 1865.

The table, placed for the sake of convenience at the end of this sketch, will show, in detail, the capital, business, and condition generally, of each of these five National Banks, and is taken from the sworn returns of their respective officers to the General Government.

RESOURCES OF THE PRIVATE BANKS.

As private bankers are not required to render any detailed report of their business to the Government, it is more difficult to give an account of them. It is well known, however, that the private bankers of Indianapolis are doing a large and prosperous business. Their capital and average deposits would probably stand about as follows:

S. A. Fletcher & Co...	$800,000
Fletcher & Sharpe...	750,000
Indianapolis Insurance Company...	550,000
Indiana Banking Company..	550,000
A. & J. C. S. Harrison...	450,000
Woolen, Webb & Co...	350,000
Ritzinger's Bank...	250,000
Pettit, Braden & Co..	80,000

Making a total of.. $3,780,000

How much of this is capital and how much deposits, we are not informed; but more than half is probably deposits.

THE CLEARING HOUSE.

The banking interests of the city reached such a magnitude as to require the establishment of a Clearing House, which went into operation in the beginning of the year 1871. The following table will show what banks constitute the association, and the amount of capital and average deposits reported by each bank at that time, viz:

First National Bank..	$1,000,000
S. A. Fletcher & Co...	800,000
A. & J. C. S. Harrison...	450,000
Fletcher & Sharpe..	750,000
The Indianapolis National Bank..	700,000
Indianapolis Insurance Company..	550,000
Citizens' National Bank...	800,000
Woolen, Webb & Co...	350,000
Ritzinger's Bank...	250,000
Pettit, Braden & Co..	80,000
Indiana Banking Company...	550,000
Merchants' National Bank..	200,000
Indiana National Bank..	500,000

Total.. $7,580,000

The Officers of the Clearing House are: President, William H. English; Vice President, F. M. Churchman; Manager, Jot Elliott; Executive Committee, A. G. Pettibone, William H. English and F. M. Churchman.

COMPARATIVE STATEMENT *of the Condition of the National Banks of Indianapolis, Indiana, at the close of business, March 18, 1871, as officially reported to the Comptroller of the Currency.*

RESOURCES.	First National.	Indiana Nat.	Merchants' Nat.	Ind'pls Nat.	Citizens' Nat.	Total.
Loans and Discounts	$1,059,082 94	$460,986 15	$147,194 67	$447,612 67	$549,696 76	$2,665,473 09
Overdrafts		7,714 39	4,631 66		1,082 38	13,348 43
United States bonds to secure circulation	890,000 00	404,107 00	200,000 00	500,000 00	500,000 00	2,494,049 00
United States bonds to secure deposits	100,000 00			100,000 00		200,000 00
United States bonds and securities on hand	7,700 00	36,400 00		47,000 00	13,250 00	106,350 00
Other stocks, bonds and mortgages	16,000 00	26,378 82	1,090 00			43,978 82
Due from Redeeming and Reserve Agents	68,382 00	23,649 19	26,266 14	146,735 19	49,131 48	315,064 00
Due from other National Banks	36,136 52	50,072 52	3,405 75	859 07	40,723 70	140,177 56
Due from other banks and bankers	61,561 52	315 59		28 01		61,904 82
Real estate furniture and fixtures	9,811 52	2,773 17	4,311 69	4,569 41	63,570 22	84,566 01
Current expenses	5,168 48	1,122 16	1,713 71	2,082 47	3,636 63	13,123 47
Taxes paid	3,743 17	642 42		2,730 36	2,656 51	9,772 46
Premiums	39,812 35	5,139 45	7,349 96	1,760 96	146 11	43,487 47
Cash Items (including stamps)	6,959 26	2,883 49	3,471 68	8,298 60	16,771 35	33,846 64
Bills of other National Banks	102,455 00	12,222 00	8,415 00	336 33	5,502 00	136,850 00
Fractional currency	1,396 71	2,640 74	198 60	3,234 10		8,306 08
Specie	274 00	6,191 40	5 15	132 25	870 84	7,473 64
Legal Tenders	175,000 00	71,500 00	24,700 00	80,000 00	19,600 00	459,840 00
Total	$2,578,151 57	$1,120,587 97	$434,025 95	$1,342,114 72	$1,350,032 28	$6,821,912 49

LIABILITIES.	First National.	Indiana Nat.	Merchants' Nat.	Ind'pls Nat.	Citizens' Nat.	Total.
Capital stock	$1,000,000 00	$400,000 00	$200,000 00	$500,000 00	$500,000 00	$2,518,000 00
Surplus fund	140,000 00	66,000 00	9,390 00	95,000 00	70,000 00	380,390 00
Undivided profits	65,192 48	14,634 97	3,993 65	8,182 44	17,765 96	110,589 50
National Bank notes outstanding	800,000 00	349,000 00	90,000 00	441,421 00	443,589 00	2,127,010 00
Dividends unpaid			179 15			179 45
Individual deposits	352,918 94	182,259 62	130,466 94	241,055 00	310,350 82	1,469,121 32
United States deposits	27,103 11			38,996 15		66,018 95
Due to National Banks	18,518 90	21,944 95	85 91	12,472 85	197 60	53,250 21
Due other banks and bankers	4,288 14	86,748 43		1,167 28	8,068 99	100,362 75
Total	$2,578,151 57	$1,120,587 97	$434,025 95	$1,342,114 72	$1,350,032 28	$6,824,831 49

BROWNING & SLOAN,

DRUGGISTS

AND DEALERS IN

Pure Drugs, Chemicals,

PAINTS, OILS, WINDOW GLASS, GLASS WARE,

Dye-Stuffs, Spices, Brushes of all kinds, Combs,

FINE PERFUMERY, AND TOILET ARTICLES,

SURGICAL INSTRUMENTS, FROM THE BEST MANUFACTURERS,

TRUSSES OF ALL KINDS,

Shoulder Braces, Supporters,

Suspensories, Elastic Stockings,

And all articles usually found in a First-Class Drug House, and in variety and detail not surpassed
by any House in the country, and at lowest figures.

APOTHECARIES' HALL,

7 and 9 East Washington Street,

INDIANAPOLIS, IND.

INDIANAPOLIS MANUFACTURES.

EARLY MANUFACTURES.

The earliest manufactures of Indianapolis, as of most new Western towns, were rather assistants to, than substitutes for, home-made work. The mills that ground grain and sawed lumber frequently also made woollen rolls for the farmer's wife's spinning and weaving. The first of these belonged to William Townsend and Earl Pierce, and was connected with the grist-mill of Andrew Wilson and Daniel Yandes, on the Bayou. It was put in operation first in June, 1823. But one set of machinery could hardly supply all the work needed for the stockings and woolsey "wamuses," coverlets and dresses of a community which made most of the material for its own clothes. Other carding machines were set at work; some, like the first, in connection with grist-mills, others by themselves—these latter being usually run by horse power. As late as 1832 or '33, the ruins of one of these latter stood on the northwest corner of Illinois and Maryland streets, and another was at work at a still later date on Kentucky avenue, about where the old Tobacco Factory afterwards stood. The addition of spinning machinery marked the introduction of what may be fairly called "manufactures." This was the effect of the impulse created by the canal, though the Old Steam Mill Company of 1832 may have contemplated some such development if it had succeeded better at the outset.

In 1839, Scudder & Hannaman built a mill on the canal "race," at the foot of Washington street, and in a little while, (if not at first,) added spinning and weaving to carding, and really "manufactured" as well as did custom carding and spinning. Nathaniel West, about the same time, established his mill at what was called Cotton Town, at the crossing of the Michigan road over the canal, doing much the same kind of work, but with an added attempt at cotton spinning.

The first of these establishments passed into the hands of Merritt & Coughlen in 1844 or 1845, and, under the railroad impulse, has developed into the large and flourishing mill near the same site, notwithstanding the "backset" of a fire in 1851.

West's mill made Cotton Town a busy place for some years, but cotton spinning was a little too long a step for the time, and though Mr. Yount, in 1849, still kept up the woolen business, there was a steady decline of the prosperity of this promising suburb.

In 1847, G. W. and C. E. Geisendorff leased the old steam mill, and renewed the wool manufacture there; but it was not a promising business at the start. Subsequently they built the frame portion of their present mill on the canal "race," and, prosperity following perseverance, they added the larger brick portion.

In 1830, or thereabout, the late James Blake built a little house on the high ground on Alabama street, near South, for the "manufacture" of ginseng—that is, its preparation—for the Philadelphia market, whence it was shipped to China. This root, which is a favorite condiment and medicine in China, used to abound in the woods about the city, especially in the vicinity of the grave yard pond and back of Samuel Merrill's residence, and was collected by the boys and sold to druggists long after Mr. Blake's house was abandoned. It has now disappeared almost entirely, even from the woods where no innovation of city influence has reached. The old "sang factory," as it was called, was a noted place for shooting doves before the railroads cut up and built up that part of the city.

In 1834, John S. Barnes and Williamson Maxwell began making linseed oil in an old stable, or a building very like it, on the alley south of Maryland street, just in the rear of the present Fifth Ward school house. They sold to Scudder & Hannaman the year after, and the latter moved the business to their new mill in 1839.

MITCHELL & RAMMELSBERG,

Furniture Company.

Wholesale and Retail Dealers in

FURNITURE,

Nos. 41 And 43 SOUTH MERIDIAN STREET,

INDIANAPOLIS, IND.

CHARLES MAYER.   **(ESTABLISHED 1840.)**   WILLIAM HAUEISEN.

CHARLES MAYER & CO.,

IMPORTERS AND JOBBERS OF

TOYS, NOTIONS, AND FANCY GOODS,

Children's Carriages, Fancy Willow Ware &c.,

29 WEST WASHINGTON STREET,

Indianapolis,   -   -   *Indiana,*

A long horizontal log, working against another, as a lever, was the press used. When hydraulic pressure came into use, Mr. Hannaman found that the Cincinnati manufacturers could buy his "cake" and make oil of it at a lower price than he could sell the first "pressing" for, and he "quit."

About the same time, and near the same place that oil was first made, Frank Devinney carried on the first mattress making establishment.

About the same time, John L. Young established the first brewery, on Maryland street, just west of the line of the canal.

The first manufacturing of tobacco was done by a man generally known as " Bill " Bagwell, in a little cabin on the South-west corner of Maryland and Tennessee streets. He made only cigars, and those of the "common," or "unsoaked" kind. This was as early as 1830, possibly earlier.

In 1835, Scudder & Hannaman began the manufacture of tobacco, on a considerable scale, in a building on Kentucky avenue, below Maryland street, in the rear of 'Squire Henry Bradley's house. They employed quite a number of boys in "stemming" or "stripping," and several cigar and "chewing" hands. The cigars were all made of soaked tobacco, and called "melee." The chewing tobacco was mostly the heavy black plug, once so well known in the West, but now driven out by "navy" and a dozen other varieties of cheap stuff. But "fine cut" was made occasionally, as well as "twist," and smoking tobacco was still more frequently made. It was chiefly sold in the north and along the lake, and wagoned away. It was raised in Marion, Morgan, Johnson, Hendricks, and Bartholomew counties. In September, 1838, the sweat-house—a little, close, wooden building for heating the heavy plug tobacco after pressing—caught fire, and it and the whole structure adjoining were burned down, causing a total loss—for in those days nobody insured anything—of $10,000. The establishment was sold to John Cain in 1843, and was carried on by him till his failure a few years after, when Robert L. Walpole took it and conducted it on the part of the creditors for a short time. Then the tobacco manufacture disappeared from the city till it was renewed by George F. Meyer, in July of 1850. It is now a very important interest.

Pork packing, another interest still more important than the last, was first attempted about 1835, by James Bradley and one or two associates. They bought slaughtered hogs of the farmers, and cut and cured them in an old log building on Maryland street, where the residence of L. B. Wilson now stands. It had formerly been the pottery of George Myers. The speculation did not pay, and no more was done in the pork trade till 1841, when John H. Wright, (the first "cash store" man,) who had come from Richmond some time before, bought slaughtered hogs at his store for "half cash, half goods," and in connection with his father-in-law, Jeremiah Mansur, and brother-in-law, William Mansur, packed them, in an old frame building that had once been the blacksmith shop of James Van Blaricum, on the northeast corner of Maryland and Meridian streets, the "Opera House" site. They continued in this fashion of business quite successfully till 1847, when the completion of the Madison railroad opening new facilities for shipping their product, they concluded to enlarge, and, to speak appropriately, "go the whole hog," killing as well as packing. They built a packing house on the west side of the Madison depot, and a slaughter house at the west end of the National road bridge, and hauled the dead hogs from one to the other. Mr. Isaiah Mansur joined them in that year, and continued till 1854–5, when William and Isaiah joined together, and Mr. J. C. Ferguson and Frank Mansur joined Jeremiah, (Mr. Wright had died some time before), and formed two establishments.

In 1847 Benjamin I. Blythe and Edwin Hedderly built the house north of the bridge, on the Fall Creek race, and killed and packed for some years. Elisha Mc-Neeley and Mr. McTaggart were concerned with them a part of the time. Mr. Hedderly carried on the manufacture of lard oil here in the latter part of his occupation of the premises. In 1854 W. & I. Mansur bought this house, and went on successfully till they quit business in 1861. They had a severe fire in their smoke house in 1858, in which a great deal of meat was lost. Wheat, Fletcher & Coffin have this house now. In 1852–3, Macy & McTaggart established a house on the river near the Terre Haute railroad bridge. It was torn down some years ago. Tweed & Gulick began, in 1854–5, in a house just north of the last; were succeeded in a short time by Messrs. Patterson, who built a brick to pack beeves; and they were succeeded by the present superb structure and business of J. C. Ferguson & Co. Col. Allen May began killing and packing in 1855, in a large building which he erected on the west side of the river, near the Crawfordsville ford. He soon failed, and his house was burned in 1858. In 1864, Messrs. Kingan—as related in the general history — built their house, then, and probably still, the largest single building of the kind in the country. It was totally destroyed by fire in the spring of 1865, with a loss of $240,000. It was re-built promptly, two attic stories lower than before, but still a large and impressive structure.

The pork packed by Wright and the Mansurs, till 1848, was shipped on flat boats to New Orleans. For some years this now-forgotten mode of transportation was no trifling item of the city's commerce. The boats were built here and at Broad Ripple, and sent down the river in the spring freshets, or whenever there was a rise in the river. They were forty or fifty feet long, ten or fifteen wide, and six or seven deep, and would carry a pretty good tonnage. They were covered in their whole length, except sometimes a little section at one end where the "cabin" was. They were steered by a huge oar at each end, and helped along by another on each side. Arrived at their destination, they were sold for lumber, sometimes very advantageously. The great peril of their navigation was a dam, and about one in every four would "break its back," or be ruined in some other way, at the Waverly dam. A pilot was valuable till the Ohio river was reached; and "Old Beth (Bartholomew) Bridges," as he was called, was much in request for this service. Besides pork, baled hay was sometimes shipped in boats; and one year Wm. H. Jones (of Coburn & Jones) and Cadwallader Ramsey sent a cargo of chickens to New Orleans. The hay was pressed in two or three places in the city, chiefly in a press north west of the State House, owned, if the writer is not mistaken, by Dr. G. W. Mears.

Somewhere about 1838 or 1840, Nicholas McCarty, Sr., began the manufacture of hemp, growing most of the stock himself, on the "Bayou farm." The "rotting vats" were excavated between the canal and the creek, some little distance below the present line of Ray street. The remains of them are still visible—conspicuous even--to the stroller in that vicinity. A little frame mill for breaking and hackling the rotted hemp was built at the bluff near the creek, and the "race" of it can still be seen. The enterprise was not profitable enough to justify a long continuance, and it was abandoned after a few years.

A dense wood at this time covered that portion of the city, except a small clearing about and below the hemp works, and a break in the canal, near Ray street, poured a considerable stream into the western part of this woods for a long time, making a regular swamp and lake of it, and covering a long line of the creek bluff with little cascades.

STEWART & MORGAN,

Wholesale Druggists,

AND DEALERS IN

FRENCH AND ENGLISH PLATE GLASS,

PITTSBURG WINDOW GLASS,

—A N D—

DRUGGISTS' GLASSWARE,

No. 40 East Washington Street,

INDIANAPOLIS, = = = **INDIANA.**

The first mills, as noticed in the general history, were those of Linton, for saw-ing, on Fall creek, near the City Hospital, and of Isaac Wilson, for grinding, on Fall creek bayou, northwest of the old Military Ground. Yandes & Wilson, in 1823, built a second grist mill on the river bayou. These seem to have sufficed till the old steam mill was erected and put in operation, in 1832. After that the Patterson mill, formerly Wilson's, on Fall creek bayou, seems to have done most of the grind-ing for home use, and no attempt was made at any other work till the canal was opened, or later. Then Nathaniel West built his mill at Cotton Town, and later, John Carlisle built his, on the canal race, near Washington street. This was burned in 1856, but immediately rebuilt. Robert Underhill built another, in 1851, on the bluff of the "glade" or prairie, south of the donation, at the "wooden locks," and ran it by water from the canal. It is still in operation, though considerably dilap-idated. In' 1848, Morris Morris and his sons built a steam mill on Meridian street, at the Union Depot, on the site of Fitzgibbon's building, which was entirely destroyed by fire in 1851. Of the mills now in operation more is said in another place.

In 1838, William Sheets established the first paper mill here, on the canal at the Market street crossing, and conducted it with great success for many years. It is now abandoned. Its successors are elsewhere noticed.

Besides the manufactory of ginseng and hemp, which were among the earliest enterprises that have never been renewed, there was another that flourished for a time, and disappeared permanently. That was plane making. This was carried on by Messrs. Young & Pottage, in what is now Hubbard's Block, in connection with their hardware store, but the work was done by Mr. John J. Nash. This was about the year 1837.

Pottery establishments were early put in operation here. One by Geo. Myers, on the corner of Maryland and Tennessee streets; another on the corner between Kentucky avenue and Illinois street, by Robert Brenton, which was displaced by the old State Bank; and a third was maintained for a long time on the corner of Washington and New Jersey streets, in the deep cut of the ravine.

The early tanneries were those of Yandes & Wilkins, on Alabama street, just where Maryland ran into it, but did not cross,—the old bark mill and building of this tannery were long visible near the site of the present Station House,—and that of some one whom the writer cannot now recall, on Pennsylvania street, on the site of Haugh's iron railing factory.

The first soap factory was built about the year 1838 or '40, on the canal, near McCarty street. Mr. Protzman, the leader of the old City Band, conducted it awhile.

David Main and a Mr. Spears, two Scotchmen, did the first regular stone cutting here, on the site of Blake's block. about the year 1835. They were succeeded by Peter Francis, on the west corner of Kentucky avenue and Maryland street.

Christopher Kellum was the first saddler, coming here in 1823. Jas. Sulgrove, his apprentice, succeeded him, followed later by Isaac Roll, Wm. Eckert, and J. J Pugh.

George Norwood was the first wagon-maker, 1822. His shop was on Illinois street, on the site of the Exchange building. Arnold Lashley did wagon and car-riage work on Pennsylvania street, on the site of the Post Office, till 1836, when he killed Collins, and had to leave. Mr. Fultz then took it, and soon after Hiram and Edward Gaston established themselves here in carriage making exclusively.

Amos Hanway was the first cooper, 1821; Wilkes Reagan, the first butcher, 1821; John Shunk, the first hatter, 1826; Andrew Byrne, the first tailor, 1820; Matthias Nowland, the first brick-layer, 1820; his widow Elizabeth, the first board-

TRADE PALACE

ing house keeper, 1823; James B. Hall, the first carpenter, 1820; Isaac Lynch, the first shoemaker, 1821; William Holmes, the first tinner, 1822; Conrad Brussel, the first baker, 1820; Milo R. Davis, the first plasterer, 1820; Caleb Scudder, the first cabinet maker, 1821; Henry and Samuel Davis, the first chair makers, 1820; Isaac Wilson, the first miller, 1820; George Pogue, the first blacksmith, 1819 or '20—soon followed by James Van Blaricum; James Linton, the first mill wright, 1821; Nathaniel Bolton, the first printer, 1821; George Smith, the first book binder, 1821; Daniel Yandes, the first tanner, 1821; John Ambrozene, the first clock and watch maker, 1825; William P. Murphy, the first dentist, 1829; John Smither, the first gun smith, (the writer thinks,) but Samuel Beck was early in the work, 1833, and keeps at it; David Mallory, a mulatto, the first barber, 1821; Samuel S. Rooker, the first house and sign painter, 1821.

The most important industry has been deferred to this point, as its consideration leads directly to the manufacturing facilities of the city — the manufacture of iron. As early as 1832, R. A. McPherson & Co. established a foundry on the west side of the river, near the end of the present National Road bridge, and maintained it for some years. In 1835 Robert Underhill and John Wood established another on Pennsylvania street, just north of University Square, and kept up the casting, at irregular intervals, of small hollow ware, plough points, mill castings, and the like, for twenty years, when Mr. Underhill built a large house on Pennsylvania street, near the creek, and started into a business on a scale commensurate with the growth of the city; but he failed, and his building was first used as a hominy mill, and then burned. A foundry was built north west of the State House, in 1837 or '38, but was never used, except as a theatre. From this time the iron manufacture ceases to belong to the early history of the city, and must concern itself either with existing establishments, or their immediate predecessors.

The iron interest, as above remarked, is now the most important in the city, and bids fair to increase in importance, not only with the growth of the city, but far in advance even of that rapid development. The facilities for this manufacture here, are unsurpassed; and a brief statement of these, and the manufacturing prospects of the city, is appended.

THE PROSPECTS OF THE CITY.

It is not placed beyond the reach of mortals to prophesy in probabilities. By combining facts, we may draw conclusions that will approach the value of prophecies in proportion to the range of facts and the correctness of the deductions from them. In this fashion of vaticination, let us see what the future promises for Indianapolis. She started a feeble inland village, planted in the midst of a wilderness and surrounded by swamps. She had no roads and no navigable water courses. She was cut off from all the means by which prosperity is attained or commerce established. She had no advantages of situation or of natural resources. Yet she has grown to be probably the largest entirely inland city in the Union. She had a population, by the last complete census, of 51,200, with a development of trade and manufactures so great and so deeply rooted, that it is inconceivable that it should not grow at least as rapidly as it has grown. The means by which this result has been effected are as fully within her command now as ever. Her central position in the State, or rather in the North-West, brought to her from all directions the new lines of communication opened by the locomotive, and in these she has found the advantages by the energetic and sagacious improvement of which

she has attained her position. These are the work of man's intelligence and energy, and are, therefore, in no way dependent on the accidents or changes of nature. They are as easily kept as got, and more, for as population attracts population and business attracts business, the concentration of railways attracts or compels the addition of railways, when new outlets to markets are needed. She will, therefore, in all probability, continue to grow from the roots already sent out, as she has grown in sending them out. But to this probability must be added others of even greater promise. No city in the West, or even in the world, offers such opportunities for illimitable and easy expansion. There is not a foot of ground within ten miles, in any direction, that cannot easily be built upon and added to her area. Cheap lots are therefore possible for more years and growth than would suffice to make her as big as London. There is no cramping of hills, or streams, or unhealthy localities, to huddle up settlements in any quarter and raise real estate to figures inaccessible to poor men. Her health is not surpassed by that of any city in the country, or any country. There is nothing in that direction to offset the advantages offered by a flourishing town, with an inexhaustible area of cheap building lots. Her schools are equal to any in the country, East or West, and have been suppported with unfailing liberality and unanimity. Her public improvements are in good part completed, or advancing to completion, so that the heaviest expenses of fitting her for comfortable and profitable residences have been incurred, and will not need to be renewed. Thus she offers the four best inducements to the emigrant—cheap residence, ample means of education, light taxes and assured health. Without these, her unequaled railroad advantages might have left, might still leave, her merely a flourishing town, but not a large commercial and manufacturing center.

But to all the advantages enumerated there must added another equal to either, if not to all together. This is the city's vicinity to the *best coal field in the world* for all classes of manufactures. Fuel is the prime necessity of manufacturing in these days, and is likely to remain so until electricity or Ericsson's concentrated sunlight replaces it. Raw material goes to power to be worked up. The philosophy of this movement need not be considered here. It is enough, in tnis connection, to state the fact. Power exists here in such abundance as all the developments of England cannot equal. Within two or three hours run of us lies a coal field of nearly eight thousand square miles. We enter it by four, and soon will by five, different lines of railway, making a monopoly, and consequently a heavy cost of transportation, impossible. The dip of the strata is to the west, thus turning up the outcrop in the direction nearest to us, and making that part which is most easily mined also the most easily reached. The seams, in many cases, are mined by drifting in from hill sides, sometimes by shallow shafts, sometimes by merely stripping off a few feet of the surface soil. The ground above is all capable of cultivation and can support all the men, and more, necessary to work them. Mining, therefore, can be carried on at the lowest possible cost. But more than this, the character of the coal itself increases the facility and consequent cheapness of mining. It is soft and easily broken; its laminations are easily separated; it breaks easily *across* the line of stratification—in fact, is seamed with lines of breakage crossing those of cleavage. It can thus be knocked out of the seam in large, square masses, or chunks, as one might knock bricks out of a dry piled wall. This again assures easy mining. It is almost entirely free from the dangerous gases that produce such fearful calamities in deeper mines of different coal. It is not saying too

INDIANAPOLIS

much to say that no coal has yet been found anywhere in the world so easily accessible, so cheaply mined, or so free from danger to the miner. These facts alone are enough to assure our city all the advantages that belong to the possession of inexhaustible fuel and illimitable mechanical power.

But there are other facts besides these that "make assurance doubly sure." This coal, called "Block Coal"—from the peculiarity above alluded to of breaking into blocks—is really a sort of mineral charcoal. It contains *no sulphur,* or so little that no analysis has been able to detect more than a trace of it. It contains enough naptha to kindle almost instantaneously, and it burns *without caking,* or melting and running together, as most bituminous coals do. These two qualities—freedom from sulphur and burning without caking—every man accustomed to using coal for steam, or for smelting or working iron, will understand at once to make the Indiana "block coal" unequaled for all manufacturing purposes. For iron it is unapproachable, being but little different from charcoal. In fact, much of it *is* charcoal, as any one can see by breaking a lump. The whole surface will be found mottled by alternates lines of bright and dull black, and the latter are laminations of mere mineral charcoal. It will rub off on the fingers or clothes like charcoal, and it can be scraped up in little heaps of charcoal dust. The brighter laminations are a sort of cannel coal. The whole mass, instead of the glossy, polished look of Pittsburg coal, is dull and dark, rather than black, with frequent splotches of greyish hue, like an underground rust, upon it. It is, in all respects, different from the ordinary bituminous coal, which has to be coked before it can be used to smelt or work iron. To its singular adaptation to iron manufacture, is due the enormous development of that interest in the city within the past ten years.

The field is calculated, from the facts so far ascertained, to contain over twenty thousand millions of tons of this "block" coal. This is more than will be worked up by all the population that can be collected on the vast plain about Indianapolis in five hundred years.

Besides the "block," the field contains many seams of the ordinary coal, though varying less from the other than does the Eastern kind. There is every variety for all kinds of work, and all can be obtained with equal ease and cheapness. The whole field is calculated to contain sixty-five thousand millions of tons, much of it close to the surface, none of it so deep as to need the costly shafting and machinery of the English or Eastern mines.

In the possession of this amount of fuel, Indianapolis offers to the manufacturer, and especially to the iron manufacturer, these advantages:

1st. The *best* coal that has yet been found in the world, to make or work iron, and as good as any—better than most—for making *steam.*

2nd. *Cheap* coal, made cheap by ease of mining, freedom from danger, facilities for approach in mining, and by the capability of the covering country to support the miners.

3d. *Cheap* transportation of coal from the mines to the city, assured by the actual operation of *four* lines of railway penetrating the field in four directions, with the certain addition of a *fifth,* already on the way to completion. Added to these is the probability of a cheap *narrow gauge* line, which the recent developments as to the value of that mode of transportation have suggested to men not likely to abandon it. The competition of these lines makes high prices impossible. These are the Indianapolis, Bloomington and Western; the Indianapolis and St. Louis;

the Indianapolis and Terre Haute; the Indiana and Illinois Central, (in progress), and the Indianapolis and Vincennes.

· 4th. *Choice* of coal. Standing at the junction of five or six lines of coal transportation, each bringing a different variety or different grade, the manufacturer at Indianapolis can choose that which suits him best, at a price regulated by strong and steady competition. Right in the coal field, he would have to take what was near him, or obtain better at a cost that would make profit impossible. Iron men know well the necessity of adapting coal to ore, and the uncertainty there is of finding one kind yielding an equal product with another. The city is, therefore, a better point for smelting, as well as puddling, rolling, casting, or any other process of iron manufacture, than any other point in the State.

5th. The numerous railway lines centering here, afford all possible facilities for obtaining necessary raw material, or shipping completed products. We have twelve lines entering the city, and will soon have thirteen. There are only about eight counties in the State that are not in direct railway connection with us, that is, that cannot send a passenger from there here all the way by rail. This can hardly be said of another State in the Union, except some of the New England States. There are only these eight from which a merchant may not come here, do business, and return in the same day, with suitable arrangement of connections and trains. This places every dealer in the State at the doors of our manufacturers, virtually.

6th. Besides these advantages, offered to the iron manufacturer especially, the advantages of cheap fuel and unequalled transportation are offered to every class of manufacture. To wood workers, we can show hardly less capabilities of profitable labor, than to iron men. We are in the centre of the "hard wood" region of the North-West; and no State in the Union possesses so much of the now valuable black walnut, as this. Eastern manufacturers have come here to obtain the benefit of this abundance. Their branch establishments have become quite a feature of business, within two years past; and it is a feature that must become more and more prominent as these valuable woods become more valuable.

7th. We offer plenty and cheap building stone, brick, and other building materials.

Now, seeing what Indianapolis has grown to, by means still as fully at her command as ever, and enlarged by many additional developments, what may we fairly conclude her prospects to be? More and more rapid growth — wider reach of trade — greater accumulations of individual wealth by individual energy and industry — a greater sweep of influence — a higher place in the commerce and productive industry of the nation. Since 1860, her population has grown from 18,000 to over 50,000; her aggregate of taxable property from $10,000,000 to over $30,000,000. If there is any dependence to be placed in the prophecy of indications, fairly interpreted, she is likely to grow in 1880 to 100,000 inhabitants, with a total of taxables of $100,000,000. This is large guessing, but it is not larger than the developments of the last ten years will make safe guessing, as well.

RAILROADS.

The railroad fever was taken early in Indiana, but its energy was expended idly because applied prematurely. If the lines at first proposed could have been built they would have languished, and possibly have died, before the development of the country could have supplied them with profitable business. It is true that they would have contributed largely to that development, and to the creation of the

sources of their support, but all they could have done, added to all that would have
been done any how, would hardly have saved them from inanition for the first few
years. In 1830, as noticed in the general history of the city, six railway lines were
projected from various points on the borders of the State, mainly on the southern
border, all centering at Indianapolis. These were the Lawrenceburgh and Indianapolis, Madison and Indianapolis, New Albany, Salem and Indianapolis, Harrison
and Indianapolis, Lafayette and Indianapolis, and the Ohio and Indianapolis.
They were chartered in February, 1831. Surveys were made on some of them, and
with some little or nothing was done. Grading was attempted in spots on the Lawrenceburgh line, and years afterwards the remains of embankments were to be
seen near Shelbyville. They may be visible yet. The Madison was surveyed and
started, and a rechartering of some of the others in 1835 indicated a continued
purpose to prosecute them. But in 1836 the "Internal Improvement System" superseded private effort, and all were abandoned but those taken in hand by the
State. The chief, in effect the only one, of these was the Madison road, with a brief
notice of which may be introduced a sketch of our railway system. Before entering upon this, however, it is due to Ex-Governor Ray to allude to his project of a
railway system which was ridiculed in his day as the dream of a disordered intellect. In fact, the old Governor was not as sound in mind as he had been, but the
system into which the separate railway enterprises have combined runs so closely
parallel with his that his dream would have been voted a prophecy some centuries
ago. He proposed a series of lines to all points of the compass; and we have it
a village every ten miles—and we have pretty nearly that; a town every twenty—
and we can come very close to that; and cities at a certain other distance (the
writer does not remember what) which, whatever it may have been, has been
practically realized. These radiating lines were all to have a common central depot—and we have *that*, and the only city in the world that has. It may detract
from the good old Governor's powers as a prophet, but it will add to his repute as a
shrewd speculator, that he wanted that central depot on his property opposite the
Court House, which, he contended, was the only proper place for it.

MADISON ROAD.

The Madison road, began as above stated, was taken by the State in 1836, and carried through the "deep diggings" at the Madison hill, in which was sunk enough
money to have brought it nearly to the Capital, and completed with a flat bar to
Vernon in 1841, at a cost of $1,900,000. There it stopped till after the echoes of
the great financial crash had died away. It was leased to Branham & Co. in 1839
for sixty per cent. of its receipts, the State furnishing engines and making repairs.
In 1842 it was sold to the Madison and Indianapolis Railroad Company, and completed to Indianapolis October 1st, 1847. Nathan B. Palmer, Samuel Merrill, John
Brough, E. W. H. Ellis, and F. O. J. Smith were Presidents till the absorption of
the road by the later born and stronger Jeffersonville road. In 1854 it was consolidated and "run" with the Peru road. In March, 1862, it was sold by the United
States Marshal for $325,000, taken by a newly organized company, and sold shortly
after to the Jeffersonville Company. It was, at first, the best paying road in the
country, as may be easily conceived, when it is remembered that it was the only
outlet and inlet to the whole center of the State. Its stock sold in 1852 for $1.60.
But it ran wild in a sort of intoxication of prosperity and wasted money in every
way. A new and round-about extension to avoid the "cut" at Madison was un-

dertaken, prosecuted at an enormous expense, and abandoned. Branch lines were
made or projected. Nothing was checked for fear of the cost. But rival lines followed it, and they, co operating with its extravagant management, sunk it till the
stock sold in 1856 for 2½ cents on the dollar. The State never got anything worth
naming for all she expended on this pioneer line of railway. It is eighty-six
miles long, passing through five counties, most of them rich in stock, corn lands and
timber, some in stone, and each containing a flourishing center of local business,
Franklin, Edinburgh (in the same county) Columbus, Vernon and Madison. Since
its absorption the lower end, from Columbus, has become a mere local road, the main
line running to Jeffersonville. Lime and building stone of excellent quality constitute one of the most important contributions of this old line to the business of
the city. Buhr mill stone is also found in Jennings county, but it is hard to say
what the value of the trade in it may be, or may be made.

JEFFERSONVILLE ROAD.

The Jeffersonville road, which by its connection with the Madison may be
more properly noticed here than elsewhere, was one of those that helped to break
up the monopoly of the Madison, and open to the city an improvable connection
with the south. It was begun in 1848, one among the earliest, and completed to
Edinburgh, 78 miles, in 1852. In August, 1853, a lease of the Madison road, with
its appurtenances, was obtained, and in 1863 the whole concern was bought and
amalgamated with the Jeffersonville. The latter was run from the Madison to
Columbus, and thence on a separate line to the Falls of the Ohio, one hundred and
ten miles from Indianapolis, traversing from Columbus four counties, and connecting with the Ohio and Mississippi road at Seymour. Until the completion of the
gigantic bridge at the Falls, this line could make no very advantageous connection
with southern lines, the transhipment of freights involving serious cost and considerable delay, but now the Ohio river interposes no obstacle, and Indianapolis can
make as complete and safe and cheap connection with Louisville as with Cincinnati. Dillard Ricketts has long been President of this road, but Mr. John Zulauf
preceded him. A controlling interest in it, and its interest in the bridge over the
Ohio, have recently been purchased by the Pennsylvania Central Railroad.

BELLEFONTAINE ROAD.

The Bellefontaine road was projected in 1847-'48, by Hon. Oliver H. Smith, to
whom it owes its existence nearly as wholly as if he had built it with his own
money. It was chartered in 1848, and by Mr. Smith's energetic endeavors, in pushing on the solicitation of stock subscriptions, and making speeches along the line
showing its undeniable but unappreciated advantages in a lake and eastern connection, it was put under way within a year, and in the winter of the next year, 1850,
cars were running to Pendleton, 28 miles. In the winter of 1852 it was completed
its full length, 84 miles, to Union City on the State line, where it connected with
a line simultaneously carried on to Bellefontaine, in Ohio. A few years later it
was given a connection at the same point with Dayton, through Greenville. A depot and other buildings were erected here, in what was then the extreme north-
eastern suburb of the city, but they were found to be too far away, and in 1853
others were built on the creek at Virginia Avenue. The old ones, with a large section of track, were sold in 1853 to Mr. Farnsworth, and occupied by him and Mr.
J. Barnard as a car factory for about six years. New freight and car houses were
built in 1864 in the eastern part of the city. In 1859 it was consolidated with the

Ohio line, and in 1808 with the Cleveland, Columbus and Cincinnati line, and the old name, with Indianapolis added, is its present name, but it goes usually by the name of the "Bee line." The Indiana end of it passes through four counties well populated and agriculturally rich, and connects with other roads at Anderson and Muncie as well as at Union. Its eastern connections give it an immense business, though for a time it languished greatly and its stock run low. Besides Mr. Smith it has had John Brough, Alfred Harrison and Calvin Fletcher for Presidents, and since its consolidation it has been largely controlled by the Ohio and Eastern interest.

TERRE HAUTE ROAD.

The Terre Haute and Richmond road was originally, as the name imports, projected to run from one side of the State to the other, but it was deemed too heavy a contract, and only the western end was proceeded with by the original organization. It was chartered in 1846, with a provision which the State has never availed itself of, allowing the Legislature, after the dividends have fully returned the original investment, to regulate the tolls and freights and to take for the school fund all dividends above fifteen per cent. It was surveyed and the contracts let in 1849. Work began in 1850, and was completed in May, 1852, at a cost, including the mortgages, of $1,154,000. The freight depot, the largest in the city, was built in 1850-51, in anticipation of the completion of the road, and for a time was used as the passenger depot too. It was thus used by several roads as late as 1853, till the Union depot was completed. It was enlarged in 1857, and was considerably damaged in 1865 by the explosion of a locomotive in it. Chauncey Rose was the first President, and is yet the principal owner. Edwin J. Peck and W. R. McKeen have been Presidents. It is now called the Terre Haute and Indianapolis road, and connects at Terre Haute with a new line to St. Louis through Vandalia. It passes through four counties, the eastern rich in agricultural, the others in mineral, wealth. It is seventy-four miles long. The coal trade has hitherto been carried on over it exclusively, and its general freight and passenger business has been probably equalled by no other in the city. It connects at Greencastle with the Louisville, New Albany and Chicago road. Its first President, Mr. Rose, with Mr. Smith of the Bellefontaine, and Mr. Peck and General Morris, devised and carried through the great project of a Union track and depot.

CINCINNATI ROAD.

A railway connection with Cincinnati was early seen to be important, and one of the first railroads projected in 1830-31 was one to effect this object. It was frequently renewed afterwards, but its direct conflict with the interests of the Madison road made that then powerful corporation a determined enemy, and no fair charter could be obtained. It was not until 1850 that it was begun in a disjointed way, in a series of sectional roads, which the Madison thought would create a less dangerous rivalry by their lack of consolidated organization. It was finished to Lawrenceburgh, 90 miles, in 1853, and the following spring, the Ohio and Mississippi road having been finished, an accommodation rail was laid upon its track for our road, then changed to the "Indianapolis and Cincinnati" from the "Lawrenceburgh and Upper Mississippi," and a continuous line made to Cincinnati. In 1855, the abandoned White Water Canal having been bought, a track was laid in the bed of that for the road. A branch road was built through the White Water Valley

some ten years ago, and another from Fairland to Martinsville. In 1866 it was consolidated with the Lafayette road, and in 1868 obtained the control, by lease, of the Vincennes road. This last arrangement has since been broken up. The shops of the road were first built here, burned in 1855, and rebuilt, and then removed to Cincinnati. For some time past the company has been greatly embarrassed. Its affairs have been placed in the hands of a receiver, and quite recently an attempt has been made to force it into bankruptcy. George H. Dunn was the first President, but H. C. Lord is best known in connection with that position. It passes through five counties, and is 115 miles long. Valuable quarries of building stone, largely used in Indianapolis, as well as a very productive agricultural country lie on this line.

LAFAYETTE ROAD.

The Indianapolis and Lafayette road was begun in 1849 under the Presidency of Albert S. White, and finished in the winter of 1852. It is 65 miles long, cost $1,000,000, and passes through four counties of great agricultural wealth, and was for a long time immensely valuable as the connecting link between the southern roads and Chicago. In 1866 it was consolidated with the Cincinnati road, to make a connection for Cincinnati with Chicago, and the consolidation in attempting too much broke down. Its freight depot was built in 1853, in the north-west corner of the city, near the canal, burned in 1864, rebuilt in 1865, and has been measurably abandoned since 1866, the consolidation having little use for it. Besides Mr. White, W. F. Reynolds, of Lafayette, was President of the separate road for several years.

CENTRAL ROAD.

The Indiana Central road was organized in 1851 and contracts made in the fall of that year. It was completed to the State line, 72 miles, in December, 1853, at a cost of $1,223,000. It was consolidated with the Ohio end of the line in 1863, and called the Indianapolis and Columbus road. In 1867 the road was consolidated with the Pittsburgh, Cincinnati and St. Louis line. It does a large business as a through line, and a good deal in the local way, traversing four of the best, and best cultivated, counties of the State. Samuel Hannah was the first President, succeeded by John S. Newman, the most efficient contributor to its construction.

PERU ROAD.

The Peru and Indianapolis road was chartered in 1846, and a company organized the year following. Work was begun in 1849 and the road completed with a flat bar to Noblesville, 21 miles, in the spring of 1851. It was finished to Peru in 1854, 73 miles, at a cost of $700,000. In a few months after its completion it was consolidated with the Madison road, but it was found to be a rather premature enterprise, as it had no through connection to the north, and the local trade was inadequate to make a paying route. It was disposed of for the benefit of the bondholders in 1857, and has since been worked for them, and having gained through connections is proving a good line. The flat rail was replaced with the T within a year after its completion to Peru. It traverses four counties which are now fast improving, but a portion lying in the old Miami Reserve was long in being brought up to the average level of other counties. It has had a number of Presidents, of whom Wm. J. Holman was the first. Dr. E. W. H. Ellis, John D. Defrees, John Burke and David Macy have also been Presidents.

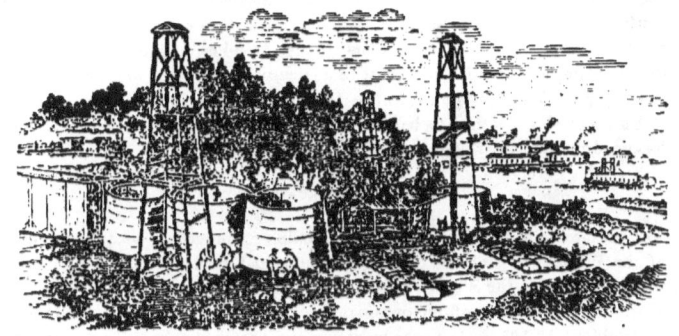

JUNCTION ROAD.

The Indianapolis and Cincinnati Junction road was began in divisions from Hamilton, Ohio, to this city, in 1850. A good deal of work was done, when the two companies concerned, the Ohio and Indianapolis, and the Junction, united in 1853 and prosecuted the enterprise with ample means and excellent prospects till they were overtaken by the embarrassments of 1855 and compelled to stop, till about five years ago. Work was then resumed and the road brought to this point in 1868. The city voted it a subsidy of $45,000, on condition that its shops were placed here, a condition that has not been complied with, though within a few months past there is a reasonable prospect of its being done. It is 124 miles long, traverses five counties in this State, all among the richest in agricultural property and prospects. It has recently passed under the control of the Cincinnati, Hamilton & Dayton Railway. Its successive Presidents have been: Caleb B Smith, John Woods, Samuel W. Parker, Jonathan M. Ridenour, and L. Worthington.

VINCENNES ROAD.

The Indianapolis and Vincennes road, opening a connection with the navigable end of the Wabash, was one of the earliest projected roads of the second era of railroad enterprise in the State. It was proposed in 1836, and again in 1850 or '51, and advanced to the point of the organization of a company, with John H. Bradley as President, in 1853. It never went further, however. In 1865 a new effort was made by an Eastern Company, organized under General Ambrose E. Burnside. Indianapolis voted it a subscription of $60,000, on condition its shops were located here. No shops have yet been established anywhere of any considerable consequence, so that the condition can hardly be deemed violated. It was finished to this city in 1868, and almost immediately on its completion was leased to the Cincinnati road. That lease was not allowed to stand long, however, and the road is now running on its own account, though controlled by the Pennsylvania Central, and is doing well. It passes through five counties, the upper section being wholly agricultural, the lower fully stored with mineral wealth of immense value, including the best qualities of coal, stone of many varieties, and "cold short" iron in abundance of good quality to mix with the "hot short" grade of Iron Mountain and Lake Superior.

CRAWFORDSVILLE ROAD.

The Indianapolis, Bloomington and Western (Crawfordsville) was organized some years ago, but after survey was checked by pecuniary embarrassments, so that the last of the work has been done upon it within the past four years or less. Its most active advocate and manager has been Mr. Sam'l C. Willson, of Crawfordsville. It runs through five counties of abundant agricultural resources, those to the West lying in the great coal field, and sure to develope, sooner or later, a vast amount of mineral wealth. It connects at Danville, Ill., with extended Western lines, and forms a valuable link in one of the Great Western chains. When first completed it entered the city over the Terre Haute and Indianapolis track, for a while, but it has since made a shorter connection with the Indianapolis and St. Louis, and established its car houses and shops on the west side of the river.

ISAAC DAVIS & CO.,

WHOLESALE and RETAIL DEALERS IN

Hats, Caps and Furs,

ROBES, Etc.,

No. 12 East Washington Street,

INDIANAPOLIS.

COLCLAZER'S

New Jewelry Store

No. 14 East Washington Street,

Everything new and direct from the Manufacturers and Importers,

AMERICAN AND FOREIGN WATCHES,

Diamonds, Fine Jewelry, and Silverware.

Special attention given to watch repairing.   All goods sold are engraved free of charge by an experienced engraver.

J. H. COLCLAZER,

No. 14 East Washington Street, Indianapolis, Ind.

ST. LOUIS ROAD.

The Indianapolis and St. Louis road, completed within a year, is the most rapidly constructed line that enters the city. It was meant to be a connection westward for some strong eastern lines, and they put their money, experience and energy upon it with such success that it really came upon the town with a shock of suddenness. It traverses the same counties as the Terre Haute road, and will be the most formidable rival of that in the coal trade, for which it offers abundant facilities. It was frequently remarked during its progress that it was the best built new road ever seen in the West. It connects at Terre Haute with the old Terre Haute and Alton line, and thus makes a single route to St. Louis. Its business, especially of through freight, is already enormous, although its coal transportation has hardly begun yet.

These twelve lines are completed. Besides these the Indiana and Illinois Central, which also penetrates the coal field, has, after many years of suspension and difficulty, been put in progress to completion, and it may be confidently expected to add its contribution to the city's business in a year or two. It will have through connections westward, and undoubtedly do a large business. All these western lines, except the Lafayette, run through the coal fields, and make it sure that no monopoly or dangerous ascendancy of one line can ever occur in supplying the city with fuel.

There have been several other lines projected, but as they have all died, for a time at least, it is not deemed necessary or advisable to extend this work by notices of them.

THE UNION DEPOT.

The importance of a Union depot and track became apparent as soon as it became settled that there was to be more than one or two roads entering the city. Oliver H. Smith, Chauncey Rose, General Morris and E. J. Peck were the active promoters of the enterprise. In August, 1849, the Union Company, composed at first of the Madison, Bellefontaine and Terre Haute Companies, was organized, and the Union track laid the year following. Subsequently other companies were admitted, and now it is composed of some half dozen or more of the different railroad managements of the city. It owns all the railway tracks in the city as independently as each company owns its own out of the city. It also owns the Union Depot. This large structure, 420 feet long by 200 wide, was planned by General Morris and completed in 1853. It was at first but 120 feet wide, but in 1866 was enlarged, an eating house placed in it, and the offices transferred to the south side. In 1871 a fire occurred in it which seriously damaged the Eating House. It now accommodates over eighty trains a day, but the crowd at times is so great that the accommodation is very indifferent, as vast and empty as the place looks at other times. A larger depot is needed, and the company understand this quite as well as others, but the difficulty is to determine how to get a larger one. Shall it be by enlarging the present one, or getting ground further west for a new one? The former will be hard, the latter will be removing public accommodations possibly so far to make them no convenience. But sooner or later there must be more depot room, come by it how the company may. Mr. Dillard Ricketts, of the Jeffersonville road, is the present President of the Union Company. Mr. E. J. Peck, of the Terre Haute road was President for a long time. Mr. Wm. N. Jackson has been Secretary all the time.

INDIANAPOLIS CINCINNATI AND LAFAYETTE RAILWAY—TONNAGE STATEMENT FOR 1870.

FREIGHTS.	Total Tonnage of Whole Line.	Forwarded from Indianapolis, 1870.	Received at Indianapolis, 1870.
Bushels of Corn................................	737,020	111,684	53,854
Bushels of Wheat..............................	1,124,085	146,253	339,879
Bushels of Oats...............................	197,186	72,519	13,600
Bushels of Rye and Barley................	202,953	17,755	18,009
Tons of Iron....................................	14,333	2,958	7,427
Cars of Coal....................................	3,211	207	497
Cars of Lumber................................	4,901	499	2,080
Cars of Staves.................................	2,235	104	1,083
Cars of Shingles..............................	225	4	88
Cars of Hoop Poles...........................	90	8	45
Cars of Stone and Lime......................	3,723	22	1,873
Cars of Horses.................................	413	99	177
Cars of Cattle and Sheep...................	1,328	499	179
Cars of Hogs....................................	3,195	945	367
Barrels of Flour...............................	292,298	68,754	42,927
Barrels of Whisky.............................	61,367	6,182	12,347
Barrels of Salt.................................	74,326	1,718	24,187
Barrels of Pork and Lard...................	9,887	949	794
Tierces of Pork and Lard...................	9,842	3,154	181
Barrels of Tallow and Grease.............	6,410	2,252	88
Tierces of Tallow and Grease.............	1,363	824	1
Pounds of Freight.............................	923,763,050	134,994,653	243,001,022

CLEVELAND, COLUMBUS, CINCINNATI, AND INDIANAPOLIS RAILWAY—TONNAGE STATEMENT FOR 1870.

FREIGHTS.	Total Tonnage 1870.	Forwarded from Indianapolis, 1870.	Received at Indianapolis, 1870.
Pounds of Butter.............................	1,333,140	4,875	1,899,603
Pounds of Cheese.............................	13,097,678	18,201	4,454,197
Pounds of Wool	4,618,082	1,061,026	33,433
Pounds of Forest Products.................	253,737,510	61,679,156	17,743,790
Pounds of Building Stone..................	116,081,672	121,300	2,029,726
Pounds of Grind-stone......................	10,042,822	....	1,547,308
Pounds of Dressed Hogs....................	1,801,666	19,606	1,700
Pounds of Tobacco	47,928,803	36,552,417	307,504
Pounds of Cotton.............................	46,381,811	35,013,992	....
Pounds of Pork, Hams, and Lard........	21,066,094	5,125,184	21,601
Number of Hogs and Sheep................	324,665	59,950	5,100
Number of Horses and Cattle.............	155,029	60,532	378
Bushels of Wheat.............................	1,558,751	200,354	647,264
Bushels of Corn, Oats, and Seed.........	2,709,201	1,329,883	36,037
Barrels of Flour...............................	743,002	556,980	4,785
Pounds of Merchandise......................	741,776,801	52,639,346	228,076,733
Number of tons of Freight Carried......	851,644	....	....

ABSTRACT OF TONNAGE OVER INDIANA DIVISION OF ST. L., V., T. H., & I. R. R DURING THE YEAR 1870.

		Equivalent in pounds.
Pounds Merchandise...		227,700,603
Bushels Corn..	968,305	54,228,293
Bushels Wheat..	342,568	21,554,129
Bushels Oats...	58',181	18,597,727
Barrels Beef, Pork, and Lard..	34,233	11,297,524
Barrels Flour..	340,800	68,160,000
Barrels Cement..	7,060	2,117,500
Barrels Oil...	23,634	8,508,240
Barrels Salt..	19,235	5,770,500
Barrels Whisky..	4,960	1,763,000
Hogsheads Tobacco..	22,348	37,415,680
Bales Cotton...	49,920	23,771,397
Bales Hemp..	2,549	990,890
Number Horses and Cattle..	46,766	48,116,000
Number Mules..	2,015	1,996,000
Number Sheep..	36,200	5,792,000
Number Hogs...	70,070	29,384,000
Cars Staves...	752	15,040,000
Cars Lumber...	2,105	42,060,000
Cars Shingles and Lath..	145	2,646,000
Cars Cooperage..	116	2,138,000
Cars Machinery..	580	10,440,000
Cars Stone..	1,781	35,630,000
Cars Lime...	200	4,000,000
Cars Pig Iron...	1,774	35,480,000
Cars Brick and Clay...	340	6,800,000
Cars Iron Ore...	2,226	44,520,000
Cars Coal...	19,431	388,620,000
Cars Coke...	281	5,620,000
Cars Cinders..	.171	3,420,000
Cars Scrap and Castings...	129	2,580,000
Cars Meal, Bran, &c...	190	3,800,000
Cars Stone Ware...	9	180,000
Cars Slate..	5	100,000
Cars Ice..	323	6,460,000
Cars Logs...	276	5,520,000
Cars R. R. Materials..	446	8,920,000
Gross Tons R. R. Iron...	31,160	92,198,400
Number Box Cars...	335	5,360,000
Number Passenger Cars...	62	1,550,000
Number Flat Cars..	118	1,416,000
Number Coal Cars..	44	528,000
Number Stock Cars...	8	96,000
Number Engines..	34	1,360,060
Total		1,284,654,692

THE RAILROADS OF INDIANAPOLIS—CAPITAL, DEBTS, INCOME, Etc.

A Blank Space (——) across the Line signifies "Not Ascertained."

NAME OF ROAD.	Capital Stock.	Funded Debt.	Floating Debt.	Cost of Road and Equipment.	Gross Earnings.	Net Earnings.	Year Ending.
*Cincinnati and Indianapolis Junction	$3,132,235	$2,052,000	$1,042,798 41	$6,187,644 62	$361,276 05	$26,712,510 00	June 30, 1870.
Cleveland, Columbus, Cincinnati, and Indianapolis	11,420,400	3,000,000		12,160,930 00	3,232,109 64	1,058,439 55	Dec. 31, 1870.
†Columbus, Chicago, and Indiana Central	12,636,772	19,473,174	822,713	32,713,540 00	†3,329,411 00	†267,452 00	June 30, 1870.
Indianapolis and St. Louis	600,000	2,670,400	265,456				Dec. 31, 1870.
Indianapolis, Cincinnati, and Lafayette	5,750,000	8,000,000	1,500,000	13,720,057 00	1,850,000 00	††450,000 00	Jan. 29, 1871.
¶Indianapolis, Peru, and Chicago							
Indianapolis, Bloomington, and Western	5,400,000	6,560,000					
‡‡Indianapolis and Vincennes					†290,000 00	403,486 00	Dec. 31, 1869.
Jeffersonville, Madison, and Indianapolis	2,400,000	3,100,000	587,179	6,027,342 00	1,140,099 00	469,465 05	Nov. 30, 1870
§§Terre Haute and Indianapolis	1,988,150	800,000		2,650,782 94	1,087,526 49		

*The Fort Wayne, Muncie, & Cincinnati R. R., from Connersville, Ind., to Fort Wayne, Ind., having been leased to the Junction R. R. Co., under contract to build and operate it, the indebtedness of the Junction R. R. Co., includes everything pertaining to the Fort Wayne Railroad. The Junction road has since been leased to the Cincinnati, Hamilton & Dayton R. R. The statement of the earnings is for the year ending June 30th, 1869. ‡‡This road having since been leased by the Pittsburg, Cincinnati & St. Louis Railway Co., its earnings are no longer reported separately. ¶Information refused. †Operated by the P. C. & St. L. Co. †Estimated. §§Does not include the Vandalia Division.

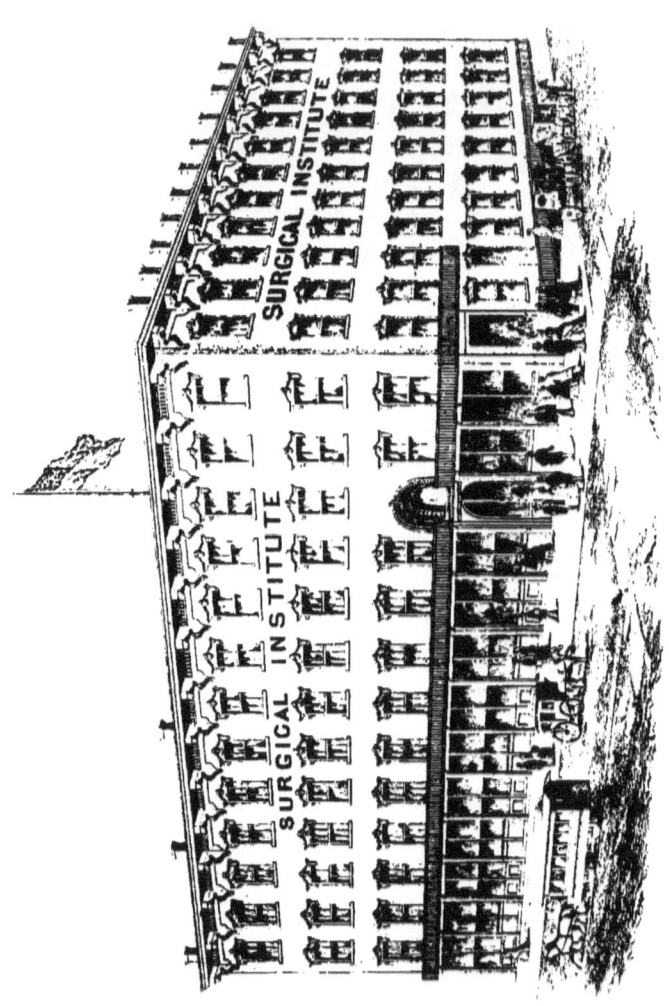

NATIONAL SURGICAL INSTITUTE.

National Surgical Institute,

FOR THE TREATMENT OF

ALL CASES OF SURGERY,

Deformities, Chronic Diseases, Etc.

ONE SQUARE NORTH OF THE UNION DEPOT, INDIANAPOLIS, IND.

THE NATIONAL SURGICAL INSTITUTE is located on the corner of Illinois and Georgia streets, and is one of the largest and most imposing buildings in the city. There is no institution, of its kind, in America, so extensive in its several appointments, and so great a reputation has it gained throughout the continent, that patients from all parts of the United States can always be seen there availing themselves of its benefits. All deformities of the Face, Spine and Limbs; diseases of the Eye and Ear, Paralysis and Chronic Diseases, are among the most prominent of the specialties here treated, and to any one affected with any of these afflictions, greater relief is offered here than anywhere else. More than four thousand cases made application for treatment during the past year, and the great good which has been accomplished within that time, is beyond estimate. Its facilities for the treatment of all deformities and Surgical and Chronic diseases surpass anything ever before attempted in this country

All kinds of Apparatus and Surgical appliances are furnished to order, to suit every known deformity, and, unlike other Surgical Institutions, the Surgeons attend personally to their manufacure and adjustment to the deformity.

The Medical and Surgical Staff is composed of Surgeons and Physicians, the most eminent in their profession, and skilful in their chosen specialties.

Many new and strange inventions have been made available through the superior genius of Dr. Allen, and to him must be ascribed the highest honors for the great and valuable assistance he has rendered in this respect to the Science of Surgery, by means of which thousands of cripples heretofore deemed incurable have been fully restored.

Hundreds of cases of Paralysis owe their restoration to the treatment as administered at this Surgical Institute, and any one thus afflicted, should make no delay, but haste to be made partakers of the greatest relief ever offered for the cure of this terrible affliction. One large department is devoted exclusively to the treatment of this class of cases. In it is found the Swedish Movement cure, perfect and complete in every particular, which with its machines for producing artificial motion in limbs and joints—and for the use of vacuum or compressed air, with the aid of steam generators, all of which are absolute and indispensable in the treatment of these cases—will, upon examination, convince the most skeptical and incredulous, of the merits of this treatment in preference to any other.

The proprietors have spared neither pains nor expence in fitting the several apartments for the reception of their patients, and the most fastidious lady or gentleman, if afflicted, will find every necessary attention and want speedily and promptly satisfied.

The institution is provided with spacious and elegant bathing apartments, with superior faculties for administering the various baths, including the Turkish, Electro Thermal, Medicated and Sulphur baths. The Electro Thermal Bath, is a great remedy for nervous diseases—diseases of Females, General Debility, Sexual Weakness, &c., &c.

The other Baths are especially adapted to the cure of Rheumatism, Venereal Affections, Scrofula, &c., &c.

The Institution is most eminently successful in the prosecution of its most noble calling, and no one afflicted will ever regret a visit there and a treatment at its hands.

Send stamp for general or illustrated circular; also for special treatices on Club Feet, Paralysis, Spinal Disease, Hip Disease, Piles and Fistula, Private Diseases and Diseases of Females.

Address—Secretary National Surgical Institute, Indianapolis, Indiana.

THE RAILROADS OF INDIANAPOLIS—MILEAGE, ROLLING STOCK, DIVIDENDS, ETC.

A blank space (——) across the line signifies "none," and running dots (.....) signify "not ascertained."

NAME OF ROAD.	Mileage.			Rolling Stock.			No. of Employees.	Dividend Periods.	Dividend last paid.	Market value of Shares July 1, 1871.
	Main Line.	Branch Line.	Second Track and Sidings.	Engines.	Passenger Cars.	Freight, Bag-gage, Mail, Express and Express Cars.				
	M.	M.	M.	No.	No.	No.				
Cincinnati and Indianapolis Junction............	98	68	56.2	16	12	279	1750	....		
Cleveland, Columbus, Cincinnati and Indianapolis	340.5	40.9	61.7	90	47	1632	1684	February and August	Aug., 1871, 3½ ℔ ct.	89¾
*Columbus, Chicago and Indiana Central............	588	12.5	67.9	135	76	1719	1884	....		19¾
Indianapolis and St. Louis............	260.6	5	....	61	51	1018	800	March and September	Sept., 1867, 4 ℔ ct.	None in market.
Indianapolis, Cincinnati and Lafayette............	179	110	23	52	40	1032	800	....		6¾
Indianapolis, Peru and Chicago............	161	——	3.7	14	10	286	160	....		None in market.
*Indianapolis, Bloomington & Western	202.05	——	——	30	18	488	786	....		
*Indianapolis and Vincennes............	116.5	——	4.5	8	7	225				...[St. L., & C. R. R.
Jeffersonville, Madison & Indianapolis............	114	110	17.9	37	28	564	290	January and July.	July, 1871, 6 ℔ ct.	Owned by P., C., &
Terre Haute and Indianapolis............	238†	16	....	90	25	1233	800	....		None in market.

†Includes length of St. Louis, Vandalia and Terre Haute Railway, operated by this company, and called the "Vandalia Division"—length 168 miles.   *Operated by the Pittsburg, Cincinnati and St. Louis Company.

PRESENT MANUFACTURES.

To the foregoing review of our early manufactures, and observations on the manufacturing resources and prospects of the city, we append a necessarily brief sketch of the principal manufacturing enterprises of to-day, and a tabular statement at the close.

AGRICULTURAL IMPLEMENTS.

The development of this manufacturing interest here is not commensurate with the demand, the advantages of situation, and the opportunities for profitably engaging in the manufacture of agricultural implements at this point.

Five manufactories—exclusive of those where parts only of certain implements are made, and exclusive of wagons, classed under the title of carriages, wagons, etc.—are reported by the census, employing an aggregate of seventy-five hands, and their products last year aggregated $105,750. Adding to this aggregate the exceptions stated, would probably double it; with a corresponding increase in the number of hands employed.

As before stated, the opportunities for profitable investment in this description of manufactures are inadequately utilized. One considerable move in this direction was the establishment in 1865, by a stock company, of the *Indianapolis Agricultural Works*, with J. A. Grosvenor as president. Various changes of stockholders and officers have occurred since the inception of the enterprise, and the establishment has been diverted from its original scope of production to the manufacture of heavy wagons, carts, drays, and the like. This caused it to be rechristened *The Indianapolis Wagon Works*, its present title.

The establishment is located directly south of the depot of the Terre Haute and Indianapolis railway; is quite extensive, and is well supplied with approved and valuable machinery. The amount of capital stock is $80,000; number of hands employed, fifty-three; value of products last year, $78,000.

There is an unoccupied field here for the manufacture of plows, threshers, reapers, mowers, and of the various other leading agricultural implements generally. In respect to these, the area of agricultural territory that should be tributary to this market is of great extent and opulent in agricultural capacities; the best of materials for their manufacture are cheap and abundant, and the facilities for shipment unrivalled. These advantages can hardly be much longer neglected. The reported sales of agricultural implements by dealers in this city, during the past year, aggregate $755,687. The total value of agricultural implements manufactured here during the same period, was but $105,750. These figures illustrate how great is the field here for engaging in this agricultural interest, and how it is almost totally unoccupied.

BAKERIES.

The census shows fifteen establishments of this description, covering the whole range of products coming under this head. They employ sixty-seven hands, and their aggregate production last year is valued at $349,386. Of these, the largest establishments are those of Parrott, Nickum & Co., and the *Aerated Bread Company*. The former has a very extensive wholesale trade, chiefly in crackers. The latter manufactures all the different descriptions of bakers' products, using the well known and approved process of "raising" the dough by charging it with car-

bonic acid gas.' The figures above given show this branch of industry to be well represented here, and prosperous.

BOOTS AND SHOES.

The census reports over fifty manufacturers of boots and shoes, employing an aggregate of one hundred and thirteen workmen, and their products last year aggregating $137 672. This manufacturing interest is yet in a primitive state of development, being confined to custom work, or individual orders, and to the manufacture in a small way, by some retail houses, of boots and shoes for their own trade. What is yet wanting to give this branch of industry its proper importance, and what could evidently be very profitably conducted here, is the manufacture of boots and shoes, on a large scale, for the wholesale trade, as in the East.

BREWERS.

The business of manufacturing malt liquors is extensively engaged in here. The principal breweries are those of C. F. Schmidt, J. P. Meikel, P. Lieber & Co., Casper Maus, Sponsel & Bals, Harting & Bro. and Frank Wright. Of these, that of Mr. Wright is devoted to the manufacture of ale exclusively. The aggregate capital employed is reported at $276,500; number of hands, fifty-six; value of annual products, $286,670. The products of our breweries are in excellent repute with the trade.

BUILDERS.

The census report shows thirty-four firms engaged in the business of carpentering and building. Aggregate capital employed, $134,800; aggregate number of hands, two hundred and twenty-nine; aggregate value of products last year, $391,075. This is exclusive of the products of the planing mills, elsewhere reported, and of building improvements not included in the returns of these builders.

BROOMS.

The manufacture of brooms at this point is engaged in by ten firms, employing twenty-one hands, and producing last year manufactured products to the amount of $23,932.

CARRIAGES, ETC.

This manufacturing interest is represented by a number of manufactories; the largest and best known of which are the Shaw & Lippincott Manufacturing Company, S. W. Drew, and George Lowe & Company. The range of production is very comprehensive, and the facilities for making superior work, at the lowest cost, are unsurpassed. Every kind of spring vehicle can be obtained here, from the simplest spring wagon to the most costly carriage, rockaway, landau, or what not style of vehicular architecture. Specimens may be seen at any time that bear comparison with the work of any similar manufactory in the United States. For reasons already stated, this point affords extraordinary advantages for profitably engaging in this species of manufactures: easy and cheap access to the best lumber, and unequaled facilities for shipment of the manufactured products.

Including the several grades of vehicles not elsewhere classed under the head of agricultural implements, and the extensive establishment known as the *Wood-*

burn Servin Wheel Company, this interest represents a capital of $585,000; gives employment to four hundred and fifty-one hands, and yielded last year products to the value of about $450,000.

CEMENT DRAIN PIPES.

The Indiana Cement Pipe Company was organized in the fall of 1869, with a capital of $15,000—commenced operations in the spring of 1870, and employed through the year from eight to twelve men. The sales for 1870 amounted to about $10,000.

The officers for 1871 are: T. B. McCarty, President; J. W. Dodd, Secretary and Treasurer; Henry Willis, Superintendent.

The company manufacture cement pipe from three to thirty inches diameter, for house drains, sewers, land drains, culverts under streets, railroads and gravel roads. They also manufacture wrought iron water pipe, lined with and laid in cement, which preserves the iron and insures the consumer pure water. This pipe can be made to stand any pressure, is cheaper than cast iron pipe, and is rapidly growing in favor wherever it is used.

The company own the exclusive right to use a patented process for carbonizing or hardening manufactures of cement, lime and sand, and are now making a handsome, durable and cheap stone for building and paving. By the use of this process, cement pipe can be so hardened as to stand a great degree of heat, making it available for chimneys, flues for green houses, air pipes for furnaces, etc.

COTTON MANUFACTURES.

This interest is represented by but one establishment, the *Indianapolis Cotton Manufactory*, devoted to the manufacture of cotton warp. This enterprise was started in October, 1866, by a stock company composed of C. E. Geisendorff & Co., John Thomas, Henry Schnull, W. W. Leathers, T. B. McCarty, and R. B. Duncan. The erection of the building—located on the canal, just inside the city limits—was completed in the winter of 1867. Upwards of $100,000 have been expended in machinery. The establishment has about forty-one thousand spindles and forty cards. It gives employment to fifty-six hands, and the value of its products last year was $300,000.

The warp manufactured here finds a ready market on account of its quality and the favorable prices at which it can be made. The only changes in the original ownership, we believe, have been the transfer of the interest of C. E. Geisendorff & Co. to General Nathan Kimball, and the admission of several new stockholders by reason of an increase of the capital of the association.

The capital stock of the company, originally $100,000, has been increased to $200,000. The officers of the company are: President, John Thomas; Secretary, William Wilson; Treasurer, Wm. Roe.

This enterprise, whose success was doubted by many at its inception, has proven a remunerative investment, and its prosperity invites further investments in cotton manufactures at this point.

CLOTHING.

The manufacture of clothing in this city, like that of boots and shoes, is chiefly confined to what is called "custom work," there being no extensive manufactory

SPIEGEL, THOMS & CO.,

Manufacturers, Wholesale and Retail Dealers in

Furniture, Chairs & Mattresses,

Warerooms 71 & 73 West Washington Street   Factory, South East Street.

INDIANAPOLIS, INDIANA,

INDIANAPOLIS LIGHTNING ROD WORKS.

MUNSON'S

Tabular Copper Lightning Rod,

WITH SPIRAL FLANGES.

The Cheapest and Most Complete Protection against Disaster by Lightning ever Invented

This Rod has been erected on more than **Five Thousand Buildings** in and around Indianapolis during the past few years; and in many cities of the country similar success has attended its introduction. Wherever it is known its sales increase each succeeding year.

Also, Manufacturers of Cable Rods, at Wholesale and Retail.

ORDERS FROM THE TRADE SOLICITED.

And others who would be inclined to take hold of a business like this. Address

DAVID MUNSON,

Manufacturer and Patentee, Indianapolis, Ind.

Patented August 6, 1856.	Patented November 17, 1868.
Patented November 1, 1864.	Patented January 3, 1871.
Extended August 5, 1870.	Patented February 11, 1868.
Patented March 8, 1870.	Point Patented February 1, 1870.

of clothing for the wholesale trade. The census reports twenty-seven establishments, whose products last year aggregated $460,940. These employ, in the aggregate, two hundred and fifty-six workmen. Among these are several merchant tailoring establishments of the first class, with respect to the qualities and styles of their work. The manufacture of clothing, in a large way, for the general trade, could doubtless be profitably carried on here.

CONFECTIONERY.

This interest has attained, within a few years, a very respectable magnitude comparing favorably with other manufactories in proportion to the relative consumption. The census shows twelve manufacturers of confectionery, employing thirty-four hands, and producing candies to the value of $135.192 last year. The leading establishments are those of Daggett & Co., and Dukemineer & Co. The candies manufactured here are of high repute among the trade, because of their freedom from unwholesome adulteration.

COOPERS.

By reason of an abundant and cheap supply of the best lumber in the country, of extraordinary facilities for shipping the manufactured products, as well as of the extensive local demand, the manufacture of coopers' products here is an extensive and prosperous business. The census returns fourteen establishments of this description, employing one hundred and ninety-eight hands. The aggregate value of their products last year to was $310,160.

COFFEE AND SPICE MILLS.

There are two large, substantial, and prosperous establishments in this city engaged in the business of grinding coffee and spices, and putting them up in that form for the wholesale trade, namely: H. H. Lee and Maguire & Gillespie.

Mr. Lee's establishment is located at the intersection of Meridian street and Madison avenue, and is complete in all respects. It was opened in June. 1871. The celebrity previously held by its proprietor as a dealer in teas and coffees in this city, the completeness of the establishment, and the reliable quality of the goods, secured for the new venture an immediate recognition and an extensive patronage; and already, in the first few months, it has attained a fixed prosperity and high standing among the manufacturing enterprises of the city.

The coffee and spice mills of Maguire & Gillespie, No 31 East Maryland street, were established in 1862 by A. Stephens & Son, who retired in 1864. Their successors were Messrs. Judson & Dodd, who were succeeded, in 1869, by the present firm of Maguire and Gillespie.

The amount of capital invested is $25,000; ten hands are employed; and the value of products last year was about $70,000. In the rear of the store room is located the mill, operated by steam, in which all the coffee is roasted and ground, and in which the spices are ground.

FERTILIZING PRODUCTS.

An establishment of considerable magnitude, entitled the "Indianapolis Hair and Bristle Works," located on the corner of West and Wisconsin streets, was

begun in 1864 by Lewis F. Lannay. It occupies about three acres of ground, and employs from thirty-six to forty-two hands.

Since 1868, its productions have been ground bone and other fertilizers. Prior to that time the establishment was also engaged in dressing bristles and preparing hair for upholsterers' purposes. As now conducted, there is no other similar manufactory west of the Allegheny mountains. The capacity of the concern is about three hundred tons of fertilizing products per annum.

FLOUR.

The first flouring mill in this city was built by John Carlisle, in 1840. Like most other branches of trade and manufactures, the manufacture of flour has grown in proportion to the growth of the city in population and commercial and manufacturing importance. Indeed, the growth of this particular interest has been relatively greater than the growth of other interests, and for obvious reasons.

Favorably situated in a highly productive agricultural region, with railways radiating in every direction, facilitating the importation of grain directly and at the lowest cost, and affording ready outlets to the markets for the products of its mills, and having abundant water power, the manufacture of flour has grown and prospered here in obedience to the plainest natural laws.

The value of the products of our city mills, representing a capital of $371,500, during the past year, was $1,656,300.

The year 1870 was one of but moderate prosperity to flour manufacturers; the market being without animation, and trade being depressed throughout most of the year. This low state of vitality kept prices uniformly low, affording scant margins, and frequently no margins, for profits. The supply was generally in excess of the demand. The European demand was less than usual; and even the Franco-Prussian war, which was expected to stimulate the market in this country, depressed it rather.

FOUNDRIES, ROLLING MILLS, MACHINE SHOPS, METAL MANUFACTURES GENERALLY.

For the sake of brevity, the different manufactories in this city comprehended in the above caption, are here grouped under one head. Combined, these constitute the most extensive manufacturing interest in the city, representing an aggregate capital of $1,791,700 employing an aggregate of 1,427 operatives, and yielding products, during the past year, to the aggregate value of $2,961,065.

Rolling Mills.—There are two large manufactories of this description: " The Indianapolis Rolling Mill," and the " Capital City Iron Works."

The former is devoted to the rolling and rerolling of railroad iron; the latter, to the manufacture of the various descriptions of merchant iron.

In respect of the capital and number of operatives employed and of the value of products, this is the leading manufacturing enterprise in this city. It was established in 1858, by R. A. Douglas. At a later date, the late James Blake was associated with Mr. Douglas in the concern. It has gone on increasing in magnitude from year to year, until it is now owned by an incorporated company, and has a capital stock of $600.000, is capable of rerolling one hundred tons daily, and employs an average of three hundred and sixty-five operatives. The value of its products yearly is about $800,000. It has the reputation of producing the best iron rails in the United States—claimed to be superior to the English rails.

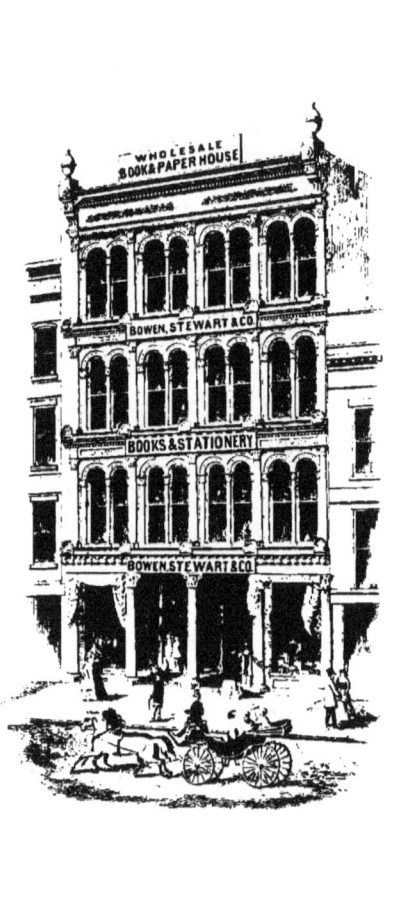

BOWEN, STEWART & CO.

Its present officers are: President, John M. Lord; Secretary, C. B. Parkman; Treasurer, Aquilla Jones, Sr. The most of the capital is owned by resident stock holders.

The Capital City Iron Works are owned by Messrs. Valentine Butsch, James Dickson, Fred. P. Rusch, J. C. Brinkmeyer, and Wm. Sims, and were established in 1867.

This enterprise had to encounter the usual opposition of similar Eastern establishments; which was at first successful. For a time they sold their iron in this city cheaper than it could be produced here. But this practice was of brief duration; and presently it came to pass that the home establishment could offer superior inducements, in respect of both qualities and prices. It has followed as a natural sequence that this rolling mill has obtained all the demand it can supply. Its products find a demand in a large area of western territory—are sold in considerable quantities in such large and remote cities as St. Louis, itself situated in an extensive iron and coal region. The superior advantages of this city for manufactures of this description are manifest: coal peculiarly adapted for the purpose, speedy access to the ore, and extraordinary facilities for the shipment of the manufactured iron in every direction.

Of the once mooted question whether such a manufactory could be profitably conducted here, in competition with the extensive and long established manufactories of the East, the success of this enterprise affords conclusive proof in the affirmative.

The possible producing capacity of the Works is about twenty tuns daily, or products to the value of $480,000 per annum. The number of hands now employed is about seventy, and is soon to be increased to one hundred and forty. The capital employed is about $150,000. The Works have twelve puddling and two smelting furnaces.

Iron Foundries and Machine Shops.—Under this head is grouped an extensive range of products, and several establishments of the first rank. Of these the principal are: The Eagle Machine Works; Sinker & Davis; D. Root & Co.; Greenleaf & Co.; Chandler & Taylor (Phœnix Machine Works); Hetherington & Co.; Frink & Moore (Union Novelty Works); Mothershead & Co.; the Dean Brothers.

The Eagle Machine Works were established here in 1848 by Watson, Voorhees & Co., under the name of the Washington Foundry. Two years later the property was purchased by Messrs. Hasselman & Vinton. Under this new firm it outgrew all resemblance to its primitive condition. By fires in 1854 and 1855, or thereabout, the firm lost property worth nearly $100,000, on which there was no insurance. These losses were repaired; the scope and extent of the establishment were rapidly enlarged; and in 1865 it passed into the ownership of a joint stock company, Mr. Hasselman retaining a one-third interest. It is still owned by a joint stock company, and its extent, the range and quality of its productions, its resources and prosperity, attest the sagacity and prudence of its management, and the advantageousness of its location. The principal articles manufactured at the *Eagle Machine Works* are engines, boilers, saw mills and threshing machines, the latter being made a specialty.

The firm of Sinker & Davis have for many years been the proprietors and conductors of a well known and extensive establishment, occupying the same field of production—except as to threshing Machines—as the *Eagle Machine Works*, and like the latter has grown to be an extensive and important establishment, with an excellent reputation for the quality of its products. The death of the senior member of the house, E. T. Sinker, Esq., in April last, was followed shortly after by a fire; the one producing a change of the firm, and the other operating a temporary interruption of business. Mr. Alfred T. Sinker has succeeded to his deceased father's interest in the establishment, and the destruction by the fire was promptly repaired.

The Stove Foundry of D. Root & Co. was established in 1850 by Deloss & J. K. Root. Through several changes of the firm Mr. Deloss Root has remained the senior and principal propietor. Advantages of location have been utilized by capable management. The establishment has grown from year to year in resources and extent, and its capacities are quite up with the times. About eighty different patterns of stoves for various uses, everything in the way of "hollow ware," and cast iron fronts for houses, sufficiently outline the products of this foundry.

The foundry of Greenleaf & Co. was established in 1865 by Wm. E. Greenleaf. It was a small concern at the start, but has since become a very extensive establishment. In May, 1870, the property passed to the ownership of a stock company, and was styled the *Greenleaf Machine Works.* The specialty of this establishment is heavy castings. A cylinder manufactured here in 1868 was extensively noticed at the time in the public prints as being the largest ever cast in the State, and, with one or two exceptions, in the West. Line-shafting, rolling-mill and blast-furnace castings and machinery, railroad turn-tables, steam engines, &c., are prominent classes of the products of this foundry.

The Phenix Machine Works were established in 1859 by Messrs. T. E. Chandler and C. P. Wiggins. After several changes of firm we find Messrs. Chandler & Taylor the present proprietors. The history of the establishment has been one of continuous increase in resources and prosperity. Messrs. Chandler & Taylor are manufacturers of engines, saw mills, and the various kinds of smaller machinery.

The foundry of Hetherington & Co. was established in 1864 by Mr. B. F. Hetherington. It was a small affair at first, but has grown to be a large establishment now. This establishment makes a great variety of the smaller grades of castings and machines.

The Union Novelty Works were established in 1862 by Dr. S. C. Frink, E. O. Frink and H. A. Moore. An establishment of no great magnitude at first, it flourished so well that by 1868 it had grown to the dignity of a joint stock company, with Dr. Frink as President, Mr. H. A. Moore as Superintendent, a large capital stock, and an extensive business. It was now named the *Union Novelty Works.* The leading articles manufactured by the company are bed irons, sad irons, Frink's safety hinge, the Novelty gate latch, gate hinges and Frink & Moore's patent street box for gas and water. In addition to these articles they have some fifty others on their list for which there is a growing demand, and the company are enlarging their works and manufacturing facilities as rapidly as means will admit.

The foundry of Mothershead & Co., established in 1864, is an extensive institution, devoted principally to the manufacture of stoves and hollow-ware.

The latest addition to the list of foundries and machine shops, located in this city, is the extensive manufactory of the Dean Brothers, located at the junction of the Jeffersonville Railroad and Madison Avenue. It was built during the summer and fall of 1870, and was opened on the 1st of January, 1871. The amount of capital invested in this manufactory is $30,000. The average number of hands employed is fifty. The range of production embraces woolen machinery, steam engines, baling presses, trucks, shafting, machinery castings of every description.

Boiler Yards.—The only firm exclusively engaged in the manufacture of boilers is Dumont & Roberts; but this branch of manufacturing is extensively engaged in by some of the establishments named under the head of "Foundries and Machine Shops," particularly by the Eagle Machine Works, and by the firm of Sinker & Davis.

Iron Railings, etc.—B. F. Haugh & Co., whose establishment was founded in 1850, employ forty workmen in the manufacture of iron railings, all descriptions of iron work used in the construction of public and private buildings, iron fronts, and, especially, iron jails; in which last respect this house has gained a widespread reputation and patronage.

Saw Works.—This interest is represented by the extensive and well known establishment of E. C. Atkins & Co. and George W. Atkins & Co. (late Alfred T. Sinker), whose range of production covers everything in the line of saws. Their capacities and prosperity are too well known to require extended mention here. The value of the products of these establishments, for the year ending June 1st, 1870, was $150,000.

Engine Governors.—Charles A. Conde & Co. are proprietors of an establishment devoted exclusively to the manufacture of steam governors.

Files.—The manufacture of files is represented by the establishment of Dratz & Steinhauer, 258 South Pennsylvania street.

Cast-Iron Mail Boxes.—Reitz & Allen, owners of the patent, are manufacturers of a patent cast-iron mail box, an invention for which superiority over other similar devices is claimed, and for which an extended demand is reported.

Brass Foundries.—The "Eagle Brass Works" and the "Phenix Brass Foundry" are two well known and prosperous establishments of extensive resources and capacities, devoted to the manufacture of plumbers' goods, gas and steam fittings, bells, and so forth, throughout the nomenclature of brass manufactures.

Copper.—The manufacture of the various descriptions of copper ware, exclusively, is carried on by William Langenskamp, at No. 96 South Delaware street. The manufacture of copper products forms also a part of the business of each of the under-mentioned tin and copper ware manufacturers.

Tin and Copper Ware.—The manufacture of tin and copper ware is carried on by a large number of establishments, principal among which are: E. Johnson & Co.; D. Root & Co.; Tutewiler Bros.; Johnston Bros.; R. L. McOunt; Jacob Vœgtle; Charles Cox; Wolfram Bros.; and Meyers & Martin. The number of workmen employed and the amount of capital invested in the business, and value of the products, make this a prominent branch of Indianapolis manufactures.

FURNITURE.

The present furniture-manufacturing firm of Spiegel & Thoms was the pioneer establishment of this description, and began its prosperous career in 1855. This manufactory has outgrown all resemblance to the diminutive establishment of 16 years ago, and this interest in general has grown in the same proportion. For the manufacture of furniture this location has an unusual combination of advantages—peculiar advantages in the respects of abundant supplies of cheap material, cheap production, and a ready outlet for the manufactured products.

The census reports show eighteen establishments of this description, representing an aggregate capital of $409,050; employing 326 hands, and producing furniture last year to the value of $475,290. Of these, the heaviest establishments are: Spiegel, Thoms & Co.; Indianapolis Chair Factory; and Cabinet Makers' Union These are very extensive and prosperous establishments.

GLASS.

The establishment of the *Indianapolis Glass Works*, in February, 1870, was as well a prudent investment for its proprietors as a valuable and needed addition to the productive industry of Indianapolis. For, by reason of the proximity, in abundance and cheapness, of the requisite materials for the manufacture of glass, of the shipping facilities for the manufactured articles, and of the large field of trade naturally and readily supplied from this place, the manufacture of glass can be more profitably engaged in here than at most of the points celebrated for this class of production.

The present establishment is owned by Messrs. Butsch & Dickson, F. Ritzinger, Charles Brinkman, and Jos. Deschler. It is an extensive concern, having a capital of $100,000, and employing eighty-one hands. The value of its products last year was $135,000. The range of production is hollow ware—such as druggists' green glassware, various sizes and descriptions of bottles, fruit jars of different patterns, and so forth.

This undertaking is only a *move* in the right direction. It has confirmed by experience what was theoretically apparent before—that the manufacture of glass can be profitably engaged in here in competition with the older and more recognized manufacturing points. With all the conditions of prosperity for manufactures in this field, with the early and large success of the present initial undertaking, it follows that this interest should, and will at an early date, occupy the whole field of glass manufacture.

GLUE.

The manufacture of this article is engaged in by John H. Goss & Co. The establishment—the *Indianapolis Glue Manufactory*—is located on the Michigan road, opposite Camp Morton. This manufactory employs twelve hands.

This initial experiment in the manufacture of glue here has been a success, and invites further investments in the same manufacturing interest. It is shown that a superior article can be made here and profitably sold at the best rates offered by competing manufacturers elsewhere located.

SADDLES, HARNESS, ETC.

This interest is represented by thirteen establishments, according to the recent census, employing an aggregate of sixty-eight hands, and producing, last year, merchandise to the value of $161,690. The leading establishments are those of James Sulgrove, A Hereth, George K. Share & Co., James M. Huffer, Frauer, Beeler & Co., D. Sellers & Co. The products of the Indianapolis harness manufacturers are in excellent standing with the trade; and it is generally known that the business can be profitably conducted here, in competition with other prominent manufacturing points.

HUMAN HAIR MANUFACTURES.

There are five establishments of this class: F. J. Medina, Mrs. S. L. Stevens, M. H. Spades, Muir & Foley, and J. T. Mahorney. The aggregate value of their products last year is reported at $40,000; and the total number of hands employed, at twenty-four.

The range of articles made by these establishments embrace the entire list: such as wigs, toupees, switches, curls, chignons, braids, puffs, front bands, etc., the material used by all of them being human hair only. None of them are en-

LEATHER AND BELTING.

gaged, either wholly or in part, in the manufacture of articles out of the various
substitutes for and imitations of human hair.

The census reports six manufactures classable under the above title, having an
aggregate capital of $60,000, and employing sixty hands. The aggregate value of
the products of these last year is reported at $200,000.

Leather.—John Fishback, corner of Sixth street and Michigan road, is extensively engaged in the manufacture of the various descriptions of shoe and saddle
leather. The products of his tannery rank with the best in the west and northwest.

Frederick Will, East Washington street, also manufactures good qualities of
shoe and saddle leather.

Sheepskin Tanners.—M. Doherty & Co. and G. W. Borst, are extensive tanners
of sheep skins, and manufacture what are known to the trade as pink linings and
pad skins. Their products are of superior quality.

Leather Belting.—The houses of Moony & Co., and the Hide, Leather and
Belting Co., are manufacturers of this article; and the merits of their goods are
attested by the great demand for them, which is almost always ahead of the supply.

LIGHTNING RODS.

This interest is represented here by the *Indiana Lightning Rod Company.* In
1856, Mr. David Munson invented and patented a copper, tubular, spiral, flanged
lightning rod. The necessary steps to secure him in his invention having been
taken, a manufactory was opened at No. 62 East Washington street. In 1857, Mr.
Munson took into partnership Josiah Locke, and for two years the business was
most successfully carried on. The succeeding three years, at the end of which the
partnership terminated, were not marked with the success of the former two, and
after the dissolution of the firm in 1863, the disturbance of trade resulting from the
war, nearly destroyed Mr. Munson's enterprise. Subsequently he was enabled to
revive his manufactory and restore it to a prosperous footing. In 1866, when the
business was established, the capital of the concern was only $1,000, which was
increased to over $10,000 in 1863, when the dissolution of partnership took place.
Recently Mr. Munson has invented and patented an improvement on all the other
rods, which he calls the "Diamond Elliptic," and the superiority of which, fitted
with his patent tip, he is ready to demonstrate. Mr. Munson's manufactory employs seven hands. Value of products last year, $18,000.

LINSEED OIL.

This interest is represented by the extensive and flourishing manufactory of
I. P. Evans & Co., located on south Delaware street, and established in 1864.

It is furnished with the machinery and appliances of a first class establishment,
and has the capacity to crush eight hundred bushels of flax seed daily. During
half of the year about fifty hands are employed.

The value of the products of this manufactory, last year, is reported at $160,000.
This was less by at least $75,000 than the business done in the previous year, by
reason of a short flax crop.

LUMBER.

The lumber manufacturing interest of the city is divisible into two classes—
the saw mills, which manufacture hard lumber from the logs direct; and the planing

mills, which take the undressed soft lumber and fashion it into the regular forms and styles for building purposes, into doors, sash, blinds, and other portions of the wood-work of structures.

There are a number of saw mills here for the manufacture of lumber from the logs brought into the city from the surrounding neighborhood; but as logs are most profitably sawed in the near vicinity of the place where the timber grows, or where water transportation can be employed, the saw mills here occupy a limited field compared with the lumber trade of the city. Five manufactories of this description are reported, employing 29 hands, and sawing lumber last year to the value of $213,800.

The *Planing Mills*, working in imported soft lumber, occupy a larger field. there being a number of extensive establishments of this kind in the city. The reported product of our planing mills last year was $515,646. Number of hands employed, 213.

MARBLE WORKERS.

This branch of manufactures, or rather of art, is represented by seven firms. The capacities of some of these are equal to the highest requirements of art in the fashioning of tombstones, monuments, etc. There are employed by these establishments 47 workmen; the aggregate value of their products last year was $160,300

PAPER.

This interest is represented by two large establishments—the *Indianapolis Paper Mill* and the *Caledonia Paper Mill*. The former, devoted to the manufacture of printing and wrapping paper, was started in 1863 by J. McLene and John McIntyre, Esqs., and is now owned by Messrs. H. Saulsbury, M. E. Vinton, W. H. Talbott and J. McLene, under the style of H. Saulsbury & Co.

The *Caledonia Paper Mill*, devoted to the manufacture of wrapping paper, was established in 1864 by Messrs. Gay & Braden. It is now owned by Messrs. Field, Locke & Co.

Both of the above undertakings have proven profitable, and their products are in ready demand. The following shows the resources, extent, and value of the products of these two establishments during the past year:

Caledonia Paper Mill, capital, $40,000, average number of hands employed 27; value of products, $50,000. H. Saulsbury & Co., capital, $50,000, average number of hands employed 55; value of products, $110,000.

PIANOS.

The Indianapolis Piano Manufacturing Company, of which W. J. H. Robinson is manager and principal stockholder, established in 1862, is now the only representative of this branch of manufacturing industry in this city. The other ventures, which were afterwards discontinued, were by J. H. Kappes & Co., George F. Trayser & Co., and C. A. Gerold & Co.

The *Indianapolis Piano Manufactory*, an extensive, successful, and permanently established institution, is located on the corner of South New Jersey and Merrill streets, having been removed to this location during the past year from its previous site on East Washington street. This enterprise has had rather an eventful and chequered history, but has been carried safely through its "dark hours," and is now entirely "out of the wilderness."

The advantages of this point, by nature, for such an undertaking were superior from the first, and have since been greatly augmented by increased shipping facilities. The best of lumber for the manufacture of pianos was directly at hand, giving this enterprise a large advantage over the Eastern manufactories, whose distance from the source of lumber supply greatly enhances the cost of production. But the advantages in respect of materials and shipping facilities were long neutralized by the stubborn impression that superior pianos could only emanate from an eastern manufactory. There was a magic in the familiar names of eastern pianos that a home enterprise had not, and which it has not been easy to dispel.

The conductors of this manufactory have resolutely persisted in their undertaking; have paid liberally for the best skilled labor attainable; have been sedulous to make their pianos speak their own recommendation; and at length have the satisfaction to know that a great many people are no longer skeptical as to the ability of a home establishment to make a good instrument. This establishment is thoroughly supplied with approved machinery and the requisite appliances and facilities for the manufacture of pianos. Nothing essential to the production of a superior instrument—one requiring so much of nicety in construction—seems to be neglected here. Great care is taken that the wood shall be thoroughly seasoned, and that the several parts of the instrument shall be scientifically and durably joined together. While due attention is given to finish, and ornamentation—to the *appearance* of the instruments—the more important consideration of music-producing quality and capacities is not neglected.

For the reasons stated, the *Indianapolis Piano Manufacturing Company* are quite justified in their pretensions of ability to furnish to western patrons pianos equal in quality to those of eastern manufacturers, and at less cost. The freight on a piano from the East to this section is no slight addition to its cost; for which reason, chiefly, we are assured that as much as $75.00 can be saved by purchasing a piano made at this establishment instead of one of eastern manufacture.

The capital of the concern is $75,000; number of workmen employed, thirty-five; value of products last year, $120,600. The recent ratio of increase indicates a business of $250,000 to $275,000 during the present year; and the number of workmen will be increased to about forty-five.

PUMPS.

There are several establishments devoted to this branch of production in this city. The principal manufactory of this kind is that of R. A. Durbon & Co., on South Meridian street. This establishment is devoted exclusively to the manufacture of the several parts of a patent pump owned by Mr. Durbon, and having a national reputation for its superior excellence. Its prominent points of superiority are: durability, neatness, ease with which it works, however deep the well; immunity from freezing in the coldest weather, and comparative cheapness. As before stated, the demand for this pump extends all over the country.

SEWING MACHINES.

The first, and as yet the only, Sewing Machine company to take the benefit of the superior advantages of this city for locating a manufactory here, is the Wheeler & Wilson Company. Their manufactory, a branch of the principal manufactory at Bridgeport, Connecticut, is located in the north-eastern suburb of the city half a mile from the corporation line. It was completed in March of last year and occupies a site six acres in extent, of which the building covers about two acres. The cost of the site and improvements has been about $50,000. A projected enlargement of these buildings, to be completed during the present year, will cost about $30,000 more. The number of workmen now employed is seventy-five; which number will be increased, when the proposed enlargement shall have been completed, to two hundred. The present scope of the manufactory is the sawing and cutting of the wood work of the machines, which is then shipped to the principal manufactory at Bridgeport, Connecticut, for the finishing operations, and to be united with the other parts of the machine. After the enlargement of the manufactory, before mentioned, all the cabinet work of the machines will be fashioned and finished here, and then shipped to the principal manufactory. The annual value of the products of the enlarged manufactory will be about $500,000.

That this is the best point in the West for a cabinet manufactory is corroborated by the prosperity of this enterprise. Easy access is afforded to all the best walnut and poplar lumber regions of the State, and the facilities are equally as good for shipment of the manufactured products.

SODA AND SELTZER WATER, ETC.

The census returns give three establishments engaged in the manufacture of soda water, seltzer water, etc., employing an aggregate of twenty-two hands. The value of their products last year is reported at $35,000.

RECTIFICATION OF DISTILLED SPIRITS.

There are no distilleries here (but one is course of erection three miles west of the city), and comparatively few rectifyers. There are three rectifying houses: Huhn & Bals, Thomas F. Ryan, and D. Martin. The capital employed by these is reported at $65,000; the number of hands, at twelve; and the value of their products for the past year, at $116,000.

STARCH.

This interest is represented here by one extensive establishment: the *Union Starch Manufactory.* This enterprise was inaugurated early in 1867, by an association composed of W. F. Riel, Charles F. Wishemeyer, Edward Mueller, and Henry Burke, with a cash capital of $75,000. An appropriate site was secured at the east end of New York street; and by the end of the year 1867, the buildings had been erected and fitted with suitable machinery, and the manufacture of starch begun.

The enterprise thus instituted had a prosperous existence until October 1868, when the establishment was destroyed by fire, involving a loss of $15,000 in excess of insurance. The company at once rebuilt and restocked the works, and the business was resumed within a few weeks after the fire. Prosperity has attended the undertaking.

The products of this manufactory have found a ready demand, and by this experiment it has been clearly shown that a superior quality of starch can be profitably made here, at prices as low as any competition can afford.

VARNISH.

The *Capital City Varnish Works*, corner of Mississippi and Kentucky Avenue, were established in 1866, by H. B. Mears. The firm name is now Mears &

Lilly (H. B. Mears and J. O. D. Lilly). The range of production covers everything in the way of varnishes, Japans, stains, &c. The establishment has been a success from the first; and though there are about twenty-two similar manufactories in the West, the products of this are in such good repute that they are sold throughout a large area of territory—from Eastern Ohio to the remote far West, and from Michigan to New Orleans. They are sold largely in Cincinnati, where there are four similar manufactories, and in Chicago, where are three or four. The capital of the concern is about $40,000; number of hands employed, five; value of products last year, $52,000. Mr. Mears recently made an extensive tour of observation of the more celebrated English varnish manufactories, for the sake of improving the products of his own.

Another varnish factory, on a smaller scale, has recently been established by Ebner, Kramer & Aldag.

STONE.

The business of dressing limestone, of which unlimited quantities, of the most desirable qualities, are cheaply and readily obtained from surrounding quarries, for building, masonry, and like purposes, is represented by a number of establishments in this city. The principal establishments of this kind are those of Scott, Nicholson & Co., S. Goddard & Sons, Smith, Ittenbach & Co., and F. L. Farman.

Artificial Stone.—Two manufactories of patent artificial stone have recently been inaugurated in this city by J. T. Macauley & Co. and H. B. & D. R. Pershing.

The first named establishment is devoted to the production of the *Lefler* patent cement stone, which is moulded into any desired shape, and is used for all sorts of building purposes, plain or ornamental. It has the color of finely dressed granite, can be made at somewhat less than half the cost of the dressed granite, and, it is claimed, will resist all the effects of time and of the elements.

Pershing & Pershing manufacture the *Freer* patent artificial stone, for which like virtues and cheapness to those ascribed to the *Lefler* patent are claimed. It is of the color of sand stone. These interests, natural and artificial stone, represent a capital of about $75,000, and employ about ninety-five hands. Reported value of products for the past year, $150,000.

TRUNKS.

The manufacture of *Trunks* is yet a young interest; but the obvious advantages of this site for the cheap production of this class of articles, cannot fail to attract the investment of capital on a much larger scale than has yet been the case. There are six establishments of this kind, giving employment to about thirty hands, and producing last year about $50,000 worth of trunks.

WHITE LEAD AND COLORS.

The fact that there was no manufactory of paints in the State, the facilities for profitably making them here, and the extensive market that could be more readily and cheaply supplied from this point than from any other, led Messrs. T. B. McCarty and Horace Scott, less than two years ago, to establish the *Indianapolis Paint Works.* There was no risk in the undertaking; the "opening" for such an investment was particularly apparent; and the wonder is that it did not sooner attract the investment of capital, and that it has not been more fully occupied.

The manufactory was equipped in a first class manner, the best quality of skilled labor has been employed, and almost from the first the establishment has been unable to supply the demand for its products. The white lead and colors ground and prepared here are in request over a wide area of country, alike because of their merits and the favorable prices at which they can be sold and shipped. Number of hands employed, twelve; value of products last year, $90,000. The extensive trade which could be most cheaply and readily reached from this point invites additional and larger investments here in this branch of manufactures.

THE WOODBURN "SARVEN WHEEL" FACTORY.

This manufactory is one of the most extensive of the kind in the country. It is located on South Illinois street, one square south of Union Depot, and is the oldest manufactory in the city. It was started in 1847 by C. H. Crawford & J. R. Osgood, for making lasts and other shoemakers' implements, and was then located near the site of the Union Depot. Six years later Mr. Crawford retired from the establishment, leaving Mr. Osgood as the only proprietor. The latter shortly afterward added the manufacture of staves and flour barrels to his other business. Finding his building too small, he erected on the present site of his establishment a three-story brick building, twenty-five by one hundred feet. This location, now in the heart of the city, was then in the open country, and it was deemed a hazardous investment in that day to locate so considerable an establishment so far from the business portion of the city. The manufacture of wooden hubs was added in 1866, when Mr. L. M. Bugby was admitted into the firm. Mr. S. H. Smith was admitted as an equal partner in 1866, and the manufacture of wagon and carriage materials was added. Thus began what has grown to be a very extensive business, not only in this city but in the State at large, employing more than $1,000,000 capital. In February, 1864, their establishment was destroyed by fire, involving a loss of $20,000. Within ninety days the manufactory had been rebuilt on a larger scale than before. In the year 1865 Messrs. Woodburn & Scott, of St. Louis, who had been doing a large business in the manufacture of wheels of various kinds, and who, in connection with a New Haven firm, had the exclusive right to manufacture the celebrated "Sarven Patent Wheel," and had expended large sums in its introduction, disposed of all their patents and business to Messrs. Osgood & Smith. In order to obtain the requisite capital to conduct this extension of their business, Messrs. Osgood & Smith disposed of a one-third interest to Messrs. Nelson & Haynes, a wealthy house in Alton, Ill., who opened an establishment in St. Louis for the manufacture of wagon materials. The St. Louis house was known as *Haynes, Smith, & Co.;* the Indianapolis firm, as *Osgood, Smith & Co.* Subsequently Mr. Woodburn purchased the interest of Messrs. Nelson & Haynes, and the St. Louis house then took the firm name of *Woodburn, Smith & Co.*

At different times since, J. S. Yost, V. Rothrock and J. F. Pratt have been promoted from employes to members of the Indianapolis house. In 1869 the establishment obtained a controlling interest in the manufactory at Massac, Ill., for making carriage materials, a step that was taken for the purpose of supplying the St. Louis house with materials.

In the same year they bought a large tract of timbered land in Orange county, Indiana, and erected a saw mill there to supply the Indianapolis manufactory with lumber.

In 1870, the concern was transformed into a joint stock company, under the name of the *Woodburn "Sarven Wheel" Company,* with a capital of $250,000, making no change in the proprietorship, other than before stated. Since then the manufacture of the *Sarven Patent Wheel* has been a specialty.

A busy and useful life was terminated by the death of the senior proprietor, Mr. J. R. Osgood, in June, 1871. The present officers of the Company are: Jacob Woodburn, President; S. F. Smith, Vice President and Treasurer; J. S. Yost, Assistant Secretary and Treasurer; J. F. Pratt, Secretary; V. Rothrock, Superintendent.

The *Woodburn "Sarven Wheel"* Company are now making wheels of all kinds, from those for the lightest buggy, weighing no more than eighty pounds, to those for heavy omnibuses and wagons; and now propose to apply the principle of their patent to railway cars. Their wheels find their way in large quantites to all parts of the United States. In addition to wheels, they manufacture carriage materials of all descriptions, plow handles, etc.

The success of this establishment is due as well to the advantages of its location as to the efficiency of its management. Indiana occupies a peculiar position not only to this country, both East and West, but to other parts of the world, in its ability to supply to so great an extent such splendid timber for carriages, wagons and agricultural machinery. The supply in the Eastern States of timber for fine carriage work is being rapidly exhausted, so that the best manufacturers are now getting their choice timber from the West. It is a noteworthy fact that there is no carriage and wagon timber to be found in all the vast extent of country between the Mississippi river and the Rocky Mountains; and that the supply for this immense prairie country, so rapidly filling up and developing, must come from a small belt of country of which Indiana is the center. This fact, in its bearings upon the future, is now engaging the serious attention of manufacturers.

We have dwelt upon this enterprise at some length because of its being so triumphant an illustration of the great advantages of this point for manufacturing purposes; and because Mr. Woodburn may be considered the pioneer of this business in the West. In 1848, he and a fellow workman left Newark, New Jersey to seek their fortunes in the West, each bringing with him a spoke lathe. One settled in Cincinnati and the other in St. Louis. Commencing business without means they worked their way up. They made the first spokes ever manufactured by machinery west of the Alleghany Mountains, and thus started the immense business now being done throughout the entire west; and the substitution of machinery, thus introduced, for hard labor, has diminished the cost of this class of products from fifty to seventy-five per cent. The capital stock of the concern is $350,000; number of hands employed, one hundred and eighty; value of products last year, $250,000.

WOOLEN MANUFACTURES.

This interest in Indianapolis has shared the general prosperity of its manufacturing interests due to advantages of location, superior shipping facilities, and so forth. In addition to these it has had a special cause of prosperity in the great improvement of recent years of the wool product of this region; so that the woolen fabrics manufactured here have acquired a high repute throughout the country This increase in the prosperity, capacities and resources of our mills, has created an increased demand for wool, and thus built up an extensive wool market here.

The present extensive woolen mill of Merritt & Coughlen, at the west end f Washington street, was established by them in 1856. Its growth is a type of the growth of the city. From an affair of small consequence, it has become an establishment of the first class. It has been enlarged from time to time, and now has three sets of machinery, of the largest size, and of the most recent and approved patterns. Forty hands, on the average, are employed. The products are cassimeres, flannels, jeans, blankets etc. These rank with the best products of the principal woolen mills of the country. The present investment of capital is about $100,000; value of products last year, $200,000.

The *Hoosier Woolen Factory*, located near that of Merritt & Coughlen, established in 1847 by Messrs. C. E. & G. W. Geisendorff, is now owned and operated by C. E. Geisendorff & Co. Successive improvements and enlargements have made their establishment extensive and complete. Its range of production embraces the various descriptions of woolen fabrics, several of which have obtained great celebrity for their peculiar points of excellency. The investment of capital is about $125,000; number of hands employed, fifty; value of products last year, $125,000.

STATISTICAL EXHIBIT

SHOWING THE VALUE of the Products of the principal Manufacturing Industries of Indianapolis, the amount of capital invested and number of hands employed, as obtained from the late Census returns and other sources, for the year ending June 1st, 1870; compared with the like exhibit of the Manufactures of *Indianapolis and Marion County* for the year ending June 1, 1860, as shown by the Census of the latter date.

MANUFACTURES.	Amount of Capital Invested.		Number of Hands Employed.		Value of Products.	
	Year ending June 1, 1870.	Year ending June 1, 1860.	Year ending June 1, 1870.	Year ending June 1, 1860.	Year ending June 1, 1870.	Year ending June 1, 1860.
Agricultural Implements	$292,000	$41,400	75	28	$105,750	$33,000
Bakers' Products	58,880		67		349,396	
Blacksmithing	35,040	4,674	45	10	75,600	11,560
Boots and Shoes	50,890	2,400	113	7	137,672	6,565
Book-binding, etc	57,433	23,000	114	12	245,000	30,000
Boxes	7,800		34		42,540	
Brooms	18,000	1,500	53	2	23,932	800
Brass Founding	28,000	5,060	17	3	38,000	4,000
Brick	150,000	12,560	325	80	225,000	90,430
Carpentry	334,800	250	229	8	391,075	5,300
Confectionery	64,275		34		135,192	
Cigars and Tobacco	116,400		161		290,660	
Carriages and Wagons	569,607	5,590	351	19	715,250	13,000
Cement Pipe, etc	15,000		10		28,500	
Clothing	135,200		256	12	460,910	7,000
Cooperage	150,400	2,000	164	12	496,900	
Cotton Manufacture	150,000		56		300,000	
Coffee and Spices	20,000		5		76,000	
Dentistry	30,500	1,000	35	1	60,000	
Fermented Liquors	274,500		56		286,670	2,000
Fertilizing Products	25,000		7		21,500	
Furniture	409,650	44,000	395	70	475,290	110,000
Fur Goods	10,400		15		16,550	
Flour	371,500	83,100	74	29	1,636,360	198,590
Iron Castings, Machinery, Engines, etc	660,000	150,000	687	119	1,180,353	150,000
Gas	400,000		75		250,000	
Glue	10,000		12		12,000	
Glass	60,000		81		135,000	
Harness and Saddlery	45,000	750	68	2	162,050	2,350
Human Hair Goods	10,000		59		40,000	
Lightning Rods	4,000		7		18,000	
Leather and Belting	160,000		69		280,000	
Linseed Oil	100,000		17		168,000	
Lumber (sawed)	44,000	49,100	29	79	412,800	67,315
Millinery	9,500		45		30,000	

Malt	44,000		18		85,000	
Newspapers and Printing	435,600		264		597,600	12,000
Paper	90,000	20,000	82	9	160,000	
Railroad Cars and Car Repairing	160,400		99		211,512	
Rolling Mill Products	765,000		435		1,100,000	
Rectified Spirits	65,000		12		116,000	
Roofing (Slate and Tar)	15,000		16		42,916	
Patent Medicines	10,600		10		29,500	
Paints and Colors	25,000		12		90,000	
Pianos	75,000		35		130,600	
Plaster	10,000		36		45,700	
Plumbing and Gas Fitting	61,000		33		66,800	
Pork Packing	1,251,000		239		2,161,750	
Pumps	30,000		50	20	137,000	60,000
Sash, Doors, Blinds, etc	225,400	50,000	213	3	515,646	10,000
Saws	110,000	5,000	40	5	160,000	10,000
Stone and Marble Work	105,000	3,000	142		310,300	
Soda Water, etc	20,000		22	6	35,000	
Starch	65,000		40		130,000	13,300
Tin, Copper and Sheet Iron Ware	95,700	6,000	95		173,200	
Trunks	18,900		37		76,410	
Varnish	40,000		10		75,000	
Woolen Goods	225,000	85,641	108	55	459,000	102,820
Miscellaneous	105,730	76,400	188		248,421	
Total	$8,420,614	$671,366	5,929	587	$16,283,359	$890,470

TRADE.

AGRICULTURAL IMPLEMENTS.

This branch of merchandise is represented by sixteen dealers and manufacturers, not including manufacturing establishments where parts only of certain agricultural implements are made.

As the commercial center of an extensive agricultural region, this city does a large business in agricultural implements; which is rapidly growing in proportion to the increasing use of labor-saving machines by agriculturists. The aggregate transactions of the past year are reported at $755,687. Principal dealers are the following: W. L. Sherwood, reapers, mowers and threshers; J. George Stilz, agricultural implements generally, seeds, etc.; Carlos Dickson & Co., woollen factor findings, etc., etc., Case & Parker, a general business in agricultural implements; A. L. Webb, agricultural implements, seeds, etc; J. Braden, agricultural implements generally; H. J. Prier, reapers, mowers, agricultural implements in general; Houck, Spencer & Co., agricultural implements generally; R. L. Lukens, ditto.

BOOKS AND STATIONERY.

Though the introduction of the book trade of the city dates back to an early period in the history of the latter, it is but a few years since it attained to any considerable magnitude. The first house that made any pretensions in the wholesale way, was that of H. F. West & Co., located on the site of the present extensive house of Bowen, Stewart & Co.

In the last year of the firm of West & Co.—1853—their aggregate sales reached $80,000. In 1854, as before stated, the establishment of West & Co. passed into the possession of Stewart & Bowen in September. The old and well-known house of Merrill & Co. was founded by Samuel Merrill in 1850; that of Todd & Carmichael in 1863. As late as 1860 the wholesale trade had grown but little; its aggregate for that year not exceeding $45,000 to $50,000. Its growth since that time has been large, continuous and permanent in its character. The aggregate of the transactions during the past year was $550,000; an increase of about 15 per cent. over the previous year. The increase in the *bulk* of the business done was considerably more by reason of the decline in prices. The shrinkage in values—which set in after the close of the war, and continued during the past year—has applied to all descriptions of paper stationery, and so forth; and to imported articles, in proportion to the steady decline in the gold premium. As to books, etc., where the chief value is not imparted by the materials used, but grows out of the cost of contents and of the skilled labor requisite to their production, the decline in prices, has been less, partly by reason of the loss, not yet repaired, in skilled labor on account of the war; and partly through the influence of trades' unions and other combinations to keep up or advance the cost of the manufacturing. Nevertheless the business of the year has, upon the whole, been prosperous. The shrinkage in values has been so gradual that, with prudent management, financial " breakers " have been avoided, though profits have necessarily been smaller. Collections here averaged well during the year; but are more difficult in the beginning of the present season.

Bowen, Stewart & Co., Nos. 16 and 18 West Washington street; Merrill & Co., Blackford's block; Todd, Carmichael and Williams, Glenns' block; and J. H. V. Smith, Yohn's block, are the principal houses in this branch of trade.

The fields occupied by these establishments are not alike. That of Bowen, Stewart & Co. covers the whole extent of the general book and stationery business; but current publications and educational text books are made special features. That of Merrill & Co. embraces the general book and stationery trade; but especial prominence is given to law books, etc. Messrs. Todd, Carmichael & Williams give especial attention to works of a religious and denominational character, and to publications designed for the religious and general education of the young—school and Sunday-school books, etc. Mr. Smith does a general business; with educational and religious works, especially Methodist denominational publications, as a specialty.

BOOTS AND SHOES.

The present large jobbing trade in this branch of merchandise is almost entirely the growth of the last ten years The first exclusively wholesale house that of E. C. Mayhew & Co. (E. C. Mayhew and James M. Ray), was established in 1855. In 1860 the wholesale business was limited to two houses: E. C. Mayhew & Co., and V. K. Hendricks & Co. The aggregate sales at wholesale that year did not exceed $175,000. As late as the year 1865 the wholesale trade had made but little headway. Business was obtained with difficulty, confined within a limited area of territory, and embraced the least desirable class of patronage within that limited area. Since then the improvement has been remarkable. The field of operations has been greatly extended in all directions. Within these extended limits it is now the *rule* of retailers to purchase their stocks here instead of the *exception*, as was formerly the case. In other words, a large and desirable trade comes here without special solicitation, because it is profitable to do so; while a few years ago extraordinary efforts were necessary to secure a small and inferior patronage. The great growth of the Boot and Shoe business is shown in the transactions of the past year, which aggregate $1,709,000. The jobbers here have no difficulty in competing with any of their rivals; offering at least equal, frequently better, inducements as to styles and prices. The additional claim is made by them, and is sustained, that they surpass competitors in the respect that their stocks are peculiarly adapted to the wants of the market in Indiana and Illinois.

During the past year trade has been active, and there has been a gradual decline in prices. The estimated increase of business during the year is about 15 per cent., attended by a like increase in the aggregate capital invested. For the greater part of the year collections were moderately well kept up; but during the winter more difficulty was experienced. On the whole the year has been a prosperous one, and the prospect ahead is promising. The number of dealers reported is twenty-four.

The principal houses are: J. C. Burton, Vinnedge & Jones, Mayhew, Branham & Co.; Hendricks, Edmunds & Co., Mayhew, Warren & Co., Kingsbury & Co.—chiefly located on South Meridian street.

CARPETS, WALL PAPER, ETC.

The carpet trade, unlike most other branches of business, has few exclusively wholesale dealers anywhere. The heaviest dealers therein, in New York and other large cities, do a retail as well as a wholesale business. The nature of the article, and of the demand resultant therefrom, compels dealers to fill individual orders as well as orders in bulk.

Wholesale operations, of noteworthy account. in carpets, may be said to have

(24)

been instituted in 1866, by the present extensive and well-known house of Hume, Adams & Co. The growth of the business here has been sudden and rapid—in harmony with the growth and progress of the carpet-manufacturing interest in this country.

In no respect have American skill and resources been shown to better advantage, and with better results, than in the manufacture of carpets—not of the cheaper grades, but of the better kinds. In the manufactories at Philadelphia, Lowell, Hartford, Yonkers and other points are produced "Axminster," "Brussels" and other varieties of woolen carpets, that are equal in every way—frequently superior in point of style—to the best specimens of English and French manufacture. The progress made in this species of American manufactures has been very gratifying. For once it is useless to buy a foreign article in order to obtain a superior article. One effect of this successful competition of the American manufacturer has been to greatly stimulate the purchase of the better grades. More or less of fine carpets is now found in a majority of dwellings.

Prices during the past year steadily and largely declined—a continuance of the shrinkage in values that began after the close of the war. It is believed that the decline has reached its minimum. The present prices, at which the market is firm, seem to be as low as the articles can be produced, and no further natural shrinkage of values can therefore reasonably be expected.

Prices of wall-paper were generally steady during the year.

The business of 1870, under this head, was one of great prosperity. The estimated increase was 33 per cent. over that of the previous year. By reason of the decline in prices, profits were often very slender; but, on the other hand, collections were very good. The future prospects are promising in a high degree. The stocks kept here, in respect of magnitude, varieties, styles, qualities, prices, and so forth, are quite capable of withstanding competition; and the ancient practice of going somewhere else than here, when a particularly elegant pattern might be wanted, or in expectation of getting better terms, has gone out of date.

The aggregate transactions of 1870 are reported at $510,000.

Principal houses are: Hume, Adams & Co., 47 and 49 South Meridian street; A. Gall, 101 East Washington street; W. H. Roll, 38 South Illinois.

CLOTHING.

The wholesale clothing trade in this city had its beginning about eight years ago—the pioneer house being that of Dessar, Bro. & Co. The growth of these eight years is full of encouragement. The trade that has been built up covers a wide extent of territory, within which the Indianapolis dealers secure their full share of patronage. The business of the past year shows a good increase. Prices during the year were steady as to the better grades; medium and the lower grades declined slightly; French cloths advanced on account of the war.

The sales last year aggregated $1,779,805.

The principal wholesale houses are: Dessar, Bro. & Co., Hays, Rosenthal & Co., Mossler Bros. (wholesale and retail).

COAL.

Of the peculiar merits and adaptation of the Indiana coal to the purposes of manufacturing, mention is made in the observations upon manufacturing on another page. The receipts of Indiana coal in this city have increased many fold during the past few years, consequent upon the better development of the coal fields. The traffic in anthracite coal is, for the most part, the creation of but a few years past.

The receipts of Indiana coal in Indianapolis for the year 1870 aggregated about eighty-eight thousand tons. Of this about thirty thousand tons were shipped to other points; the remainder was consumed in this city and vicinity. The prime cost, by the car-load, including freight, delivered in this city, during the past year, has averaged about $6,50 per ton. The present price, compared with that of one year ago, shows a decline of about 25 per cent.

The receipts of Pittsburg and anthracite coal in this city during the year 1870 were about thirty-five thousand tons.

The average price of Pittsburg coal during the past year has been about $5.00 per ton; and the price was quite steady during that period.

The present price of anthracite coal, compared with that of a year ago, in this city, shows a decline of about $1.50 per ton.

The coal trade of this city during the past year may be stated in round numbers at $550,000.

The current year will bring a largely increased importation of Indiana coal; a ratio of increase that will be maintained for a number of years.

In the past the measure of this importation has been the carrying capacity of but one railway—the old *Terre Haute & Indianapolis* line. Recently three new railway lines, radiating from this city, have been opened through the coal fields, and a fourth is projected. The development of the coal resources in the regions penetrated by these lines will rapidly follow—will go on increasing for many years, and the amount mined and shipped to and through this city will multiply in proportion.

CONFECTIONERY.

The wholesale business in confectionery was begun, in any noteworthy degree, by Daggett & Co. in 1856. The increase of this business in the succeeding years has been commensurate with that of most other branches of commerce.

The products of our confectionery manufactories are noted for their exceptional freedom from unwholesome impurities, imparted by the use of injurious chemicals; and for this reason, particularly, command a ready and extended sale. Every variety of confectionery can be found here, as well as excellent qualities.

The past year was one of great prosperity to this interest. The increase in the amount of business was about 30 per cent. During the early part of the year there was a considerable decline in values; afterward prices were steady to the end of the year. Profits were generally better than during the previous year. Collections were fair up to Christmas; but since then have been more difficult.

Principal houses are those of Daggett & Co., 26 South Meridian street; Dukemineer, Scott and Johnson, 100 South Meridian street—both of whom are manufacturers and dealers.

DRUGS.

The jobbing trade in this branch of commerce has a greater antiquity than that of most others in this city; though, as in the case of all others, it is but a few years since it attained any considerable magnitude. The wholesale transactions of any consequence may be said to have been inaugurated by the house of William Hannaman & Co., in 1832. The next considerable venture in this respect was by

Craighead & Braden (afterward Craighead & Browning), in 1842 and 1843. The subsequent increase in this trade is one of the best illustrations of the commercial growth of the city; which can now show some of the most extensive and prosperous establishments in the West.

The business of the past year shows an increase of 12 to 15 per cent. over that of the previous year, and a healthy increase of the capital invested. There has in some exceptional articles, been a steady shrinking in values during the year. By consequence, profits were small; but as the collections were good, the business of the year was, upon the whole prosperous.

The destruction of the extensive perfumery establishments in the neighborhood of Paris by the German army, caused an advance in that class of goods in the summer; but this advance has not been sustained.

The transactions of last year foot up $1,661,600.

Principal houses are those of Browning & Sloan, 7 and 9 East Washington street; Stewart & Morgan, 140 East Washington street; Kiefer & Vinton, 68 South Meridian; Haskit & Morris, 14 West Washington; Patterson, Moore & Talbott, 123 South Meridian street.

DRY GOODS.

Of comparatively recent introduction here, the wholesale trade in Dry Goods has attained to a leading prominence in the commerce of the city. Prior to 1860 several houses in the wholesale Dry Goods trade had been established, and after unprosperous existences of greater or less duration, had disappeared; so that in that year the only exclusively wholesale house was that of J. A. Crossland. The aggregate wholesale transactions of 1860 (both of dry goods and notions) did not exceed $200,000. Within the past five or six years this business has had an extraordinary development and increase.

The transactions of the past year aggregate $4,542,000.

A very large area of territory, extending into Michigan and Illinois, and occasionally much further, has been largely supplied by this market. This foothold has been gained by the simple superiorty of the inducements offered, and over the old-time prejudices that led retailers to assume that the advantages offered here must necessarily be inferior.

In whatever respect, whether as to variety, styles, qualities, prices, and so forth, dealers here can look with great composure on outside competition. The business of 1870 was generally prosperous. The increase in the money value of the transaction was fully 20 per cent.; and the increase in the bulk of goods sold was considerably larger, by reason of the shrinkage in values. One feature of the business was a partial interruption of the supply of eastern fabrics, resulting in a transient advance in prices, owing to the suspension of many manufactories for want of water.

One effect of the war in Europe was a depression of prices, particularly of cotton goods; as the foreign demand for cotton was very light, and prices declined here in proportion.

The demand for flannels has been active, stimulating production by western mills. The products of these mills are in growing favor with the trade. Woollen cloths have been in good demand. Western mills are manufacturing them in larger quantities than ever before, with a marked improvement in quality which is surely bringing them increased favor. Their shawls, especially, are unsurpassed. The West is now manufacturing knit goods. shirts, drawers, hosiery, and all these meet with ready sale. There has been a steady demand for cotton fabrics during the year. The sales of dress goods show a very large increase. In prints the market has been steady, and demand fair throughout the year. The increase of capital during the year was about 30 per cent. Profits were fair; but collections were unsatisfactory and difficult.

The present year opened with an improvement on last year's business; but it is yet too early in the season to speak more particularly of the current year's trade.

Principal houses are: Murphy, Johnson & Co., southeast corner of Meridian and Maryland streets; Byram, Cornelius & Co., 104 South Meridian street; Hibben, Kennedy & Co., 97 and 99 South Meridian street; Pettis, Dickson & Co., Glenns' block; N. R. Smith & Co., 26 and 28 West Washington street.

FURNITURE.

The growing wealth and population of the region supplied by this market, have greatly multiplied the demand for the finer descriptions of furniture; and this class of merchandise is largely represented in this city, by both dealers and manufacturers.

The total sales of the past year aggregated $749,000.

This has now become an important supply market for a large area of territory, embracing not only this State, but extending into Illinois, Missouri, Kansas Nebraska and other Northwestern States.

The business of the past year, as to the amount of furniture sold, exhibits an increase of about 25 per cent. over that of the previous year; and the increase of capital was about the same. The greater part of the business is represented by manufacturers; for so great are the facilities in this respect that the manufacturer of furniture here can make a fair profit at prices which leave a very slender margin for the competing dealer who purchases his stocks here or elsewhere. Prices were steady during the past year, profits fair, and collections well kept up.

The present year opens with every assurance of a decided improvement on last year's business.

The principal establishments representing the furniture interest are those of Spiegel, Thoms & Co., Cabinet Makers' Union, Burk, Earnshaw & Co., Western Furniture Company Philip Dohn, Indianapolis Chair Company, N. S. Baker & Co. Of these the last two are dealers; the others manufacturers and dealers; and they represent among them every description of furniture.

GRAIN.

By reason of the location of this city, in an essentially agricultural region tributary to it by nature, and made more securely so by the railways that radiate from this city at every point, our grain trade is very large. But the want of the "Elevator system" here has retarded the growth of the Indianapolis grain trade; has been, and still is, the one great obstacle hindering the city of Indianapols from rising to an eminent rank among the grain markets of the country. A want so serious in its consequences, and so readily remedied, will hardly be much longer neglected by the grain dealers and breadstuff manufacturers of this city.

Wheat.—The crops of 1868 and 1869 were very heavy, leaving a large surplus in excess of the home consumption. The foreign demand for the surplus of 1868 was but limited, and for that of 1869 only moderate. Prices ruled so low in 1869 that a large stock was carried over to the next year in expectation of an advance. The crop of 1870 was less than its predecessors as to yield; but at the same time grain was unusually good. Thus when the crop of 1870 was ready for market, the stock of wheat in the United States was far larger than at any previous date. Early in the month of June, 1870, prices advanced suddenly and considerably. There was a continued improvement throughout the next two months; the quotations of March 1st, and July 1st, 1870, showing a difference in favor of the latter date of about 25 cents per bushel. "This advance was caused in the first place by a large demand from France, where the crop had proved short beyond doubt, and afterward by the commencement of war between France and Prussia, which, it was supposed, would lead to an increased demand for breadstuffs from Europe; and this feeling was strengthened by the rapid advance in gold, which took place in July. But all these anticipations proved incorrect; the demand for breadstuffs did not increase when hostilities began, but really diminished; and the overwhelming successes of the Prussians, with a decline in gold, flattened the market, and caused general disappointment." The advance was soon lost, and prices receded lower than they had been during the year; reacted again on the conclusion of peace between Germany and France, and during the past spring became nearly as high as at any period in the past two years. The aggregate purchases of wheat in this market, for local consumption and shipment, during the year 1870, were about two millions, five hundred thousand bushels, of the aggregate value of about $2,550,000.

The following will show the price of prime red wheat in this market on the days named:

January 3d, 1870	$ 95@1 00
February 1st, 1870	1 00
March 1st, 1870	1 30@1 35
April 1st, 1870	1 25@1 30
May 1st, 1870	1 00
June 1st, 1870	1 05
July 1st, 1870	1 12
August 1st, 1870	1 27
September 1st, 1870	1 10
October 1st, 1870	1 06@1 08
November 1st, 1870	1 05@1 07
December 1st, 1870	1 05@1 08
January 1st, 1871	1 05@1 10
February 1st, 1871	1 13@1 18
March 1st, 1871	1 20@1 25
April 1st, 1871	1 25@1 30
May 1st, 1871	1 26@1 28
June 2d, 1871	1 20
July 28th, 1871	new red, 1 05@1 10; old red, 1 25@1 30

Corn.—The crop of 1869 was very deficient both in quantity and quality, and prices were correspondingly high. The crop of 1870 was the largest ever raised in the country, and of excellent quality; and prices ruled accordingly. The aggregate receipts during the year 1870 were about one million, eight hundred and fifty thousand bushels; and the average price about fifty cents per bushel. The price on the 31st December, 1869, was 65 cents; on the 1st August, 1870, 80 cents, for shelled; on the 1st, January, 1871, 42@43; on the 1st May, 1871, 47@48, for shelled; on the 30th June, 1871, 50@51, for shelled

Oats.—The crop of 1869 was good; that of 1870 large, but inferior in quality. The receipts at this market for the year 1870 are estimated at six hundred thousand bushels. The average price for the year 1870 was about 45 cents. Quotations in 1871: April 6th, 50@53; May 4th, 50@53; June 1st, 48@50; June 30th, 60@65; July 28th, new, 30@35; old, 58@62.

GROCERIES.

The beginning of the jobbing trade, in this department of merchandise, antedates that of any other in this city. The first wholesale grocery house was established almost seventeen years ago; but, as in all other branches, it is but a few years since the jobbing trade in groceries obtained to any considerable dimensions . In 1860 the firms engaged in this trade were: Andrew Wallace, J. W. Holland, Mills, Alford & Co., Wright, Bates & Maguire, M. Fitzgibbon & Co., A. & H. Schnull. At this time, and for some time after, the patronage of Indianapolis jobbers was circumscribed within extremely narrow limits indeed; and even the patronage of country merchants within these limits was exceptional instead of being the rule—the better class of custom going to Cincinnati.

Now all this is changed: the trade has extended in every direction—as far west as Central Illinois; south to the Ohio river, and beyond; east into Ohio; and north to an equal extent. Furthermore, the trade within these extended limits, naturally tributary to this city, comes here. This is now the rule, not an exception, as used to be the case.

The inducements being equal, or superior, the retailer naturally seeks the most convenient supply market. The Indianapolis jobber having demonstrated his ability, by reason of the extraordinary advantages of the location and railway communications of this city, to compete on equal terms, in respect of qualities and prices, with opposition from the eastern cities, the retailer within reasonable distance of this city has more reasons for purchasing here than elsewhere.

The aggregate wholesale grocery trade of Indianapolis in the year 1860 did not exceed $400,000. The sales in 1870 foot up $6,443,150. This comparison effectively illustrates the great improvement that has been made in ten years.

The increase during the past year was quite satisfactory—perhaps 15 per cent. in the aggregate. The extension, both in trade and capital employed, shows that the onward march still continues, and the prospect is promising as the retrospect is gratifying.

The shrinking in values that set in after the close of the war, has gradually continued ever since—not so violently as to derange business or produce bankruptcy, but in a healthy, gradual way, enabling jobbers to adapt their business to the tendency of values. Profits were good, collections well kept up, and but few losses have been sustained. Consequently a judicious as well as a large and increasing trade has been, and is now being, done.

Briefly, the advantages of Indianapolis, as a wholesale trading point, as to groceries, may be stated thus:

It has a superior location, by reason of an unequaled system of railways, radiating at every point, and penetrating or connecting with all parts of the State and adjoining States, rendering it speedy of access, and facilitating the quick and cheap delivery of goods. The same superiority of location enables its jobbers to take advantage of competition in freight rates, and deliver goods to their patrons on better terms than the latter could obtain elsewhere. The stocks are equal to any possible demand in extent and variety.

The more prominent *exclusively* wholesale grocery houses in this city are: Crossland, Hanna & Co., southwest corner of Meridian and Maryland streets; Wiles, Bro. & Co., 149 South Meridian street; Alford, Talbott & Co., 123 South Meridian street; Severin, Schnull & Co., 55 and 57 South Meridian street; Foster, Wiggins & Co., 68 and 70 South Delaware street; Andrew Wallace, 52 and 54 South Delaware street.

HATS AND FUR GOODS.

Prior to the year 1863 there was no exclusively wholesale house of this description in the city. Early in that year J. M. Talbott & Co., and Donaldson & Carr opened wholesale establishments. Since then the growth of the business has been very rapid—covering much the same extent of territory as other departments of the wholesale business of the city. Of the great inducements offered here the best proof is found in the large patronage that has been secured; for trade, being selfish, bestows its favors where the inducements are greatest.

The business done during the past year shows a considerable increase in bulk; but not in the pecuniary aggregate realized, owing to the decline in values. The estimated increase of capital employed during the year is 15 to 20 per cent.

The principal firms are: Donaldson & Stout, Ryan & Talbott, Lelewer & Bro., (fur goods exclusively); Isaac Davis & Co., (wholesale and retail).

IRON AND HARDWARE.

The first exclusively wholesale iron house in this city—that of Burt, Metcalfe & Over, was established no longer ago than 1865. For several years prior to that date, the establishments of W. J. Holliday & Co., and of Pomeroy, Fry & Co., had been doing a mixed wholesale and retail business in this line of merchandise. The trade has had an extraordinary increase in the past few years, and has permanently occupied a large area of territory.

During the past year the estimated increase has been $33\frac{1}{3}$ per cent.; but owing to the considerable and continuous decline in prices, profits were very small. The average decline in prices during the year was about $16\frac{3}{4}$ per cent. The decline in the gold premium facilitated British competition and reduced profits to a narrow margin. The addition during the year to the aggregate capital invested is estimated at 15 per cent.. Collections were reasonably good. The present season has opened out with good prospects of a large increase over last year's business

The principal establishments are those of Maxwell, Fry & Thurston, 34 South Meridian street; E. Over & Co., 82 and 84 South Meridian street; W. J. Holliday & Co., 59 South Meridian street.

In hardware, the wholesale trade was inaugurated in 1856, by J. H. Vajen, who had opened a retail establishment five years before. As late as 1861 Mr. Vajen was still the only representative of the wholesale trade in hardware, and his sales during the year were about $75,000. The field has been liberally occupied since, and the business has grown to be an extensive one.

During the past two years the shrinkage in values has been so constant and considerable that profits have been greatly curtailed. This shrinkage in values appears to have reached its lowest point. Prices are once more on the advance, and the outlook is more encouraging than for several years past.

Leading houses are those of Anderson, Bullock & Schofield, 62 South Meridian street; Kimball, Aikman & Co, 110 South Meridian street; Fugate & Hildebrand, 21 West Washington street; Layman, Carey & Co.; 64 East Washington street.

The aggregate transactions in iron and hardware during the past year are estimated at $3,500,000.

JEWELRY, WATCHES, &C.

The trade in the various articles usually comprehended in the term "Jewelry," has grown to be a very extensive branch of the commerce of the city. The first considerable venture in this line was that of E J. Baldwin & Co., (E. J. Baldwin and J. McLene), in 1851.

The present well-known house of W. P. Bingham & Co. was established in 1859; and it was about this time that wholesale operations of any considerable extent were begun. Since then the trade has grown rapidly and extended in all directions. Stocks embracing every conceivable description of article in the nomenclature of watches, jewelry, precious stones, gold and silver ware, fine cutlery, clocks, and so forth, are now maintained here; affording the amplest and best inducements to purchasers. The business of the past year, as to the amount, shows an increase of perhaps 25 per cent. over the previous year. Imported articles advanced, on account of the war, about 10 per cent.; but now that peace has returned, the prices are returning to their former standard.

On gold and silver articles of domestic manufacture there was a small decline during the year; also on solid and plated silver ware. The profits were small considering the amount of business done. Collections were rather difficult; and in this respect the present year does not start out auspiciously. The aggregate value of transactions in this line last year was $195,000.

The principal houses are: W. P. Bingham & Co., 50 East Washington street; J. McLene, Bates House block; Craft & Cutter, 24 East Washington street; F. M. Herron, 16 West Washington street; J. H. Colclazer & Co., 14 East Washington street; Henry Daumont & Co., 15 West Washington street. (The business of the latter does not comprehend watches, jewelry, &c., but embraces clocks, paintings, pictures, picture frames, &c.)

LEATHER, BELTING, HIDES, &C.

The first wholesale business, of any moment, in leather, hides, &c., was inaugurated by D. Yandes & Co., in 1850. Like most other branches of trade, this has grown in a few years to large proportions. The transactions last year aggregated $458,297.

In some respects the business of the past year was quite profitable to those engaged, and in others only slightly so. Unlike the previous two or three years, 1870 brought considerable profits to tanners of sole leather. Production was much smaller; and the market was kept in light supply at quite remunerative prices. Manufacturers of upper leather found it a less prosperous year. The high prices of previous years had so stimulated production that the supply has generally been greater than the demand. To tanners of rough leather also, the year was not a profitable one. Jobbers of leather did a large business during the year; but profits were at no time better than moderate; often very slender.

The rapid advance in French stock, by reason of the war between France and

Prussia, did not benefit dealers, as might be supposed, because the stocks held at the breaking out of the hostilities stated were generally small, and the advance in prices here has been fully equalled by the advance at the sources of supply.

In domestic leathers, calf-skins were affected by the rise in the French article, and advanced in price. As to heavy leathers, the prices declined somewhat during the year.

As to hides, there was an advance in prices up to July; since that time prices have been steady and well sustained.

Bark ruled higher than for several years past. As to belting, the market was steady, without material alteration in prices.

The principal dealers are: D. Yandes & Co., dealers in leather, hides, &c., 76 East Washington street; J. E. Mooney & Co., dealers in leather hides, leather and rubber belting, &c., 147 South Meridian street; Hide, Leather and Belt Co., 125 South Meridian street; J. K. Sharpe, dealer in leather, hides, boots, shoes, &c., 47 and 49 South Delaware street.

LIQUORS.

The beginning of the wholesale trade in distilled liquors, in this city, may be dated about the year 1846. Among the earlier wholesale dealers was Patrck Kirland, succeeded by Kirland & Fitzgibbon. The first house that made systematic efforts to establish a wholesale trade, by sending out traveling agents, etc , was Kirland & Ryan, in the year 1859.

In 1860 there were in the city the following wholesale dealers: Kirland & Ryan, Ruschaupt & Bals, and Elliott & Ryan. The aggregate sales at wholesale that year were not far from $100,000. This business has increased many fold in recent years.

The principal establishments at this date are, T. F. Ryan, Gapen & Catherwood, Ryan & Holbrook, Hahn & Bals, John C. Brinkmeyer, J. P. Stumph & Co., C. Kaufman, Schwabacher & Selig, Rikhoff & Co. The aggregate transactions of the year 1870 are reported at $2,807,087. The business of the year was a considerable increase, in bulk, over that of previous years, though the aggregate sum realized was less, by reason of the reduction in the government tax from $2 to 50 cents per gallon. The effect of a more thorough collection of the tax on spirits has had the effect to prevent violent fluctuations in prices. For this reason dealers have been able to do a safe business. The seven hundred and seventy grain distilleries of this country have a producing capacity of over two hundred millions gallons annually; while the consumption is not over eighty millions gallons. Consequently there has been an excessive production; the market has been overstocked, and prices brought down below the remunerative point. The aggregate losses of distillers during the year 1870 would considerably exceed their aggregate profits; though these losses have, to some extent, been compensated by the profits on the hogs fed by the distillers.

The price of raw highwines reached its lowest decline late last summer; when it was 75@76 cents. Since then it has rallied to 98 cents, and is now about 90 cents, and steady at that figure.

In imported brands of whisky, brandy, etc., the readjustment of the tarriff has brought an average decline in proportion to the average reduction of the duties on these articles. As to imported wines, the European war interfered with their exportation to this country, producing considerable advances in prices. On champagne wine there was a temporary advance of nearly one hundred per cent. The conclusion of peace between France and Germany has removed the restrictions upon exportation, and prices have about returned to the old standard.

LIVE STOCK.

By location, this city is entitled to be one of the leading live-stock markets of the West; that it has not that prominence is due simply to the failure to employ adequate means to utilize natural advantages; and the prominence that has been attained has been in spite of the latter default. Without adequate yards for the reception of live stock, there can be no market of consequence.

In 1865, Mr. E. W. Pattison established the first yards in this city for the reception of live stock. With no previous provision of this character, it is readily understood that prior to that date there could be no live stock market here. Local purchasers secured their supplies in the country, and as no provision was made for sellers, there was nothing here for shippers to buy. The live stock that would naturally have been unloaded and penned here, passed through the city to such points as had the requisite conveniences for holder and purchaser.

The effect of Mr. Pattison's enterprise was to supply, through his yards, sufficient stock for the city demand, with now and then a surplus of a carload or so for purchase on Eastern account. The improvement in receipts was in proportion to the improvement in accommodations, both far short of what they might have been. In 1867, Mr. Pattison disposed of his yards to J. C. Ferguson & Co., for many years extensive pork packers at this point. About this time, at the solicitation of the butchers here, Messrs. Kingan & Co., opened more extensive yards near White River, between Maryland and Georgia streets. The firm of Kingan & Co., who still own these yards, is composed of Samuel and Thomas D. Kingan, who, by the extent of their investments and operations, their extensive Eastern and foreign connection, and comprehensive knowledge of the trade in live stock, and the products thereof, were well qualified to inaugurate and carry out the necessary measures for bringing the holder and purchaser together here—to make the city, in a larger sense than before, a live stock market. The location selected for their yards was advantageous; especially easy of access for shippers from the West, whence come nearly all the stock brought here; easy of access for stock driven in to the city on foot; convenient and cheap of access for butchers; and sufficiently commodious for all the demands upon them.

Early in 1871, the *Pittsburg, Cincinnati & St. Louis Railway Company* purchased a site of twenty-two acres, at a cost of $40,000, in the Eastern suburbs of the city and have since occupied a portion of the ground for live stock yards, which are now in operation, but owing to their greater distance from the center of the city, the bulk of the stock sold here are yarded at Kingan's pens. The effect of the establishment of these yards has been to make a live stock market of Indianapolis, but still a local market chiefly.

What is yet needed to give this city the true place among the live stock markets of the country, to which it is naturally entitled, is the opening of extensive Union Stock Yards, like those at Chicago, St. Louis, and Cincinnati, in which each of the railroads converging here should have a proprietary interest, and to which should be shipped all the live stock sent in this direction over those roads—just as all the live stock sent to market from the North-west for instance, are sent to

Chicago, and there sold for local consumption and shipment to the East. This would make Indianapolis a prominent shipping and receiving point, instead of, as now, a receiving point on a small scale, compared with what it might be.

The establishment of such an enterprise has several times been attempted, but without success, because of the opposition of two of the Railway Companies, who objected to benefiting the city in this way at the expense of losing a supposed monopoly in the bulk of the carrying trade in live stock.

The resultant benefits of such an enterprise to our financial and commercial interests would obviously be very great; and for this reason it would be liberally aided by our merchants. Even if the Western railway companies, who carry four-fifths of the live stock shipped from the surrounding country, should combine in such an enterprise, self-interest would impel the other roads to come into the combination.

Beef Cattle.—The foregoing observations on the live stock market here sufficiently indicate the past and present magnitude and needed improvements of the cattle market. The establishment since 1865 of the several live stock yards before mentioned, has brought to the city the supply needed for the local demand, with something of an excess, at times, for the eastern demand. With improved accommodations and facilities in the way of yards will come proportionally augmented receipts and shipments. The year 1870 was characterized by increased receipts and a steady market. The variation in prices from the beginning to the end of the year was not more than 1 cent per lb. The higest price for prime was 8 cents; the lowest 7. Fair butchers' stock ranged from 3½ to 5 cents. During the first four months of the present year prices, as compared with those at the close of last year, have declined on an average about ½ cent per lb. The quotation of 8 cents given above applies to the best grade seeking this market. The grade quoted as "extra" in Chicago, represents the very choicest selections from the cattle brought there, a quality that is not shipped to this point, and is worth about 1 cent per lb. more than the best grade of the offerings here. The price of beef has not receded toward the ante-war level as rapidly as those of other commodities. This has been due to the excessive consumption during the war, a waste that it has taken years to repair. The figures appended will show the approximate business in cattle at this point for the year ending November 1, 1870:

Beeves: sold for city consumption, 16,000; valued at $960,000. Shipped, 5,000 head; valued at $400,000. Veal calves: sold for local demand, 2,000 head; valued at $20,000. Total value, $1,380,800.

Hogs.—In spite of the wants mentioned in the previous remarks on the live stock trade in general, this city has for a number of years been a prominent hog-slaughtering and pork-packing point. For the reasons mentioned it is not a shipping point to a commensurate extent, but chiefly a receiving point for supplying the wants of local packers and butchers. Surrounded by an extensive agricultural and stock-growing country, largely developed, and with the most complete railway system on the continent, this city is entitled to be one of the largest live stock markets and packing points in the West; and could readily command a supply of 250,000 to 300,000 hogs annually if it had the requisite packing establishments and requisite inducements and opportunities in the matter of yards, &c. The packing establishments at this point are:—

Kingan & Co.; J. C. Ferguson & Co.; Wheat, Fletcher & Coffin; Lesh, Tousey & Co. These establishments employ and represent an aggregate investment of $1,250,000, and employ an average aggregate of 239 hands.

There were packed here for the year ending November, 1870, about 75,000 hogs; worth about $2,000,000. To this add about 30,000 head slaughtered and packed by butchers for city consumption, and worth about $75,000. Total number for the year, 105,000. Total value, $2,750,000.

The hog crop of the past season throughout the West was an increase of about 56 per cent. over that of the previous season. The increased per cent. of the crop handled here was much greater than even this. The number packed here during the past season (beginning with November, 1870, and ending April 28, 1871) was 112,500, against 59,600 for the same time the previous year.

The average weight the past season was 240 lbs.; for the previous season, about 210 lbs. Consequently the increase in pounds this season over the season before was more than 100 per cent. The average weight during the past season was the heaviest for ten years past. The average price was about $6.00, live weight, against $10.00 for the previous season. The number yet to be packed up to November 1st will probably reach 45,000 head, making the aggregate for the year 157,500 head, against 75,000 for the year ending November 1,1870.

The past year and the opening months of the present year have, generally speaking, been profitable to those who promptly disposed of their products, and unprofitable to persistent holders for higher prices. The Southern demand has not been what was anticipated, and the war in Europe failed to bring the expected foreign demand and advance in prices. In the aggregate operators lost more than they made.

Sheep.—From the reasons given in the foregoing remarks concerning live stock in general, it will appear why transactions in sheep here chiefly relate to supplying local wants. The annual shipments from this point are probably 10,000 head per annum. The sales for home consumption here during the year ending November 1st, 1870, aggregated 75,000 head; value, $150,000. To this add 10,000 head shipped, valued at $20,000. Total number, 85,000 head; total value, $170,000.

The range of prices for sheep during the year 1870 was $2 00@4 00 per head lambs, $1 25@2 50. Prices were steady for the greater part of the year, with an upward movement toward the close. Comparing the closing prices of last year with those current at the end of the fourth month of 1871, an advance of fifty cents to one dollar is shown.

LUMBER.

This city is known as the greatest "hard lumber" market in the country. It is situated in the center of a large area of territory heavily set with valuable timber whose resources in that respect have but recently begun to be utilized for purposes of commerce. While the timber of the older states approaches exhaustion, or has already reached that state, an extensive area in this State possesses an affluence of lumber wealth that has, in many sections, only commenced to flow into the channels of commerce. As each new railway has been built, new lumber regions have been penetrated, and outlets for the resources opened. Nature and the railroads have thus made this the leading market of the country for the more desirable grades of hard lumber—walnut, oak, ash, etc., and for poplar. Enormous quantities of these varieties of lumber are shipped from this point to supply the demand from the Atlantic cities and other points.

As to pine and similar species of soft lumber not indigenous to this region, this is an importing rather than a supply market. Large quantities of pine lumber are imported here, chiefly for local building and manufacturing purposes. The carrying trade in pine lumber of the railways connecting this city with Chicago and Michigan City is very large, amounting to between four and five thousand car loads from the latter point alone.

The aggregate transactions of the lumber dealers of this city last year are reported at $1,294,469. Principal lumber dealers are the following:

Streight & Wood, McCord & Wheatley, Bunte & Dickson, Coburn & Jones, Emerson & Beam, Warren Tate, H. W. Hildebrand, Isgrigg & Bracken, Cornelius King, George W. Hill, Charles Donellan, Eberts & Owens, Long & Carter, J. Marsee & Son, J. T. Presley.

METALS AND TINNERS' STOCK.

This business—disconnected from the kindred merchandise of stoves, tinware, etc.—is of quite recent establishment in this city—the pioneer house—that of Thomas Cottrell, having been established but a few years ago. Prior to that time, and in a considerable degree yet, this branch of trade is conducted by the stove and tinware houses.

Being yet a young business, the annual transactions therin have not yet attained the magnitude of other departments of the city's commerce. The transactions of last year are estimated at $420,000—a considerable increase over the business of the previous year. The range of prices was lower than during the previous year. Quotations are steady, and the shrinkage in values has evidently pretty nearly reached the minimum.

The leading houses are, Thomas Cottrell and Messrs. Ransdell & Grubbs. Everything in the nomenclature of this branch of business can be found here, in qualities and prices equal to the best inducements of outside competition.

MILLINERY, &C.

The present large and growing business in Millinery goods, and the few years in which it has been established, is an eloquent representative of the commercial growth of the city

The first wholesale house—that of J. W. Copeland—was established in 1856.

The area of territory now occupied by Indianapolis dealers in this department of trade corresponds very nearly with that occupied by other leading branches of trade, dry goods, groceries, &c.; and this area is constantly being extended.

The business of the past year has been, in respect of amount, encouraging; showing an increase of about 20 per cent. The increase of capital was about the same. Generally, prices at the close of the year showed an advance over those at the opening of the year. In domestic goods, there was an advance in most articles; particularly in straw goods. As to imported goods, the advance was quite appreciable, owing to the war in Europe.

Profits during the year were fair, but collections were more difficult, though the *per cent.* of bad debts made was judiciously small. The present year augurs an improvement on last year's trade.

The principal wholesale establishments are those of J. W. Copeland & Co., 116 South Meridian Street; and Fahnley & McCrea, 131 South Meridian Street. The transactions of 1870 in this department of trade aggregated $400,554.

MUSIC AND MUSICAL INSTRUMENTS.

The trade in music and musical instruments has grown to be a very considerable feature of the general commerce of the city. In 1844 the first piano was sold in this city. In 1850 the first music store was opened by Albert E. Jones. The present extensive house of Willard & Co., was established in 1853. The next important addition to this interest was the opening of the present well known house of Benham Brothers, in 1862. For many years the business was altogether in the retail way, and chiefly local. In recent years, sharing the general prosperity of the city, and aided by the greatly increased popularity of musical science, this business has multiplied many fold, and an extensive jobbing trade, covering a large area of territory, is being done. Recently, too, the manufacture of pianos, etc., was instituted and is now prominent among the industries of the city. Every variety of musical instrument and of musical merchandise, a list far too long to be mentioned in this place, can be obtained here at wholesale or retail, with the best inducements as to prices and qualities that can be anywhere offered. The aggregate value of reported transactions last year in this branch of business was $394,000. The principal houses are Benham Brothers, 36 East Washington Street; Charles Soehner, 36 East Washington Street; A. G. Willard & Co., No. 4 Bates House Block; M. A. Stowell, No. 46 North Pennsylvania Street. Manufacturers, *Indianapolis Piano Manufacturing Company,* 297 South New Jersey, and salesroom Ætna building, North Pennsylvania street.

Benham Brothers and Professor Soehner occupy the same location. The former do a general business in all descriptions of musical instruments (except pianos) musical merchandise, musical publications, etc. Professor Soehner deals in pianos exclusively, and is the State agent in this city for the *Steinway* and *Knabe* Pianos.

NOTIONS.

The Notion trade in this city, though young in years, is extensive in amount and importance. For the most part, it is the creation of the past ten years. The aggregate of sales last year was $1,083,656; which shows a very gratifying growth.

The business of the year last past has been, in the main, one of prosperity: showing an increase of about 20 per cent. over that of the previous year, and a corresponding increase of capital. The shrinkage in values continued throughout the year: for which reason profits were, on an average, rather slender. It is believed that the downward course of prices has about reached the lowest point; and that prices will be steady during the current year at the present figures

The leading houses engaged in this branch of trade are: Byram, Cornelius & Co., Fahnley & McCrea, Fortner, Floyd & Co., L. Ludorff & Co., Murphy, Johnson & Co., John D. Evans & Co., Stoneman, Pee & Co.

PICTURES, FRAMES, &C.

The different grades of art productions embraced above in the general term of Pictures, are well represented in establishments here devoted to that line of trade. In some respects a better and ampler variety is offered than could be found in any other western city.

Paintings.—At the well-known establishment of Lieber & Co. there may be found the works of the more eminent artists of this and other countries. Occasionally there are auction sales of the more costly paintings that have failed to find purchasers at private sales. An extensive and costly collection of imported paintings from the celebrated Dusseldorff gallery, was thus disposed of last autumn. Patrons are yet comparatively few for this class of works of art. But, as is the rule in new countries, the number of purchasers for this class of works of art would admit of a considerable increase.

Engravings—In this respect there is claimed for the dealers in this city a better and more various display than is offered by any other western city. There can be seen here at all times full collections from France, England and Germany, as well as from our own country.

Chromos.—In this respect it is sufficient to observe that about every chromo known to the trade may be had here.

Lithographs.—Of this cheaper class of pictures, plain and colored, there is the fullest display.

Photographs.—There is nothing in this line that cannot be found here.

Frames, etc.—The stocks contain pretty nearly everything in this line that can be found in the market in this country. The reported transactions for the past year were $110,000. The principal houses are: H. Lieber & Co., Daumont & Co., R. P. Crapo. The former two are wholesalers and retailers of pictures, frames, etc.; the latter is a dealer in frames, mouldings, photographers stock, etc.

QUEENSWARE, GLASSWARE, ETC.

The wholesale trade in this branch of merchandise was begun, in a small way, fifteen or sixteen years ago, by Jacob Lindley. So slow was the growth of the business that in 1860 Mr. Lindley was still its only wholesale representative. The business is now represented by the following leading establishments: Hawthorne, Morris, & Gorrell, 38 South Meridian street; Patterson & Co., 127 Sout Meridian street; John Woodbridge & Co., 36 South Meridian street; Hollweg Reese, 96 South Meridian street; Geo. H. West, 57 West Washington street. The increase of capital invested, and extension of the trade during the past seven or eight years has been very great.

The area of territory tributary to this market has been greatly extended on every hand, and within these limits a large, desirable, and constantly increasing trade has been permanently established·

The business of the past year shows an increase over the previous year o bout fifteen per cent.

In queensware, the greater portion of which is of foreign production, th shrinkage in prices was in proportion to the decline in the gold premium.

In glass ware, prices were steady during the year. Collections during the year were not so readily made nor so closely kept up as might be. The sales for the year amounted to $365,000.

This year's business opens out with promising indications of a prosperous year.*

---

* In the foregoing remarks concerning Trade, the expression "the past year," relates to 1870 and references to the business of "the present year," relate to the opening months of 1871.

SEWING MACHINES.

Within a very few years the sewing machine, from being esteemed by the mass as a fanciful article, of doubtful utility, and destined only for a privileged few, has became one of the cardinal necessities of every family. Having now become indispensable to the family and to the manufacturer of clothing of whatever kinds the trade in sewing machines at this point has come to be a commanding feature of its commerce.

The growth of the business here is even considerably greater than the relative growth of the business generally. For the commercial advantages of this city have made it a central distributing point, supplying and controlling the trade of most of this State and of portions of adjoining States.

The earliest agencies established here were by the *Wheeler & Wilson* and *Singer* Companies, about the year 1857. As new inventions multiplied, and the sewing machine became popularized, agencies were established from time to time, until now all the better inventions are represented here—generally by agencies having control of a large area of territory, extending in some instances into adjoining States. The magnitude of the sewing machine business in this city may be seen from the re-ported sales for 1870—about $600,000. The following companies have agencies here:—

The Singer, by Messrs. Wm. R. Nofsinger and A. K. Josselyn; the Wheeler & Wilson, by Messrs. L. B. Walker & Co.; the Grover & Baker, by Wiley & Van Buren; the Howe by Messrs. Olin & Foltz; the Florence by J. W. Smith; the Weed by Jas. Skarden & Co.; the Button-Hole, C. E. Cardell & Co.

The sewing machine trade, which is destined to attain a far greater magnitud, in the country at large than it now has, is sure to have a much larger proportionate increase here. For apart from the superior location of this city in a commercial way for the distribution of the machines over a large extent of territory in every direction, the facilities for obtaining suitable lumber for the cabinet work of machines at the cheapest figures, is attracting the establishment of manufacturies here. The Wheeler & Wilson Company have already established an extensive branch manu-factory in the eastern suburb of the city, and others are likely to follow. The course of prices as to the more meritorious inventions has been steady, ranging from $65 to $165, according to style of finish. Prices of sewing machines did not par-take of the general inflation during the war; consequently there has been little or no shrinkage in values since.

STOVES, TINWARE, ETC.

The first manufacturers and wholesalers of stoves and tinware in this city were the firm of J. K. & D. Root, who began operations in 1851. In that year their aggregate sales were about $10,000. In 1860 the same firm was still without con-siderable opposition, and that year their transactions reached $103,000.

If during the first ten years this interest prospered but indifferently, its growth in the past few years has quite compensated for the slow progress of the former period. By comparing the transactions of 1851, amounting to no more than $15,000, with those of 1870, aggregating $850,000, a remarkable increase is shown.

By the above caption is embraced a great variety of articles usually classed under the heads of "stoves, tinware, and house-furnishing goods"—stoves and the numer-

(25)

ous products of iron, tin, etc., too numerous to be detailed in this mention, but made or sold here in the widest variety, and of the most approved qualities and styles.

In nearly every class of goods of this general description there was a steady, decline in prices during 1870, averaging ten per cent. Collections were better than the average during the year, but the present year opened with a change for the worse in this respect. The principal establishments are: D. Root & Co. manufactory 183 South Pennsylvania street; salesroom 66 East Washington street; Tutewiler Bros., 74 East Washington street; Johnson Bros., 62 East Washington street; Charles Cox, 57 West Washington street; R. L. McOuatt, 61 & 63 West Washington street; Frankem & Kline, 34 East Washington street; Meyers & Martin, 257 West Washington street; J. Voegtle, 103 East Washington street C. Zimmerman, 35 South Alabama street; Wolfram Bros., 197 East Washington street.

TOBACCO, CIGARS, ETC.

The first to engage in the wholesale tobacco business and in the manufacture of cigars exclusively, of whom we find any record, was George F. Meyer, at his present place of business, in 1850.

Though this branch of commerce and manufactures developed slowly for a number of years, it has in recent years risen to great consequence. The bulk of the business in cigars is now represented by dealers who are also manufacturers. The manufacture of tobacco in any considerable degree is represented by two establishments: Smith & Thomas, and Thomas Madden & Co. The former firm makes plug tobacco, which meets a ready demand, not only from Western dealers, but from jobbers in the principal Eastern cities. Mr. Madden manufactures fine-cut tobacco which has already attained great favor with the trade. The transactions of 1870 aggregated $1,659,301.

The various grades of tobacco and cigars are abundantly represented here by a great number of manufacturers and wholesale dealers. The business of 1870 shows a good increase—10@15 per cent. Profits, however, for the last two or three years have been very small, smaller perhaps than those of any other branch of manufacture, and too small in proportion to the amount of capital employed, and to the magnitude of the transactions. The heavy government tax on these articles, much larger than their separate value, necessitates a very large capital for the handling and carrying of stocks. The government tax, the high price of labor maintained by the operatives' Unions, and the enhanced cost of the leaf, have kept up prices and diminished profits. This is particularly true of the common grades of cigars, on which the profits of manufacturers have not greatly exceeded 7 per cent.

As to imported cigars, prices were well sustained during 1870, but afterward slightly declined. As a compensation for diminished profits, collections were good during the year.

The following are the principal establishments in this line: Manufacturers of cigars and dealers in cigars and tobacco—A. W. Sharpe, Geo. F. Meyer & Co., Mayer & Bros., Charles C. Hunt, C. M. Raschig, C. C. Hunt, Solmon & Garratt, George Reswinkle, A. W. Reynolds, Clemens Back, Uhl & Durham, S. F. Reynolds, Peter Kretsch.

Tobacco Manufacturers—Smith & Thomas, Thomas Madden, Charles Oliver Dealers in Tobacco and Cigars—J. C. Green & Co., J. W. Lines & Co., J. A. McGaw.

The greatly increased consumption of wool by the mills in this city has propor-

WOOL.

tionally augmented the bulk brought to this market. The aggregate receipts fo 1870 were about 5,000,000 lbs.; worth about $200,000.

This article has shared the general shrinkage in values since the close of the war. The average prices in 1870 were: for washed and picked, 48 cents; unwashed, 30 cents. Though the price of wool has been gradually declining during the past few years, its price is still comparatively higher than the prices of the products made from it.

Agriculturists and stock-growers in this State have of late taken great interest in improving the breed of their sheep, and they have had an excellent return for their trouble and outlay. The average sheep in Indiana to-day is a very different animal from that of ten years ago, securing a breed that unites superior size and quality of mutton with a fleece double the usual quantity, and best adapted to the manufacture of the grades of woolen fabrics most in use. Merino sheep are comparatively few in number in this State, because unprofitable. Indiana is noted among wool dealers and operators for its clean, tub-washed wool of the common and medium grades, being in general much more thoroughly washed before it is sent to market than is the rule, and therefore more acceptable to purchasers.

STATISTICAL EXHIBIT,

Showing the aggregate value of sales of leading articles of merchandise by Indianapolis dealers for the year 1870:

Agricultural Implements	$755,687
Beef Cattle	1,380,000
Books and Stationery	556,000
Boots and Shoes	1,709,000
Bakeries	193,700
Carpets and Wall Paper	510,000
Clothing	1,779,805
Coal	550,000
Confectioneries	190,508
Cigars and Tobacco	1,659,300
Dry Goods	4,542,000
Drugs and Medicines	1,661,600
Eggs	291,580
Furniture	749,000
Grain	3,745,000
Groceries	6,443,151
Hardware and Iron	3,500,000
Hogs	2,750,000
House Furnishing Goods	850,000
Hats and Caps	412,000
Jewelry	195,000
Leather and Belting	438,290
Lumber	1,294,469
Liquors	2,807,087
Music and Musical Instruments	394,000
Millinery and Fancy Goods	400,558
Notions	1,083,651
Paints, Oils, &c	726,150
Pig Iron	771,600
Poultry	207,000
Queensware	365,000
Saddlery Hardware	318,000
Sewing Machines	563,753
Sheep	170,000
Wool	200,000
Total	**$44,182,889**

REAL ESTATE.

The rapid, steady advance in the value of real estate in and near the city is the best index to its present prosperity, and to the confidence felt by business men in its future growth. This advance is a marked feature in the recent real estate transactions, and prices for years have almost constantly tended upward.

The selection of this place as the State Capital in 1821, temporarily inflated the values of real estate; but as no highways to the town then existed, prices receded and few transfers were made, until the internal improvement scheme, in 1836. This caused a feverish activity in transfers and a rapid rise in prices for a year or two; but on the failure of the public works values again declined, and no demand existed for property till the opening of the Madison and Indianapolis Railroad, in 1848, at last gave the city an outlet. The improvement may be said to date from that year; but it was not until the completion of the State Railway system, in 1853-4, that the advance became sufficiently great to attract attention.

Up to that time business had been confined to two or three central squares on Washington street, and the choice locations there did not command more than $75 to $100 per front foot, while the remainder of the city plat was held only for residence or farming purposes, and most of it valued at not more than $100 per acre. Under the effects of the railway system, however, prices soon doubled in the central parts of the city, while the advance in outside property was very much greater. Subdivisions of the various out-lots in the old plat were rapidly made, and many additions were laid off outside of it, and the advance in price continued quite steadily; for though checked by the bank failures in 1854-5, and the commercial panic of 1857, the values attained before these checks were at once increased as soon as the pressure was removed.

This lasted till the war brought business matters to a dead stop, and for two years prices were comparatively unchanged, transfers were few, and little activity existed in the trade. The best business locations on Washington street would command $400 or $500 per foot, while outside property had gone far beyond the advance in the central portions. In the year 1863 a rapid increase again began, and by the end of the war prices on Washington street, for choice locations, had reached $1,000 per front foot, and in many portions of the suburbs values were ten fold higher than three years before. These figures received a decided check on the sudden cessation of the war, and values, especially in the outside property, receded to some extent, while the transfers—except to settle claims—rapidly diminished in number; but this was an experience felt in all the cities of the country; and in none other was the check so temporary as at this point. The figures prevailing at the beginning of 1865 were soon resumed in most parts of the city, and though not much activity prevailed, there was little or no diminution in the prices asked for lots.

In 1868 another advance began, which has steadily continued to the present time, and has recently been so marked and startling as to awaken the fears of many persons that it is unhealthy and feverish, and that a rebound must ensue. This advance has mainly been in outside property, for though choice locations on Washington street would probably bring $1,500 to $1,800 per foot, the advance on former figures there is trifling compared with that in the suburbs, where, in many places, 100 per cent. advance is asked and given in a few months.

Sub-divisions comprising over two thousand two hundred building lots have been made and put in market thus far in 1871, and the demand seems to anticipate the supply.   The activity in real estate transfers has been constant from the beginning of the year, averaging thus far, probably, $160,000 per week; and the excitement seems increasing as time rolls on.

The comparative activity of the real estate trade at the different periods hereinafter stated, may be inferred from the aggregate amounts of the transfers for the several years. These were for 1850, $217,991 61; for 1860, $1,111,492.08; for 1870, $5,223,865.18; and for the first six months in 1871, $3.992,175.70.

The assessment of real property, in this city, for taxation has always been much below the selling prices, and of late years, by reason of the rapid advance, the discrepancy—especially in the newer parts of the city—is too glaring to admit of any defense, other than that the improvement is too rapid for an annual assessment. The following table, therefore, does not give the actual values at any period, and especially at the present; for we may safely say that the selling rates would almost double the aggregate values reported for 1870—but the tables will show how steady and decided the improvement has been during the last twenty years:

The assessment of real and personal property in 1847 amounted to about $1,000,000

In 1850..	2,326,185
In 1853..	5,131,582
In 1856..	7,146,670
In 1858..	10,475,000
In 1860..	10,700,000
In 1862..	10,250,000
In 1863..	10,750,000
In 1864..	13,250,000
In 1865..	10,144,447
In 1866..	24,231,750
In 1867..	21,943,605
In 1868..	23,593,619
In 1870..	25,981,267
In 1871..	28,516,215

The foregoing table, and the facts above mentioned, will show that the advance in real estate at Indianapolis is no evanescent matter, but that it has been steady, solid, and permanent. The rapidity in the late increase may be considered by many as an unsound indication, but the facts thus far do not seem to point that way; but on the contrary, would indicate that the city has but just entered on its full career, and that its future greatness is assured beyond all doubt.

Vandalia Route

WEST.

23 MILES THE SHORTEST.

3 EXPRESS TRAINS leave Indianapolis daily, except Sunday, for **ST. LOUIS** and **THE WEST.**

The ONLY line running PULLMAN'S celebrated DRAWING-ROOM SLEEP-ING CARS from NEW YORK. PITTSBURG, LOUISVILLE, CINCINNATI, and INDIANAPOLIS, to

ST. LOUIS WITHOUT CHANGE.

Passengers should remember that this is the GREAT WEST BOUND ROUTE for KANSAS CITY, LEAVENWORTH, LAWRENCE, TOPEKA, JUNCTION CITY, FORT SCOTT and ST. JOSEPH.

EMIGRANTS TO KANSAS, for the purpose of establishing themselves in new homes, will have liberal discrimi-nation made in their favor by this line. Satisfactory commutation on regular rates will be given to Colonists and large parties traveling together; and their baggage, emi-grant outfit and stock, will be shipped on the most favorable terms, presenting to COLONISTS AND FAMILIES such comforts and accommodations as are presented by no other Route.

Tickets can be obtained at all the principal Ticket Offices in the Eastern, Middle, and Southern States.

ROBT. EMMETT.
Eastern Pass. Agt., Indianapolis.

C. E. FOLLETT.
Gen. Pass Agt., St. Louis.

JOHN E. SIMPSON,
Gen. Supt., Indianapolis.

www.ingramcontent.com/pod-product-compliance
Lightning Source LLC
Chambersburg PA
CBHW022023110726

47901CB00006B/1642